THE DROW GREW STRONGER

THE DROW GREW STRONGER

GOTH DROW™ BOOK FOUR

MARTHA CARR

MICHAEL ANDERLE

Copyright © 2020 Martha Carr and Michael Anderle
Cover Art by Jake @ J Caleb Design
http://jcalebdesign.com / jcalebdesign@gmail.com
A Michael Anderle Production

LMBPN Publishing
PMB 196, 2540 South Maryland Pkwy
Las Vegas, NV 89109

First US Edition, August, 2020
eBook ISBN: 978-1-64971-109-0
Print ISBN: 978-1-64971-110-6

THE DROW GREW STRONGER TEAM

Thanks to the JIT Readers

Angel LaVey
Daniel Weigert
Deb Mader
Diane L. Smith
Jackey Hankard-Brodie
John Ashmore
Kerry Mortimer
Larry Omans
Paul Westman
Peter Manis
Veronica Stephan-Miller

If we've missed anyone, please let us know!
Editor
The Skyhunter Editing Team

CHAPTER ONE

This can't be real. None of this is actually happening right now, is it?

Cheyenne Summerlin stalked through the corridors of black stone, blinking at the bright code scrolling across the walls. Grimacing at the distraction, she reached behind her ear and ripped off the silver activator coil. The code flickered and disappeared with the buzzing pinch that still made her eyes water. She jammed the activator into her coat pocket and kept moving.

Beside her, L'zar Verdys moved with long, purposeful strides away from the Heart at the center of Hangivol. The drow thief stood tall, his hands clasped behind his back and a daring, infuriating smirk on his dark-gray lips.

"Look at this," he muttered, gesturing toward the crowd of snarling magicals gathering in the wide archway of a branching corridor on their left. "They look happy, don't they?"

Cheyenne stared expressionlessly at the Crown's servants and attendants cramming into the archway, who were shoving each other against the black walls. "Happy enough to jump out and try to rip us to shreds."

"Oh, they could *try*, yes." L'zar raised his eyebrows at the sneering, hissing magicals glaring at them, a multitude of races, skin colors, and facial features. He didn't even bother to lower his voice when he passed a foot from the archway. "Then they'd find themselves at the foot of the deathflame with nothing but oblivion to greet them there."

A slavering rat-faced skaxen drew her head back and spat violently at L'zar. The drow's fingers flicked toward the furious servant in a fraction of a second, sending the foamy wad of spittle flying back toward its owner, where it landed with a grotesque smack. The skaxen screamed and reeled away from the corridor, clamping both clawed orange hands to her eye and pushing through the crowd to withdraw the way she'd come. No one else said a word.

L'zar clasped his hands behind his back and kept up his brisk but unhurried pace through the Crown's inner fortress in the center of Ambar'ogúl's capital. "You know, for the first time, I think I like the way things are headed in this place."

On the other side of Cheyenne, Ember Gaderow snorted. "Because no one can do anything to stop you."

The drow chuckled and cast the fae girl a sidelong glance. "They wouldn't have been able to anyway. The only difference is they know it now. It's about time the willing slaves in this place pulled their heads out of their beloved Crown's ass and opened their eyes to the truth."

And he thinks the truth is that he's much better than she is. I'm still not buying it.

Cheyenne and Ember shared a quick glance, and the fae girl shrugged.

They followed L'zar down too many twisting corridors for Cheyenne to count until they finally stopped at two broad metal doors the same black as the walls, stretching a full twelve feet up to the equally black ceiling. The drow turned toward his daughter and her fae *Nós Aní* and dipped his head in acknowledgment. "Ladies, I believe our reception awaits."

"What are you talking about?" Cheyenne stopped when he slammed both hands against the doors and pushed them open into the room beyond. *The Crown might not be able to do anything to him, but I sure as hell can.*

L'zar marched into the room as the massive doors thumped against the walls. Dozens of low black metal tables lined the wide, tall room, each of them with matching benches like picnic tables. Every surface was cluttered with every type of magical and non-magical weapon imaginable, daggers, maces, clubs, swords, throwing stars, axes spears. Mixed in with these were the same floating metal orbs the Crown had sent out into the city's multiple rising levels, both for the affluent and the lower-class citizens alike, to keep her not-so-loyal subjects in line. Cheyenne's fingers slid around the cold metal coils of the activator in her pocket, but she didn't need to put it on again to know that these pieces of weaponized tech were dead. *For now.*

Standing around all the tables and benches, either cleaning the weapons or testing them or simply hefting them in their hands, were at least fifty O'gúl soldiers, all orcs. Some looked like they'd been a part of the fight in the Heart's courtyard less than twenty minutes ago. Others were fresher-looking as if they'd joined the party in the weapons room and had missed all the fun before Cheyenne returned her drow coin to the altar. All of them glared at L'zar, practically skipping down the center aisle between the metal tables toward the double doors on the opposite end of the room.

The first orc they passed thumped a metal club against his meaty palm and snarled. *"Nilsch úcat."*

L'zar looked quickly at the orc and feigned insult, leaning away and placing a mocking hand to his chest. "Who, *me?*"

"Nobody wants you here, Weaver."

"She'll grind you to dust before the end."

"Blood and fire, *nilsch úcat.*"

"The next time any of us see your face, it'll be in the halls of the unmarked dead!"

The snarling, growling curses flew faster from the orcs' mouths, growing in volume until they were all shouting after L'zar, spit flying from between their protruding tusks with the force of their hatred. The drow didn't change his pace across the room, meeting many of the soldiers' gazes and dipping his head in approval, grinning as if they were congratulating him for his efforts instead. One orc at the far end of the room got so worked up, he swung a wickedly sharp ax back in a wide arc and sent it crashing into the metal table in front of him with a roar. Sparks flew, and the table dented significantly beneath his blow. By the time L'zar reached that table, the orc's chest was heaving as he scowled at the drow, thick spit flying in strands around his tusks.

L'zar stopped, looked the orc over from head to toe, and dipped his head. "Nice arm."

The weapons room echoed with unintelligible curses and O'gúleesh obscenities. Cheyenne and Ember stopped behind L'zar as his gaze wandered over the other set of doors in front of him. The halfling turned to glare right back at the enraged soldiers and raised an eyebrow. "They're gettin' worked up over this. Over *you*."

"Ah." L'zar passed his hand over a section of the metal doors, then looked over his shoulder at his daughter. "This is nothing. Wait 'til we get outside."

Great.

Cheyenne glanced at Ember, who flinched when another orc pounded some heavy metal weapon into a table or a bench with an echoing clang. Then she looked at the halfling with the ghost of a smile. "Even *you're* not this much of a sore loser."

"At least we can make that distinction."

An unseen heavy metal lock slid aside within the doors' mechanism, and L'zar pressed his hands against the metal surface before leaning back to peer at the screaming, roaring soldiers behind them. "You only have a fortnight. Don't waste it."

Then he shoved open the doors, and the mid-afternoon light from the open streets of Hangivol's inner circle spilled into the weapons room. The instant L'zar, Cheyenne, and Ember stepped outside, the orcs launched their weapons at the heavy doors that were slowly swinging back inward. The blades smashed into the slabs, glancing off with deafening echoes of metal on metal. A spear struck the door and stuck fast, the shaft quivering at the impact. The deadly blade of a war ax stuck into the very edge of one slowly closing door a second before a black metal dagger whistled through the air, spinning hilt over point as it passed through the last four inches of space between the doors and sailed over Cheyenne's shoulder.

On instinct, she slipped into drow speed and turned slightly to snatch the suspended dagger from the air. When she returned to normal speed, the doors of the Crown's fortress shut with a resounding boom behind her. She scowled at the dagger in her clenched fist.

L'zar glanced at it and raised his eyebrows. "Feels like you just reached into a frozen body and ripped out an icy heart, doesn't it?"

"Quit saying crazy shit like that." Cheyenne chucked the dagger at the ground and stuck her hand in her jacket pocket to hide her urge to wipe it on something.

"Honor, *Cu'ón!*" A drow man in a dark-blue, shimmering suit cut at weirdly sharp angles lifted a fist in the air and shot a blast of silver and black light toward the magical dome stretching high above the entire city of Hangivol. The spell raced toward the dome and the gray-filtered light and crackled against the shielded wall with a muted hiss.

L'zar met the other drow's gaze, stepped forward on his heel with the toe of his borrowed Earthside shoe pointing straight up, and spread his arms in an exaggerated bow.

The other drow chuckled as his cry of recognition was taken up by the dozens of other drow stepping out of dark, shimmering doorways. They each sent a blast of their magic into the dome until the filtered light dimmed beneath the hissing crackle of impact and the dark streaks of magic racing across the curving wall of the shield for every citizen of Hangivol to see.

Cheyenne's mouth popped open at the sight of so many other drow gathered in the square outside the Crown's fortress. She immediately forced it shut again but couldn't help but stare at all the glowing eyes and bone-white hair and slate-gray skin like her own. They were all well-dressed, standing tall and dipping their heads toward L'zar and his daughter as the *Cu'ón* led the way through the square. *I had no idea there were this many.*

A drow woman with white hair falling past her hips, wearing a gauzy dress so low-cut it might as well have been a halfway-open robe, grinned at Cheyenne. The feral hunger in the drow woman's gaze made the halfling look quickly away. *Apparently, L'zar's not the only one who's mastered that look.*

The drow in the low-cut dress slammed the heel of her fist against the closest wall with a metallic clang. One by one, the other drow took up the weird greeting, wordlessly striking dark fists or open hands on the metal walls, doors, and doorframes. It wasn't nearly as unruly and chaotic as the other times O'gúleesh had gone full-creepy on Cheyenne by banging on metal. The magicals here struck over and over in a slow rhythm as they grinned at the two drow and the fae crossing the square to make their way to the outer rings of the capital.

L'zar threw his head back and laughed. Then he stepped sideways away from Cheyenne and spread his arms again, gesturing toward her like a crier clearing the streets in front of some medieval lord. "The *Aranél* returns!"

The other drow took up the cry.

"Honor, *Aranél*!"

"She is seen!"

"*Mór úcare!*"

Cheyenne frowned when she heard the last one. "Why are they calling me that?"

"That's what you are." L'zar grinned. "Cheyenne, the Weaver's daughter. Dark child returned. Princess of Ambar'ogúl!" The drow spread his arms and pranced across the square, turning in a slow circle as he moved and laughing back at all the drow who'd come to see them both.

Ember grimaced. "He's much crazier than I thought."

"Tell me about it." Cheyenne frowned at her father and snorted when he delivered bow after exaggerated, moronic bow to the drow in every direction. "The loyalists called me that. *Mór úcare.*"

"I'm guessing that's the 'dark child returned' part."

The halfling scrunched her nose and watched her drow father's crazed antics as they reached the other side of the square. "And *Aranél* is 'princess.' They keep throwing these words around in front of me, and I'm too dense to pick up on any of it."

"Oh, *that's* right." Ember rolled her eyes. "You should've spent more time learning the language so you could've picked up on all the secret messages. I bet there's a whole section on O'gúl history at the library."

Cheyenne gently elbowed her friend in the side and kept walking.

The fae girl squinted in thought and glanced slowly around the square. "And I'm just noticing for the first time how weird it is that everybody here speaks English with random O'gúleesh tossed in."

"Huh." Cheyenne blinked at the realization. "Guess we'll have to ask about that one."

When they reached another wide archway of dark, shimmering metal on the other side of the square, L'zar spun again to face the gathered drow. They still pounded in unison. The slow, steady rhythm vibrated through the ground and the air, and Cheyenne clenched her jaw to keep her teeth from feeling like they were rattling around in her head.

"Brothers! Sisters!" L'zar spread his arms, his golden eyes wide and glowing with a sharper light than usual. "A new Cycle turns in fourteen days. Be ready for the end. I know *I* am."

A collective, wordless shout rose from the other drow, and L'zar took a deep breath as he grinned at his people paying tribute to him right outside the Crown's lair. Both hands shot up to his head as his long, slender fingers smoothed the hair away from the sides of his face and his forehead. Then he spun smartly again and raised his eyebrows at Cheyenne, gesturing toward the arch. "This is the beginning, Cheyenne. There's so much more than what you've seen."

Cheyenne glanced at the dozens of drow keeping up the pounding rhythm on the metal walls. "Am I supposed to be impressed?"

"Not in the slightest." L'zar leaned farther toward the dark archway and waited for Cheyenne and Ember to pass through ahead of him. "I'd be quite disappointed if you were."

CHAPTER TWO

The passage leading through the wall around the Crown's inner city containing nothing but drow subjects was so long, Cheyenne couldn't see the other end of it. The noise coming from both ends of the dark tunnel was quietest at the very center, though she was more focused on the erratic flashes of yellow and blue light streaking through patterned grooves in the tunnel's walls and ceiling. "What's that?"

L'zar gazed at the blips. "No activator to answer that question for you?"

"I don't need it for everything. Unless you have no idea, and I should write you off as clueless."

The drow laughed and ran a hand along the grooved wall. "You're still in a touchy mood, I see."

"I just found out I'm the O'gúl Crown's niece and that I have to come back here in two weeks to order her off the throne of a world she's been poisoning for who knows how long." Cheyenne cocked her head and shoved both hands into her jacket pockets. "'Touchy' is a bit of an understatement."

"Let it go for now." His voice was surprisingly soft when he said it, and she almost turned to look at him in surprise. Then he chuckled and slapped a hand on the wall, which resulted in a cracking echo up and down the tunnel. "You've earned your right to feel however the hell you want, Cheyenne, but moping about it is a waste of everyone's time. I'm not a fan."

"Sure, let me just change my moods to suit you."

L'zar gave her a small, amused smile and pointed at the flashing lights along the ceiling. "And *that*, by the way, is the city code rewriting itself."

"Wait, what?"

He nodded once and clasped his hands behind his back. "All part of the interim hold on magic if you will. The Crown's preparing in whatever way she can for your next meeting in two weeks. So are all her marvelously expendable subjects. *Her* words, once upon a time. And this is Hangivol, the most technologically advanced city and the heart of Ambar'ogúl, preparing for the new Cycle."

Cheyenne gazed at the crackling flashes across the otherwise dark surface. *The activator's staying in my pocket for now. I don't think I could handle reading a bunch of crap about myself, if that's even included.*

The metallic banging coming from the drow inner city behind them faded, replaced by a growing ruckus from up ahead. Cheers, shouts, bawdy laughter, and much more chaotic pounding in sporadic bursts came from whatever circular level they were about to enter at the end of the slightly declining tunnel. "Why do they do that?"

"I *know* you understand what a celebration is, despite the fact that I haven't yet seen you participate in one."

She gave her father a deadpan stare, and he shrugged before turning away from her. "I'm talking about all that banging. They did it at Rez 38 and then in Peridosh. *You* did it the day I came to talk to you about—"

"The traitor in the FRoE, yes." L'zar's head bobbed from side to side as strange, ululating O'gúleesh music filtered through the tunnel toward them. "It's a sign of immense respect, Cheyenne. They're paying tribute."

"To *me*?"

"Unless they're staring at someone else while they're doing it, yes."

She frowned at the bright end of the tunnel quickly approaching. *I guess all the Earthside O'gúleesh won't have much of a problem with me ruling over there. If I even do. Seems like they already approve.*

When they stepped out of the tunnel and into the dazzling light reflecting off every bright, shining surface, Cheyenne recognized

Upper Tech. It wasn't the same courtyard she'd visited with Persh'al, but it was definitely the same district. And the people here were unhinged.

Magicals of every race danced in the glistening streets, their fine jewelry and expensive clothing whirling around them in bright flashes and ridiculous patterns. An incredibly tall, thin woman with skin the lightest shade of pale blue and four arms twirled between high-flying leaps, slamming her hand against a metal bench every time her bare, hand-shaped feet touched the ground. An orc with a high, stiff collar on his black dinner jacket and five gold rings inlaid in each tusk swung his head from side to side, kicking the metal walls of a building in rhythm to the strange music.

Expensive scarves and capes swirled in a kaleidoscope of shimmering patterns as the once entirely proper denizens of Upper Tech danced and whooped and roared in victory.

Cheyenne straightened, glancing back and forth across the square at the maddened celebration. "This place was a *lot* different the last time I was here."

Ember backed away from a goblin who lunged toward her, his tongue hanging out of his open, grinning mouth as he shook his head wildly and snatched the odd-shaped top hat that was split down the middle off his head. The fae girl widened her eyes as he cackled and whirled away again, throwing his weird hat into the air, not caring where it landed as he danced across the square. "What was it like last time?"

"Like everyone had a stick up their ass."

Ember chuckled wryly. "Maybe the sticks finally made it up to their brains."

"That does sound like an accurate assessment."

"L'zar!" A skaxen man wearing a sparkling green bodysuit limped toward them, spreading his arms in greeting. "Took you long enough, eh? We all thought you'd been rotting in the ground for the last two hundred years."

L'zar gave the skaxen a tight-lipped smile as they passed. "That's hardly long enough to cause concern."

The skaxen did a little jig in his delight, his bad leg making him look like he was trying to skip on one leg as he shook his clawed orange fists in the air and kept dancing.

Cheyenne forced herself to look away and caught up with L'zar. "Who was that?"

He looked slightly over his shoulder to raise an eyebrow at the dancing magicals. "I have no idea."

Ember floated beside them, unable to decide between frowning at the strange celebration or laughing at it. "You know, after everything I've heard about the shitty direction things have taken over here, I honestly expected this place to look a lot worse. Is the whole city like this?"

L'zar barked a laugh. Cheyenne ignored him and shook her head. "No, Em. Upper Tech's like Windsor Farms, with slightly more sticks up asses."

"Okay." Bobbing her head, Ember gazed around and blinked against the glare reflecting off the glittering white metallic surfaces everywhere. "So, this is the fancy level without drow."

"Pretty much."

L'zar turned toward another tunnel leading out of Upper Tech and paused when a fae man with violet skin and dark-blue hair falling over his shoulders floated into their path. Ember took a sharp breath and stared at the first of her kind she'd seen in this world, but she quickly covered her surprise.

"You shouldn't have returned." The fae man's expressionless face and his calm, even tone were totally at odds with the celebratory air spilling through Upper Tech, and his shimmering violet eyes were cold. "Nothing good will come of this."

The prodigal drow pointed at the fae and squinted. "I'm trying to place your name."

"The last thing I'm giving you is my name, thief."

"If we're throwing names around, I prefer 'Weaver' while I'm here." L'zar spread his arms and offered the fae man a flashing grin. "*Cu'ón* does fairly well too."

The fae man pointed across the square in no particular direction but away from the tunnel he currently blocked.

L'zar chuckled. "Come now, that's not very celebratory. If not for me, you can at least step aside for the *Aranél*, can't you?"

The only reply he received was a slow blink from the fae's luminous eyes and a highly judgmental glance up and down.

The drow thief winked at the fae, then stepped aside and gestured for his daughter to enter the tunnel. "Cheyenne."

She studied the fae man, who only gave her a brief and dismissive glance, then looked at the rest of the dancing square again. *I'm not about to start fighting magicals who don't appreciate L'zar Verdys in their city.* "There's more than one way out of this level."

"No." L'zar's grin disappeared, and his golden gaze bored into the fae's violet eyes. "You step aside for no one, Cheyenne. Not today. Enter the tunnel."

The warning in her father's voice sent an involuntary shiver down the halfling's spine. She exchanged a quick glance with Ember and blinked slowly. *We're doing things differently than the last time I was here.*

"Excuse us." Cheyenne nodded at the fae man and slipped around him into the bright tunnel leading out of the district square.

Ember followed, smiling briefly at the other magical until the fae man turned his gaze on her and narrowed his eyes. She swallowed and raised her eyebrows as she floated past him into the tunnel.

L'zar dipped his head toward the fae, a smile flickering across his lips before he followed his daughter and her *Nós Ani*. The blue-haired fae turned slowly to watch the trio make their way down the tunnel and out of the upper level beyond the drow inner city. His silver-slippered feet didn't touch the ground once.

When L'zar caught up to walk at Cheyenne's side again, she shot him a sidelong glance. "Apparently, not everyone's happy to see the rebel Weaver return to Ambar'ogúl."

"That brooding fae is one of the outliers. I think." L'zar shrugged. "It doesn't mean he's loyal to the current Crown or that he won't celebrate the new Cycle when it turns. The second he steps inside his opulent quarters on the top floor of some high-rise penthouse, he'll be dancing himself into a purple fae sweat."

Ember leaned forward to look at him. "So why'd he try to block us?"

"Not us, just me." L'zar brushed his hair away from his face with a nonchalant chuckle. "I probably did something a thousand years ago to piss him off, and he's still holding a grudge. That happens a lot."

Cheyenne snorted. "Doesn't sound like he's just 'one of the outliers,' then."

"I'm talking about total numbers in Ambar'ogúl, Cheyenne." The drow lifted his chin with a sneer and clasped his hands behind his back as they moved through the tunnel. This one also sparked and crackled with visible light in the grooves in the walls. "Most of the magicals here are only too happy to see change, even if it comes merely because I stepped back over the Border from the human realm you and I love so much."

The halfling's eyes widened, but she kept walking straight ahead without turning to look at him. "They don't like that you were over there for so long."

"Mostly, they don't like that I was over there at all. Or that anyone goes Earthside, though it's been happening for as long as any of us can remember. By the way, let's keep that little nugget of truth to ourselves for the time being."

Cheyenne glanced at the flashing ceiling of the tunnel in exasperation. "And what little nugget is that?"

"The one about where you come from. It's not common knowledge, as I'm sure you've noticed by now." L'zar hummed a humorless chuckle. "We have to approach it gently when the time is right."

"Oh, yeah? As gently as you approached barging through the Heart so I could throw myself off a balcony for that stupid coin?"

"Naturally. That's about as gentle as we get, isn't it?" He shot her another grin and raised his eyebrows.

Cheyenne shook her head. *More secrets about who I am. I guess it's better to be keeping them this time instead of being the clueless one.*

"Stop." The urgency in L'zar's voice made Cheyenne and Ember spin to look back down the tunnel. He ignored their surprise and reached a hand straight out in front of him, eyes wide, before whirling around and slapping his hand against the wall on their left. The tunnel echoed with the smack of flesh on metal, then the wall flashed yellow light. A section of metal burst out of the wall two inches in front of Cheyenne and Ember, making them both jump back before a hollow clang signaled the sliding metal hitting the other side of the tunnel and blocking them.

Cheyenne glared at her drow father, who merely grinned and

stepped away from the wall he'd slapped, hands clasped behind his back again. "What the hell are you doing?"

"Testing my memory." He scanned the ceiling and the solid obstacle in front of them. "I'd step back if I were you."

Ember quickly did as he said, and Cheyenne narrowly avoided dropping through the hole that opened in the floor a second later. She leaped away, slamming a hand against the wall to steady herself as the metal floor shifted and folded in tiny clinking squares. When the movement stopped, the trio found themselves standing at the opening of a short stairwell leading into the underbelly of the city.

The halfling peered down the dark staircase. "A heads-up would have gone a long way, you know?"

"I told you to step back."

"Yeah, *after* you almost took my face off when you cut the tunnel in half."

L'zar clicked his tongue. "The surprise is half the fun."

"Okay, agree to disagree." She gestured toward the stairs. "Why don't you go ahead and meet all the other surprises first, huh?"

"With pleasure." The drow thief stepped forward with a little jig, gave his daughter a mocking bow, and headed briskly down the staircase.

Ember bit her lip to stifle a chuckle and shrugged when Cheyenne shot her a warning look. "At least his memory works."

"I'm not sure I trust that either." With a snort, Cheyenne stepped down after her father, followed closely by Ember. The second the fae girl's head descended below the level of the tunnel's floor, the small metal squares unfolded and sealed themselves back up to cover the hole in the floor. Cheyenne glanced at the ceiling. *Why do I feel like he doesn't have any idea where we're going?*

CHAPTER THREE

L'zar led them through a confusing series of twisting corridors and descending stairwells. Twice, they passed open chambers where magicals had gathered under Hangivol's various city levels in private. The first time, L'zar paused outside the chamber entrance and gave the three ogres inside a full bow, sweeping low over the upturned toe of his forward foot.

None of the ogres were amused by his antics. The closest one glared into the corridor and snarled before waving a huge, thickly scarred hand at the chamber entrance. A metal door slid out of the wall and cut off L'zar's view of the room with a sharp clang.

"Hmm." He chuckled and kept moving. "I expected more of a reaction."

Cheyenne rolled her eyes. "You almost sound disappointed."

"You know, I just might be."

The second chamber they passed was visible only through a narrow slit in the wall, but the magicals' enraged voices filtering through it into the corridor made it easy for Cheyenne and L'zar to pinpoint where this second gathering was held. The halfling noticed the narrow opening in the passage wall immediately. *Nobody considers drow hearing down here when all the drow have been living the high life in the inner city.*

"I say we put an end to this *now!*" A hissing, snarling skaxen woman pounded a fist into her clawed hand. "I won't stand for seeing that low-life piece of *nilsch úcat* scum sitting on the throne when the Cycle turns."

L'zar came to a silent stop in the narrow underground passage when he heard those words. He cocked his head toward the slit in the wall and turned that way.

"Shut your mouth, Raesh." A huge magical stepped in front of the opening and blocked the rest of the chamber from view. "That's bordering on treason, and you know it."

Cheyenne wrinkled her nose at the stench of rotting meat and body odor that wafted into the passage. She looked at L'zar and pointed down the hall.

The drow lifted a finger for her to wait and faced the chamber opening, folding his arms while listening intently to the argument.

"It's only treason once the new Cycle turns, Folreg," the skaxen hissed in reply. "You were singing prettily about the unending rule three days ago. Don't tell me you're changing your tune *now*."

"I don't sing." The massive shadow covering the slit in the wall moved aside again, and the thin light from inside the chamber threw a yellow line down the center of L'zar's grinning face.

"You two need to pull yourselves together." The high, nasal pitch of the third speaker's voice made Cheyenne think of nails on a chalkboard. "I'm as prepared to see the new Cycle turn as the rest of us. The Crown's had Hangivol on its knees for longer than anyone wants to accept anymore. If L'zar Verdys truly returned to take the throne for himself, I say we sit back and watch the threads unfold."

"If L'zar Verdys came here to sit the throne, he brings the deathflame for all of us!"

The huge magical named Folreg growled. "Just because he set you back a few hundred years with that flight scheme of yours doesn't mean he's here to kill his own."

"Set me back? Set me *back*?" The skaxen leaped across the chamber in a flash of orange flesh and snarled. "That blood traitor took *everything* I had! For what? So he could power some fell-damn experiment he stole from the tinkerer in Qi'woc."

"He must have had his reasons."

"He only needs one! His own greed and insatiable desire to watch the rest of us flail while he skirts by without consequences."

"Raesh, I said—"

"So it's treason! I have nothing left to lose." The skaxen woman pointed a glinting claw at the unseen magical with the nasal voice and shouted, "*You've* been spending too much time in the Goldsmile dens, Hivara. As long as those stay open, you'd be happy with a *radan* sitting the throne. If I see that Weaver scum in this city before the Cycle turns, I'll show him a side of O'gúleesh loyalty he's never seen before."

L'zar chuckled and raised a hand toward the thin opening in the wall.

The magicals in the chamber fell silent, and more than three bodies shifted uneasily inside the room. "What was that?"

Cheyenne leaned toward him to mutter, "Don't."

"I can't help it." L'zar waved his hand at the opening, and the narrow slit widened as both doors slid slowly apart to reveal the chamber beyond. "My name's been invoked."

When the doors stopped opening with a shudder and an echoing boom, the trio in the passageway looked on a gathering of over a dozen magicals, all of them crouching in surprise and wariness. Half of them had summoned attack spells in their hands, and all but one of them immediately killed their magic when they saw L'zar Verdys standing in the corridor, his arms spread wide as he gave them that feral grin that had given him such a reputation even in prophecies.

"You called, and I answered." The drow scanned the shocked faces in the corridor. "I wasn't aware there was a side of O'gúleesh loyalty I haven't had the chance to examine, but I have to admit I'm remarkably curious."

The huge magical who smelled like rotting meat—a cross between the gargoyle-like Golra and a rhinoceros—grunted. "You skaxen moron."

The skaxen woman's yellow eyes widened at L'zar, her entire body trembling as she raised a handful of hissing orange sparks in her upturned hand. "How *dare* you?"

"Me?" L'zar gestured toward himself and chuckled. "I merely want to give you the opportunity."

The skaxen hurled the ball of sparks at him, intentionally aiming for the space beside his head and the far wall of the passageway instead of the drow's grinning face. Her spell exploded against the metal wall disguised as stone and crackled across the grooved lines spanning the hallway. Cheyenne and Ember stepped toward each other in the middle of the corridor and stared warily at L'zar.

The drow cocked his head and blinked. "Come now, Raesh. That's no way to greet an old friend. They were only minor damages. I hear you recovered quite nicely."

The trembling skaxen woman shrieked in rage, her open mouth lined with fangs contorting her already rat-like face. Then she lunged toward the drow in the passageway.

L'zar danced away from her and cast a spell with a quick, one-handed gesture. Raesh careened into an invisible wall before she could set foot out of the chamber and shrieked again, ignoring the dark blood spraying from her broken nose as she clawed at the shield he'd cast around her. "I'll kill you! I swear it. I'll kill you myself! Do you hear me?"

"In a fortnight, my dear, you can do whatever you want." L'zar headed down the corridor again with an extra spring in his step. "Until then, I'd be careful about making promises you aren't sure you can keep."

The skaxen shrieked again, fighting both the shield and her fellow conspirators, who were trying to draw her back into the chamber as someone inside activated the doors to slide shut again. L'zar looked over his shoulder at Cheyenne and widened his eyes. "And everyone thinks *I* have anger issues."

The halfling slowly shook her head and shot a final brief glance into the chamber before the doors fully shut. Some of the magicals stared at her, their faces lined with a mix of disgust and fear. Then the doors clanged shut, muffling Raesh's furious screams on the other side.

Ember floated beside her as they continued after the drow thief, intent who was on stirring up trouble. "That was intense."

Cheyenne snorted. "Yeah. *That* is why everyone wants to kill him."

"Not everyone, Cheyenne." Ten feet ahead of them, L'zar thrust a slender finger in the air but didn't turn around. "Just those who think they're better than the rest of us."

"Like you?"

He laughed. "Oh, don't be so dramatic. I have a special set of skills, and it takes a rare mind to fully appreciate their scope. I most certainly don't fall into the category of O'gúleesh who want to kill me."

Chuckling softly as they came upon another branching set of corridors, L'zar pointed at various places in the walls, illuminating bright flashes of yellow and blue in the grooved metal before doors and walls in places Cheyenne couldn't see opened and closed and responded in whatever way he commanded. Frustrated shouts rose from one branching corridor on their right, followed by bursts of raucous laughter from a passage coming up on their left.

"Get back here and face me, Weaver!"

"The Crown should have killed you when she turned the Cycle!"

"Rot in the abyss!"

Cheyenne looked straight ahead as the shouted curses of enraged magicals echoed after them down the hall. The laughter on their left came from a group of yellow-skinned gremlins streaked with black grease and soot. They raised tankards of a thick drink that looked like blackened oil in a toast as L'zar danced past them.

"About time someone closed off that bridge."

"Honor, *Cu'ón!*"

"Where you goin', L'zar? You missed two other lounges back down that way."

L'zar stopped in front of the snickering gremlins and pointed behind him. "The doors to the safes are wide open. It would be a shame to leave them unattended for so long."

The gremlins started cackling, spilling their oozing black-sludge drinks all over themselves as they fell into each other and tried to raise more toasts at the same time.

Ember laughed with them, and the gremlins raised an indecipherable shout with something about a fae at the end. She elbowed Cheyenne in the side and stuck her thumb over her shoulder as they followed L'zar away from the gremlin celebration. "That sounded a lot like he was telling those yellow guys to go rob the magicals who hate him."

Cheyenne glared at her father's back as he pointed randomly at different areas in the wall and hummed a careless tune. "He can play drow Robin Hood all he wants. I'm not buying it."

L'zar laughed. "Such a warm welcome home, don't you think?"

"Not really. Do you have to screw with everybody like this?"

He whirled around and pointed at her. "Yes. Yes, I do. You have no idea what I've done and how long I've waited for this day, Cheyenne. Stop trying to ruin it for me."

She peered behind her at the still-echoing shouts of the angry magicals behind them. "This isn't how you get people excited about you being back and your daughter challenging the Crown."

L'zar blinked slowly and stopped before a final turn in the hallway. When he turned, his smile was gone. "Stop talking about any of this like you understand a fraction of it. This is *my* city, Cheyenne. It'll be yours soon if you want it enough, but I wouldn't blame you if you didn't. I certainly don't, but I suggest you embrace what's happening. You don't want to make them think you're ungrateful, do you?"

"What?"

Holding her gaze, L'zar cast another spell on the wall in front of him. It shimmered with green and orange light that converged into the four-pointed star symbol. The illusion covered by the wards fell away, and two massive metal doors studded with two-inch bolts down either side stood at the end of the corridor. "They're waiting. I did all this for you, *Aranél*. Don't forget."

Leaping backward, L'zar threw his full weight onto the metal doors, and they burst open into the main room of his secret bunker below the capital city of Ambar'ogúl. Without another word, he turned and strolled through the open doors like he owned the place.

Technically, I guess he does.

Ember peered through the doors at the short staircase leading into the room beyond. The dozens of voices inside faded into an eerie, expectant silence. "That last part sounded pretty genuine."

"He's had thousands of years to practice sounding genuine, Em. Come on." Cheyenne headed through the doors down the staircase. "We better be done with surprises today."

CHAPTER FOUR

When Cheyenne and Ember descended the short, wide staircase into the room beyond, the entire crowd of L'zar's rebels stared up at them in silence. The doors swung shut on their own with a boom.

Maleshi Hi'et raised a fist into the air and shouted, "The heir returns!"

The room exploded with voices echoing the cheer and shouting greetings of their own. Ember laughed and floated down the rest of the stairs toward the celebrating crowd. Cheyenne stood frozen on the second-to-last step and stared at the dozens of bruised, bloody, battle-torn rebels pounding their fists on the giant metal table in the center of the bunker's main chamber. "What?"

"Don't just stand there, kid," Corian shouted, waving her forward. "Get your ass down here and join us. It's *your* party."

She took a halting step down the stairs.

"First real O'gúl win, huh?" Laughing, Lumil stepped onto the stairs beside the halfling and clapped a hand on Cheyenne's back to guide her down the stairs. "I remember my first battle, halfling. Didn't think I'd be able to move again. I mean, it didn't help that I got stuck right here by a fell-damn spear, but hey." The goblin woman thumped a fist against her side below the ribs and laughed again.

"I didn't get stabbed," Cheyenne said blankly. *I didn't even fight.*

"Of course you didn't! It's shock. That'll clear out in no time." Lumil led Cheyenne toward the other rebels, who gathered around L'zar Verdys' daughter to clap her on the back and thump their fists to their chests.

"Well done, Cheyenne."

"You did what you had to do, and you did it right."

"This is the start, *Aranél*. The chains are broken and the Cycle will turn, with you at the helm."

"Wait, no." Cheyenne shook her head at the orc nodding vigorously, his bottom lip pulled down as he grinned around giant tusks painted with black rings. "I'm not at the helm of anything."

"Ha!" The orc snorted and pounded a fist into his other hand. "You already are."

Staring blankly at the far wall of the main room, Cheyenne swallowed and tried not to flinch away from all the congratulatory pats and thumps and shakes of her shoulders. *If they don't stop touching me, I'm gonna lose it.*

Standing back from the crowd beside the metal table, Maleshi watched the halfling barely putting up with all the attention. The nightstalker raised her hand again and shouted, "Sakrit! Last time I checked, you had a hundred barrels stashed in this dump."

"You been counting my supplies, General?" A huge light-gray ogre with dried blood streaked down both bulging arms turned away from the crowd and pointed at Maleshi.

The nightstalker dipped her head toward him, the stiff collar of her military jacket rustling with the movement. "You can't expect me to come back to this shithole and not seek out the most important part first."

"Yeah, you came back for the swill. That I'll believe." Sakrit laughed and stalked across the wide room. A quick spell from the ogre opened a door in the stone wall barely big enough for him to squeeze through into the tiny hidden room beyond, but he did.

Maleshi's closed-lipped smile grew as she turned back toward Cheyenne, who hadn't moved an inch while nearly every member of the Four-Pointed Star gave her a congratulatory thump. *We'll start a brand new battle in here if somebody doesn't save her from all that.* "Cheyenne!"

The halfling blinked when Maleshi called her name and bent forward through the wall of jeering, shouting, beaten-up magicals to get a better view.

"Get over here." The general waved her toward the other side of the table. "We'll celebrate this victory in what little style we have left, huh?"

"Right." Cheyenne grunted when a rebel she recognized from her last visit materialized beside her in a swarm of tiny black flecks before grabbing her forearm for some kind of comrade's handshake.

"This is where it all starts." Only a deep blackness existed within the hood of his black cowl, although his black hand was clenched tightly around her forearm. "With L'zar Verdys's daughter. I had my doubts, sure. We all did in one way or another. You proved us wrong."

"Thanks," Cheyenne muttered. "Excuse me." *I'm done. I gotta get out of here.*

She shouldered her way past the circle of rebels gathered around her, all of whom reached out again for a thump on the back or a fist nudged into her shoulder.

A goblin woman stepped in front of Cheyenne to get her attention, still cackling at a wartime joke from the snickering orc behind her. "That's something for the *Aranél* to decide, isn't it?"

"I saw you jump off that wall, kid. Wouldn't have been my first choice, but impressive all the same."

"You've already put your terms together, haven't you? The Crown won't stand on her mountain of skulls for much longer."

"See this right here, Cheyenne? Bull's Head bastard stabbed me right in the thigh. I knocked him over the balcony seconds before those walls went up. Stings worse than an imp bite, and I'll show this scar to every young pup born to my line after today. You can count on *that*."

"Like you could find a mate willing to put up with you long enough for that to happen, you big-mouthed greenskin."

Laughter erupted around her as she tried to march through the bodies pressing in on her and shoving each other too. A flare of extra heat churned in Cheyenne's belly and raced up her spine and across her shoulders, mixing with her intense physical discomfort. She clenched both fists, and a flare of purple light blazed behind her eyes. Without knowing what she was doing, the halfling unleashed a wave of dark, shimmering energy all around her. The shockwave knocked the raucous magicals away from her in a wide circle, sending those closest to the Crown's challenger barreling backward into their neighbors and clearing a ring of space around her.

The main chamber fell silent again, and Cheyenne took a deep breath. She caught a glimpse of Maleshi standing on the other side of the table before her gaze fell on the surprised expressions of the other Four-Pointed Star rebels. *I should explain that one, right?* She cocked her head and centered her gaze on Maleshi again. "I don't like being touched."

A roar of approval and victory-drunk laughter filled the chamber. Every magical standing within striking distance of a metal surface started banging on it again, and those who had been blasted into their friends were jostled around, jeering at each other and themselves.

Maleshi dipped her head toward Cheyenne in acknowledgment, and the halfling chuckled. *Not the reaction I expected, but at least I can breathe again.*

"Hell of a way to kick off the toasting, eh?" A dark-purple troll with a blood-soaked bandage wrapped around his throat pumped a fist in the air. "Where's the fell-damn grog when we need it?"

"Deathflame take your grog, Kayal." The ogre Sakrit squeezed back out of the magically hidden pantry with two large dark-green glass bottles in each hand and a massive metal barrel strapped to his back with coils of hardened rope. "If you're gonna mention that swill in my presence, I say whoever started to slit your throat should've finished the job!" Another round of laughter rose at that as Sakrit trudged across the chamber and clinked the four bottles down on the table. The metal keg followed shortly after with a heavy clang. "Don't tell me you brainless mutts need to be told to get the tankards."

"I've got you covered there, friend." L'zar appeared again from some other area of the bunker, wheeling a heavy metal trunk behind him in each hand. "Who else thinks all this would be much easier if we took down the tech-eaters?"

"Ha! Never thought I'd live to see the day when you made yourself *useful*, L'zar."

"Never thought I'd hear intelligence fall out of your mouth, either. I guess only one of us was surprised today."

L'zar's rebels roared with laughter as the drow hauled one huge trunk up onto the metal table, slid it away from the edge, and thumped the second down beside the first. He flicked his fingers at the trunks' latches, which flashed briefly before flying open. The trunks' open lids hit each other with a loud bang, and the magicals gathered around to pull out empty metal cups, tankards, and goblets.

Cheyenne reached Maleshi as the drinking vessels were passed around with more playful insults and friendly scuffles. After shrugging out of her backpack and setting it on the floor against the wall, she brushed her drow-white hair away from her forehead and turned to watch them from beside the nightstalker general, folding her arms. "The ogre brought out four magnum wine bottles and a keg. Doesn't seem like nearly enough."

Maleshi snorted. "That's more than enough fellwine to last us a week, kid."

"Oh, shit." Cheyenne stared at the green glass bottles and chuckled. "Seriously?"

"I wouldn't turn my nose up at a barrel of Bloodshine either if I were you." The general shot Cheyenne a sidelong glance and subtly nodded across the chamber toward Ember, who had been pulled into a conversation with Lumil, Byrd, and two battered orcs. "Sakrit made a good call on that one too. You might not know about it."

"Fae don't drink fellwine." Cheyenne pressed her lips together to keep from laughing and nodded. "We already figured that one out."

Maleshi grinned. "Aren't you just privy to all the nuances of O'gúleesh drinking customs?"

"Spent a lot of time in Peridosh. Where else am I supposed to go out on a weeknight to get in a barfight or two?"

"Earthside?" The nightstalker shook her head. "I couldn't tell ya. *Here*, though, for the next two weeks, you can go just about anywhere to get the same results, and you won't find a single O'gúleesh reveler trying to fight you. No war machines tunneling into the marketplace, either."

Cheyenne watched the cups being passed around and finally let herself smile. "Promise?"

"Ha. Once those bottles open, kid, I won't be able to promise you a damn thing." Maleshi leaned toward her and lowered her voice, though no one would have heard her over the rowdy conversation and the rising shouts coming from Byrd and Lumil as they argued about who slashed up more Crown soldiers. "Good way to deflect from the *real* issue, though."

Cheyenne looked slowly across the chamber. Almost all the rebels had a drinking vessel of one kind or another, but Sakrit still hadn't popped the corks to let the O'gúleesh liquor flow. "I have no idea what you're talking about."

"Have an issue with large crowds, huh?"

Cheyenne focused on Ember and the goblins again and slowly exhaled through her nose. "I do when the whole crowd's touching me and shouting my name."

"Who else's would they be shouting, kid?"

The halfling swallowed. "I don't need to be put on a pedestal, Maleshi. I didn't fight those magicals, and I almost didn't finish what I came here to do."

"Bullshit." Maleshi straightened the front of her military jacket, sending a shower of dust and what looked a lot like flecks of dried blood to the floor around her. Then she lifted her chin and clasped her hands behind her back. "You put yourself on the line as much as the rest of us to get to the Heart. Every O'gúleesh in this ridiculous bunker would make the decision to stand behind you and fight a thousand times over just to get to where we are at this moment. It might not seem like much right now, Cheyenne, but what you did today was impossible until a few hours ago. They were ready to give their lives to make the impossible happen, and they'd do it again in a heartbeat, no questions asked." The general turned to face the halfling princess and raised her eyebrows. "So would I."

Cheyenne shook her head and had to look away. "How many of them did?"

"Two." Maleshi didn't skip a beat in answering. "They'll be sent off in O'gúl warrior fashion before the end of the week. Thanks to you, it wasn't any more than two. I can't say I enjoy losing the use of my own body for an extended period of time, but it was quick thinking."

Cheyenne snorted. "I told her to call off the fighting, not freeze the whole damn courtyard."

The general threw her head back and let out a deep, unhindered laugh. "That drow bitch wants every thinking mind in this world to believe she's got everything under control, but she's as fond of stretching the truth as her brother."

Catching sight of L'zar beside the open and almost empty trunks of metal drinking cups, Cheyenne wrinkled her nose. "Still weird to think of that connection. I did *not* see that coming."

"If you'd known all that before you agreed to come here and return your *marandúr*, would it have swayed your decision?"

The halfling blinked quickly and shook her head. "I don't know. But I should've been given all the facts first."

"I agree, you should have. You deserved to know the truth like the rest of us." Maleshi dipped her chin and took a deep breath. "But we couldn't take the chance that telling you would drive you away from your birthright. That's part of being a leader, Cheyenne."

The halfling snorted. "Being lied to?"

"Letting what you deserve take a back seat to doing what's right for those you're responsible for protecting."

"Wow. You sound almost as philosophical as Corian right now."

Maleshi's smile tightened as she turned toward Cheyenne and shot her a quick wink. "I've had thousands of years to ruminate on my choices, kid."

"And last but not least!" The huge orc with the black bands of paint around his tusks stomped toward them with a metal goblet in hand. "For you, *Aranél*."

Cheyenne gave him a deadpan stare as he bent low in a semi-mocking bow, delivering the goblet with his other hand behind his back. He chuckled and stared up at her with narrowed yellow eyes until she took the thing and turned it over in her hands. Made of black metal, the goblet seemed to suck away the light around it and funnel it into what looked like rubies studded all over the cup above the long, thick stem. "I get the fancy cup, huh?"

The orc's laughter rumbled through his chest. "It's a replica. The gems are fake. Sorry to disappoint."

"Wonderful."

"So feel free to smash it at the end of the night. It's been done before."

Cheyenne couldn't help her wry chuckle as she stared at the dark goblet. *Not that many times if they've been waiting this long for something to celebrate.*

The orc straightened and fixed his gaze on Maleshi. A hush fell over the bunker's main room when the other rebels realized what was happening. Some of them nudged their neighbors to interrupt the conversation and point out the next interesting moment.

"And for the Hand of the Night and Circle," the orc's lower lip turned down as he grinned around his thick tusks, "a token of our undying gratitude for the spark of this fell-damn revolution."

Maleshi lifted her chin and stared him down. Despite the orc having at least six inches on her, the general could have been the tallest magical in the room. "Well?"

He whisked his other hand out from behind his back and thrust a mangled, glinting silver shape twice the size of his palm under her nose. Maleshi blinked. The quiet rebels around them sniggered and tried to fight back their amusement. It took Cheyenne two seconds to realize the unusual shape was a creature's skull with the bottom jaw removed.

Maleshi's nostrils flared as she looked up from the silver skull and scanned the tensely waiting magicals scattered around the chamber. "Which of you brainless morons went through my personal effects when I made my great escape?"

No one said a word. On the far side of the chamber, L'zar cleared his throat and nodded toward Corian, who was standing behind him. The nightstalker blinked in surprise at the skull in the orc's outstretched hand, one tawny, tufted ear twitching above his light-brown hair. Then he laughed and slowly pressed a fist to his heart as he met Maleshi's gaze. "My blood for the Hand of the Night and Circle."

"In battle or the bedroom, *vae shra'ni?*" jeered a goblin with his arm in a makeshift sling.

The rebels exploded in boisterous laughter again, pointing at Corian and falling over themselves in their mirth. Feet stomped on the stone floors as the rebels pushed each other around and laughed harder. Corian grinned at Maleshi, and she snatched the silver skull out of the orc's hand with a half-joking hiss. "And you sent Jara'ak to return it to me for you."

"I wasn't planning on returning it at all," Corian shouted above the howling laughter and the pounding echoes. He turned slowly toward L'zar, who looked at his nightstalker *Nós Aní* with a mocking shrug.

Maleshi laughed and stormed toward the bottles of fellwine and the metal keg on the table. "Dahal would be rolling in his grave if he saw this skull empty in my hand. What are we waiting for?"

The rebels lifted their mismatched metal goblets, tankards, and simple cups in a cheer of agreement. The general snatched one of the fellwine bottles, ripped out the cork with her teeth, and spat it onto the floor with a roaring cheer. The shouts and snarls of approval rose in a deafening roar as General Maleshi Hi'et poured a splashing stream of fellwine into the overturned silver skull in her hand. Sloshing the sparkling green liquor all over the place, she handed the bottle off to the magical beside her and raised the skull, whirling to face Cheyenne. "To the *Aranél*!"

The rebels lost it when she guzzled from the silver skull, fellwine splashing down the front of her military jacket and bubbling in small pools on the stone floor. The other fellwine bottles were snatched up and uncorked, and Sakrit cranked open the spout on the metal keg before filling whatever goblet was thrust his way to catch the shimmering golden Bloodshine spilling out of it.

Cheyenne's eyes widened at the unbelievable amount of fellwine Maleshi put away, and she forced herself to shut her mouth when she realized it had been hanging open. *Yeah, Mattie Bergmann and Maleshi Hi'et are two different people, all right. Shit's about to get real.*

CHAPTER FIVE

Once every cup was filled and the real party got started, Cheyenne found herself staring at the golden liquid poured from the keg into her fake-fancy goblet. Ember laughed at a toast one of the rowdy rebels tossed her way and approached her friend's side, grinning from ear to ear. "Honestly, I thought the fighting was crazy, but this?"

Cheyenne said, "I know, right?"

"It doesn't even seem real."

"Tell me about it."

Ember peered over the lip of Cheyenne's black goblet. "No fellwine for you either, huh?"

"Are you kidding?" The halfling snorted and gestured at the revelers with her drink. "These guys make everything we did at Peridosh look like a bunch of kids on a playground. And Maleshi's drinking out of a freakin' *skull.*"

"You think it's real?" Ember lifted her heavy metal tankard of Bloodshine and raised her eyebrows as she slurped.

"I mean, it could be, for all we know. Dipped in silver or something. Or it could be a gag."

"You should ask her."

Cheyenne laughed. "*I* should ask her?"

"Don't look at me like that. No way in hell am I going up to the psychotic nightstalker warlord to ask if her drinking skull is the real deal or a prop."

"Ha. You're forgetting one important detail, Em."

The fae girl cocked her head and shot her friend an exasperated look. "Enlighten me, then."

"You're *Nós Aní* to the *Aranél* of Ambar'ogúl." Cheyenne fought back a shudder. "You can ask anyone anything you want, and they can't do a damn thing about it."

"Oh." Ember found Maleshi in the crowd of drinking rebels. The general had propped one blood-splattered boot on the closest pulled-out chair and leaned forward over the table, laughing and drinking out of her silver skull with the others. "Still, *you* should ask her."

"I think you care a lot more about the story behind that one than I do. Might as well use your high status while you can. Your best friend's drow royalty, apparently." Cheyenne snickered and lifted her goblet in a sarcastic toast before taking her first drink of Bloodshine. She wrinkled her nose and sniffed at the burst of tingling bubbles sailing both down her throat and somehow up to her head. "I don't know what to say about this stuff."

"Like champagne on steroids." Ember took another long drink and smacked her lips. "I love it."

Cheyenne laughed and looked at her friend in surprise. Then she caught sight of Foltr for the first time and lowered her goblet.

The gnarled old raug had made his appearance at the celebration without anyone noticing his arrival through one of the dozen archways leading into the bunker's main chamber. He shambled toward the partygoers with a heavily wrinkled scowl on his gray face, orange-brown eyes blazing beneath the thick ridges of his furrowed, hairless eyebrows. The heavy walking stick in his clawed hand clacked on the stone floor, but it wasn't loud enough to draw anyone else's attention. When he stopped at the end of the huge black table, he propped both wizened hands on the top of his stick and lifted his chin. Then he cracked the base of the stick against the floor and sent strobing orange light in every direction.

The rebels turned toward him with their smiles frozen on their faces. Foltr lifted his stick and pointed at the table. "It's been a long time, but I assumed you lot were smarter than a pen of bare-assed pups still sucking on their mothers' teats. Clear the table. Give the seats to those who earned them. And somebody better pour me a drink before I have to come after it myself."

Laughing, Sakrit grabbed the last tankard from the open chest before hurling the empty box behind him. It clattered to the floor, quickly followed by the second, and he grabbed a half-empty bottle of fellwine to fill the tankard to the brim. He turned back toward Foltr with a grin. "For the ancient one."

"The ancient *sleeping* one," a troll man shouted, raising his goblet. "You missed all the action, raug!"

"I miss nothing." Foltr snatched his drink from Sakrit's hand with a grunt and moved toward the closest chair beside the head of the table. He took a moment to upend his drink in a long guzzle, then slammed the tankard to the table before lowering himself into the chair. "But the lot of you seem to be missing the point entirely. Don't make me say it again."

A cheer rose from the surrounding magicals as a select few removed themselves from the crowd to head toward the table. Maleshi slid her boot off the chair and sat where she was. Corian and L'zar approached the end of the table, where the drow sat at the head beside Foltr and the nightstalker took the chair on L'zar's other side. Jara'ak, the buzzing magical made of swarming black specks, Lumil, and Byrd joined them.

"Cheyenne." Foltr stretched his arm toward her and nodded. "I would be honored if the *Aranél* sat beside me. Both of you, of course."

"Right." Cheyenne and Ember exchanged confused glances before making their way toward the table. The halfling sat in the chair beside the ancient raug, who sniffed and nodded curtly before propping one hand on the top of his crooked cane and grabbing his tankard with the other. Ember sat on her other side and gazed at the others at the table while the rest of the magicals stood or lounged about on stacked crates, drinking and laughing in their own private conversations and ignoring the little meeting the raug had called.

The troll woman Elarit Masharun took a seat directly across the table from Cheyenne. The silver chains draping across her purple nose from one eyebrow to the other were flecked with someone else's blood, and she widened her eyes at the halfling with a small, approving smile.

Cheyenne nodded back and took a sip of her drink. *She's sitting right next to Corian like nothing ever happened. No idea Persh'al's been lying to all of them.*

"Foltr." L'zar sat back casually in his chair at the head of the table and smiled at the raug. "I know you're a stickler for details, but I'm sure this can wait until we've all had our fill of victory."

"You've already *had* your fill, Weaver." Foltr looked the drow thief up and down. "You've been having your fill since you opened your mouth for your first lie. Do us all a favor and shut it now unless someone asks you a direct question."

"Your bite hasn't aged a century." L'zar laughed and thumped his fist on the table. "I've missed you."

"That makes one of us." Foltr grunted, but a small smile flickered at the wrinkled corners of his gray mouth. "The last time the *Aranél* sat at this table with a less complete assembly, she was clueless about her part to play in this grander scheme."

Cheyenne choked on her Bloodshine and tried to play it off as choking on a laugh. "Thanks. It was that obvious, huh?"

Across the table, Elarit leaned back in her chair with a knowing smirk. "Glaringly."

Foltr waved aside the troll woman's comment and fixed Cheyenne with his scrutinizing gaze. "You walked through a river of fire to be here for our city. For this world, which is the only world most of us in this room have ever known. You know another, Cheyenne. Whatever knowledge you carry with you of our kind on Earth differs vastly from what you know of Ambar'ogúl and its history. Which is next to nothing, it would seem."

She pointed at the wizened raug and raised an eyebrow. "I *do* know the Crown is my aunt."

L'zar chuckled. Corian dipped his head and stared at the black metal surface of the table, unsuccessfully hiding a small smile. Maleshi slurped fellwine from her silver-plated skull.

The old raug grunted. "That discovery was by necessity, yes. A good thing to know. It changes nothing." He thumped his stick on the stone floor again and settled both gnarled, clawed hands over the round knob on top. "Tonight, you'll learn what you're fighting for, *Aranél*. Not because you asked, but because you are owed the truth. After what you've accomplished today, *we* owe you the truth."

While the rest of the rebels drank and laughed and got into half-playful skirmishes, an expectant silence hung over the magicals sitting at the central table. Foltr gazed at each of them with narrowed orange-brown eyes, daring anyone to challenge the decision he'd made for everyone.

"I'll start then, eh?" L'zar steepled his fingers and rested both hands on the table, leaning forward with a feral grin. "I never had my doubts that we'd reach this moment."

Corian barked out a laugh. "I believe the raug wanted to start and end this conversation with the truth."

"If you're looking for a heartfelt confession from me tonight, brother, you'll be disappointed. I don't lie and tell."

Corian rubbed his mouth, his tufted, catlike ears twitching as he shook his head. Elarit rolled her eyes and buried a smart remark in her tankard of fellwine.

Maleshi's chair scooted backward with a screech of metal on stone before the general stood, swinging her skull cup to the side to avoid spilling it on the line of magicals sitting at the table. Hooking her boot around the metal chair leg, she pulled out the empty chair on the other side of Ember and thumped down into it. She narrowed her eyes at the other members of the Four-Pointed Star across the table, then leaned forward to peer past Ember at Cheyenne. The silver curve of the skull-shaped cup didn't leave her hand. "I think we should start at the beginning."

"For the love of everything I despise, General!" L'zar thumped back in his chair. "I didn't come all this way to listen to how Ba'rael Verdys filled her throne room with shit."

Ember snorted, and when L'zar turned his golden eyes to her, she stared at the table and hid her smile with another long drink from her tankard.

Maleshi fixed her gaze on the drow at the head of the table and cocked her head. "And *I* didn't come all this way to listen to you tell me what I can and can't say in your royal presence, *Cu'ón*. Keep at it, and there *will* be another battle tonight. And you won't have your daughter to do the heavy lifting for you."

L'zar raised an eyebrow and nodded once.

"Prince among thieves, huh?" Cheyenne muttered. "Literally."

Foltr hissed and raised his tankard to his lips. Only when he'd finished drinking did she realize he'd been laughing too.

Slurping from her skull again, Maleshi met Cheyenne's gaze. "The only true beginning to the story that has anything to do with anything these days is how the Crown turned the new Cycle herself and put all this into play."

"To be clear," Corian added, "L'zar's always been a dick. That goes all the way back to the beginning."

The table erupted in laughter. Foltr thumped his cane on the floor as he chuckled in grunting bursts. Maleshi and Corian raised their drinks toward L'zar in another toast and drank. The drow joined them, his golden eyes glowing as he gazed at every face at the table.

Except mine. Cheyenne smiled with the others as they made their infuriating leader the brunt of more jokes. *He hasn't looked at me once since we sat down.*

"The drow Crown K'laht sired two offspring," Foltr began.

"Two fell-dawn spawn," L'zar added quickly with another toast to no one.

"L'zar's the baby brother." Maleshi swirled the dregs of her fellwine around and around in the bottom of the silver skull. "Which explains quite a bit, when you think about it."

"I've earned my titles, thank you very much."

"Dark Smiling Weaver." Cheyenne stared at her father, who gave her a sidelong glance for half a second before dipping his head and taking another drink.

"That's one of them, sure. *I* was referring to Royal Bottom-feeder. The Scoundrel Prince."

"Endaru's balls, L'zar. Don't hurt yourself." Maleshi shook her head and shot the drow's feral, predatory look right back at him. "This conversation isn't about *you*, anyway. Give it a rest."

"I've suddenly lost interest, then. Should I excuse myself?" L'zar scooted back in his chair like he meant to get up.

Maleshi leaned sideways against the edge of the table, barely sitting in her own chair anymore. "Ask the raug. I don't give a shit."

L'zar eyed Foltr and gave the old magical a mocking half-bow from his chair. "By your leave, Aged One."

"If you need my permission to remove yourself from that chair, you'll be sitting here all night," Foltr grumbled. "I'm not giving you a fell-damn thing."

With a low chuckle, L'zar ran a hand through his hair and sat comfortably back in the chair again. "Lovely to be surrounded by such loyal friends again."

The magicals around the table chuckled and raised a silent toast. Once everyone had set their cups back down on the table, expectant glances passed between L'zar's core group of rebel leaders.

"Don't look at me." Foltr set both hands on the knob of his cane again and shook his head. "I'm just here to correct the embellished *carako* waste bound to spill out of one of your mouths."

"You've made your point, Grandfather." Maleshi turned in her chair and thrust her silver skull in the air. "Dahal's thirsty again. Don't make my predecessor come after you. Where's the fellwine?"

Lumil turned from the group of magicals swapping battle stories and raised another cheer when she hoisted a sloshing green bottle in her fist. She trudged toward Maleshi's outstretched empty skull and poured the fellwine from so high, it spilled over the edge of the skull and splattered to the floor in a glowing green fizz. "For the general. And the general." The goblin woman gave Maleshi a mocking bow, then thumped the bottle onto the table and spun. "Where were we? Oh, yeah. Blood and glory!"

The magicals cheered as Lumil returned to the small group, one of many around the chamber.

With a self-important smirk, Maleshi took a sip from her skull, smacked her lips, and turned toward Cheyenne again. "It's our lucky night, kid. While they talk about blood and glory, we get patricide and shitty life skills."

The halfling sputtered into her goblet, then forced herself to swallow the small bit of Bloodshine left in her mouth. "Sounds like fun."

L'zar grinned and lifted his tankard. "You have no idea."

CHAPTER SIX

"As the oldest, Ba'rael was next in line for the Crown's new Cycle," Maleshi continued. "If your Weaver father ever had plans of ruling, those plans were screwed from the moment he entered this world."

L'zar thumped a fist against his chest. "With a full head of hair and an already honed sense of how to take what's mine."

"You mean, how to take what's everyone else's," Corian corrected, raising an eyebrow.

The drow shrugged. "Same thing."

Maleshi snorted. "Knowing he was born with that sense of entitlement, kid, I'm sure you can imagine your father as the little shit he was in his formative years so very long ago."

"Yes, General. Because you spent so much time studying me in my formative years."

"I did," Foltr grumbled. "She's not far off the mark."

Another round of laughter rose at that, and L'zar dipped his head toward the raug. "Well-played."

"K'laht Verdys served as the O'gúl Crown for centuries," Corian added. "As far as drow go, he had a good head on his shoulders. To this day, I still can't fathom how he sired two of drowkind's most disappointing specimens."

"I blame our mother." L'zar raised his tankard. "To Ulahel and her final journey through the deathflame."

The magicals around the table ignored the drow's spiteful comment. Corian's smile faded somewhat, but he looked at Cheyenne with his silver nightstalker eyes and nodded. "Ba'rael always knew she would turn the new Cycle as the next Crown. It was her right from the beginning, and there is little that can stand in the way of a rightful heir claiming what's theirs. Or at least there was, back when Ambar'ogúl was a world I recognized."

"Save the self-pity for after the real party." L'zar stared at his *Nós Ani,* and Corian's upper lip twitched in irritation.

"So." Maleshi thumped a hand on the table and raised her skull, fellwine spilling over her hand in streams. "While L'zar was off screwing over every poor bastard who crossed his path, Ba'rael grew impatient. It's an interesting thought, isn't it? To have absolutely everything at your fingertips, nothing withheld, and *still* want more."

"The bitch will stay true to her nature 'til the very end." L'zar shook his head. "I remember it like yesterday. The day my rotting sister told me she didn't intend to wait for the Cycle to turn on its own. As many times as I've tried to drink myself into oblivion, hoping *that* memory would be the one siphoned out of my head by morning, I've apparently been cursed into never forgetting that excellent gem."

Cheyenne glanced quickly around the table. "You think you should be joking about curses right now?"

L'zar fixed her with his golden eyes, which were narrowed in warning. "It was a figure of speech in this instance, Cheyenne."

Corian leaned away from the drow at the head of the table and eyed L'zar. "But in another instance?"

"We can talk about that later."

The nightstalker looked at Cheyenne next, who gave him a small shrug and barely shook her head. She didn't miss it when Corian and Maleshi shared concerned gazes as well. *Right. It's all fun and games in the rebel bunker until somebody brings up the literal curse L'zar failed to mention. That'll be a fun conversation.*

L'zar took a long drink of his fellwine and sucked in a hissing breath, cocking his head as the strong liquor burned down his throat and swam up into his head at the same time. "We *were* talking about me.

Briefly. And my rot-hearted sister coming to me personally to try to draw me into her secret and highly unnecessary plan."

At those words, the multiple prophecies Cheyenne had heard from Oracles and in her own dreams came back to her. *Cut out the heart. Cut out the rot. Christ, it's all tied together even as we sit here telling stories.*

"What did she say?" Ember asked, her luminous violet eyes fixed intently on the drow.

"She wanted to challenge our father before her time," L'zar replied simply, "Ba'rael had convinced herself she could do much better than the unprecedented era of peace under his Cycle."

"She thought K'laht was too soft on our people." Maleshi snorted. "Too content to let Ambar'ogúl run itself unless the Crown's intervention was absolutely necessary. Hell, that's how I got *my* job."

"You served under L'zar's father." Cheyenne gazed at the war general. "For how long?"

"Longer than any of us care to think about right now." Corian raised his tankard toward Maleshi and drank.

"Wait, wait." Ember pressed both hands on the table and glanced for a second at the silver skull in Maleshi's hand before looking back up at L'zar. "I still wanna hear about this plan of hers. She told you she was going to overthrow your dad?"

"No." A thin smile tugged at the corners of L'zar's lips. "She told me she meant to challenge him. By the old laws, of course. Her *marandúr* hadn't yet been returned to the Rahalma altar, and, I suppose, she wanted my full support."

Elarit snorted, the thin silver chains draping across the bridge of her nose jingling when she shook her head. "It worked out so well for her."

Sitting beside her, Jara'ak chuckled and widened his eyes at the troll woman's rare facetious comment. "You have a way with words, Lady Masharun."

"Don't call me that." Elarit buried her face in her goblet but looked up at Cheyenne.

"She's not wrong." L'zar sat back in his chair and looked at the ceiling of the bunker. "It didn't work out anything like what she'd planned."

Ember nodded. "Because you didn't support her."

"Ha." Corian waved his hand over the table, shaking his head.

"Ba'rael didn't give a shit whether or not she had L'zar's support. She assumed giving him that information would goad him into making a fool of himself."

"Which I'd already done a thousand times over at that point," L'zar added dryly.

The magicals chuckled and kept drinking like their cups would never empty.

"She goaded him all right." Maleshi raised her silver skull toward L'zar. "Right into making herself look like an idiot."

Cheyenne frowned at her father. "What did you do to her?"

L'zar rolled his eyes. "Trust me, Cheyenne, if I'd wanted to physically hurt my sister, I would have done it centuries ago. Psychological damage, on the other hand, is a different game, at which I naturally excel."

Jara'ak thumped a fist on the table. "You've been building up for centuries is what you've been doing. Give the damn punchline."

Ember's eyes widened as she gazed from one magical around the table to the next. "This is a joke?"

"Only in the sense that I still find it highly amusing," L'zar replied blankly.

Corian blinked, swaying forward in his chair before turning toward the drow and pointing a fur-tipped finger at L'zar. "If you don't tell her, I will."

"Everyone's in such a hurry." L'zar set his drink on the table and tipped his chair backward on two legs, smoothing his long white hair away from his face. "I ruined all her plans, Cheyenne, by returning my *marandúr* to that altar before she grew enough of a spine to do it herself."

Ember shook her head in disbelief. "Why?"

L'zar grinned. "Because I could."

Jara'ak barked out a laugh. "Just to fuck with her head. She should've been used to it at that point, eh?"

Maleshi took another long drink. "It gave L'zar first right to challenge K'laht for the throne and turn the new Cycle for himself if he so chose."

L'zar pointed at her. "That was never my intention."

"Anyone with half a brain knows that," Foltr added with a grunt.

Cheyenne narrowed her eyes at Maleshi. "You said patricide."

"I did." The general gestured toward L'zar and raised an eyebrow. "I'll leave that elaboration to your royal drow ass."

Cheyenne's father gazed around the table, then rolled his eyes. "Ba'rael doesn't have half a brain, and she never did. To keep me from the throne I never wanted, she snuck into the Heart like a coward in the middle of the night and returned her *marandúr*, then slit our father's throat in his sleep and turned the Cycle by force."

"Jesus." Cheyenne slumped in her chair and grimaced at the Bloodshine in her goblet. "And that was it? No one tried to stop her?"

"There was no one *to* stop her. I certainly wasn't going to."

She looked quickly at L'zar again. "But it was your fault."

"Oh." He feigned surprise and gazed around the table, chuckling. "I didn't realize you had any interest in defending the Crown's actions, especially not after you defied all the odds stacked against you in the very fabric of fate by challenging her yourself."

"I'm not defending her." Cheyenne's fingers tightened around the black metal stem of the goblet. "I'm saying you should have taken responsibility."

Elarit's high laughter filled the bunker. "That ship sailed long before the last Cycle ended, Cheyenne."

"And it doesn't weigh on you even a little?" The halfling's hands slid off the edge of the table into her lap as she stared at her father. "That your own father died because you wanted to screw with your sister's head?"

"In a perfect world, that would seem abhorrent, wouldn't it?" L'zar grinned back at her and spread his arms. "As you so aptly put it about a week ago, Cheyenne, I dropped a coin on a table. Ba'rael did the rest. I didn't challenge the Cycle, and I most certainly didn't guide her hand when the tip of the blade it held pierced K'laht's throat. I have my own crimes to pay for if the day ever catches up with me, but that is not one of them."

Cheyenne clenched her jaw and couldn't bring herself to say anything else about it. *L'zar's always looking out for number one, and that's it. He seriously doesn't care what he's done.*

"What about, like, trying to get vengeance or something?" Ember asked, staring blankly at the table as she tried to make sense of the situation. "For your dad. You didn't even try to step in and fight against *that?*"

"It comes down to their respective feelings about me, little fae."

"Watch it." She pointed at him, the tip of her pink-tinged finger glowing with violet light.

"I'd listen to her, L'zar," Maleshi said through a full-throated laugh. "Every magical in this room has seen what that one can do."

The rebel leaders gathered around the table fell into another fit of laughter, raising their glasses toward Ember this time both in jest and as a sign of respect.

"Look at that," Jara'ak roared. "A *Nós Aní* who has no issues taking a bite out of L'zar Verdys if she has to!"

"I'm assuming that's meant to be an affront to my honor," Corian muttered as the orc howled with renewed laughter. "Nice try."

L'zar leaned toward Corian and clapped a hand on the nightstalker's shoulder. "This one only bites in private."

Corian scowled at the drow and shrugged L'zar's hand away.

"And I'm pushing all the wrong buttons today. Damn, this *does* feel like home." Chuckling, L'zar smoothed his hair away from his face again and turned back to Ember. "As I was saying, the rest of my royally obnoxious family did have one thing in common. They were finished with me long before I ever returned my *marandúr* to the Rahalma altar. The only difference is that my father never made his lack of love for me anywhere near concrete with an official banishment."

"You banished *yourself*," Foltr grunted.

"Yes, it was all voluntary. Until a few hours ago." L'zar's wide golden eyes roamed around the table, drinking in the reactions of his loyal followers as each of them realized what he was saying.

Cheyenne didn't look away from him. *He's loving watching the truth sink in and ruining the mood for everyone. Dude's got serious issues.*

"L'zar." Corian set down his tankard and shifted in his chair to face the drow squarely. "Did she really?"

"Cheyenne was there too, you know. This is *her* party, after all."

The halfling closed her eyes in irritation. "I wouldn't want to steal your spotlight."

L'zar threw his head back and roared with laughter. "You *are* my daughter. Yes. Yes! Ba'rael banished me from Ambar'ogúl and made it official with her fancy little curse. That's neither here nor there."

"Of course it is." Maleshi's smile had vanished. "That's an important piece of information we all deserved to know the second you stepped through those doors."

The drow chugged the rest of his drink and slammed the tankard on the table, shaking his head. "This is a *celebration*. And no, I don't feel bad about *this*, either. How you choose to feel about what's happened is on each of you, not me. When I make the crossing again, I'll be happy never to return. I fell in love with the other side on the very first trip, and since we're all being honest and fucking open with each other, I despise what this side has become. I always have, and this has been a phenomenal reminder of why I stayed away as long as I did."

With that, the drow prince lurched from his chair, sending it flying away behind him and clattering across the stone floor. He swayed a little and steadied himself by pressing the tips of his slender fingers on the black tabletop. "I'll take this as being excused from the conversation."

"Stop." Foltr stretched a long, gnarled claw at L'zar.

"Say what you have to say, Grandfather, but make it quick."

The wizened raug pushed himself to his feet with a grunt and peered into L'zar's drunken eyes. Faster than his gnarled body seemed capable of moving, Foltr swung his walking stick back in both hands and cracked the hard knob against the side of L'zar Verdys' head.

The deafening sound drowned out the noises of dozens of other conversations around the bunker as every magical turned to see what had happened. L'zar stumbled sideways, his white hair flying around his face beneath the force of the blow. When he finally caught his balance and straightened, he smoothed his hair back with both hands and took a deep breath through his nose.

Foltr thumped his cane on the floor. "Now you are excused."

L'zar whirled and stalked across the chamber toward one of the dozen archways leading into branching tunnels. He waved a hand behind him and shouted, "Don't even think about stopping now, you ingrates. I'm just takin' a piss!"

Someone raised their drink in the air and cheered as L'zar opened the door with a motion of his hand and stumbled through.

Foltr groaned as he lowered himself into his chair and grabbed his drink. "He's a fell-damn ingrate."

Corian burst out laughing, that crazed, animalistic grin sharpening his features. Jara'ak, Elarit, and Maleshi joined him. The booming voice of the flickering dark magical rose above it all. Then he whisked away in a burst of black specks and materialized in front of the Bloodshine keg to refill his drink.

Cheyenne and Ember stared at each other. "That went well."

Ember snorted. "You gotta admit neither of us has any idea of what a fucked-up family really is."

"Can't argue with you there, Em." The halfling raised her goblet to her lips and took a small sip. "I'll take Bianca Summerlin over this any day of the week."

"Yeah, me too."

Catching Corian's gaze across the table, Cheyenne tilted her head. "He doesn't hate this whole world, does he?"

The nightstalker kept laughing. "You mean, you can't tell?"

"It's not like he gives anyone or anything special treatment."

Foltr laughed, propping his hands on his cane and shaking his head.

"L'zar had less to do with the way things turned out in our world than you might think. Sure, he hasn't done much to improve the situation."

"No, he went in the opposite direction." Elarit stared at the arch where L'zar had disappeared.

Corian glanced at the troll woman. "Until you, Cheyenne."

"I haven't improved anything, either."

"You have. More than you know. And things will continue to improve."

Cheyenne shrugged and stared at her drink. "Only after the Crown steps down in two weeks."

The nightstalker wrinkled his nose. "*If* she steps down."

"What?" The halfling's glowing golden gaze cut toward him again. "Nobody told me there was a loophole to our loophole."

"In two weeks, you'll bring her your terms. Once we've hashed out the details, of course. But she has the option not to accept them."

"You've gotta be kidding me." Cheyenne turned to Maleshi, not having to lean forward since Ember sat stiffly back in her chair in disbelief. "What happens if she doesn't accept?"

With her elbow propped on the table, Maleshi lifted a finger from around the silver skull and extended one slicing, glinting four-inch claw from the tip. "You get to fight again. Alone."

"I have to fight her again," Cheyenne said. "Great."

"To the death," Jara'ak added with a sneer.

"Oh, even better."

"Which is why we'll be focusing on arranging the terms in a way Ba'rael Verdys can't possibly refuse." Corian stared at Maleshi's extended claw until she retracted it with a sharp sound. "A fight for the Crown isn't an option any of us are willing to entertain, but know that it exists."

"And you'd win," Maleshi added before burying her face in the silver skull and chugging noisily.

Ember snorted. "Sounds like someone's entertaining the option."

"After the Crown steps down," Corian continued, "we'll turn our resources to washing out all the O'gúl filth lining Hangivol's streets. Things *will* change around here, but now that I've seen what's going on, it'll probably take us as long to clean up Ba'rael's mess as it took her to shit all over everything. Or longer."

"Wonderful visual. Thanks." Cheyenne raised her eyebrows and stared at the table. *I haven't had nearly as much to drink as the rest of these warmongers. Why am I so dizzy?* She felt Ember's gaze on the side of her face but couldn't bring herself to look at anyone.

"Okay, if Cheyenne's not gonna ask it, I will." The fae girl took another long drink of her Bloodshine. "Say we go back in, the Crown accepts the terms and steps down, and Cheyenne doesn't want to take her place?"

The halfling grimaced but didn't stop her friend.

Corian took a deep breath. "Then someone else will take it."

Cheyenne looked at him. "Someone like L'zar?"

The table burst into raucous laughter again. Maleshi pounded the metal surface so hard her fellwine sloshed all over her other hand, the edge of the table, and her lap. "No fucking way, kid. The last thing that drow thief wants is to sit on a dead O'gúl throne."

"Right." The halfling let herself grin as the howling laughter grew around her. "Because he could've taken it if he wanted to." *So why the hell did he need me for any of this?*

Foltr leaned toward her and cleared his throat. "If you do not want the rule the of new Cycle for your own, *Aranél*, there is a way to hand it off to someone else."

"What? You mean I can give someone the throne and say 'Here, have fun?'"

"There is a bit more involved, but yes."

"Of course there is." Cheyenne ran a hand through her hair and sat back in her chair. "Does it have to be a drow?"

Maleshi shrugged and stared thoughtfully at the tabletop. "Nothing in the old laws says a thing about *who* the Crown should be."

Corian laughed. "But show me a drow who doesn't want all the power and control for themselves, eh? You can't." When he turned his silver eyes on Cheyenne, Ember pointed at the drow halfling and cocked her head. "Oh. Your circumstances are a little different, kid."

"Why? Because I'm not full drow?"

"Probably."

Cheyenne tossed a hand toward him. "Fine. What about you then, Corian? Why don't *you* be the nightstalker to defy ages of drow rule and sit on that throne your own damn self?"

"Hmm. Tempting. Also, no."

She rolled her eyes. "Of course not."

"I go where L'zar goes, Cheyenne. You understand that a lot better now with your own *Nós Aní* sitting beside you."

Ember raised both hands in front of her and shook her head. "I didn't tell her to give *you* the throne."

"Trust me, that wouldn't have made a difference." He fixed the fae girl with a tight-lipped smile and drank from his tankard.

"Then who the hell am I supposed to shuck this whole Crown thing onto, huh? Seriously." Cheyenne leaned over the table and raised her voice. "Who here wants to sit on the throne of Ambar'ogúl as the Crown of the new Cycle? Anyone? Speak up now. I'm making a list!"

"To the *Aranél*!" Sakrit bellowed.

"The *Aranél*!" The other rebels took up the cry, swinging toward the table with sloshing tankards and cheering Cheyenne, daughter of L'zar Verdys.

Beside her, Foltr snorted into his tankard.

Cheyenne slumped back in her chair again and shook her head. "I don't want it. This is ridiculous."

"For now, this is what you have to work with, kid." Corian shrugged. "Besides, even if you promised to abdicate right now, it doesn't mean shit until we sit down with Ba'rael and turn the new Cycle officially. The old laws don't include promises made at a drinking party underground."

"Ha!" Jara'ak pounded the table. "Maybe they should!"

"Feel free to rewrite them to suit your needs, orc." Foltr narrowed his eyes at the orc with the black bands around his tusks. "You wouldn't make it past the first two words."

"Bah." Jara'ak guzzled his drink noisily and reached for the nearly empty bottle of fellwine before emptying the rest of it into his tankard.

CHAPTER SEVEN

Cheyenne frowned at the few empty seats left at the table, then turned to scan the drunken magicals around them. *Two of them didn't make it. Why didn't I put this together sooner?* "Where's Nu'ek?"

Corian blinked heavily and leaned far back in his chair, scanning the chamber. "I know she was with us."

The halfling caught Maleshi's gaze, and the general shook her head. "Wasn't the Golra, kid. You can relax."

Corian asked, "How the hell do we lose one of our own *that* size? She was right."

A furious bellow burst into the chamber, followed by a laughing L'zar being thrown across the room through one of the open arches. Thunderous footsteps followed as the drow scrambled to his feet and smoothed back his hair. Nu'ek's broad shoulders tufted with red fur squeezed through the archway, followed by her massive head and the two horns protruding from her long red hair. She snorted and stomped toward L'zar, fists clenched at her sides. The bat-like wings that looked so strange on a creature her size stretched to their full span, sending a buffeting wind across the bunker's main room that spilled as many drinks as the rebels had been tossing all over themselves.

"I'm just playing, you overgrown bat." Grinning, L'zar stuck his hands in his pockets and shrugged. "I'd tell you to work on your anger issues, but you've already made considerable improvement."

"You *are* my anger issue, drow." Nu'ek loomed over him and stabbed a huge, claw-tipped finger into his chest. "My quarters are off-limits, and I don't care if I'm lying dead in them. Got it?"

"Well, *now* I do." Laughing, L'zar turned back toward the table, his mischievous air back in full swing. "Touchy."

"What the hell is that?" Ember muttered, staring at Nu'ek's hulking form as the Golra brushed dirt, plaster, metal parts, and dried blood off the front of her leather vest.

Cheyenne grinned and pushed herself up from the table. "Come on. I like this Golra, and I'm pretty sure she likes me. I'll introduce you."

"Pretty sure?" Ember floated out of her chair and moved hesitantly behind the halfling.

"Yeah. I mean, hey. Compared to L'zar, I'm like the tame drow everybody appreciates."

Ember snorted. "Wonderful."

Nu'ek saw them approaching and jerked her chin at Cheyenne. Folding her wings behind her back, she gazed across the chamber and scowled. "Sakrit! You said you were prepared."

"I am!" The ogre laughed and headed for his secret pantry of O'gúl alcohol. "You take so damn long doing whatever it is you do after a fight. I never know when you're ready to show up."

"The only thing you need to know is that I'm here and need a drink." Nu'ek glared at the ogre until he shot her a rude gesture. Then she laughed and turned her attention to Cheyenne. "Well done, halfling. You returned to do the impossible."

"I didn't do it all by myself." Cheyenne smiled up at the huge Golra and stuck a thumb out toward Ember. "This is Ember."

"A pleasure. Not many fae come down into these tunnels."

Ember's eyes widened, and she chuckled in disbelief. "Yeah, I'm not sure many fae become a drow's *Nós Aní* and suddenly have the magic they thought they were born without, so it's a day of firsts for everyone."

Nu'ek laughed deeply and nodded. "A good day. Excuse me. I think Sakrit needs a good reminder of how easy it would be for me to rip his head off his shoulders if he doesn't hurry up with my refreshments."

The Golra stomped toward the ogre, pretending to ignore the cheers from the other rebels she passed.

"That is one seriously gigantic magical," Ember whispered.

"Not even the biggest I've seen on this side, Em, but yeah. She's pretty big."

L'zar stepped up behind his daughter and the fae girl and bent toward the space between them to mutter, "And a thousand times more reliable than the scurrying little bastards you can't keep tabs on no matter how hard you try."

Cheyenne stepped away from him and shot him a deadpan stare. "Were you planning on telling me I might have to fight your sister if she refuses our so-called terms?"

"Oh. Not necessarily."

"Come on, L'zar. Can we cut through all this bullshit of what not to tell Cheyenne unless she calls everyone out on it?" His daughter frowned at him.

He laughed and shrugged, his hands still in his pockets. "There are so many other immediate things to think about right now, it honestly slipped my mind."

"Oh, yeah? It slipped your mind that I might have to fight her to the death, and if I end up losing, the rest of you are screwed?"

"That won't happen." L'zar grinned and set a hand on her shoulder, squeezing tightly. "My daughter slapped her coin down on that altar without lifting a finger. She's got a hell of a lot more up her sleeve."

"She also thinks it's stupid to talk about her in the third person."

Chuckling, he let go of her shoulder and gestured around. "Just in case anyone else was listening."

"I doubt it. Me almost getting my ass handed to me in that courtyard is hardly as exciting as all the drinking going on."

L'zar's smile faded. "The forces that met you when you threw yourself over the edge of that balcony into the Heart did not belong to Ba'rael. Not her magic. That was everyone she's been feeding off of for centuries. *If* you end up having to fight, it'll be your power against hers. Only hers. You could take her with one hand tied behind your back."

"And you can't?"

"That's not how this works, Cheyenne. My time has passed. I'm freely handing it all over to you, and I will find that perfect combination of offer and pressure to make my sister step down off her decomposing pedestal. She can't do anything for two weeks. That's more than enough time to find her weak spot."

"You say that like you know she has one."

"Everyone does. Even you." L'zar spread his arms and shot her a mocking wink as he turned away to join the raucous party again. "Even me."

"It better not take longer than two weeks."

"You might not believe it, but I work best under pressure." He snatched his empty tankard from the head of the table and walked casually across the bunker, raising his cup at every toast thrown his way until he reached the new bottles of alcohol.

Ember leaned toward Cheyenne and muttered, "That kinda sounded like he was challenging you to find *his* weak spot."

"Yep. I'm sure if he had to pick one, he'd say it's me." The halfling shook her head and watched her father celebrating with the others like all their hard work was over and none of them had anything to worry about anymore. "I doubt he even knows what it is."

Ember glanced down at her tankard and shrugged. "I'm outta booze."

"Go for it, Em. Drink the night away with these weirdos. Who knows? Maybe all your magic will help you keep up."

"I am *not* trying to drink anyone under the table." Ember pointed at her friend as she floated toward the new keg spouting sparkling gold Bloodshine into empty cups. "Especially not Nu'ek."

The Golra held another keg in both gigantic hands, laughing at some crude joke before she upended the spigot into her mouth and drank right from the metal barrel.

Cheyenne snorted and shook her head, content to watch everyone else celebrate their first victory. Then her gaze fell on Elarit again, still sitting at the table and occasionally rolling her eyes at something Jara'ak said to the magical made of swarming black specks. Corian was now on the other side of the chamber, shaking his head as L'zar pointed at him and continued his story.

Probably an account of all the horrible things they did together in the name of chaos. Laughing, Cheyenne headed toward Corian's empty seat and sat down beside Elarit. "Hey."

The troll woman lifted her goblet to her lips. "Cheyenne."

"Thanks again for the activator."

"Oh, sure." Elarit chuckled. "Didn't take you long to learn to use it. That last message today was from you, right?"

"Yeah. Kinda came as second-nature, I guess." Cheyenne leaned back in the chair and watched the other revelers. "What the hell are they doing?"

The troll woman stared at the small ring of magicals gathered at the far end of the chamber. Lumil stepped into the center with a fist held in front of her, leering at an orc, who quickly drank the rest of his fellwine before crouching in a ready stance. "Looks like a fight."

"We just got done fighting."

"This is for fun. I know that goblin woman would say that about every battle, but this is what happens when O'gúl warriors open their bottles and get down to serious business."

"You mean, a staged fight in front of their friends is the O'gúleesh version of a drinking game?"

Elarit cocked her head and set her drink on the table. "Sure. It's evolved a little. Used to be the loser had to cut off a finger or a toe and hand it over as the victor's prize."

"You're screwing with me."

"As fun as that would be, Cheyenne, I'm not."

Not sure whether to grimace or laugh, Cheyenne watched Lumil and the orc circle each other in the ring, calling out ridiculous insults to the howling of laughter as the other magicals pushed them toward each other.

Jara'ak and the swarming magical rose from their seats to watch the games, and Cheyenne took her chance. "You know, Persh'al *wanted* to be here."

Elarit turned slowly toward the halfling and raised her eyebrows. "I'm curious why you think now is the right time to bring up Persh'al. He's safe and warm in his Earthside tech cubby, isn't he?"

Okay, so she's a little bitter. I could've read that better.

"Yeah. He's still at the warehouse."

"Then I wouldn't waste time at *this* celebration worrying about what he's doing over there by himself."

"I'm not worried about anyone. I just thought you'd like to know he wanted to be here, and he *didn't* come with us because of you."

The troll woman's eyes narrowed. "Because of me."

"You know, so L'zar wouldn't find some reason to kick you out or whatever." *This isn't going the way I wanted.*

"Why would he do that?"

"I mean, with Persh'al here, and everyone else all crammed together celebrating this."

Elarit pushed herself up from the table, and Cheyenne found herself staring at the long bloody gash in the side of the troll woman's tunic instead of her face. "I'm glad you enjoy the activator, Cheyenne. Don't mention Persh'al Tenishi around me again."

"I was trying to help."

"Stick to revolutions and saving this world from itself." Elarit snatched her drink off the table and stared across the chamber as she pushed in the chair with a metallic clink. "That's what you're good at."

Cheyenne stared after the troll woman as she stalked across the bunker. Elarit stopped once to refill her cup, then headed through one of the arched doors lining the room and disappeared. *That went well. Jesus, the magicals over here are all insane.*

The table jolted beneath her hand when Maleshi stomped onto the opposite end of it, stepping precariously over the newly opened bottles and waving her silver skull. A round of cheers and bellowing laughter rose from the onlookers. "You all wanted to see General Maleshi Hi'et's return, didn't you?"

"The Hand of the Night and Circle!"

Maleshi spun around on the table and snarled. "The Hand of the Night and Circle can eat the deathflame torch, for all I care! But Blade of the Untouched Eye? The Blade is alive and well!"

The rebels roared again, stomping their feet on the stone floor and pounding whatever metal they could find. The most readily available of that down here beneath the city was the table. Cheyenne pulled her hands away from the shuddering tabletop and caught Foltr picking up his tankard with a snarl of disgust before drinking for a long time.

Maleshi let out a wild howl, her head thrown back as she staggered across the surface. Then she drank deeply from the silver skull and snarled, "I marched through the fires of Azercól and drank from death-flame bowls!"

Cheyenne stared at the nightstalker woman stomping on the table in rhythm with her words, and the other rebels quickly took up the butchered tune. *No way. She's singing war songs on the table. At least she's not slitting anyone's throat.*

Barking a laugh, the halfling took a long pull from her goblet of Bloodshine and scrunched her nose at the bubbles that hadn't calmed since she'd poured her one and only drink.

Maleshi howled the ridiculously violent, bloodthirsty O'gúleesh song and thrust her fist at Corian when he walked alongside the table toward Cheyenne. Chuckling, he shook his head and waved the general's antics off before taking the empty seat beside the halfling.

"A part of me should've expected things to turn out like this tonight." He practically tossed his half-empty drink onto the table and slumped in his chair. "And I'm still surprised."

Cheyenne snorted. "Because Maleshi isn't usually the 'get up and dance on the table' type? Or because she is?"

"Who knows?" When Corian turned to look at the halfling, his body moved with his head, swaying in his chair. "We might not have another chance to talk like this after tonight, depending on how things go in the next few days."

"Oh, good. So get your deep, philosophical time in now while you still can."

"No philosophy tonight, kid," The nightstalker said, "I aim to drink myself into the depths of the abyss and fell-damn the rest."

"I can see that."

He chuckled and picked up his tankard again, pausing with it halfway to his lips. "I wanted to tell you I'm proud of you, Cheyenne. You did everything that was asked of you. Sure, you complained a little, but who wouldn't?"

She laughed. "You can stop the compliments right there, man. I get it."

"I'm serious. I'd stand behind a halfling who complains sometimes but follows through with everything she has any day. I do, and I will for as long as I can. It's a hell of a lot better than trying to back someone who talks themselves up too much and can't pull their own weight. Not saying you ever did that, by the way."

"I know. I'm not a big talker."

Corian hissed and bowed his head. "Am I crashing your private party over here?"

Cheyenne sat back in her chair, watching Maleshi's riotous, drunken march across the other end of the table as the rebels sang with her. "Nah, you're good. For a wasted nightstalker."

"Tonight, that's exactly what I am."

"Let me ask you something, though."

Corian lifted his head and shot her a crooked grin. "You picked a good time for it, kid. I'm an open book."

"Okay." Chuckling, Cheyenne nodded across the chamber at L'zar, who'd propped himself up with a hand on the wall and was pumping his tankard to the rhythm of the song, grinning the whole time. "That promise you made to L'zar…"

The nightstalker stuck a finger in the air. "The promise I *kept*."

"Right. The promise and the secret were the same thing, weren't they?"

Corian swiveled his head toward her and raised his eyebrows. "You'll have to be a little more specific, halfling. That list stretches to eternity and back again."

"Of course it does." Cheyenne grabbed the tankard from him and took a small sip of fellwine, squeezing her eyes shut as the green liquor burned down her throat and instantly into her veins. "Your promise to L'zar not to tell me who I really am. The daughter of an O'gúl prince. The Crown's niece and heir to the throne. That was why you wouldn't answer half my questions, wasn't it?"

Corian slowly took his drink back from her and managed to look sober enough to hold her gaze. "He didn't want you to know because he didn't want it to go to your head."

She leaned away from him with a dubious look. "Why would it?"

"Ah." The nightstalker lifted his tankard in L'zar's general direction and hissed out a laugh. "Because he let it go to *his* head. And because the asshole loves surprises."

"Yeah, no kidding." They chuckled, and Cheyenne folded her arms.

"That's the most straightforward, honest answer you've given me since we met."

"In this world, kid, the truth isn't the great equalizer all you humans seem to think it is. Well, not *you*. You're obviously not human."

"I get it."

He hissed out another laugh and set his cup in his lap. "The truth in Ambar'ogúl has to be earned. We all have a right to it, but not everyone deserves it. If anyone in this room deserves the truth tonight, it's you."

"Damn straight it is."

Corian laughed and shook his head. "You earned it, plain and simple. It won't set you free, either. Shit's gonna get a lot more complicated after this."

"I can handle complicated." The halfling cracked a smile as Maleshi thrust her silver skull in the air with a roar, raining fizzy green fellwine down on everything around her. The rebels started chanting something Cheyenne couldn't understand and the general leaped off the table, caught by the outstretched arms of L'zar's followers thumping her on the back and toasting General Hi'et's return to Ambar'ogúl.

Just as long as I don't have to turn against what I believe in. Still not sure that isn't part of the deal.

CHAPTER EIGHT

Cheyenne had no way to tell how long she sat at that table watching L'zar's rebels drink themselves into a stupor, but by the time she started feeling tired, it couldn't really be called a party anymore. Some of the magicals, like Nu'ek and Foltr, had removed themselves some time ago to turn in. Most of them, though, had drunk until they couldn't drink anymore and sprawled on the table, the chairs, the floor, and in heaps on top of each other.

L'zar filled his tankard one more time from the dregs of the last metal keg on the table, whistling to himself. He took a drink and raised his eyebrows, then walked down the table toward his daughter. Someone snorted and rolled over when he nudged them out of the way with the toe of his shoe. "Come on. I have no idea what time it is, not that it matters, but if you sit there any longer, you'll end up just another passed-out magical who couldn't pull it together long enough to find a bed."

Cheyenne rolled her shoulders and grimaced at the ache in her neck. "I think I fell asleep at some point already."

"It happens. The beds are better, I promise. Even all the way down here." Chuckling, he stepped around a pair of legs sticking out from beneath the table and waved the halfling toward one of the archways in the wall.

"Hey, Em."

"Yeah." Ember looked up from her conversation with the magical made of swarming black specks and smiled tiredly.

"I guess we get beds."

"That's all you needed to say." Ember excused herself from the conversation and floated across the chamber as Cheyenne pushed to her feet.

"We're following His Royal Highness." The halfling gestured toward L'zar and let out a huge yawn as she went to collect her backpack. Somehow, it had lasted all night without being disturbed.

The drow chuckled as he passed a hand over the door. It slid aside to reveal a passageway beyond. "Not as satisfying to crack jokes about my lineage now that you know how far it extends, is it?"

"Oh, no, it's still perfectly satisfying. We all know I'm not talking about myself."

He entered the dark passage and walked slowly enough for the tired halfling and the floating fae to keep up. "The best thing to do now is sleep it off. Which I'm hoping those other idiots can manage relatively well."

"I'm not drunk, L'zar."

His golden eyes flashed in the semi-darkness when he looked over his shoulder at her. "Not on fellwine and Bloodshine, maybe. Victory is just as intoxicating, in my experience."

"Uh-huh." Cheyenne and Ember exchanged dubious glances, then the fae girl snorted and choked back a laugh.

"Tomorrow's a big day too. Different but big. We'll take a walk around the city, huh?" L'zar pointed at each door they passed in the hall, counting them silently in his head. "You'll get the grand tour of the grandest dump this world has to offer. What you and Persh'al saw the last time was like pulling up a picture of Greece on Google Images and trying to convince yourself you've been there."

Cheyenne snorted. "Not the comparison I would've picked, but okay."

"If my comparisons annoy you, I promise that's at the bottom of my list of things to work on in the future. I want to show you the *real* Hangivol, Cheyenne. Give you a taste of what the capital and the O'gúleesh here are like when everyone's not too chickenshit to be themselves, scared of being sucked up by the walls and spat out into a bowl of the Crown's magic-sludge soup."

Cheyenne grinned at L'zar's back and stuck her hands deep in the pockets of her black trenchcoat. *Wasted L'zar sounds slightly more lucid than sober L'zar, and then he pulls out something like that.*

"And by 'be themselves,' I mean taking this city into their own hands again."

Ember's eyes widened. "You mean, like riots?"

"Of course. That's expected of every coup, isn't it?" He stopped at a door on the left, his finger frozen and pointing at it. "Let me tell you, there's nothing like an O'gúl riot. Beauty in one of its purest forms. Here we are."

The door crackled with blue light before sliding aside into the stone wall. A soft glow illuminated the room beyond, mostly hidden by L'zar standing in the doorway and grinning at the two young magicals, his golden eyes half-concealed by heavy lids. "I hope neither of you has a problem with sharing quarters for the night."

"We already share an apartment." Ember floated past Cheyenne into the room when L'zar stepped aside, her curiosity too great to ignore.

"Then that's settled." L'zar nodded firmly and turned toward his daughter. "Enjoy the rest of your night. Oh. And just so I don't spring it on you tomorrow, when we find the right time, I want to take you somewhere special. Just the two of us."

Cheyenne folded her arms and raised an eyebrow. "If you say 'father-daughter date,' I'll punch you again."

"You only *tried* to punch me last time." He clasped his hands behind his back and scanned the walls of the hall before chuckling. "Though I wouldn't be surprised if you managed it on a second attempt. I want you to go into tomorrow with an open mind. We'll go cheer and fight the power with the citizens for a while, and then you and I will take a little detour. If I'm never coming back after this, I plan to make the most of my final hurrah in this world."

She stepped toward the open door and squinted at him. "Why do you need me for that?"

"Because you'll love it. Goodnight, Cheyenne." With a small bow that looked oddly genuine, L'zar spun on his heel and marched farther down the hallway. His lilting whistle echoed behind him until the halfling advanced into the chamber and the door slid closed behind her.

"Because I'll love it." She laughed and shook her head. "Probably not."

"Okay, maybe you can help me with this one." Ember floated in the middle of the room, pointing at the massive bed along the far wall. It was draped in satin and finely embroidered velvet, and a mound of shimmering pillows covered half the bed from the center to the headboard. "What the hell size bed is that?"

"Whoa."

"Yeah. It's like two California Kings smooshed together, but it's not. It's all one fucking mattress." Ember drifted across the stone floor toward the bed and launched herself onto the pile of pillows. "Oh, my God."

Cheyenne laughed and slipped off her backpack before shrugging out of her trenchcoat. "You know what? I bet they call this an O'gúl Prince."

The fae girl snorted and sat up. "You're stuck on this whole royalty thing, aren't you?"

"I'm pretty sure I'm handling it fairly well."

"True." Ember shrugged and flopped back onto the pillows, propping herself up with cushions beneath both arms. When Cheyenne dove onto the bed from the side, her outstretched arms didn't even make it to the halfway mark. "Jesus, this bed is gigantic."

"Might as well have our own separate rooms." Kicking off her black Vans, Cheyenne rolled onto the bed and sank into the pillows too. "I can't believe we did this, Em."

"I know. This whole day!" The fae cracked up. "And you! You're a drow princess! What the hell is happening?"

The halfling closed her eyes and sank even deeper into the pillows until they formed puffy, embroidered walls around her head. "Right now, we're lying on a giant bed in a medieval-looking bunker for tech-less magicals talking about my not-so-imminent rule as the next O'gúl Crown." This time, saying the words aloud did make her shudder. "That's not anything close to what I wanted."

"I know."

"I wanted to stop that psycho on the throne from making things worse everywhere and bringing her screwed-up war to Earth."

"Yep." Ember took a sharp breath and yawned, throwing her forearm over her eyes.

"So many things make sense now. I mean, I thought this was L'zar's attempt to overthrow a ruler and take everything for himself, but it's… Shit, I don't even know. It *is* about me, and I walked right into the middle of it, thinking I could drop a coin in a fucking bowl, go back home, and call it good. Ugh." Cheyenne snatched the closest pillow and pressed it onto her face. She waited in the muffled darkness for Ember to make a remark that would pull the halfling out of her own head, as usual. It didn't come. "Em?"

Slowly pushing herself up, Cheyenne thumped the pillow down by her friend's hand. Ember's mouth popped open, and she let out a loud, rumbling snore.

"Right. Apparently, I'm the only one who cares so much about what's happening that it's keeping me awake. Or I'm the only one who didn't get shitfaced."

She had to crawl almost four feet toward the foot of the bed to grab the extra velvet blanket folded on top of the heavy quilt beneath them. She dragged it back with her and tossed half the blanket over Ember, then fell back into the mountain of pillows and closed her eyes.

I'm the next drow heir. So what? It won't change a thing about me as long as I make the right choice, whatever the hell that is.

The next morning, Ember and Cheyenne woke to the sound of hurried footsteps, shouted commands, laughter, and the smell of food cooking. The halfling sat up in the huge bed, ran a hand through her mussed hair, and quickly changed into fresh clothes before gathering everything up again and slinging her backpack over her shoulder.

"Smells like breakfast, Em."

"Right. And I realized we didn't eat a single thing yesterday after breakfast."

"Huh." Pulling a hair tie from the pocket of her jacket, Cheyenne twisted her hair back into a loose bun and shrugged. "All the better to get wasted with, I guess."

"Very funny. I will eat anything right now if it doesn't run away."

"You sure?" Cheyenne studied the closed door to their guest quarters as Ember quickly changed and collected her things too. "I told you about the last time I ate on this side, right?"

"Oh." Ember straightened, her green backpack dangling from her fingers. "You mean that Jell-O shit with the eyes?"

"Yep. And that was the fancy food."

The fae swallowed thickly and grimaced. "I take that back. I'll eat anything that doesn't watch me as I stick a fork into it. Wait, do they use forks here?"

"Kinda. Hey, did you see what L'zar did to get this door open last night?" Cheyenne pulled the activator out of her pocket and stuck it behind her ear, but the ensuing pinch and sync with her magic didn't come. *Of course not. We're in a bunker of magic only, no tech.* She dropped the silver coil back into her pocket and waved a hand over the door.

"What are you doing?"

"Trying to open the damn door." Cheyenne passed her hand over it again, then waved faster and finally dropped her hand on her thigh. "Why are you laughing at me?"

"Because you're waving at a door."

"You know, I could blast a hole in this thing right now, and we wouldn't have to have this conversation."

"Relax, Princess."

Cheyenne snorted and folded her arms. "Don't ever call me that."

"Just testing it out to see if it sticks. I know it won't." Ember stopped beside the halfling with a grin and passed her hand in front of the door. It lit up with blue lines and slid into the wall. "You might be L'zar's daughter, but you couldn't pass as a thief in any world."

"What are you talking about?"

"Sleight of hand, Cheyenne." Ember looked down at her left hand, her wrist pressed against her thigh as her fingers moved in a quick spellcasting gesture while she waved her hand in front of the door again.

It started to slide closed, and the halfling leaped forward. "Okay, I get it. You guys master spells easily." She grabbed the edge of the sliding door with both hands and shoved it back into the wall with an echoing boom. A shower of stone chips and dust rained down around the doorway, and Cheyenne turned to her friend. "We all have different skills."

Laughing, Ember rolled her eyes and followed Cheyenne down the semi-dark tunnel toward the bunker's main room.

When they stepped through the arch into the huge chamber, Cheyenne's mouth popped open. "They're all awake. *Working.*"

Ember adjusted the straps of her backpack and stared at the dozens of magicals bustling around the chamber, stacking crates, passing plates piled high with food, packing, and unpacking who-knew-what. "How great would it be if hangovers didn't exist in this world?"

Cheyenne chuckled when her gaze fell on the keg at the end of the black table, much larger than any from the night before. "Sorry to burst your bubble, Em. Smells like straight-up grog this morning."

"Oh." The fae's shoulders sagged. "I *knew* it was too good to be true."

"Did you drink too much last night too?"

"Definitely not. I was thinking about the future."

Maleshi approached them from the other end of the table, her face buried in her upturned tankard as she gulped down the entire thing. She stopped in front of the young magicals, wiped her mouth with the back of her hand, and grinned. "Nothing like this O'gúl piss to get you moving again in the morning. You want some?"

Ember leaned away from the general. "O'gúl what?"

"Nah, it's just grog. The real kind, not the shit I've heard about them serving in Peridosh." Maleshi turned and slammed the tankard on the table. "Does the job right. I heard you, by the way. We still get hangovers on this side, but the hangover cures are hard to beat."

Cheyenne eyed the nightstalker woman. "Yeah, you're looking peppy."

"Thank you very much." Maleshi gave her a goofy little bow. "You two enjoy yourselves last night?"

"In weird ways, yeah."

Ember pointed at the general and cocked her head. "You definitely had fun."

Maleshi picked her teeth with an extended claw and shrugged. "I guess it was a long time coming. I'd like to say I got it out of my system. I'm back, which I never thought would happen. Just making the most of a weirdly nostalgic situation. There's breakfast over there if you want any."

"Does it have eyes?"

The general snorted. "Not that I know of."

"Perfect."

Ember elbowed Cheyenne in the side and muttered through clenched teeth, "Ask her."

"What?"

"Ask her about the thing."

Maleshi turned her wide, glowing silver eyes on the fae girl and grinned. "I'm standing right here, Ember."

Ember glared at the halfling until Cheyenne stepped back and gestured at the general with both hands. The fae girl asked, "Okay, fine. Is that thing real?"

Maleshi glanced over her shoulder and chuckled. "I don't follow."

Ember pressed her lips together and rolled her eyes when Cheyenne didn't step in to help her. "The fancy skull cup. That was, like, a symbol or something, right?"

"Oh." The general threw her head back and laughed. "No, that's a very real skull from a very dead magical."

Cheyenne stuck her hands in her pockets and nodded. "Let me guess. His name was Dahal. Don't look *that* surprised. You said it like five times last night."

"Caught me." Maleshi gave them an exaggerated grin. "He was my mentor once upon a time. One of the fiercest warriors I've ever met, and he taught me almost everything I know. The rest of it I taught myself, and that's why he's dead. Any other questions?"

Ember swallowed. "Nope. That about sums it up for me."

"Great. Get some food while you can. When we head out of here, we're going in style."

"That's right!" Byrd straightened from where he crouched over a plate of food and slurped something noodle-like into his mouth before pumping a fist. "General Hi'et's finally getting her warlord's procession!"

"Shut up." Lumil shoved the goblin man in the back and Byrd stumbled forward, his arms outstretched to keep his breakfast on his plate.

Maleshi raised an eyebrow. "That's not what we're doing."

"Sure it is." Corian lugged a crate toward the other side of the bunker and grinned at them as he passed. "The O'gúleesh in Hangivol need to see their hero return."

"Uh, no. If anyone's the hero, it's Cheyenne."

The halfling pointed at her and shook her head. "Don't put that shit on me."

Maleshi laughed. "No procession for this warlord. I had my fun yesterday."

Jara'ak dusted off his hands after moving another crate and leered at the general from the other side of the bunker. "Should've known so many centuries on Earth would make you soft, Maleshi. You won't even take your moment, huh? It's gotta be shoved down your throat instead."

The general scowled at him. "Okay, fine."

"The Blade of the Unseen Eye returns to raze the streets of Hangivol!" The rebel who'd raised the cry ducked behind a group of magicals gathered around the breakfast spread, but they all echoed the cheer with grins and pumped fists.

Maleshi rolled her eyes. "I'm done listening to these idiots. Eat. Then we're getting the hell out of this place."

"Not a fan of long periods underground, huh?" Corian chuckled as he headed back toward them.

"Says the nightstalker who could've set himself anywhere in the world and chose an unfinished basement apartment with concrete walls." The general put her hands on her hips and stared after him with a raised eyebrow when he walked past. "That's right. It didn't take me long to find your not-so-secret lair, *vae shra'ni.*"

Corian laughed but didn't continue the banter.

"I need more grog." Maleshi snatched up her tankard and spun toward the far end of the table, wagging her finger between Cheyenne and Ember. "I'm serious. Eat something. You're gonna need it."

Cheyenne cocked her head. "She almost sounds like how I imagine most people's moms talk to their kids. I'll know there's something wrong when she starts telling us to wash our hands and not to play with fire or knives." Snorting at her joke, she turned toward Ember. "What's wrong with you?"

"She killed her own mentor." Ember grimaced. "And she drinks out of his skull."

"Nightstalkers, right?" Shrugging, Cheyenne headed toward the other side of the bunker and the strong scents of something at the very least edible rising from a table against the wall. "Still a good idea to eat, though."

"Is it? Is it really? 'Cause now I'm expecting to be handed a fork made from the bones of their enemies."

The halfling grinned. "That would be cool as hell."

CHAPTER NINE

Half an hour later, the surviving rebels of the Four-Pointed Star surged through the huge iron double doors out of the bunker and headed toward the upper levels of the capital. The stone halls echoed with their shouts and rowdy laughter, jests flying through the air as the magicals speculated on what they'd find when they reached the surface. Cheyenne found herself caught up in the excitement, not caring where they were headed first as the cheering, shouting rebels swept her along in the center of the procession.

They made their way through the underground tunnels beneath the city, passing the occasional pocket of O'gúleesh citizens meeting privately where others were least likely to look for them. Some groups cheered and launched spells through the tunnels in celebration, making everyone duck and call out jests about fighting each other after the Crown came crashing down. Some of the wayward groups even joined the procession, squeezing in on the sides and filling the passages even tighter with bodies crammed against magical bodies.

Everywhere, the whispers traveled through the halls, both toward the boisterous procession and away from it.

"It's Maleshi."

"General Hi'et. She's back."

"Endaru smiles on the Blade of the Unseen Eye."

Cheyenne's drow hearing picked up the fading echoes of surprise and awe the other magicals thought they were keeping hidden from the unwieldy parade. *They love their bloodthirsty nightstalker warlord, don't they? Good to keep in mind.*

Whether L'zar opened the blocked tunnels to them or someone else at the front of the line guided their procession, she couldn't tell. It didn't matter by the time the swelling river of sweaty, shouting, enlivened magicals burst through the final opening into the open air of one of Hangivol's outer circular levels.

Cheyenne paused beneath the pale gray glow of light muted by the dome around the city. Howling, roaring, cackling magicals streamed around her out of the tunnel, shouting and pumping their fists and sending magical bursts into the air as they followed the procession.

The lower levels of the capital were filled with chaos.

L'zar wasn't kidding about O'gúl riots.

Hangivol's citizens streamed through the open, crowded, dirty square, drinking and fighting each other, dancing and racing through the streets and in and out of buildings. From the rooftops of high-rise metal buildings around them came the clanging of at least a dozen magicals pounding on some kind of metal drums. Spells flew through the air like fireworks, most of them without aim or purpose.

A crackling ball of blue flames soared over the crowd from an upper level of one of the tall buildings and headed straight for Cheyenne. She stepped quickly aside and spun to watch the flames bash into a storefront on the street level right next to where they'd emerged from the tunnels. A second blue fireball careened into a metallic window two levels above, and the halfling whirled again to face the attacker. "Hey!"

"Relax, kid." Lumil's green hand came down on Cheyenne's shoulder and the goblin woman laughed, tossing her hair out of her yellow eyes. "Take a little time to check things out. I promise no one's getting hurt in all this. Not unless they want to. Ha!" With an exaggerated wink, Lumil removed her hand and went marching after the rest of the procession. She took off at a run when she saw two other magicals starting to fight each other, wanting to get in on the action.

"Check things out?" Cheyenne walked hesitantly after the procession and looked over her shoulder at the first storefront hit by the blue flames. Nothing was on fire, no windows or doorways destroyed, and the orange flash of protective wards reinforced by O'gúl technology faded into nothing. "Oh."

Ember floated up behind her with a wide grin. "You look *way* too interested in a shop. Fine, I can't read the symbols on that sign, but whatever it is, it can't be nearly as awesome as whatever's happening right now."

"They warded all the shops," Cheyenne muttered.

"Okay. Come on."

The halfling picked up the pace beside Ember and got a better look at the other unintended targets of wayward spells as the procession grew with every block they passed. "Em, when you hear 'riots,' what do you think of?"

"I don't know. Burning buildings and people breaking stuff and going insane. Maybe cops."

"Yeah. That's not happening here."

"You didn't expect the police to show up on this side when you challenged the Crown, did you?" Ember snorted and wiped the smile off her face when she caught her friend's exasperated glance. "Come on, it's funny."

"L'zar said there would be riots. I think this is it."

"Huh. Doesn't look very riot-y to me."

Cheyenne grinned. "I know. They're not rioting against the city, just everything it stands for. You see any metal balls flying around?"

"Like the kind you fought at the binding ceremony?"

"Yep. That kind."

Ember looked at the high-rises and laughed at a group of magicals dancing on the rooftops. "Not one."

"The whole city shut down to keep itself running while the O'gúleesh flood the streets and party."

"I feel like that would be forever ago."

"Probably."

They quickly caught up with the main body of the procession, where the rebels had taken up some other battle song and were shouting it at the tops of their lungs. Citizens of every race flooded the main avenue from within shops and homes and dark alleys between buildings, all to get a glance at Maleshi Hi'et.

"Look where they're going!" An orc standing in the doorway of a darkened building grinned at his neighbor and pointed farther up the square.

"To Vedrosha!"

"Maleshi Hi'et's heading for Vedrosha!"

The metallic drumbeats grew faster and louder as the procession picked up the pace. Cheyenne grunted when a wide-eyed, snarling troll knocked into her on his way up the parade. Ember floated sideways to avoid the halfling barreling into her too. "Persh'al didn't happen to show you this Vedrosha by any chance, did he?"

"Didn't even mention it." Cheyenne tried to peer over the heads of the magicals in front of her but couldn't see a thing. "We're about to find out."

It was impossible to tell from inside the lower-level ring that the buildings stopped as suddenly as they did about a mile inside the outer wall rising around the city. Cheyenne's eyes widened when she stepped from beneath the looming shadows of the buildings into the only wide-open space she'd seen in Hangivol.

"So we found out." Ember folded her arms and frowned at the celebrating magicals leaping and running about. The rest of the procession headed to the left across the bare ground, with nothing between them and the curving shield dome signifying the outer line of the capital. "It looks like a giant parking lot."

"No, the parking garage is outside the wall and underground."

Ember laughed. "Wait, are you serious?"

"Yep. The walls ate our ride and everything."

"This place keeps throwing punches left and right."

Cheyenne smiled and nodded toward the crowd gathering around one section of the open ground. "Come on. I gotta see what they're pulling out next. There's nothing here."

"Okay. I'm gonna call it." Ember floated along beside her friend, unable to keep her smile from widening at the sight of so many O'gúleesh dancing and whooping in the open space, clinking tankards together and jostling each other in excitement. Somewhere behind them, the drummers had come down from the rooftops and now approached. "They're gonna build a giant bonfire and burn everything that makes them think of the Crown."

"Right. That would pretty much be the entire city, and it's made of metal."

Ember shrugged. "Fine. Debunked. Do *you* have a better guess?"

"Nope."

The drumming grew louder and closer behind them, but Cheyenne couldn't see the magicals approaching through the crowd, which had doubled in size in the last two minutes. She did, however, get an open view of Maleshi standing on a large square of metal that was much lighter and cleaner-looking than the ground around it.

The general spread her arms and lifted her chin. "We're here to take back what has always been ours!"

A cheer rose from the crowd, magicals roaring and cramming closer together to get a better look.

"Come on." Cheyenne grabbed Ember's wrist and practically pulled her through the crowd. It surprised her to find a path opening up in front of her when the O'gúleesh saw the drow girl in the black trenchcoat, followed by the fae girl hovering an inch off the ground. *Do they know who I am already? Not the halfling part. That would make this a whole different kind of crowd.*

They stopped at the edge of the crowd gathered around the fifteen-foot-square metal square on which General Hi'et stood. Maleshi's silver eyes flashed in the muted gray light when she met Cheyenne's gaze. Her lips parted in a feral grin, and she stepped off the brighter square. "Blood and glory, brothers. Rip this fell-damn thing apart!"

Two ogres stepped through the crowd from different directions, each carrying what looked like a pickaxe over their hulking shoulders. Cheyenne squinted at the tools-turned-weapons. "What are they supposed to do with those?"

A troll woman with thick bands of tattoos racing up both bare arms nodded at Cheyenne and leaned toward her. "They're breaking the seal."

Ember snorted. "How nice."

"On what?" Cheyenne asked.

"Come on. We're done pretending we've forgotten. For now, at least. It's in our blood."

"Right." *And if I keep asking, someone's gonna notice I'm not from around here.*

The ogres grunted and swung the deadly-looking pickaxes at the square of metal. The weapons hit the ground with a grating shriek and a burst of sparks. Maleshi shot a bolt of silver lightning at the metal square, and in five seconds flat, the entire panel blew away like ash on the wind to reveal a ten-foot pit in the middle of so much nothing.

A crazed, emboldened roar exploded from the crowd. Magicals jumped up and down, shoved each other forward, snarled and hissed, with the occasional word of O'gúleesh thrown in for good measure. Cheyenne removed the activator from her pocket and stuck it as covertly as she could behind her ear. After the sharp pinch of syncing tech subsided, she flicked her finger beside her thigh and managed to turn down the noise before she got a migraine.

They opened a giant pit outside the city, and there's hardly any tech out here.

Lines of code scrolled across her vision here and there, difficult to see through so many bodies and spread out far more than she'd seen with the activator feeding her information in Hangivol.

Maleshi howled and drew a thin, glinting silver dagger from a sheath at her hip before thrusting it over her head. "We let that bitch pin us down for far too long, but we know the old ways. The Crown wouldn't last two seconds in here, but I know every one of you bastards can hold their own in the ring that binds us all!" Grinning, she grabbed the blade with her other hand and sliced a deep cut into her palm, hissing at the pain. Then she raised her clenched fist over the ten-foot drop and let her blood patter onto the sand below for everyone to see.

The crowd erupted in wild, animalistic grunts, hisses, roars, and bellows. Cheyenne stared at Maleshi's blood, sinking into the white sand at the bottom of the square hole. *I thought we were done with sacrifices. And it sounds like a damn zoo out here.*

She recognized Jara'ak's bellowing laughter and stepped past two other jeering magicals to get to him. "What is this?"

Jara'ak brought his heavy hand down on her shoulder and gave her a quick shake in his excitement. His hand disappeared again before she had a chance to warn him about losing it. "The true heart of Ambar'ogúl, Cheyenne. The O'gúl fighting pits are officially open again, eh?"

"The fighting pits."

"By the blood of Op'paro, I've been counting the days." The orc slammed a huge fist into his opposite palm and chuckled darkly, glaring across the open pit at anyone who met his gaze and sucking in the drool pooling around his tusks.

"Jesus." Cheyenne stepped back toward Ember and shook her head. "Fighting pits."

"Seriously?"

"Yeah. Apparently, they're a real hit."

Ember grinned. "Awesome."

"All right, bloodletters, listen up!" With her dagger sheathed again, Maleshi ignored her bleeding hand and shrugged out of her military jacket before tossing it into the magicals gathered behind her. A troll man caught it, shook it in the air, then balled it up and dropped it at his feet. "We're celebrating a new turn today."

"And General Hi'et's return to the Glinting Eye!" someone shouted from the back.

The nightstalker woman pointed in the direction of the cry. "So I've been told."

Laughter cut through the snarls and roaring cheers.

"Who's gonna kick this off with me, huh?" Maleshi spread her arms and turned in a slow circle, her silver eyes glinting as she grinned like a lunatic. "Who's stupid enough to take me on in the first open fighting pit since K'laht the Everbright fell?"

Magicals shoved each other into volunteering, laughing and stomping on the metal floor beneath them.

Corian stepped forward, rolling up his shirtsleeves to reveal the tawny fur covering both arms. The general straightened and lowered her arms when she saw him, her eyes wide with amusement. Corian pressed a hand to his chest and dipped his head. "By your leave, General."

"Shit." Cheyenne stared at them, waiting for Maleshi to unleash her pent-up wrath at the other nightstalker, given the jaded history between them.

"What do you think?" Maleshi called to the crowd. "Is Corian Vedi'im a worthy sacrifice today?"

The crowd roared with laughter and approval, stomping and howling even louder now.

"Get the nightstalkers in the fucking pit!" someone shouted.

"Yes." Maleshi held Corian's gaze and nodded toward the gaping hole beside them. "Into the pit, *vae shra'ni.*"

Corian bowed and spun to head for the opposite side of the square while Maleshi did the same. He caught Cheyenne's gaze at the last moment and winked.

Ember leaned toward the halfling, her mouth open in surprise. "What's happening?"

"They're gonna fight each other." Cheyenne couldn't help a sharp laugh of disbelief. "Like I said. Nightstalkers."

CHAPTER TEN

By the time Maleshi Hi'et and Corian Vedi'im dropped into the fighting pit, the crowd of Hangivol's lower-level citizens had quadrupled. Magicals spilled across Vedrosha, the flat, open area at least the size of a football field. Many climbed onto the surrounding rooftops for a better view. Those who could fly or levitate did so, and the others got creative with stacking crates or unleashing their tech into the air to view the fight for them.

Cheyenne scanned the crowd, her activator highlighting the different tech pieces worn and operated by the O'gúleesh of Hangivol. Most of them were basic models compared to hers. *Makes sense. Elarit said she modified this one herself.*

A swarm of floating metal orbs headed toward Vedrosha from the inner circles of the city. Cheyenne watched them carefully, but the other magicals either didn't notice or weren't that concerned. When the halfling's activator picked up the data stream from the flying orbs, though, it made sense.

These aren't tech-dark like the Crown's police spheres.

With a quick flick of her finger to select the activator's offered command, Cheyenne's sight magnified the data streams flowing through the orbs as the blinking blue and yellow lights in the metal spheres rotated in multiple directions, capturing everything down here outside the O'gúl fighting pits.

So the fancy magicals in Upper Tech want to be part of this without leaving their shining upper-class streets. Might be as united as these guys are gonna get today.

The self-appointed drummers scattered throughout the crowd and produced deep, booming echoes from every direction around the open pit. Cheyenne stared down into the drop as Maleshi and Corian circled each other, grinning, and the gathered magicals erupted in a crazed chant punctured by snarls and bellows, feet stomping in rhythm with the drums.

The general spread her arms and extended glinting silver four-inch claws from all ten fingers. "I'm glad it's you, *vae shra'ni.*"

Corian crouched and extended his own claws, his silver eyes burning into hers. "I've been waiting a very long time for this."

"To get your ass kicked and finally settle everything between us? Oh, yeah. I know."

Cheyenne shoved her hands into her pockets to hide her clenched fists, despite the thousands of spectators who were coming undone in their excitement in much more obvious ways than clenched fists.

"Hey, you okay?" Ember leaned toward the halfling with a concerned frown.

"Not really." Cheyenne couldn't take her eyes off the nightstalkers circling each other in the pit. "You've seen a nightstalker fight before, right?"

"Briefly, yeah. I mean, I was a little busy trying not to get killed." Ember's chuckle stopped short when she realized how tense Cheyenne was. "From what I've seen, this'll be good."

Cheyenne gritted her teeth. "They're gonna kill each other."

"No way. This is all just for fun." Ember glanced at the hissing, growling, stomping spectators and cocked her head. "I think."

The pounding drumbeats had become such a part of the background out here in Vedrosha that when the drummers stopped all at once, it was startlingly silent.

The nightstalkers took their cue and began the fight. Silver flashes erupted from within the pit as Maleshi and Corian slipped into enhanced speed and raced toward each other, to the crowd's rising cries of approval. Cheyenne couldn't help herself. She slipped into drow speed to watch the nightstalkers fight so she could follow it.

Maleshi's swiping claws came down toward Corian's face, and he raised his own to block her attack, resulting in a shower of sparks when their natural weapons collided. Grinning, the general disengaged and sent a swift kick with the sole of her boot into Corian's chest. He flew backward across the pit and out of enhanced speed, his back slamming against the metal wall as sprays of sand burst on either side of him and hung suspended in the air. Then Maleshi dropped into regular speed, and Cheyenne was the only one watching a fight that hadn't yet continued.

This is ridiculous.

She fell into regular time again, and the roar of the crowd crashed back in. Corian finished thudding against the far wall as the sand fell back to the bottom of the pit and the flash of silver nightstalker light faded. He dropped into a crouch, the tips of his blade-like claws pressing gently into the sand as he stared up at Maleshi and chuckled.

The general spread her arms and gazed at the crowd with battle fire raging behind her silver eyes. The O'gúleesh magicals roared with primal excitement. Two separate fights broke out in the crowd away from the pit, but they were quickly dispelled so the spectators could focus their attention on the nightstalkers in the pit.

"Blade of the Unseen Eye! Blade of the Unseen Eye!" The chant grew louder and Maleshi snarled in appreciation, soaking it all in.

Corian sped toward her again in a brilliant silver flash, preceded by a burst of lightning crackling across the sand. In that split second, Cheyenne forced herself not to slip into drow speed again. *I can't keep up with this anyway.*

The nightstalkers' streaks converged, then Maleshi stopped on the other side of Corian, one arm wrapped around his middle with her claws pressed against his belly, the other hand holding the tips of her deadly blades against his exposed throat. She hissed in his ear and pushed him away.

The crowd went wild.

Corian spun and leaped toward her again, sending blinding streaks of silver lightning at her as he charged. Maleshi deflected each attack with a swipe of her claws, her eyes widening as a crazed laugh escaped her open-mouthed grin. Then Corian was on her again, slashing and swiping too quickly to follow without going into enhanced speed. The general blocked every attack, sparks flying up second after second as the air filled with the shriek and clang of nightstalker claws meeting, scraping against each other, and freeing themselves.

He ducked her next swing, blocked a second with his forearm, then brought his left hand slicing down toward her face and leaped away.

A lock of black hair separated from those hanging over her shoulders and drifted to the ground, scattering into individual hairs across the sand. Maleshi looked down at the hair he'd sliced from her head and grinned. "That's a first."

"First time for everything, *ma gairín.*" Corian crouched again in a ready stance and jerked his chin at her.

With a dark chuckle, Maleshi advanced again, and this time, she didn't hold back.

The general's silver streaks of light flashed in strobing brilliance as she slipped in and out of enhanced speed too quickly for Corian to follow. Five seconds later, he was meeting her nightstalker speed as nothing more than a defensive tactic, but General Hi'et was too quick. Unbelievably quick.

She darted around him again and again, pausing in regular time for half a second to give the spectators the show they wanted. A spray of blood erupted from Corian's back, and he staggered forward, roaring. The next second, Maleshi's dark fist cracked against the side of his face. Corian toppled sideways, and she reappeared on his right to slash his thigh and spray more blood across the sand before shoving him in the opposite direction.

Corian limped in a circle, blinking in and out of his brilliant silver speed to catch her. But he couldn't.

Over and over again, Maleshi darted around her opponent, claws glinting in the muted light one second, more blood spraying from a new wound somewhere else on Corian's body the next.

She is gonna kill him.

Cheyenne found L'zar standing at the edge of the pit, arms folded and a satisfied smirk on his face as he watched General Hi'et demolish his *Nós Aní* in the ring.

He's loving this. Of course he is. He doesn't give a shit about anyone else.

The halfling looked urgently back down into the pit in time to see Corian drop to his knees in the sand, snarling, his chest heaving as he raised his arm to feebly block Maleshi's next downward swing. She darted in a bright flash to his other side and sliced her claws across his ribs. Corian roared and lurched away, but Maleshi appeared in front of him again in the blink of an eye, claws retracted, and sent a vicious uppercut into the underside of Corian's chin. His eyes rolled back as he skidded on his back across the sand.

The crowd cheered and bellowed their approval, stomping and screaming the general's name. Maleshi ignored them all and tossed her hair out of her eyes, laughing through panting breaths as she stalked toward a prone Corian on the pit floor.

No way. Cheyenne's jaw ached from how hard she'd clenched it. *No way he is going to keep going after that.*

The general set one foot on either side of Corian's body, then dropped to her knees and straddled his chest. He coughed through a trickle of blood spilling from the corner of his mouth. Maleshi's claws extended again, and she pressed their tips into the side of his neck at the jugular. "Do you yield, *vae shra'ni?*"

Corian let out a gurgling laugh that turned into a cough. He lifted one hand to her thigh beside his chest and gave it a little squeeze before picking his head up off the sand as far as he could. "Are you kidding? Finish it."

His head thumped back into the sand with another wet, dangerously choking laugh. Maleshi's lips twitched as she grinned down at him with battle-crazed eyes.

"Maleshi!" Cheyenne shouted.

Whether the general heard the cry above the roar of the spectators didn't matter. Maleshi drew her claws across Corian's throat, the crowd lost it, and Cheyenne roared in fury and horror.

Instantly, General Hi'et leaped to her feet as Corian's blood spilled into the sand and went quickly to the closest wall of the pit. She pounded it with her fist, and a tall drawer slid out of the wall toward her. From it, she withdrew a thick torch of black metal that flared to life with green fire the second it left the drawer. Laughing, Maleshi thrust the torch in the air and screamed, "The O'gúl deathflame, brothers and sisters. For blood and glory!"

Then she swiped the eerily flickering flames of green and black across Corian's body and stepped back. His body erupted in flames, consuming him until the center of the pit was filled with green and black, turning the fallen nightstalker into a pillar of flame shooting four feet above the walls of the pit.

"What the fuck!" Cheyenne pushed magicals aside as she raced toward L'zar. "How can you just stand there? Do something!"

L'zar slowly removed his gaze from the flames, shot her a brief glance, and lifted a hand for her to wait.

"Fuck you." Cheyenne spun toward the edge of the pit, meaning to leap down into it.

Her father's cold, slender fingers clamped around her wrist and jerked her back.

"Let go of me!"

"Just wait." L'zar's golden eyes were filled with a calm but fierce warning. "Watch, Cheyenne. This is important for you to see."

"To watch him die?" She jerked her wrist from his grasp and turned to face the blazing pit again. L'zar's hand settled on her shoulder instead, maybe as a warning, maybe to hold her in place. Cheyenne didn't try to shrug it off this time because she saw movement in the flames.

The green and black fire spewed higher into the air, illuminating the faces around the pit with an eerie green glow. A warm wave of heat and magical energy passed through the crowd and funneled deep underground, spreading around everyone and beyond the city limits. The spectators chanted and stomped their feet in rhythm again, tossing their heads back to howl at the sky as they watched the green blaze intently.

The deathflame shrank, flickering slowly until it died and winked out. In its place stood Corian, palms turned outward and slightly raised beside his thighs, his eyes closed. A hush fell over the crowd when they saw him standing unscathed in the center of the pit.

Then the nightstalker's eyes flew open and settled on Maleshi. "Blood and glory."

She threw her head back and laughed before jumping up the wall out onto the flat ground, surrounded by cheering O'gúleesh. Then she spun and reached back down to help Corian up and out. Hands clapped his shoulders and back as the nightstalkers clasped forearms and grinned at each other.

"Think you got it out of your system?" he asked.

"Maybe. Maybe not." Maleshi squeezed his hand even tighter and cocked her head. "The pits are open now, *vae shra'ni*. We'll just have to let things play out."

Laughing, Corian released her and headed around the open pit toward L'zar and Cheyenne. The halfling stared at him in disbelief, a chill racing down her spine even as her eyes told her he was fine.

She slit his throat. She killed him. And the fire?

L'zar and Corian clasped forearms and shared a brief, sturdy hug, slapping each other on the back. The drow chuckled. "Looks like you needed that."

"Maybe I did." Corian turned toward Cheyenne and raised his eyebrows. "You're looking a little pale even for a drow, kid."

Cheyenne looked him up and down. "You're okay."

"Better than okay. I know you felt it. The deathflame."

"I don't know what the hell I felt." She lurched toward him and grabbed his arms, staring at the spot on his neck Maleshi had sliced open minutes before. A hard lump formed in her throat, and she forced it away as she stared at the nightstalker. "I thought you were dead."

"I could have been. If I'd yielded." Corian tapped the underside of her arms and cocked his head. "I'm pretty sure this is the closest you get to giving hugs, but you're digging into my arms."

"Shit. Sorry." She released him immediately and ignored L'zar's laughter. All around them, the liberated magicals got back to their celebration. The drums kicked up again, and the sound of metal slicing through metal ripped through the air as the metal covers over the other five fighting pits in Vedrosha were ripped off and destroyed. Cheyenne ignored it all. "Will someone please tell me what the hell happened? I can't wrap my head around this."

Smiling, Corian stood beside her and looked down into the fighting pit. "That was the deathflame, kid. One version of it, at least. You might say it's a kind of lifeforce running through this world. Keeping us sane. Whole."

She snorted. "You didn't look whole when you were bleeding out in the sand."

"That's part of the tribute." Corian tugged his rolled-up shirtsleeves back down over his arms. "The fighting pits have been fueling the life-force magic of Ambar'ogúl since the beginning. We fight. We spill each other's blood in the pits. Those of us willing to walk through the death-flame heal the land, which heals us in turn."

"Wait." Cheyenne scanned the sandy bottom of the pit, from which Corian's dark blood was gone without a trace. "Fighting. That's what keeps this entire world running?"

"Something like that, yeah. In the pits, at least. We all get an extra boost when a fighter refuses to yield and chooses the deathflame instead."

"And you have to almost *die* for that to happen?"

"It varies." Corian chuckled. "Maleshi doesn't end any battle without giving the people a good show."

"Jesus." Cheyenne rubbed her mouth and stared at the perfectly white sand.

Laughing and cheering with the other citizens around them, Maleshi joined Cheyenne and Corian and thumped a hand down on the nightstalker man's shoulder. "What a way to kick off these two weeks, huh?"

"It's relatively satisfying, sure."

Maleshi grinned at Cheyenne. "What do you think?"

"I think you're all insane."

"Ha! Probably. But we stay true to who we are, and that might make us saner than anyone else. That bitch should never have sealed these up."

Cheyenne frowned and glanced at the magicals dancing past them, whooping and roaring in excitement as they headed toward the other open pits to watch more fights. "That added to the mess the Crown made of this place, didn't it?"

"Oh, you told her?" Maleshi shot Corian a sidelong glance, and he dipped his head in humble acknowledgment. "I bet he didn't mention who came out of that fight with another victory under his belt, huh?"

"*Corian* won the fight?" Cheyenne's eyes widened as she glanced at them.

"I would have if he'd yielded. He never does." Maleshi tossed her dark hair out of her face and folded her arms. "Takes a lot of balls to get your ass whooped by an opponent and then *again* by the deathflame. The victory's his. I'd say he earned it."

"How does that even work?"

Corian cocked his head and grinned at the halfling. "Imagine the darktongue salve spread all over your body, kid."

"Yeah, I remember when that happened pretty clearly, thanks."

"And *inside* your body. Swimming through your veins and up into your head. If you're willing to choose that for the benefit of Ambar'ogúl."

Cheyenne nodded slowly and glanced into the pit again. "Of course you get the victory."

"Cheyenne."

She looked at Maleshi, who was smiling at her. "What?"

"You look a little pale."

Cheyenne rolled her eyes. "That's what happens when nobody tells me not to worry about my friends trying to kill each other. Hey, leave it up to the green flames turning Corian into a bonfire. No big deal."

"Okay." Corian chuckled. "Admittedly, we could have prepared you for that. Can't blame us too much for getting caught up in the moment."

"That's what you call it, huh?" Cheyenne snorted. "I almost lost it."

"I appreciate the sentiment, kid, however unnecessary."

"Obviously."

Maleshi lifted her chin and studied Cheyenne. "I'm more interested that she called us friends."

The halfling brushed away locks of white hair that had fallen out of her bun and folded her arms. "Yeah, don't let it go to your head. You're already swimming in deathflame insanity."

The nightstalkers burst out laughing.

"Come on. The whole day's a celebration, Cheyenne. Might as well make the most of it." Corian turned and nodded in the direction of the crowd swarming toward the other newly opened fighting pits. "Maybe you'll appreciate our O'gúl brand of beauty if you're not worried about two friends killing each other in the ring."

"That's a hell of a maybe." With a final glance into the pit beside them, Cheyenne followed the nightstalkers toward the other pits to join the celebration. *This world is ass-backward sometimes, but those two are looking especially chummy right now.*

"Cheyenne!" Ember floated through the streaming magicals, grinning and shaking her hands beside her head in excitement. "Did you *see* that?"

"Corian getting his throat slit? Totally."

"Oh, my God. That was amazing!" Ember laughed when Cheyenne scowled at her. "Not that Corian got this throat slit. That part sucks. I mean the fight. The fire. All of it. *That's* the fucking deathflame!"

"Apparently, yeah." Despite her shock, Cheyenne couldn't help but laugh at her friend's passionate reaction. "*You* look like you're enjoying yourself."

"Of course I am! Come on, don't tell me you don't feel all this. I don't even know what to call it." The fae pointed at her friend and chuckled. "Happiness isn't the right word, but holy shit."

"They're free, Em."

"Yeah. I think I was going for 'connected,' but free works too. This whole thing is a lot bigger than I thought. What you did yesterday. Ah!" Ember pumped a fist and bobbed over the heads of the crowd before settling back down into her hovering position an inch above the metal floor.

"Was that a jump?"

Ember rolled her eyes. "I'm still working on that part. Doesn't quite feel the same as doing it with my own leg muscles, but I can't complain."

Laughing, Cheyenne moved through the crowd with her friend, leaning away when Ember let out a shout of excitement with everyone else. *Guess battle rage is contagious on this side. Can't be all that bad as long as nobody takes it too far.*

CHAPTER ELEVEN

A goblin and what looked like a giant hamster with bat wings and fangs got the first fight in the closest re-opened pit. The crowd of celebrating magicals had split among the six fighting pits in Vedrosha to watch the show. Others left the excitement to take to the streets of the lower levels again, dancing and drinking and celebrating in their own way now that they'd been satisfied by watching the first pit fight in centuries.

Cheyenne grimaced at the flying hamster thing darting around the goblin. "Any idea what *that* is?"

Ember grinned at her and shrugged. "Who cares? They're about to start!"

The fae girl pumped her fists, surprisingly into the fight and the raucous energy spilling through Hangivol. Cheyenne shoved her hands in her pockets and found herself studying the magicals around her fulfilling some primal O'gúleesh instinct. *Instinct for madness. That was the legacy I claimed yesterday with that damn coin.*

A hand settled lightly on her shoulder, and she turned to see L'zar behind her, gazing over her head at the crowd. "Perfect time for us to slip away, Cheyenne. They won't even notice we're gone. Come on."

"Yeah, okay." *Pretty much anything sounds better than being caught up in this right now.* Cheyenne nudged Ember's arm. "Em."

"Yeah." The fae girl turned her head but didn't look away from the fight.

"I'm stepping out with L'zar for a second."

"Yeah, sounds good. Have fun." Ember roared with everyone else when the magicals started fighting. "Get him!"

Cheyenne slipped away from her friend and followed L'zar's tall, erect figure as he practically floated through the spectators without a levitation spell. The magicals parted around them as they made their way out of Vedrosha and back into the main metropolis of the lower levels. *Like they know we're coming and step away without even seeing us. I bet he's got some kind of spell for that too.*

When they emerged from the crowd, L'zar paused to let her catch up. He rolled his shoulders, took a deep breath, and smoothed his hair away from his face before it fell around his shoulders again. "Gets loud out there, doesn't it?"

"I didn't think you'd have a problem with crowds."

He cast her a sidelong glance. "Only when they stop serving a purpose. This way."

They walked down the main avenue circling the lower level, where O'gúleesh freely brawled, drank, danced, and gathered in the street without fear of the Crown's ever-watchful gaze. A yellow-skinned gremlin leaped in front of them, cackling, and removed a ratty top hat from his head of frazzled gray hair. "A drow in Ritfarrin." The gremlin bowed low, leering up at L'zar and Cheyenne.

"And a gremlin." L'zar mocked the other magical's low bow, wiggling his head in lieu of removing a hat.

The gremlin cackled again and raced away from them, firing green sparks into the sky.

L'zar chuckled. "I like the ones who don't bother to remember who I am."

"Because they either love you or hate you, right?"

"Or they make fun of a drow in the lower levels and count themselves lucky to get away with it." L'zar clasped his hands behind his back and walked swiftly down the avenue. "Have you been to the Goldsmile dens?"

"I've seen them." Cheyenne stared at his profile and slowly shook her head. "If you're taking me to a drug den in the middle of an O'gúl riot, I'd rather jump into one of those fighting pits."

"Good. If you were anyone else, I might have given you the option of trying out one of Hangivol's finer vices. I hear the service has improved since the last time I was here."

"Yeah, because everyone's getting wasted on whatever they can to forget about how shitty things are."

"How shitty things *were*." L'zar raised an eyebrow when he glanced down at her. "You're changing all that now."

"I'm not doing anything."

"Really?" He swept his arm in a wide gesture toward the celebrating streets, every store empty or nearly empty as Hangivol's citizens forgot their everyday grind to revel in the turning of the new Cycle. "Does this look like nothing to you?"

"This looks like magicals taking a hard-won break from being ground into the dirt by the drow who are supposed to protect them."

"And *you* are changing all that." L'zar kept moving, dipping his head and smiling at the magicals who crossed their paths.

A hunched ogre wearing more scars than clothing stepped out a doorway in the shadows between the metal buildings and held out a sealed flask. He wiggled it so they'd hear the liquid sloshing and leered at them. "Two drow beyond the Heartland, eh? Either of you care for a little augur spice?"

"Ooh. Tempting." L'zar danced away from the ogre with a little bow, then peered into the darkened doorway behind the magical. "You open for business?"

"Making the most of this fortnight before we see how the Cycle turns." The ogre chuckled darkly. "You're welcome to come in and look around."

"Hmm." L'zar bit his lip, paused, then shook his head. "Another time, perhaps. I know where to find you."

"You always do." The ogre bowed at the waist and disappeared into the darkened doorway again.

Cheyenne watched until even his bright yellow eyes disappeared, then hurried to catch up with her father. "I'm gonna take a wild guess here and say he was hawking illegal stuff."

"That wasn't hawking, Cheyenne. That was astutely seizing a business opportunity." L'zar said, "He's a darkseller. Deals in stolen items."

"Oh, so you'd be a regular customer, then."

"Stolen *organic* items."

She snorted. "What, like nightstalker blood and gremlin toes? Maybe skaxen whiskers just for fun?"

"Don't be ridiculous. Skaxen whiskers are useless."

"You're serious."

They veered around three brawling trolls on the side of the street, and L'zar looked over his shoulder to watch them a little longer before facing forward again. "Of course I'm serious. You hit the other two right on the head, though."

Gross. Cheyenne grimaced and tried not to think about a jar of severed yellow toes being rattled around in the ogre's hand instead of the flask.

L'zar stopped abruptly, leaned back, and peered into another dark alley between buildings. "Here we are."

He didn't wait for her to realize he'd doubled back, and Cheyenne spun to look for him before catching a fleeting glance of his white hair disappearing. Rolling her eyes, she hurried after him. "You gotta give me a heads up before you disappear into dark spaces."

"You won't need a heads up if you keep up." L'zar turned another corner, winding his way through the maze of dark alleys.

Gritting her teeth, Cheyenne jogged to catch up with him and had to keep jogging so she wouldn't lose him after every turn. *How can he be moving this fast and walking normally at the same time?*

Her activator pulled up fewer and fewer data streams from within the metal walls as they moved deeper into the lower levels. Then L'zar stopped beside a wall on their right and reached out to press his hand against it. Metal sections peeled away beneath his touch, clinking and folding together like a slinky made of square pieces before a doorway revealed another covered dark passage beyond.

Cheyenne looked at the thin lines of gray light filtering through the tops of the buildings around them. "We couldn't have walked here from the *outside?*"

"What, you don't enjoy navigating a maze?" L'zar gestured toward the opening. "You get points for a keen sense of direction, Cheyenne, but this does *not* lead back to the outer limits."

She eyed the dark passage and lifted her chin. "Where does it lead?"

"I'm about to show you, aren't I? Hurry up. The wall won't stay open much longer." He stepped into the passage, and the metal pieces started to unfold and close up the hole.

Cheyenne leaped forward and squeezed through the moving pieces with half a second to spare before the wall sealed once more. A ball of pale violet flames burst to life in L'zar's hand to light the way for them as they continued down another series of twisting, turning corridors. Shadows danced across the walls, and Cheyenne slid her hand along them when she realized the activator wasn't picking up anything here. *Feels like stone.*

"No tech in the walls down here, huh?"

"No magicals, either." L'zar lifted his hand to illuminate the walls, peering closely at one before continuing. "No one wants to go where we're going."

"Oh, wonderful."

He chuckled. "Why waste technology on a place you know no one's going to visit? Of course, there's not much on the outside stopping others from getting *in*."

Cheyenne rolled her eyes. "Right. Just what's on the inside that makes them wanna stay *out*. Care to enlighten me about that?"

"Not really."

The tunnel headed slightly downward but nowhere near as far as the tunnels leading into the Four-Pointed Star's secret bunker. Then L'zar snuffed out the purple flames in his hand and exited the tunnel, stepping aside to let Cheyenne through.

"Whoa."

They stood in a small courtyard made entirely of black stone. It looked much like the courtyard in the heart of the Crown's fortress, but this one was the size of a small house. Two twisted, gnarled trees grew from the cracked stone floors, their branches coiling in every direction. From the branches hung potted plants, tendrils, and leaves overflowing from the tops in shriveled black threads. Bottles of dark-colored glass dotted the courtyard, filled with shimmering liquids and lights of every color, though they were all muted and tinged with a darkness that made Cheyenne's skin crawl.

"Looks like someone failed at their gardening attempts."

"Not at all." L'zar clasped his hands behind his back again and walked slowly across the courtyard, reaching up with one extended finger toward the closest potted plant hanging from a tree branch. The shriveled black vine pulsed with sickly green light like an electrical current and lifted away from the pot toward L'zar's finger. He smiled thinly and removed his hand before the plant could make contact. "This is how they're supposed to be. The magical responsible for flora in here is very good at what she does."

"So." Cheyenne turned slowly around, eyeing the dark corners of the courtyard and the tattered, frayed black cloth draped over one wall. "Who is this magical, exactly?"

L'zar chuckled softly. "I wouldn't call her a friend, but if there's one magical in this fell-damn world my sister truly fears, it's Ur'syth."

"Ur'syth?"

"Say it three times, and she'll appear in front of us."

She snorted. "They let you watch *Beetlejuice* in Chateau D'rahl?"

L'zar merely smiled and turned to casually stroll across the courtyard.

Cheyenne followed him, ducking when the branches of the gnarled tree shivered and creaked, reaching out toward her. "What does she do?"

"All sorts of things, Cheyenne. Be quiet." L'zar peered into a dark corner of the courtyard, then straightened and turned slowly around again. "Ur'syth! Dark Mother. I can't say I expected to find you in the Heart, but I'm sure you didn't expect me to find you here either, did you? Come out and see what I've brought with me." He stuck his hands in his pockets and shot Cheyenne a playful wink.

She stepped away from the tree, scowling at it as the branches returned to their original positions. *This better be one of those quick in-and-out visits. I like creepy stuff, but this takes it to a whole new level.*

CHAPTER TWELVE

"Ur'syth?" There was laughter in L'zar's voice as he strolled across the courtyard. "I'll summon you if I have to, but we both know you and I are past that point. Don't keep me waiting too long."

The black cloth hanging over the wall whipped in a wind that didn't blow through the rest of the courtyard. L'zar's eyes widened when he saw the fabric move. He met Cheyenne's gaze and nodded toward the tattered black sheet before it billowed out into the courtyard as if the wind came from the wall itself.

"You're early." A grating voice like sandpaper came from behind L'zar, and he whirled, laughing when he saw the hunched, shriveled figure draped in black rags.

"So, you *were* expecting me."

A shrouded arm rose from the tattered folds, and a dark-gray finger poked from the end of the sleeve toward L'zar's face. The crone's features were invisible in the thick blackness within her hood. "I expected you at the end of days, Weaver, when the deathflame takes us all and Ambar'ogúl sails upon the tides of all its dead. Which basically means never. So yes, you're early."

The figure sidled forward and returned her hand to the folds of her tattered rags. "Show me what you've brought, then. Is it a gift?"

"Of sorts." L'zar stepped aside and turned to gesture toward his daughter. "Cheyenne, come meet Ur'syth."

Cheyenne straightened and stared at the shriveled figure. She raised an eyebrow. "I'm good."

The crone wheezed with laughter, batting L'zar aside with a flapping hand to approach Cheyenne. The drow stepped easily out of her path and watched her limp toward his daughter.

Cheyenne glanced at him and stuck her hands in her pockets. *I was seriously hoping to leave the creepy stuff behind today.*

"You." The crone lifted both hands to her hood and pulled it back in a puff of dust and black particles that danced behind her in the still air.

The halfling's stomach clenched when she saw Ur'syth's face—wrinkled lines in dark flesh, beady black eyes, black paint flaking on her face from forehead to chin, and sharp, pointed teeth within a mouth as red and glistening as freshly spilled blood. The face from her dreams. "*You.*"

The sharp teeth glinted at her when Ur'syth's lips twitched into a sneer. "I am always myself, *hinya.* You are something else half the time, are you not?" The crone raised a hand toward L'zar and waved him forward. "Who is this?"

"Cheyenne."

"You gave me her name already, you grinning idiot. Who *is* she?"

L'zar clasped his hands behind his back and straightened, that feral glint in his golden eyes giving him a disturbingly hungry look. "My heir. My daughter, Ur'syth. Why else did you think the new Cycle turned when you felt it like the rest of us? The Rahalma has already received her *marandúr.* It's done."

Ur'syth gazed at Cheyenne's face, or at least her fully black eyes glinted with movement. *No pupils. I can't tell what the hell she's looking at.*

The crone nodded at her, her blood-red tongue poking out between her lips. The spittle left behind on her lips and teeth looked a lot like blood too. "As it was foretold."

"No." L'zar stalked toward them, his smile widening into a twitching grin. "Your prophecy was shit, Oracle. Sure, it took me a thousand years or more to prove it, but I did. That's *my* daughter standing before you. The Crown's newest challenger."

"Yes, you said that too." Ur'syth turned to peer up at the drow, one shoulder hunched to the side. She cocked her head and sneered. "Did you bring her here to label me a heretic, or to prove to yourself that you've achieved whatever victory you sought?"

He stared calmly down at her and shrugged. "Both, most likely."

The crone narrowed her eyes at him, then burst into wheezing, gasping cackles.

L'zar's golden eyes flickered toward Cheyenne's. Her nostrils flared and she shook her head. *Proof for me too. No one in this world is sane.*

The drow thief pressed his lips together and stared down his nose at the Oracle hag cracking up in front of him. Ur'syth flapped a wrinkled, mottled gray hand in front of her face, the black rags fluttering around her bony wrist. One cloth-wrapped foot thumped softly on the stone floor, and the crone shook her head as quickly as her deteriorating body would allow.

"I'd love to share the jest with you," L'zar muttered, his smile thin and tight now in irritation.

"You would, wouldn't you?" Ur'syth fell into a fit of hacking coughs and spat out a nasty black ball of phlegm. It landed in one of the potted plants, and a black, shriveled O'gúleesh version of a Venus flytrap snapped its brittle mouth closed around the unexpected offering.

Cheyenne wanted to spit herself and clenched her jaw instead. *No wonder the Crown hates this creature.*

Ur'syth cleared her throat, her sharp, pointed teeth glinting in her red grin. She wagged a finger at L'zar. "It's all fun jests and playful mischief for the Dark Smiling Weaver until he realizes what a fool he's been. Until he discovers he made himself the center of a universal jest much larger than himself."

L'zar's nose twitched. "And what might that be?"

"My prophecies are always fully and completely true, you drow-headed buffoon."

He gestured at Cheyenne again. "Clearly."

"*Clearly*, you didn't take my interpretation of the threads at the full value with which I delivered them. *Clearly*, you came out of my circle that day already assuming I was wrong."

"You were."

"All this time, and you're still dumber than my plants. Ha!" Ur'syth moved around Cheyenne again and peered up at the halfling. "I told you every child of yours you pursued would perish before their time. This one only lived because you abandoned her from the start. Quite a blow to your overinflated ego, isn't it?"

L'zar snorted and eyed the crone up and down. "I suspected you already knew where the loophole was."

"Not the prophecy's loophole, *Cu'ón.* Mine." The crone hissed out another laugh, pricking her shiny red tongue with her sharpened teeth. "I merely failed to spell it out for you. Wouldn't be much of an Oracle if I had, eh?"

"Now you know I found it."

"Oh, sure. She knows too. Don't you, Cheyenne?"

Hearing her name on the crone's tongue, slightly accented at the end with growling O'gúleesh sounds, sent a chill down the halfling's spine. She forced herself not to back away from the beady eyes inching closer despite Ur'syth being at least two feet shorter.

"If he left you to suffer in our sister world, to grow into what you are now standing here before me, tell me how you came to my front door together."

Cheyenne stared at what she thought were the centers of the Oracle's all-black eyes. *Maybe the whole thing's one giant pupil.* "I followed him through the streets."

"Oh. You think you're as amusing as he thinks *he* is. I can't say I'm surprised." Ur'syth's tongue ran over her sharpened teeth. From within the folds of her tattered robes came the sound of nails scratching dry flesh. Cheyenne's nostrils flared. "Did you seek him out, then? Did you pine after your nonexistent father and search the threads for him like he searched for you? Eh? Did you blaze a trail of scorched earth and broken promises like he did?"

Cheyenne pursed her lips, fighting back the spitting snarl she wanted to shove in the old Oracle's face. *She's goading me. Don't get pissed and stupid, Cheyenne.* "No. I didn't seek him out."

"And yet here you are together, yes? Here you've returned, to Hangivol, the seat of the O'gúl Crown, to claim your birthright and turn the new Cycle toward you, a fully acknowledged drow in all her glory. Don't be obtuse, girl. I know you couldn't have done it without him."

The halfling took a deep breath. "I went after an orc who almost killed my friend. Then I found L'zar safe and snug in a half-assed Earthside prison, and he took it from there."

"Oh, is *that* all?"

"Long story short, yeah."

"Very simple. Very amusing." Ur'syth hissed out more laughter and tilted her head from side to side. A black-nailed finger stabbed toward Cheyenne's face. "And you didn't once go looking for the man who sired the magic running through your veins?"

"I stopped wondering who my father was when I was six, so no. It's more like he fell into my lap."

"Ah!" The crone shrieked with laughter, which cut off abruptly when another coughing fit wracked her.

Cheyenne closed her eyes and turned her head away. *Please don't spit again. Jesus, I can smell her breath.*

"L'zar Verdys does have that tendency, doesn't he? *Falling* where everyone else least wants him to land." Ur'syth winked at Cheyenne and looked her up and down again. "And here you are now. The youngest of how many dead, L'zar?"

"That doesn't matter."

Cheyenne looked at him sharply and bit her lip, glaring at him. *All his dead kids, and he says they don't* matter?

"Perhaps not to you, Weaver. Perhaps not to the rest of us. But they mattered." Ur'syth nodded slowly. "Oh, yes. But not as much as this one." In a blur, the Oracle's hands lashed out from under her robes. Clammy, ice-cold hands clamped around Cheyenne's wrist while the crone jerked up the sleeve of the halfling's jacket.

Cheyenne immediately yanked her hand away in disgust and rubbed her wrist on the side of her jacket.

Ur'syth cackled. "Oh! Did I startle you?"

"I don't like being touched."

"Of course not. That's the easiest way to see the truth, isn't it?" The Oracle pointed at the thick silver band around Cheyenne's wrist. "Especially when someone went through such pains to hide it from the rest of us. Born Earthside to a human mother, I see."

"My mother has nothing to do with this," Cheyenne snarled, her composure snapping as her drow magic burned up her spine. Purple light flared behind her golden eyes.

Ur'syth grinned. "Not yet." She pointed at the metal cuff and turned toward L'zar. "I should have known *your* hand was the one to snatch up that little trinket."

The drow thief smiled back at her with a shrug of fake humility. "I've got a reputation to uphold, Ur'syth, and we both know you wouldn't have given it to me."

"It's been put to an acceptable use." The Oracle stepped away from Cheyenne, giving her another once-over with those glistening black eyes. "L'zar's halfling heir, eh? It *shouldn't* make a difference in the matter of a new Crown turning her own Cycle. But it might. Or it might not."

Cheyenne gave the old magical a bitter smile. "It hasn't stopped me so far."

"Indeed."

"Ur'syth." L'zar lifted his chin when the Oracle turned to face him again. "Read the weave for my daughter."

"What do you bring as an offering?"

He removed his hand from behind his back and held out a small vial filled with a dark liquid that looked like muddy water. Wiggling the vial at her, L'zar raised his eyebrows. "Right off a darkseller."

"Ah. Come then." Ur'syth waved her hand for L'zar to approach, and he set the vial gently in her wrinkled gray palm. Her hand and the vial disappeared into her tattered robes, and she sneered up at the thief.

"Make it a good one, Oracle."

"That's for *her* to decide." The crone sidled past Cheyenne toward the base of the gnarled tree on the right and grunted as she lowered herself to the stone floor.

L'zar headed toward his daughter and dipped his head. "This will be fun."

"What?" Cheyenne glanced at the haggard gray face emerging from the pile of tattered black rags on the ground and shook her head. "No. No one said anything about more prophecies. I don't need any more of that kind of crazy in my life."

"Too bad, Cheyenne. It's already been paid for." He leaned toward her and lowered his voice. "You don't change your mind once the offering's been accepted. Not in Ur'syth's house." L'zar nodded, then stepped past his daughter and calmly sat in front of the crone, crossing his legs beneath him.

Cheyenne let out a deep, frustrated sigh and swallowed. *I already know this is gonna be bad.*

CHAPTER THIRTEEN

U r'syth reached out for the closest potted plant on the ground beside her. The courtyard echoed with the grating crunch of small stones scraping across the ground beneath the metal pot. The dead-looking plant inside it shrieked when the crone's hand plunged into the pot and ripped out a large, blue-pulsing root. The thing squirmed in her tight grip, mewling like a baby animal. Ur'syth scooted the pot aside and raised the root to her mouth. Her pointy teeth tore into its flesh, and it let out a piercing scream as glowing bright blue sludge squirted from its center. Most of it dribbled down the Oracle's open mouth as she laughed, but a handful of wayward specks splattered the hem of Cheyenne's trenchcoat where she sat beside her father.

"Ugh." She leaned away from the crone, her drow sense of smell picking up the thick decaying odors mixed with the scent of copper and the stench of rancid fish.

Beside her, L'zar chuckled.

"Shut up, both of you." Ur'syth thoughtfully chewed the piece of root in her mouth and used the other half of it like a paintbrush, drawing the blue sludge down the line of paint on her face from forehead to chin. Grinning, she tossed the other root away and spat a purple-blue wad into her gnarled hands. Once she'd rubbed that into her palms like skin lotion, she set the backs of both hands on her knees and closed her eyes.

Cheyenne shot L'zar a sidelong glance. He gestured for her to keep watching. *Maleshi was right about Oracles. I'm done with them.*

A low, crackling moan came from Ur'syth's slightly parted lips. When her eyes fluttered open, they were white, rolling around in her head. Her voice rose in volume, not in thousands of tones like the raug Oracle's voice but just hers, grating and gravelly.

"The Cycle turns."

The crone was silent for so long, Cheyenne snorted. "Is that it?"

L'zar raised a finger to his smiling lips and stared at the Oracle.

"Crowns rise and fall. Tides of power raise all bloodlines into the Everweave. The bright is no more, and the darkness abides. The sword will pierce the heart. Shackles unbinding. Shackles pinned to pillars of hidden dreaming. A Crown is not a Crown without the blood of all. The blood of one will consume the Crown. The blood of one will lift the tides. The blood of one will sway the doorways into endless flux, and the gates will fall to ruin. To tear, to grieve, to unite the rift between what has always been and what will never be. But only here."

Ur'syth swayed where she sat, her voice lowered again into mumbled words Cheyenne couldn't make out. Then she sucked in a deep breath, her eyes rolling back in her head, and slumped against the tree. When she opened her eyes again, they'd returned to their unnatural all-black shade.

"Really?" L'zar stroked his chin and frowned at the crone, who was struggling to push herself away from the rough bark at her back. The tree shuddered and groaned in protest. "I said, make it a good one."

"And *I* said it was up to the *Aranél* to decide whether or not it's *a good one.*" Ur'syth coughed and pointed weakly at the halfling. "You are the only one who can make the decision, Cheyenne. Choose wisely."

Cheyenne blinked. "I have no idea how to tell if a prophecy is good."

The old crone wheezed with laughter again and shook her head. "Not *that* decision, *hinya.* The blood of one will do many things, yes? You must choose the one."

"I have no idea what you're talking about."

Ur'syth cocked her head abnormally far toward her shoulder and grinned. "Ask your father to help you with that one, eh? He's had thousands of years to practice the art."

A thunderous, bellowing explosion rose from the center of the city.

All three of them saw a shimmering mushroom cloud of strobing colors peeking above the highest wall of the courtyard. "What was that?"

L'zar slowly lowered his hand to the stone floor to push himself to his feet. "I don't know."

The ground bucked beneath them without warning, making the trees creak even louder and the hanging plants swing violently from their ropes.

The muted gray sky beneath Hangivol's domed shield flashed with brilliant colors one right after the next, and another explosion wracked the center of the city. Ur'syth's glass vials and jars toppled over onto the stone and rolled in every direction. The ground shook so violently that the second tree ripped half its roots from the ground and lurched forward, suspended sideways when the rest of its root system held fast however many feet below the surface.

Ur'syth shrieked at the sky. Cheyenne looked again and only saw colors. *What's making her freak out?*

The old Oracle convulsed where she sat, her pointed teeth chattering and her wrinkled hands flapping away from her lap over and over as if she tried to shoo away a cat. Streaks of black light pulsed from her fingers.

Cheyenne and L'zar leaped to their feet to avoid being blasted by the Oracle's magical fit. "Seriously, L'zar, what's going on?"

"I said, I don't know. Can't tell you any more than that."

"What's wrong with her?"

Ur'syth trembled on the stone floor, her arms jerking in awkward directions. A thick choking sound burst from her mouth.

"We can at least do something to help her!"

"If you want to get close to whatever magic she's letting off right now, Cheyenne, be my guest." L'zar staggered sideways across the trembling stone floor and caught himself with a hand on the sideways-leaning tree. Roots snapped with an earsplitting crunch, and the tree fell the rest of the way to the ground.

"Ur'syth?" Cheyenne shouted over the next round of rumbling explosions from the city center. "Can you hear me?"

The ancient Oracle shrieked again, whipped both hands out to either side in a moment of lucidity, and disappeared.

"What?"

"Come on." L'zar snatched her wrist and dragged her across the courtyard, ducking beneath the rocking potted plants and the dangling vines now lashing out toward the fleeing drow.

"You guys get a lot of earthquakes on this side?" Cheyenne shouted.

He pulled her into the stone passage leading to Ur'syth's courtyard and finally released her wrist as she hurried after him. "Not really."

"How about new portals opening up when and where you least expect them?"

L'zar snorted. "This isn't a new portal, Cheyenne. This is the city."

"Really? 'Cause I've been around *twice* when those things opened up Earthside, and it looks and feels exactly like this."

"Those new portals are overflow. The real problem's right here. Stop talking and move faster."

Gritting her teeth, Cheyenne stumbled when the tunnel bucked and shifted. She and L'zar caught themselves against opposite walls and pushed into a run. A minute later, L'zar passed his hand over an indiscriminate metal wall, which vanished instantly and led them right into the main avenue of Hangivol's lowest level.

The halfling gazed at the open area and glanced back once before the wall shimmered into place again. *Did he take a shortcut?*

L'zar stopped in the center of the avenue, his golden eyes wide as he craned his neck to take in the bursting, churning magic spilling into the sky from the center of the city. He ran a hand over his mouth and took a deep breath.

"So, who's blowing up the Heart?" Cheyenne stopped beside him. Screams echoed down the avenue from far away, growing louder as the magicals on the outskirts of the city realized what was happening.

"Who do you think?"

"The Crown wouldn't blow up her own—"

"Not on purpose, Cheyenne. That doesn't make her any less of a fell-damn idiot. Let's go." He reached for her arm again, but she leaped out of the way.

"We have to do something."

"There's nothing to be done!" he snarled and pointed at the dome. "This place is about to rip itself apart."

A splintering crack rent the air, followed by another massive tremble in the ground beneath them. Then a bright line of multicolored light raced down the center of the outer level's main avenue, zigzagging in a jagged fissure and spewing magical light into the air.

Cheyenne's activator was working overtime to analyze everything that was happening within and below the city. It responded to each of her thoughts as if she were processing it all, and she pointed at one of many cracks splintering outward across the ground from the Heart of Hangivol. "We can fix this."

"Don't be an idiot."

"Fine. I'll do it myself." She took off down the avenue, darting away from the magical blasts shooting up from the crack in the ground and trying to keep her balance as the entire city shuddered in an endless quake.

"Cheyenne!" L'zar roared. "Get back here!"

She flipped him the bird without stopping and disappeared around the bend in the street.

With a snarl, L'zar whirled toward the outer edge of the city. A mile away, the shouts and screams of the O'gúleesh at the fighting pits rose above the constant rumble beneath the streets. *We could've been out of here by now and left this whole thing behind us.*

Hissing, he turned back and took off after his daughter. *You're gonna get us both killed, Cheyenne. And you won't be able to climb out from under that debt to be paid.*

CHAPTER FOURTEEN

Cheyenne leaped away from a branching crack splitting off from the main fissure. Her activator pulled up a huge, blinking yellow arrow. *Right around the corner. That's where we can put it back.*

A shrill scream came from her right, and she skidded to a stop to see a group of magicals running out of an alley toward her, their eyes wide with terror. One of the buildings behind them started to sink, crumbling in on itself as the ground buckled beneath it. Cheyenne scanned the stats the activator gave her and nodded. *I can make it.*

"Stop!" L'zar grabbed her wrist again and jerked her back.

Cheyenne whirled and slammed her fist into his face, powering it with a sphere of crackling black energy balled in her hand. L'zar grunted and staggered backward, blinking against the daze as she shook out her hand. "Either help me or get the fuck out of here, but don't try to stop me again."

"Wait!"

She darted toward the slowly collapsing alley where the screaming magicals still spilled out of the space between buildings. "Over here!" She waved them toward her, and the frightened O'gúleesh headed her way without a second thought. "How many more are in there?"

"I don't know." The troll she asked barreled past her as he answered, looking over his shoulder.

The buildings crashed against another, spewing sparks and shrieks as metal ripped into metal. Cheyenne ran toward the collapsing alley and threw up a shield of dark, shimmering drow light. The force of the top half of the building toppling onto her shield made her cry out in an effort to keep it up. Marching closer, she raised her hands above her head and sank to her knees when more of the building toppled onto her broad shield. *A little heavier than that construction site. No problem.*

O'gúleesh raced past her, dragging each other along. A wide-eyed goblin dropped his tankard on the ground, and Cheyenne snarled at him when he stopped to pick it up. "Go!"

He jumped and scurried around her. With a deep breath, Cheyenne slipped into drow speed and released the shield. As soon as she got to her feet, L'zar barreled into her, and they both went flying away from the collapsing building and the spray of unleashed magic spewing through the closing alley faster than either drow could move.

Grunting, Cheyenne rolled across the cracked metal and pushed herself to her feet.

"Are you okay?" L'zar scanned her as he approached.

"So you decided to help. I'm fine."

"We need to go."

"Not yet." She spun and scanned the avenue for the source of the bright yellow arrow in her vision. "I can turn all this off. Probably temporarily, but it's something."

"Cheyenne, I can't risk it."

"You don't get to decide for me!" She stalked toward the yellow arrow blinking in her vision, ignoring his growl of disapproval.

"You're making this incredibly difficult."

"No, that would be you."

The ground bucked beneath them again, but she managed to keep her balance this time. When she finally reached the blinking yellow arrow, the activator displayed brand new lines of code and overlapping diagrams along the wall of a short, squat building another block off the main avenue. She studied the data and pressed her hand to the wall.

"We don't have time for you to play around with this shit," L'zar snarled. Right on cue, another explosion came from the center of the city.

"Shut up." Cheyenne selected the best of the activator's next presented options, and with a swipe of her finger against the wall, the O'gúl version of a breaker box opened in a recessed square in the wall. She bent over and reached inside as far as she could, feeling for the lever the wall should have created on its own under her command.

"What are you doing?" L'zar ran his hand over his head and looked between her and the mushrooming cloud of volatile magic spewing toward the top of the dome-shaped shield.

She ignored him and finally found the lever, giving it a quick jerk as she poked the illuminated symbols on the wall. A loud, pressurized hiss filled the avenue. When she looked up, she saw the muted gray dome above Hangivol shimmer, flicker, and disappear. The released magical cloud caught inside burst from the top of the city and rose straight into the sky like a beacon.

Metal and earth groaned around them, and Cheyenne removed her hand from the hole in the wall before it sealed itself.

L'zar's mouth popped open as he stared at the clear sky above them. "Did you just do that?"

"That and other things, yeah."

"How? You know what, never mind. Let's go."

"Wait." Cheyenne glared at him as she stalked down the block again and entered the main avenue. The spewing magical light dimmed beneath the giant crack in the ground, then tiny metal squares folded and unfolded themselves along the fissure, drawing the floor slowly back together and sealing the crevasse in less than a minute.

The ground stopped trembling, and a deep groan rose from beneath the city before everything was still and quiet again, except for the column of magic still spewing from the center of Hangivol into the sky.

Cheyenne gestured toward the mended ground. "Told you."

"Incredible." L'zar chuckled, slowly shaking his head. "You instinctively knew how to do whatever that was?"

"This activator is no joke." With a flick of her finger, she dimmed the scrolling data feeds on every metal surface so they wouldn't distract her. *Better keep it on just in case, though.* "What idiot thought keeping a magical shield around a city filled with brewing magic was a good idea?"

He spread his arms. "Again, nearly every bad choice in this place can be traced back to Ba'rael. That shield was one of the first things to go up when she started making changes."

"It was part of the damn problem. Those fellfire pits outside the city. No one would be working those today, right?"

"Not a chance. No one's working."

"Good, 'cause I just let off a whole bunch of magical pressure through them. That's what this was, right?"

L'zar blinked at the magic shooting from the city center as his daughter stormed past him and back down the avenue. "If you're talking about all the magic my moronic sister was storing in her torture chambers, I'm inclined to agree with you. Yes."

"Good thing the moron gene ended with me."

The drow thief spun and followed her, laughing. "And I had nothing to do with that, huh?"

"No, I don't think you did." Cheyenne stopped and whirled on him, shoving a finger in his face. "The Crown isn't the only one around here I can blame for making stupid choices. What the hell *was* that back there?"

He tilted his head. "Which part?"

"The part where you kept running away like a coward to save yourself. The part where you tried to drag me with you when I clearly knew what I was doing and could save this city and the people *you* told me I'm here to protect!" She shoved his chest with both hands, and L'zar staggered backward.

His smile disappeared. "I don't want to lose you too, Cheyenne."

"This isn't about me, this is about your self-righteous power games. You're willing to let everyone else fend for themselves, even if they end up dead, because they aren't part of your master plan."

"Cheyenne!"

"Shut up!" She launched a crackling sphere of black energy at his face, and he ducked but didn't step back. "If you want me to do any of this, giving the Crown her terms, taking the throne or not taking the throne, helping to put this screwed-up world back together, don't even think about telling me I'm wrong or that I don't understand. I get how you work, L'zar. It's great that you wanna protect me, but it's too late to think I'll start listening to you now over what *I* know I can do."

He pressed his lips together. "I did get you out of the way of all that magic shooting through the alley."

"Please." Cheyenne rolled her eyes and turned away from him to stalk down the avenue again. "I wasn't even close to being in real danger."

With a deep breath, L'zar took one more look at the pillar of dazzling, churning magic spilling into the sky and hurried after his daughter. *She's not exactly like me, not in this.* When he caught up with her, he stuck his hands in his pockets and easily matched her agitated stride. "You know, you would make an *excellent* Crown if you decided to stay. I'm inclined to think your human blood is responsible for that."

She snorted. "You're not a selfish asshole because you're *not* human, L'zar. Me being half-human doesn't make my decisions for me either."

"Maybe. Maybe not." The drow thief chuckled and didn't say another word.

Cheyenne snuck a quick glance at him and found him staring at the blue sky as they walked down the avenue. *Looks like I got my point across. Maybe you* can *teach an old drow new tricks.*

CHAPTER FIFTEEN

They met up with the others at the fighting pits in Vedrosha. Most of the magicals had scattered and returned to their homes and stores on the lower levels. Some O'gúleesh remained to help with the cleanup, which mostly amounted to getting the magicals lying on the ground back on their feet and inspected for serious injuries.

Cheyenne found Ember surrounded by magicals holding bleeding faces and arms, clutching whatever hurt and waiting their turn. The fae girl reached toward the next injured magical in line, her palms glowing with a slightly brighter violet light than her other spells before fading again.

The healed magicals stared at their mended wounds and bowed to the fae girl, muttering their thanks before heading out of Vedrosha to regroup somewhere else. Cheyenne waited for Ember to tend to the last of them, then approached.

"So you're whipping up healing spells now after magical disasters, huh?"

Ember grinned when she saw the halfling and raised her pink-tinged hands. "I don't even *need* spells. It just happens."

"You know, I've heard things about the fae's innate healing." Cheyenne snorted. "The only things that come out of my hands are magical bombs and whips."

"Everybody's got a calling, right?" Ember's smile faded as she glanced at the column of magic at the city's center. "What happened?"

Cheyenne looked over her shoulder at L'zar, who had joined Corian, Maleshi, and some of the other rebel magicals to explain his version of events. *Probably downplaying his panic to get the hell out, too.* "Remember that room we fought our way through yesterday? With the pool of black whatever and the bubble of light in the ceiling?"

The fae girl frowned. "Yeah. They were stealing magic in there."

"That magic had to go somewhere, right? I'm pretty sure the Crown sucked up too much of it and overloaded the city somehow. I fixed it for now. I think."

"That was you, huh?" Maleshi's strained smile made her look incredibly tired when she approached them. "You just happened to find the O'gúl breaker box to turn off the dome shield and let off the extra pressure."

"No, I found *one* place where I could access all those things. I'm sure there are more on different levels."

Maleshi briefly set a hand on Cheyenne's shoulder and nodded. "Whatever you did, it seems to have worked. We can't be sure how long it will last, though."

"I know. That's a problem."

Corian joined them with a concerned frown. "And it could quickly turn into a large, very dangerous problem. You made the right call, kid. Honestly, I'm glad this happened. Now we know what else we have to deal with when your two weeks are up."

"You mean, getting all that extra magic back under control, so it doesn't rip up the city?"

"Forget ripping it up." Corian scratched behind his tufted ear and grimaced at the pillar of shimmering light. "Hangivol could be blown off the map entirely, and millions of citizens with it."

"What about dampening wards like Maleshi cast on the portals?"

Maleshi shook her head. "Those new portals were apparently just overflow."

Cheyenne cast a scathing glance at L'zar, who conveniently chose that moment to turn away from the group and study the escaping magic. "So I heard."

"Dampening wards or binding spells are only a temporary patch, anyway. I'm not sure they'd be any more effective than what you did. Obviously, we can't keep trying to hold this magic *in*. The Crown's attempt at that already failed."

Ember rubbed her arm and shrugged. "What about evacuating the city? Get everyone out of here, and then if something happens…"

"I like where your mind's headed, Ember." Maleshi shook her head. "But that would make things even worse. It's a small part of the bigger picture, but the last Nimlothar tree still stands at the center of the Heart. At least, I hope it does after this, and it won't do any good for this world if the capital disappears off the face of it. The Crown and the Heart will both be gone. That leaves a massive power vacuum around here, and Ambar'ogúl will become the biggest battleground any of us have ever seen. Bigger than anything in the world's history, I'd bet. Hangivol isn't just a city. It has a power of its own."

"Like, it's alive?" Ember watched the nightstalkers.

"In its own way." Corian dipped his head, clasping his hands behind his back. "The kind of explosion that could very well take out this entire city won't be contained. Imagine someone nuking Washington DC and taking out the entire eastern half of the US with it. Not something we can afford to let happen."

Cheyenne folded her arms. "So, what do we do?"

"That's what we need to figure out." Corian glanced at L'zar's back as the drow thief watched the magical pillar and listened in on the conversation at the same time. "And quickly. We can't afford a long deliberation about this."

L'zar's rebels gathered around one of the open fighting pits, everyone sitting down at the edges and dangling their feet, claws, or hooves over the white sand below as they discussed their options.

Cheyenne fought back a smile as she gazed around the square of deliberating rebels. *Not as sophisticated as sitting around a table, but I guess it works.*

"So, a hold's out of the question, then?"

"Of course it is. It would take all of us combined to hold back a fraction of what's seeping out of the Heart as we speak."

"I don't suppose Ba'rael's alchemists came up with a way to distribute magic to more than one individual."

L'zar snorted. "She must be furious right now."

Corian shot him an exasperated glance. "I'm normally fond of your ability to find amusement in every situation. Now's not one of those times."

"Just an observation, *vae shra'ni*." The drow shrugged and set his hands behind him on the metal floor to lean back and look up at the clear blue sky.

"Do we know any conjurers?"

"Not closer than three days from here, and you know they won't accept a journey by portal. Impossible to pinpoint them anyway."

"What about our alchemists?"

"We don't *have* any alchemists, Jara'ak. She took them all."

A dozen more options were offered, and the conversation grew into a shouting match as the Four-Pointed Star realized they were wasting time and still couldn't come to a satisfying conclusion. L'zar raised his eyebrows at Cheyenne and leaped away from the edge of the pit, shoving his hands in his pockets and pacing across the open metal ground.

"All right, stop. Stop!" Maleshi raised both hands, and when the magicals around her kept arguing, she sent two bolts of silver lightning into the opposite wall of the pit. They stopped immediately and looked at her.

"Well?"

"I'm not sure yet. I can't think when you're all squabbling like these two." Maleshi tossed a hand toward Lumil and Byrd, who were sitting along the adjacent wall of the pit. Lumil elbowed Byrd in the side, and she bumped her into her other neighbor with a grunt.

Corian lifted his head. "We could take a request to the *Sorren Gán.*"

L'zar spun toward the pit and shook his head. "Absolutely not. Keep thinking."

"None of us wanted to say it, brother, but it's the most obvious solution."

"There's always a way around the obvious solution, Corian. Cheyenne's proof of that." L'zar nodded at his daughter and picked up his pacing again. This time, it was tense and aggravated.

"L'zar." Foltr smacked his stick against the pit wall beside his dangling legs. "You know how that could help us. Follow that knowledge and set your cowardice aside, will you?"

The drow thief whirled on the elderly raug and snarled, "I'm *not* going. That's my final word, and if I have to order each and every one of you not to mention it again, I will."

Foltr laughed deeply and swung his cane up to point at Cheyenne. "You gave up the right to give us orders when you handed over your blood right to your daughter. Unless *she* orders me to be silent, I'll sing about the *Sorren Gán* all night if I have to."

L'zar's eyes widened, and he sneered at the shriveled raug. Foltr raised his thick brows, and the drow snarled before spinning away into more pacing.

"I think that's our best option at this point." Corian nodded and pushed himself up. "Does anyone disagree with me?"

The rebels exchanged wary glances but didn't offer any protest.

"Then we'll send out a party. I'm happy to make the journey again."

"I'm not," L'zar spat. Corian ignored him.

"There's a first time for everything." With a wry chuckle, Maleshi stood and dusted off her pants. "I wouldn't miss this trip for the world. Hell, for both of them."

"Anyone else who wants to be part of this is welcome." Corian nodded at the rebels slowly rising from their makeshift seats. "L'zar's coming, of course. Ember, you're free to stay here with the others if you like, though I'm sure you won't because Cheyenne, we need you with us."

"Okay." Cheyenne accepted Ember's hand for a boost to her feet when the fae girl floated instantly off the edge of the pit. "What do I have to do?"

"Whatever you do, don't look forward to it." L'zar snorted and headed away from the pit.

"All right. Whoever's with us, get ready to move out. We're leaving now." Corian shot Cheyenne a wary glance, then nodded and headed after L'zar.

"What's a *Sorren Gán*?" Ember muttered.

"I'm the last person to ask about that, Em."

"Sakrit." Maleshi approached the orc and clasped his forearm. "On

General Hi'et's orders, get these pits closed up for the time being. It hurts to say it as much as it hurts to hear, but we can't risk overloading the city with power until we've cleared out the worst of it."

"They'll understand. We had a good few hours with the pits for the first time in centuries. They can wait a little longer if it means they can use them the way they were meant to be used. I'll take care of it."

"I know." Maleshi clapped a hand on his shoulder and nodded before joining the rest of their party following L'zar.

Cheyenne hurried after her father and Corian. "Hey, wait a minute."

Corian looked over his shoulder at her and Ember, who was floating closely behind. L'zar showed no sign that he'd heard her.

"We talked about the whole 'no more secrets' thing, so who's gonna tell me where we're going and what the hell a *Sorren Gán* is?"

L'zar snarled. "I'm so *sick* of hearing that name!"

"At least tell me why I have to go. I mean, not that I wouldn't, but nobody even *asked* me."

Corian slowed to fall in beside her. "You and L'zar are the only ones it will listen to."

"Why? Because we're *royalty?*"

In front of them, L'zar snorted. "No. Not even close." He stepped aside and let them pass, fuming at the ground and refusing to meet his daughter's gaze.

Corian put a hand on Cheyenne's back and urged her to keep moving.

"What the hell's wrong with him?"

"We might have a chance to talk about it on the way there, kid. Just leave it alone for now. When L'zar's ready to stop throwing a fit about it, he'll fill you in."

***

The group of rebels made their way underground to the Four-Pointed Star's hidden bunker. The place had suffered a little damage from the magical earthquake, but it wasn't enough to make it dangerous. Cheyenne grabbed her pack from where she'd left it beside the wall that morning and stared at the fallen chunks of stone scattered across the huge metal table. "One more downside to not having any integrated tech down here, huh? Can't just patch the holes in the wall with a bunch of smart metal."

Maleshi moved her fingers in a quick spell. The stone chunks on the table and scattered around the main chamber illuminated with silver light and whisked toward the opposite side of the room, where they fell in a neat heap against the wall. "It's an easy enough fix."

Ember grabbed her own backpack and slung it over her shoulders. "I would've said you could use your fancy earth magic and stick it all back up where it goes."

Cheyenne shot her friend a brief smile and shook her head. "I can rip the ground apart and shove it back together again, Em. Not sure it's refined enough for filling holes in the ceiling."

Maleshi, Corian, L'zar, Byrd, and Lumil quickly packed and got ready to head out. A handful of the other rebels darted between them, dispersing prewrapped packages and small metal boxes. A grinning goblin handed these to Cheyenne and Ember too. Cheyenne frowned at the box. "What's this?"

"Drow eat like everyone else, don't they?" Chuckling, the goblin hurried away to take care of some other preparation.

When the journeying party had gotten everything together, Corian pointed at a large arch on the far right side of the chamber. "We'll take the transport shuttle out to Ki'uali. That's the farthest point."

"No objection to that." Maleshi hefted a pack onto her shoulders and nodded at Cheyenne. "Let's move out."

Foltr cracked his cane against the floor, the sound amplified by a spell to get everyone's attention, which it did. L'zar turned to shoot the old raug an irritated glance. "What?"

"I'm coming with you."

"Foltr," Corian started, "this isn't—"

"We're heading a lot closer to the dens than most parties ever go, and I've been where we're going."

L'zar snarled. "We both have, Grandfather. At least *you* get to stand there and watch." The drow spun back toward the arch and disappeared into the corridor beyond.

Foltr smacked his wrinkled lips and hobbled after him, his cane clicking on the stone. "Don't let this place fall to ruin while we're gone."

"Depends on your definition of ruin, old one!" a rebel shouted. A handful of others laughed, and the aged raug waved them away before joining the rest of their party and entering the tunnel.

Ember leaned toward Cheyenne in the semi-dark tunnel echoing with over half a dozen pairs of footsteps. "So, we're taking a tunnel?"

"To a transport station, I guess. Like a subway."

"Oh." Ember frowned. "You'd think they would've come up with a more sophisticated way to get places on this side, right?"

"I said, *like* a subway. Trust me, it's sophisticated enough."

"L'zar," Corian called after the pissed-off drow leading the way.

"Say another word, and I'll bring this tunnel down on top of us."

Corian cleared his throat before muttering, "And we press on."

Cheyenne watched the nightstalker shake his head, and those in the tunnel fell into a tense silence, punctured only by their quickening foot-steps. *They're all putting up with massive drow mood swings 'cause that's what they've been doing forever anyway. Guess L'zar's got more to teach me than I thought, like how not to be that drow throwing tantrums.*

Ember chuckled softly and whispered, "Little tense in here."

The halfling snorted. "Yeah. This is what it's like to be around me when I'm pissed all the time, isn't it?"

Ember shrugged. "At least we know who you get it from."

"Fair enough. I'm working on it." Cheyenne raised her voice enough for everyone in the tunnel to hear, including L'zar. "Someone told me meditating has a lot of great benefits."

In front of her, Corian snorted and shook his head.

CHAPTER SIXTEEN

The high-speed shuttle waiting for them in Hangivol's lowest level, Halter's Deck, was a lot more modern than the one Cheyenne had ridden with Persh'al. The doors opened seamlessly without anyone having to poke and prod the commands, and they filed into the compartment.

"Wow. Somebody sprang for the luxury seats in this one, huh?"

Corian went to the control panel at the front of the compartment. "The transports that get used the most are the ones that need the most updates. Honestly, if I were the one in charge of updating these things, I'd get rid of the one-track-per-shuttle system. It's a complete waste."

While everyone else flopped down on the roomy seats covered in soft, cool fabric and arranged like a lounge in the back half of the cabin, Cheyenne set her backpack down on the closest seat and joined Corian in the front. "It is a little weird that something with this much juice only goes one way."

"Juice." The nightstalker laughed dryly and scanned the blank panel in front of him.

Cheyenne watched his indecision and leaned forward to catch his gaze. "Having trouble figuring out where to start?"

"I spent all this time getting ready to bring you here for one reason.

Didn't expect to be heading out of Hangivol with an alternate purpose, and I seem to have forgotten the need for an activator of my own."

"I'd offer to lend you mine, but…"

"No, thank you," Corian said to her. "You sure you know how to drive this thing?"

"It does go in a straight line."

"Very funny."

"I got this." Cheyenne nodded toward the seats in the back, and the nightstalker turned swiftly to take one for himself, scratching the back of his head. "Everyone good to go?"

"No." L'zar slumped in his seat at the very back, both legs stretched out in front of him with his ankles crossed and arms folded, and glared at the slick metal floor. "It's not too late to open those doors again."

Cheyenne slid her finger along the starter sequence the activator neatly lit up for her on the control panel. A low whine filled the shuttle, quickly rising to a high pitch that faded into silence again. Lights blinked on, the device powering the cabin with a mix of magic and tech thrummed to life, and the doors let out a soft hiss as they sealed from the inside. "Whoops."

L'zar looked at her and narrowed his eyes. "Don't pretend to make mistakes, Cheyenne."

"Why not? Does it insult you?" She turned back to the control panel and activated the rest of the powering sequences.

"No, it makes you look like you're trying too hard. Insulting me is a lofty goal, though."

Cheyenne chuckled and braced her feet before swiping the panel one last time. The shuttle hummed louder and tore out of the transport station at top speed.

"Whoa." Ember slid against Maleshi, gave her an apologetic smile, and shifted back into her own seat. The general grinned at her before sharing a glance with Corian across the compartment.

"Way smoother than the last one." Cheyenne's eyes widened as the activator pulled up the hundreds of extra commands her first transport shuttle hadn't offered. She played around with it, swiping up on the display and changing the walls from shiny silver to black, then white, then a panoramic view of a forest wrapping around the shuttle.

"Hey!" Byrd cringed in his seat and stared at the trees around them.

Lumil burst out laughing and pointed at the goblin. "You thought this shit was *real?*"

He chuckled nervously. "Some updates. Damn, it *looks* real, though."

"I'm pretty sure no one would build one of these things through a forest," Cheyenne called from the front, now fiddling with the ambient lighting. "Or if they did, the forest wouldn't exist after a shuttle's first trip through. Anybody know how fast we're going?"

"Do enlighten us." Maleshi leaned forward and propped her forearms on her thighs, grinning at the halfling who was enjoying herself so much up front.

"No problem." Cheyenne wiggled her fingers over the control panel and shrugged. "I mean, seeing is believing, right?"

She selected the shuttle's invisible walls, and almost everyone in the party let out shouts of surprise when the floors, walls, and ceiling disappeared around them. Even L'zar sat up straight in his seat, drawing his feet back toward himself to peer beneath the shuttle at what looked like nothing but dirt and dry grass whizzing past beneath them.

"This is so cool," Ember muttered, her luminous violet eyes locked on the wall behind Corian's head. He turned slightly to see what she found interesting, then clenched his eyes shut and shook his head.

Cheyenne turned, and her smile faded when she saw the massive pillar of magic bursting out of Hangivol far behind them. "Wow. That looks bad even from here."

"The decision's been made, Cheyenne." L'zar waved his hand, feigning indifference and failing to pull it off. "No use in looking behind us if we're not headed that way."

"Uh-huh." She turned back to the console and managed to return the opacity to the back wall alone while the rest of the shuttle remained transparent.

Foltr chuckled, both gnarled hands resting on the top of his cane. "Your daughter's skills rival your own, L'zar."

Cheyenne stuck her hands in her pockets and stepped slowly toward the back of the cabin to take the empty seat beside Ember. "Old-world magic versus the new generation of tech advancement, huh?"

"The two aren't comparable." L'zar stared at her, but the corner of his mouth twitched in a tiny smile.

"I don't know." Maleshi sat back against the cushion and crossed one leg over the other. "I never saw *you* pull up anything quite like this, and we've taken plenty of shuttles."

"Just the two of you?" Corian looked sharply at Maleshi and raised an eyebrow. "When?"

She shook her head and waved him off.

L'zar's smile widened as he stared at his daughter. "When Cheyenne's abilities rival my own, I'll be the first to bend the knee. I don't need to stick a piece of metal behind my ear to manipulate the threads *I* see."

Corian snorted. "No. You have to hole yourself up in a vacuum and meditate for four hours minimum. I agree, it's much more convenient."

Byrd and Lumil sniggered and stared at the drow thief, who was slowly being pulled out of his brooding. L'zar interlaced his fingers and set them on his lap. With a final smile at Cheyenne, he dropped his head back against the cushion of his seat and closed his eyes.

Corian pointed at him. "See?"

***

They rode the transport shuttle long enough to get hungry and pull out the so-called lunches packed in metal boxes. Cheyenne lifted the square of dark-green chewy-looking something and narrowed her eyes.

"Don't eat that all at once." Corian pointed at it and popped a bright-red nut into his mouth. "That's better left for when we run out of everything else."

"Yeah, I'm pretty sure I know what this is." Cheyenne sniffed the square and dropped it back into the box. "Energy bar, huh?"

"Something like that."

"Yeah, the FRoE has something like it on the other side." She opted for what looked like a strawberry except for being a deep, shiny purple with heart-shaped leaves. *Doesn't taste like a strawberry either, but it's way better than that bar.* "How do those people over there have the same recipe for a brick of stinky magical fuel?"

Maleshi and Corian exchanged knowing glances. The general shrugged and picked at the food in her rebel lunchbox. "Those friends of yours."

"They're not my friends." Cheyenne shook her head and dropped the berry leaves into the box. "Associates, maybe. That's it."

"Whatever the case, when they see something they like when the refugees cross over, they put their own spin on it. Let me guess—their version is mass-produced and comes in a plastic wrapper."

"Huh." Cheyenne closed the metal box and stuck it back in her pack. "You know a lot more about them than they know about you."

Corian chucked. "That's the way we like it."

Despite the shuttle's high speed, they traveled for at least another three hours before Cheyenne's activator sent her an alert that they'd be slowing down soon. "Looks like we're almost there."

Byrd scanned the empty open land around them and frowned. "What part of the nothingness gave you that impression?"

She stood and went to the control panel, bringing the walls, ceiling, and floor back to their usual shining metal. Then she pulled up a map on the front wall for everyone to see. "Wow. We're way out in the middle of nowhere."

"Oh, yeah. Look at that." Byrd snorted. "Could've said you saw it on a map."

Shortly after that, the shuttle applied its braking system and decelerated to a smooth, efficient stop. The doors hissed and slid open on their own, and the traveling band of magicals pushed themselves out of their seats, groaning and stretching as they filed out of the shuttle.

Ember gave a mocking grimace as she floated out of the shuttle. "What area of town are we in again?"

"Ki'uali," Lumil muttered behind her. "Not a town. More of a waystation." The goblin woman's eyes widened when they stepped around the front of the train. "Ghost town, I guess."

The shuttle doors closed again, and the bullet-shaped O'gúl train powered up to head toward the capital with zero passengers. Cheyenne didn't turn to watch it leave. "What happened here?"

"Looks like the same thing that's been happening everywhere else." Corian readjusted his pack and nodded for everyone to follow him. "Persh'al painted a clear enough picture of what you saw the last time."

Foltr scowled at the abandoned village surrounding the transport station, the end of his cane digging into the dirt at his feet. "Four hundred years."

"What?" Maleshi looked at him over her shoulder and stopped when she saw the old raug's trembling lips curl into a grimace.

"I was last here four hundred years ago, and the Ki'uali station was an active village. Full of trade. Pups scurrying around underfoot."

"A lot happens in four hundred years, right?" Ember gazed at the rotting buildings falling apart.

"Not here." Maleshi approached the raug and clapped a hand on his shoulder. "Come on, Grandfather. We need to keep moving."

Foltr snarled but didn't protest, thumping his cane with unnecessary force into the ground as he fell in line.

"Watch out over here." Corian pointed toward the closest slanted building on their way up the wide dirt path that led into the mountains behind the village.

"Yeah, that looks like what Persh'al and I saw." Cheyenne leaned toward the building to peer at the dark lines of black sludge climbing the walls of the building like snaking vines. *Shiny vines that pulse like worms.* Wrinkling her nose at the mixed scent of decay and old urine, she kept moving after the others.

Lumil's boot squished into a puddle of thick sludge off the path, sending out black ooze in rivulets like a scurrying swarm of maggots before she lifted her foot again. Beside her, Ember scowled and floated away from the mess. "Ew."

"Oh, yeah. It's not always the case, but right now, I'd say 'ew' and the death of the land go hand in hand."

"Wait." Cheyenne stopped and sniffed at the air. *Definitely urine. How did I let that one go?* "Anyone else smell something?"

"Yes." L'zar spun and eyed the abandoned buildings. "We're not alone."

Byrd snorted. "Really? I know half of us here can smell fae, but I doubt we'll find any here."

"Not fae." L'zar stepped back down the path, his eyes darting from one rotting building to the next. "But the smell of piss doesn't hang around for four hundred years."

A howling shriek split through the air, and a dark shape darted between the buildings. Grunting and sharp, warning hisses followed, then more dark blurs moved across the village.

Corian pressed his lips together. "If we keep walking, we're not a threat."

Lumil snorted. "Yeah, great idea. Let's turn our backs on those. What the hell are they?"

The closest building on their right shifted and collapsed the rest of the way, then a snarling, rabid skaxen leaped from behind the next building over and charged at Byrd.

Byrd unleashed two balls of green fire at the skaxen, hitting it in the chest and stomach. The other magical staggered backward and looked down at its chest. Loose rags hung from the skaxen's skin, and beneath them, the same black sludge oozed from its pores, giving it an eerie sheen as if the magical had slathered itself in black oil. The skaxen thumped its chest, sending a spray of sludge in all directions, then attacked again.

"Seriously, what the hell?" Byrd sent out more green fire, stopping his attacker long enough to step away from the snarling, flailing creature.

"What happened to him?" Cheyenne asked.

"Anyone wanna help first and ask questions later?" Byrd shouted as the skaxen just kept coming.

Lumil conjured the spinning disks of blazing-red runes around her fists. "I gotcha."

A mottled black-orange skaxen leaped from the ruined village and landed on Lumil's back. The goblin woman roared and flung her attacker away, then stalked after that one instead. "Come back here!"

A dozen more skaxen wearing rags and covered in oozing black sludge swarmed from the wreckage toward the traveling party. Black sludge dripped from their fangs and ran beneath their orange skin in thick lines like veins. Cheyenne took a step back. "Jesus, look at their eyes."

"They might look the same, Cheyenne, but those are not the eyes of Oracles." L'zar hissed at the oncoming swarm of rotting skaxen while Byrd and Lumil finally managed to put down the first two.

"They're gone." Corian's blade-like claws extended in a glint of silver. "We're fighting animals now."

If I couldn't smell them dying, I'd say he was wrong. Cheyenne summoned two sparking black orbs and nodded. "This sucks."

When Lumil's fist came up into her attacker's face and sent the skaxen-thing flying back into a rotting building, the rest of the crazed pack turned to look at the damage. Then they charged.

Cheyenne sent blast after blast into the oncoming horde, knocking them back into each other. Orange-black bodies flew, spraying black sludge in every direction, but they kept coming.

Maleshi and Corian darted around the attackers in flashes of silver light, going as close as they dared to the sludge-soaked grass and the rotting village. Their claws glinted in the light as they came down on any mottled body part in their way. The skaxen screamed and clutched bleeding stumps. One kept crawling toward Maleshi's foot with one hand as it clutched its eviscerated stomach with the other. She put it down with another swipe of her claws and kept moving.

Foltr raised his staff and swung it at the creatures, making contact every time with thick smacks and blasting them back with red light from his gnarled, outstretched hand.

Ember froze behind the line of fighting, staring at the bleeding, burned, or disemboweled skaxen clawing across the ground to get at the magicals standing against them. "Holy shit. We're fighting magical zombies."

Cheyenne flung black tendrils from her fingertips, which coiled around the neck of a skaxen leaping right toward Ember and jerked the creature backward. It let out a strangled choking sound and Cheyenne stepped aside, releasing her tendrils to send two black energy spheres into the thing's throat. "Can't really say *we* if you're just standing there, Em."

"Right." The fae girl blinked and stepped forward, shoving outward with both hands. A wall of brilliant violet light shot away from her and spread across the scrambling, snarling lines of rotting skaxen. The force of her attack threw them back like bowling pins, and the lost creatures convulsed on the ground before lying still.

"Whoa." Cheyenne spun around toward her friend. "That one new?"

Ember shrugged. "I think so."

L'zar dodged a skaxen's swiping claws, stepping around the thing with his hands clasped behind his back and watching it move.

Cheyenne turned with the others to watch the drow not fight the creature. "What is he doing?"

As if to answer her, L'zar flicked his hand toward the creature. A concentrated burst of white light hit the skaxen in mid-air as it leaped toward him and blew the blighted magical to smithereens. Thick, sludge-covered chunks of skaxen rained down around the drow, who'd raised a shield around himself and held it until the revolting deluge subsided.

Byrd and Lumil guffawed in surprise, pointing at the mess and shaking their heads.

Ember doubled over and turned away, dry-heaving at the side of the path.

Grunting, Foltr watched the path beneath him as he trudged onward, thumping his staff into the dirt. "A waste. Pure waste is what it is."

Corian headed toward L'zar, frowning at the bodies littering the ground between them and the not-so-abandoned village. "That was a little excessive."

"In the end, perhaps." L'zar's fingers moved quickly to lower his shield, then he stepped toward the closest intact body and bent over it for a closer look. "I wanted to see how this worked."

"What, you mean, how an entire village of skaxen mutated with the blight over four hundred years?" Cheyenne stopped beside Ember and set a hand briefly on her friend's back. "You okay?"

"Yep." Ember straightened and swiped her violet-streaked hair away from her face. "I can't believe I didn't puke. I'm good."

"This wasn't a generational mutation." L'zar straightened again and stepped back to study the black-oozing bodies. "No skaxen village would have a new population in only four hundred years, if it's even been that long since these were tainted."

Corian said, "So, they were infected."

"That's one way to look at it. Touched, perhaps." L'zar strode up the path and scanned the foothills ahead. "The wildlife Persh'al mentioned were mutations. I would've said these skaxen contracted this from the water or a tainted food supply, but I can't, can I?"

Maleshi shook a glistening black chunk off the toe of her boot and joined the rest of the party. "The rot found them in their homes. It's still the Outers, but at a different point of the O'gúl compass. This shouldn't be possible."

"No, it shouldn't." L'zar stared straight ahead and picked up the pace. "We're running out of time a lot more quickly than I expected."

CHAPTER SEVENTEEN

After fighting off the tainted skaxen, the group's mood was considerably dampened. Even Lumil and Byrd agreed to an unvoiced truce and didn't nag each other as they moved up into the mountains. The path rose steadily, and the mood only worsened.

L'zar eventually led them off the path and through the mountains in a direction only he knew. They passed a small pond in a clearing, but it was filled with the same oozing black sludge, every tree and bush and blade of grass around it shriveled into blackened husks. Farther on, a flock of strangely squawking birds dove toward them from the sky, intent on attacking despite hardly being able to fly straight. Their bloated bodies smacked into tree trunks and overhanging branches, throwing some of them off course or to the ground. Most of the birds exploded on impact, raining bird parts and chunks of sludge. Those on the ground flapped around miserably, croaking in denial of their circumstances before Cheyenne put them out of their misery.

"That's probably the only good way to handle it," Ember muttered, staring at bird carcasses oozing black sludge. "Don't beat yourself up."

"I'm not." Cheyenne trudged after the others, gritting her teeth. "I want to figure out how to stop this while we still can."

The next time the group came upon a village, they were cautious of approaching too close. The magicals living up here in huts in the mountains weren't blighted like the skaxens at the transport station, though it took longer than it should have to discern that the dark smudges on their faces and bodies were from dirt instead of the cursed ooze eating away at Ambar'ogúl.

"If we're moving farther away from Hangivol into the Outers," Cheyenne muttered as they passed the village, "how did those magicals skip out on getting infected?"

Corian shook his head, warily eyeing the troll youngsters staring at him from where they sat on the ground in front of the village's adults. "Doesn't seem to be any rhyme or reason for this, and we can't afford to assume there is one."

A troll elder hobbled toward the strangers, squinting so harshly her scarlet eyes practically disappeared within the folds of her wrinkled violet skin. She thrust a finger toward L'zar and moved it between him and Cheyenne. "Black spirit you bringin' out to us, nah. Keep movin'. Keep out them no-light *wadeen*."

With a hiss, the old troll waved the travelers away, shouting after them in a combination of the Outers dialect and old O'gúleesh Cheyenne didn't try to understand. She stepped toward Corian and looked over her shoulder at the entire troll village staring after them. "I'm guessing there's some story about drow being evil spirits."

"Nope." He shook his head. "Just O'gúleesh so far removed from civilization, they've forgotten what a drow is."

"For real?"

"You saw the inner city, kid. All the drow holed up close to the Crown and the Heart. Drow aren't freely roaming around in the Outers anymore. Not like they ever did in large numbers, but it's obviously been a lot longer for this tribe."

Maleshi fell behind the party and stopped, facing the old troll head-on and spreading her arms in supplication. "Do you know me, Grandmother?"

The troll elder scoffed, her long, washed-out scarlet braids swinging over her shoulders. "Ha! Nightstalkers lookin' like all the same, dem, yeh. I know one pushed mine out far back in these hills. Now we pushin' yours, yeh. Run quick. These pups want nothin' with claws and hush-hush lyin'. Shoo!"

The general swept her gaze over the three dozen trolls staring silently at her, many with fearful curiosity in their eyes but most of them with pure hatred. Pressing a hand to her heart, Maleshi gave the old troll woman a small bow, then hurried to catch up with the others.

Cheyenne didn't notice Maleshi had fallen behind until the nightstalker stepped in line beside her as the party followed L'zar up the next rise into the mountains. "Why'd you stop?"

"Just to talk." The general grimaced and clenched her fists. "I've seen that old troll before."

"What?"

"Long time ago, kid. Not long enough for me to forget the tattoos on her arms. Apparently long enough for her to forget *my* face."

"Who is she?"

"A hell of a fighter, that's for sure." Maleshi cleared her throat and took one last look at the edge of the village through the trees behind them. "I don't know her name. I should, though, shouldn't I? I'm the reason her tribe's all the way out here."

Ember floated along quickly behind them. "I know General Hi'et comes with a long line of titles and honors, but I'm sure your leaving this world for Earth doesn't make you responsible for what's happening on this side."

The nightstalker smiled bitterly. "I am well aware of that, Ember, and I appreciate the sentiment, but I am responsible for this specifically."

Cheyenne stared at Maleshi's profile and waited for the general to keep going. *She'll say more. She wouldn't have brought it up if she didn't want to talk about it.*

"I can feel you staring at me, kid."

"I can feel you about to explode, General."

Maleshi snorted. "Maybe. After Ba'rael turned the new Cycle, she didn't waste any time putting all her grand plans into action. I served the Crown back then. Got my orders and carried them out unquestioningly, not thinking about what kind of Crown would give those kinds of orders."

Up ahead, Corian cleared his throat without turning around to look at them. "We all had our parts to play."

"Oh, sure. And I played mine very well. That's not an excuse."

"Whatever it was," Ember said, "it can't have been that bad. The magicals in the capital went crazy when they saw you this morning."

"The magicals in the capital only saw a fraction of what I did in the name of the Crown." The general looked into the upper branches of the stunted trees dotting the mountainside as they climbed after L'zar. "I led more war parties than I can count into the Outers right after Ba'rael took the throne. We cleared out the valleys and farmland first. Took the livestock, then the forests, then the mines. Everywhere we went, everywhere she sent us, O'gúleesh had been living their lives relatively peacefully for ages. We all knew that, and we moved them out without a second thought."

Foltr grunted and thwacked his staff against a tree trunk. "It's all in the past, *hinya.*"

"Sure, until the past looked me right in the eyes five minutes ago and had no idea who I am." Maleshi shook her head. "That troll was one of the few who fought back. Very few did, and she was one of even fewer I didn't cut down for standing up to the Crown to protect what was theirs."

Cheyenne swallowed. "Shit."

A bitter laugh escaped the general. "Yeah. That tribe is all the way out here because of me. Who knows, maybe they've been here the whole time, but probably not. If this blight is moving as quickly as we think, I'm sure they've relocated more than once."

"Ambar'ogúl will heal itself," Corian muttered. "We'll make sure of it."

"After how many lives are taken, *vae shra'ni?* Huh?" Maleshi hissed. "I should've stopped her when I realized what she was doing. I could've taken her back then before she started stealing more magic than even she can handle."

At the head of the line, L'zar stopped short and spun to face them, propping one foot on a boulder set into the hillside. "Then you would have started this war way before its time. Maleshi Hi'et would have fallen from her high horse as our greatest warlord, the factions would have turned against each other *and* you, and nothing would have changed. What would have happened then, hmm? *I* would've had to stand up and take a throne I never wanted, and I'm not even sure L'zar Verdys as the Crown of Ambar'ogúl would have been any better than

Ba'rael the Spider. Feeling sorry for yourself doesn't suit you, General. Keep moving."

Without waiting for a reply, he spun back and trudged farther up the hillside.

Maleshi stared after him for a long moment before shaking her head and moving on.

"I hate to say it," Cheyenne muttered, "but he might be right."

The general laughed bitterly. "Don't let him hear you say that."

"I've heard enough to know that when you left, it gave everyone here the hope they needed. That it was possible to escape from all this. That at the very least, you weren't dead, and in the best-case scenario, you might come back."

"Best-case scenario. Ha. That turned out to be me branding myself as a traitor to the Crown and taking up arms against her at *his* side." Maleshi nodded toward L'zar. "And it took *this* ragtag group shoving their way through my front door to get me moving again."

Foltr grunted. "Don't include me in the band of misfits, Blade of the Unseen Eye."

"Of course not." Maleshi glanced at him over her shoulder and smiled thinly.

"Sometimes, we have to live through the worst-case scenario to pull ourselves out of complacency. It's ugly and effective, isn't it?" The raug chuckled as he thumped his staff into the leaf-strewn mountainside. "I heard you made a comfortable bed of lies for yourself in our sister world."

"Yes, thank you." Shaking her head, Maleshi scoffed. "I was quite comfortable. Maybe someday I'll return to it."

Foltr's sharp laugh echoed through the trees. "But not today."

"No. Today, I'm following a mad drow into the jaws of the *Sorren Gán*."

Ember gulped. "Jaws?"

"A figure of speech. Mostly."

CHAPTER EIGHTEEN

"So, I have a question." Ember swiped her hair out of her eyes, floating easily over the increasingly difficult terrain. The rest of the party was breathing heavily as they finished the last of their climb over a fallen mound of boulders L'zar had refused to take them around.

Cheyenne wiped sweat from her forehead and readjusted the straps of her backpack. "Might as well go for it, Em."

"I'm thinking. It was, what, mid-morning when we left the city? We had that ridiculously long train ride or whatever it was, and now it feels like we've been hiking through these mountains for just as long."

Maleshi let out a winded laugh. "None of those are questions."

"No, I know. But it makes me wonder how long the days are here."

"Still not a question."

Cheyenne snorted. "Don't tell me General Hi'et can't infer the question anyway."

"Oh, I can infer plenty. For one, this fae over here has the time and energy to contemplate elongated daylight in Ambar'ogúl while the rest of us are focused on marching with our actual feet on the ground."

Ember scowled at the back of the nightstalker woman's head. "Hey, believe me, if I *could* march with you, I would in a heartbeat."

"I know." Maleshi shifted her pack on her shoulders and nodded. "I'm messing with you. The days are longer over here, and that's the best answer I can give. Not much of an issue coming into this world, but I tell you what. When I went Earthside, it took me months to get used to the days cut short by at least a third."

"A third?"

"At least. It might even be half."

"Stop." L'zar's order cut sharply through the woods around them, and the group instantly halted. He peered through the sparse trees as they gave way to more rocks and eventually cliffs in the distance.

Cheyenne looked around and waited for the explanation. "Something on your mind, L'zar?"

"You couldn't handle half of what's on my mind," he spat, turning around, not to look at her, but to scan the way they'd come and the mountainside below them.

"Right, because you have such a clear understanding of what I can handle."

"Shut up." The drow's gaze flickered past her as if he didn't even see his daughter standing in line with the others following him.

Cheyenne frowned. *He looks like he's losing it. If he goes all space-drow on us again, I'll lose it too.*

Lumil glanced at L'zar and tried to follow his gaze. "Anything in particular we're looking for?"

L'zar hissed and stepped away from the party, peering through the trees. A rustle in the short, scruffy bushes on his right made him turn, and he launched a blazing dart of white light at them.

An angry, frightened squeal erupted from the shrubbery, followed by a creature with mottled dark-brown skin and three horns protruding from an elongated snout. It scrambled across the loose earth, yellow eyes wide before L'zar's next attack caught it squarely in the side and dropped the creature on the spot. The animal snorted once, sending up a spray of leaves away from its snout, and lay still.

Ember stared at the thing. "Is that a pig?"

Corian raised an eyebrow at the dead creature. "Something like one, yeah." He looked at L'zar. "And apparently such a threat that L'zar had to deal with it for us."

L'zar grunted. "It was moving."

"Not a good excuse," Cheyenne muttered.

"It's mutated too." The drow tossed his hand toward the O'gúl version of a wild boar and kept moving. "Wouldn't want that thing attacking us and spreading the blight, would we?"

Corian stared after him and slowly shook his head before exchanging concerned glances with Maleshi.

Five minutes later, L'zar spun wildly and sent a wave of blinding white light at the tallest tree they'd seen in half an hour. The branches exploded, and startled gray birds shrieked as they fluttered down the mountainside. The furry dark-purple body that fell from the tree squeaked once and lay still on the ground.

Ember looked from the purple thing to the tree again and blinked. "I don't even know what that might be."

"Not a threat, L'zar," Corian warned.

"You don't know that," the drow hissed. "You don't know anything out here. *I* do."

"Jesus, you need to chill out." Cheyenne walked steadily across the shallow incline and tried to get L'zar to look at her. "Pigs and birds and whatever the hell that purple thing is aren't our main concern right now."

L'zar whirled on her, his eyes wide and maddened with the first sign of fear she'd seen in him since he'd projected himself into her head, trying to make sure she wasn't dead. "You have no idea what we're about to face, Cheyenne. If I feel like losing my shit, there's a damn good reason for it. Enjoy your ignorance while it lasts. You'll understand soon enough."

Kicking up a spray of leaves, dry twigs, and fallen pine needles, the drow thief stalked toward the destination only he knew. The rest of the party exchanged silent, wary glances.

Corian said, "I think we're getting close."

Maleshi scoffed and gestured toward L'zar, who was storming off ahead of them. "Really? How could you tell?"

Cheyenne looked at Ember, who offered a clueless shrug. *He better pull himself together before we need him for something dangerous.*

Not long after that, L'zar led them down a steep ravine into a valley. Cheyenne noticed how quiet the valley was—no birds, no animal noises, not even the wind rustling through leaves. A cold tingle prickled down her spine. She finished sliding down the last of the loose shale behind Maleshi as the nightstalker offered Foltr a hand. He took it for a moment, then brushed her away from him before moving on with his staff.

The halfling looked at the sprawling valley in front of them and felt dark, grieving anger boiling up inside her. "What the hell?"

The valley was filled with the gnarled, twisted shapes of nearly a hundred trees towering into the sky. She could feel the power that used to be here and knew it had been stripped from the empty husks stretching in front of them. *Nimlothar trees. A whole forest, and they're all dead.*

"Keep moving," L'zar muttered with a grunt, passing the dead trunks as if he didn't notice them.

Like he's been here before. Cheyenne clenched her fists as they moved through the dead forest. The Nimlothar trees towered above them, every branch bare of leaves and devoid of life. A trace of the power that had once connected them to the drow race still hung thick in the air.

She stopped and reached out to touch the twisted black bark. A chunk fell away beneath her fingers and crumbled to dust that fluttered away in the low breeze. Her fingers stung with the residual pain in the ruined tree's memories, and she sucked in a sharp breath. *This is what losing an arm feels like. It has to be.*

"Cheyenne," Maleshi said her name softly, but there was a warning in it. "Keep moving."

Blinking back the tears welling in her eyes, the halfling gritted her teeth and pressed on. The weight of so much dead, stolen power in the forest pressed on her like a physical force. "What happened here?"

Corian looked at the branches with a pained frown. "I'm sure your first guess would be right on the mark."

"The Crown killed them." Cheyenne felt the truth in her bones and forced herself to keep her rage under control. *Hold it together, at least until we're out of here. This place doesn't deserve any more damage or pain.* "Just so she could have the last Nimlothar all to herself in the Heart."

L'zar scowled and kicked up the dry, dead soil like a spoiled child who didn't get the candy he wanted. "I mourned them too when I first saw this place. I don't like it any more than you do, but she honestly did our kind a favor when she wiped out this forest."

"*What?*" Cheyenne glared at her father. "How could this possibly be a good thing?"

"This place was a living snare, Cheyenne."

"A snare for what?"

L'zar briefly paused and turned as if to finally look her in the eye. His gaze drifted upward instead, and his lip curled in a sneer. "Drow."

"That doesn't even—" Cheyenne started to say when Corian put a hand on her shoulder and slowly shook his head.

"Not here. Later."

She swallowed thickly and stormed away from him, staring at the ground because she couldn't bear the sight of so many dead husks stripped of the power they didn't deserve to lose. *This place was sacred, not a snare. L'zar's still keeping his damn secrets. That'll end soon, even if I have to* make *it end.*

The dead, still silence was overwhelming as they moved through the Nimlothar forest. When they emerged on the other side, the ground dipped into a bowl-shaped clearing made entirely of stone. Flames flickered across the clearing like light dancing across water. Small plants, sparse bushes, and short trees with narrow trunks dotted the curving stone floor, but everything burned with continuous flames of green, red, and purple. Ash blew across the clearing amid the constant crackle and the occasional burst of sparks from the endlessly burning plants. Even the wind was silent.

Cheyenne studied the strange phenomena with a pit of hesitation in her stomach. "I don't get it. Stone doesn't burn."

L'zar shot her a quick sideways glance like he'd forgotten she was there and scowled. "It does here. Everything burns." He jumped down into the bowl-shaped clearing and stared at the massive cave on the opposite side. The stone mouth of the cave burned too, mostly with yellow and orange flames of natural fire, but with random bursts of white fire and purple sparks.

Cheyenne studied the cave but couldn't see anything past the raging fire that shouldn't have been able to burn without fuel. *It's magic. That's all the fuel anything needs on this world.*

L'zar headed toward the closest burning plant, a withered lily, casting a quick spell before reaching down and plucking the whole thing from the stone. Scowling, he moved to the next plant and the next, harvesting burning stems and leaves and flowers. Foltr grunted and handed his staff to Maleshi before heading into the center of the clearing to help L'zar with his task.

"What are they doing?"

Corian leaned toward Cheyenne and nervously licked his lips. "It's an old ritual, kid, to call out the *Sorren Gán* for a little chat, more or less. It guarantees a certain protection for us. Walking into that cave without it would end our journey right here."

She looked up at him and raised her eyebrows. "Seems a little strange that we'd have to protect ourselves if we're coming to this thing to ask for help."

The nightstalker grimaced. "This *thing* has a fondness for drow."

L'zar spun toward them, his eyes wild and his arms full of burning plants. "Don't downplay what we're facing, Corian. It likes the way we taste, plain and simple."

Cheyenne blinked and stared at the flaming mouth of the cave. "The *Sorren Gán* eats drow?"

Corian dipped his head. "When it can."

Ember swallowed. "Holy shit."

"We're here for a bargain," L'zar spat as he broke a flaming green branch off one of the trees with a sharp snap. "To come to an agreement so it'll stomp its fiery ass all the way to the capitol. We may be a delicacy for the *Sorren Gán*, but its main food is magic."

"Magic." Cheyenne folded her arms. "It eats drow and magic."

"I don't have time to listen to my damn echo, Cheyenne." L'zar trudged across the clearing, dropping his fiery armful in the very center before moving on to another plant.

"What's spilling out of Hangivol right now should be a decent feast for the *Sorren Gán*. One would think that in and of itself would be enough to entice it out, but these things don't leave their lairs if they can help it."

"So beyond dangling an exploding magical carrot in front of it, how do we get it to leave?"

"We make the trip worth its time. Placate it however we can, and in return, it should agree to make the journey and take care of the most immediate problem at the capital."

With a snort, Cheyenne shook her head and watched her father and

Foltr gathering flaming tribute to the *Sorren Gán*. "'Should.' That means none of you is sure this will work."

"We don't have any other options, kid. We're asking the *Sorren Gán* for help as a last resort. No way to hide that from the creature either, because we only have this one card to play. It's always a gamble with them."

L'zar's bitter laughter came out as a snarl. "Gamble. We're just full of fell-damn euphemisms today, aren't we?"

Corian leaned closer to Cheyenne and lowered his voice. "This one is best known for a willingness to put its appetite aside and at least listen to offers. Countless drow have tried to make deals with this particular *Sorren Gán* if they get that far. Very few of them make it out alive to see the deal fulfilled, but L'zar did. Once."

"Shut the fuck up," L'zar hissed. "I need to concentrate, and you running your mouth about the past isn't helping."

Ignoring his touchy mood, Cheyenne widened her eyes at her father as he bustled around the stone clearing. "You've done this before?"

"No. The last time, I didn't have a bunch of idiots buzzing in my ears while I was trying to focus."

She turned toward the nightstalker. "Corian, what are we getting ourselves into here? Seriously. I need to know before I go barging in there like a clueless moron."

He blinked at her above a small, cautious smile. "Sounds like you're finally coming to understand the importance of being prepared."

"I blame you for planting that seed." Cheyenne raised her eyebrows. "Tell me."

Corian took a deep breath, then turned his back on L'zar and the stone clearing as if that would keep the drow thief from overhearing the conversation. He leaned toward Cheyenne's ear and whispered, "I've only seen your father truly scared on two occasions. The first time was before he walked into that cave thousands of years ago."

As she studied the cave, Cheyenne muttered, "And the second time?"

"When he came back out. Honestly, Cheyenne, that one was worse. I think that's when he started to lose his mind."

When he leaned away from her, Cheyenne looked into his glowing silver eyes. He gave her a reassuring nod, but his concerned frown expressed what he really thought. The nightstalker turned away and jumped down into the stone clearing, standing with his feet spread wide and his arms folded to watch L'zar and Foltr preparing for their *Sorren Gán*-summoning ritual.

Shit. The drow prince who doesn't care about anything is about to take us to the one thing in two worlds that terrifies him. Won't this be fun?

Ember floated toward the halfling and gave her a weak smile. "Everything okay?"

"I have no idea, Em. After all this is over, I'll let you know, okay?"

"Yeah, sure. Anything I can do?"

"Cross your fingers, maybe?"

Ember raised both hands and crossed her fingers. They smiled at each other, but it didn't make either of them feel better.

L'zar returned to the pile of burning plants in the center of the clearing and knelt to rearrange them in a pattern for his ritual summoning. Foltr grunted and started to lower himself to his knees beside the drow, but L'zar grabbed the ancient raug's arm to stop him and shook his head. "You've done enough, Grandfather. This one's on me."

Foltr snorted. "It won't help *you*, but I'm relieved to hear you say it. For my sake."

L'zar chuckled humorlessly and went back to work arranging the burning twigs, branches, and long flowering stems. When he'd finished creating the O'gúleesh symbol with the flames, he stood and cast a summoning spell, his lips moving in a barely audible whisper. Then he spat on the symbol, and every patch of fire, flickering flames, and burning plant flared with renewed strength. The multicolored flames roared to three times their normal height, the burning cave most of all. The fires flickered in and out of different colors, favoring green and black, and a roar like howling wind and crumbling stone came from the mouth of the cave.

A low, rumbling laugh filled the clearing, and the fires settled back to their normal size. The voice coming from within the cave and echoing maddeningly within the bowl-shaped stone clearing was deeper and far more sinister than any voice had a right to be. "Come now, little drow. I told you two thousand years ago you and I would become good friends. It didn't take nearly as long as I thought."

L'zar grimaced at the mouth of the cave and lifted his chin. "I've come back with another proposition for you, *Sorren Gán*. Will you hear it?"

The *Sorren Gán's* growling laughter made Cheyenne's eyes water, the sound vibrating in her head and chest. "I will always listen to *you*. I see you've brought another of the dark ones with you this time."

"Yes."

Cheyenne clenched her fists. *It's talking about me.*

"Only the two drow on my doorstep may enter today," the *Sorren Gán* rumbled. "I can't stand the smell of the rest of you."

The flames around the cave changed to dark light and shrank to reveal the unimpeded entrance. It was pitch-black inside.

Baring his teeth in a silent snarl, L'zar turned to the rest of the group and gestured toward Cheyenne without looking at her. "Let's go."

"I thought we were all supposed to go talk to this thing together?"

"Clearly the plan has changed." L'zar bowed his head, grimacing at the stone. He couldn't bring himself to look at any of them. "I'll drag you in there if I have to, but this will be a lot easier if you come willingly."

Right. Willingly into the private cave of a thing that eats drow. Perfect.

Clenching her jaw, Cheyenne glanced at Ember, nodded, and hopped down into the clearing. Behind her, Byrd swallowed and muttered, "Good luck."

What do I say to that? "Thanks."

She walked past Corian, who dipped his head in acknowledgment.

Even the nightstalker doesn't think we'll make it out of this one in one piece, and here I am, following L'zar into the fire.

When she reached her father, L'zar lowered his arm to his side again and turned to the cave entrance. The second they reached the mouth of the cave, the flames burst to life again, seemingly blocking their path. L'zar rolled his eyes. "It's fucking with us. Let's go."

"Uh-huh." Cheyenne stared at the flames licking inches from her face and let her father step through first. When he didn't scream or shrivel into a drow crisp, she rolled her shoulders and entered behind him.

CHAPTER NINETEEN

The multicolored flames were cool against Cheyenne's skin, but on the other side, the cold permeating the pitch-black cave made her pause. *If the cold's bothering me in here, it'd probably kill the others—that or the smell.*

As her eyes adjusted to the darkness, she realized the cave was much larger than it looked from the outside. It stretched endlessly in front of them, the stone walls rising into the side of the mountain until she couldn't see the top. Flames flickered across the walls, black smoke wafting in the frigid darkness. *Looks a lot like the in-between if you ask me.*

On the far side of the cave was a massive lake, the surface covered in endless purple flames. The crackle and hiss of unnaturally burning stone and the occasional spark tossed into the air punctured the silence. L'zar took three steps forward, Cheyenne at his side, then dropped to one knee without warning.

She frowned down at him. "What are you doing?"

He didn't lift his bowed head. "We're not here to fuck around. Kneel."

"Yes," the *Sorren Gán* roared in its overwhelmingly brutal voice. "You learned that lesson the first time we met. Didn't you, L'zar?"

Cheyenne quickly scanned the dark cave and couldn't see a thing. *Where the hell is it?*

L'zar's cold fingers clamped around her wrist and he jerked her to her knees. She pulled her hand away and scowled at him.

"What's wrong with you?" she whispered.

His golden gaze burned into the black stone floor of the cave in front of them. "Right now? Everything."

From the back of the cave, a yellow-orange glow grew within the darkness. Cheyenne looked up and watched the massive creature made of fire and thick black smoke emerge from some hidden recess in the cave's walls. It was at least thirty feet tall and had tongues of fire dripping from its broad shoulders. Four arms extended at its sides, two of its hands splayed out, the fingers tipped in black claws that trailed thick lines of smoke behind them. The *Sorren Gán* might have had horns, but then again, they might have been smoke. Clawed feet stomped across the ground, making it tremble beneath them. The lake of fire shuddered, and two massive, fiery wings spread from the Sorren Gán's back with a fan of more black smoke before settling against its sides again.

L'zar kept his head bowed, clenching his jaw so tightly he thought his head would explode. *The first time was for me. This time, it is for Ambar'ogúl. Fuck taking the throne, but I won't let the place burn before I leave it forever.* His balled fists ached, and still he didn't look up at the *Sorren Gán* stalking toward them. He sure as hell could feel it.

The fiery beast let out another low, ominous chuckle. "I enjoy this sight very much. Now tell me why you're here."

"We need your help." L'zar swallowed. "*I* need your help."

"With the afterbirth of the foulness your sister spawned." The *Sorren Gán* stopped yards in front of them, casting burning light over the kneeling drow. The smoke wafting off its body was so thick, Cheyenne expected to choke on it at any minute. "Tell me why you wish to have this threat subdued, L'zar. We both know you do not seek the O'gúl Crown."

"No." L'zar bowed his head even lower and pressed his fists against the stone.

Cheyenne shot him a sideways glance and tried looking at the *Sorren Gán* but couldn't face the blazing light. *L'zar is bending the knee. Why?*

"I don't want to rule," the drow continued. "But I don't want to see Ambar'ogúl destroyed, either."

A flaming tail lashed out from behind the *Sorren Gán* and struck the stone floor with a burst of sparks. "Why?"

"Because I don't want to be remembered as the Weaver thief who brought an entire world to its knees. Not like this."

"Wrong." The beast stepped closer and snorted a thick plume of rancid black smoke into both drow's faces.

Cheyenne turned her head away from the worst of it and caught a glimpse of her father's fists and arms through the dispersing smoke. *Shit. He's shaking.*

"You've had time to practice your lies, little drow," the *Sorren Gán* rumbled. "But not nearly enough to make them convincing. Tell me why you want to save this world."

L'zar's lips trembled when he opened his mouth. He pressed his lips together and glared at the floor in humiliation. "It's my daughter's legacy. She deserves all of it. I owe her that much, at least."

Cheyenne's eyes widened despite the smoke stinging her eyes. *First time I've heard him own up to anything, even if it's under duress.*

"Hmm. Yes." The *Sorren Gán* chuckled again and stopped looming over the kneeling drow, taking a step back. Its wings shot out again, fanning more smoke through the cave, and its other two fists opened to stretch clawed fingers in anticipation. "Honesty is your weakness, isn't it, little drow? Your inability to humble yourself makes you weak. That is why you've come to me again. Someone has to make you face your trembling terror. We made you strong before, did we not?"

L'zar glared at the floor, his jaw clenching and unclenching.

The flames around and within the *Sorren Gán* erupted with a roar. "Did we *not*?"

"Yes!" L'zar breathed heavily now, pressing his fists into the stone floor so hard they bled.

Cheyenne wrinkled her nose at the smell. *What the hell happened between these two?*

"And now you return for more of the same." The *Sorren Gán* extended a hand toward L'zar as if it meant to rest the fiery paw on the drow's hand, but it didn't. "Why should I travel such a long way to Hangivol? It means nothing to me if the wealth of magic your sister pilfered destroys one city or a thousand. The magic will find me anyway."

L'zar's head lifted an inch, and he managed to settle his gaze on the creature's clawed, burning feet. "Name your price."

"You know I require something now."

"Yes."

Cheyenne flinched away from an unnaturally long tongue of flame licking toward her face.

"This daughter of yours is different," the *Sorren Gán* growled. "You knew I would want her."

L'zar straightened and turned toward Cheyenne. "That's not what I had in mind."

"Nor is it something you would refuse me, hmm?"

Cheyenne stared at her father. *He better say something.*

L'zar swallowed and opened his mouth, but nothing came out.

"L'zar." She raised her eyebrows.

His upper lip twitched as he stared into his daughter's eyes. "You'll be fine."

"Are you fucking kidding me?"

The *Sorren Gán* thundered with dark laughter. The sound echoed through the cave and made the floor tremble as much as the creature's footsteps. "Your loyalty pleases me very much, L'zar."

"You can't bring me in here and toss me to this thing as a quick snack!" Cheyenne leaped to her feet, blinking away the tears against the smoke spewing from the *Sorren Gán*'s body. "I'm not doing this."

"You have to, Cheyenne."

"No, I don't. *You* have to grow a conscience and a goddamn spine. Look at you. You won't even get off your knees to give me up. I came in here willingly, but not as a fucking sacrifice."

"You don't have to be willing," the *Sorren Gán* growled. "*He* wasn't the first time."

"What?"

The fiery beast laughed again, shaking the cave around them.

"I'm done, L'zar. You can follow me out or stay here and die on your knees. I don't give a shit." She whirled toward the mouth of the cave and stormed off.

The flames around the entrance flared in blinding brilliance and a wave of smoke barreled toward her, pushing her back across the stone floor even as she dug her feet in. Coughing and gasping for breath,

Cheyenne let her rage fuel the drow magic building inside her. *Think of the Nimlothar seed. And the dead forest.*

Cold pressure coiled around her leg and whipped it out from under her. She crashed to the stone and spun onto her back, glaring up at the *Sorren Gán* as a coil of black smoke extended to drag her toward it. Purple and black light burst from her body, glowing brighter from behind her golden eyes, and her magic burned through her veins with renewed force. *Yeah, that's more like it.*

She fired countless rounds of black energy spheres at the *Sorren Gán*'s flaming head. It only laughed harder, dragging her with it as it retreated from L'zar. Cheyenne lurched upward and grabbed the coil of black smoke before summoning two more energy spheres, and the smoke burst into black shards that caught fire as they flew through the air.

The *Sorren Gán* roared in fury, its barbed tail lashing the ground as it stepped toward her and reached out with one of its four hands. Cheyenne raised a shimmering black shield as a roaring column of fire shot toward her. The shield stopped it, but the freezing cold that enveloped her when she expected heat made her pause.

"You *will* give me what I seek," the *Sorren Gán* roared as the column of flames subsided.

Cheyenne lowered the shield, her fingers numb, and reached out with her connection to the earth to find that ledge of resistance. "Fuck you."

When she pulled with both hands, the stone floor erupted in front of the *Sorren Gán*. A massive slab of earth broke free and hurtled toward the flaming beast, knocking it back across the cave.

"Cheyenne."

"And fuck *you*. Trying to give me up like this." She stormed toward the cave entrance again, but before she took two steps, black smoke ballooned from every dark crevice of the cave and enveloped her. Cheyenne couldn't see a thing as she stumbled forward blindly, waving the smoke away and trying to catch a breath as it seared into her lungs and muddled her thoughts.

The next thing she knew, she was flying through the air, sailing out of the black smoke and high above both L'zar and the *Sorren Gán*, who was staring up at her with blazing eyes of smoke and fire. There was nothing to grab, nothing to wrap her black lashing tendrils around even when she released them and tried to find purchase. The last thing she saw before she plunged into the hissing, raging lake of fire on the other side of the cave was the *Sorren Gán*'s mouth splitting in a wide grin, spewing flames and smoke. Its laughter echoed through her head as she fell into the lake.

The unbearable cold coursed through her before her drow magic took over. Cheyenne's body erupted with black fire that rushed across her skin, blocking the cold as she sank into the bright, burning substance. *This shit is definitely not water.*

Something told her she could take a breath, and when she did, her lungs were free from the burning smoke. Black flames burst from her eyes as she gazed at the terrifying images coalescing around her in the fiery substance. Screaming faces contorted in terror and anguish. Humanoid shapes fighting each other, burning, destroying, wailing.

Cheyenne kicked out at the fire surrounding her, but it didn't get her anywhere. Finally, her feet touched the bottom of the lake, and she took a tentative step forward. Flames moved around her, propelled by the drow fire racing across her skin. Gritting her teeth and clenching her fists, she took step after slow step up the incline of the lakebed back toward the shore.

When I get up there, those bastards are in for it.

CHAPTER TWENTY

"The ultimate test, is it not?" The *Sorren Gán* loomed over L'zar, who sat cross-legged on the cave floor, his head hanging between his slumped shoulders. "Does L'zar Verdys truly hold within his insignificant hands the ability not to show restraint, but to relinquish everything?" Another thunderous laugh rose from the beast's chest. "You are a slow learner, little drow. Once I break her as I broke you, perhaps your daughter will be capable of withstanding what you cannot."

L'zar stared at the ground, clenching and unclenching his jaw. *If I'm right, she already does.*

He leaned away from a tendril of smoke the *Sorren Gán* extended to caress his face. "You're so emotional, L'zar, not a trait I envy in any of you. With time, I see that withering away with all your other weaknesses. You will see."

A burst of flame erupted from the lake on the other side of the cave, and the purple fire fell away as Cheyenne, covered in black drow fire, stormed out of the lake and headed for L'zar and his unlikely master. Purple flames fell like water behind her with each step and burned like scattered pools of ignited oil.

L'zar lifted his head and watched her, wide-eyed, with the ghost of a smile.

The *Sorren Gán* stepped back, stretching its wings wide again and roaring with laughter. "I seem to have been mistaken, L'zar. Between the two of you, her blood flows much stronger."

L'zar gazed up at the beast's face, constantly shifting in the flames, and grinned. "You gave me what I was missing, didn't you?"

"I gave you what you *needed*," the *Sorren Gán* hissed. "You came to *me*. *You* begged me for the cleansing, and I poured everything I had into your soft flesh. Surprise or not, little drow, do not be ungrateful."

"*I* am." Snarling, Cheyenne raised her hands toward the *Sorren Gán* and unleashed a column of her own flames, hissing and black as they crashed into the beast's chest.

The thing turned to face her and spread its four arms. "Here she is."

Cheyenne roared and fired again, blasting the *Sorren Gán* over and over with drow fire as the flames flared around her body and flashed behind her eyes. Every attack was swallowed by the beast's form, and it laughed again.

L'zar could barely see his daughter beneath the flames, but he leaped to his feet and hurried toward her. "Cheyenne."

"No!" She kept attacking as she stormed toward the thing that ate drow and had tossed her into the burning lake. "I told you I was done."

"Cheyenne, it won't do anything."

"No, *you* won't do anything."

"I can explain."

Shouting in rage, Cheyenne whirled on her father and sent a ball of black flames hurtling into his chest. It threw him toward the cave wall, and he pulled the same trick he'd used before. The black fire consumed his body and he spread his arms, slowing himself before hitting the wall and hovering over the cave floor before lowering himself to the ground. The flames curled inward and almost sank into his skin, then they were gone.

Cheyenne summoned a churning sphere of black energy and stormed after him. "Don't tell me you can explain."

"I can."

"You *sacrificed* me! Just like that." She launched the energy sphere at him, and he batted it aside with a flash of white light. "You didn't even try to find a better way. All you did was tell me I'd be fine!"

A chuckle escaped him and he shrugged. "And so you are."

"Stop laughing!" Cheyenne hurled two more attacks at him. L'zar deflected the first, but the second caught him in the shoulder and spun him off-balance.

Finally, she reached her father and took a black-flaming swing at his face. He ducked and tried to grab her wrist. Cheyenne brought her other elbow up toward his throat, but L'zar blocked it with a quickly raised forearm and stepped aside. "I'm serious, Cheyenne."

"You're never serious. That's the problem!"

"Stop." He parried another punch and tried to pull her against him. "Stop trying to fight me and listen."

"Stop pretending you give a shit about me!" Cheyenne snarled as she kept up the attack, launching punches that would send most magicals crashing through the walls. L'zar was too quick.

The *Sorren Gán* watched the squabbling drow for a moment before its fascination dwindled. It snorted another cloud of thick black smoke and flicked two of its hands toward the mouth of the cave.

Cheyenne and L'zar were ripped apart by the *Sorren Gán*'s magic and went sailing through the wall of fire blocking the cave entrance and out into the stone courtyard beyond.

The halfling braced herself for the fall and tumbled across the stone, rolling as much as she could.

Lumil leaped up from where she'd been sitting in the clearing, eyes wide. The other magicals in their party got to their feet to watch L'zar sliding on his back into the center of the bowl-shaped clearing too. Both drow trailed thin wisps of smoke behind them. Cheyenne's black flames had been snuffed by the *Sorren Gán*'s disposal of her and her father.

"Shit." Cheyenne slapped the real fire igniting the hem of her trenchcoat and two spots on her sleeves. *Dammit, I just bought this thing.*

L'zar scrambled to his feet and slapped at the fire singeing his pants and the front of his shirt. When he finally got it all out, he straightened his shirt and smoothed his long white hair away from his face with both hands.

"So." Maleshi folded her arms and blinked at the drow. "How did it go?"

L'zar lifted a hand and opened his mouth to answer. Words escaped him, so he gestured at Cheyenne.

The flames blocking the cave entrance flared brighter, and the *Sorren Gán*'s voice boomed across the clearing again. "You have amused me, at the very least. This I will accept as payment. For now."

"Endaru's balls." Byrd smiled in relief. "I didn't think that would happen."

"In three days' time," the beast roared, hidden behind the flames guarding its cave, "I will make the journey to Hangivol, and I will feast on the product of Ba'rael Verdys' stupidity. Do not wait another thousand years to visit me, L'zar. I did miss you."

L'zar spun and shot the cave the middle finger as the *Sorren Gán*'s terrifying laughter faded.

"Three days?" Corian rubbed his mouth. "I guess it's better than never."

Cheyenne whipped the back of her trenchcoat around, looking for any errant fire she might have missed. L'zar approached her and reached out toward her face. "Are you all right?"

She slapped his hand away. "Don't touch me."

"I want to make sure you're all right."

Another churning sphere of crackling black energy flew from her hand. He stepped quickly away to dodge the attack, and her magic cracked into the stone behind him, sending black and purple sparks everywhere.

"Whoa, whoa." Corian rushed toward them. "What happened?"

"Ask *him*." Cheyenne launched another energy sphere, but Corian threw off her aim when he pushed her arm down.

Then he grabbed her shoulders and turned her around to look at him. She tried to struggle out of his grasp, but he gave her a quick shake. "Cheyenne!"

"What?" she snarled.

"Cut it out."

Breathing heavily, she tried to look over her shoulder at L'zar, who merely straightened his shirtsleeves before clasping his hands behind his back and turning away from them.

"Don't look at him, kid. Look at me."

"You're not the one I want to kill, Corian, but if you don't let go of me, I'll fight you too. I already punched you once. Imagine what I can do *now*." Cheyenne jerked his hands off her shoulders and spun toward L'zar.

"What happened in there?" Maleshi asked, stopping hesitantly beside Corian.

Cheyenne jabbed a finger at L'zar. "That asshole sacrificed me to the *Sorren Gán*."

Maleshi unfolded her arms. "What?"

Corian bared his teeth in a snarl. "L'zar."

The drow thief slowly turned around and spread his arms. "I wouldn't say that's an accurate recounting."

"Bullshit! That's exactly what happened. You didn't even try to fight for me. You're a fucking coward, and I think ripping your head off your shoulders would do more good for all of us than any of your shitty plans."

"Cheyenne, I understand you're upset."

She roared and lunged at him. Corian and Maleshi went after her in twin flashes of silver light, and Cheyenne found herself struggling against both nightstalkers holding her back. She tried to slip past them, snarling, but they held her shoulders and yanked her back.

"You need to stop, kid," Maleshi growled. "This isn't the right way to handle it."

"Sure feels right." The halfling jerked against their hold, and they pulled her back even farther.

"We'll figure it out," Corian muttered, "but you have to let this go. Right now."

Cheyenne sneered and shoved her face up to his. "You weren't *there*. You have no idea what I saw!"

"Hey."

Cheyenne turned at the sound of Ember's voice and shot a quick glance at her friend before the fae's hand smacked the halfling's cheek. Cheyenne's head barely moved, but the shock of it took the fight out of her for two seconds.

"Oh, shit." Byrd sucked in a breath and pressed his knuckles against his teeth. Beside him, Lumil ran a hand through her mop of yellow hair and watched silently.

"Ember."

"Get it the fuck together already. What's wrong with you?"

"Hey, I'm not the one who tried to feed my daughter to a—"

"Shut up." Ember pointed at Corian and Maleshi. "Let go of her. She's not one of your prisoners."

Corian cleared his throat and slowly slid his hands off Cheyenne. Maleshi released the halfling's other shoulder and raised her hands, backing away.

The halfling rolled her shoulders and lifted her chin. "What happened back there was—"

"Inexcusable. Horrifying. A massive betrayal. Yeah, I get it." Ember grabbed her friend's shoulders and squeezed. "We can talk about it later. Right now, you're starting to sound a lot like the drow you're so set on blowing to pieces. Got it?"

Cheyenne blinked. *Jesus, I probably do look like a raving lunatic.* She glanced at L'zar, who had his hands in his pockets and was staring at the ground.

Ember shook her gently. "Got it?"

"Yeah. Yeah, Em. I get it."

"Okay." Ember released her and asked, "So what now?"

"If it's all right with Cheyenne," L'zar muttered, slowly looking up at his daughter with a small frown, "I would very much like the chance to explain what happened."

"You can't leave it alone for five minutes, can you?"

"It's important."

Cheyenne spun and stormed past the nightstalkers. "Give me five minutes."

L'zar looked at Corian and gestured toward his daughter. The nightstalker pointed at him in warning. "Don't push it."

"Okay." The drow raised his hands in submission. "I'll wait."

Cheyenne walked across the bowl and slumped against the slope, her back curving with the shape of the smooth stone. Light tapping sounded on her right, and she snorted when she saw Foltr sitting on the lip of the stone bowl, swinging his staff over the edge and hitting the rock.

"Time heals many things, *Aranél.*"

"Yeah, well, I don't think five minutes is enough to patch up this mess." *Not even five lifetimes. I should never have trusted him.*

The old raug nodded slowly. "We shall see."

CHAPTER TWENTY-ONE

"Can I sit?"

Cheyenne glanced at L'zar's shoes beside her. "You were timing me, weren't you?"

"Only with an internal clock. It's pretty accurate after the first thousand years."

She snorted and didn't protest when he lowered himself to the stone beside her. The rest of their party had gathered on the other side of the clearing to give the drow space for a much-needed chat.

L'zar kicked out his legs in front of him and said, "I'm sure you've picked up on the fact that I was here once before."

"Yeah, two thousand years ago. And you found yourself a master. Sounds like some kind of messed-up drow BDSM without any of the benefits."

He slowly looked at her with a growing smile. "And those would be?"

"I don't know, it just came out. Say what you need to say."

"Ba'rael wasn't the only one looking for more power, Cheyenne." L'zar wrapped his arms around his bent knees and hooked his fingers together. "We shared the same brand of youthful stupidity back then. Honestly, I wonder sometimes if it's changed much."

She scoffed. "How observant of you."

"Most days, I like to think my stupidity is slightly less prevalent these days." L'zar shot her a sidelong glance and smiled. "My sister was too much of a coward to leave the safety of her precious city and risk everything she had to get what she wanted. I was too much of an idiot not to consider that coming here the first time would give me everything I wanted in all the worst ways. But I came. The Nimlothar forest was still thriving then. The rest of this place is unchanged."

"What's your point?"

"My point." The drow chuckled. "I came here wanting power from the *Sorren Gán*, and it showed me how to get what I wanted. I know exactly what it's like in that fell-damn lake, Cheyenne. I spent more time down there than I care to remember all at once, without coming up for air."

"You know you can breathe in there, right?"

"No. You could. I could not." L'zar turned his head toward her, then looked away. "I died in those flames. The part of me that makes me myself died, and when I did, I saw the threads right there in front of me, laid out in perfect order and with such clarity."

Cheyenne shifted her position and frowned across the clearing. "I have no idea what you're talking about when you bring up threads and weaving and whatever."

"Hmm. What you see with that activator, lines of code and data and the various outcomes of a single command, I see with magic. Those are the threads. The bonds tying us to every living thing in this world and Earth. To *ourselves*." He shrugged. "As I died, I found the threads to pull myself out of the flames. Maybe it was only a return from the brink of death and not real death. Who knows? L'zar Verdys, the O'gúl *Cu'ón*, fell into the fire, and L'zar Verdys the Smiling Weaver walked out of it, the same and not the same. Sometimes, I wonder how far from myself I've gotten since that day."

"Everyone says you were an annoying little shit from the beginning, so it can't be that far."

They both laughed, and L'zar nodded. "There is that. But we're talking about you."

"Right."

"When I walked out of that lake, Cheyenne, the *Sorren Gán* told me something I never expected to fully understand. I had the power I wanted, sure. I'd survived. I rewrote what would have been the end of my story and transformed it into something like the middle, or at least the end of the beginning. I had the *Sorren Gán's* full approval and what it called 'my power,' but it told me I would not be the last one to use it."

"Meaning me." Cheyenne nodded. "I get it. I'm your kid, I got your drow powers. Sure."

"No. I'm sure you've noticed our abilities are not the same." L'zar chuckled. "And you can't read the Weave like I do."

"Well, you can't handle computers."

"That's a fair assessment. The day you told me you'd unlocked your final ability and used the black fire, though?" L'zar said, running a hand through his hair, "That was the moment I understood what the *Sorren Gán* meant."

Cheyenne waited for him to continue, but the pause felt far too long. *He's still stalling.* "I have a feeling there's something more to this. Otherwise, you lost me."

"You get your drow fire from me, Cheyenne. *And* from the *Sorren Gán.*"

"Wait, what?"

"In plainer words, drow fire was not one of my abilities when I passed my trials. I'm fairly certain that came from my time spent in the lake, under the *Sorren Gán's* control in its domain. To save myself, I took a piece of that beast's magic as my own and came out with a new fierce power I couldn't explain. No one would have listened anyway, except for you. You were born with it."

Cheyenne leaned away from him and frowned. "That's crazy. You're telling me I'm part-*Sorren Gán*?"

"Hardly. You just have its magic in your blood."

"Magically speaking, L'zar, I'm pretty sure that's the same thing."

He looked her in the eyes, a small frown flickering across his eyebrows. "It most certainly is not." With a grunt, he pushed to his feet and walked across the clearing toward the others. "And now I need a drink."

Cheyenne stared after him, trying to make all the pieces fit. *It sounds like total crap, but it makes sense. I could breathe in the lake, didn't lose my mind, and couldn't hurt the damn thing with my most powerful ability.*

She shook her head. "Later. I can think about that later."

She stood and headed after her father. Corian gave her a wary smile. "Everybody good?"

"'Good' is probably a little strong, but I don't want to kill him anymore."

L'zar smirked but didn't look at her.

"That's acceptable." Corian rubbed his hands together and gazed around the gathered circle. "Time to figure out what happens next."

"Don't we go back to the capital and wait for that thing to come and suck out all the extra magic?" Ember asked.

"We could."

L'zar lifted his chin. "I can't think about what happens next until we get out of here. And I'd prefer not to waste another day at the very least traveling the way we came so I can find a quiet place to put my head together."

"Right." Corian glanced at the cave entrance and cocked his head. "We have plenty of that to do still."

"And if possible, I would prefer to return to Hangivol with much more of a plan than we have now when it comes to the terms of Ba'rael's secession and Cheyenne taking the O'gúl Crown. If she wants it."

Maleshi shrugged. "The plan we have now is nonexistent."

"What exactly do we have to sit down and think so hard about?" Cheyenne asked.

L'zar's smile widened. "Where my sister's weakest point is and how to exploit it."

She gestured toward the burning cave. "After everything that happened in there, you want to talk about exploiting weaknesses?"

The other magicals glanced around in confusion, but L'zar and his daughter stared only at each other.

"You make an excellent point." The drow nodded, and his smile bloomed into his trickster grin. "You can't tell me it's not extraordinarily effective."

She laughed. "No, I guess not."

"We can go to Hirúl Breach." Foltr lifted his staff and gestured farther into the mountains. "Another few hours through the next pass."

Lumil snorted. "Hirúl Breach? You know, I heard they call that place the Crown's Bastion."

The old raug grunted and stuck his stick into the ground. "The *last* Crown, yes. K'laht traveled there often, and Hirúl Breach welcomed him with open arms and everything they had to give. There is no love lost between them and Ba'rael."

L'zar narrowed his eyes. "No love lost, or they hate her?"

"They despise the Crown of this Cycle, L'zar. As they should."

The drow clapped his hands together and pointed in the direction Foltr had indicated. "Then by all means, that needs to be our next stop. A few hours is much better than an entire day. Lead on."

"I'm not leading us anywhere," Foltr blustered. "But I can get us inside."

L'zar leaned toward him and shook his head. "I don't know where it is."

"Of course you don't." The old raug thumped his staff against the drow's calf. "You never went farther into these mountains than *this* cursed stinkhole."

"We should go somewhere else." Maleshi folded her arms and squinted into the woods.

L'zar cocked his head. "Come again?"

She rolled her eyes and glared at him. "Do I have to spell it out for you, L'zar? Hirúl Breach is the closest hub to the den at Felagtrok."

"Ah, yes. And this is apparently an issue for you." L'zar tapped a long, slender finger on his lips. "Care to elaborate?"

"You know exactly what I'm talking about."

Foltr patted the general's arm and nodded. "If there were survivors, Maleshi, they would most likely be there. And yes, they might be uncomfortable with our presence."

"Uncomfortable?" The nightstalker woman closed her eyes. "You know that's not the way those raugs see it."

"They will see past what you have done as Hand of the Night and Circle, *hinya*." Foltr nodded and thumped his staff on the ground. "They will not forget, but they will understand."

Lumil snorted. "Yeah. Raugs understand with their fists."

"Just like you, eh?" Foltr pointed the end of his stick at her legs. "Don't make me use this."

"I've been to Hirúl Breach," Corian muttered, giving Maleshi an apologetic smile. "It's a good idea, and it'll help us, whether or not they enjoy a visit from General Hi'et."

Maleshi grimaced. "Fine. What's done is done, and everyone's made up their minds."

Corian nodded. "I'll open a portal."

Foltr looked at him. "You can port that far, eh?"

"I've connected two spaces a lot farther apart than that, Grandfather," Corian said, "Though I'd be a lot more comfortable with it if we got away from this cave first. The last thing I want is a *Sorren Gán* feeding on my trail."

"Excellent point. It would follow you and ask for more." L'zar chuckled and stepped out of the bowl-shaped clearing to trudge through the slowly thickening forest on the other side. "Things are already looking up. I can feel it."

Cheyenne nudged Maleshi with her elbow. "I don't need to know the details, but if I got sacrificed on purpose to make a point, I'm pretty sure you can handle a few raugs who recognize you and might hold a grudge."

The general scoffed. "You just keep broadening your horizons, don't you, kid? Here's hoping you're right." Maleshi stalked after the others, and Cheyenne sighed.

Ember leaned toward her. "Talk about mood swings."

"Right? I think I understand a little better where they're coming from now."

"Oh, yeah?"

"I mean, most of it's still 'cause he's losing his mind, but there's a reason for that too."

Ember folded her arms and eyed the halfling. "When we get more than a minute, you have a hell of a lot to tell me, don't you?"

"More than I can even think about right now, Em." Cheyenne stepped onto the lip of earth above the clearing and headed after the others. "I might need a little more time to sort it all out in my head."

"Sure. While you're doing that, how's your face?"

Cheyenne snorted. "You hit like a fae."

"Huh. I have no idea if that was a compliment, but thanks."

"It definitely was." The halfling cast her friend a sidelong glance. "Good thing I have you to slap some sense into me, right?"

"That's exactly why I'm here. Friends don't let friends kill their crazy-ass fathers."

"Ha. Hopefully it won't be a thing again, but you might have to remind me of that once or twice."

Ember raised her hand and shook it in a goofy wave. "I'll be ready."

CHAPTER TWENTY-TWO

After a half-hour hike through the mountains, Corian stopped to open a portal for them into Hirúl Breach. They stepped through the dark window of light and found themselves on a stone plateau at the edge of a mountainous canyon. Natural rock walls stretched high all around them, and in the center was Hirúl Breach.

"Well." Foltr frowned at the rising towers of stone and dark metal tech. "The place has certainly changed since I last came through."

Corian nodded slowly. "Tell me about it."

"For a tribe opposed to technological advancements, I'd say they're doing pretty well for themselves." L'zar bowed to Foltr and gestured toward the wide staircase carved into the stone of the plateau, which descended to the front gates of the city. "How about now, Grandfather?"

"If it gets you to stop making a mockery of yourself, Weaver, I'll lead the fell-damn way." Foltr thumped his cane with each step as he approached the staircase, and the party moved from their vantage point toward the raug city below.

"Not sure what he means by technological advancement," Cheyenne muttered. "There's tech here, but it's not like anything in Hangivol."

Corian looked at her over his shoulder. "For Hirúl Breach, it's a huge step forward. They're stonemasons, or at least they *were*. Looks like they've taken it upon themselves to add old-world tech to the mix. The buildings are a lot higher, and they *have* front gates this time, so it must be doing something for them."

Ember peered over Corian's head to look down at the whirring, rumbling machines of black metal rolling slowly across the open area in front of the gates. "Old-world tech as in war machines?"

"Same look, different purpose." Corian chuckled. "It's pretty ingenious of them. The Crown can't hack into their machines with her fancy new gadgets that won't sync up. They've made themselves as autonomous as anyone can get out here."

"They're protecting themselves." Cheyenne eyed the machine of black, glistening metal passing in front of them when they reached the bottom of the staircase. *That one looks way too much like those diggers.*

"That's what it looks like, doesn't it?" Maleshi gazed at the high metal gates in front of them. "And they built a city."

"A trade city, looks like," Corian said, "It wouldn't house nearly as many magicals, but if something *did* happen to Hangivol, we might be looking at the runner-up for a new capital."

L'zar scoffed. "Right. Everyone in Hangivol will throw out their activators and come swarming out here to live in the dark ages of O'gúl tech. Brilliant analysis." He thumped the back of his hand against Corian's chest and shook his head. "Hangivol will be fine."

"Sure."

"*Salut!*" The gruff shout came from atop one of the towers beside the gate. "*Qui êtes vous?*"

Foltr extended a hand toward the traveling party and nodded. "Let me speak to them first, eh? Just a few minutes, and I'll get us inside."

Cheyenne and the others waited halfway between the bottom of the stairs and Hirúl Breach's front gates.

"A word, brothers!" Foltr shouted at the towers.

A lot of banging and clanking came from within the gates, then a door opened at the base of the tower, and two raugs in matching gray uniforms marched out to meet with the old magical wielding his trusty staff.

Cheyenne cocked her head as she listened to the conversation. The only words she could pick out were *Aranél* and *Cu'ón*, but she recognized the language. She turned toward Maleshi and pointed at the raugs. "Are they speaking French?"

"*Oui.*" The general chuckled at Cheyenne's confusion. "Don't tell me you never wondered why a separate world full of magic and every race under the sun except the human race was full of magicals speaking English."

"Of course I wondered." Cheyenne folded her arms. "I guess I figured it was because of the portals or something. I don't know. You guys travel back and forth all the time, don't you?"

Corian snorted. "Only some of us, kid."

Maleshi shot him an exasperated glance but couldn't help a smile. "It has something to do with the portals, sure. Our worlds are connected. Nobody can argue that. Very few O'gúleesh magicals speak the old O'gúleesh tongue day-to-day, minus the few colorful words thrown in for fun."

"So, what? Everyone just speaks English and French instead?"

"Try *all* Earth languages." With his hands clasped behind his back, L'zar wiggled his eyebrows at his daughter and grinned. "Earthside portals exist all over the world. It wouldn't make sense if we only spoke English and French over here, now would it?"

Cheyenne shook her head in disbelief. "How long has this been a thing?"

Corian shrugged. "As long as the portals, I assume. It's anyone's guess."

"The only pure O'gúleesh language still intact is our alphabet." Maleshi chuckled and stared wistfully across the small courtyard in front of the gates. "Let me tell ya, kid, it took me a hell of a lot longer than I expected to nail down reading and writing after I made the crossing. Just one of those things you don't think much about when you're abandoning your post and a dying world to start over fresh."

Ember slid her hands down her cheeks and let out a surprised chuckle. "Raugs speaking French. Now I've seen it all. What else is there?"

Corian smiled at her. "The Golra have a fluent understanding of almost every Chinese dialect."

Cheyenne barked a laugh, then cleared her throat. "Nu'ek too?"

"Probably."

Foltr nodded at the raug guards and turned slowly toward the group, shambling back with his staff clicking on the stone.

L'zar dipped his head toward the ancient magical. "Well?"

"It's a start." Foltr looked at Ember and raised his thick brows over wrinkled eyelids. "They need your help."

"*My* help?" Ember glanced at the others. "You're not talking about just me."

"Yes. Just you." Foltr grumbled something unintelligible, then looked at Maleshi. "They don't want us here. Especially you, General."

"They recognized me, huh?"

"Yes. They also made it perfectly clear they have ended all ties with the capital and whatever fate befalls it." He lifted a crooked gray finger at Ember. "But they need you."

"To do what?"

"They need a fae. A healer. There's a dying raug inside those gates who stands to meet the final deathflame far before his time. If you can save him, these gates will open for all of us. They'll give us a warm raug welcome, and we can sit down with whomever we like to discuss how they can help us."

L'zar chuckled. "'Warm raug welcome?' There's a term you don't hear every day."

"If it didn't exist before, it will after this." Foltr waved Ember forward. "Let's get it done."

"For real?" Ember looked at Cheyenne. "Is he serious?"

"It's healing, Em. No spells. You just do it, right?"

The fae glanced at Foltr, who was shuffling away again. "I guess."

Cheyenne nodded. "You got this."

L'zar sat down outside the front gates, stretching his legs out in front of him and propping himself up with his hands. "We'll be waiting for you. Try to be quick about it."

"Oh, sure. I'll just rush the healing of a dying raug. No problem." Rolling her eyes, Ember floated after Foltr, clenching and unclenching her fists at her sides.

L'zar chuckled. "I like a fae who talks back to me."

Corian snorted. "You like anyone who talks to you at all."

"Not true, but nice try."

Cheyenne watched Ember and Foltr follow the guards through the door at the base of the massive gates. "So we wait."

Maleshi set a hand on the halfling's shoulder and dipped her head. "We're not storming into *this* stronghold, kid. I can tell you that much."

"As long as they let her back out."

"If she heals this raug, they will."

When the small door shut behind the raug guards, Cheyenne sat down on the ground too and crossed her legs. "There's no if. She'll get it done. That's what fae do, right?"

"It certainly seems that way."

CHAPTER TWENTY-THREE

Ember floated behind Foltr and their raug escorts into Hirúl Breach. She didn't get to see much of it after they passed through the gate, but it was enough to convince her she'd walked into one more giant city she knew nothing about. *And I'm here playing magical doctor. Okay. I can do this.*

The guards led them into a long, low building built against the wall of the canyon. They climbed three sets of narrow staircases and stopped in front of a heavy wooden door. One raug pressed his palm to the door and nodded at her. "Don't let him kick you out, fae. He does that."

"Okay."

He shoved the door open and gestured for her to walk in. She floated through the door, and the other guard held out his hand to block Foltr from entering as well. "Only the healer, old one."

Foltr grunted and lifted his staff, preparing to knock the guard's hand aside. "I'm old, brother. Not useless. I can help."

"Not if you catch what eats this one."

"Hmm." Foltr stepped back and called through the door, "I'll be outside, girl. Call if you need anything."

"Right." Before she could say anything else, the guards pulled the heavy door shut with a bang. Wrinkling her nose, she scanned the room. One wall was open to the outside air, pulling in a small breeze that made the lanterns sway on their hooks in the ceiling. *They could knock down all the walls, and it still wouldn't improve the smell.*

Grimacing, she floated toward the large bed on the other side of the room, where a mottled gray hand poked out from beneath layers and layers of thick blankets. "Hello?"

A wheezing cough greeted her.

That doesn't sound good. What am I doing? I'm not a raug doctor.

"I came here to help."

"Get out." The voice was raspy and dry, more like a croak. The red claws at the tips of the raug's nails flicked toward the door. "Let me be."

"See, that's not an option. You need help, and that's what I'm here to do." She floated slowly along the side of the bed, fighting not to wrinkle her nose.

The raug lying beneath all the blankets and furs didn't look old enough to be so sick or on the edge of death. *He's huge. Bigger than Gúrdu.* Ember stared at the bulging muscles of his arms and shoulders. Her eyes widened when she saw the black lines snaking up his arms beneath his gray flesh. *Just like the skaxen. How the hell am I supposed to fix this?*

His chest rose and fell with a constant wheeze, his large eyes closed over a grimace of pain and determination.

"What's your name?" she asked.

"If you don't know my name, you shouldn't be here." The raug slowly rolled his head toward her, and his eyes fluttered open. "No. Send the other healers, girl. I don't want a fae in here." He broke into a fit of hacking coughs. The bed groaned beneath him as his huge body lurched, and he thrust his hand toward the door. "I said, get out."

"You don't want a fae in here, huh?" Ember waited for the coughing to subside, then reached for the edge of the blankets and cautiously peeled them away from his chin to expose his chest. "I don't wanna be in here either, so it looks like we both have to do something we don't like. Deal with it."

The raug growled at her, his glowing orange eyes narrowing. "Where are the other healers? *My* healers?"

"I don't know, and I don't care." Folding the blankets over his legs, she fought not to grimace at the thicker lines of black streaking across his chest and meeting in a dark stain over his heart. *Assuming raug hearts are in the same place as human hearts.* "Doesn't look like *your* healers had much luck. Just think of me as a last resort."

He sputtered and clenched his eyes shut, and for a minute, Ember thought he was choking. Then a grin split his lips, revealing sharp, pointed teeth and a black tongue behind them. She rolled her eyes.

"Last resort or last rites? The deathflame's calling my name, either way."

"Which you still haven't given me, by the way."

"Bah." He turned his head away from her and lay still, breathing quickly and shallowly. "Do your best, then."

"What happened?"

The raug grunted. "Apparently, I didn't think to have a fae on hand every damn place I go."

"Okay. I get it." *Big guy got tainted by the blight, and now he's punishing himself for it.* "Has it happened to anyone else?"

A low growl escaped him, and he kept his eyes closed. "No. I got this on a mining expedition, fae. Been in this room for three fell-damn days since I returned."

"Then let's hope I got here fast enough."

He started to chuckle and fell into a fit of coughing even worse than the first one. Ember glanced at the stone shelves cut into the wall beside the bed and picked up the metal pitcher there to give it a quick sniff. *Smells like water. Decent chance it's safe.*

She poured some into a copper cup and set that gently in the raug's open hand. He grasped the cup, his nails clinking on the metal, and brought it to his lips without lifting his head from the thick pillows. Water spilled from the side of his mouth and down around his shoulders. When it was empty, he tossed the cup away. Ember started at the harsh clang of copper bouncing on the stone floor.

The raug twirled a finger in the air before his hand dropped to the bed with a thump. "Get on with it. If I'm at the end, I'd rather get there sooner than later."

"You've got an awfully cheery view of things, don't you?"

He grunted and said nothing.

"Try to relax, I guess." Ember slowly reached out to hover both palms above the raug's broad, black-streaked chest. She focused on her healing magic, and a faint purple light glowed between her palms and the sick raug. After a full minute with no effect, she frowned. *I'm tasting bananas, so I know it's the healing and not the throw-things-across-the-room kind of magic. What am I missing?*

The raug wheezed. "See? No use for a fae."

"Shut up." Gritting her teeth, Ember placed her hands on the raug's chest.

He gasped and lurched, his orange eyes flying wide open as he gaped. Ember almost pulled away from the instant burning in her hands but forced herself to keep pressing on his chest. *I'm a full-blooded fae and the drow princess's goddamn* Nós Aní. *This is gonna work.*

The burning heat traveled slowly up her wrists and forearms, intensifying as it spread. Ember grunted against the pain and kept at her healing, even when the raug gasped again and started cursing in French. She would've laughed if she wasn't so focused.

An unseen force propelled her away from the raug. Arms flailing, Ember tried to keep her balance and focused on the levitation spell Corian had taught her, but it winked out the next second, and her feet dropped an inch to the floor. Her legs crumpled beneath her and she landed on the stone floor with a thud, shouting in surprise and pain.

The room was eerily silent.

Ember rolled as much as she could onto her side and pushed herself up to sit four feet away from the bed. She stared at her legs, willing them to move, and slapped a hand against her thigh for good measure. *Great. Almost no feeling. I'm right back to being a useless fae lump.*

A low chuckle came from the bed, and it quickly grew to a roar of laughter that made her want to cover her ears. The raug's hands shot into the air and he flipped them over and over again, staring at the scarred flesh free of black streaks. "*Hishmál.* Would you look at that?"

He bolted upright in the bed and swung his legs over the side, grinning at the space five and a half feet above the ground where he expected Ember to be. Then he looked down at the fae on the floor and cocked his head. "What's wrong with *you*?"

"Oh, you know. Just the usual."

"Let me see your hands."

Ember pursed her lips. "I didn't *take* your sickness if that's what you're wondering."

"Fae don't sit around on the floor, girl. Show me your hands."

Rolling her eyes, Ember lifted both hands and turned them back and forth as he had. "See? No black streaks. No blight. I'm just regular old me."

"Ha!" The raug leaped to his feet and smacked his bare chest, now gray again. "We *both* underestimated you. Vingat! De'garu!"

The heavy wooden door burst open on the other side of the room, and the two raug guards thundered in. They stopped short when they saw the healed raug standing over the fae girl on the floor. "What is this?"

"*This* is your chief returned!" The raug pounded his chest again and spread his arms. "It's done."

The guards grinned at him and thumped fists on their chests in response. "It worked."

"What's this?" Foltr came into the room, his cane clacking across the floor. "What's all this now?" The same surprise and confusion flashed behind his widening eyes when he saw the raug and Ember, and he nodded. "Yes. Well done, girl."

"Just doing my fae thing, I guess." Ember patted the floor beside her. "Lost my mobility, though."

The healed raug laughed and stomped toward her. "We will fix that for you, Healer."

"I'm not really a healer. Wait, what are you doing?"

"Helping you." He bent down with a snort and scooped her up in his arms.

She tried to push him away. "No, that's okay. You don't have to pick me up."

"Ha! No fae enjoys the floor, and you most certainly do not deserve it. De'garu, find a crawler for this one."

One of the guards nodded and left the room.

"A crawler?" Ember stared at the raug's huge face right next to hers as he cradled her like a child in his bare arms.

"But you won't be doing the crawling." He chuckled. "What's your name, girl?"

She laughed and shook her head. *This is absurd.* "Ember."

"Ember. I am Cazerel. Welcome to my home."

"You were talking about yourself when you mentioned a chief, weren't you?"

"Ha. I thought I wouldn't be soon enough. Everything we have here is yours, Healer. You've done us a great service. Me, specifically."

"I figured I could help." Ember shot Foltr a nervous smile, and the old raug chuckled. "I don't need everything you have. Just the crawler, I guess."

Cazerel roared with laughter, bouncing her up and down. Ember tried to keep her arms from rubbing his rough gray skin but ended up laughing too. *Weirdest thing I've ever done. Cheyenne's gonna lose it when I tell her about this one.*

CHAPTER TWENTY-FOUR

Cheyenne folded her arms and watched the half-dozen raugs standing between L'zar's traveling band of rebels and the outer gates of Hirúl Breach. "Huh. Call me crazy, but this doesn't feel like a very friendly greeting."

The raugs prowled in the front of the massive gates, glowing eyes in various shades of orange narrowed as they scrutinized the newcomers. Most of them glared at General Hi'et, but some of their gazes turned toward Cheyenne and L'zar too.

"They're not doing anything," Corian muttered and glanced at L'zar, who was still sitting on the ground beside him. "And neither are we."

The drow chuckled. "I didn't say a thing."

Corian looked back at the agitated raugs. "You didn't have to."

Behind them, Maleshi had taken up pacing in jerking steps, occasionally stopping for five to ten seconds before she couldn't help but look at the raugs again. Then she'd walk three or four feet, pause, and do it all over again.

The next time she passed Corian, he reached out to touch her forearm without turning away from the raugs. "You need to stop doing that."

Maleshi glared at his hand on her arm and brushed it off before continuing in her halting, irritated march. "Sure. *You* try being the target of all this hatred and standing still. Look at you, a perfect night-stalker statue, all proper and composed."

"Maleshi."

"I'm *trying*," she hissed, lunging toward him from behind to snarl in his ear. "You have no idea what this is like for me. I'm doing the best I can."

"It's not ingrained in you to kill them, and it's not ingrained in you to lose control of yourself when things get dicey."

Maleshi scoffed. "It is when I'm the one to blame for all of it."

Cheyenne caught the general's gaze and grinned. "I know exactly how you feel right now."

That caught the nightstalker woman off-guard, and she stopped to stare at Cheyenne. "Yeah, I guess you do." She picked up her pacing again.

One raug growled something in French, and Maleshi spun toward him and hissed.

"Okay, what was that?"

The general glanced briefly at Cheyenne and rolled her eyes. "More jokes about cats. Without claws."

Then the raugs switched to English and started pounding their chests. "The Hand of the Night and Circle couldn't push us all out, could she?"

"We stayed *true*, nightstalker!"

"Doesn't matter how long you've been gone, Hi'et. Our memories are *long*."

The raugs chuckled and snarled, stalking in front of the gates with their shoulders hunched and their hands outstretched to show how sharp their red claws were.

"Hey, maybe we'd be better prepared for this if we all knew why they're so pissed off at you," Cheyenne suggested. When Corian and the goblins shot her confused looks, she shrugged. "Okay, I guess I'm the only one who doesn't know."

"They're the last of Gúrdu's tribe," Maleshi hissed. "I led a siege against Felagtrok under the Crown, and apparently, these are the ones I didn't manage to get my hands on before they fled."

Cheyenne narrowed her eyes. "What happened to the rest of them?"

"I gave Gúrdu the option to make the crossing. Perks of being an

Oracle, I guess. And then I killed everyone else." Maleshi stopped, looked at the halfling, and shrugged. "It was a different time, kid. *I* was different."

"I sure hope so." Cheyenne watched the general pace, then had to look away. "You're making me nervous."

"I don't give a shit about your fragile composure right now. I'm too busy with my own."

Cheyenne and Corian exchanged quick glances, and the night-stalker man shook his head. "We'll hold right here. That's all there is to it."

"And if they attack us?"

"Relax." L'zar lifted his forearm from his knee to wave his daughter's concerns aside. "They're not going to attack."

"You want a sliver of your honor back, *nilsch úcat?*" The shouting raug thumped his fist on his chest over and over. "Let's see how you fight when I rip those fancy little whiskers right out of your coward's face!"

Maleshi hissed again and vanished in a flash of silver light. A second later, she'd stopped two feet from the line of raugs and snarled at him. "I dare you, grayskin. Anyone who holds onto the past this long has nothing else worth their time."

"Smashing you into the ground would be worth my time."

The raugs behind him chuckled darkly and snarled at the night-stalker. Two of them stepped forward, and Maleshi cocked her head. "Don't."

"Why not, Hand of the Night and Circle?" The closest raug licked his gray lips with a shiny black tongue and sneered, eyeing her. "You look so *soft.*"

The general lifted her arms away from her sides and extended four-inch claws from every finger. "Wanna bet?"

"Maleshi," Corian shouted. "Not here."

"This looks like the perfect place to me, *vae shra'ni.*" The general spread her arms wider and lifted her chin at the sneering raugs in front of her. "Unless every one of you wants a repeat of the Felagtrok. I didn't tell anyone about the cowards who ran off and abandoned their tribe that day, but now we have witnesses."

Another raug hissed a bitter laugh. "I thought this was the General

Hi'et who abandoned her post for a world full of weaklings. What a convenient way to avoid paying for what you've done!"

Maleshi snarled and took a step toward him, pulling her arm back and holding it there, ready to strike.

"I said, not here!" Corian came toward them in a flash of silver light and grabbed the general's shoulder. "If it comes to it, let *them* strike first."

The raug in front of Maleshi lunged forward and swung a powerful uppercut into the general's stomach. She flew across the stone courtyard, and in nightstalker fashion, landed in a crouch, sliding across the stone and glaring at the raug with a wild hiss.

The raug looked at Corian. "Thanks for the invitation."

The nightstalker glared at him. "That's not what I meant."

Maleshi flashed past him in a blaze of silver light and barreled into the raug, slashing across his chest with her claws. The other five gray-skinned magicals roared in approval, shouting insults at Maleshi and encouragement to their fellow raug as the two battled it out with their fists and claws.

"This isn't why we're here!" Corian shouted over the noise. "Maleshi, call it off."

She darted around the raug, who spun in the opposite direction and knocked her out of her enhanced speed when his left fist cracked into her jaw.

"Dammit, Hi'et!" Corian ducked when another raug swung at him. Then he hissed, rolled his shoulders, and blasted the attacking magical with a bolt of silver lightning.

"Jesus." Cheyenne jogged toward the nightstalkers, who were in furious single combat with two raugs. *It's gonna be two against six pretty soon. I thought I was the one who got pissed-off and stupid.*

"Hey!" She stopped four feet away from the cheering group of raugs and summoned a crackling black sphere of energy in one hand. "I know all of you can hear me. We have bigger problems to deal with right now, and this isn't helping."

L'zar stayed where he was, his forearms dangling over his knees, and chuckled.

"Fuck this." Lumil clenched her fists and summoned the red, spinning runes around them. "No way am I sittin' this one out."

"Nope." Byrd's hands filled with green flames, and both goblins raced toward the fight.

"You're all a bunch of idiots," Cheyenne shouted, trying to be heard without getting closer.

"Kiss my goblin ass, you beefy shits!" Lumil raced past the halfling and punched the closest raug where a human's kidney would have been. The raug stumbled forward with a grunt, whirled toward the goblin woman, and snatched the front of her leather jacket before tossing her away with one hand.

Byrd ran screaming into the fray, ducking huge, swinging gray arms and blasting green fire in all directions.

Every raug roared and focused on a new target. One of them hooked a claw through the back of Byrd's collar and lifted the goblin off the ground, swinging him from side to side and grinning. The hulking magical beside him burst into thunderous laughter until Lumil launched at him and smashed her spell-enhanced fist into his mouth.

"Dammit." Cheyenne gritted her teeth and quickly scanned the fighting magicals. "Guess it's a full-on brawl now." She launched the crackling sphere of magic at the raug swinging both fists toward Lumil and knocked him back enough that he missed. Lumil cackled and dropped to her knees to bring her fist up into his muscular gut.

The halfling sent her lashing tendrils toward the raug dangling Byrd by the collar. Despite his odd position, the goblin man kept blasting green fireballs at the other raugs while he swung left and right. Cheyenne's black tendrils coiled around the raug's outstretched arm, and she pulled hard. Byrd's collar ripped, and he dropped to the ground and shot two fireballs into the huge magical's face. Cackling, he scrambled away and headed after someone else.

Blinking and snorting against the residual green flames, the raug's orange eyes settled on Cheyenne. He grinned and stomped toward her. "Shit."

Cheyenne slipped into drow speed and raced toward him. Just before she reached the gray-skinned magical, he turned with surprising speed for someone that size and lowered his shoulder toward her with a quick step forward. She couldn't stop in time and crashed into his muscular frame. It knocked her out of enhanced speed and sent her flailing across the stone.

He straightened and grinned at her. "Surprise."

Raugs don't have superspeed. How the hell do they move that fast? She cocked her head at him and spread her arms. "That all you got?"

The raug lumbered toward her. "No."

Metal hinges creaked at the base of the wall, and the smaller door opened. Foltr lurched through first, the clack of his cane unheard beneath the din of the brawl. "What is this? Not even an hour."

Cazerel ducked through the door with Ember in his arms and snorted, his eyes widening when he saw what was happening. "Excuse me, Healer."

Ember stared at the brawl. "For what?"

"What I am about to do." The raug chief stalked toward a short ledge of stone jutting from the wall of the canyon against which Hirúl Breach's outer wall was built and set her down with a firm nod. "My apologies."

He didn't wait for her to say anything but whirled and stormed toward the fight. "Enough!"

His booming voice cracked across the courtyard in front of the gates. At their chieftain's angry shout, every raug stopped immediately and straightened. The nightstalkers fell out of their enhanced speed with silver flashes. Cheyenne stepped away from the raug, who was no longer coming at her. Too far gone to her battle rage, Lumil charged her opponent with a roar. The raug reached out with one hand and wrapped his long gray fingers around the top of the goblin woman's head, holding her away from him at arm's length while she snarled and swung uselessly with her spinning red fists.

"Lumil," Cheyenne muttered. "Hey, cut it out."

The goblin woman grunted, then reached up with both hands and jerked the raug's palm off her head. "Get the hell off me."

The raug lowered his arm and stared at his chief, ignoring her like an elephant ignoring a fly.

L'zar finally stood and clasped his hands behind his back to watch the raug chief with a knowing smile.

"Who is responsible for this?" Cazerel boomed. None of his magicals replied, so he stalked down the line of raug men, who were all at least a foot shorter than him, thumping a hand against his bare chest. "You see this? Do you see your chief standing here before you? I lay ready to face the end, and I come to greet new friends, only to find you thick-headed beasts thanking them with your fists. Tell me what happened!"

"*Zokri.*" The raug whose loose tunic was shredded to ribbons from Maleshi's claws stepped forward and pounded his chest. "This was vengeance."

Cazerel snarled. "For what?"

"Felagtrok." The raug gestured at Maleshi. "General Hi'et returns."

The chief turned toward Maleshi. Under his gaze and finally catching her breath, the general straightened and clasped her hands behind her back, lifting her chin.

"So she does." Cazerel nodded with another grunt of acknowledgment. "Felagtrok was a long time ago. Consider this battle the only vengeance you will have, Bru'uga."

The raug snarled at Maleshi but lowered his gaze when the chief looked at him. "I am not satisfied."

"Neither am I." Cazerel pounded his chest again. "See this! Your chief stands tall outside Hirúl Breach's gates because General Hi'et's party brought a fae to our door." His massive arm swung toward Ember, who was still sitting on the rock ledge beyond the gates. She coughed, then cleared her throat. "The healer has claimed victory over the deathflame for me. Maleshi Hi'et's debt to you has been paid with my life. Leave it."

"*Zokri.*" Bru'uga dipped his head and stood perfectly still as Cazerel headed toward Foltr.

The chief leaned toward the aged raug and muttered, "You and yours are welcome in our city now, old one. Bring them. We have much to discuss."

"We do." Foltr nodded at the raug towering almost two feet above his shoulders.

Cazerel headed toward the open door at the base of the gates and muttered something in French to a waiting guard. The guard nodded and disappeared inside, then the chief followed, stooping to squeeze his massive frame through the doorway.

Foltr cracked his cane on the stone floor and glared at the subdued raug warriors. His scowl turned on Maleshi and Corian next, and he moved slowly back through the open door, muttering and shaking his head.

"Well." L'zar chuckled and strolled casually across the small court-yard. "Hell of a welcome, huh?"

Grinning at the gathered raugs, he dipped his head and slipped through the door after Foltr.

Corian stepped away from the warriors and nodded before taking his leave. The raugs glared at him and then Maleshi when she followed Corian into the city.

Cheyenne nudged Lumil and muttered, "I'll go get Ember."

"Yeah. Get the chief-healing fae." The goblin woman scoffed at the warriors and stomped off, rubbing her hand vigorously through her mop of yellow hair until it hung over her eyes. Byrd jumped and headed after her, looking between the open door and the raug warriors growling at him.

Weird to not be the center of everyone's hatred, but I'll take it.

CHAPTER TWENTY-FIVE

Cheyenne headed quickly across the stone square toward Ember, who propped herself up on the ledge with her hands behind her and started coughing again.

"Hey." Cheyenne stopped beside her friend and turned to eye the raugs again, folding her arms. "Looks like you did it."

"Yeah, I did it." Ember sucked in a wheezing breath.

"You okay?"

"No." With another cough, Ember doubled over and shook her head. "I think I short-circuited my magic with that one."

"What?"

The fae looked at Cheyenne with a fiery violet gaze. "You think I'm just sitting here without getting up to follow everyone else for fun?"

"Shit. No floating spell?"

"Nothing." Ember snapped her fingers and opened her hands again. "Not even a spark."

"Must've been some seriously intense healing."

The fae girl scoffed. "He had the blight, Cheyenne. So yeah, it was pretty intense."

Nothing personal. I'd be pissed too if I couldn't walk after helping someone. Or float. Nodding slowly, Cheyenne sat beside her friend on the ledge and bumped her shoulder against Ember's. "Two good things out of this, though."

"Since when did you become the silver-lining drow?"

Cheyenne snorted. "Since the silver-lining fae went all dark and broody and could use a pep talk. Maybe."

"Whatever. Go for it."

The halfling watched the disgruntled raug warriors, who had gathered and were grumbling at each other, trying to find another outlet for their rage. "You saved a raug chief's life, apparently. And we were clearly only getting inside this place with the approval of a chief who doesn't want anything to do with Hangivol or the Crown."

"You mean, you couldn't have stormed the gates and blasted your way inside for another chat with a city leader?"

"Very funny." Cheyenne rubbed her hands up and down her thighs. "But we're in, thanks to you."

"No problem." Ember rolled her eyes. "I'm not accepting donations. You know, 'cause I can't walk *or* float around anymore. This is as good as it gets again."

"Nah. You still look like a fae. Your magic probably needs a reboot."

"It better come back."

"It will, Em. I still need you around, so you don't have a choice."

Ember snorted, and they both laughed softly. "Okay, so what's the second good thing?"

"Now we know it's possible to reverse the whole blight thing, at least when it's starting to take over magicals."

"Huh." Ember tossed a hand in the air. "Hope for healing Ambar'ogúl, right? I'd honestly settle for healing my own legs and leave it at that."

"You'll get there." They sat in silence for a moment, then Cheyenne slapped her thighs and leaned toward her friend. "If I know those guys in there, they're probably *not* waiting for us to get started with their chief-to-chief chat, but I don't wanna miss it."

"By all means, drow." Ember gestured at the open door in the gates. "I'm not going anywhere."

"I'm not leaving you here. I was gonna offer to carry you with me. You know, drow strength and everything without having to worry about humans freaking out if they see it."

Ember grimaced. "I'm not a fan of being carried."

"Hey, I'm not a giant, bare-chested raug chief."

"Oh, jeez." The fae laughed and rolled her eyes. "That was one of the weirder things I've experienced. The guy's got, like, sharkskin."

Cheyenne snorted. "Sounds fun."

"At least he wasn't sweaty." Ember shrugged. "Dammit, just carry me."

"Yep."

Cheyenne stood and bent over so Ember could hook her arm around her neck. Before she could scoop the fae girl into her arms, a raug guard whistled sharply from the open door and shouted something at them in French. Cheyenne straightened again and shook her head. "English."

The guard frowned and banged the open door with another shout in French to someone up in the tower. "The healer's not forgotten, drow. Don't carry her. The *Zokrí* has a gift."

"A gift." Cheyenne turned toward Ember and raised her eyebrows. "From your hulking chief admirer."

"Shut up."

The grating creak and rumble of mechanisms turning in the huge metal gates echoed across the stone square, then a square section of metal at the base of the closest gate tower lifted like a garage door. The guard who'd called to them headed toward it and waited for a machine of black metal to fully emerge from the base of the tower.

"What the hell is that?" Ember muttered.

"I think that's your gift, Em."

"Oh, jeez."

The raug guard reached into the center of the old-school O'gúl tech machine and tapped the controls. Eight legs unfolded from the undercarriage with a clang of metal on stone, and the main body lifted three feet off the ground. When the guard headed toward Cheyenne and Ember, the machine scuttled after him like a giant headless spider with a depression in its huge abdomen.

Ember grimaced. "No. Please, no."

The guard stopped in front of them and offered Ember a sleek, two-inch bar of flattened black metal. "For you."

The fae took it and turned the item over in her hand. "Looks like the barrettes I used to wear in grade school, without the clip."

Cheyenne fought back a laugh and tapped behind her own ear. "Activator, Em."

"Oh." Ember lifted the piece of metal toward the raug and raised her eyebrows.

"Wear it." The guard looked at Ember and Cheyenne, his thick brow flickering in and out of a confused frown as he tried to keep a straight face.

He's gonna be wracking his brain forever, trying to figure out why a fae in Ambar'ogúl doesn't know how to use an activator.

"Behind your ear," she muttered.

"Yep." Ember lifted the metal piece to the back of her ear and gasped when the tech synced with her vision and her magic. Her eyelids fluttered, and when her violet gaze fell on the black metal machine behind the raug, her mouth dropped open. "Oh. My. God."

The guard grunted. "Until the healer regains her strength." Thumping a fist against his chest, he bowed and quickly spun to march back to the small door in the gate.

"This is *insane*." Ember studied the old-tech machine, her eyes flickering back and forth as she took in all the information the activator fed her.

"Told you you'd love it." Cheyenne folded her arms. "If that one came with the spider chair over there, I'm guessing it's one of the older models."

"I couldn't care less." Ember leaned over the edge of the rock ledge but caught herself before she fell off. "I totally get why you love yours."

"You haven't even tested it yet."

"I don't need to."

Chuckling, Cheyenne reached toward her friend. "Want a boost?"

"That's a seriously dumb question." Ember draped her arm over Cheyenne's shoulders and let the halfling pick her up and set her in the seat-shaped depression in the center of the machine. "Jeeze, getting in and out of your car would've been a hell of a lot easier if you could run around freely like a superdrow."

"Not an option back home, but yeah. Would've saved us a lot of time." Cheyenne straightened and gave her friend time to shift around and get comfortable in the machine.

Ember's gaze moved slowly across the smooth surface of the control panel at her fingertips. "I can't believe this. It's so easy."

"That's the point. Try it."

The fae girl swiped the panel, and the machine's legs lifted her higher off the ground before turning back toward the gate. Ember grinned, absorbed in the novelty of her first O'gúl activator.

Cheyenne snorted, tried to hold it back, then burst out laughing.

"What?"

"You." The halfling doubled over and howled with laughter, stomping her feet. Every time she looked at her friend, she lost it all over again and had to turn away.

"All right, spit it out." Ember folded her arms and chuckled despite trying to look fed up. "What, am I doing it wrong?"

"No," Cheyenne squeaked through another laugh, waving her hand in front of her face. She sucked in a huge breath. "You're rocking the Doc Ock look like a pro!" She barely got the last word out before she cracked up all over again.

"Oh, so we watch one *Spiderman* movie, and now you're throwing around Marvel references?"

"I can't help it." Cheyenne wiped the tears from the corners of her eyes with the back of a hand and sniffed. "I totally blame you."

"He called it a 'crawler.'" Ember wrinkled her nose. "Does it really look like Doc Ock?"

Cheyenne pressed her lips together and nodded vigorously. Then she barked out another laugh. "Yeah, if he was sitting in a chair."

"Didn't you say you wanted to get inside and be part of the meeting with the chief?"

"Yeah, I do."

"You're wasting a lot of time laughing at me." Ember rolled her eyes and turned the machine toward the gates. "It's cooler than a wheelchair."

The machine lifted again on its mechanical legs, and with a swipe of her finger across the controls, Ember took off in the scuttling contraption. Cheyenne tried not to laugh and ended up laughing anyway as she followed her friend toward the gates.

Six feet from the small open door, Ember stopped, the metal legs clinking against the stone. "Crap. How the hell am I supposed to get through there?"

Cheyenne fell into another fit of laughter, holding herself around the middle while Ember glared at her over her shoulder.

"You're not helping."

"I'm sorry, Em. Oh, man. I wish you could see what I'm seeing right now."

A raug peered out of the open garage door in the base of the tower and whistled sharply. He waved them toward him, and Ember lifted her chin. "Always a way, Cheyenne."

"Yeah, you have your own private entrance and everything."

The fae tossed her head and steered the crawler toward the beckoning raug. Cheyenne followed and finally managed to pull it together. *Just watch her head. Don't look at the legs.* Chuckling, she stepped into the base of the tower and pressed her lips together as the garage door groaned shut again behind them.

CHAPTER TWENTY-SIX

Cheyenne and Ember passed through the tower onto a wide stone walkway that ran around the perimeter of Hirúl Breach. The rest of the city was depressed into the canyon floor another ten feet, making the rising buildings of metal and stone even taller now that they could see their full height. The less-advanced metropolis was a quarter the size of Hangivol.

Most of the magicals here were raugs. The occasional goblin's green skin stuck out against so many hulking gray bodies, and as Cheyenne and Ember traveled down the stairs at the end of the walkway, the sound of steel pounding on stone grew louder from almost every direction.

The raugs gave them passing glances, but none of them stared at either the girls or the crawler. *This can't be a normal sight around here.*

The guard who'd brought Ember the crawler shouted from a doorway in the wall beneath the walkway. "Healer! This way."

They followed him through the door, which was thankfully wide enough for the machine to get through with only the occasional scrape into the long hallway beyond it. Ember gritted her teeth as she tried to guide the crawler in a perfectly straight line, her head jerking sideways when the wide base of her seat got too close to the wall and knocked her away.

"You good?"

"I'm fine," Ember hissed. "Still better than a wheelchair."

Cheyenne focused on the back of Ember's head.

The guard led them to another door on the left and stepped aside to let them enter. He had to press himself against the wall to avoid getting crushed by the scuttling crawler, but he nodded firmly at Cheyenne when she followed Ember into the room beyond and closed the door behind them.

The magicals sitting around an intricately carved stone table stopped the discussion when the clink and whir of Ember's crawler echoed along the back wall. The meeting included all of Cheyenne's party, the raug chief, and three older, skeptical-looking raugs taking up the chairs closest to their leader. Cazerel's orange eyes lit up when he saw Ember, his pointed teeth flashing in a wide grin. "Healer! Join us."

"Thanks."

"How does the crawler suit you, eh? You won't find the sniveling-fancy spark in Hirúl Breach like they have in Hangivol."

"It's great. Thanks." Ember steered the machine toward the corner of the huge table and positioned herself between Lumil and Corian.

"Good. *Good.*" Cazerel nodded vigorously and took a moment to grin at the fae.

Cheyenne headed for the empty chair beside Maleshi, gauging the others' reactions. *Nobody else thinks it's funny? Guess I'm the only asshole who laughs at a fae in a spider machine.*

She slumped onto the thick cushion lining the heavy wooden chair and gazed around the table. "What did I miss?"

"Not much," Maleshi muttered.

"Ah, yes." Cazerel turned his orange gaze onto L'zar. "I still do not understand why you need *our* help, Weaver. She's *your* kin."

"She's the worst part about me." L'zar set his folded hands on the table and leaned toward the chief. "Why do you think I've spent so much time away from her?"

Cazerel stroked his chin, his long red claws rasping his gray flesh. "Indeed."

"I know you lost all love for the drow when the last Cycle turned. K'laht did his part for you and Hirúl Breach in his time, did he not?"

"The Everbrite did more than *his part*." Cazerel sat back in his chair. "He was and is our Crown."

L'zar's eyes widened. "Sounds like you hate my sister as much as I do."

"I do not know the extent of your feelings, *Cu'ón*, but perhaps you are right."

"One has to know their enemies as well as their friends to protect themselves from that enemy." The drow spread his arms. "You've done well here in Hirúl Breach. I think you've also done well in drawing out as many dark truths about my sister as you possibly can. I need your help because I'm looking for the one thing that will make Cheyenne's terms of secession impossible for the Crown to refuse. I'm looking for leverage."

The chief's orange eyes narrowed. "I find it hard to believe the Weaver thief does not already have leverage."

"Oh, I have plenty, but it's not enough. If you tell me what *you* have, we can compare notes." L'zar grinned and sat back in his chair, feigning casual indifference despite how intently his golden eyes were fixed on the raug chief.

Cazerel studied the drow for a moment longer, then kept his gaze on L'zar as he turned his head toward one of the raug elders and muttered something in French. The elders shifted in their seats.

Cheyenne was acutely aware of the wary glances Maleshi and Corian exchanged across the table.

L'zar's eyes widened. "What don't I know?"

Cazerel growled and sat back in his chair, shifting his shoulders as if scratching an itch on his back. "Ba'rael Verdys has a child."

Cheyenne held her breath. *Holy shit.*

L'zar broke into a predatory grin and leaned forward. "Where?"

Corian shifted uncomfortably. "L'zar."

The drow cut him off with a raised hand without looking away from the chief. "Tell me."

"Somewhere not even the *Cu'ón* thief would find him," Cazerel replied evenly. "I expected you to know."

"Clearly I did not." L'zar set a slender slate-gray hand on the table and raised his eyebrows. "If you want to barter for this information,

Cazerel, name your price. Whatever it is, you know I can and will pay it."

"Yes." The chief glanced at Ember and nodded. "I believe you paid in advance. It is no small thing to keep a healer at your side."

"I'm sure she's very good," L'zar muttered dismissively. "So, if the price has been paid, tell me where he is."

Corian hissed softly. "Don't you think the bigger issue is why we didn't know about him?"

"Not at all."

"If Ba'rael hears so much as a whisper about us going after her son, she won't wait for the rest of the fortnight, L'zar." Corian gripped the edge of the table. "She'll break as many of the old laws as she can to get to him before we do if she hasn't already."

"She has not." Cazerel dipped his head toward Corian and folded his arms. "And she will not. The child was sent away from her at birth. He has spent the first four hundred years of his life hidden, and not even his mother knows where to find him. On her own orders."

"Damn," Cheyenne muttered. "And I thought *I* had it bad growing up."

Ember snorted but immediately wiped off her smile when Corian shot each of them a warning look.

"The Olforím look after him now, or perhaps he looks after them. Either way, he is impossible to find." Cazerel's thick gray lips twitched into a grim smile. "But not for us."

A low chuckle rose from L'zar's grinning mouth. "That will work beautifully, *Zokri*."

"What? No." Cheyenne slapped her hands on the stone table and raised halfway out of her chair. "You are *not* gonna use her kid as bait or leverage."

L'zar turned slowly toward her and cocked his head. "I just want to *talk* to him, Cheyenne. I want to see this nephew of mine with my own eyes. A conversation won't hurt anyone."

"If he's sitting down to talk to you, L'zar, yeah, it might."

He chuckled and waved her off before turning back to the chief. "Will you take us to him?"

"L'zar, I'm serious," Cheyenne spat.

"Hush."

"Don't," she began, then Maleshi's hand clenched painfully around her wrist. The nightstalker woman nodded at Cheyenne's chair. The halfling seethed with contained anger, but she forced herself back into her seat.

Cazerel's tight smile widened. "If a new Cycle is to turn, I would say it's our duty to take you."

"Yes. We all have our own duties to perform, don't we?"

The chief stood, his chair scooting noisily across the floor. "Tomorrow, we will fulfill it."

The raug elders stood, quickly followed by L'zar and the rest of his party. "Thank you." He thumped a fist against his chest and nodded. "I look forward to it."

"I'm sure you do. You're welcome to stay in our city tonight." Cazerel walked swiftly around the table and stopped beside Ember. "If you think of anything else you need from us, Healer, my clansmen will provide it for you."

Ember stared up at him from her seat in the crawler. "Thanks."

He grinned at her, nodded brusquely, then pulled open the door and left, followed by the three raug elders, who didn't say a word.

When the door closed behind them, Cheyenne leaped to her feet. "You can't use this kid against his mother."

The drow brushed invisible dust off his shirtsleeve and rolled his shoulders. "I wouldn't keep calling him a kid, Cheyenne. He's *much* older than you."

"That doesn't matter. In a world where everybody lives practically forever, he's still a kid, and this is crossing a line."

"There *is* no line." L'zar stalked around the table. "If there were, I'd say *you're* crossing it right now. Don't speak against me like that again."

"I don't take orders from you."

"Oh, that wasn't an order." L'zar's smile faded as he pointed at her. "That was a warning. We do what we have to do, so my sister doesn't rip this world apart from the inside out. I'm not going to *hurt* him. He's family. Nothing better than family, isn't that right?"

Cheyenne scowled at him. "So far, my O'gúleesh family has been pretty disappointing."

"Aw." He cocked his head and winked. "We'll grow on you."

Without waiting for anyone else to share their opinion, the drow thief strolled past her and slipped into the hall. He was gone before the wooden door stopped swinging toward the wall.

Cheyenne looked at Corian. "He can't do this."

"I know. And so far, he hasn't," The nightstalker said, "It's the only option we have right now. He's right, though. Talking won't hurt the kid."

"It will if he's lived four hundred years, not knowing *anything* about this world."

"Can you honestly say living hidden and in ignorance is the better path, even when the truth is hard to swallow?"

She clenched her fists. "It's not the same."

"It's close enough, Cheyenne. Maybe you'll feel differently about it when you wake up in the morning."

Ember stuck a finger in the air. "Hey, does anyone remember we're on a time limit here?" The other magicals stared at her. "I mean, Cheyenne and I have a life to get back to Earthside. You know, after the weekend's over. Maleshi too, probably."

Maleshi gave the fae girl a sympathetic smile. "Time doesn't run quite the same way over here."

"No, but we have to go back, right?" Ember looked at the nightstalkers on either side of the table. "I mean, we *are* going back."

"Try not to worry about that right now, huh? We have slightly more important things to think about before we make another crossing. We'll make this as quick of a trip as we can." Maleshi exchanged glances with Corian, then the nightstalkers headed toward the door.

Corian paused when he passed Cheyenne, leaned toward her as if he wanted to say something, then nodded with a weak smile and stepped out of the room.

Lumil clapped her hands together and rubbed them vigorously. "All right. Time to see what kinda luxury suites these raugs are hiding behind all this dead stone, huh?"

Byrd chuckled. "I heard they're pretty good cooks."

"Not if we're talking about Foltr."

"I didn't say Foltr. Just raugs in general." The goblin man pumped a fist in excitement. "I bet they know how to party, too."

Cheyenne stared at them. "You were just fighting them outside the gates."

"Yeah, that was fun, huh? Come on." Laughing, Lumil waved her toward the door before she and Byrd disappeared down the hall.

Cheyenne looked down at Ember. "We're running all over the place trying to fill in this hole, and it keeps getting deeper."

"Corian's right. Nothing's happened yet." Ember swiped the control panel on the crawler, the edge bumping against the table as the legs lifted in response. "Honestly, the only thing on my mind right now is finding something to eat in this place. I don't know if it's the long day or dumping all my magic into a raug chief, but I'm starving."

Cheyenne snorted. "One step at a time, huh?"

"Exactly." Ember slapped the side of the crawler, producing a metallic echo. "Or eight."

CHAPTER TWENTY-SEVEN

The raugs had given Cheyenne and Ember adjoining guest quarters that shared a central room and a small terrace overlooking the center of Hirúl Breach. Cool air spilled through the open stone wall connecting the terrace to the main room, bringing with it the scent of strange cooking spices, sweat, and ground stone.

Just as Cheyenne set Ember down on one of the giant cushioned lounges in the shared room, there was a knock on the door. "Yeah?"

The door creaked open, and a comparatively skinny raug with tattoos on his face bowed slightly. "The *Zokri* sends a meal with his gratitude."

Ember grinned. "Food."

"I wouldn't get too excited until we see what it is," Cheyenne muttered out of the side of her mouth.

The raug flicked his clawed fingers into the room, and a metal table walked through the doorway on four mechanical legs, carrying a massive lidded tray, a pitcher of water, and two cups.

"Okay." Cheyenne hesitantly approached the table and handed the cups and pitcher to Ember before grabbing the tray. "Thanks."

The raug nodded. "Anything else, Healer?"

"Oh. No, thanks. I think we're all good here."

With a final glance at Cheyenne, the raug recalled the table machine and waited for it to walk out ahead of him before he closed the door again.

Cheyenne sat on the low lounge stacked with pillows in front of the low table. "It's like they threw out the idea of wheels altogether."

Ember snorted and poured them each a glass of water before setting everything on the table beside the tray. "Why use wheels when everything you need gets up and walks on its own?"

"Not completely on its own." Cheyenne tapped the back of her ear, where her activator was placed. "It's a little weird."

"This whole place is weird. I like it." Ember leaned forward to remove the lid from the tray and paused. "Maybe I spoke too soon."

The dish was piled high with a steaming mix of what looked like rice and noodles with various colorful chunks layered throughout. Cheyenne leaned closer. "Huh. Smells like—"

"Chili dogs." Ember set the tray down and wrinkled her nose. "The kind you slop out of a can."

"Not the whole thing."

The fae playfully rolled her eyes and studied their meal. "Obviously just the chili, but *this* smells like the whole thing. Why are there chunks of glowing blue in there?"

"Oh, yeah. That's, uh...you know, I can't remember the name because it's weird, but my troll-neighbor friends cooked it for me one time. Some kind of plant, I think. It moves. Sometimes."

"Okay, so nothing with eyes, but the plants still move after they're cooked. Excellent." Ember shook her head. "I don't even care. I'm starving."

"Dig in, then."

The fae burst out laughing. "They didn't bring any silverware."

Cheyenne grinned. "Can you imagine raugs cutting into something like this with a dainty silver utensil in each hand?"

"No, but I can *vividly* picture them cramming handfuls into their mouths." Wrinkling her nose, Ember reached toward the steaming mound of raug delicacy. "We're going to eat this with our hands, aren't we?"

"I mean, you could always opt for the magical energy bar in your lunchbox."

Ember snorted. "I heard those were better to save for emergencies."

"Okay, then." Cheyenne plunged her fingers into the top of the pile. Thick, drooping noodles plopped back onto the tray when she tried to lift the whole thing to her mouth.

"Oh, jeez. Come on, I knew you had weird eating habits, but this is going a little too far."

The halfling chewed, nodding slowly, then swallowed and grabbed a cup to wash it down. "Okay. After a chaser, it's not that bad."

"Awesome."

"I'm staying away from that blue stuff, though."

Outside below the small terrace, raugs shouted at each other and knocked something over as the closest onlookers laughed and cheered on the fight.

Ember looked through the open wall toward the terrace. "These guys like their fights, don't they?"

"I hadn't seen raugs fighting before today." The halfling sucked left-over pieces of whatever it was off her fingers. "I mean, besides Gúrdu that one time. Those warriors outside the gates? They were pretty brutal and way too fast for something their size."

"What do you mean?"

"I mean, moving at superspeed isn't exactly an advantage." Cheyenne snorted and scooped up another bite. "Maleshi got punched out of hers."

"No way."

"They were all egging each other on. Hopefully, they got it out of their systems."

Ember laughed. "Listen to you, being all diplomatic and frowning at the brawlers in the streets."

"I mean, I ended up fighting them too, but you'd be proud of me, Em. I tried to break it up with words first."

"You're learning."

"I'm trying not to be that pissed-off drow who gets stupid when something goes wrong. L'zar doesn't lose it the way I do, at least most of the time, but spending so much time with him definitely makes me realize how much I *don't* want to be like him in a lot of ways."

"Was he fighting too?"

Cheyenne almost sprayed her next sip of water all over the table but managed to swallow it and laughed. "Are you kidding? He sat there and watched the whole thing like it was his own private show. Could've pulled out a bowl of popcorn, and it wouldn't have been weird."

"There's one thing you don't have to actively avoid not to be like him." Ember slurped a long, dangling noodle into her mouth, spraying sticky sauce all over her chin. She snorted, looked around for a nonexistent napkin, and used the back of her hand instead. "You've never been the kind of person who sees someone needing help and stands there watching."

"Not after the first time, anyway." Cheyenne buried her face in her cup for a long drink. *My friends get shot when I don't step up and do something.*

"L'zar could use some pointers from you that way."

"Right. Like he'd listen to them." The halfling shook her head. "I lost it on him when the capital exploded. He wanted to run away. That's all he ever does. And then he tried to stop me from helping a whole bunch of other magicals who would've been flattened by a falling building if I hadn't stepped in. I mean, I'm not saying I always make the best decisions, but at least I'm trying to be better about it."

"And you think L'zar's too stuck in his ways to even bother trying, huh?"

Cheyenne looked up from the tray and frowned. "He is."

Ember pressed her lips together and looked back down at the tray. "Maybe you're paying too much attention to what you don't like about him."

"Oh, come on. Don't try to tell me L'zar's a good guy with a big heart who had a rough time growing up, and all he needs is a little love."

"I didn't say that."

"That's what it sounds like."

Something heavy and metal clattered to the floor outside below the terrace, followed by cheers and snarls of encouragement.

"Okay." Ember leaned away from hovering over their weird dinner. "You guys had a little heart-to-heart after you got thrown out of that cave, right?"

"Just casually, huh? The *Sorren Gán* threw out the drow trash." Cheyenne laughed.

"Hey, that's an excellent description." Ember looked around unconsciously for a napkin again, couldn't find one, and settled for sucking the sauce off her fingers. "But I'm serious. A few weeks ago, you would've fought every single one of us to avoid sitting down with him like that. It looked like a pretty intense conversation, and no one left it bleeding or looking pissed."

"Yeah. I guess it was." *Pretty sure that's something L'zar wants to stay a secret. I can't believe I'm gonna keep it for him.*

"While you two huddled on the other side of that clearing, Corian had a lot to say about L'zar's sudden decision to start making better choices."

Cheyenne cocked her head. "Corian doesn't ever have a lot to say."

"It felt like a lot for him, okay?" Ember leaned back against the lounge. "He said he'd never seen L'zar show so much restraint toward another magical coming at him like you did."

"He was trying to protect himself, Em. Not by fighting me back, by trying to convince me I was wrong and he was right the whole time." Cheyenne shrugged. "Which might technically be true, but that goes back to the whole 'don't lie to Cheyenne if you want her help' issue. Which hasn't stopped."

"He explained everything to you, didn't he?"

"Yeah."

"And you didn't ask for it."

With a wry chuckle, Cheyenne folded her arms and stared at her friend. "You're diving deep into this, aren't you?"

"Hey, I'm not trying to convince you L'zar's a great guy. I'm not sure anyone believes that one hundred percent. I'm just saying he's changing. All the magicals who've known him forever can see it."

"They told you that explicitly, huh?"

"Yeah." Ember raised an eyebrow. "They were pretty worried about the whole thing."

"They shouldn't have been. I was pissed, but even if Corian and Maleshi hadn't gotten in the way, I would've run out of steam eventually. That tends to happen."

"Cheyenne, they weren't holding you back to protect L'zar."

The halfling wrinkled her nose. "What?"

"They were protecting *you*. Which apparently didn't need to happen because L'zar's been working on *not* killing the wrong people when he gets angry. You know, like his daughter."

"Huh." Cheyenne blinked at the pile of food on the table and shrugged. "I could still take him."

"Oh, my God." Ember laughed and rolled her eyes. "You're not even willing to say it's *possible* that he's trying to be better?"

"I don't know, Em. Not something I wanna think about right now. The guy basically killed himself for power no one else had, and I don't know what that says about how much he can change."

"What?"

Crap. "Nothing. It doesn't matter. I can't let my guard down around him, not all the way. I mean, however many thousands of years he's been alive, he's been Ambar'ogúl's trickster thief the whole time. Why would he stop that now?"

"Hmm. I hear people do weird things when they have kids."

Cheyenne snorted, then a cheer rose from outside, followed by a growling chant of, "*Cu'ón! Cu'ón!*"

"What the hell?" Cheyenne stood and quickly went out to the terrace. Below, a crowd of raugs had gathered around a cleared circle in the square. L'zar squatted on one side of the ring they'd formed, grinning at a huge raug sitting cross-legged on the other side. The raug cast some sort of spell, and L'zar copied the gestures almost exactly. Bright light strobed from their hands, and Cheyenne blinked against the glare before heading back into the room.

"Okay, you can't stand there watching without telling me what's going on down there. Immobile fae girl, remember?"

"He's down there competing in some kind of spell-off with a raug. I have no idea what they're doing."

"Oh." Ember perked up. "That sounds cool."

"If your magical battery recharges before we leave, I'm sure you'll have a chance to try it out for yourself." Cheyenne plopped back down onto the lounge, then turned and kicked up both feet to stretch them out in front of her. "I'm totally fine with sitting here and doing nothing for a while. Things feel okay right now, you know? I mean, if we ignore the whole part about this entire world falling apart under the Crown's shitty ruling habits."

"Ha. Delicately phrased."

Cheyenne widened her eyes and shrugged. "You know *me*, Em. Super-eloquent halfling."

"I know what you mean, though. Not always running around trying to fight off the next thing coming for you. I mean, I don't know what it's been like for you, but I can imagine."

"It is what it is. It's kinda nice to sit back and know that at least right now, nothing's coming after me, and no one's gonna open a portal into our apartment and tell us to get ready for something *right now*."

Ember glanced around and grimaced. "I'd knock on wood right now if there was any."

"Not trying to jinx it."

"I know."

"Don't get me wrong. I know how much work it's gonna take before anything in this world looks even *half* right again. I don't think I can even say things have ever been right with a drow on the throne."

"Maybe not *our* version of right." Ember sipped at her water. "But right for this world. Like the fighting pits."

"Oh, yeah. Everybody goes crazy for the chance to smash each other up for fun and call it honor and glory." The halfling chuckled and closed her eyes. "Not to mention purposely slicing each other to the brink of death."

Ember laughed. "Can't say a little fun never hurt anybody anymore, can we?"

"Not in Ambar'ogúl."

"No, I'm talking about the deathflame and the healing part. This place runs on violence. That's obvious. But it seems to balance itself out, you know? Violence as a way of enjoying peace. Or getting seriously fucked up for a purpose. Get healed in the fighting pits and spread more life magic to this entire world."

"Hey, good idea." Grinning, Cheyenne swept her hand in a wide arc around the room. "Let's set up a giant fighting pit and have everybody go at each other at once. Giant deathflame bonfire on millions of dying bodies, and *bam*. All the blight gone, everybody healed and happy, and we go home."

"In theory, that sounds like a promising solution." Ember refilled her copper cup and sat back again, cradling it in both hands. "Not sure how great it'd work out, though. That's a lot of deathflame torches on a lot of bodies."

"We could figure it out."

They were silent for a moment, then Ember added, "You planning on going back home and picking up right where you left off after all this is over?"

"Probably. I mean, no, not *right* where I left off. That'll be impossible after getting the Crown to step down. L'zar said I had two options: stay as the Crown here, or go back home and be Earth's drow royalty there instead."

"Everybody needs a leader, right?"

Cheyenne said, "Not everyone, but all those O'gúleesh who made the crossing to get away from this mess? Probably. The FRoE isn't enough to handle things over there anymore. They don't even know *what* they're handling, or how to help those magicals beyond sticking their names in a stupid database and giving them a tiny house until they think they're ready to move into the brave new human world on their own. But they're not. They're missing huge pieces about how to get by over there, and they don't have anyone there to show them. The FRoE doesn't give a shit what they do after they leave the reservations."

"Sounds like you've already made your choice."

"Not quite. I'm hyper-aware of what those choices are. I mean, there *is* a third choice, which is going back home without being the Earth-drow monarch but still knowing what I know. It won't be the same as before, but I won't be wearing a damn crown, that's for sure."

Ember laughed. "Now *that* I'd like to see."

"Sorry, Em. Not gonna happen." Cheyenne looked at the ceiling and brushed loose hair away from her face. "The only thing I know is that I'm not gonna be the Crown here. That's just too much. I don't want it, and I can't leave my mom behind."

"What, you don't think she'd follow you across the Border and find herself a cozy little tower?"

They burst out laughing. *At least we can still find the parts of this to laugh about.* Her smile faded.

"I still need to find someone to be the new Crown over here. I'm not leaving this place in a giant power vacuum, and I have less than two weeks to figure out who the hell that's gonna be."

"Maybe your cousin will want the throne."

"My what?" Cheyenne sat up and frowned at her friend, then made the connection. "Oh. Jesus, that's weird."

"Should I call him Ba'rael's secret heir instead?"

"Very funny. I don't know what's gonna happen with him, Em. If he's anything like me, he won't want to be a part of this either, and if he's anything like either of our parents, he's not the right drow for the job."

Ember leaned sideways against the lounge and pursed her lips in thought. "Or maybe the right drow for the job isn't a drow."

"What, do *you* want it?"

"Ha. Nice try."

"Didn't think so." Cheyenne kicked off her black Vans and crossed one ankle over the other, lacing her fingers behind her head. "I guess we'll just have to find out."

"You don't seem like you're in much of a hurry."

"I'm not. Not right now. Tomorrow's a whole different story." *And L'zar sure as hell better keep his word. A talk, or I don't think I'll be able to hold back.*

CHAPTER TWENTY-EIGHT

Maleshi poured herself a glass of Bloodshine and took a long drink. The fizzing bubbles made her swallow quickly before she let out a satisfied sigh. *Totally worth arguing with three different raugs to get a bottle. Nobody ever said I wasn't persistent.*

Sitting in the large pile of cushions that served as a raug armchair, she dropped her head back and enjoyed the relative silence. She could still hear the cheers and laughter from the square outside and briefly imagined herself out there with the crowd. *Nope. I have everything I need right here, though a bath with hot water would be excellent.*

A gentle knock sounded on the door to her guest quarters.

Frowning, Maleshi set her cup on the low table and stood. *I told them to leave me alone for the night, and I know how good raugs are at remembering.*

She went to the door and pulled the iron-ringed handle. "If you're here to get the Bloodshine back, it's already gone. Oh."

Corian stood in front of the open door, his hands in his pockets, and cocked his head. "I always knew you could handle your booze, but that seems a little excessive."

Maleshi gave him an exasperated look. "It's a lie. I just opened the damn thing, but the raugs in charge of guarding the alcohol supply here take their jobs seriously. Why are you here?"

He shrugged. "I was hoping you had time for a chat."

The general frowned and shifted her weight onto one hip. "Why?"

"Oh, I don't know. Not having had the chance to talk to you about anything without interruption for the last few centuries feels like a good place to start."

"Hmm." Maleshi leaned into the hall and quickly glanced up and down. Then she shrugged and pulled back in. "Close the door behind you."

"Yes, General."

"Cut that out, huh? The loyal soldier crap is getting old."

Corian closed the door behind him and stood in front of it, his hands in his pockets again.

Maleshi flopped onto the mound of pillows and picked up her cup again, then saw him standing there and snorted. "You're obviously not standing at attention, so what are you waiting for? I already invited you in."

"I'm giving you enough time to change your mind."

"Change my mind." She snorted and took a long drink of Bloodshine. "I know exactly what I want, not that I'm gonna get it here. Duty before desire, right? And the way I remember it, you're the one who had problems making up his mind."

Corian chuckled and dropped his gaze to the floor. "All right. I suppose I deserved that."

"That's the least of what you deserve, *vae shra'ni.*" She studied his bowed head. He still hadn't stepped farther into the room. "I'm not going to change my mind. Come sit."

Glancing at her briefly, Corian moved swiftly across the room and pulled an extra-large cushion toward the low table.

Maleshi grabbed an extra cup, filled it to the brim with bubbling Bloodshine, and handed it over. "What's going on?"

"I'm concerned." Corian took the drink and held it over his crossed legs, frowning at the golden liquid.

"Interesting."

"Ha. That's all you have to say?"

"I didn't come here to talk to myself." She eyed him with a smile. "What task did L'zar give you that you can't figure out this time, huh?"

Corian shook his head. "Not a task. I'm concerned about him and where this is headed."

"And you came to *me* for advice?"

With a self-conscious smile, Corian dipped his head and stared at the cup as he raised it to his lips. "More like comfort, honestly. I'm starting to think I knocked on the wrong door."

Maleshi swallowed and watched him try to hide his embarrassment behind the cup. *After centuries,* now *he needs comfort from me. Something's wrong.* "Where is he right now?"

"In the square playing king of spells with the raugs."

"Are you sure?"

Corian looked at her, his jaw clenching. "Maleshi, I wouldn't have come to you like this if I didn't know exactly where he was and what he was doing. I don't want him to know I'm here."

"Neither do I." She set down her cup and sat up straighter on the mound of pillows. "But you obviously need to get something off your chest, and I think you should stay to do that."

"Thank you."

"You're welcome." She spread her arms and gestured to the pile of cushions around her. "I *am* very busy right now, so just know this bottle of Bloodshine is going to feel particularly abandoned until I can give it my full attention again."

He snorted. "By all means, drink while you listen. We might both need it."

"Corian."

"Yeah."

"You're stalling."

Corian took another drink and reached for the bottle to refill his cup. "All this about Ba'rael having a child and us going to find him. It doesn't feel right."

"I thought you agreed we should speak to him?"

"I do. Cazerel didn't say a thing about where he is. About where we're going."

"You don't trust the raugs?"

"No, I do. I don't think they trust us. We only got into that meeting because of Ember, and that says enough on its own. I'm not worried about the raugs, but L'zar seems way too excited for a family reunion and a quick chat about the future." Corian rubbed the back of his neck. "He won't tell me what he plans to do with this newfound nephew of his, and I'm not sure I can predict his intentions anymore. Not as well as I used to, at any rate."

"You think he's lying to you?"

"Lying and avoiding the whole truth are one and the same for him. You know that."

Maleshi frowned. "I do. I also don't see a reason why he'd keep anything from you. Not now, when we're so close to finishing all this."

"Neither do I, but I can *feel* it." He rubbed a hand over his mouth and stared at the ceiling. "Now I know how Cheyenne felt before she learned the rest of what she needed to know."

"You're comparing two very different things, *vae shra'ni.*" Maleshi dipped her chin and stared at him from beneath her darkened brows until he met her gaze. "Neither of them knows how to fulfill their role with the other. Is it strange to see L'zar Verdys loosening up around the halfling daughter he's known for all of a month? Absolutely. Can we trust that he's trying to do all this for her and for the world he despises as much as some O'gúleesh despise him? Maybe."

"That's the thing. I thought I did." Corian bit his bottom lip, his nostrils flaring as he tried to put his thoughts into words. "I'm not sure I do anymore. I think he's hiding things from me *because* we're this close to the end, and he no longer thinks it's necessary to keep me informed."

"That's not the way you two operate."

"Yes, I'm well aware."

Maleshi scooted closer to the edge of the pillows. "Do you think he's noticed that you feel this way?"

"No. He knows I agree with Cheyenne that using Ba'rael's son against her is not the route we want to take. He also knows I stand with him in heading out to wherever they're keeping him to see him for ourselves and make our judgment call then."

"Then leave it at that. Make the judgment call then, and don't spend time worrying about it until we get there. That won't do any of us any good."

Corian closed his eyes. "I can't lie to him, Maleshi."

"You have to. If L'zar thinks you're questioning him, you know how he'll react. He hasn't had nearly enough time to recover from the Weave he spent all that time cloaking around himself, and then he returned to the *Sorren Gán*. If I had to guess, I'd say he's as unstable now as he was the first time he made that journey. Don't set him off."

"You think I want to?" Corian set his cup on the table, rubbed his lips, and stood. "It was a mistake to come here. I'm sorry."

"Corian, you brought me into this by coming to talk to me *now* of all times. Don't walk away from this conversation before it's finished."

"Why, because you're the only one who gets to do that?"

Maleshi leaped from the cushions and hissed, "Don't you dare compare that to *this*! I told you exactly what was happening. I laid everything at your feet. All her plans. All the orders I'd been given to carry out. Every single speck of information, yours and L'zar's to do with however you saw fit. You had a *choice*."

"I know." Corian stared at her and raised both hands in submission. "I know. I'm sorry."

"No, sorry isn't good enough, especially not now. He *told* you to leave. He saw what you wanted, and he handed it to you on a fell-damn tray. You turned away from all of it."

"Maleshi."

"Don't do that." She pointed at him and shook her head. "Don't try to talk your way out of this. You've been skirting around it for centuries, Corian, and you're trying to do the same thing again, right here in front of me! L'zar *knew* he'd be going Earthside again. He *knew* he'd be spending as much time over there as he did, and he told you to come with me. You turned against *both* of us when you stayed here, and then what? You made the crossing centuries later, settled into a world full of humans, and didn't once try to find me? I am *here* for you now, *vae shra'ni*, and you still owe me."

"You're right."

"I know I'm right!" Maleshi balled her fists, glaring at him and breathing heavily through her clenched teeth. "Don't talk to me about walking away like you know what that means."

His jaw clenched, Corian stepped toward her and paused. "I should have come with you. I didn't have all the pieces before you left, and L'zar didn't give them willingly to me then. That's what I'm afraid of, *ma gairín*. It feels like it's happening all over again, only this time I know the consequences of *not* seeing what he sees." He took a sharp breath and grimaced at the ceiling. "Maybe the consequences of knowing what he plans to do are even worse."

"Maybe they are." Maleshi smoothed her dark hair away from her face and regained her composure. "There's a good chance that if he hasn't told you to do something, there's nothing to do but wait and watch. And if he *does* give an order, no matter how insane it is, I hope you follow it. Sometimes I want to rip that drow limb from limb, but as long as I've known him, he's never been wrong."

"*I* was, though." Corian slowly approached her and lifted a hand toward her face. Maleshi tilted her head away slightly and stared at him. He nodded, ran his fingers briefly along her cheek, and dropped his hand. "And I *am* sorry."

"So am I." Maleshi closed her eyes and took a deep breath. "I think we're finished with this conversation."

"Right." A pained frown creased his eyebrows, and he nodded. "I'll let you get back to your drinking."

"I didn't tell you to leave." When he turned back toward her, she gave him a soft smile. "You said you came looking for comfort, didn't you?"

A wry chuckle escaped him. "That's not what I found, but I'll be fine."

"Or you could stay. Find comfort without L'zar Verdys being at the center of it." Maleshi nodded toward the bottle on the table, still three-quarters full. "That Bloodshine won't drink itself."

The corners of Corian's mouth flickered into the hint of a smile, and he turned to eye the bottle. "Are you sure?"

"As I said, I know what I want. Just waiting for you to make your decision."

He studied her silver gaze, then dipped his head and returned to the table to fill both their cups. When Maleshi joined him, Corian handed her a drink and raised his for a toast. "To Maleshi Hi'et, who always gets what she wants."

"And Corian Vedi'im, who somehow always wants what he gets."

They knocked their metal cups together, staring at each other, and drank.

CHAPTER TWENTY-NINE

Shut up, already! I'm trying to sleep.

With a groan, Cheyenne Summerlin rolled over in the massive bed and tossed the thick, itchy blanket off her shoulders. The muffled shouts and raucous laughter spilling through the substantial door to her private room quieted enough to let her slip back into unconsciousness.

Ten seconds later, something huge crashed into a bunch of metal and stone, followed by uproarious laughter and growling voices shouting in French.

The sound startled Cheyenne out of her sleep again, and she pounded a fist into the thick, hard pillow beneath her to push herself up. "What the hell is *wrong* with those guys?"

More shouts and laughter carried into her room. Someone else grunted and fell against more metal, then a deep, rough voice broke out in tuneless song.

With an aggravated grunt, Cheyenne sat upright and pushed herself off the side of the huge bed before striding barefoot across the room. She flung open the heavy, creaking wooden door and stumbled into the living room connecting her guest quarters in the raug city to Ember's.

The ruckus outside was much louder now, echoing up the stone walls of the building and spilling into the main room through the open balcony. She blinked at the darkness of the sky beyond the balcony, not quite the black of night but nowhere near late enough for everyone to be awake like this.

So, the raugs get up and fight for no reason when it's barely even dawn, huh?

Cheyenne stepped groggily toward the open balcony but stopped when another crash came—from Ember's room this time.

"Damnit!" The fae grunted in frustration. "Come on. Just get this stupid... No, no. Wait!"

Metal clinked against stone, and the crawler bashed into the doorway of Ember's room before scuttling through and darting wildly across the living area toward Cheyenne. The temporary O'gúl wheelchair on eight legs wobbled when two of its pointed feet struck the large pillow scattered across the floor. It almost fell over but paused, as if the old-school tech was aware of the danger if it kept moving.

"This sucks," Ember muttered from her room.

Trying not to laugh, Cheyenne headed for the crawler. "Want me to herd this thing back in there for you, Em?"

"Oh, shit. Did I wake you up?"

"Nope." Cheyenne pulled the silver activator coil from her front pocket and slipped it behind her ear. The pinch of the O'gúl tech syncing with her magic and her brain had faded at this point to little more than a fleeting itch, though her eyelids fluttered from the buzz of tech-induced magic.

"Okay, then yeah. Bring the stupid thing back in here so the magic-less fae can depend on a machine again to move around." Ember groaned. "Please."

The lines of code scrolling across the crawler's flat, unlabeled control panel translated the O'gúleesh symbols to readable English in under two seconds. Cheyenne stopped in front of the crawler and quickly scanned the panel. *They weren't kidding about the old-school part. This thing isn't half as complicated as any machine in Hangivol.*

She swiped the control panel and directed the crawler off the pillows and back across the living area. The machine moved quickly and easily this time, avoiding the doorframe altogether before it slowed to a stop beside Ember's huge bed, which was built for a raug's dimensions, not a fae's.

"Oh, sure." Ember rolled her eyes. "The thing has no problem avoiding obstacles when the drow gives it commands."

Cheyenne walked slowly into the room. "Looked like you were getting the hang of it yesterday."

"Yeah, when I had *you* to pick me up and stick me in that thing. If I had my magic back, I wouldn't need you *or* this stupid machine."

The halfling stuck her hands in her pockets and raised an eyebrow. *Someone woke up on the wrong side of the O'gúl bed.*

Ember stopped glaring at the glittering black machine long enough to flick her gaze at the half-drow. "Sorry. I think I'm still half-asleep."

"Yeah, me too."

Right on cue, another crash and round of boisterous laughter rose from the courtyard outside the balcony. Immediately after that came the thump and slap of flesh hitting flesh.

Cheyenne closed her eyes. "Whoever those idiots are out there, they're gonna wake up the entire city with that crap."

"Yeah." Ember ran a pink-tinted hand through her violet-streaked brown hair and reached for the crawler, but drew her hands away again, thumped her thighs, and shot her friend an exasperated glance. "I think I made this thing freak out when I tried to climb in. Feel like lifting a fae into a machine this early in the morning?"

The halfling smiled. "If that's what the fae needs, sure."

Ember gave her friend a thin smile and reached out to wrap her arms around Cheyenne's neck. The halfling scooped her up and set her in the depressed seat in the middle of the crawler's main body. The fae grabbed each of her thighs in turn to shift them around more comfortably in her seat. "Thanks."

"No problem." Cheyenne stepped away from her friend and stared at the mottled dark-gray splotches with barely visible black lines snaking across Ember's forearm. "Shit, Em. Your arm."

"What, this?" Ember lifted her forearm with wide eyes, then rubbed it with her other hand and shook her head. "I'm fine."

"That looks a hell of a lot like the blight on those skaxens."

"I didn't *catch* the blight from Cazerel if that's what you're wondering." Ember's head wobbled in indecision as she looked back down at her arm. "It's like, you know how when you throw a rock into a pond, and the water keeps moving and rippling for a long time after the rock's at the bottom?"

The halfling snorted and folded her arms. "That's not a rock, Em. That's a mutating magical plague eating this entire world and spilling across the Border. And you're not a pond."

"Cheyenne, you're making way too big of a deal out of this."

"So far, you're the only person who can heal this thing in magicals, and now your magic has taken a back seat for however long."

"Trust me, it was a lot worse than this last night. Kept me up for hours."

"Seriously?" Cheyenne stepped toward the so-far-motionless crawler, frowning at the dark splotches on her friend's pink skin. Ember didn't even try to hide them. "Why didn't you tell me?"

"Because it got better." Ember shrugged. "And there's nothing you could've done about it, right? If I am the only one who can heal this crap."

The room was silent after that. Ember might have had a chance at setting a record for a staring contest with the drow halfling, but a small cough escaped her and grew quickly into a full-blown fit.

"Jesus, Em."

"I said I'm fine." Ember lifted a hand to stop Cheyenne from coming any closer. "Seriously. I'm fairly sure last night was the worst of it."

When the fae girl seemed to have her breathing back under control, Cheyenne nodded. "Okay. But I need you to promise me that if those black lines get worse again or show up in different places, you'll tell me."

"Sure."

"Hey, I'm serious. I don't know about you, but I sure as hell didn't expect you to have to heal a raug chief from the blight and lose your magic in the process. That wasn't part of the plan when we came here."

"I didn't *lose* my magic." Ember raised an eyebrow. "It's not working the right way. No spells yet, and I'm still a half-assed noob with this activator."

Cheyenne laughed wryly. "Right."

"I still *look* like a full-blooded fae, so I know my magic isn't gone."

"Obviously. I'm saying we can't screw around on this side." Ember opened her mouth to argue and Cheyenne stepped back, raising both hands in concession. "Hey, I know. That probably makes me a hypocrite. I've ignored way more injuries than I probably should have at the time because I figured I'd be fine, but things are getting serious over here. And seriously weird. I learned my lesson about sitting back and letting things play out when it comes to you, Em. Not gonna do that again."

Ember slowly folded her arms, and her chin dipped almost to her chest as she studied her gray-blotted forearms. Then she looked up at Cheyenne again without moving her head. "Even Foltr said this is temporary."

"Still." Cheyenne shrugged. "We have no idea how long 'temporary' will last, and I don't like the odds."

"You don't even know what they are."

"Exactly." Cheyenne nodded curtly, trying not to look too freaked out, only the right amount. *Last time I didn't pay attention to the consequences, Ember got shot. Wasn't that long ago, either.* "I'm trying not to make the same mistakes, Em. Especially with you."

"Yeah, I get it. Thanks." Blinking quickly, Ember glanced down at the control panel on the crawler and lifted her hand to attempt another command, then paused. "You can play drow bodyguard, Cheyenne, but the last thing I want is—"

Someone roared in anger down in the courtyard as another heavy something caused what sounded like an entire stone wall to topple over. The magicals who'd been laughing and egging on the good-natured brawling outside now growled and snarled. Muted red light flashed in the main room of Cheyenne and Ember's shared quarters and the doorway of Ember's room.

The halfling rolled her eyes. "Sounds like somebody doesn't know when to hold back."

"*That's* what woke me up." Ember glared through the doorway. "Seriously, if they don't cut it out, I won't be the only pissed-off magical who didn't wanna be up this early."

"You aren't." Cheyenne spun and stormed across the main room toward the open balcony.

Something thudded against the wall of the building, making the floor beneath her tremble. Deep raug voices echoed around the courtyard, roaring with renewed excitement and the contagious battle rage they shared in Hirúl Breach.

"Show him, Barlek."

"Smash his head in!"

"Blood and honor, brother!"

Cheyenne slammed both hands on the balcony rail and peered over the edge as the only voice she recognized came from below.

"You think you can handle *this*?" L'zar spread his arms and grinned, sucking in a sharp breath through his teeth as he swayed on the stone floor of the courtyard. "I've eaten radan hooves that fought back better than that. How long have you been hiding here, wondering who cut off your balls?"

"Jesus Christ," Cheyenne muttered. "Why am I not surprised?"

CHAPTER THIRTY

The raug L'zar had hurled against the wall of the building bellowed and charged the drow thief. L'zar staggered back but somehow wasn't fast enough to avoid a massive hard gray head ramming into his chest. The drow flew across the courtyard and toppled into two other raugs who were cheering their clansman on as another half-dozen of the giant gray magicals snarled their approval.

One raug snatched the front of L'zar's shirt in a meaty fist, red claws scraping the drow's slate-gray flesh, and sneered in his face. "Not so big *now*, are you?"

Blinking heavy eyelids, L'zar tried to steady his wobbling head and meet the leering raug's burning gaze. "Bigger than you where it counts, I imagine."

The second raug he'd stumbled into swung a fist into the drow's jaw. L'zar's head whipped to the side, the rest of him held in place by the other raug's fistful of his tunic, and dark blood splattered on the stone floor.

L'zar snickered. "You call that a hit?"

The raug holding him shoved the drow away and sent his fist crashing into the other side of L'zar's face. The drow spun beneath the blow, then whirled back toward his attacker with wide, furiously glowing golden eyes.

"I wasn't finished!"

"You will be." Both raugs charged him at once, their pounding footsteps making the ground tremble beneath them as they kicked up bits of stone splattered with drow blood.

L'zar darted into drow speed and brought his fist up into the first raug's gut of solid muscle. The gray-skinned magical staggered backward with a roar, and his clansman stepped toward the blur of gray and white and swept his muscular arm aside in a smashing arc. L'zar flew out of drow speed and gained his footing before the raug he'd slammed into the wall stepped up behind him and punched him in the lower back.

The other magicals gathered to watch the fight roared in approval and stomped their feet, pumping their fists in the air and snarling. Spit and blood and sweat flew everywhere as L'zar whirled under the simultaneous attacks of three raugs, none of whom looked likely to take mercy on the drow thief.

Even from where she stood at the balcony, Cheyenne could smell the fumes of Bloodshine and fellwine as if she'd downed a whole keg of it on her own. *Of course, he's drunk. He's gonna get himself killed.*

L'zar darted into drow speed again and clambered onto one raug's back. The raug roared and pounded his fist against the drow's forearm, which was squeezing his thickly muscled throat. Another raug cracked an elbow between L'zar's shoulder blades, then grabbed the drow around the middle and swung him fiercely away from his kinsman before slamming him to the ground. The crack of L'zar's skull hitting stone echoed through the courtyard.

Ember scuttled toward the balcony in the crawler, weaving as she swiped at the control panel and tried to get the machine to do what she wanted. "Did I hear L'zar screaming?"

Down below, the crouching drow spun in a streak of gray and black and white, hissing and baring his teeth. Then he leaped at the closest raug and pummeled the magical's muscular torso with both fists. The others closed on him and took turns smashing their knuckles into L'zar Verdys' face, back, ribs, and shoulders.

Cheyenne gritted her teeth. "That's it."

"What's happening?" Ember stabbed a finger on the control panel and made the crawler totter off in the wrong direction. "Cheyenne, if he's stupid enough to start a fight, let him."

"He's wasted, and they're gonna kill him."

"Why is that suddenly your problem?" Ember stopped and stared in exasperation at the empty balcony and the flash of bone-white hair fluttering toward the courtyard below. "Right. 'Cause jumping off balconies is her thing now."

Cheyenne landed in a crouch, steadying herself with her fingertips on the stone, then rose to her feet. "Hey! What the hell's wrong with you?"

L'zar ignored her. So did the raugs. One of them reached out when the drunken drow thief darted past in a blurred streak. L'zar was ripped out of his enhanced speed when the raug's fist buried itself in the drow's long white hair. His roar of pain and fury cut off when the raug jerked him back by his locks and smashed his other fist into L'zar's gut.

The drow hit the ground and slid away on his back, firing flashing red bursts of magic that went everywhere but at his attackers. Cheyenne ducked a stray burst and it hit the wall behind her, resulting in an explosion of stone chips and black dust. "Come *on*."

The raug closest to L'zar charged the drow with a crazed sneer, his black tongue hanging out of his mouth in drunken excitement. L'zar lashed out with a booted foot and connected squarely with the gray-skinned magical's kneecap. Something crunched, and the raug bellowed as he crashed down on his other knee.

"I'm serious." Cheyenne darted forward when the second raug lunged toward L'zar with both fists raised high above his head. "You guys need to cut this shit out! Hey! I'm talking to you!"

The raug only had enough room in his Bloodshine-addled head to focus on his target. As his arms swung toward L'zar's chest, Cheyenne reached out. Lashing black tendrils burst from her fingertips and whipped around the raug's forearms. She yanked back, he jerked down toward L'zar, and both were whisked off their feet to stagger toward each other.

Cheyenne's coils slithered away from around the raug's wrists when she looked up and found his face inches from hers. The raug snarled in battle-maddened glee.

"No." She pointed at him. "I came down here to break this up."

His thick gray forehead cracked against hers, and she reeled back-ward with a grunt. The raug's drunken roar of laughter cut off when L'zar jumped onto his back and swung wildly with both fists.

Cheyenne rubbed her forehead and scowled. *This isn't even a real fight.* "L'zar! You're not doing yourself any—whoa!"

The third raug had come up behind her and now lifted her with one hand clenched around the back of her shirt and the other arm wrapped around her waist. The next thing she knew, she was flying through the air toward the wall of the building. She caught a glimpse of Ember's furious glare at the edge of the balcony before the halfling aimed her black lashing tendrils at the railing. They coiled around it before Cheyenne struck the wall, and she managed to pull herself up and hit that wall with the soles of her feet instead of her face.

Ember moved forward in the crawler and raised an eyebrow. "Didn't think you were into fighting this early in the morning."

"I'm not." Cheyenne released the black whips of drow magic from her fingertips and dropped to the ground. *I'm done with everyone fighting raugs at the worst possible time.*

She summoned a crackling black orb of energy in one hand and tossed it at the raug swinging his fist at L'zar's face again. Her attack hit the magical in the shoulder and sent him spinning away from the drow thief, but another raug came up behind L'zar and sucker-punched him. L'zar staggered toward Cheyenne, briefly lifting a hand to his jaw.

"Time to call it." She put a hand on his shoulder to draw him away from the growling raugs. L'zar's elbow shot up and cracked into her nose before he realized he'd made contact with his daughter instead of a hulking grayskin.

Cheyenne's back thumped against the wall, tears filling her eyes at the overwhelming pain, and gingerly prodded her nose with a hiss. "Are you fucking kidding me?"

L'zar spun and peered at her, his golden eyes unfocused as he stag-gered sideways. "Don't get in my way."

All her attempts to be the voice of reason disappeared. With a snarl, she shot two black energy spheres at the drow thief, who ducked one and took the other in the shoulder. Cheyenne's first orb glanced off a raug's head as he lowered it and charged the only two drow in Hirúl Breach.

The third raug appeared from nowhere and snatched Cheyenne away from the wall before throwing her into the fray. She was caught up in a flurry of flying fists and snarling teeth as three raugs and L'zar Verdys exchanged blows aimed at anything that moved.

"End them!" the spectators shouted.

"Hey, we're not ending anybody!" Cheyenne ducked a red-clawed gray fist and stepped under the flailing raug's swing before kicking him away. "Cut it out!"

The gray-skinned magicals around them jeered and stomped their feet, roaring in excitement. L'zar darted into enhanced speed over and over but was forced back out of it every time by a raug's outstretched foot or lowered shoulder or the swing of a massive arm.

When two raugs sent their fists hurtling toward L'zar at the same time, Cheyenne gritted her teeth and raised a translucent black shield around her father. The raugs' fists glanced off it with echoing cracks like they'd struck metal and the magicals staggered away, bellowing. L'zar threw his head back and cackled. Cheyenne ducked another swing by the third raug as her father backed away from behind the shield and darted back into the fight.

All around them, voices rose not from the gathered raugs who'd been up all night partying with the Weaver, but from those who'd gone to sleep when they should have and were now awakened by the brawl.

"*Tais-toi!*"

"*Ce n'est même pas l'aube!*"

"*Putain d'idiots!*"

Cheyenne didn't need to speak French to get the gist of the angry shouts as raugs glared sleepily from open balconies around the courtyard. "Hey, I'm trying to help!"

L'zar flew over her shoulder and bashed into the wall. It took him two seconds to pull himself off the ground, shake himself off, and dart back toward the raugs.

Cheyenne clenched her fists and was about to reach after him with her lashing tendrils when two darting streaks of blazing silver light entered the courtyard.

Corian and Maleshi appeared on either side of L'zar and grabbed his arms to hold him back. The drow thief struggled against them and lunged at the three raugs leering at him. Despite everyone being covered in hours-old blood and O'gúl booze and dirt, none of them was ready to back down.

"Stop it," Corian whispered harshly, his fingers digging into L'zar's upper arm. "This isn't why we're here."

L'zar ignored him and hissed at the three raugs, who were debating whether or not to keep going. "You're all useless. If you want to fight me, Barlek, then fight me!"

"Hey!" Corian shook the drow thief by the shoulder when L'zar lunged.

Maleshi kept a firm hold on L'zar's other arm and stepped in front of him. "I think it's time to call it a night."

The closest raug hurled a snaking attack of orange light at the trio. Cheyenne raised a shield around L'zar and the nightstalkers, sending the bolt into the air above the courtyard. It bashed into the wall of another building, and snarled French shouts rained down around them.

Corian tightened his grip on L'zar and bared his teeth. "Cheyenne."

"Yeah, as long as you keep him out of it." The halfling shot both nightstalkers exasperated glances, then darted into drow speed toward the three raugs still intent on kicking L'zar Verdys' ass.

CHAPTER THIRTY-ONE

Cheyenne loomed over the last drunken raug she'd just put on his back and summoned an energy sphere in warning. Black and purple light flickered across the raug's scarred gray face. "You wanna try that again, or are you done?"

The raug spat a glob of blood-stained saliva, then laughed and waved her off. "I looked forward to ripping the Weaver's head off his shoulders."

"Yeah, I bet you did." She stepped back, still cradling an energy sphere, and glanced at the other two raugs helping each other up off the stone floor. "Anyone else?"

The raugs turned away, wiping blood and spit and dirt off their faces before joining their kinsmen. The spectators roared in approval and welcomed their clansmen back into the small crowd with fresh cups of Bloodshine and hard thumps on the back.

The other citizens of Hirúl Breach glared down at the brawlers, muttering in French and casting even dirtier looks at Cheyenne.

She stared right back at them and spread her arms. "Sure. Next time I'll let them kill each other."

"They can try," L'zar hissed behind her.

Cheyenne spun and stormed toward him, fighting to keep her magic under control as it burned through her. "What the hell's *wrong* with you?"

L'zar made a poor attempt at wrenching himself free from Corian's and Maleshi's grasps. The nightstalkers instantly let go and stepped back when Cheyenne approached her father, her glowing golden eyes blazing. "Just my self-righteous spawn getting in the way."

The energy sphere crackled, briefly flaring to twice its size in the halfling's hand. "Say that again."

"Not the time," Corian warned in a low voice.

"I know it's not the time. Why do you think I came here? We're supposed to be heading to wherever the Crown's secret kid is, and he's out here making an ass of himself." Cheyenne killed the black orb and scowled at L'zar. "You look like shit. Did you get any sleep?"

He scoffed and flung his hand toward her in a dismissive wave. "I don't need to sleep. Not now."

"You can barely stand."

"A minor setback, easily fix—" L'zar staggered across the ground, his eyes wide and unfocused. "Easily fixed by another drink. Where's the damn Bloodshine?"

"Not here." Cheyenne folded her arms. "Bet I could find a bucket of water for you, though. I'd be happy to hold your head under it for you."

He hiccupped, blinked heavily at the nightstalkers, then spun away from his daughter and stumbled toward the other side of the courtyard and the open streets of the raug city beyond. "Whenever you assholes are ready to leave, I'll be at the gates."

His footsteps echoed through the stone alley between buildings, and he gave a huge belch before wiping away the blood trickling from the corner of his mouth and another cut at his temple. A raug hissed another curse at him in French from an open balcony, and L'zar shot him the O'gúleesh version of the middle finger and stalked away.

"I don't get it." Cheyenne turned toward Maleshi and Corian and spread her arms. "Does he have some kind of hidden agenda for drunken street fights, or is he finally showing his stupid side?"

Pursing her lips, Maleshi shrugged.

Corian stared after the drow thief even after L'zar disappeared around the corner and shook his head. "I'm not sure *I* want to know the answer to that. We need to give him time, kid. He'll be fine."

"Uh-huh." Cheyenne glanced at the nightstalkers and finally had the chance to take in their appearance. Maleshi's black hair was tangled and mussed in a dark halo around her feline face. The white shirt hanging off her frame looked oddly loose and big on her. Conversely, the black jacket with the gray stripe running down the side looked way too tight on Corian, the sleeve cuffs ending two inches above his wrists because it was the general's.

Looks like L'zar wasn't the only one getting into trouble last night. The halfling folded her arms and met Maleshi's gaze. "I'd ask if it was against the rules to lend your uniform to civilians, but I guess he's not technically a civilian, huh?"

Corian's eyes widened, and he looked down at General Hi'et's unfastened military jacket hanging off his shoulders. "Shit."

Maleshi chuckled.

"Not funny." With a final warning glance at Cheyenne, Corian whirled and disappeared in a flash of silver light. Inside the building where they'd all been put up for the night, a heavy door slammed with an echoing boom.

"Well." Cheyenne met the general's gaze again and raised her eyebrows. "You can spare me the gory details. Please tell me the two of you worked out whatever it was going on between you."

The corner of Maleshi's mouth twitched into a smile. "Gory, huh?"

"Come on. I know enough about nightstalkers at this point to be sure there was at least a little violence involved."

"You can think whatever you want, kid. What Corian and I work out in private is none of your business."

"Right." Cheyenne stared at the nightstalker woman for a moment longer. *Stand here and wait. That's all some people need to open right up.* Maleshi stared across the courtyard at the alley leading into the city streets of Hirúl Breach. The halfling nodded. "Okay, good talk. Wanna change the subject and tell me what's going on with the shit-faced drow who fought like it was his first time?"

Slowly, Maleshi turned her gaze to Cheyenne and pursed her lips. "I'm leaning toward scrambled brains."

"You're talking about L'zar too, right?"

"Yeah, kid," The general said, "Look, I get how frustrating it is to see him go through these mood swings."

"Nice euphemism."

"He needs time, Cheyenne." Maleshi stared at the sleeves of Corian's button-up shirt hanging past her wrists before she focused on rolling them halfway up her forearms. "The Weaving he cast on himself to hide his return to Ambar'ogúl was bound to take its toll sooner or later. Very few magicals know how to cloak themselves like that, and even fewer can pull it off."

"So, it made him lose his mind?"

"Pretty much." The general pushed her rolled sleeves even higher, then stopped fidgeting with them and folded her arms instead. "That and paying the *Sorren Gán* another visit. The way I heard it, his first meeting with that thing took him as close to the brink of madness as he's ever been without falling off the edge."

"Yeah." Cheyenne glared at the corner around which L'zar had disappeared, fighting the urge to run after him when another flashing burst of red light flickered against the stone walls. "That's the way I heard it too."

"From him?"

The halfling shrugged. "It was a weird conversation."

"I'm sure. Two maddening endeavors in the last two days, kid. I'd say he pulled himself together a hell of a lot better than the rest of us expected. He wanted to make sure everything went as planned in Hangivol, which it did. For the most part." Maleshi gestured toward the blood splatter, chunks of broken stone, and crushed metal crates strewn across the courtyard. "All this? Well, this is how L'zar Verdys made a reputation for himself in the very beginning."

Cheyenne snorted. "As a drunken asshole?"

"Yep."

"I couldn't care less about his reputation, Maleshi. He needs to pull himself together before we head out to find this other drow."

The general leaned toward her, her close-lipped smile barely growing. "You mean, your cousin?"

"You know what? Let's stick to calling him the secret prince or something, okay?" Cheyenne rolled her eyes when Maleshi chuckled. "I'm not looking to strengthen my family ties over here right now, especially when I'm already dealing with L'zar."

"I imagine he feels very much the same way, kid."

"Whatever he's feeling, he needs to work that out too and fast. A fighting, pissed-off, wasted L'zar Verdys trying to talk his recently discovered nephew into helping us doesn't build a lot of confidence."

Maleshi raised an eyebrow and dipped her head. "Neither does a daughter who loses her faith in him."

Cheyenne scoffed and turned toward the arch in the courtyard that led into the building holding their guest quarters. Shadows played along the wall in the tunnel, growing closer with the echo of half a dozen pairs of footsteps and the telltale click of Foltr's staff smacking the stone floor. "Kinda hard to lose faith when I didn't have any to begin with. But if he can prove me wrong, I won't say I'm not open to the possibility."

Maleshi chuckled. "What a compromise."

The sharp retort that hadn't fully formed on Cheyenne's tongue disappeared when the raug chief stepped through the arch into the courtyard, followed by five of his hulking guards. Foltr trailed after them, the old raug's shoulders hunched as he slowly walked along with a deep frown, leaning on his staff for support.

Cazerel eyed the bloody stone floor, took a deep sniff, and turned toward Maleshi and Cheyenne. "I would ask if you and your party are prepared to set out, but something tells me you've been held up."

"Not quite." Maleshi gave the raug chief a respectful bow of the head and ignored the gray-skinned magicals behind him, who still didn't bother to hide their disdain for General Maleshi Hi'et taking refuge in their city.

Cheyenne had no problem eyeing the raugs right back, those who were sober and stoic and way more prepared to set out on the journey that lay ahead of them. *Even the ones coming with us hate her. This will be a fun trip.*

"Make it quick, then. Our supplies are ready and waiting for us at the gates. Gather the rest of your party. We'll wait for you there.'

"We'll be there shortly, *Zokri*."

A raug guard snarled at the general's use of that moniker for their chief. Maleshi met his gaze without any expression, and Cazerel thumped a hand against his guard's chest to pull him out of the staring contest. "We leave in ten minutes, General. With or without the rest of you."

With another glance around the destroyed courtyard, Cazerel

snorted and took off toward the open streets in the same direction as L'zar.

Cheyenne said, "Ten minutes for us, but I bet he'd wait all day for Ember if she needed it."

"He does seem oddly fond of her, doesn't he?" Maleshi shrugged. "Guess I would be too if she drew that poison out of me."

Foltr turned away from the raug chief's disappearing procession, eyed the general, and snorted. "And you seem oddly fond of wearing clothes that don't belong to you."

She lifted her chin and shot the old raug a sidelong glance. "With all due respect, Grandfather, that's none of your business, either."

"I should say not. But you're the one standing here like that for everyone to see." When the general didn't move or open her mouth to retort, the old raug snorted again. "Whatever it is, Hi'et, settle it before L'zar clears his head. I can smell the liquor in his blood from here." Foltr shot Cheyenne another glance and nodded. "Eight minutes now." He cracked the end of his staff on the stone and went after Cazerel and his hulking raug entourage toward Hirúl Breach's front gates.

Cheyenne ran a hand through her hair. "Weird way to start a quest for the Crown's secret kid."

"Agreed. Better hurry."

"I'm already—"

Maleshi disappeared in a flash of silver light without a real end to the conversation.

"—packed." The halfling rolled her eyes and looked up at the open balcony of the main room she shared with Ember.

The fae girl stared down at her with luminous purple eyes, her arms folded as she sat motionlessly in the crawler.

Cheyenne spread her arms. "What?"

Ember merely tilted her head and raised an eyebrow.

"Yeah, okay. I'm coming."

CHAPTER THIRTY-TWO

"Got everything?" Cheyenne slung her backpack over her shoulder and stopped at the wooden door to their guest quarters. When she glanced over her shoulder, she found Ember grimacing at her.

"Right now, I'm pretty sure the only thing I need is this stupid hunk of metal." The fae girl slapped the edge of the crawler's control panel in exasperation. The machine lurched forward and tilted drastically to one side. "Whoa, whoa. Sorry. Okay. Got it."

Cheyenne watched her friend's fingers swipe across the control panel and waited for the machine to wobble back into balance. "You good to drive that thing to the gates?"

"What? Totally." Ember gestured at the door and leaned forward. "By all means, *Aranél*, lead the way."

"You don't have to keep it up with the stupid title, okay?"

"I think it kinda suits you."

Cheyenne snorted and pulled open the huge door. "Cool. Then I'll call you 'Healer' from now on too."

Ember rolled her eyes and drove the crawler in an awkward, slightly sideways scramble through the doorway after Cheyenne. The O'gúl machine had a knack for smacking into walls just when she thought she'd gotten the steering down.

They wound their way through the wide stone halls, and the halfling paused when they reached Maleshi's quarters from the night before. *I'd clear this room pretty damn fast too if I were her. I can still smell her. And Corian.*

Cheyenne wrinkled her nose and took a final glance around the empty room.

"What's wrong?" Ember asked as she slowed the crawler, the pointed ends of its mechanical legs plinking on the stone floor.

Cheyenne leaned away from the open door and headed down the hall again. "You picked up on the whole nightstalker situation back there, right?"

"You mean, the one where they showed up before dawn, wearing each other's clothes?"

The halfling snickered.

"Yeah, kinda hard not to notice, honestly."

"Well, that's it." Cheyenne shrugged and turned left down a wide, uneven stone staircase toward the city's outer streets. "Nothing wrong with it as long as L'zar doesn't start thinking there's something going on, apparently."

"What?" Ember gently moved her fingers over the control panel to steer the crawler into a slow, bumpy descent down the staircase one metal leg at a time. "Why would he care? I thought the nightstalkers were already a thing."

"They *were*, I'm pretty sure." Cheyenne stopped at the bottom of the stairs to wait for Ember and adjusted the straps of her backpack. "I mean, there's no way all these O'gúleesh have been cracking jokes about those two from the very beginning if there wasn't something there. And it would *definitely* explain how excited they were to battle each other in the fighting pit."

The fae girl snorted, staring with unblinking eyes at the control panel and navigating the crawler as gently as she could until it reached the bottom of the stairs. For two seconds, the entire metal body leaned dangerously sideways, three of its legs still propped awkwardly on the second-to-last stair. Cheyenne opened her mouth to offer a suggestion, but Ember jabbed a finger at her friend without looking away from the panel.

"Don't. If I'm gonna be on this side of the Border, I need to figure out how to do this on my own."

Cheyenne smiled. "We need to get you a better activator."

"There's nothing wrong with the activator." Ember's finger hovered over the panel, then she swiped up. The crawler skittered sideways, still leaning dangerously forward and to the side. Ember braced herself against walls of the depression where she sat and gritted her teeth. "What *I* need is to get my damn magic back. Can't move without it, and apparently, I can't use this stupid, creepy machine the way I'm supposed to, either."

A second before the crawler would have crashed into the wall of the stairwell, Ember smacked her palm down onto the control panel and turned her hand two inches clockwise. The machine groaned, shuddered, jerked away from the wall, and brought the rest of its eight legs down to the ground floor. When it stopped, the sharp point of its closest foot clicked on the stone half an inch from the toe of Cheyenne's black Van.

Ember slowly looked up at the halfling. "But I guess using it at all is a plus. Barely."

Cheyenne turned away from the machine with a small smile and headed down the hall again. "You'll get it down."

"I've had this thing for twelve hours, Cheyenne. At the very least, I should be able to keep it from slamming into walls. That wasn't an issue with the levitation spell."

"Well, your magic and a piece of super-old-school tech are two totally different things. I'm honestly hesitant to check how out-of-date that activator is."

"You wouldn't have any problem with it." Ember released her frustration and split her focus between keeping the crawler on a course toward the building's main doors and holding a less-aggravated conversation. "Persh'al gave you an outdated activator the first time, didn't he? You used it to do stuff he didn't even know was possible."

Cheyenne shot her friend a sidelong glance. "How do you know that?"

"Come on." Ember returned the glance and smiled. "I'm part of this whole crazy-ass band of magical rebels now. When you're off fighting a *Sorren Gán* or skipping through Hangivol with your mad ol' dad, people talk."

"About Persh'al and how much he hates what I can do with O'gúl tech?"

"Well, mostly about you." Ember tried to keep a straight face, but a chuckle escaped her. "Persh'al might've mentioned it a few times before we made the crossing. A few being five, I think."

Cheyenne ran a hand through her bone-white hair and shook her head. "I wouldn't start comparing your ability to use the magitech with mine, Em."

"Oooh. Magitech. I like it."

The halfling playfully rolled her eyes. "Sounds good, yeah. But seriously. I highly doubt I'm the standard for what anyone can do with the activators and their magic synced up with the weird machines in this world. Or on Earth, apparently."

"I'm not *comparing* myself to you." Ember gave her friend an exaggeratedly formal bow of the head when Cheyenne pushed the heavy wooden door open and held it for her. One of the activator's legs knocked against the doorway before correcting itself, and both girls held back stifled laughter. "That's another exercise in futility, isn't it?"

"Yeah." Cheyenne stepped into the wide stone street in the blue-gray light before dawn. "I'm a freak that way, I guess."

"That's one way to put it, I guess." The girls oriented themselves toward the massive rise of Hirúl Breach's front gates stretching high above the rest of the city. "Or we could go with the undeniable truth that you're L'zar Verdys' daughter. He's a freak with 'reading the threads,' which I still don't get. You're a freak with reading lines of code and smashing it all together to do exactly what you want. Forget what being a whatever-you-are means in either world, Cheyenne. The freak part's in your blood."

With a wry chuckle, Cheyenne cocked her head in acknowledgment. *Still have to skirt around calling me as a halfling over here. A bunch of raugs hiding out from the capital are even more likely than most to tear me apart if they knew. At least for now.*

Already, the almost-techless haven's raug citizens were moving slowly about the streets, groggily shaking their heads and shuffling across the stone to get to whatever duties their day required. A select few, those coming from the same direction as the halfling and her fae friend, cast Cheyenne wary, disapproving glances.

She stared right back at those who didn't immediately look away in aggravation. *I'm not the one who started that fight and woke up half the city, but something tells me they don't give a shit.*

They had to climb another set of stairs leading to the upper-level walkway inside the gates, which were slowly opening with a trembling groan and the creak and click of metal and stone gears moving against each other in the gate towers on either side. Cheyenne quickly scanned her side of the gate towers, but even with the activator, all she saw was stone and metal and a flicker of movement from the raug guards inside. *They are as low-tech as it gets here. Manual gates and everything.*

The rest of their party had already gathered in front of the gates. Lumil caught Cheyenne's gaze and jerked her chin in greeting. "We were starting to wonder if you guys were even coming."

"Who's 'we?'" Byrd folded his arms and cast the goblin woman a disapproving look. "*I* knew they were coming."

"Oh, yeah. 'Cause *you're* always right."

"I didn't say that. I'm tellin' you to speak for yourself, man. You can't read my mind."

Lumil slapped a green hand against her forehead, making her hair flutter around her face. "Because there's nothing *in* there. I don't have to read your mind to know *that.*"

Cheyenne ignored the goblins' bickering, trying not to laugh when Corian raised an eyebrow at the green-skinned magicals and stepped away from them.

Cazerel straightened from stooping over one of the two black metal machines piled high with supplies, which were covered by thick canvas tarps stretched taut and hooked to iron loops on the machines' sides. His orange eyes widened when he saw Ember and Cheyenne approach, and he spread his arms. "Healer! Now we can depart."

"Looks like you already started," Ember muttered as the gates stopped halfway open with a groan.

"It is a process." The raug chief chuckled and thumped a fist against his muscular chest before gesturing toward the canyon beyond the gates. "I would not dream of leaving without you. Darkness descends on the fool who abandons his greatest gift."

Ember and Cheyenne looked at each other in confusion. "Great. He thinks I'm a gift."

"I think he's talking about your healing skills, Em."

"Those have been lost. What is left?"

"Come." Cazerel nodded at the raug warriors awaiting his orders to move out. Then he glanced at L'zar, sitting two feet from where the gates rested when they were fully closed. The chief's hairless brow furrowed, and his black tongue flickered over his razor-sharp teeth. "Before I change my mind."

The warriors beside the supply machines swiped across the panels on the front of each contraption. The machines shuddered and wobbled as they lifted from the ground on only four legs, then the procession headed after Cazerel.

"Travel beside me for a time, Healer." The chief waved Ember toward him and grinned, his yellowed teeth flashing in the first light of sunrise. "That would please me."

"Great." Ember shot Cheyenne a quick glance, then plastered a smile on her face. "Now I'm playing court jester to a raug chief."

"Again, I think he's talking about your skills, Em. Not the admittedly hilarious way that thing moves around."

Shaking her head, Ember swiped the crawler's panel and successfully made a straight run toward the raug chief. He laughed as she approached, nodding before turning to lead the way out of the canyon.

The warriors and their machines followed closely. Cheyenne studied L'zar, who was still sitting on the ground, his legs crossed beneath him as he swayed from side to side. His muttering voice rose softly, though the words were indecipherable.

Lumil shrugged and stalked off after the raug, Byrd close on her heels. Foltr gave the halfling a sharp nod and walked through the open gates, his staff clacking on the stone.

"L'zar." Cheyenne stopped between her father and the nightstalkers, both of whom had changed back into their regular clothes. Corian and Maleshi gave her warning looks, but she ignored them. "Hey, we're leaving."

The drow didn't respond.

"Awesome." She raised an eyebrow at Maleshi and spread her arms. "He's still drunk and unresponsive, huh?"

L'zar stopped swaying. "I've had centuries of practice fine-tuning my mental condition, thank you very much." He pushed himself halfway to his feet, paused with a heavy sigh, then straightened all the way and moved with long strides after the rest of their party. He only stumbled twice before disappearing through the open gate.

Corian rubbed his forehead and passed Cheyenne without a word.

"Fifteen minutes isn't what I meant by 'give him time,' kid." Maleshi gestured at the courtyard beyond the city and waited for Cheyenne to move after the others.

"What about the time it takes us to get to wherever the Crown's kid is?" They walked out of the city together and quickly joined the rest of their group to bring up the rear. Corian kept at least three yards between himself and the stumbling L'zar. "If he doesn't pull himself together by the time we get there, we might as well not even go."

"He'll be fine." Maleshi straightened one of the pins on the left shoulder of her military jacket and nodded. "Right now, kid, we're a bunch of magicals trekking through the mountains and hoping a certain other mad drow in Hangivol doesn't get word of where we're headed before we get there. Anything else is an unnecessary focus."

"Oh, yeah? Including the very high possibility that L'zar's officially insane now and might never come back from it?"

"Yeah, kid." Maleshi stared straight ahead and shoved her hands into her pockets. "Even that."

CHAPTER THIRTY-THREE

"Ow. Hey!" Byrd darted away from the large mechanical wagon on legs carrying their supplies. "You guys gotta work on the programming for this stuff, man. I'm not losing a foot to this thing and have to ride *in* it the rest of the way." He glanced at Ember with a sheepish smile. "No offense."

The fae girl shrugged. "I still have my feet."

"If the old one thinks you'll recover," Cazerel said and looked quickly over his shoulder at Foltr, "I'm inclined to believe him. He led you to me, after all."

Ember gave the raug chief a tight smile. "I'm trying to believe it too."

"The crawler is yours to use for however long you need it, Healer. It is the least I can do."

The walking metal cart beside Lumil struck an uneven patch of stone and lurched sideways into her, nearly knocking her over. The goblin woman snarled and slammed a fist into the side of the cart, which squeaked and instantly righted itself. "The least you could do, huh? What about putting these things together so they work? You know, get with the times and make some updates already."

Beside her, one of Cazerel's warriors rolled his eyes and shook his head.

"Our tech works the way we prefer it to work," the chief replied. "The new entanglement of magic and Hangivol's updates? It goes against everything we believe, greenskin."

"You don't believe in tech?" Ember looked over her shoulder at Cheyenne, who shrugged and turned her attention to the chief again.

Can't wait to hear how he explains that one.

"It is not a lack of belief in the technology, Healer." Cazerel eyed the wobbly cart stepping up on his other side. "It is an aversion to what that technology makes of us when used the way most O'gúleesh have been using it for centuries."

"Like, side effects?" Ember stared at the control panel of the crawler and briefly touched the cold metal of the outdated activator behind her ear. "I have enough of *those* to deal with."

"Not for you, Healer. You did not need metal and code to restore my life." The chief grinned down at her and nodded. "You are purely of your own magic, as it should be."

"You've obviously been doing fine here on your own without the most recent updates," Cheyenne muttered. *Or updates from three thousand years ago, probably.*

"Yes. We thrive in different ways." Cazerel scanned the rising cliffs and jutting stone in front of them as he led them farther into the mountains. "Magic and technology can work together. We know this. To say it does not alleviate the heavier burdens for my kind would taint my words with lies, Healer. A chief who lies is not fit to be saved, even by one such as you."

Corian's ears twitched, and he turned toward a flock of small brown birds darting over the next ridge in front of them. "I assumed Hirúl Breach refused the updates to stand against the Crown or to stay hidden from her."

Cazerel laughed mightily and slapped his belly. "We do not need faulty machines to stand against the Spider. But it helps, yes. These things should not rely on each other, *vae shra'ni*—magic and the machines that serve it. For most of this world, they are so intertwined that a magical has no mastery over their own abilities because they have given themselves over to the system, which is quietly weakening them day by day."

Ember wrinkled her nose and tried not to look at her legs resting beneath the crawler's control panel. "Like muscle atrophy."

The chief smiled down at her. "Like a raug in his prime lying useless in his bed while the deathflame calls his name."

"Or like building up a drug tolerance." Cheyenne removed her activator and stuck the silver coil into the pocket of her trenchcoat. "Makes sense."

Ember gave her friend a playful frown. "What do *you* know about drug tolerance? An elephant's dose of morphine wouldn't take you out."

"Elephant?" Cazerel's eyes widened.

Cheyenne tried to keep a straight face. *Nobody knows Ember's from Earth either. He'd change his tune really quick if he knew his Healer set foot on this side for the first time two days ago.*

Ember caught her slip and shrugged. "A saying we picked up."

"Whatever you mean, Healer, I have full faith in your knowledge. And drow are particularly difficult to understand, eh?" The chief chuckled and shook his head. "And prone to madness."

"Hey, don't lump us all in the same category." Cheyenne looked back at L'zar, who stared at the ground as he followed the procession, his eyes wide and his jaw working. "I'm trying not to be prone to weakening my magic with an activator, if that's even possible for drow."

"That won't be a problem, *Aranél*. Trust me." Cazerel swept his beefy arm through the air, gesturing toward the range of mountains in front of them that still seemed far away. "Where we're headed, there won't *be* any high tech. Perhaps not even as low as these wobbling carriers." His gray hand smacked down on the rim of the cart walking next to him. The machine staggered under the weight, then righted itself and continued unaffected. The warriors keeping their eyes on their supply machines sniggered.

"Not surprising." Maleshi stepped around L'zar when the drow stopped suddenly in mid-stride and tilted his head back, closing his eyes against the morning sunlight. She glanced at Corian, who shook his head and continued past L'zar. "The world without high tech is expanding, isn't it? Has been since the last Cycle turned."

"It continues as we speak." The raug chief grunted in disapproval. "I cannot say how far the Spider's reach has extended while the *Cu'ón* endeavored to make his mark. In some ways, it has shortened more than I expected."

"You mean the Outers, right?" Cheyenne stepped lightly over the loose chunks of rock in their path, warily avoiding the cargo machines as they staggered across the slippery shale. "Because that line's been changing too."

"More than any of us realize, I think."

Cheyenne looked at Maleshi with raised eyebrows. The nightstalker woman pressed her lips together and looked at the mountain range. *The skaxen village was just the beginning. Persh'al and I saw the dead land for ourselves, and now we're following this raug chief with no idea what we're getting into. Awesome.*

The raug warriors barely spoke as the party climbed steep rock walls and slid into valleys, following Cazerel on his secret path toward a secret location. After the first two hours, Foltr climbed onto a supply cart and set his staff across his lap, grimacing at the ache in his legs. Ember had a good laugh, seeing the wizened old raug wobbling with the cart machine's unsteady gait.

They stopped for a meal an hour after that. L'zar refused to stay with the rest of them, opting instead to stomp away and sit alone on a boulder beside the clearing in the jagged stone. He crossed his legs beneath him, closed his eyes, and entered a much steadier meditation session than earlier that morning.

The warriors rummaged around in the supply carts and pulled out flat dark-gray rectangles of something edible wrapped in cloth. These were passed around quickly to the chief, Ember, Cheyenne, the goblins, and Foltr, who remained sitting on the supplies. No one asked the oldest magical among them to move aside.

Maleshi eyed the last two bricks of traveling food with a raised brow. The warrior closest to her unwrapped one of them from its cloth, sneered at her, and bit into it before chewing noisily. The other four warriors did the same, chuckling among themselves and stepping away from the carts to sit in a small group. They glared at the general with glowing eyes in various shades of orange and muttered to each other in French.

"Gah!" Byrd pulled his brick of chewy sustenance away from his face and scowled. "I tell you what, man. The original recipe might've started over here, but the guys across the—"

He grunted and wheezed when Lumil shot an elbow extra-hard into his gut. "We're not talkin' about that. Or the recipe, you moron. Just eat the damn bar."

The goblin wrinkled his nose as he brought the magical energy bar up to his mouth again, rubbing his gut with the other hand. "Easy for you to say. You don't have any taste buds left."

"But my brain cells are all intact, *dae'bruj*." Lumil snorted and ripped away a huge chunk of her bar with her teeth, nostrils flaring.

Cheyenne nibbled the sour yet earthy-tasting bar in her hand, feeling it slide a little beneath her fingers through the cloth. *He's right. At least the FRoE improved on the worst-tasting meal ever invented.* She gazed around the clearing, ignoring the goblins muttering curses at each other and ducking angry, half-assed blows. Ember was a much paler shade of fae pink as she swallowed her bar and tried to focus on the story Cazerel was telling her about the first time he'd ventured this far northeast into the mountains.

Not a conversation meant for me to hear, probably.

Then the halfling turned her attention to Maleshi and Corian. The nightstalkers stood on opposite sides of the clearing, and while Maleshi gauged what she'd be risking by stalking toward the carts to grab food for herself, Corian stared at the general.

"Something wrong, General?" A warrior lying with his back against a boulder with his thick legs splayed in front of him sniggered and looked Maleshi up and down. "You look like you forgot something important."

"I haven't forgotten anything," Maleshi snarled. "And neither have you." The nightstalker's clenched fists trembled at her sides.

"Ah." Another warrior stood, stalked toward the cart without an old raug sitting on top of it, never taking his burning gaze off the general, and rummaged to pull out a drinking gourd that looked like it could've been made either from a sturdy O'gúleesh plant or some kind of animal hide. He sneered at Maleshi, uncorked the gourd, and took a long, messy drink. Then he stoppered it again and tossed the gourd to the other warriors. Laughing, they passed the water around, all of them shooting General Hi'et warning, challenging glances.

Corian finally stepped toward Maleshi and paused to lean toward her. "Keep ignoring them. It's for a reason."

"I know what it's for, *vae shra'ni.*" The general's long black hair twitched around her face and shoulders since her head trembled in rage now too. "I don't need your counsel."

Corian licked his lips in thought, glancing quickly at Maleshi's profile, but she didn't look away from the raug warriors who found General Maleshi Hi'et's rage over their little prank hilarious.

If Cazerel had picked up on his kinsmen's blatant disregard for his orders to drop their grudge against the nightstalker woman, he ignored it in lieu of sharing his drinking gourd with Ember.

Corian stepped over to the closest cart and flipped up the canvas tarp, then reached inside to pull out two more energy bars. As he walked back around the cart to Maleshi, his silver eyes flickered up to meet Cheyenne's gaze, and his eyebrows quickly drew together.

Great. Cheyenne swallowed another nasty bite with an aftertaste of mildewed laundry crusted in sour milk and didn't move. *We're all relying on these raugs to get us where we need to be, and Corian would rather play at saving the general in distress. If they start fighting again...*

"Hungry, *vae shra'ni?*" another warrior called, glaring at Corian's profile as the nightstalker headed cautiously toward Maleshi. "If one unit is enough for a raug, it's enough for you."

Corian ignored the glares burning into his back and offered one of the bricks to Maleshi with a nod.

"*Dae'bruj.*" Another warrior chucked the gourd on the ground and rose swiftly to his feet. "That is not for you to give."

"I saw what's in the cart, raug." Corian cast the warriors a fleeting glance. "We're not running low."

"Not your decision."

"I already made it."

The warriors snarled and sneered at the nightstalkers, either sitting up straight or standing to add to the threat. On the other side of the clearing, Byrd smacked Lumil with the back of a hand and nodded at the growing tension. Lumil crammed the rest of her bar into her mouth and chewed fiercely, barely managing to keep it all from spilling out as she stared at another brewing battle.

"The Hand of the Night and Circle eats from the Crown's hand, nightstalker. Not from ours."

Corian shook the bar at Maleshi again. She snatched it from him and whirled around, gritting her teeth as she turned her back on the warriors to eat in silence.

"Will you pay for her crimes too?" The warrior who'd stood first stormed toward Corian. "That's a high price."

Corian darted toward the warriors in a flash of silver light and stopped mere inches in front of the snarling raug. One long, deadly sharp claw pressed against the raug's belly right below his sternum. Looking calmly up at the gray-skinned magical, Corian flashed a feral grin beneath blazing silver eyes. "*I heard the debt was already paid, brother. It's rare that my hearing fails me, but if you think I'm mistaken, by all means, take it up with your Zokri.*" He nodded toward Cazerel, who'd hunkered down beside Ember and her crawler and was gazing up at her in admiration.

The raug, facing a mortal slice to his core, growled deeply and stepped back. "Not all debts can be paid with one life. Try this again when we are alone, nightstalker."

Corian lowered his hand, and the blade-like claw retracted with a silver flash. "If you and I are ever alone, it means we've already failed. Don't hold your breath."

He shot another warning glance at the warriors growling and muttering threats in French and the occasional O'gúleesh curse before turning his back on them. One of the raugs spat in Corian's direction, then flung the rest of his bar over the edge of the ridge where they'd stopped.

Cheyenne watched the nightstalker head toward Maleshi, and he sat down beside her to eat the meal he'd had to fetch for them on his own. The general's nostrils flared as she chewed, but she finally looked up at him and gave him a brief smile. The only magical in their group who didn't see the exchange between them, other than Cazerel, who was laughing heartily at something Ember said, was L'zar.

"Hey," Lumil croaked. She swallowed heavily and nodded at the stationary carts. "Any more water in all that crap?"

"I'll check." Cheyenne headed toward the carts, eyeing the raug warriors the whole time. They'd gone back to talking in French and laughing at each other, casting spiteful glares at the nightstalkers. They ignored the halfling heading toward their supplies. *It's a problem with nightstalkers, then. Awesome.*

CHAPTER THIRTY-FOUR

Cheyenne reached under the canvas, pulled out two full drinking gourds, and tossed one across the clearing to Lumil. The goblin woman caught it and guzzled half of it down with loud, slurping gulps. Cheyenne opened the other to wash down the worst of the energy bar's aftertaste and approached the other cart.

Foltr still sat atop the heap of provisions, sucking the chewy gray meal out of his sharp teeth. A shouted punchline of some joke in French and the ensuing roar of raug laughter drowned out any other conversation around them. The old raug shook his head when Cheyenne offered him a drink. "If it's not ale, *Aranél*, I'll fall asleep up here."

The halfling snorted and leaned against the cart so she could see everyone in the clearing at the same time. She took another long drink, stoppered the gourd, and tried not to stare at Maleshi and Corian. Lumil and Byrd started another fight over the other water gourd, and Cheyenne turned toward Foltr. "Is it just me, or are they getting careless all of a sudden?"

"The goblins have always been careless," Foltr grumbled, "Someone should give them a good bash over the head. You can tell them it's from me if you like." He slid his staff toward her and dipped his head.

"You know that's not who I'm talking about."

"Yes. I know." Taking a deep breath, the old raug picked energy-bar goo out of his teeth with a red claw. "For now, it's none of our business."

"You know who'll make it his business if he catches on, right?" Cheyenne glanced at L'zar, who hadn't moved an inch in his meditative posture.

"L'zar is busy plotting his own course, as always." Foltr made it a point to look away from both the drow thief and the two nightstalkers sitting closer than normal to each other at the other end of the clearing. "No doubt another one of his plans to carry out when we find this nephew of his."

"And when he's done plotting?" Cheyenne dropped her elbows casually over the side of the cart behind her. "I've heard a lot of stuff lately about keeping things from L'zar. Don't draw attention to it. Don't wave anything under his nose. Leave him alone and don't fight him when he starts acting like a lunatic. Nobody seems to be following their own advice, especially those two."

Corian whispered something to Maleshi and the general grinned, bowing her head in an attempt to hide the expression from everyone else.

"Leave it alone, Cheyenne." Foltr sniffed and readjusted his staff on his lap. "The *Cu'ón* has a weakness for those who pledge their life and loyalty to the Four-Pointed Star and the cause we've all taken up as our own. *His* cause. That weakness includes conjuring threats where no threat exists."

"Seriously?" She looked up at the old raug and frowned. "He thinks they're a threat to *him?*"

"Not yet, but he might if his awareness changes."

"They've both put everything on the line to follow him into this mess, and they haven't seen each other for what? Centuries before this?" The halfling glanced at her father, so deep in his Weaver meditation that he could have been a statue cut from a boulder the same color as his skin, and shook her head. "I don't think I could stand behind someone who forces everyone else to give up on everything they care about except for him."

"Many of us have made sacrifices to force the new Cycle's turning." Foltr sucked his teeth again, scowled, and swallowed loudly. "Whatever you've heard from others, their personal stories are not unique."

Like Elarit and Persh'al. Now it's Corian and Maleshi. Cheyenne shook her head. "And no one's stood up to him about it?"

"In their own ways, they have. And still do." Foltr nodded at the nightstalkers and shrugged. "What L'zar doesn't know at this point won't hurt him, *Aranél*. Not right now. What he could know, on the other hand…well, that would end up hurting everyone around him, wouldn't it?"

"If you're using that as a euphemism, it's not working."

"It's happened before." The old raug stared at her and lowered his head. "That's all you need to know before I tell you this conversation is best left buried. Do not dig it up again."

Cheyenne snorted and shook her head. "Digging stuff up is one of my specialties."

"Perhaps, but here and now is not the time and place, *Aranél*. L'zar might be distracted, but the rest of us cannot afford such a luxury." He glanced at the nightstalkers one more time. "Either they will come to the same understanding, or they won't. Lending them your focus helps no one."

Staring at the stone at her feet, Cheyenne nodded slowly. *Never thought I'd get this wrapped up in keeping secrets from L'zar. If anyone deserves some personal time, it's the magicals who gave it all up to watch that crazy drow's back. They better get it out of their systems before he comes back down to reality.*

"*Hishmál!*" Cazerel threw his head back and roared with laughter, pointing a red-clawed finger at Ember. "Such tales, Healer. I could listen to you all day and not understand half of it!"

The fae girl chuckled in surprise. "At least I'm amusing."

"Ha! Far more than that." The chief slapped his thigh and pushed himself to his feet. "Another day, when time has grown long again, you and I will sit together again to finish these stories. Perhaps you can teach me how to understand a Healer's metaphors, eh?"

"Well, they're not metaphors, but okay."

"We move out now!" Cazerel raised a massive arm and flicked his hand in the air. "The journey isn't long, but it leaves us with more than enough time to be ensnared."

Ember swallowed. "By what?"

"By the end from which you saved me, Healer." He nodded firmly and headed down the incline out of the rocky clearing. "And I would rather not confront it again so soon."

The warriors stood quietly and jammed whatever items they'd taken from the carts back into place before swiping thick gray hands across control panels to send the carts after their chief once more.

With a startled glance at Cazerel's retreating back, as if he'd forgotten anyone else existed in the clearing, Corian stood abruptly and cleared his throat. "Back to it, then."

"One day, *ma gairín*," Maleshi said. She finally noticed the goblins staring at her and Corian across the clearing and narrowed her eyes at them.

Lumil turned and shoved Byrd after the raug chief and his warriors, ignoring the goblin's shout of protest.

The general stood and stormed past Cheyenne. "Don't say anything."

"I wasn't gonna."

"Good."

Corian sniffed and turned toward the meditating drow. "L'zar."

"Why is everyone always *shouting*?" L'zar snarled and waved away his *Nós Aní* with a dismissive flick of his wrist. "Always beneath the surface. Buzzing, buzzing…buzz the fuck out of my head, huh?"

The nightstalker suffered the strange outburst without expression. "We're heading out again."

"Telling me what I already know doesn't make you useful, Corian. Just annoying." L'zar stood and jumped off the boulder before brushing past the nightstalker with a scowl. He muttered unintelligibly as he stalked after the rest of their traveling party and didn't look at Cheyenne when he passed her.

Corian scratched the back of his head and crossed the clearing.

Cheyenne folded her arms when he approached her. "It's almost like you enjoy the abuse."

"I have to pick my poison, kid. Right now, it's the venom on his tongue." The nightstalker shot her a warning glance. "Better than being tied up in one of his webs for the rest of eternity."

"His what?"

"Doesn't matter."

The halfling followed him and slowed down when she reached Ember waiting in the crawler at the edge of the clearing.

The fae girl stuck her thumb out after Corian and wrinkled her nose. "Is it just me, or does everyone seem tense right now?"

"It's not just you, Em, but we might be the only ones weirded out by this new normal."

Ember swiped her hand over the control panel, and the crawler dipped forward to carry her down the incline after the rest of their raug escort. "Do I even wanna know what's going on right now?"

"You want to be complicit in keeping L'zar in the dark and tiptoeing around him until he's lucid again? *If* he's ever lucid again."

"No, I'm good."

Cheyenne snorted. "Trust me, I'm starting to think I prefer everyone keeping secrets from me over being a part of whatever this is, pandering to a five-thousand-year-old drow toddler with more magic than half of Ambar'ogúl combined."

"Five thousand? Really?"

"Give or take, Em. I don't know."

"Hmm." Ember shifted in the crawler's seat and frowned at the travelers ahead of them. L'zar kicked huge chunks of loose stone over the ridge down which Cazerel led them, snarling and hissing curses at something or someone no one else could see. "He looks like the kind of drow I'd want to lock up tight right now."

"Yep." Cheyenne waited for the clunky, awkward crawler to scrabble its way over a steep drop in the path before she jumped down after her friend. "At this point, I think the only prison that can keep him locked up is the one he's building inside his head."

"Makes sense. The drow Weaver, former heir to the O'gúl throne, practically unstoppable…and then he goes insane. That would be game over for us, wouldn't it?"

"No." Cheyenne grimaced when L'zar's next wild kick sent him reeling dangerously close to the edge of the ridge. Corian moved in a flash of silver light and grabbed the drow's shirt to jerk him back onto the path. "I have a feeling he's almost done being able to help us."

"Almost, huh?"

"Yeah. As soon as we figure out what the hell terms I'm supposed to use for the Crown, it wouldn't surprise me if L'zar dipped out early and left the rest of us to pick up the pieces without him. That's what he does."

"Or maybe he'll stick around as long as you do. 'Cause the next time he makes the crossing Earthside, he can't come back."

"I know." Cheyenne shook her head. "Looks like he's getting exactly what he wanted."

"Except for you on the throne."

"Well, that's not happening, no matter what side of the Border he's on." The halfling shot her friend a sidelong glance and smiled. "It looked like you and the chief were having a nice little chat."

"Sure, I guess."

"I thought you'd still be up there with him, enjoying your place as honored Healer."

"Shut up." Ember playfully rolled her eyes. "I need a little break from a giant raug falling all over himself, asking if I need anything and planning our super important conversations after this little detour's over."

"Did he offer you all the stone riches of Hirúl Breach yet? You know, to stay with him forever."

"Very funny."

They chuckled, but it was tense and distracted.

"What stories were you telling him, anyway?"

"Well, they weren't about you, so you can relax. Your secret's still a secret."

Cheyenne raised an eyebrow. "Uh-huh."

"He wanted to know about where I come from." Ember shrugged. "So I tried to describe Chicago without giving anything away."

"Wow. He didn't understand any of it."

"Yeah. If you wanna make a raug laugh, confuse him, I guess."

"Or suck the blight out of his chest."

Ember steered the crawler carefully over a rotting fallen tree trunk in the path and shrugged. "Honestly, I'm a little worried about what's gonna happen once we head back to the capital after this. Like, am I gonna have a raug chief following me around everywhere because he feels like he owes me his life? Can't exactly take him home with me."

"Right. He'd break the elevator."

CHAPTER THIRTY-FIVE

Despite the sun shining directly down on them and the lack of shade as they passed through the rocky mountain range after Cazerel, the air was cool. The wind whipped up every time they crested another rise on the path the raug chief seemed to recognize. It made conversation harder, and the magicals traveled with a stoic concentration when they hiked over the top of another narrow ridge with long, straight drops on either side.

"Whew." Byrd stopped to wipe a sheen of sweat off his green forehead. "You know, I think I'd take a freakin' Stairmaster over this. Can't we have one of the nightstalkers port us into this secret place and get it over with?"

Lumil smacked the back of his head as she passed him. "You don't think we would've done that if it was an option?"

"Hey, I dunno. Everything else around here is freaking out and doing weird shit. Case in point right there." He nodded over the side of the ridge at the valley below and narrowed his eyes. "Kinda seems like the worst place to build a town, but again, the whole world's lost its mind."

"A town?" Corian stopped near the edge of the ridge. "*Zokri.*"

"Nightstalker." Cazerel turned around with an amused look, but it faded when he saw Corian's darkening frown. The raug chief looked in the same direction and sucked in a sharp breath. "So it's come this far."

"How long has that town been there?" Corian's jaw clenched and unclenched quickly.

"Last I knew, there was no town there."

Cheyenne peered over the edge and barely made out the rising blocks of stone buildings interspersed with shacks that looked a lot like the skaxen village. *And every magical there turned into some kind of O'gúleesh zombie.*

Ember shielded her eyes with a hand, trying to get a better view of the small town nestled in the valley far below them. "Wait. Are you guys saying a whole town popped up out of nowhere? That is new."

"The Outers have been shifting around for a long time, like Cheyenne and Persh'al told us they were." Corian's silver eyes blazed in his frowning face. "Wouldn't surprise me if that included whole settlements shifting with them."

"Looks like something else is shifting too." Byrd's eyes widened, and he leaned over the edge of the ridge, trying to get a better look.

Lumil stared at the dark wave of shadow moving steadily across the valley below toward the small town. Her arm shot out to thump Byrd's chest, making him stagger backward instead of falling over the cliff. Her eyes widened too, and she looked slowly up at Corian. "What the hell *is* that?"

Cazerel grunted. "Out of our control. Keep moving."

As the raug chief continued across the ridge, an echoing crack like thick ice splitting rose from the valley. Within the moving shadow, Cheyenne finally realized the rest of what she was seeing. "It can move."

The blight rolled down the valley toward the town, splintering stone and felling trees—the ones that didn't shrivel under its touch into hollow, twisted husks.

Maleshi nudged Cheyenne softly with her elbow and nodded. "Come on, kid."

"What? No." Cheyenne stared at the jagged black lines of magical destruction racing across the valley floor. An outcropping of boulders split apart as if it had been blasted and crumbled toward the town, leading the way. "We can't leave them down there."

"We have to." Grimacing, Corian ran a hand through his tawny hair and hissed. "Doesn't mean we have to like it, Cheyenne."

The halfling turned toward L'zar, who stood on the higher side of the ridge and stared at the blight creeping down the valley. His glowing golden eyes widened, and the only sign that he wasn't off in his own world again was that he stroked his chin and tilted his head when the streaking lines of his sister's unchecked dark magic reached the outskirts of the town.

Cheyenne scowled at him. "So everyone's suddenly—"

A scream rose, echoing madly across the stone valley. It was joined two seconds later by more screams and shouts of alarm, and the magicals meeting the blight below darted through the buildings were tiny moving specks within the black shadow sweeping across their homes.

"We have to do something. Seriously, does no one else give a shit?" Without waiting for a reply, Cheyenne took off toward the other side of the ridge.

"Cheyenne!" Corian took two steps toward her, but the screams from below made him stop to watch the devastation in morbid, guilt-ridden curiosity.

She raced past the staring goblins and the slowly trudging raug warriors, scanning the descent into the valley. *I can make it. Just a few long drops, but I've jumped from higher.*

Cazerel stepped in front of her to cut her off. "No."

"We can't stand up here and do nothing!" The shrieks and screaming grew louder, punctuated by more cracking stone and the buildings higher up the valley crumbling in on themselves. "I've seen what that shit does to villages. No one deserves that."

"You are correct." Cazerel's eye twitched. "No one survives it, either."

"Yeah, we'll see." Cheyenne darted past him and slid on the loose layer of gravel and dirt, trying to gauge where she'd land before getting back to her feet.

"Cheyenne!" Maleshi and Corian exchanged glances.

"That's something else, isn't it?" L'zar muttered, unable to pull his gaze away from the destruction.

"So are you." Maleshi's scowl was ignored before she took off across the ridge to get to the halfling scrambling down the steep incline. "Cheyenne, stop!"

Cheyenne ignored the warning, paying attention only to the screams in the valley far below her. *If I go to drow speed now, I'll flatten myself at the bottom of this thing.* Just when she got her footing and thought she'd try anyway, the ground lurched away from her, and she was flying back up the mountain toward the far side of the ridge. She landed with a grunt at Cazerel's feet and scrambled away from him with a snarl. "What the hell?"

The bright white light of the raug chief's spell crackled around his hand as he pointed at her. "Try it again, and I will drag you along like this until we reach our destination."

She glanced down at the town caving in on itself, the magicals' screams growing louder as they panicked and darted away from the blight taking everything from them. A burst of green light flared at the center of the village before the growing shadow snuffed it out.

"So, that's your answer. Just let everyone else die."

"No, *Aranél.*" Cazerel's hand stopped glowing, and he offered it to the halfling to help her up. "It pains me to see anyone fall beneath that poison as well. You have seen what it does to villages, but I have felt what it does to the flesh."

Trying to block out the screams, Cheyenne swallowed and pushed to her feet without taking his hand. "Then of all people, you should want to help them."

"I do want to. I cannot. Neither can you." Cazerel glanced quickly down at the town and scowled. "It's too late for them, as it was almost too late for me. If you wish to kill yourself, by all means, die with them."

Cheyenne clenched her fists. "There has to be something we can do. And maybe the blight doesn't do anything to drow."

"If the Healer were recovered, I might be willing to let you take that risk. Perhaps it would even be possible to save one or two of them, but without her, our only option is to stay above the darkness, yes?"

The screaming in the town suddenly changed to gurgling croaks and gasping breaths that echoed up to the ridge. Cheyenne clenched her eyes shut and forced her anger back down. *Now it's definitely too late.*

"You cannot blame yourself for this, *Aranél.*" Cazerel nodded as the rest of their party crossed the ridge. Even L'zar had turned away from the destruction below to join the raug chief and his warriors, casting occasional glances at the town that now looked as abandoned as the skaxen village. "That same darkness nearly brought me to the death-flame. I've fought many battles and survived more wounds than I can count, but that?" The chief shook his head. "There is no coming back from that."

Cheyenne opened her eyes and glared at him. "Unless you're a raug who was healed by a fae."

"Correct. You cannot say the same, and you have much more work ahead of you to bring the Spider to her knees. I also wish to see that come to pass."

As the chief turned away from her to continue the trek, the valley fell silent. Cheyenne shot one more glance at the destroyed town and forced herself to breathe. *It's like nothing happened, and there's nothing left.*

She looked back at Ember, who was focused intently on navigating the ridge with all eight of the crawler's stiff metal legs. Maleshi reached her and set a hand on the halfling's shoulder.

"Don't." Cheyenne shrugged out from under the general's hand.

Maleshi eyed her, nodded, and followed the rest of their group. Corian passed the halfling next, but he didn't try to offer any comfort. There wasn't any.

Cheyenne stared down at the destroyed valley. *I should've been able to do something. What's the point of kicking Ba'rael off the throne if I can't help the magicals she left out here to die like this?*

"Now you know what it's like."

L'zar's voice in her ear made her step quickly away from him. "Are you here, or is this more drunken crazy coming out of you?"

Her father shrugged. "I'm merely trying to put things in perspective for you."

"All the perspective in the world can't fix this, L'zar."

"No, but maybe it'll help you understand what's in store for you. And understand me, however difficult that is."

"What are you talking about?"

"This is how it feels, Cheyenne, to *not* step in when others think you should. When others recognize the danger and see you doing nothing because even though they're begging for help, you're the only one who knows how much worse the consequences would be if you were to get involved."

She narrowed her eyes at him, gritting her teeth. "You mean, the way you stand back and let everyone else do the hard work for you?"

"There are reasons."

"Sure, but you're still missing one huge difference between us." Cheyenne gestured at the destroyed town in the valley but couldn't bring herself to look away from L'zar's golden eyes. "I tried to help. You've had plenty of time to explain to everyone else around you why you're doing what you're doing, or why you hang back and do nothing when it counts but can't stop yourself from taking on a gang of raugs in the streets. You still haven't told me or anyone else what you're planning next."

"When the time is right, Cheyenne, you will know what steps to take."

"Right. Just like I knew who I was challenging when I dropped my coin on the altar."

"That was different." L'zar held her gaze for a moment longer, then took a deep breath and ran a hand over his head. "I'll settle for agreeing to disagree. But I do recommend chewing on it for at least a few minutes if you can spare that." He stepped closer and lowered his face toward hers, his eyes roaming over her features as if he'd find someone else there instead of his daughter. "You and I are too much alike for you not to understand what I've told you, and we both know that when it counts, you will do what you have to do. Even if that means letting a few O'gúleesh fall to a fate none of them deserve. It's about the bigger picture, Cheyenne. We can't all be heroes all the time."

"Not your best pep talk."

"Hmm." He pulled away from her, looked down into the valley one more time, and passed her to head after the rest of their group.

Cheyenne stared daggers at her father's back and stiffly pushed herself forward. *He has no idea what he's talking about. L'zar Verdys doesn't do anything for the sake of helping someone else.*

Still, somewhere in the back of her mind, she couldn't quite convince herself he was wrong.

CHAPTER THIRTY-SIX

Cazerel's path through the mountains flattened out noticeably, and the rocky passages gave way to forests. These had already been touched by the blight that spread with no direction and no warning across Ambar'ogúl. The raug chief grumbled and scowled at every area of scorched earth and clump of twisted, lifeless trees they approached before steering their party around the devastation.

Cheyenne stared at the huge, jagged cracks splintering the dead ground fifty feet away. Most of them glistened with thick black ooze, the occasional bubble bursting with a wet, slurping pop. *No one is gonna suggest passing through it, not after seeing what it does in real-time.*

The chief stopped and cocked his head. A husk of a tree groaned in the gentle wind cutting through the dead forest, then a branch snapped and fell to the blackened earth, shattering in a puff of glittering black dust. Dark sludge oozed from the hole in the tree's trunk and dripped to the ground.

"Ugh." Byrd stepped farther away from the edge of the blighted landscape and wrinkled his nose. "And here I was, thinking I'd gotten used to the smell."

"That'll keep you up at night, huh?" Lumil snorted and kept moving.

The goblin man blinked at her, surprised she hadn't smacked or punched or shoved him, and hurried after her.

"I didn't know it had come this far." Cazerel sighed heavily and turned toward Ember. "Have you seen this elsewhere, Healer?"

She raised her eyebrows and shook her head. "No, but Cheyenne has."

When the raug chief turned to stare at her, Cheyenne shrugged. "Like I said, the Outers are moving in. So is the blight, I guess."

"But we are not."

"Yeah." Cheyenne glanced at Ember, who'd taken her hand off the crawler's control panel and paused to watch the raug chief and the halfling. "That's one of the weirder parts to wrap your head around. The farther we are from the capital, the worse it gets."

"And it's crossing through the portals," Corian added. "Bit by bit."

Cazerel looked at the nightstalker with a confused frown. "You have seen this on the other side as well?"

"A different version of it, maybe. Yeah." Corian pressed his lips together in thought. "Apparently, this darkness is squeezing its way Earthside and opening new portals. At least, that's as good a guess as any of us can make."

The chief grunted. "And if that is *not* the cause?"

"Then we have a lot more to worry about, don't we?" The nightstalker spread his arms and dipped his head at their escort. "Which, of course, none of us would ask you to involve yourself in. Leading us here is more than enough."

"I know." With a quick glance at L'zar, who'd stepped closer than any of them to the ring of blackened earth to study it with his usual objective apathy, Cazerel grimaced and ran a glistening black tongue over his needle-sharp teeth. "When my clansmen and I return home, I mean to close the gates and keep them closed."

Cheyenne cocked her head. "I don't think that's gonna do much good if this poison makes it back to Hirúl Breach."

Corian shot her a sharp look, and she shrugged.

"The walls of my city have stood against the Spider's venom for centuries, *Aranél*." Cazerel snorted. "They will continue to stand."

"How do you know?"

Corian clamped a hand around Cheyenne's wrist to stop her as the chief gave the scorched, oozing forest a wide berth. "Not now."

"He knows exactly what can and can't stand against the blight." The halfling frowned at him. "Unless he has some kind of protective ward we don't know about, he's delusional."

"That's his choice. Until we find a way to clear the sickness out of this world, kid, it's not our place to tell anyone else what to think."

She blinked at him. "You're kidding, right?"

"Magicals have their own ways of dealing with what they don't understand over here. When we find a way to stop the blight from spreading, we can offer them that knowledge and our opinions. Until then, trying to argue with a raug will only make it worse." He raised his eyebrows, then clasped his hands behind his back and followed the chief and the group of warriors leading the carts on legs.

Cheyenne stared after him and shook her head. *I know everyone here is nuts. Why does it keep surprising me?*

Ember waited for the halfling to catch up before she commanded the crawler to move again. "Okay, I get that no one wants to believe what's happening here, but did I hear him say the stone gates are gonna keep the blight out of his city?"

"Trust me, Em. You lost your magic for a bit, not your hearing."

"That's insane."

"Yep. You haven't agreed to go back with Cazerel after this, have you?"

"No. He hasn't asked."

"Good." Cheyenne gripped the straps of her backpack and stared at the raug chief stomping around the edge of the destroyed forest. "If he does, tell him no, or don't give him an answer."

Ember bit her lip and stared at her friend as they turned east beyond the edge of the scorched earth to get back on course. "Cheyenne?"

"Yeah."

"I don't want to assume anything, but if you're saying what I think you're saying, I might be freaking out."

"Sorry, Em." Cheyenne gave the fae girl an apologetic frown and lowered her voice. "He had no idea what happened there. He probably thought getting the blight was bad luck or some kind of debt he had to pay. I still haven't figured these guys out."

Ember swallowed. "But?"

"But now that he's seen what this crap is doing to this world all the way out here in the middle of nowhere, I wouldn't put it past him to try to keep you in his city."

"Like blackmail?"

"Maybe. Or like keeping the only cure anyone knows about right at his side." The halfling leaned toward her friend. "That's you, by the way."

"I know it's me," Ember hissed, then ran a hand through her violet-streaked hair. "Jesus. You think he'd do that?"

"Until we figure out how to reverse this, or at the very least keep it from spreading, I think every O'gúleesh is gonna do whatever they think it takes."

"Shit." Ember stared ahead blankly. "Right when I thought I could get over the weirdness of being friends with a raug."

"It's all weird, Em. We have to be careful."

Two hours later, with the sun still high above them and the last stretch of blight-stricken forest miles behind them, Cazerel raised a meaty gray fist in the air and stopped. "Here."

"Here what?" Lumil spun, her yellow hair fluttering away from her head before flopping back down over one eye. She blew it out of her face and frowned. "There's nothing here."

"So it would seem, hmm?" The chief turned and raised his eyebrows at the travelers. "And yet, here we are."

For the first time since they'd stopped to eat their tense meal, Foltr stirred on the top of the cart and cleared his throat. "Would you accept an extra pair of hands, *Zokri*?"

"If you wish, old one." Cazerel nodded at the hunched, wizened raug, then turned toward his warriors and spread his arms. "We open the doorway here, *Lugah'wo*."

The raug warriors gathered silently around their chief. When Foltr struggled to lower himself from the top of the cart, Corian stepped toward him and offered a hand. The old raug slapped it away and grunted. "I'm not as useless as I look, *vae shra'ni*. If I need your help, I'll ask for it."

Fighting back an amused smile, Corian clasped his hands behind his back and nodded before stepping away again.

Foltr jammed his staff into the dirt and clung to it as he slid unceremoniously from the top of the cart. To drive his point home, he smacked the end of his staff against the nightstalker's shin and rolled his eyes. Then he moved toward Cazerel and his warriors, muttering through clenched teeth. When the old raug's back was turned, Corian grimaced and bent over to rub his shin.

"So, what kind of doorway is this?" Ember gazed at the raugs, who were situating themselves in a semi-circle facing the trees.

Byrd shrugged. "Raug doorway, raug spells, right?"

"Oh. Better stay outta this one, Cheyenne."

The goblins burst into snorting laughter.

"Oh, yeah, thanks." Cheyenne playfully rolled her eyes. "Very funny."

"Definitely don't want the spell-dud drow gettin' her sparking hands on this one, do we?" Lumil grinned and nodded at the halfling. "I still can't believe it. L'zar's daughter and all that drow magic doesn't mean shit when it comes down to the technical stuff, huh?"

"Hey, at least I don't have to physically hit something to make a dent."

The goblin woman raised both fists and summoned her spinning red runes. Her yellow eyes reflected the bursts in orange-tinted light. "But what a dent, huh? Wanna know how I got these babies to work so well?"

"Not really." Cheyenne shot Ember a sidelong glance. The fae girl stifled a laugh. "But I have a feeling you're gonna tell me anyway."

"Just one big badass *spell*, kid."

Byrd guffawed and doubled over. Lumil stared at him, and when he looked up and saw her fists inches from his face, he choked back the rest of his laughter and leaped away.

Cazerel turned away from his warriors with a curious grin. "Is this true, *Aranél*?"

"Is what true?" Cheyenne tried to look clueless. *I don't need the raug who thinks his gates are all-powerful to start making fun of me too.*

"That you cannot cast spells?"

Lumil folded her arms and nodded. "Pretty much, yeah."

"No," Cheyenne said, shooting the goblin woman a warning glance.

"I can cast spells, no problem. They just don't always work the way I want."

Corian chuckled. "That's one way of putting it."

"All right. Don't you raugs have a door to open or something?"

Ember grinned at the chief, momentarily brushing aside Cheyenne's warning about him. "Even if she had better luck with spellcasting, she doesn't need it. When she's got an activator, Cheyenne Summerlin's unstoppable. On both sides of the Border."

"Ah." Cazerel stroked his square, hairless chin, then chuckled and pointed at Cheyenne. "Perhaps there are exceptions to my personal rules for the appropriate use of tech, eh? I believe it would be best for the *Aranél* to wear hers at all times."

The goblins cracked up again and quickly got into another shoving match.

"Thanks for the advice." Cheyenne folded her arms and raised an eyebrow at the raug chief. "But I've been doing fine with nothing but drow magic. So far, that's all I need."

Cazerel shrugged and stuck out his huge bottom lip. "Until it isn't."

As he turned away to rejoin his warriors and Foltr in setting up for their spell, Ember met Cheyenne's gaze and burst out laughing. "Sorry. Sorry, I'm just…"

"You're enjoying this as much as everyone else, aren't you?"

Ember tried to hold back her laughter, and a squeak of effort escaped her.

Maleshi stepped up beside the halfling and leaned toward Cheyenne's ear. "If you're going to take the Crown's place when you turn the new Cycle, kid, spellwork is kinda one of the prerequisites."

"Well, good thing I'm not planning on taking anyone's place."

"Haven't changed your mind about that after everything we've seen, huh?"

Cheyenne folded her arms. "I'm not the only one capable of sitting on some dumb throne and keeping things running."

"True." Maleshi shrugged. "But so far, the only name drawn from the proverbial hat is yours."

"I'll find someone."

"Sure. Finding someone else and offering the job is the easy part. It's finding someone who gives a shit and won't run away screaming that's gonna be a little tricky."

Cheyenne shot the general a sidelong glance and scoffed. "Thanks. I hadn't thought of that."

CHAPTER THIRTY-SEVEN

I t took Cazerel, his warriors, and Foltr nearly half an hour to set up for their spell, complete with finding a perfectly sized stick for drawing runes in the dirt and weighing out the required amount of crumbled bits of stone they'd packed in one of the carts.

After gnawing impatiently on the inside of his cheek, Corian stepped forward and nodded at the chief. "Is there anything we can do to help, *Zokri*? Merely in the interests of time, of course."

"No, *vae shra'ni*." Cazerel straightened from where he'd bent over to toss a handful of the glittering black rock pieces onto a rune in the dirt. "I prefer to keep the casting of this one fueled by raug magic. You understand?"

Cheyenne cocked her head at the runes and squinted. "Only those who created the doorway and hid the Crown's secret kid can open it again?"

"We did not create this doorway, *Aranél*."

She looked quickly up at him and found him smirking at her. "Oh."

"But we *are* the only ones on this side of it who know the Spider's heir lies beyond." The chief slowly tilted his head, his smile disappearing as he held Cheyenne's gaze. "I prefer not to hand my clan's secrets over to every curious magical. Especially her." He nodded at Maleshi and narrowed his eyes.

The general glanced at the sky in exasperation and turned her back to the raugs gathered to create the spell. She spread her arms and stared back in the direction they'd come. "I'll wait."

With a low growl of approval, Cazerel rejoined his warriors, speaking French to them in low tones.

"Great." Cheyenne approached Corian. The nightstalker folded his arms and watched the raugs, slowly shaking his head. "I thought he said the general's debts had been wiped clean?"

"Debts, sure." He shrugged. "Doesn't mean they have to be best friends."

"We're all working toward the bigger picture though, right? Not that hard to let go of a grudge if it helps get the job done."

Corian turned slowly to look at her and raised an eyebrow. "That's a bit hypocritical of you, don't you think?"

"Hey, what Maleshi did thousands of years ago and whatever daddy issues I have with L'zar are *not* the same thing."

"Of course not. But we've all had thousands of years to do things we regret, make mistakes, and condemn ourselves with the reputations we built serving under the Crown's ever-watchful gaze."

She snorted. "Speak for yourself."

"I am, kid. And for everyone else, minus you and Ember. Obviously." Corian shoved his hands into his pockets and rocked back on his heels, watching the group of raugs finally get down to the spellcasting. "It's hard to let go of that much history in one day, especially when raug memory stretches almost as long as drow memory and extends way before drow rule."

"That's not an excuse to…wait. Before drow rule?"

"That *was* what I said."

"Well, let's stay on that topic for a second, huh? 'Cause I'm hearing you say the drow didn't always rule Ambar'ogúl."

Corian's gaze flicked toward her before settling on the raugs again. "Correct."

Cheyenne stepped in front of him to block his view and waved a hand in his face. "Let them do their raug thing, man. I'm sure they can handle it without you watching them. I wanna hear about all this 'before the drow took the throne' stuff."

Wrinkling his nose, Corian met her gaze. "I take it a spark of inspiration is waiting to catch fire."

"Hey, if you're better at teaching me O'gúl history than spellcasting, then yeah. Probably."

He chuckled through his nose and nodded. "All right. Drow haven't always ruled Ambar'ogúl, and it wasn't always one Crown on the throne over all of it."

Behind the nightstalker, L'zar picked dirt from under his fingernails and snorted. "Whoever thought *that* was a good idea couldn't see any farther than their own lifetime. Or didn't care."

Corian rolled his eyes. "You can't blame everyone else for not being able to see the future."

"Of course I can. *And* I can see the future." L'zar widened his eyes and flipped his fingers back and forth for a different view of his nails.

Cheyenne frowned at the drow thief and shook her head. "We can ignore him."

The corners of Corian's mouth twitched in amusement. "We can try. It depends on how much detail you want me to go into."

"The CliffsNotes version is cool."

"Mm-hmm." Corian briefly closed his eyes to gather his thoughts. "As far as any of us know, this world started with a handful of different kingdoms, each ruled by a different race, and their capital cities inhabited mostly by the same race as their sovereign. If we're basing any of this on what the records say—"

L'zar snorted. "Whatever records still exist and haven't been tampered with."

Corian ignored him and continued in a flat, unamused tone. "These kingdoms enjoyed a lot more peace and prosperity than any of *us* have experienced, especially in the last few thousand years."

"I wonder why?"

Cheyenne peered around the nightstalker to shoot her father a deadpan stare, but L'zar was busy with a last-minute self-manicure on his other hand. "Peace, huh?"

"Regulated by the fighting pits, yeah. As I'm sure you noticed, that's another of Ba'rael's glaring mistakes during this Cycle. This is an inherently violent world, kid. We take our outlets where we can find 'em."

"Sure. So, peace and prosperity. Lots of different rulers. No one's singing *Kumbaya*, but they're all playing nice enough. I get it." The halfling looked back up at the nightstalker and nodded. "What happened?"

"The drow weren't satisfied."

"Hey, big surprise."

Corian smiled. "The records name him as Sylra Nightflame. Obviously not his real name, but I guess that doesn't matter this long after the fact. He started rounding up others of his race, pulling them out of hiding and bringing as many drow together as he could to build their own little kingdom."

"Hiding," L'zar hissed with a humorless laugh, "Those drow didn't *hide*, Corian. They were relegated."

"They made decisions and stuck with those decisions until they found someone who would make a different choice *for* them." The nightstalker folded his arms and gave Cheyenne a wide-eyed look.

Surely that was meant for L'zar, not me. The halfling tried to ignore her father's comments, but it was impossible not to pick up on Corian's last words. "What decisions?"

"The decision to rise up and claim their fate."

L'zar finally stopped pretending he was far more interested in his fingernails. "That's the mildest version in existence, *vae shra'ni*. Don't sugarcoat it. By the deathflame, she's my daughter. If anyone can handle the truth, it's the drow standing in front of you."

Seriously? He's suddenly fighting to give me all the pieces of the puzzle?

As Cheyenne blinked dumbly in surprise, Corian lost his tense composure and whirled to face the drow thief. "Would you care to explain to your daughter the origins of your race's authority in this fell-damn world?"

L'zar spread his arms, kicked one heel out to bow low over his extended leg, and grinned. "If my *Nós Aní* permits."

Corian rolled his eyes and stepped aside, gesturing for L'zar to join them. The drow thief's golden eyes flickered toward Cheyenne as he stepped into their circle of three now. She leaned away and scanned him. *Same crazy grin. I think that's his lucid face.*

Behind her, a low, guttural chant rose from Cazerel, his warriors, and Foltr. Soft yellow and orange light flashed slowly, reflected in

L'zar's golden eyes. At this point, both drow had abandoned any interest in the raugs' spell.

"Our kind rose from the darkness, Cheyenne." L'zar tilted his head, studying her reaction. "You know our other name, don't you? *Mór edhil.*"

"Dark elf." The halfling narrowed her eyes. "That doesn't mean we *are* the darkness."

"No. We were merely born from it." His mad grin widened. "You of all people should understand we are not the source of our existence. We are not those who came before us, yet we can't untie ourselves from the threads that birthed us, hm?"

Cheyenne leaned slowly toward her father. *Jesus, this feels like talking to a toddler. If I even knew what that was like.* "If you're gonna keep talking to me in riddles, *Weaver*, I'd rather listen to Corian's version."

The nightstalker laughed and looked at the drow thief.

L'zar raised an eyebrow, his opposite eye twitching into a squint.

Okay, that's either annoyance or approval. Here we go.

He leaned toward her until their faces were inches apart, chuckled, and withdrew. "It's easy to forget you are exactly the age you look. So young."

"And so not interested in being talked down to because of it."

Corian dropped his gaze to the ground between them with a smirk.

L'zar took a sharp breath through his nose and smoothed his hair back with both hands. "Then let me spell it out for you, Cheyenne. We drow were created to live in shadow, you understand? *Mór edhil.* All the dark corners of this world were ours. All the darkened threads of the Weave. All the magic no one else had the balls to touch. We thrived in the darkness and the fear; it was our birthright. For the rest of Ambar'ogúl, the spaces drow inhabited, physically and with the magic running through our blood, were reserved only for the mad."

Cheyenne tilted her head. "Sounds like you would've fit right in back then."

"Indeed." He wiggled his eyebrows.

The flashing lights of the raugs' spell grew brighter as the gray-skinned magicals' voices increased in volume and strength.

"We're all a bit mad, aren't we?" L'zar dipped his head. "I suggest you embrace it."

"Maybe, after you get back on track and finish this illuminating history lesson."

He chuckled. "It might make you feel sane. Sylra wanted to bring the darkness and the light together. Not in harmony, but to lift our race higher than we were ever meant to be. His wish was well-timed. The drow were pulled toward his idea like moths to the flame, only these moths did not burn. They *consumed* the fire."

Cheyenne rolled her eyes before her gaze landed on Corian. "Is he even capable of giving me a straight answer?"

The nightstalker shrugged. "Ask *him*."

"Oh, I'm perfectly capable. What you *should* ask is if I'm interested."

"Okay, forget it." Cheyenne tossed her hands into the air and let them drop against her sides. "I'll ask someone whose brain cells haven't been fried by their own magic."

She started to turn around.

"Cheyenne."

The sharpness in her father's harsh whisper made her pause.

"Hangivol is *the* drow city, the capital Sylra and his followers created from within the darkness. The metropolis they worked together to raise from the crumbling shadows of a world that always had and always would prefer not to see us. It's our legacy. Ba'rael's. Mine. Yours."

She glanced at Corian, but the nightstalker didn't look up from the particularly interesting patch of thin, drying grass at their feet. "So, they built the city."

"They built the city. And their forces grew. Drow surged from the underbellies of every other O'gúl kingdom, from their eternal existence in madness and unseen power." L'zar's grin widened even more as a dark, longing chuckle escaped him. "Then Sylra led our people across this world and razed every other kingdom to the ground."

"What?"

"We are *conquerors*, Cheyenne. One by one, the other thriving cities of every race in Ambar'ogúl fell to Sylra's forces and his mad dream. When he was finished, Hangivol remained, the bastion of drow power, ruled by one *mór edhil* at a time with their *Nós Aní* by their side." Giving his daughter a moment to let the information sink in, L'zar took a deep breath and spread his arms. His dark grin faded slightly, and the crazed glory burning in his golden eyes snuffed out. The raugs' combined spell flashed brighter still, and the pace of the chanting picked up. "It's the ultimate underdog story if you ask me."

"I wouldn't call it that." Cheyenne frowned. "Sounds more like a bloodbath."

"Oh, I'm sure it was." L'zar closed his eyes. "I would have loved to see it with my own eyes."

Of course he would. She snorted and shook her head. "So, there's nothing special about drow that keeps Ambar'ogúl running, right? Like, the whole world won't fall apart if a drow doesn't sit on the throne?"

Corian cleared his throat and looked at her. "Absolutely not, except that a drow has ruled as the Crown for as long as any of us have lived. Even Foltr."

"Then I *can* choose someone to take my place, and they don't have to be a drow."

L'zar chuckled. "I assumed you already realized this."

"Well, now I know for sure."

"It's possible." Corian scratched his neck beneath one twitching ear. "We might find ourselves hung up on a few technicalities, changes we'd have to make to reorient the source of magic from the drow to any other race. Keep in mind, kid, Hangivol was built *by* drow *for* drow. The last Nimlothar lives within the Heart."

"I'm *not* cutting down that tree so someone else can sit on the throne without it."

The nightstalker gave her a gentle smile. "No one's asking you to."

"Good."

"The old laws would still stand for anyone who took your place if they agreed."

Cheyenne said, "Yeah. Apparently, that's gonna be the hard part."

"Indeed." L'zar chuckled, half growl and half hum of amusement. "If the next drow in line to turn their own new Cycle doesn't want to claim it, I can't imagine anyone else who would."

She stared at her father and his crooked smile. *Someone will want it. There* has *to be someone else, 'cause it sure as hell won't be me.*

When neither offered anything else, she shrugged. "I'm open to suggestions."

"Hmm." Corian pressed his lips together and fought to hold in a laugh. "I'll have to get back to you on that one."

"If we're looking at changing the ruling race for this entire world, are the O'gúleesh gonna have a problem with a Crown who isn't a drow?" A massive crack split the air, and Cheyenne looked over her shoulder to see the group of raugs blasting pulsing yellow and orange light at a central point in the air in front of them. The spellcasting wasn't finished yet. She turned back toward her father to continue.

"Not particularly." Corian stroked his chin.

L'zar clasped his hands behind his back and dipped his head. "No, I imagine most would be thrilled by the prospect at this point."

"Right."

"No one expected the drow to excel in their rulership, kid." The nightstalker glanced briefly at the growing spell behind her. "As it turned out, once the chaos settled after Sylra's rule, of course, every drow Crown since has done a remarkable job of running this world, with a surprising knack for maintaining balance. Justice and violence. A measure of tolerance for dark magic amidst maintaining the lifeforce of Ambar'ogúl, not to mention that all the technological advancements were made under drow rule. It didn't take long for the rest of the O'gúleesh to fall back into their regular pattern of going about their daily lives and not giving a shit who sits on the throne."

"Seriously?" Cheyenne snorted. "Those raugs over there have been holding a grudge against Maleshi for centuries, and you're telling me nobody cared about the drow conquerors staying in power?"

"You're comparing a personal slight with a world-wide shift, kid. Not the same." Corian wiped another smile off his face and nodded. "The past Crowns generally leaned toward letting what used to be the other sovereign kingdoms run things however they wanted, just as separate territories instead."

"Generally." L'zar scoffed. "Until Ba'rael the Spider."

Cheyenne shot him an exasperated look. "Then everything went to shit."

"Obviously."

"So that's what I need to do." A small smile flickered at the corners of the halfling's mouth. "Abdicate to someone who *isn't* a drow and make sure this doesn't happen again. Break the cycle and turn a new Cycle with someone else."

"If that's still your decision when we get to that point, then yeah." Corian nodded. "But I'd *strongly* recommend putting it up for a vote among the Four-Pointed Star at the very least. Putting someone on the throne to wash your hands clean is one thing. Putting the *right* magical on the throne takes a bit more finesse."

"What makes someone else the *right* magical? 'Cause I'm clearly not."

L'zar clicked his tongue. "I disagree. Of course, that's my personal opinion."

"Yeah, you have a lot of those."

"The right magical for the job is someone who can hold their own, Cheyenne." The nightstalker raised a fist between them. "In a fight. I'm sure you've noticed by now how important that is to O'gúleesh everywhere, no matter where they come from or what they've been doing for the last few thousand years."

Cheyenne shrugged. "Goes without saying."

"Almost. Anyone who can stand against a challenge from their seat in Hangivol will make the magicals in this world fairly happy. For a few hundred years at least, give or take. If it's not a drow, maybe that's even better. But if some power-hungry O'gúleesh gets it in their head that the next Crown isn't strong enough to face a challenge—and there *will* be challenges—we could end up with another new Crown who forced their way onto the throne through violence, instead of someone who stood up because they wanted to serve Ambar'ogúl, not themselves."

With a frown, the halfling nodded. "Then we're right back where we started." She turned to look at Maleshi, who prowled back and forth behind Lumil and Byrd. All three of them stared at the growing raug spell.

L'zar laughed. "Absolutely not."

"What?" Cheyenne peered at him. "I didn't say anything."

"You didn't have to."

"It's written all over your face, kid." Corian glanced at the sky and shook his head. "The general returned to help us tear Ba'rael off the throne, and hopefully, she'll stay to help us clean up this mess the Crown left behind, but she's done too much as Hand of the Night and

Circle to get more than half the magicals' support. The other half would despise her as much as they despise Ba'rael, if not more."

"You don't know that."

"I'm fairly certain." Corian raised an eyebrow. "Feel free to make her an official offer, but you'd be wasting your time."

Cheyenne studied his amused expression and jerked her chin at him. "What about you, then?"

"Nice try." He nodded at L'zar beside him. "You know I'm tied to the Weaver. Wherever he goes, I go, and once he steps foot across the Border again, he's never coming back here."

L'zar snorted. "A day that can't come soon enough."

"Fine. Then I'm working with narrowed options, aren't I?" Cheyenne folded her arms and gazed blankly at the empty air between Corian and L'zar. *Minus the physical ability to fight, Bianca Summerlin would make the best Crown this world has ever seen. But she'd strangle me before stepping foot in this place.* The thought made her hiss a brief laugh, then she looked at Corian again.

His silver eyes flashed. "If you want advice on how to choose your replacement, kid, we can sit down and hash that out later."

"Later better be soon, right? I have less than two weeks to find someone who wants this enough to take it."

"Or you'll be stuck here, ruling Ambar'ogúl on your own until you *do* find someone else." L'zar widened his eyes, his head wobbling as he fought back a laugh. "That'll be a lot harder to do with all the extra responsibilities resting squarely on your shoulders."

"What the hell does that mean?"

"Don't spend your energy worrying about that until it comes to pass, which I'm confident it won't."

Corian shot L'zar a sidelong glance, and his brow darkened with a concerned frown. "Cheyenne, you have to keep in mind that any of this is only possible if the Crown accepts your terms."

"She will." L'zar tossed a dismissive hand toward his *Nós Aní.* "When I'm finished putting those terms together for you to offer her on a silver fucking platter, Cheyenne, she won't have a choice."

"Not true." Corian scowled at the drow thief. "And you know it."

"She could still choose to fight me, right?" Cheyenne glanced at them. "If she refuses the terms?"

"Yes, and we need to avoid that possibility at all costs."

"Why?" The halfling tilted her head. "You don't think I can take her?"

Corian chuckled wryly. "Do *you*?"

"Your spellwork is atrocious, Cheyenne." L'zar smiled and nodded like he was congratulating her instead of calling out her faults. "That needs to change."

"Sure. Any takers on a mentor for *that*?"

Both the drow thief and his nightstalker *Nós Aní* looked away from her. Corian's lips twitched in and out of a smile. "Maybe you should go to your first mentor for that one. She did, after all, pen the most user-friendly spellbook I've ever seen."

Cheyenne glanced at Maleshi again. "She gave me that stack of spells and told me to go home and figure it out on my own time."

"Mattie Bergmann told you that. I think Maleshi Hi'et will have a different answer."

"Great." Cheyenne studied the general's slow pacing, which was clearly fueled by an anxious urgency to get to their destination. *Yeah, I'm ready for this long-ass spell to be over too.* "Then I guess I'll have to ask for some pointers."

"It's a good start." Corian ran a hand through his hair. "And this time, you two know enough about each other to hopefully make that training a little easier on you both."

She shot him a scathing glance. "I can learn."

"I look forward to seeing you prove it."

Without warning, the flashing lights of the spell and the raugs' chanting, which had grown to a chorus of shouted words in O'gúleesh, stopped.

Cheyenne turned around to see a dark, shimmering oval of light spreading in the air where the raugs had been concentrating their focused blast of magic. "Is that the doorway?"

L'zar rubbed his hands together and stepped past her toward the raugs. "I sure hope so."

CHAPTER THIRTY-EIGHT

Foltr rested both gnarled gray hands on the twisted knob at the top of his staff. "Nothing quite like tapping into the source with your own kind."

Cazerel turned from the shimmering window of dark light in front of them and smiled crookedly at the aged raug. "Has it been long for you, old one?"

"Longer than I care to admit," Foltr rumbled, then nodded at the open doorway, "Thank you."

"No need to thank me. We've reached the end. Healer!" Cazerel's massive frame spun quickly to face Ember. "Come. I want you at my side to lead these friends of Hirúl Breach through the doorway."

Ember's wide violet eyes flicked from the dark window to the raug chief's face. "Go ahead. I'm right behind you."

A booming laugh escaped him, and he thumped a fist against his chest before waving her forward. "Come, come. I wouldn't lead you to the deathflame willingly. There's no danger for you, Healer. Only honor."

When Ember shot Cheyenne an unsure glance, the halfling nodded slowly. "While we're here."

"Right." The fae girl swiped her fingers across the crawler's control panel and moved the skittering machine toward the raug chief.

Cazerel grinned at her, his chest quivering in silent laughter. "This pleases me very much, Healer. Now you will see what no one has seen for centuries. Excluding me and mine, of course."

"Of course." She widened her eyes and looked at Cheyenne one more time before she disappeared through the doorway at Cazerel's side.

The raug warriors snickered and shook themselves like huge, hairless horses twitching beneath buzzing flies before they followed their chief through the open portal.

Maleshi growled and stalked toward Cheyenne, Corian, and L'zar as the goblins and Foltr passed through the portal and disappeared. The general scowled at the dark window of light and shook her head. "This feels different."

"It's a raug portal, General." L'zar dipped his head toward her in a mocking bow and gestured toward the doorway. "Of course, a nightstalker wouldn't recognize it."

"I thought only nightstalkers could open portals." Cheyenne stared at the doorway, the other side of which was shrouded in darkness and impossible to make out.

"On their own." Corian shot her a quick glance and shrugged. "Another reminder not to mess with more than one raug at a time. Especially not a whole tribe."

Maleshi hissed at him, "Keep your reminders to yourself." She didn't give him time to respond before stalking toward the portal and disappearing.

Cheyenne nudged the nightstalker's shoulder with a loose fist. "Nice one."

"I misspoke." He cleared his throat. "She knows that."

"Clearly. Hence the pissed-off storming away from you." When she noticed Corian's warning glance, she took a deep breath and turned toward the portal. *Here I am running my mouth and screwing up the nightstalkers' little secret. Shut up, Cheyenne.* "Guess they're waiting for us on the other side."

"Then let's not keep them waiting, hmm?" L'zar strode casually toward the portal and disappeared.

Corian licked his lips in restrained agitation and stared at the doorway. "Don't let yourself slip up like that again."

"He didn't pick up on anything." Cheyenne waved toward the portal. "He's too excited about blackmailing his sister with his surprise nephew. Honestly, don't you think you'd both feel better if you let it out in the open and *told* him?"

The nightstalker swallowed thickly and didn't look at her. "I won't tell you again."

He took off. Rolling her eyes, Cheyenne headed quickly after him and stepped through the raug portal as Corian's back foot disappeared in front of her.

The same squeezing pressure she'd felt every time she'd crossed the Border between worlds overwhelmed her. Cheyenne gasped for a breath that didn't come and her mind reeled. *No way those raugs opened a brand-new Border portal. No one said anything about crossing the in-between.*

Then she was through, stumbling forward and wheezing when her lungs finally filled with air again. When she looked up, she knew immediately that she wasn't in the in-between, but everything had changed.

"Whoa."

Corian cleared his throat beside her and tilted his head. "Not what I expected either if we're being perfectly honest."

She frowned at him. "Are we?"

He shook his head and headed after their party. Everyone else had slowed down to let the rest of them catch up, and the group now stepped cautiously across the ground as a single blob of magicals in a sprawling valley hidden from the rest of Ambar'ogúl.

Cazerel turned around to grin at the band of rebels who'd followed him here. "Now you see. Only the raugs could bring you here. Remember."

Ember gazed around the open valley that had replaced the forest on the slanting mountainside where they'd waited for the portal to open. Her mouth fell open. "This wasn't here before."

"It is always here, Healer. Only accessible to those who know the way in."

"Which now includes us," Cheyenne muttered. "Where are we, exactly?"

"A different plane." Maleshi's silver eyes moved slowly across the sprawling valley. "Don't get too cocky about it, kid. It doesn't include us."

"What?"

"That isn't a portal we can open whenever we want," Corian added. "The chief speaks only for the raugs."

"You can't get back here on your own?" Cheyenne walked beside him, squinted against the bright sunlight reflecting off the white stone surrounding the valley and running through the center of it.

"Not without a band of raugs and that spell."

"Which he refused to give us." She grimaced. "Awesome."

The magicals made their way down the gently sloping hillside toward the center of the valley. Cheyenne would have thought the place was empty if it weren't for the squat buildings of white stone scattered around them, interspersed with huts made of white mud and straw. Huge columns of stone rose in an unrecognizable pattern across the valley, some of them supporting stone roofs without any walls. Around the central ring of buildings were massive statues carved in more white stone, O'gúleesh magicals in various poses of welcoming, warning, and suspended battle.

Looks like Ambar'ogúl's version of ancient Greece.

Cheyenne looked at the closest statue as they passed it—a fae woman draped in flowing silk, one hand extended toward the sky as the other pointed straight at the place where the raug portal had spat them into the valley. "Who are these guys?"

L'zar snorted, though his golden eyes shimmered in delight as he looked everywhere but at the statues. "A bunch of dead O'gúleesh meant to remind the living of what's better left forgotten. For most of them, anyway."

"What's that?"

When he turned toward his daughter, the eager, crazed grin had returned. "That this place exists."

Ember drummed her fingers on the rim of the crawler's body as it moved slowly one leg at a time. "I'm feeling out of place here in this thing."

"No one will hold it against you, Healer." Cazerel chuckled. "And when you no longer have need of a machine, you'll forget all about it."

"Uh-huh."

Cheyenne glanced at the back of the crawler and her friend's purple-streaked hair. *She's right, though—no other tech in this place. No metal.* She reached up to touch the activator coil attached behind her ear to make sure it was there. *I'm not picking up on anything.* "Kinda feels like we went back in time."

Corian slowly shook his head. "More like this plane has fallen behind. Or never changed with the times."

That assessment felt like the truth. The stone buildings and the statues didn't show signs of normal wear over the centuries. Nothing looked old, but none of it matched anything Cheyenne had seen on either of her visits to Ambar'ogúl. *A different plane, all right. One that doesn't even look like the same world.*

The hair on the back of her neck bristled and the sharp, astringent taste of vinegar and some kind of fruit she couldn't quite place settled on her tongue, tingling through the back of her throat until it bloomed up through her nose. She smacked her lips and snorted. "That's funky."

"That's magic." Maleshi fixed the halfling with her silver eyes and ran her tongue over her teeth. "Strong magic."

Corian licked his lips and wrinkled his nose in discomfort. "Been a long time since I've felt the source like this, and it wasn't anywhere near as strong."

Cheyenne tried to rub the furious tingle out of her nose, blinking through the shimmer of tears the sensation had brought to her eyes. "I'm not a fan."

Lumil stuck her tongue all the way out and grunted in disgust. "Tastes like someone pissed in the grog barrel."

Byrd repeatedly wiped at his mouth. "How would *you* know?"

"Tell me I'm wrong, asshole. You can't."

L'zar stopped, blinked slowly, and burst into shrieking laughter.

The other magicals in their party, raugs included, turned to watch the drow thief fall deeper into madness. Cazerel's orange eyes narrowed.

"L'zar." Corian's low voice was barely audible beneath the drow's cackling.

"Ha!" L'zar slapped a hand on the nightstalker's shoulder and shook it roughly as his golden eyes flickered across the valley. "Ba'rael's son living out his life in Nor'ieth. This is way too good."

Even as Corian and Maleshi turned disbelieving stares on the drow,

L'zar fell into another fit of laughter. He slid his hand off Corian's shoulder and shook his head, howling.

"Nor'ieth." Maleshi frowned. "That's a myth."

Cheyenne turned away from her father's explosive amusement and gazed at the other magicals. "While he's battling his inability to make any sense, anyone wanna explain what the hell he's talking about?"

"An origin story, kid." Corian vigorously scratched the back of his head, trying to rid himself of the tingling itch of so much concentrated magic in one place. "Every world has its own. More than one on Earth. Only one here."

"The source of magic," Maleshi muttered. "Where everything begins and ends."

"You're kidding."

"Not about the story." The general's eyes twitched and watered slightly when she met Cheyenne's gaze. "Whatever this place is, we can't prove it's Nor'ieth."

"Oh, yes, we can." L'zar's laughter died to a soft chuckle and he grinned like a lunatic at the empty air around them. "I can *see* it."

Cheyenne wiggled her lower jaw, trying to fight off the growing pressure in her ears. "Lemme guess. This is another one of your 'reading the threads' moments, huh?"

"Every moment is one of those moments. What idiot thought to hide the child *here?*"

Cazerel grinned at the drow thief and pounded a fist on his chest. "I did."

The raug chief's dark chuckle filled the air, then he and L'zar lost it all over again. Their booming laughter echoed across the valley in one obnoxious wave of amusement after another.

Cheyenne grimaced at them and shook her head. *Apparently, insanity's contagious.*

Corian looked at them, his nostrils flaring. "I fail to see the humor."

"You know the high regard in which I hold you, *vae shra'ni.*" L'zar burst out laughing again and tried to cut it short, waving a long, slender gray hand in front of his face. "But you fail to see a lot."

Foltr shot an annoyed glance at the raug chief, then stepped toward L'zar and cracked the end of his staff against the drow thief's ribs. It only made L'zar laugh harder, despite his attempt to flinch away from the blow. "Pull yourself together, Weaver. If you have an explanation, give it."

The drow's laughter simmered down to a chuckle, and L'zar wiped the corners of his eyes. "Honestly, I expected you to share my amusement, Grandfather."

"You have high expectations for a lunatic," Foltr spat. "Out with it."

With a deep breath, L'zar held the old raug's gaze and nodded. "My sister's child is here, old one, secluded within the walls of Nor'ieth for his entire life. No word in or out of this place but for the few instances, like today, when travelers open the doorway and cross through. No knowledge of the outside world. Ever."

Cheyenne blinked in realization. "He has no idea he's the Crown's son."

L'zar whirled toward her and pointed at her with a sharp thrust of his finger. "No idea there even *is* a Crown. No idea that anything exists beyond this place. For those passing their days in Nor'ieth, there *is* no other place. This is all there is."

Despite the six feet between her and her father, Cheyenne glanced at his finger and leaned away. *He's enjoying this way too much.*

"How is this useful?" Corian turned in a slow circle, gazing intently at the empty valley, the empty buildings, and the empty courtyards of white stone between the rising pillars. "If Ba'rael sent her son away for no other reason than to keep him safe from *you*, L'zar, she sure as hell accomplished that."

"Ah, but if she sent him away with the hope of someday calling him back home to join her?" L'zar said, chuckling wildly again. "To stand beside her against me? That makes this the Spider's greatest mistake. She has no idea where he is, Corian. She has no idea her *son* has been raised at the source, making him useless to her as a bargaining chip." He laughed. "She fucked up *royally*, didn't she?"

No one else found his play on words nearly as amusing as he did.

Cheyenne shook her head and couldn't keep watching her father's ridiculous display. "She wouldn't do that, would she? Use her own kid as leverage to stay in power."

"Cheyenne," Corian growled. "Ba'rael Verdys slit her own father's throat to step into power and keep L'zar out of it. That drow would do *anything* to get what she wants. She already has."

"And she thought she had the upper hand by secreting this child away, even from her own awareness." L'zar clapped his hands together. "She thought she had a hidden ace up her sleeve, but the card's not even in the deck!"

The halfling stepped away from her cackling father. "If he starts jumping up and down and squealing, I'm done."

Corian grinned at her. "Ten seconds. If he doesn't snap out of it, I'm happy to offer you the first shot."

Cheyenne laughed and lifted a fist in preparation. "Deal."

CHAPTER THIRTY-NINE

Holding Corian's gaze, Cheyenne counted silently to ten but never got the chance to punch her father out of his insane laughter. By the time she reached eight, L'zar's sudden recovery and immediate silence made her turn to look at him again, and she forgot all about her impromptu pact with the nightstalker.

The valley was filled with luminous magicals heading toward the travelers in their midst. Cheyenne squinted against the glare of so many shimmering bodies growing brighter as the strangers approached.

She leaned toward Corian and whispered, "Who are they?"

He stared at the newcomers and shook his head. "I have no idea."

A crack echoed across the valley, and the bright halos of light disappeared from around the magicals' bodies. The closest one, a tall, startlingly thin magical with skin nearly as white as the stone around them, spread his arms after clapping his hands together and bowed a smooth, hairless head toward the travelers. "Welcome."

His voice rang out in numerous tones at once, as if all the magicals surrounding L'zar and his rebels had spoken at the same time, although only the tall male's mouth moved. A small smile split his pale lips. Blue eyes so light they were almost colorless flickered from face to face among the travelers.

Cheyenne couldn't stop staring. *He doesn't even blink.*

Byrd's mouth fell open.

Beside him, Lumil opted for her usual jab in the goblin's ribs, but it was a weak attempt without any real effort behind it.

Cazerel stepped toward the magical who'd addressed them all and bowed his head. "The first time for my companions, Yilas."

The ridiculously tall, thin Yilas straightened from his bow and swept his gaze over the awestruck faces staring at him and his people. "We know."

"A word, bright one. If it pleases you."

Yilas tilted his pale, elongated head and gestured behind him. "Come then."

Without another word for the rebels he'd led into Nor'ieth, Cazerel nodded and headed after the strange-looking magical.

Cheyenne watched the pair move off to have a private conversation, then she scanned the wide-eyed, softly smiling faces of the other strangers surrounding them. *If I had no idea magic and Ambar'ogúl were a thing, I would've sworn these guys are aliens.*

Corian ran a hand down the side of his face. "When he said the drow was with the *olforím*, I let it slide. Thought it was just an expression."

"That's what they are?" Cheyenne found it hard to look away from the slightly glowing magicals radiating thick magical energy despite no longer giving off the blinding light. When she did, she found the night-stalker looking as dumbstruck as she felt. "*Olforím?*"

"As much of a myth as Nor'ieth," Maleshi added, her voice barely above a whisper. "No one's seen them for…I'd say centuries, but it's been longer than that. One of those races everyone assumed died out."

"They didn't." L'zar grinned at the *olforím*. "They came here."

Ember tried to direct the crawler away from the closest *olforím*, who was stepping slowly toward her. The machine rocked sideways, lurched in a spinning half-circle, and finally righted itself before stepping quickly back the way she wanted. "Cheyenne!"

"Yeah." The halfling stepped toward her friend but couldn't look away from the pale blue eyes and the long, thin features peeking out from beneath the *olforím's* flowing robes.

Ember swallowed. "You can feel that, right?"

"All the magic?" Cheyenne stopped beside the crawler and nodded. "Yeah, Em."

"It touched me when that one got closer," the fae girl whispered. "I could feel *everything.*"

"For real?"

Ember's mouth had gone dry, but she licked her lips anyway. "Everything."

"Huh." Cheyenne rubbed the magical tingle growing beneath her nose. *This is gonna get old fast.* "If this place is a bubble with no openings to the outside, I guess the magic's been building in here."

"Like at the capital, do you think?"

Corian leaned toward them. "No. The magic in this place belongs here. I imagine it's been strengthened by having no access to the rest of the world. No tech, untouched by the blight."

"So this was what Ambar'ogúl was like before any of that," Cheyenne muttered. "Before Sylra and all his *changes.*"

L'zar dipped his head at an *olforim* woman passing fluidly by him, though she kept a distance of ten feet. "If anyone would know, *they* would."

"Oh, sure. I'll ignore the magical shockwave and ask the closest one if this is what the world was like in the very beginning." Cheyenne meant to snort at the idea, but it came out of her as a shallow, unsteady sigh. *I bet it's impossible to even think when one of those things gets too close.* Her gaze drifted toward the bottom of the sloping hill where Cazerel stood in quiet conversation with Yilas. *Or unless someone's been here before and got used to it. Raugs are full of surprises.*

As if he'd heard her thoughts, the raug chief turned back toward the traveling party and gestured at them with a wide sweep of his meaty arm. He looked like a mangled gray tree standing beside the lithe, graceful *olforim,* who was a head taller than the chief. Yilas nodded, and the pair made their way toward Cheyenne and the others.

"These, Yilas, are the drow's kin." Cazerel eyed L'zar intently. "L'zar Verdys and his daughter."

"We are all kin in this place," Yilas interrupted, sweeping his unblinking gaze across the entire party of dumbfounded travelers. "The source sweeps away all bonds of blood, does it not?"

"Blood bonds with blood." Cheyenne wrinkled her nose when the line she'd heard in more prophecies than she'd wanted to hear came into her

mind. *Not here, though. Not in a place that doesn't exist on the same freakin' plane.*

L'zar stepped toward Yilas, and while he didn't grin at the magical, his closed-lipped smile was no less eager. "I would very much like to see him. My sister's child."

"Look around you, Weaver." The *olforím* gestured toward the valley with a sweep of his thin arm. The sheer sleeves of his light-colored robes shivered with the movement, and Cheyenne noted the thumb and only two fingers on the magical's hand.

Definitely like aliens.

"Everything you see is everything he is," Yilas continued. "As are we all."

"Indeed." L'zar raised an eyebrow. "All the same, I would very much like to also see a physical body. If it's not too much to ask."

"No request is too grand, drow." Yilas pursed his thin, pale lips. "Nor is the fulfillment of it. Come. We will lead you to this physical body. Do not be surprised if you cannot see it the way you expect."

The *olforím* turned and headed toward the opposite side of the valley. Cheyenne and Ember glanced at each other, and the halfling leaned toward her friend to mutter, "I think we hit the jackpot for magicals even kookier than L'zar."

"Kookier?" Ember snorted.

"It felt right at the moment."

Corian paused on the other side of Cheyenne and nodded at Yilas and two other *olforím* walking beside him to lead yet another procession. L'zar had fallen in line behind them even before Cazerel, who rubbed his hairless gray head and nodded at the giant statues of long-dead O'gúleesh as if he approved of the unchanging state of things in Nor'ieth.

"This is it," the nightstalker muttered.

"What, the end of sanity as we know it?"

Corian met the halfling's gaze and raised an eyebrow. "Your chance to meet your cousin, kid. I wouldn't be surprised if you feel a lot saner after *that* conversation."

"I won't be surprised if I lose my mind." She'd tried to make it sound like a witty, sarcastic comment, but it didn't quite work. *I might've pinned the magical tail on the flying donkey with that one.*

Ember's attempt at a smile only made it to distracted-grimace level, but she steered the crawler down the sloping hillside as Cheyenne and L'zar's rebels headed after another guide.

Behind them, Byrd kept clearing his throat. "I can't even."

"Then shut up, already," Lumil muttered. "I'm right there with you, man."

They passed through the center of Nor'ieth, weaving through the short, squat buildings of white stone and the occasional hut erected beside them. The highest concentration of what looked a lot like ancient Grecian temples filled the right side of the valley, interspersed with longer white buildings extending beneath the shadow of the rocky valley walls. Pale, elongated faces peered at the travelers from open doorways and from behind fluttering drapes made of the same material as the *olforím*'s matching robes. None of them said a word, though they smiled softly at the newcomers with unblinking eyes.

That's how people smile at newborn babies, only five thousand times creepier.

Cheyenne blinked and forced herself to focus on the back of Corian's head as they made their way through the densest mass of buildings and curious onlookers.

"They don't look surprised to see us here," Ember whispered. "Just amused."

"That's on my list of 'how to know someone's not right in the head,'" Cheyenne muttered. *It's the same look L'zar gave me from behind bars when I met him.*

The thick buzz of concentrated magic in the center of the valley made Cheyenne's eyes water. Lumil took a sharp breath and sneezed violently, sending a shrieking echo blasting back at them from the valley's high stone walls.

"Nice one," Byrd muttered.

"You or me, *dae'bruj*." The goblin woman rubbed her forearm under her nose and sniffed. "One of us is gonna shut you up."

They could have made the trip across the valley in half the time if the procession hadn't moved so slowly. Yilas' long, thin legs moved at a careless, steady pace as if this were a stroll through a garden. L'zar matched the magical's stride easily, a thin, eager smile on his lips and his hands clasped behind his back. He looked over his shoulder at Cheyenne and widened his eyes.

Like a kid in a toy store. Or a psychopath who got away with murder.

Before she had the chance to decide what kind of expression to give her father in return, L'zar chuckled and turned around again to scan the incredibly high walls of the valley in front of them.

The taste of vinegar and unknown berries faded as they walked farther from the center of Nor'ieth. *Good to know. Wherever the exact center is, I'm staying away from it.*

Yilas stopped at the base of a steep hill rising. He watched the rest of the ragtag group of magical visitors with no expression and waited for the last of them to gather around, then swept a long arm toward the top of the hill and gazed at it. "You will find Aut Na'mor there, communing with the source."

Cheyenne felt more than saw the glances Maleshi and Corian exchanged. She turned toward them with a questioning frown. "What now?"

"It's just a name," Corian muttered, shifting his gaze to the top of the hill.

"Obviously not *just.*"

Maleshi leaned toward the halfling. "It means 'Lost One.'"

"Huh." Cheyenne eyed Yilas. "Are we sure this guy knows what he's saying?"

"Nope."

L'zar craned his neck to peer at the top of the rising hill and grinned. "Let's go ask for a moment of his time."

Foltr thumped his cane on the ground and smacked his lips. "I'll sit this one out."

"Yeah, me too." Ember brushed violet-tinted hair out of her eyes. "No offense, Cazerel, but I don't trust this machine enough to make it climb something like that."

"None taken, Healer. More time for us to sit together in peace, yes? I would hear more of your fae knowledge."

Cheyenne glanced at the raug chief. "You're not coming with us?"

"No. I've fulfilled my promise in bringing you here. The rest is up to you to decide. I have no part to play in what comes next."

"The pleasure's all mine." L'zar stepped toward the narrow path winding up the steep hillside, moving as casually as if they had all the time in the world.

But we don't. Cheyenne nodded and took off after him.

"Hey." Ember pointed at her, violet eyes narrowed. "Be careful."

Cheyenne nodded and shot another brief glance at the raug chief. "You too. We can compare notes afterward."

"After you." Byrd shoved Lumil forward. "Go."

The goblin woman stumbled forward and snorted. "Not for the deathflame, asshole."

"Oh, yeah? You get all shriveled and scared looking up at that hill?"

Lumil swiped the back of her hand under her nose and sniffed. "Yeah."

Byrd ran a hand over his bald head and shrugged. "Me too."

Corian and Maleshi passed the goblins, who shrank away when Corian leaned toward them to mutter, "I wouldn't be so sure it's safer down here than up there."

"Hey, screw you." Lumil gestured toward the mountaintop and let her hand smack back down against her thigh. "Nobody puts anything harmless at the top of a steep climb like that."

"Just sayin'." Corian headed for the base of the footpath after Cheyenne and L'zar.

Maleshi shook her head and started up the path right behind him. "That was less delicate than I would've expected from you."

He stopped and turned around. "You should stay here."

"What?" She chuckled, but it faded the instant she realized he was serious. "Not on your life."

With a soft hiss, Corian glanced over his shoulder at L'zar and Cheyenne, who were halfway to the first switchback. "Not a good idea when it's just the four of us."

"Well, you're the one making a big deal out of it."

"I'm the one trying not to make a big deal out of anything. We've made enough mistakes as it is."

"I'm coming with you whether you like it or not. Feel free to throw a fit all the way to the top." She gestured up the mountainside and raised her eyebrows. "We both know what L'zar's likely to try when he stands face to face with his nephew. Cheyenne may suspect it, but even if she does, she can't stop him on her own. Not yet."

"Maleshi."

"And *you* have already proven you're not willing to stand up to him, even if it were possible. I care a lot more about Cheyenne at this point than I do about your hesitation or what L'zar might or might not understand, so turn around and get your ass up this mountain."

Corian's silver eyes narrowed before he snorted and spun to climb the path.

Maleshi smirked and headed after him. "And before you say anything, yes, I know how insufferable I am."

He gave a resigned sigh and shook his head. "Not the most insufferable. I'd rather have *you* on this hike than the chaos twins down there."

She glanced down the hillside at Lumil and Byrd, who'd started another round of bickering, though it was whispered and faint and they hadn't started hitting each other yet. "I wonder if they see it that way? You think it's a good call to mess with their heads like that?"

"It was either that or send them both to meet the deathflame, General. If I scared them long enough to keep them from deciding for themselves, it's worth it. Trust me, if you'd spent centuries with those goblins Earthside, only to suffer their constant nagging on your first return home, you'd feel very much the same way."

"But I wouldn't call this home, *ma gairín.*"

"Me neither." Corian lifted his gaze to see the back of L'zar's shoe vanish around the corner where the path turned around the side of the mountain. "Not anymore."

CHAPTER FORTY

Cheyenne pushed herself up the steep rise. When the path curved back around the mountain again, she looked down to find the rest of their rebel group right where she'd left them, staring up at her and L'zar and the nightstalkers. *I give it five more minutes, then they'll get bored. Or they won't be able to see us anymore.*

She looked at the top of the hill, which was more of a mountain now that she saw how much more there was to go. *We're gonna be a while.*

"You good?" Corian asked from behind her.

"Yeah. Just taking it all in."

L'zar stopped at the curve of the switchback heading in the opposite direction and suggested, "You should keep your eyes and your attention that way." He pointed at the peak. "Right now, the only thing that matters is up there waiting for us."

Cheyenne kept climbing. "He's not a thing, L'zar."

"Yes, I know. You're the first to jump to everyone else's defense but mine, aren't you?"

"So far, you're the only one I have to defend against."

Behind her, Corian shook his head but remained silent. Maleshi trailed her fingers along the tops of the tall, pale grasses tinged with purple growing along the path.

"I've never attacked you, Cheyenne."

"I wasn't talking about me." *Just every other magical who trusts him too much and can't see L'zar's lunatic sucker-punch until they're on the ground.*

"Have I hurt anyone?" L'zar chuckled. "I mean, *really* hurt anyone. We're talking about since you and I have gotten the chance to get to know one another."

"We've already been over this." Cheyenne's foot slipped on the loose dirt of the path and sent a wave of gravel and dust down the mountainside. *Focus.* "There are plenty of situations where nothing is as bad as hurting everyone around you, just like saying nothing is lying through your teeth."

"Ah. You're still focused on my lack of action, is that it?"

She heard Corian's hesitant breath behind her but kept after her father up the trail. *If he thinks I'm talking about them, that's his problem.* "Yes, and I'll have a problem with it until you decide to step in and do something. Not because it's part of your plan, L'zar, and not because it serves your twisted purpose."

"Don't speak of my purpose like you have any idea what it is!" L'zar stopped and glared down at her from the next level of the trail above. "You don't see the way this all plays out, Cheyenne. If you want me to treat you as an equal, quit running your mouth like a child."

"Hey, I'm not the one who stayed up all night getting wasted and almost ripped the whole raug city out of bed to shut me up." Cheyenne put her hands on her hips and returned her father's burning gaze. "You wanna throw names around and call me a child? Great. I can hold up a mirror, L'zar. That's what kids are for, right?"

The drow thief stared at her, then his gaze flicked to Corian and Maleshi. The nightstalkers had stopped to watch the argument, and the fact that they had witnesses seemed to snap L'zar back into the present. "You excel at reflecting all my pet peeves right back at me." A humorless chuckle escaped him. "But you have no idea what I'm thinking or what I have planned. Don't talk to me like you do."

"Why won't you tell me?" Cheyenne spread her arms. "Let me in on the secret plan you've been off in your own world thinking about for the last two days, huh?"

He cocked his head, then let a slow smile bloom on his face. "Where would the fun be in that, huh? You'll know when you're meant to know, just like everyone else."

L'zar picked up his hurried pace up the mountainside, and Cheyenne snorted. "Yeah, everyone except you."

"Let him have his fun, kid." Corian shrugged. "Everything else worked the way it was supposed to when we got to the Heart. Well, mostly. In the end, what needed to happen happened. If he wants to keep his secrets, we'll wait together until he's ready to share."

Cheyenne stopped and turned to frown at the nightstalker. "So *you* don't know what he's got cooking up for his nephew either?"

The nightstalker blinked.

"He won't lie to you," Maleshi said. "But he's not gonna come out and say it."

"Interesting."

"No, it's not." Corian scowled and trudged toward the switchback, quickly gaining on the halfling. "And don't look at me like that and say, 'Interesting.' I don't have to tell you who you remind me of when you do that."

"Plenty of family traits I have no control over, I guess." When Corian grunted and shot her a warning look, Cheyenne spun to head up the hill behind her father. *Maybe I did just pull a L'zar, but I can read between the lines with the rest of them. If Corian doesn't have any clue what the drow's got up his sleeve, we all need to be a lot more careful.*

She looked up the mountain at the drow thief, who'd stopped to put his hands on his hips and take a deep breath, gazing out over Nor'ieth like he took this hike all the time to clear his head and get the endorphins pumping. Cheyenne snorted. *He could probably conjure his own endorphins if he wanted to.*

Half an hour later, they reached the first leveling-out of the mountain, though they still had another six yards at least until they reached the peak. Cheyenne squinted against the sun blazing down on them and could barely make out what looked like another Grecian temple above them. The white stone glistened in the sunlight and blocked out whatever else was up there.

When she looked down the way they'd come, Corian and Maleshi followed her gaze. "They're all still down there."

"Probably waiting for one of us to fall off or for the top of the mountain to explode." Corian heaved himself up the particularly steep switchback and nodded at Cheyenne to continue. "Can't stop now."

"Did something happen?" Cheyenne looked at Maleshi, who wouldn't meet her gaze.

"Not yet." Corian gestured up the path for her to keep moving. "And it won't if we stay here talking about it."

"Wow. Somebody's in a mood."

"It's definitely not the mood for figuring out how many different ways I can say keep going."

Cheyenne scowled at the nightstalker and nodded slowly. "Got it."

"Cheyenne, I'm just—"

"No, it's fine. If anyone can spot the signs of a magical about to lose their shit, I can. I hope you cool off before we need your head back in whatever game he's playing." She nodded at L'zar, who was busy pulling himself up over the lip of the mountain peak when the footpath just stopped.

"I'm fine, kid."

"Good." Cheyenne headed after her father. *It's reassuring to see someone else who's frustrated by L'zar and his secret plans. I wish he picked a better time to let me see it.*

She reached the end of the path and glanced up at the overhanging ledge of earth, the soil dry and crumbling, with bits of grass and protruding roots dangling toward her face. The second she got a good grip on the ledge with one hand, L'zar loomed over the edge and blotted out the sun.

"Jeeze!" Cheyenne stepped backward, away from him and his glowing golden eyes. "What?"

L'zar slowly extended a hand and grinned. "Thought you might want some help up."

"Uh-huh." Narrowing her eyes, she gripped the ledge again with one hand and accepted his help with the other. She kicked once against the loose earth and let him pull her up the rest of the way.

"There. And here we are."

As soon as he released her hand, Cheyenne wiped her palm on the outside of her trenchcoat, then stuck both hands in her pockets. "And there *he* is."

She'd been right about the white stone temple at the center of the mountaintop plateau, which still glistened under the sun and cast a glare in every direction. It was a lot easier to see what was inside the temple, which only had four stone pillars, a stone base, and a stone roof. There were no walls, curtains draped around the pillars, or an altar. Just a magical sitting cross-legged on the stone, his back turned toward them and his bone-white hair fluttering in the breeze.

Corian and Maleshi quickly climbed up over the ledge and stopped beside L'zar and Cheyenne. The general dusted off her hands and cocked her head. "Hell of a climb just for this."

"We're not finished yet." L'zar stepped silently toward the temple, his hands clasped behind his back as he considered the best way to introduce himself to the younger drow deep in mediation. He never got the chance.

"Welcome." The other drow's voice was soft, almost emotionless, but it didn't contain the same numerous tones as Yilas'.

L'zar stopped and studied his nephew's back. "Thank you."

The younger drow stood in one fluid motion without using his hands and turned to face his visitors.

Cheyenne's eyes widened; the face staring back at her looked exactly like L'zar's, only younger, thinner, and the wrong color. His skin had faded from the usual slate-gray drow color to pale, washed-out violet, but the gray was still there beneath the surface. His eyes, though, were so much lighter than her own, they were almost yellow. Even then, a soft glow emanated from them as Ba'rael Verdys' son swept his slow, discerning gaze over the four magicals who'd come to speak to him.

No way this is a trick of the light, even if I can't tell what color his eyes are. The halfling shot Corian a sidelong glance and whispered from the corner of her mouth, "That's not normal. Right?"

The nightstalker shook his head. "Not beyond these walls. But for Nor'ieth?" He shrugged and met her gaze for a split second before returning his attention to L'zar.

Great. Too much time spent in this secret plane, and we'll all get the color drained right out of us. Cheyenne took a step forward but couldn't bring herself to move any closer.

L'zar dipped his head and grinned at his nephew. "You saw us coming?"

The light-skinned drow passed his gaze over L'zar and returned it immediately to Cheyenne. "We see many things."

He talks like the olforím too. We're not dealing with a drow at this point. The halfling swallowed.

"I'm sure you do, all the way up here." L'zar looked over his shoulder. "Great view."

His nephew kept staring at Cheyenne.

"What's your name?" the Weaver asked.

"We are called Aut Na'mor."

"Sure. When the *olforím* address you." L'zar chuckled. "I mean your real name. The one you were born with."

The light-skinned drow's pale yellow eyes moved slowly back toward his uncle. "We have no name."

"Ha." Turning around to fix Cheyenne and the nightstalkers with a growing smile, L'zar gestured at Ba'rael's secret heir. "He has no name."

Corian rubbed the back of his neck and shot Cheyenne a quick glance before stepping forward to join the drow thief. "Do you know who we are?"

"If you're referring to the names you use for yourselves, then no." The drow eyed Corian now, his wide eyes and blank expression looking so much like L'zar's when he'd cloaked himself in magic that Cheyenne had a sudden urge to slap a reaction into him. "If you're asking if we know *what* you are, we have our suspicions."

"Oh, indeed?" L'zar blinked at his nephew, tilting his head from side to side as his grin widened. "What do you suspect we are?"

"Telling you would not change the truth one way or the other."

"Ah. I would still very much like to hear it from you."

Ba'rael's son blinked slowly and stared at Cheyenne. "No."

L'zar chuckled. "No. Well, then. Is there anything you *will* agree to discuss? Seeing as we climbed all this way to speak to you."

Cheyenne frowned at her father and tried to ignore the strange itch spreading across her face beneath her cousin's intent stare. *This guy's been brainwashed, and L'zar thinks it's one big joke.*

"Hello?" L'zar leaned toward his nephew and flicked his fingers in front of the other drow's face. "Should I repeat the question?"

"Her." The light-skinned drow barely lifted his chin as he studied Cheyenne. "We will agree to discuss her."

"Oh." L'zar tilted his head at Cheyenne. "Your cousin has taken a certain interest, it seems."

"Cousin." Ba'rael's son slowly tilted his head, eyeing Cheyenne again. His unsettling gaze made her eyes itch too.

"Yeah, but we didn't come here to talk about me." The halfling walked slowly toward them, frowning at the complete lack of reaction on her cousin's face. *Totally insane. There's nothing there.* "We're here to talk about you. Or to you. About your home."

The corners of the other drow's mouth twitched. "You're interested in Nor'ieth, then."

She glanced at Corian and shrugged. "Not this home. Your first one."

"We have only one existence. That is here. Cousin."

"Yeesh." Cheyenne grimaced at her father. "This isn't going the way you expected, huh?"

"I need a little time, Cheyenne."

"Yeah, I've heard that before."

L'zar shot her a warning glance, then stepped toward his nephew and placed a hand on the younger drow's shoulder, meaning to guide him toward the temple for a quick chat. A burst of magical energy traveled up the drow thief's arm at the contact, and his eyes widened. "Perhaps a good deal more time. But we have plenty of that, don't we?"

His nephew didn't budge, and L'zar removed his hand as if the other drow had threatened to remove it for him.

"Time belongs to itself, Weaver."

"Oh, so you *do* know me." The drow thief grinned. "Now we're getting somewhere."

CHAPTER FORTY-ONE

Ba'rael's son appraised L'zar with a slow, unamused glance. "We know the seeds you've sown and failed to nurture. We know the threads you've woven from one end to the next. We do not know *you.*"

"Hmm. Few do." L'zar clasped his hands behind his back again and dipped his head, still smiling and staring at his nephew like a starving dog staring at an untouched steak.

The same way he stared at me the first time. And the second. Not good. Cheyenne cleared her throat. "So, okay, look. Maybe you don't have a name, but it's weird calling you Lost One. Ever imagine yourself with a real name?"

"Neros." The drow blinked as if he'd emerged from lifelong amnesia. "You can call us Neros."

"Okay, that works. I'm Cheyenne. You picked up on the cousin part, so I'm pretty sure you can put those pieces together. The nightstalkers are Corian and Maleshi."

"Cheyenne." Her name whispered by Neros' lips made her shiver.

"Yep. That's me. And the grinning lunatic next to me is L'zar. My dad. Your mom's brother."

"You do not believe blood bonds with blood, Cheyenne. Why should we?"

She stared at Neros and leaned forward in surprise. "What did you say?"

"You heard us, bright one."

"Bright?" Cheyenne snorted. "Okay, I don't know what you're seeing right now. Maybe all this shiny stone and, I don't know, the altitude up here is making things look kinda funny, but I wouldn't call me—"

"Cheyenne." L'zar turned his head toward her but kept his golden eyes on his nephew.

"What?"

"Ask him if he's seen his mother when he searches through the Weave."

"You're standing right here in front of him, L'zar. Ask him yourself."

"He obviously doesn't want to talk to me."

"I wouldn't wanna talk to you either if you were asking me stupid questions."

L'zar's gaze flicked toward her. "Do it."

"We hear everything, Weaver. And we have seen the drow of which you speak." Neros' washed-out gaze settled on his uncle's face. "She is no concern of ours."

"Really?" L'zar's grin returned. "So you see Ba'rael Verdys in her last days on the O'gúl Crown, and you're not concerned."

"There is no reason for concern."

"Ah. Even when the drow who created you and sent you here, however unknowingly, will fight Cheyenne to keep that throne?"

Neros blinked slowly. "She will not."

"You've seen it?"

"This is ridiculous." Cheyenne shook her head and turned around. "Two drow talking in circles around each other. My brain can't handle it."

"Let her go." L'zar waved dismissively at his daughter. "If she wants to fill in the missing pieces on her own, Neros, that's on her. I want to hear more about what you've seen."

Neros took a deep breath, let it out slowly, and watched Cheyenne stalk across the plateau to put distance between them. "We have seen the pattern and the fray, Weaver. So have you. Everything turns, begins anew, and ends."

"What about the Crown?"

"The Crown will be the Crown. It's all the same." Neros turned his body toward Cheyenne, who caught the movement from the corner of her eye and folded her arms, trying to ignore her cousin's tingling stare. "We are all the same. Except for her."

L'zar broke into a wide grin again. "There it is."

Cheyenne turned back toward them. "Wait, what?"

"What do you see in my daughter, Neros?"

"Something different." Neros tilted his head. "Half of her does not exist in this world."

"No way." Cheyenne eyed her cousin warily, then glanced at the nightstalkers. "He can't know that. How?"

"How, indeed." L'zar's wide eyes flickered from Neros' face to the silver cuff peeking out from beneath the sleeve of Cheyenne's trenchcoat. "It seems Ur'syth's trinket only works on eyes that don't see through the Weave."

"Meaning?"

"Meaning we have an excellent opportunity to look farther than I've ever imagined." L'zar steepled his fingers and drummed them against each other. "Neros, I would very much appreciate your help in a certain matter. Or a few, now that I think about it."

The light-skinned drow stared at Cheyenne without moving.

"I've been searching for a few things that would greatly aid my cause. Our cause, of course. Cheyenne shares it with me."

She shook her head. "Don't put words in my mouth, especially not after your little warning about your purpose, L'zar."

"Whatever is said up here will remain between the five of us." The drow thief spread his arms. "I'm not telling anyone to leave, and I have no problem letting you stay. If you still want to know, that is."

"So, you're finally gonna reveal your master plan, huh?"

L'zar reached toward his nephew's face as if he meant to sweep the bone-white hair away from Neros' angular jaw, then thought better of it. His long, slender fingers curled into a loose fist, then he lowered his hand. "If Neros will join us in the conversation, of course. You'd be doing all of us a great honor."

"We will not."

L'zar gave a surprised laugh and shook his head. "Pardon?"

"We wish to speak to Cheyenne. Alone. Now."

"After that?"

"You may leave."

L'zar's eye twitched as he stared at his nephew's profile. "That's not an option."

"L'zar." Corian stepped toward him, gazing at the drow thief and his nephew. "This obviously isn't the right time."

"It is *exactly* the right time!" L'zar's shout echoed down the mountainside and sent a handful of small rocks plummeting down to the valley below.

No one else said a word, but all eyes except Neros' were fixed uncertainly on the drow thief. Neros didn't look away from Cheyenne.

With a deep breath, L'zar smoothed his hair away from his face, and his smile returned. "I have made the time, Neros. The least you can do is give me the same courtesy."

"Only Cheyenne."

The drow thief's eyes blazed with gold light, his mad grin fracturing into a furious snarl as his head trembled.

Corian moved toward him. "We'll give them a moment, and then we'll try again."

"No. Cheyenne knows nothing about the order of things, and I will have the answers I came for. Look at me!" L'zar's hand came down on Neros' shoulder again.

The light-skinned drow moved faster than any of them could see. His pale hand flicked toward L'zar with a flash of blinding white light. The concentrated magic pummeled the drow thief in the chest and sent him flying across the plateau. Corian and Maleshi were caught up in the same wave, and all three magicals hurtled over the side of the mountain with the crack of splitting stone and the ensuing rumble of debris tumbling to the valley floor.

"Hey!" Cheyenne darted toward the plateau's edge and peered over the side.

Corian and Maleshi were sliding down the mountainside on all fours, and they succeeded in bracing themselves and slowing to a stop. L'zar picked himself up off the footpath where he'd landed, a tangle of dry weeds and dead grass knotted in his hair, and snarled up at her. "I'm gonna kill him!"

"Oh, boy." Cheyenne turned back to Neros. "There's a good chance he meant that, at least until something changes his mind. Be ready when he gets back up here." She glanced at her cousin's pale hand hanging by his side and shrugged. "Not like you can't take care of yourself, obviously."

"He will not return until we allow it."

"What?" She laughed in disbelief and shook her head. "I know you guys just met, but believe me, if a prison built specifically for magicals couldn't hold him, I don't think—"

A loud thump cut her off, followed by L'zar's enraged roar from halfway down the mountain.

Cheyenne peered over the side again, and her mouth dropped open. "No shit."

L'zar stood on the other side of a shimmering wall of light, ignoring the blood pouring from his nose. He snarled and hissed, pounding the magical barrier to no effect. "Cheyenne! Tell him to take it down! Now!"

She stared at her father and slowly backed away from the edge of the plateau.

"No. Cheyenne! Don't you *dare!*" Another furious bellow escaped him, and he shot a useless burst of purple drow magic at the shimmering wall of light. It bounced back off and narrowly missed Corian's shoulder as it soared toward the other side of the valley. "*Cheyenne!*"

Neros snapped his fingers, and the top of the mountain quieted. Even the thin whistle of the wind through the temple of white stone was silenced, and Cheyenne found herself smiling when she turned around to face her cousin. "You know, it was starting to sink in that I've got some pretty big, bloody, not exactly comfortable drow shoes to fill after all this, but I think L'zar Verdys finally met his match. And it's not me."

"You looked pleased."

"Well," she said, chuckling, "I'd be lying if I said it wasn't satisfying." *Just to watch someone else hit that drow with his own medicine and finally shut him up.* Folding her arms, Cheyenne studied the empty plateau and the pristinely kept temple in the center. "You know he's gonna try again, right? He won't take no for an answer, so he'll keep beating the problem until it finally gives up. That's what he does."

"The Weaver is no concern of ours either, cousin." Neros' mouth flickered into a small smile, and he spread his arm to gesture at the temple. "Come sit with us. We have questions for you."

"Oh." Cheyenne spared the edge of the mountaintop a fleeting glance, then slowly made her way toward the light-skinned drow staring at her with wide eyes. "Any chance you could drop the talking in the second person? It's a little weird."

"It makes you uncomfortable."

"Well, there are varying degrees of discomfort." She shrugged. "You know what? Never mind. I'm the last person who should be trying to change anybody else just 'cause they're a little different. You talk about yourself however you want."

When she reached Neros' extended arm, he lowered it and turned with her toward the temple. "Thank you."

"Sure. Wait. It's just the way you talk, right? Like there isn't more than one of you in there?"

For the first time, her cousin's mouth drew up farther than a tiny jerk, and he favored her with a full, amused smile. "That does not have one answer, but I will try to explain."

"That's a good start, I guess. I'll take it." Trying not to shy away from the growing tingle of strong magic around her and the returning tang of vinegar and berries in her mouth, Cheyenne stepped onto the temple floor with her cousin raised by *olforím* and sat when he gestured for her to sit.

The drow no one knows about has more power in his finger than L'zar and I put together. Would that still be the case if he came with us?

She waited for a moment longer beneath Neros' intent gaze as he sat directly opposite her, then looked down into her lap and took a deep breath. "You ever wonder about leaving this place? Getting out into the rest of the world instead of being stuck here for however long it's been?"

"Four hundred years. That is what they tell us." He chuckled. "What they tell *me*."

"Right. Long time." Cheyenne leaned away a little when her cousin leaned toward her. *Not long enough to learn about personal space, appar-ently.* "But you didn't answer my question."

"I want your answers first, Cheyenne. Then I will give you mine."

"Okay." She spread her arms and tried to smile at him, but the closeness of his intense magic made her face feel tight and not quite there at all. "Ask away."

CHAPTER FORTY-TWO

On the side of the mountain, L'zar roared again and pounded his fists against the shimmering wall of Neros' spell. "No. I won't be thrown out like that and forced to *wait* while they— Cheyenne! Undo this. Do you hear me?"

"The whole valley can hear you." Corian sat cross-legged on the footpath and studied the wall of light. "Apparently, you're being ignored."

"Not when I don't agree to it," L'zar snarled.

"That's part of being ignored."

"No one asked for your useless commentary, *vae shra'ni.*" The drow stalked along the path and let off another burst of purple fire. It crackled against the shield and again ricocheted off.

Corian leaned sideways and snatched the violet flames with a silver-glowing hand. He closed his fists around L'zar's magic and dampened it, then he flicked the transformed metal star with four points into the air and caught it again. "We have two choices."

L'zar slammed a fist into the magical wall. "Shut up."

"We can sit here and spend the rest of our energy fighting a spell like *that*, which doesn't seem to have any weak points."

"Everything has a weak point."

"Or we can allow what's happening up there to unfold and go over the details with Cheyenne later."

"No. Cheyenne is not prepared to handle something this delicate on her own."

"Of course." Maleshi, who stood in front of the closest switchback, nodded. "The *Cu'ón* is far better trained in the art of delicacy."

He hissed at her and turned away again to pace back along the trail. "I don't even know why you came with us, General."

"Would it surprise you to hear I enjoy the company?"

Corian snorted and immediately wiped the smile from his face when L'zar spun again.

"Not *my* company." The drow looked at the nightstalkers. "No one enjoys that."

"I know you're speaking from personal experience, L'zar, but I'll say the same thing your daughter told you." Maleshi's silver eyes glowed, reflecting the shimmering white wall. "Don't put words in my mouth."

"And don't think I don't see what's going on here." L'zar sneered at Corian. "You two have found an awful lot of free time lately, haven't you?"

Corian cocked his head and fixed the drow with an unwavering gaze. "We're back in Ambar'ogúl, L'zar. You knew the risks associated with your return."

"Those were risks I counted on, *vae shra'ni*. If I'd known the risks of letting two feral *vaga* enter the same room, I wouldn't have allowed it."

"That's going too far." Corian remained seated on the path, though he straightened from where he'd hunched over his crossed legs. "We've already spent more time on this side than either of us expected. You and Cheyenne have come to a deeper understanding of each other in the last few days, which I can honestly say I didn't expect either. But it's starting to show."

"Ha." L'zar's hands formed open claws, and his low growl rose into another furious roar. "My own daughter. The *mór úcare* everyone else—"

"Careful." Maleshi clenched her jaw, her nostrils flaring. "If you want her to continue on this path, I'd avoid the Crown's name for her."

"I'll call her whatever I want. She's *my* daughter."

"And our last hope for finishing this Cycle now, before things get any more complicated."

L'zar glared at the general and wagged a long slate-gray finger at her. "You've grown too bold on your return, Hi'et. No one restored your rank. Don't forget who made it possible for you to step foot in Hangivol without having your furry head ripped right off your flea-ridden shoulders."

Maleshi rolled her eyes and gazed at the valley.

Corian watched the drow stalk back and forth. "You still haven't had enough time to recover from the Weave."

L'zar lifted a clawed hand again like he meant to rip something out of the air in front of him. "That bane of my existence has nothing to do with this."

"There's no use arguing with him, *vae shra'ni*." Maleshi shrugged. "Might as well let him burn himself out."

"What do *you* know of burning, Hi'et?" L'zar hissed at her. "Beyond what brought you back to my *Nós Ani's* side?"

"That's enough." Corian stood and stepped between L'zar and Maleshi, blocking the drow from storming toward the general. "Tell me what you meant to do up there with Neros."

L'zar snarled and stared into the nightstalker's glowing eyes.

"We still have twelve days, brother." Corian leaned sideways to cut the drow off when L'zar tried to sneak past him. "That's plenty of time for Cheyenne to coax whatever information you need from your nephew."

"I don't want his information. I want his *eyes*."

"His eyes."

L'zar hissed and whirled away from the nightstalker, opting to pace the other half the trail instead.

"L'zar, I can't do anything for you if you don't tell me what I need to know."

"You don't need to know anything."

"But it will help." Corian said, "Let me help you carry it. You've shared every single step up to this point with me—everything since the beginning. I don't know what you think has changed, but I stand by my vow and the binding. You know that."

"Yes. You're bound to me no matter what I do or don't tell you." L'zar stormed toward the nightstalker again and thrust a finger at

Corian. "I should have bound you to my command as well. Then you'd have no choice but to shut up."

"You need to calm down."

"You need to stop being such a pathetic waste and choose where your loyalties lie!" L'zar's gaze swung toward Maleshi. "That's what this is about, isn't it? You want to know my plans for a final time so you and the scourge of the Night and Circle can take what's mine. You want all the threads you could never touch to wrap yourselves together within them." Spittle flew from the drow's mouth as he shouted in Corian's face. "I see *everything*, Corian! Everything except your choices because you haven't made them yet!"

Corian stood firmly against the verbal assault and lifted his chin. "You think I'm choosing whether or not to betray you?"

"Well, I'll know when you do. Try to go behind my back again, *vae shra'ni*, and neither of you will make it out of this alive."

"Stop blowing this out of proportion, L'zar." Maleshi stepped toward him and ignored Corian's warning glance. "Corian chooses his vow to you over everything else, time and time again."

"You're trying to undermine me. Both of you!" L'zar's wild eyes rolled furiously in his head, and he swiped at the empty air in front of him as if trying to clear away a swarm of gnats. "After everything I've done for you, this is how you repay me?"

"Stop." Corian tilted his head in warning. "You're not thinking clearly."

The breath went out of L'zar all at once as he gazed at the thick magic in the air only he could see. "I am unraveling."

"L'zar…"

The drow burst into enhanced speed and knocked Corian against the side of the mountain as he raced down the path. Maleshi staggered against the edge of the switchback, her black hair whipping around her head as the blur of gray and white zipped from side to side and finally darted to the valley floor before disappearing into a grove of white-trunked trees on the north side of Nor'ieth. Two dozen small black birds squawked and took off from their perches in panicked flight. The entire valley echoed with L'zar's ragged, curdled scream of rage, and then there was nothing.

Corian sagged against the side of the mountain, dirt and dislodged stones raining down around him. "I knew it."

"Don't do that." Maleshi brushed her hair from her face and fixed him with a gentle gaze. "None of this is your fault."

"Not now. But I left him to his own mind for far too long." Dropping his head back against the mountainside, Corian stared at the sky. "I should have questioned him sooner. Long before he started questioning everything else."

"He's overwhelmed, *ma gairín*." Maleshi moved slowly toward him, stopped, and offered her hand. "Being here, of all places, isn't helping his frame of mind, either. You know that."

"Just one layer on top of the next, huh?" He chuckled wryly when she nodded, then finally grasped her hand and let her pull him to his feet. "I don't know what world he was made to inhabit, Maleshi. But it wasn't this one."

"Or maybe this world wasn't meant to contain him. Hm?" She gave him a wan smile and flicked a patch of dirt off his shoulder. "Once we leave this plane, he'll clear his head. You'll guide him like you always have, and we'll finish this. Whatever happens after that won't matter nearly as much as this, will it?"

"He wasn't wrong. That he's unraveling. I can't read the Weave, but I don't have to. I know he shouldn't have come back here. If we're not quick enough, we'll lose him entirely, and making the crossing Earthside again won't do a thing to help."

Maleshi replied, "Then I suggest we let the *Aranél* at the top of this mountain do what *she* came here to do. We'll guide her too. And judging by the surprising intensity of L'zar's most recent outburst, I'm willing to bet he'll write this whole thing off as a bad dream."

"He won't wake up from a psychotic break. Not one caused by an overload of magic that doesn't belong to him."

"It does belong to him. He's made it part of him, and no matter what the *Sorren Gán* might want from L'zar after this, there's no pulling them apart. Cheyenne wouldn't have half the power she does if that weren't the case." The general turned to head down the path. "I'm finished with hiking for today, *vae shra'ni*. Come find me when you're ready to talk about something else."

He snorted. "Like what?"

"Anything but L'zar and his madness."

CHAPTER FORTY-THREE

Ember stared at the white stone buildings rising around her, trying to ignore the thick taste of vinegar filling her mouth. *Not the flavor I would've paired with more magic than exists in all of Richmond.*

The crawler moved slowly beneath her as her guiding hand swiped across the control panel. The machine's metal legs had only cracked into a building's outer wall once, and when she'd recovered from the startling sound, she forced herself to pay much closer attention to where she was going and how much room the bulky contraption needed.

A strange, lilting tune filtered through the buildings in front of her. Multiple voices rose at once in a wordless song. Ember slowed the crawler to a stop and cocked her head. *That's the weirdest song I've ever heard. Like someone gave a saxophone to a whale.*

White light moved around the corner of the closest building before fading away to reveal one of the *olforim* standing calmly in front of the fae girl. Ember swallowed. "Hello."

The woman dipped her bald head and smiled, her hands clasped in front of her between the draping sleeves of her sheer, glowing robe. "We can offer you aid with your difficulty, fae. If that is what you wish."

"My difficulty, huh?" Ember chuckled and glanced around the otherwise empty grouping of buildings. "Which one?"

"The root." The *olforim* woman gestured toward her with a wide sweep of her arm. "We can help you restore it."

That didn't narrow it down. Maybe she meant all of me. Ember cleared her throat. "The root as in my magic?"

"Yes."

"You can help me get my magic back. Is that what you're saying?"

"Yes."

A barking laugh escaped the fae girl, and she clapped a hand over her mouth before pulling herself together. "No way."

"Do you accept?"

"Yeah, I accept!" Ember grinned and spread her arms. "What do I have to do?"

"Follow us." The woman turned and walked fluidly back through the buildings toward the side of the valley filled with temples.

"Just follow. Yep. I can do that." Her fingers trembled in excitement, and she swiped the wrong command on the crawler's control panel twice, nearly throwing herself from the machine in the process before she sent the eight-legged O'gúleesh wheelchair scrabbling after the *olforim*.

When they emerged from the cluster of white stone buildings, Cazerel turned away from his conversation with his warriors and raised a hand. "Healer. Are you enjoying Nor'ieth?"

"Ask me when I come back, Chief." Ember waved at him and quickly looked for the *olforim* woman leading her across the valley. "But I have a feeling the answer's gonna be hell, yes."

"I'll come with you." Cazerel handed the drinking gourd to one of his warriors and stepped after the crawler.

"I got it, Cazerel." Ember tossed her hand in the air and didn't dare look back at him. *This feels like a one-shot deal. Don't wanna screw it up by getting lost.* "Don't need a bodyguard against my own magic, thanks."

The raug chief stopped and blinked at her in surprise.

"Let it go this once, huh, *Zokri?*" Lumil took a crunching bite of a round green fruit that sprayed purple juice and red light as she chewed. "The fae girl's stronger than she looks. And how bad could it be? I mean, really. We're in Nor'ieth surrounded by *olforim*. None of this is supposed to exist. Doesn't leave a lotta room for foul play, know what I'm sayin'?"

"No." Cazerel blinked again and stared after Ember and the crawler, lurching across the valley. "I do not."

"Well, trust me. She's fine." Lumil bit into the fruit again, then stared at it and shook her head. "Man, these things are delicious. You try one yet? No? Well, damn, Chief. Forget the fae and grab yourself one of these. I'm tellin' ya, they don't grow stuff like this anywhere but here, I guess." Munching happily, the goblin woman stalked away to join Byrd in front of a huge basket of food grown in Nor'ieth's soil.

Cazerel scratched his head, grunted, and rejoined his warriors.

***

Ember's heartbeat pounded in her head as magic thickened around her. *All this power in one place? If this doesn't help me at least a little, I don't know what will.*

The *olforim* woman led her through different temples scattered across the valley, where the sounds of the old-school village—the singing, conversation, and raug laughter—were almost inaudible. Birds twittered in the trees lining the outside of the valley, and then the woman stopped and faced the fae girl.

"Your contraption must remain."

"Oh. You know what?" Ember slapped the sides of the crawler and spread her arms. "I'm done with the contraption anyway. So as soon as I figure how to get out of it. *Whoa.*"

White light engulfed her. The *olforim* woman smiled gently as she flicked her fingers away from the crawler, and Ember rose slowly from the seat depression before floating through the air toward the temple behind her guide.

"Okay. Kinda silly of me to think I'm the only one who can levitate myself." Ember tried to keep her arms relatively still, but hovering five feet above the ground made her flap her arms awkwardly as if that would keep her from falling. *You're making an ass of yourself, Em. If she can move you around and be graceful about it, you can take it gracefully and act like you know what you're doing. You're a fae, for chrissakes.*

So she focused on her thin shadow creeping across the white floor of the temple. The *olforim* woman lowered her gently to the cool stone, and Ember cleared her throat. "Thanks. That was helpful."

The tall, thin white-glowing magical stepped in front of the fae girl and dipped her head, clasping her three-fingered hands in front of herself again. "When you find what is already yours, take it."

"Okay. What am I looking for, exactly?" Ember glanced around the empty temple and raised an eyebrow. "Because believe me, I've already tried everything I could think of to…and she's walking away. Got it."

Ember shifted her hips and grabbed first one shin, then the other to pull them toward her in something resembling a cross-legged position. *So, I'll sit here and look for what's already mine. Excellent plan. If I had any idea what that was.*

A soft rustling sound on her right made her look over her shoulder. "Oh, hey. If you came to watch the fae show, I don't think there's… Wow. What is that?"

Two other *olforim* floated across the temple floor toward her, smiling and gazing at her with creepy light-blue eyes that never blinked. One of them held a silver pitcher and a small silver cup, and the other carried a small basket of O'gúleesh produce.

Ember glanced at the hems of their robes and pressed her lips together. *They have to be floating like I used to. I can't see their feet, but those are* definitely *shadows.*

"For you." A woman with a thin, intricate tattoo snaking up the side of her neck in faint violet ink knelt in front of the fae girl and set both pitcher and cup on the temple floor.

"Thanks." Ember stared at the magical's luminous eyes and couldn't think of anything else to say. When she stood, her compatriot knelt in front of Ember as well and set the basket beside the pitcher. He dipped his head and gave her a gentle, knowing smile before rising again in one fluid motion. "This is a lot of food. Anyone wanna join me?"

"We must decline." The tattooed *olforim* pressed her fingertips together and pointed them first at her own chest, then at Ember's. "To aid you in your rediscovery. Take all the time you need."

"Okay. I'm still a little fuzzy on the details." Ember sighed, her shoulders sagging as she watched the two *olforim* float away without a word and disappear around a thick pillar supporting a neighboring temple. "It's easy to walk away from a fae who can't run after you, isn't it?"

Shaking her head, she looked down at the pitcher and the basket of brightly colored O'gúleesh vegetables. *At least I hope they're vegetables. Or fruit. As long as it doesn't have eyes or move around on its own.*

Ember eyed the basket warily. "So far, so good, but I'm not even hungry." She closed her eyes, took a deep breath, and let it slowly out again. "Find what's already mine. I'm looking for my own magic. In a temple. And apparently, that doesn't qualify me for a trip to the mental ward."

When she opened her eyes again, she studied every carved surface of the pillars in front of her, then focused her attention on the perfectly smooth white stone floor. *Not gonna find it in a chunk of rock. I think.*

A roaring bellow of rage burst from the other side of the valley, echoing through the stone temples and within the high natural walls around Nor'ieth. Ember scrunched her nose and looked over her left shoulder toward the sound. A flock of birds darted out of a grove of trees, nothing more than tiny specks from this far away. *I've never heard him scream, but I'd bet the rest of my magic that was L'zar.*

She snorted, and the snort grew into a chuckle of disbelief. "This whole thing is ridiculous. This place. This food. Finding the *root*. And now a screaming drow."

Laughing, Ember leaned forward to sift through the produce in the basket and pulled out a pale-blue something that looked more like an apple than anything else. She sniffed it twice, tentatively poked it with the tip of her tongue, and lowered it to watch for movement. *No eyes. Tastes like maple syrup, but that's not the worst thing.*

The blue fruit's skin burst and sent cold juice dribbling down her chin when she took a bite. Humming, Ember chewed and gazed around the temple. Her stomach growled fiercely, and she gave it a gentle pat before swallowing her mouthful. *Guess I was wrong.*

Two minutes later, she'd eaten the entire blue maple-apple and had already gone through half a sprig of small berries that tasted like black licorice. Sucking the gooey fruit out of her teeth, she filled the cup from the silver pitcher.

She downed the whole thing and set it gently on the stone beside her. "Hey. These guys know how to set up a guest. Clean water. Privacy. Little bit of dancing fruit."

Ember stopped and blinked at the sprig of black berries in her hand. She lifted it toward her face and squinted. The berries dangling at the bottom swung back and forth, glowing intermittently like flashing Christmas lights. "No."

She swung the berries toward the basket and stopped when the light-colored woven material shrank and grew. Blinking slowly, Ember dropped the berries on the top of the produce pile, and beaded strands of bright-yellow light puffed out of the basket like dust. The lights rose steadily into the air, blinking and bobbing around the girl's head before spreading out through the temple.

"Like flies. Firefruit. Flying fruit fire." Ember burst out laughing, and she couldn't stop it even when she clapped both hands over her mouth. *Holy shit. Did they drug me?*

She lunged toward the pitcher and almost knocked it over, temporarily distracted by her outstretched fingers flapping in front of her like bird's wings. *I'm losing it.*

Her hand wrapped around the handle of the pitcher, and she drew it closer to take another sniff. Her mouth watered, but she set the pitcher aside and blinked at the dancing yellow lights swirling in front of her. *Psychedelic fruit. I'm tripping my ass off, and they call that fixing my little difficulty?*

With a strangled laugh, Ember rocked backward, gasped, and steadied herself with both hands pressed into the cold white stone. *Okay, okay. Don't freak out, find what's already mine.*

The lights in front of her coalesced into a shape that looked a lot like her. Two pale-violet eyes formed in the center of the blinking lights, then the fae-shaped figure raised one arm and swept it through the dancing lights. Ember's mouth fell open, and she raised her own arm, which felt like it weighed a million pounds.

As soon as she extended her finger, the dancing lights burst away from the fae-shaped figure. They raced toward Ember's fingertip and tingled up her arm and across her neck. *That's something.*

She closed her eyes and tried to focus on the buzzing tingle of *someone's* magic racing across her skin. Her head buzzed too. *That's just the fruit.*

With a final bright burst, the yellow dancing lights swirled faster and faster, first around Ember's body and then outward until they filled the entire temple. Her vision narrowed, darkening at the corners, and all the color around her dimmed except for one pulsing strand of lights.

No way. When I find what's already mine.

The single strand of yellow lights that stretched farther away from her than she could see flared brighter the closer her outstretched fingers approached. Then she tapped the thread, and it flashed from yellow to violet. A small gasp escaped her, then Ember pinched the thread of purple light and pulled.

Warm, buzzing energy raced up her arm and bloomed inside her chest, filling every part of her until she thought she'd explode with purple light and fae magic. "Oh, yeah. Ha! It worked!"

She took a shuddering breath and looked down at her arms and chest, pulsing with the purple light. Even her legs, legs she hadn't moved more than half an inch in weeks, glowed. The blinking purple strands raced up and down her thighs and calves, disappearing beneath her shoes and rippling back up again in an endless circle.

Holy shit. That's my magic, healing me!

Ember's mouth went dry as she stared at her legs. Then she felt the buzz warming her unused muscles and laughed. *I'm gonna walk again. Jesus, how do I know this?*

Her stomach heaved. *It's gonna happen.*

She wiped sweat off her forehead and took slow, steady breaths, focusing on her legs. *I had no idea I could do this. I can do this, however long it takes.*

The fae girl lurched forward and leaned sideways right before she vomited glowing blue fruit skin and half-chewed berries all over the temple floor. Breathing heavily, she waited for the next wave. When it didn't come, Ember wiped her mouth with the back of a hand and laughed.

"They drugged me into finding my magic. And," she said, grinning, "I'm totally okay with it."

CHAPTER FORTY-FOUR

On the top of the mountain, Neros leaned toward Cheyenne and narrowed his eyes as he scanned her face for the millionth time. "Why are you so different?"

"We went over that." She scooted back across the floor and dropped her hands into her lap. "I *am* different. At least, different from everyone else in *this* world. Apparently, halflings are an Earthside myth like Nor'ieth and the *olforím*. Now we know it's all based on truth, huh?"

"No."

Cheyenne squinted at him and cocked her head. "No, the myths aren't based on truth, or no, something else I missed?"

"Your human blood is only part of what makes you different, Cheyenne. There's something else." Neros frowned, his bone-white eyebrows darkening his pale features in an odd play of shadow and sunlight. "Something I haven't seen before."

"Well, that might also be the *Sorren Gán*'s magic that L'zar tricked himself into getting, I guess. Then he gave it to me."

"You have so many answers, cousin. None of them tell me what I want to know."

"And you have a lot of questions." With a snort, Cheyenne folded her arms. "I don't know what else you to tell you, Neros. I don't have all the answers. I can't see whatever it is you and L'zar see. Not even sure I want to. And by the way, how are *you* able to read the Weave? L'zar had to almost die and pledge his unending loyalty to a creature that doesn't give a shit about him, but I have a feeling you took a different route."

Neros spread his arms and gave her a blank, distracted smile. "We are here."

She clicked her tongue. "And you were doing so well with the first-person pronouns."

"Not just me." Her cousin gestured toward the valley with a sweep of his arm, his fingers folding in on themselves at the end. "All of us. The *olforim*, Nor'ieth, the light. Everything weaves together. If I were to leave this place, I would still be here."

"Hmm." Cheyenne nodded slowly. *Play along, and maybe he'll say something that makes sense.* "So you *can* leave."

His pale eyes narrowed. "Why would I?"

"Well, to start, there's the fairly large, looming issue of your mother, who's as crazy as L'zar but kinda still has a foot in the door when it comes to plastering her crazy all over Ambar'ogúl. And keeping me from fixing everything she's broken in the process." *Assuming she doesn't refuse my so-called terms and goes the kill Cheyenne route instead.*

"Nothing is broken."

"See, that's where I think we're hitting a disconnect. You haven't stepped out of this place once since you got here, have you?"

"Why would I?"

Cheyenne closed her eyes and forced herself not to rub her temples in frustration. "Yeah, you already asked that. And I don't have an answer for you, because I'm not...whoa, whoa." She jerked away. His pale fingers were floating through the white hair draping over her shoulders. "What are you doing?"

"I can't *see* you."

"You can see me fine, and I'd seriously appreciate it if you continued to see me from at least two feet away. At *least*."

Neros sighed, another frown flickering across his forehead. "Whatever you carry with you, Cheyenne, it is enough."

"Well, thanks." She shrugged. "I'm all for a healthy level of confidence, but I'm not sure that's gonna help me much against the Crown. She's been poisoning this world, Neros. Stealing magic from others to fuel her own. Spilling the leftover waste as far as it'll go. It's crossing over the Border now too."

"I don't care about any of that." The pale drow waved her off with a scowl, then ran his gaze across her shoulder and down her arm. "Tell me about your beginning."

"My beginning?" *I'm not sitting here, spilling my guts to this guy about the terrifying, lonely first years of my life. And I'm definitely not saying a word about Bianca.* "Anything specific?"

"Everything." Neros' eyes widened, and he leaned toward her again. "Your first memory. Your first thought. What you felt when you saw yourself in the mirror and realized it was *you* staring back through your eyes."

Cheyenne chuckled and cocked her head. "Sorry, man. I have a fairly good memory, but it doesn't go that far back."

"Why not?"

She frowned and pursed her lips. "In general, most of us don't remember any of those things."

"I do." Neros leaned forward even farther and placed his hands on the white stone floor. "I remember the doorway opening to me for the first time. I remember the light touching down from the Weave to wake me up. I remember *you*."

"Nice try. We never met before this."

"And still." He looked quickly back and forth from one of her golden eyes to the other and drew a long, loud breath. "I can't find what binds you."

"Hey, seriously. Cut it out." She slapped his hand away when he reached toward her mouth. "That's another thing, man. You can't crawl up to someone and start touching them."

"Does it hurt you?"

"What? No. It's creepy, and I like my personal space, okay?"

"Space." Neros withdrew his hand and stroked his pale, hairless chin. "How much?"

"Okay." Cheyenne pushed to her feet and spread her arms as she stepped away from him. "Like, this much. At all times. What is that, four feet?"

The pale drow placed his hands in his lap and stared up at her. "You said two."

"Yeah, I know. It doubles every time you cross the personal-drow bubble."

"Hmm." Rising slowly to his feet in one fluid movement, as if a giant hand pulled him up by invisible strings, Neros tilted his head and frowned. "I can show you things you haven't dreamed of imagining."

"And there's the offer." The halfling folded her arms. "Thanks, but no thanks. I've already listened to way too many prophecies and had all kinds of crazy dreams. Not looking to add to that list."

"Prophecies mean nothing." He stepped toward her. "Dreams are only as good as the mind around them."

Cheyenne couldn't hold back a laugh. "Okay. Nothing wrong with my mind."

"The light, cousin. And the Weave. The threads through us all." Another step closer.

"Hey, you can stop right there."

"Even those that run from me to you." Neros pinched his fingers together against his chest, then spread them toward Cheyenne's. "From you to me."

"I'm serious. Stop walking at me."

"We can find those threads together." He flicked his fingers toward her face, and she *felt* his hand brush across her cheek despite the three feet between them.

Cheyenne jerked away from the touch and scowled at him. "Don't do that again."

Neros' pale eyes blazed above a determined smile. He lifted his hand again and took one more step toward her.

"Back off!" She shoved the air between them with both hands and sent her cousin sailing backward across the temple.

He landed on his ass and skidded across the floor until the back of his head cracked against the thick stone pillar. Neros slumped over his lap, breathing slowly, and gingerly touched the back of his head.

Shit. I drew first blood, and now he's gonna come right back at me.

Neros looked at his fingers as if he'd never seen blood.

"I'm sorry." Cheyenne took a halting step toward him. "I gave you plenty of warnings. I know it's not an excuse, but my need for personal space is a very real thing." *So is failing at an apology.* "I didn't mean to hurt you. Badly."

Her cousin tilted his head and studied the blood on his fingers. "You didn't."

"Well, maybe you don't feel it now, but in the morning, you will."

The blood glowed in a halo of white light and lifted from the drow's pale fingers. It sparked and floated away like embers from a fire, dissipating into the air.

"Oh. Because you can heal yourself." Cheyenne wrinkled her nose. "Probably should've seen that coming."

Without a sound or even a grimace of discomfort, Neros stood and blinked quickly before staring at his cousin with the same intensity again. "You look surprised."

She took a step back and lifted her hand slightly. *If he goes nutso-drow on me after this, I'll be ready.* "I am. First, because I've gotten myself into a lot of situations where self-healing like that would've come in handy. And mostly because you're not angry."

"No, I'm not."

The halfling lifted her chin and shot him a skeptical glance. "And you're not attacking me."

"No."

"I saw how fast you can move. You didn't even lift a finger to defend yourself."

Neros' open, curious gaze brought another tingling wave of magical attention buzzing across the halfling's skin. "There is nothing to defend *against*, Cheyenne. Not here. Certainly not with you."

"Well, I did bash your head open. And O'gúleesh aren't famous for being peaceful and letting something like that slide."

A soft chuckle escaped the pale drow. "O'gúleesh do not dictate the ways of this world, cousin. Rather, it is the other way around."

"Okay. Either way, I'm sorry I lost it on you."

"I'm not." In a burst of white light, Neros darted across the temple and stopped inches in front of Cheyenne.

"Jesus, for *real?*" She staggered back and almost fell off the edge of the temple floor, then stepped off and backed up across the plateau. "You move fast but pick up new concepts pretty slow, huh?"

"Stay with me."

"What?"

Neros took a slow step toward her, his washed-out golden eyes flaring with intensity. "Stay with me, Cheyenne. Here, in Nor'ieth. On this mountain. I will show you everything. And you will show me what I cannot see without you."

"Uh, no." Cheyenne glanced behind her to gauge how much room she had before she'd end up falling off the mountainside. "I get it. You're intrigued. Everyone seems to have some kind of realization along those lines when they meet me. And I'm definitely not a stranger to being different. But staying here is not an option."

"It *can* be."

A dry laugh escaped her. "Oh, no. It definitely can't."

"We have a purpose, Cheyenne, you and I. We can fulfill it together, without ever 'lifting a finger to defend ourselves.' Like you said."

"That wasn't what I meant." She stuck her finger in the air, meaning to point it at him in warning, and paused. *Without ever lifting a finger. Maybe I don't have to find a different race to put on the throne. Maybe I need a different breed of drow, the kind that can knock L'zar Verdys off a mountain and keep him off but won't fight back.* "What about fulfilling your purpose somewhere else, huh?"

"I do not understand."

"Clearly." Cheyenne glanced at the sky and took a deep breath. "Look, I don't know how much you've *seen*, but here's what *my* purpose is for the foreseeable future. I basically staged a coup against the Crown of Ambar'ogúl, or at least the beginning of one. We all thought I was the only one left to inherit that throne, family ties and all. None of us knew you existed until yesterday."

"I exist here."

"Yeah, yeah, I get that. But what if you could exist at the center of Hangivol? The capital. The highest seat of power in this entire world. You have a purpose there too. A birthright, more or less. You could change everything about what it means to be a drow ruler. You gave L'zar a run for his money, Neros, and you didn't fight me. That's an insanely powerful combination, don't you think?"

"I don't *care* about the Crown." A darker golden light flashed behind her cousin's eyes, and he continued his slow, almost predatory stalk toward her. "I don't want it. I don't need it. I have no desire to be anywhere but here, where I belong. And I want you to stay with me."

"Again, no." Cheyenne spread her arms. "We went over this already."

"I can change your mind." Neros' eyes widened, and he lifted a finger toward her. Bright white light crackled and sparked at his fingertip, throwing eerie reflections into his glassy, colorless eyes. "Let me show you."

"Nope. I'm good." *So that's a no on putting a new drow on the throne. At least I can say I tried.* "I think we're done here."

"I want you to stay."

Broken record with this guy, huh? "Yeah, well, we all want things, Neros. Doesn't mean we always get 'em." She backed up toward the edge of the plateau and gauged the distance down to the footpath. "Nice to meet you. Good luck with seeing stuff. I'm glad your head's okay."

"Cheyenne."

She spun and jumped off the ledge. Her black Vans skidded across the loose dirt and gravel, then she set off down the zigzagging path a lot faster than she'd climbed it. Silence followed her down the side of the mountain.

He's not even gonna try to stop me. Would've been a pretty decent choice for a new Crown, but Maleshi was right. It's gonna be hard as shit to find someone else who wants it.

CHAPTER FORTY-FIVE

When Cheyenne reached the base, L'zar, Corian, and Maleshi stalked toward her from a grove of white-trunked trees. L'zar's golden eyes were wide with eager expectation. Corian frowned. Maleshi raised her eyebrows and stayed a dozen feet behind the others.

"Well?" L'zar caught up with his daughter as they headed back toward the central grouping of Nor'ieth's white stone buildings. "What did you find out?"

Cheyenne couldn't look at him. "He's even crazier than you are."

Maleshi snorted.

"That doesn't tell me anything, Cheyenne."

"Yeah, well, your nephew didn't *tell* me anything, other than that he's not leaving this valley. And you're not getting anything out of him that you can use against Ba'rael."

"He said that?"

"No. Not the last part." The halfling stopped and whirled toward her father, looking him up and down when he leaned away from her in surprise. "Look, whatever you thought you could convince him to do for you, it's not gonna happen. He kicked your ass without even trying."

"He did no such thing."

"Yeah, he did. You're pissed because you weren't fast enough or slippery enough for once in your life." Cheyenne pointed at the top of the mountain. "Neros is more powerful than both of us, and he didn't even try to fight me. He just healed his wound and brushed it off like it was nothing."

"You hurt him." L'zar dipped his head and studied her intently.

"Accidentally." She shrugged. "The guy has a problem with boundaries. Probably not a big deal for you. I get it. Runs in the family. No boundaries plus insanely powerful magic and no desire whatsoever to get revenge or fight back or even protect himself. L'zar, you won't be able to find anything to change his mind. The only thing Neros cares about is staying here, reading the Weave, and…"

"And what?"

Cheyenne glanced at Corian. "And me. I guess."

The nightstalker ran his fingers back and forth across his mouth and frowned. "What about you?"

"He wants me to stay here so we can fulfill some purpose together." She turned quickly and marched toward the stone village. "And that's not happening, so as far as Nor'ieth goes, we're out of options. At least we tried."

L'zar snarled and took off after her. "That's not good enough."

"Okay, then *you* go try talking to a drow who's spent his whole life being pumped with all this magic and doesn't give a shit about anything you have to say. Oh, yeah, that's right. You already tried, and he threw you off a mountain."

"What did you tell him? Did you at least explain what's happening?"

"Stop!" Cheyenne spun toward her father and shook her head. "I spent the last I don't even know how long answering Neros' questions. I can't believe I'm saying they were more obnoxious than yours, but I'm not in the mood to answer more right now. So back off."

"Cheyenne!"

"And we don't need anything from him. Just to be clear." The halfling glanced at L'zar and then Corian, who was quickly catching up with them. "You didn't even know you had a nephew until yesterday."

"Yes, but it changes everything."

"So, which is it? Huh? Either you had complete faith in me and the rest of the magicals who put everything they have on the line to give your sister these terms she can't refuse, or you've been lying to me the whole time. Is that why you wouldn't tell any of us what you wanted from Neros?"

L'zar opened his mouth and cocked his head.

"Yeah." She scoffed, "That's all the answer I need."

"Cheyenne, we can still do this, with or without Neros."

"*I* know that." The halfling stormed toward the buildings. "Time for *you* to start believing it, Weaver."

L'zar stood perfectly still. He took a sharp breath when Corian placed a hand on his shoulder but didn't move.

"She's not wrong," Corian muttered.

"You're saying I am?"

"No. It *is* possible for both of you to be right, you know."

L'zar snorted. "When did she turn into this…this force I can't control?"

Corian slid his hand off the drow's shoulder and nodded. "Looks like your head's starting to clear a little."

"What's that supposed to mean?"

"It means she's always been that force, brother. You haven't had the time to see it until now." The nightstalker took off after Cheyenne.

L'zar turned around to see Maleshi approaching behind him. "General?"

She raised both hands and stepped sideways around him, giving the drow thief a wide berth. "If it's still important later, bring it up then."

Shaking her head, the general put a little spring in her step and hurried away from him.

L'zar opened his mouth to call after them, then closed it again. *This would be the moment my own flesh and blood calls checkmate. Only she won't. She's not enough like me for that.*

He licked his lips and frowned at the dry grass beneath his feet. *One step at a time, L'zar. That's all it takes. Everything else will work itself out.*

Lifting his head, the Weaver *Cu'ón* pulled himself together before following the others toward the center of the ageless city, so thick with magic he could hardly breathe. *We're almost there. And there's always another way.*

Cheyenne didn't have a particular destination in mind as she wound between the white stone buildings, occasionally meeting the wide-eyed, unblinking gazes of the *olforim* staring at her from doorways and around corners. When she broke free of the central buildings in Nor'i-eth's valley, her eyes watered so much, she could only see vague shapes and blurred colors.

"Come on." She sniffed and wiped her eyes, trying to clear the burning itch of concentrated magic and the way it made her want to scratch her own flesh off her bones.

As she moved away from the center of the village, the tears slowly cleared, and she stopped.

Ember stood, or hovered, an inch off the ground, with Byrd, Lumil, Foltr, and Cazerel in a loose circle. The raug chief's warriors held a private conversation farther ahead, but they cast the fae girl brief glances of approval between bouts of rumbling raug laughter.

Cheyenne headed toward them. "Looks like you were right, Grandfather."

Foltr narrowed his eyes at her, surprised to hear the title from a halfling's lips, especially hers, and thumped his cane against the ground with a snort. "You don't live as long as I have only to throw empty guesses into the wind, *Aranél*."

"Obviously. You knew her magic would come back." Now that she was close enough to see through her still-watering eyes, Cheyenne eyed Ember and grimaced. "I mean, I'm glad to see you out of that machine, Em, but you look like shit."

Byrd and Lumil burst out laughing, elbowing each other in the ribs.

Ember folded her arms and gave the halfling a haughty head-wiggle. "Such kind words, *Aranél*."

"I thought we talked about you not calling me that."

"Everyone else does."

"You're not everyone else, Em." Cheyenne tried to keep a straight face, but seeing her best friend standing, even with the help of her magic and a levitation spell, made her break out in a wide grin. "Standing looks way better on you than that spider-chair."

Ember snorted. "I'm taking that as a compliment."

"What happened?"

Ember wrinkled her nose. "I'm pretty sure the *olforim* drugged me."

"*What?*"

"I mean, it was for a good cause. Obviously. But still." The fae girl leaned toward her friend and whispered, "I was tripping balls, Cheyenne. Saw my magic in the air, grabbed it, and it all came back. Then I puked."

"Uh-huh." Cheyenne fought back a laugh and nodded. "That explains the pale fae-pink and the dark circles under your eyes."

"Which I wear with pride at this point, thank you very much." Ember closed her eyes and spread her arms, basking comically in her transformation. "Oh, and by the way, I'm pretty sure my legs will heal too."

"For real?"

"*Pretty* sure." The corners of Ember's mouth turned down in mock consideration, and she glanced at her legs. "Don't know when, but I saw it."

"Oh, boy." Cheyenne ran a hand through her hair.

"You don't believe me?"

"I totally believe you, Em. No doubt. And you have no idea how glad I am to see you with working magic again. There's been a lot of *seeing* going on." The halfling shook her head at Ember's clueless expression and muttered, "I'll fill you in later."

"Huh." Ember shrugged, then she caught sight of the nightstalkers heading toward their little gathering. L'zar was striding carelessly along behind them like he didn't have a care in the world. "So, I'm curious."

"Yeah?"

"What was L'zar screaming about?"

"Huh?"

"The scream, Cheyenne. And the birds. Come on, don't tell me you didn't hear it." Ember plastered an over-eager grin on her face when Corian and Maleshi reached them. "*Hey.* Weird day, right?"

Corian eyed her briefly, then turned toward the raugs' provision carts. This time, none of the warriors gave him any trouble about it.

Maleshi nodded slowly at Ember. "So the fae *Nós Aní* regained her magic. Sorry, Ember. Are you feeling okay?"

"Yes." Ember widened her eyes and glanced at Cheyenne and the general. "Just because I look a little tired and malnourished, maybe, it doesn't mean there's anything *wrong* with me."

"Those are usually the first red flags, kid, but okay." Maleshi shrugged. "I'll take your word for it. Congratulations on the magical recovery."

"Thank you." Ember glanced at L'zar, who was taking his sweet time to join them. "Any luck with the secret drow heir?"

"Nope." Cheyenne stuck her hands in her pockets. "We can talk about that later too. L'zar's a little sensitive at the moment."

Lumil snorted. "That's a first."

"Friends."

The rebel magicals jumped in surprise when Yilas' multi-toned voice came from behind them without warning.

Cheyenne nodded at him with a tight smile. "You're talking to *us*, right?"

The *olforím* smiled and dipped his head, his pale eyes moving slowly from one face to the next. "We invite you to stay with us through the night. There is food, shelter, and plenty of room for everyone."

Byrd nodded. "Yeah, the food's not half bad."

Lumil snorted. "Like you even tasted it."

"Hey, I can eat fast *and* enjoy it at the same time, okay? Get off my ass."

Maleshi stared at the goblins until they noticed and elbowed each other into silence again. "Thank you, Yilas. We'll have to discuss it before we let you know one way or the other."

"Of course." The *olforím* bowed low, his flowing robes draping down off his slender frame until the thin fabric brushed against his forehead. Then he straightened. "What we have here is yours, should it please you to share it with us."

Maleshi nodded at him, then turned stiffly toward Corian. He stood empty-handed behind the supply carts and shrugged. "It's getting pretty late, isn't it?"

"Depends on your definition of late." The general looked at the sky, which glowed with the orange and pink hues of sunset, even in this hidden plane. "I guess that's a decent qualifier."

Cheyenne turned around to stare across the valley. "Wait, how long were we on that mountain? Or I guess just me."

"Long enough, apparently." Maleshi readjusted the collar of her military jacket and took a deep breath. "There are pros and cons to staying or leaving now, I suppose."

"Sure. I vote for leaving." Cheyenne started to nod toward the place where they'd entered Nor'ieth, then stopped. "However we end up doing that."

"We can't leave." L'zar approached their group looking calm enough, but his eyes darted away from Cheyenne's face and back again. "Not yet."

"Something else you're trying to get out of this visit and failed to tell any of us?"

"We need more, Cheyenne."

"There *is* no more." She swept her arm at the valley. "Neros doesn't want anything to do with the Crown or us. Neither do the *olforim*. We have to move on and look somewhere else. Not to mention that I have a life back home." *Neros might know what I am, but I doubt shouting it across the valley is gonna help us.*

"Yeah, me too." Ember nodded. "I mean, I can't say I'm anywhere near as busy as Cheyenne, but I definitely have things."

"Things." Corian folded his arms.

"Yeah. Stuff that doesn't have anything to do with us being *here*."

"Maleshi's in the same boat." Cheyenne raised her eyebrows at the general. "Right?"

"You have a point."

"No." L'zar shook his head but couldn't look any of them in the eyes. "There's more. We just have to find it."

"What's there to find? We didn't get what we came here for, which is fine. We'll find another way. At least we got a clear answer from someone for once. Neros refused to step foot out of Nor'ieth, and he doesn't want anything to do with the Crown or Hangivol or anywhere else, so for any of *your* purposes, L'zar, he's useless."

An earsplitting screech shattered the air in the peaceful valley. Lumil and Byrd jumped and ducked at the sound. Cazerel and his raug warriors broke off from their own conversation to turn in surprise, wondering at the sound.

Another screech and a high-pitched, trembling bellow echoed from the stone ridge on the far side of Nor'ieth, then another and another.

The crack and whip of thick fabric fluttering through the air made Cheyenne spin with a frown. *Not even a little windy right now.*

The ridge on the far side of the valley was moving.

"What the hell are those?" Ember whispered.

"I don't have a guess, Em."

CHAPTER FORTY-SIX

No way does Ambar'ogúl have dragons *too.*

But they weren't dragons. Cheyenne recognized that a second later when dozens of the massive, glowing blue beasts took to the skies over Nor'ieth and headed toward the party. Their wings cut effortlessly through the air in slow waves as the creatures swooped and dove and glided down from the top of the white stone ridge.

The two fastest cut a straight path to L'zar and his rebels, casting massive shadows over the glistening city. A small smile spread across Yilas' thin, pale lips.

Ember folded her arms and gazed at the creatures filling the sky and blocking out at least half the sunlight. "Nobody mentioned giant glowing flying *stingrays.*"

Cheyenne snorted, and the fae girl shot her friend a glance. "Took the words right out of my mouth, Em."

"The *luré*," Yilas said in his multiple ringing tones. His long three-fingered hand stretched out to gesture toward the creatures. "Aut Na'mor is fond of them, and they of him."

"Endaru's balls." Byrd clapped a hand to his bald head and rubbed it vigorously.

L'zar's eyes widened at the largest, brightest-glowing *luré* swooping across the valley. It headed right for their group, unaffected by the other creatures diving and spinning around it. "A mount fit for a drow."

"Are you serious?" Cheyenne shot her father an exasperated stare, but he ignored her. *Didn't think we'd have to fight O'gúl wildlife.* She summoned a crackling orb of black drow energy in one hand, her face illuminated by the purple sparks at its core, and turned to face the creature heading toward them. When she focused on it again, she cocked her head and snuffed out her magic. "Oh. Seriously?"

Neros stood on its back, arms hanging casually by his sides as his pale, flowing robes and bone-white hair whipped around his body and head. The *luré* slowed to a gentle glide, then hovered four feet above the ground. Its massive wings undulated like ocean waves. Two huge black eyes glistened at the front of the creature's wide, flat body as it glanced from one visiting magical to the next.

The blue light glowing in the *luré's* eyes flashed behind Neros' own as Cheyenne's cousin leaped from the creature's back. His bare feet thumped softly onto the pale grass, and he ran a hand along the *luré's* sleek body before stepping away from it to join the other magicals, who were staring at him in awe.

The *luré* gave something between a snort and a moaning call but stayed where its rider had left it.

Neros' pale gaze settled on Cheyenne, his face expressionless as he stepped toward her. "Cheyenne."

"Here we go." She shot Ember a sidelong glance. "What's up, Neros?"

"We could not let you leave without saying goodbye."

Ember leaned toward the halfling and muttered, "Please tell me you're not going all *Game of Thrones* on us with your cousin."

Cheyenne snorted. "If I didn't get that vibe from him too, that'd probably be funnier." She met Neros' unblinking gaze as he moved slowly toward her and folded her arms. *It's weird enough that he's bordering on obsession now, and he doesn't even care that we're related.*

"Neros." L'zar stepped into his nephew's path, cutting the pale drow off from reaching Cheyenne. "If you've seen enough about me in the Weave, nephew, you'll know I don't beg. This is as close as I'm ever going to get."

The pale drow's pale eyes slid slowly from Cheyenne's face to her father's. "No, it is not."

L'zar swallowed. "Come with us. Everything we need lies within you." The drow thief's mask of composure fractured when he extended his hand, his face contorting like he was about to be physically sick when he added, *"Please."*

"No."

That one word made L'zar's entire body tremble as if it were a spell instead of a refusal.

"You *have* to come with us," the drow thief snarled. "It's your duty. Four hundred years in Nor'ieth is enough for you to have seen that."

"L'zar, he's not coming." Cheyenne stepped toward them, forcing herself not to stare at the sparking purple light bursting from her father's fingers. *He's gonna lose it, and then we'll all be in deep shit.* "We both asked, and he still said no."

"I don't care." Snarling, L'zar lunged toward his nephew and grabbed Neros roughly by the shoulder. "If you can't see it, I'll *make* you see!"

"Hey, cut it out!" Cheyenne tried to wrench her father's hand off Neros' shoulder, and he spun toward her with a crazed hiss. "We didn't come here to kidnap anyone, L'zar. You can't take him against his will."

The drow thief's eyes flashed golden as he snarled at her and jerked Neros forward. "Don't tell me what I can and can't do, Cheyenne. *I'm the only—"*

Neros' hand moved too quickly for anyone to see, despite the rest of him standing perfectly still. He slapped L'zar's firm grip off his shoulder, and the drow thief stumbled sideways under the force of it. As her father stared in disbelief at his hand, Cheyenne backed away. *Staying out of this one.*

"That's how you want to do this?" L'zar whirled toward his nephew and grinned. "Fine."

Corian stepped forward and stopped. "L'zar, don't."

The drow thief ignored the warning as his hand shot toward Neros' face. Neros stepped swiftly aside to avoid the blow and stared at L'zar impassively.

"I will have what I want," L'zar roared. "Even if I have to take it!"

"Stop!" Cheyenne's shout went unheard beneath the crackle of black sparks bursting from L'zar's hand.

Neros flicked his hand aside and sent L'zar's attack sailing up and over the stone ridge beside them.

L'zar snarled and let off another attack. His nephew stepped calmly out of the way and again deflected the burst of magic. It raced into the sky instead and disappeared with a pop. Again and again, the drow thief attacked his nephew, launching spells and blows in a blur of dark-gray. Neros moved fluidly and avoided every burst of magic, stepping calmly away and lifting his arms only to block L'zar's speedy movement over and over.

Maleshi cleared her throat and looked at Corian. "Should we do something about this?"

He shook his head. "I'm not getting involved in *that.*"

L'zar snarled and fought like a starving, rabid animal but didn't once hit his target. Spit flew from his lips as black and purple drow magic flew from his hands, filling the sky with dark light.

Then Neros took one step forward and a flash of brilliant white shot from his hand. He struck L'zar in the shoulder and sent his mad uncle flying back across the grass.

The drow thief hissed and skidded to a stop on his side a foot away from Cazerel's warriors. A dark stain of blood grew quickly on his shoulder.

"Jesus." Cheyenne stepped toward him, but Corian's fingers around her upper arm made her stop.

"Just let it play out, kid."

"They're gonna end up killing each other."

"Just wait."

Cheyenne gritted her teeth and stared at her father, still lying on the ground. *I'm trying to help him. None of this turned out the way we thought.*

L'zar clamped his other hand on the wound, breathing heavily and glaring at his nephew. He grimaced and tightened his grip, then a soft golden light bloomed beneath his trembling hand. The blood on his palm and staining his shirt didn't fizzle into the air the way Neros' had, but the bleeding stopped when the golden glow on his shoulder faded.

He wrenched his clenched fist away from the healed wound and closed his eyes with a sigh, then looked at his nephew and grinned. "Okay."

"What?" Cheyenne glanced between them.

"That settles it, then." L'zar pushed to his feet. "You've shown me what I need to see, Neros. You'll live out your abnormally long life doing absolutely nothing, and we'll stay out of it."

Ember patted her cheek. "Did I miss something?"

Cheyenne turned toward Corian and Maleshi, but the nightstalkers looked as surprised as she was. *Was all that an act?*

L'zar strolled casually toward them and nodded. "We can go now."

"What are you doing?" Corian muttered.

"Getting my answer, *vae shra'ni*. And now I have it."

The nightstalker frowned at the drow thief.

Neros headed for Cheyenne, staring at her with pale, unblinking eyes. "Which of these magicals journeyed into Nor'ieth with you from the other side, cousin?"

She blinked quickly and tried to wrap her head around what had happened. "Right. Everyone but the raugs."

"I see." Neros darted forward in a white blur and pulled Cheyenne into his arms for a weirdly tight hug.

"Whoa, whoa." She struggled but couldn't get him to let go. "Hey, we talked about personal space."

"Do not be afraid of what makes you different, Cheyenne," he whispered fiercely in her ear, then took a long, deep sniff. A warm buzz of intense magic flowed into her and settled like a blaze in her core. She froze. "That is the only thing that will change the way all this plays out."

"What?"

Neros released her and stepped back, looking her over again. Then he spread his arms and closed his eyes.

The ground trembled. Pale grass and loose earth erupted between the drow cousins. Cheyenne staggered back as a thick crack split across the valley floor, and a sleek, smooth, glinting obelisk of black stone rose from the hole in the ground. It shot straight into the air, dirt and rocks crumbling away from it.

She stared at the black stone pillar and her mouth fell open. *Like a mini-portal ridge. Or the towers at every single Border rez.*

When the ground stopped shuddering and the last of the earth fell, the only sound in Nor'ieth was the slow, heavy flap of *luré* wings and the occasional screech.

Ember's luminous violet eyes didn't leave the obelisk. "What just happened?"

Cheyenne's mouth worked in surprise before she found her voice. "I think that's a—"

"Friends." Yilas' multi-toned voice rang out. "Thank you for joining us in Nor'ieth. We learn much from visitors. It is our hope that others have broadened their awareness in return."

"Thank *you*, Yilas." L'zar spread his arms and kicked up his heel to deliver a low bow over his extended leg to the *olforim*. "I won't speak for the others, but this has been my pleasure."

Cheyenne scowled at her father. *He's so full of shit all the time.*

"*Zokri* of the Hirúl Breach raugs." Yilas turned toward Cazerel and his warriors. "You and yours are welcome to stay as long as you wish. For the rest of you, we offer our blessing of good fortune. May the light of the Weave not blind you to the darkness."

All around the rebel magicals, the *olforim* joined their leader. Pale, elongated faces offered small, gentle smiles to the travelers. Lightless eyes gazed unblinkingly at Cheyenne, L'zar, and the rest of their startled group. L'zar focused intently on Neros, his mad grin widening.

Lumil stepped toward the nightstalkers with a raised fist but didn't summon her swirling red runes. "Feels like we're missing something."

Corian snorted and muttered, "What else is new?"

Every *olforim* around them raised both three-fingered hands toward the black stone obelisk in front of Neros. The pale drow didn't move.

White light burst from the *olforim*'s hands and struck the column all at once. The light flared and wiped everything else away.

Cheyenne heard someone shout her name before her body was hurled forward. The air burst from her lungs beneath the squeezing pressure of passing through the Border portal her cousin had opened for them in Nor'ieth. She tried to shout, gasping for air that didn't exist, and hurtled through the crossing.

Dark lines of black smoke flew past her in the in-between. *That has to be what this is.*

A booming crack like thunder filled her head, and the next thing she knew, she was lying on her side in a forest somewhere, her cheek pressed against cold, dew-studded grass.

Cheyenne gave a raw, shuddering gasp and started coughing uncontrollably. Her lungs burned, and dozens of tiny lights pulsed in her vision. Her head pounded furiously, sending blazing pain radiating down through her neck and shoulders. She gasped again, coughed one more time, and rolled weakly onto her back with a groan.

What just happened?

Her racing pulse and heaving breath echoed in her ears, drowning out any other sounds.

I can't move.

She stared at the night sky, stars winking at her through the leaves rustling on the branches overhead.

Cheyenne opened her mouth to shout for Ember, Corian, or even L'zar, but no sound came out.

This can't be it.

Her vision darkened.

We didn't even...

The halfling's eyes rolled back in her head, and she lost consciousness.

CHAPTER FORTY-SEVEN

The pounding agony in her head returned. Cheyenne groaned and tried to roll over, but all she managed was to slide her arm closer to her side. *That's not grass.*

"*There* she is," Corian muttered.

"Well, help her up."

"No," Cheyenne croaked. "Don't." She grimaced against the blazing pain in her temples and behind her eyes and swallowed. "Don't touch me."

Persh'al snorted. "She sounds fine to me."

Cheyenne forced open her eyes and hissed at the bright light hanging from the ceiling directly above her. "Turn that off."

A shadow loomed over her, blocking the light. The halfling found herself looking into Corian's glowing silver eyes. "Time to get up, kid."

"Shit." She pushed herself slowly off the floor and sat there for another ten seconds while the pain in her head faded to a bearable ache. "What the hell was that?"

Corian offered her a hand, and she took it without thinking. "Looks like your cousin has a knack with portal towers too."

Cheyenne swayed after she stood, blinking heavily. The nightstalker steadied her with a hand, but she brushed him off. "A portal." The room spun when she turned around, but she shook off the dizziness and gazed dumbly at the main room of Persh'al's warehouse. "Here?"

"Not quite." Corian watched her carefully as she smoothed her hair away from her face. "We didn't have a lot of time to check specifics, but Neros sent us somewhere in Michigan."

"Michigan."

"Your guess is as good as mine, kid." The nightstalker shrugged. "But we're all back in one piece."

"Where's Ember?"

The front door of the warehouse burst open, followed by Lumil and Ember, both wearing their human illusions. The goblin woman cackled and held the door open for the fae girl. "Not even close, fae. I don't care where you've been or what you think you— Oh, look who finally decided to wake up."

"How you feelin'?" Ember floated across the warehouse toward the halfling with a small, concerned smile.

"Like I fell from a ten-story building." Cheyenne rubbed the back of her neck and tried to stretch out the kinks. "Am I the only one who passed out?"

"No, but you're the only one who stayed out this long." Ember shrugged. "Even though you're the last magical I'd expect to be laid out like that. Corian ported us all back here last night. At least, I *think* he did."

"Trust me, it's a blur for all of us." Corian folded his arms. "I wondered if *I'd* make it, but we're all here."

"Yeah, it was so much fun." Persh'al scoffed and scratched his shaved blue head. "Would've been nice to have some warning before everybody came crawling right through a portal. I almost had a heart attack."

Lumil snorted. "Don't be dramatic."

"Hey, that's rich coming from the goblin who kept screaming about being turned inside out before she fainted."

"Whatever."

The front door burst open again, and Byrd barreled inside. "Five minutes! It's not too much to ask, is it?" He saw Cheyenne standing in the middle of the warehouse and grinned as the door slammed shut behind him. "Ha! The halfling lives!"

"I'm still not sure." Cheyenne clenched her eyes shut and briefly rubbed her temples. "He opened a *portal*."

Corian scratched his head. "I think I said that already."

"And we went right through. Isn't that supposed to be impossible? Portals straight from Ambar'ogúl to Earth?"

"Wasn't impossible for the Crown that one time," Ember muttered.

"It's supposed to be, yeah." Corian stuck his hands in his pockets. "Ba'rael had a lot of stolen magic fueling her portal at your binding ceremony, Cheyenne. And Neros? I think he's more tapped into *olforim* magic than we realized."

"That wasn't *his* magic?"

"Well, I'm sure it is *now*. Spending his entire life in Nor'ieth, it makes sense. But the *olforim* are allegedly the ones who created the Border portals."

"Wait, I thought no one knew where they came from or how long they've been there?"

The nightstalker shrugged. "No one knows truth from myth, kid. Until you're staring the myth in the face. Didn't think you'd put any stock in O'gúl legends anyway."

"I don't. But this is real."

He nodded slowly. "Very."

"Neros is one of them, then. Right?" Cheyenne asked, "I thought the washed-out drow look was weird, but I guess he's more *olforim* than drow at this point."

"It would seem so."

"Awesome. We wasted a whole day going after something that was useless all around, huh?"

The door to the square office at the back of the warehouse creaked open and L'zar strolled out, grinning. "Not completely useless."

"Right. 'Cause we all got to see that L'zar Verdys isn't unstoppable."

"Well, that was a minor irritation, Cheyenne, but not what I meant." He pulled his hand out of his pocket as he approached her and stopped to open it. Resting in his palm was a small metal four-pointed star, though this one glowed with a bright silver light in a way those formed from Cheyenne's magic never had.

She stared at the small piece of metal. "I thought that was a night-stalker thing."

"You learn quite a bit from having a nightstalker for a *Nós Aní.*" L'zar shot Corian a sharp glance. "Perhaps more than a nightstalker realized."

Corian's silver eyes remained fixed on the glowing four-pointed star in the drow's hand, and he swallowed.

Cheyenne glanced between them, but Corian never looked up from L'zar's palm. *Something's going on, and no one's gonna say anything about it. Again.* "So, you turned his magic into metal. How's that supposed to help us?"

"It has its uses." L'zar stopped glaring at Corian and stuck the small piece of metal back into his pocket before grinning at Cheyenne. "I'm looking forward to telling you all about it. In private."

Corian cleared his throat, then stepped back and stared at the cement floor.

Not a good sign.

"Where's Maleshi?"

"She left an hour ago," Ember said, her eyebrow raised as she studied Corian's uncharacteristic nervousness. "To go to class, I think."

"Oh, shit." Cheyenne reached up for the strap of her backpack, realized it was gone, and searched the warehouse. Her backpack rested against the far wall, and she stalked toward it. "It's Monday. I have a class too. What time is it?"

"Nine-thirty."

"Great. That would barely be enough time if I were at my apartment."

Corian opened a portal right there between them and glanced quickly at her before averting his gaze. "Then I guess you'd better go."

L'zar chuckled and glared at the nightstalker. "You'd like that very much, wouldn't you?"

"It's not about what I want."

"Oh, no? It looks very much like what you want, *vae shra'ni.*"

"We can talk about this later, L'zar."

The drow thief grinned. "Of course we can. When *I'm* ready. At the very least, you can wait for *that.*"

With her backpack slung over her shoulder, Cheyenne headed toward the portal. *Whatever's going on, it has to wait 'til I'm done teaching my students how to break all the rules.*

"So. I'm gonna go."

"Enjoy your academic pursuits, Cheyenne." L'zar didn't look away from Corian, who stared intently at the open portal, his jawing clenching and unclenching. "We all know how important *that* is."

"Please. You're the last magical to give a convincing 'stay in school' speech." Cheyenne nodded at Ember, and the fae girl floated across the floor toward the shimmering oval of light leading into their living room. With a final glance at Corian and then her father, Cheyenne added, "I'll be back after class, so don't go anywhere. Or kill each other."

"Don't worry about us." L'zar's gaze flickered toward her. "We'll find some way to occupy our time."

"Uh-huh." *This is so not the time.* "Come on, Em."

"Yep."

They passed through the portal together into the living room of their loft apartment beside the long wall of floor-to-ceiling windows. The portal closed with a soft pop, but not before they heard L'zar's furious snarl and the beginning of a shouting match on the other side.

Yeah, we're definitely gonna have a chat about whatever the hell that was.

Cheyenne headed for the front door.

"You okay?" Ember asked.

"Not really." Cheyenne patted the pockets of her trenchcoat. "And I don't have my keys."

"What?"

"Maleshi took my car before our fun inter-world adventure." Rolling her eyes, the halfling jerked open the door and looked over her shoulder. "You good? Need anything?"

"Got my magic and my own apartment again." Ember spread her arms. "I'm good."

"Right."

"Later." Ember flicked her fingers toward the door, which shot open before a wall of purple light shoved the halfling into the hall. "You're gonna be late."

The door shut quickly in Cheyenne's face. She stared at it and snorted, then headed quickly down the hall toward the elevators. *Fae magic. Looks like she got a little boost.*

The elevator seemed to take forever, and she couldn't mash the buttons fast enough to close the doors behind her. The lobby was empty when she barreled through it around black leather chairs and burst outside into the morning sunlight. *Maleshi said she'd take care of the car. I swear, if it's not here, I'm gonna...*

She stopped on the sidewalk. "What the fuck?"

The shiny black Porsche Panamera, not so shiny today, was parked diagonally across the two closest parking spaces in front of her building.

"Are you *kidding* me?" Cheyenne darted toward the car and choked as she ran her hand over the long scratch down the driver's side. Dust and dry mud were splattered all over the body, and there was a huge dent above the rear driver's side wheel well. "The general took my fucking car for a joyride. At least she didn't park it in two handicap spots!"

She wrenched open the driver's side door, tossed her backpack on the passenger seat, and slid angrily behind the wheel. Even in her wrath, she made sure not to slam the door, then she reached for the ignition and the keys Maleshi had left in the car for two and a half days.

"She's never touching this thing again." Cheyenne started the car and sniffed.

A growl escaped her when she found a burger wrapper and a paper carton of half-eaten fries spilling over the seat beneath her backpack. *Nightstalkers. Jesus. No wonder L'zar and Corian get into it all the time. And everyone wondered why I drove around in a beat-up piece of crap before this.* "Come on!"

She slammed a hand on the wheel, then shifted into reverse and peeled out of the Pellerville Gables Apartments' parking lot, cursing Maleshi the whole time.

CHAPTER FORTY-EIGHT

Cheyenne pulled into the parking lot at the VCU campus at 9:54 a.m. The little chirp flaring behind her when she locked her car did absolutely nothing for her mood. Jamming the keys into her coat pocket, she trudged across the parking lot to get to the Computer Sciences building.

I'm gonna be late. Awesome. What is this, my second week of teaching?

She stepped back and drew her hand back when a mutated troll darted in front of her, all metal spikes and black clothes and a puff of neon-yellow hair sprouting from its head.

"Hey, nice costume." A human mouth grinned at her beneath the wrinkled, grotesque rubber mask. "If you're entering the costume contest with that one, I'm screwed."

"What?" The magic that had almost flared at Cheyenne's fingertips recoiled and disappeared. The student, who was dressed up like a magical that didn't exist in any world, laughed, shot her the peace sign, and hurried toward wherever he was headed.

She glanced down at her purple-gray hand, then at the bone-white hair falling over her shoulders. *Shit. I'm still in full-on drow mode.*

More students shouted as they hurried across the campus to their next classes. Half of them were in costume.

It's Halloween. How did I miss that?

Shoving her hands in her pockets, Cheyenne trudged down the walkway through campus, staring at the cement beneath her. Students everywhere stopped and stared, pointing and calling out her costume.

"Yo, you into that cosplaying stuff?"

"Sure." She kept her head down and walked faster.

"Hey, for real, though." A kid dressed like Superman jogged toward her, his thin cape fluttering behind him as he grinned. "That's a seriously realistic makeup job you got goin' on. How did you get that color?"

"Get lost."

"Whoa. And those *ears!*" He reached toward her head with wide eyes.

Cheyenne slapped his hand away. "Back the fuck off!"

"Okay, okay." The kid's hands flew up in surrender, and he stepped back. "Hey, I'm a fan, all right?"

She looked him up and down and gritted her teeth. "Thanks. Nice cape."

He gaped at her as she stormed past him down the sidewalk. *Get it together, Cheyenne. You can't bring this other crap with you into the classroom. Forget L'zar and Corian. Forget the Panamera. Just chill the hell out. Stupid mistake not to kill the drow look, and now you gotta deal with it.*

She started jogging across the quad when the Computer Sciences building came into view. The giant mound of dirt where she'd closed the newest Border portal was still surrounded by people in uniform, who knelt and took measurements and typed on tablets. *Sir's still got agents pretending to work for someone else, huh? At least he didn't ignore the warnings on this one.*

One of the FRoE agents with an oversized baseball cap looked briefly up at her, blinked, and spread his arms. "Hey."

Of course they recognize me.

"Hey, where the hell's your *mask?*"

Cheyenne hurried toward the building's entrance and spun to face him with a shrug. "This is best I could come up with on short notice, okay? It works."

The agent glared at her and slowly shook his head.

Great. Any minute now, I'll get a call about walking around in public looking like myself. Sir can suck it.

She barreled into the building and hurried toward her classroom.

The door was open, all the lights on, and her undergrad students were already in their seats, engaged in their own conversations. Cheyenne stormed down the aisle and glanced at the clock on the back wall. *Only five minutes late. Could be worse.*

"Whoa!" The kid in the back row dressed up as the Hulk, green face paint smeared on way too thick, thumped both hands on his desk and leaned forward. "Nice costume, Professor."

"Don't call me that." Cheyenne stopped behind the desk and shrugged out of her backpack, fighting not to chuck it at the ground. The rest of the students stopped talking and turned wide eyes and awed smiles on their instructor.

"Seriously," the kid continued. "I mean, it's not as awesome as the Hulk, but you went all out."

She cocked her head and looked him up and down. "Yeah, the fake foam muscles were a great touch. Totally believable."

The students laughed, and the guy sitting next to the kid who gave Cheyenne crap every class reached out and squeezed his friend's puffy bicep.

"Cut it out." The Hulk smacked his friend's hand away and glared at him. "At least I put some effort into it. One day of the whole year when her regular look makes sense." He looked back at Cheyenne. "You could've told everyone *that* was your costume."

Cheyenne smacked the desk. "Shut up and pay attention."

The kid's smile faded, and the laughter around him died immediately.

With a deep breath, Cheyenne closed her eyes and gave herself a moment. *Just a bunch of undergrads. Definitely not the worst thing you've faced in the last few days. Figure it out.*

"Sorry I was a little late."

Her students said nothing.

Okay, think. No lesson plan. No plan at all. What the hell am I even doing here?

"All right, listen up. Today's a little different. Advanced Programming." Someone snorted, and Cheyenne stood straight and lifted her chin. *Gotta give them something. Or maybe they can get* me *something.* A slow smile spread across her face, making most of her students lean back in their seats. "Any of you heard of a company called ThomasSafe?"

Blank stares and a few shaken heads were the only responses she got.

"Yeah, I didn't think so." *This is probably breaking a bajillion rules, but I don't have time for rules. Might as well use the resources I have.* "Here's your assignment."

The blonde girl's hand shot into the air, but she didn't wait for Cheyenne to call on her. "You haven't gone over our last assignments. Or taught us anything new."

"You wanna stand up here and teach this class instead?" Cheyenne raised her eyebrows at the girl and mentally kicked herself. *Awesome. Now I sound like every other asshole professor I never liked.*

"I told you guys this class would be different, and I meant it. So here's the deal. Between now and Wednesday, I want you guys to research as much as you can about this company and its owner and CEO, Matthew Thomas. And I mean *as much* as you can. Anything. How ThomasSafe was founded, how it's structured, what technology they're using. Hell, pull up familial connections to the man. Bonus points if you can tell me what he ate for breakfast yesterday."

"Wait, how is this part of Advanced Programming?"

Cheyenne gave the large kid with the beard a pert smile. "Because ThomasSafe is one of the highest-grossing cybersecurity firms in the U.S. If you guys wanna get good at this whole tech thing, you might as well learn from the best."

"You're saying this Matthew Thomas guy is *the best*?" The girl on the end of the front row with half her head shaved folded her arms.

Cheyenne fought back a grin and pointed at her. "That's *not* what I said."

"When we find all this stuff," another student asked, "what do you want us to do with it?"

"Send it to me."

The room fell silent.

"Okay." Cheyenne clapped her hands together. "It's Halloween. I have places to be too, so I'll see you Wednesday. Now get out."

The girl in the front row snorted and slid out of her seat first, her messenger bag slapping her thigh as she headed into the hallway.

Sticking her hands in her pockets, the halfling watched her confused students gather their things to leave the shortest Advanced Programming class all semester. *Let's see which of them has the most promise, huh? If anybody takes me seriously on this one. If not, I'll find Matthew Thomas' uncle on my own. Whatever the FRoE's up to, it stops with him.*

Her fingers drummed on her thighs inside her pockets, and she raised her eyebrows at the last student turning around to shoot her a confused glance before he stepped through the doorway. *And that's how you clear a room.*

Cheyenne grabbed her backpack, slipped it on, and stalked up the aisle. The lights clicked off, the door shut with a louder bang than she intended, and she marched down the hall toward Maleshi's current class.

Through the rectangular window in the door, she watched Maleshi, human-looking once again as Professor Mattie Bergmann, gesture with a wide sweep of her arm before clicking the remote at the smartboard behind her. Her students laughed softly, and the woman's brilliant green eyes flicked toward Cheyenne's face in the window. Maleshi's eyes widened, but she continued with her lesson.

Cheyenne folded her arms. *Yeah, I'll wait.*

Fifteen minutes later, Maleshi waved at the door, and Cheyenne stepped aside before the first students pushed it open and swarmed into the hall. Most of them gave her appraising looks before heading to their next class. Maleshi followed the last student toward the door and pointed at Cheyenne with a tight smile. "Well, look at you. Went all out on your costume this year, huh?

"Guess Halloween kinda snuck up on me."

Maleshi chuckled and nodded at the last student slipping past Cheyenne into the hall. Then she grabbed the halfling's arm and jerked her into the classroom.

CHAPTER FORTY-NINE

"What the hell are you trying to pull, kid?"

The door clicked shut, and a bright burst of silver light from Maleshi's fingertip blacked out the window.

"It's Halloween. Nobody cares."

"*I* care. So does every other magical who might see you like this. Have you lost it?"

"I forgot about the cuff, okay?" Cheyenne jerked the sleeve of her jacket up to expose the thick silver band on her wrist. "And it was too late to do anything about it when I got here."

"That's a dangerous risk to take, Cheyenne."

"More dangerous or less dangerous than whatever swamp you drove my car through?"

Maleshi blinked. "Your car?"

"You told me you'd take care of it. I guess I assumed that didn't have the same meaning as when it's said about *people.*"

"I didn't *kill* your car, kid."

"You fucked it up." Cheyenne shook her head. "Anything to say about it?"

"I think a car is the least of our worries right now, don't you?"

"No. Not the least of mine." Cheyenne cocked her head. "Maybe the least of yours, though."

Maleshi hissed at her and glanced at the window in the door despite it being a long black rectangle. "What's that supposed to mean?"

"I'm talking about L'zar. He lost it on Corian before I came out here, and it sounded a lot like he knows what's up between you two."

The general's olive-skinned human face paled, her eyelashes fluttering in surprise. "Then I won't go back right now like I planned."

"So, you're gonna hide from it?" Cheyenne shook her head. "It's not like he's going anywhere. He's not even supposed to *be* Earthside right now, but the *olforím* don't give a shit, and now he's stuck here forever."

Maleshi swallowed. "Ba'rael's curse."

"Yeah. We have that awesome surprise to deal with. And now L'zar definitely won't be with me when I have to go back there to give the Crown my *terms*. That's what *I'm* worried about."

"You'll be fine." Maleshi turned around and walked stiffly toward the desk at the front of the classroom.

"Sure, if L'zar's in the right headspace to cough up whatever information he has that will help me. I mean, he's hardly ever in the right headspace, but he surely won't be if you and Corian try to clear this mess up with him."

"Corian and me." The general slipped loose papers into her rolling briefcase and turned. "If there is a mess, Cheyenne, it's between the two of them. Corian makes his own decisions, even if it looks like the exact opposite. I'm not part of this."

"Fine, but you're part of all the open ends we left in Ambar'ogúl before we got shoved back across the Border. Right?"

Maleshi grabbed the handle of her briefcase and stalked toward the door. "Like what?"

"Seriously?" Cheyenne gritted her teeth when the nightstalker walked past her, then spun and followed Maleshi up the aisle. "Like all the extra magic spilling out of Hangivol. Like the *Sorren Gán*. Shouldn't someone be over there checking whether that asshole's doing what it promised?"

"Well, you can make the crossing and check it all out for yourself if that's what you want." The general pointed at the door, and a silver flash removed the window's black color. "But I highly recommend you spend your time thinking about what *is* under your control."

"Like what?"

The door jerked open, and Maleshi turned to whisper harshly, "Like who you're gonna put on that throne if you *ever* want to step foot Earthside again. Like *how* you plan to force Ba'rael *off* that throne. Everything else is a drop in the bucket and a waste of all our time."

The general stormed into the hall and didn't look back.

Cheyenne stepped out after her. "I'm still taking suggestions. Anyone come to mind?"

"Close the door behind you." Maleshi disappeared around the corner, the wheels of her rolling briefcase squeaking and clicking across the divots in the linoleum floor.

"Great." *'Cause it's the easiest thing in the world to find someone to rule Ambar'ogúl among the limited options on Earth.* Cheyenne snorted, slammed the classroom door shut behind her, and headed down the hall toward the closest restroom. "Mondays suck."

The bathroom door opened, and a short, scrawny girl who couldn't have been taller than five feet skirted into the hall. "Tell me about it. Nice costume."

Cheyenne ignored her and slipped into the bathroom. The stall door banged shut behind her, and she twisted the lock before slapping her hands on the metal door and bowing her head between them. *Only eleven days left until I either force the Crown to step down or try to keep her from slitting my throat. No big deal.*

She jerked the cuff off her wrist and shoved it angrily into the pocket of her trenchcoat. The warmth of the magic she'd been walking around in for the last three days faded, and she smoothed her dyed-black hair away from her face with pale Goth-girl hands. *Feels like taking off all my clothes. Never thought it'd feel weird to look like a human, but okay.*

Taking a deep breath, she opened the stall door and glanced briefly at herself in the mirror. "You need food. And a shower. You smell like a raug."

The toilet in the other stall flushed, and her student with the half-shaved head stepped out to wash her hands. "I don't know what the hell a raug is, but speak for yourself."

Cheyenne scowled at the girl.

"I figured all that face paint would take a lot longer to wash off."

"Just takes practice."

"Okay."

Turning stiffly, Cheyenne hurried out of the bathroom, slamming her hand against the door to throw it open. *A university campus is not the place to talk to myself in the mirror. Or at all. Noted.*

When she got back to her apartment, she found Ember sitting on the couch, both legs propped on the cushions, watching TV. The girl looked at her and smiled. "Get caught up?"

"Maleshi owes me a new car."

"What?"

Cheyenne dropped her backpack on the floor and slumped into the black leather recliner on the other side of the coffee table. "She's why I don't have nice things."

Ember wrinkled her nose. "That might be stretching it a little. You could buy three more of those things brand-new and not even make a dent in your bank account."

"That's not the point, Em." Cheyenne dropped her head back against the headrest and closed her eyes. "It's the principle. If somebody says they'll take care of it and you can trust them, that better be what they mean." Her eyes flew open, and she bolted upright in the chair. "Shit, Em. Your PT appointment. I totally forgot." She fought with the side of her trenchcoat to get to the phone in the left pocket. "What time is it? We can still—"

"Whoa, slow down. It's okay."

"No, it's not. Here I am, talking about keeping promises, and now I'm the asshole who—"

"Cheyenne, stop."

The halfling looked up at her friend and paused with her phone halfway out of her pocket. "What?"

"I canceled PT."

"Because I didn't show up?"

"Because I'm healing *myself*, Cheyenne. I don't need the clinic anymore."

"Oh." Sitting back in the chair, Cheyenne cocked her head. "You sure?"

Without looking away from her, Ember pointed at her feet. The left one wiggled an inch, and that was it. "It's a hell of a lot more movement than I had yesterday."

"Well, that's cool." Despite her frustration, the halfling couldn't help but smile. "The healer healing herself. No wonder Cazerel didn't want to let you go anywhere alone."

"Yeah, he's probably freaking out right now," Ember said, "Maybe. I don't know. Do raugs freak out?"

"Not unless they're in rage and with a lot of exploding magic. Or prophecies, I guess."

"Yeesh." Ember lifted the remote toward the TV. Her show clicked off, and a low hum filled the apartment as the flatscreen lowered itself into the long entry table until it disappeared. "So." The remote clattered onto the coffee table. "Now what?"

"Well, we're Earthside again, so I guess we're focusing on Earthside problems for now."

"Right." Ember grimaced and wrinkled her nose. "Like 'Matthew Thomas' uncle in the FRoE' problems, huh?"

"Pretty much." Cheyenne snorted and pulled her phone from her pocket to drop it in her lap. "I kind of outsourced that one."

"To whom?"

"My students."

"Ha!" Ember rolled her eyes. "Seriously, though. You find some new hacker friends or something?"

"Seriously, though." Cheyenne grinned. "This is how I'll find them. And whoever digs up the most dirt on our friendly neighbor across the hall and his scumbag uncle gets a passing grade no matter what."

"Oh, my God." The girl laughed. "You put your students up to that?"

"As an assignment, yeah."

"You know what? I'm not as surprised as I thought I'd be."

"So, I'm predictable now. Good to know."

Ember clicked her tongue. "Yeah, that's totally what I meant."

"Hey, if my *students*, which is still weird to say, can find Matthew's uncle, it gives Matthew one less reason to come after *us*."

"He wouldn't do that."

"You don't think so?" Cheyenne pushed out of the armchair and headed toward the iron stairs to the mini-loft. "The dude lied to us twice to keep this secret, Em. I had to record Maleshi fighting a war machine for him to take us seriously."

"I don't wanna talk about Matthew right now."

"Why?" Cheyenne stopped halfway up the stairs and stared at her roommate. "Did you talk to him while I was gone?"

"What? *No.*" Ember rolled her eyes. "I don't wanna think about him *or* talk to him. Not until we find out who his uncle is. Oh, shit. You think it's Sir?"

Cheyenne snorted and continued up the stairs. "Think about both their faces for a second, Em, then tell me you think that's even remotely a possibility."

"I don't know what he looks like."

"Oh." With a shrug, Cheyenne sat in her spinning desk chair and powered up her computer. "Well, they don't look anything like each other."

"Could be his uncle by marriage or something."

"Huh."

"And not everyone looks like the rest of their family members, either."

No, just drow apparently. Creepy-weird how much Neros looks like L'zar. "I guess you have a point."

"Of course I do."

"I'll keep it in mind when I'm digging through the vast world of information at my fingertips." Cheyenne touched the activator behind her ear to reassure herself it was still there, then Glen's monitor turned on, and her vision filled with the scrolling lines of code telling her everything she needed to know about the system she'd built. "I don't know how long this is gonna take."

"Totally fine." Ember grabbed the remote again, and the flatscreen rose from its slot one more time. "I'll go back to what I was doing before you stormed in here, ready to rip General Hi'et's head off."

Cheyenne snorted. "Sounds good." *I'm gonna focus all this pissed-off energy into something useful.*

When Glen finished powering up, Cheyenne pulled up her VPN and dove into the dark web to look for things she knew none of her students would be able to find.

The Borderlands forum under *Third Quarter Projections* was as active as normal, but none of the new topic threads mentioned anything about Ambar'ogúl, a new Cycle, the Crown, loyalists, or anything remotely related to L'zar's rebels storming the Heart at Hangivol.

Weird. Every O'gúleesh on the other side knew the second I slapped that coin down on the altar, and no one over here has a clue.

She scrolled down the main page to check the topic titles over the last three days and found nothing. Sitting back, she frowned at the screen and drummed her fingers on the armrests. *I guess that means information isn't getting across the Border. Makes sense if the Crown suddenly had all her magical assets frozen—no way for the loyalists over here to get a whiff of what happened.*

"Shit."

"Found something already?" Ember called up to her.

"It's what I'm not finding. I don't think anyone over here knows what we did."

"Huh. You're not usually upset about your secrets staying secret."

"Yeah, but that wasn't a secret." Cheyenne wheeled her chair toward the iron railing to peer through the bars at her friend. "I'm mostly talking about the Crown loyalists, Em. If they think Ba'rael's still living' it up in Hangivol with *all* her magic intact, it's business as usual for them over here."

Ember's eyes widened. "Meaning all the war machines are still up and running."

"Or about to be, yeah."

"Shit."

"Yep." Cheyenne took a deep breath and rolled back toward the wobbly office desk to get back to work. *It all starts and ends with this uncle, doesn't it? Find him, and we find a way to cut out the rest of the war machines.*

Her monitor quacked, and a notification for a new email rose on the bottom corner of her screen.

"Did your computer just quack at you?"

"Yep. Best way to interrupt my focus, other than everyone else's questions." Cheyenne shrugged. "I didn't mean you. Sorry."

"No problem. I won't keep distracting you."

Frowning, Cheyenne opened her personal email and found a new message from 2youngtodie@gmail.com titled: 'Is This Enough?'

Who the hell is that?

She clicked the email and laughed as she read the message.

I figured you're more likely to check your personal email, so I sent this to both. And I'm holding you to your offer of bonus points if you were serious about that part. If this wasn't what you wanted, let me know.

—Tori

"Tori?" Cheyenne scrolled all the way to the bottom and found a picture of the girl with the half-shaved head in the email signature. "Huh. Touché."

She kept scrolling and opened the massive compressed attachment. It took thirty seconds for her system to unzip the files, but then they opened one right after the other in overlapping boxes all over the screen.

Cheyenne's eyes widened, and she grinned as the activator pulled up everything she wanted to know without her needing to read a single line of what was in the files. "Way to go, Tori."

CHAPTER FIFTY

"Nope. Nope. Interesting, but no." Cheyenne clicked the boxes closed one by one, her eyes darting frantically back and forth as she picked up bits of information flagged by her activator, only to read the files and find them useless.

Come on, Tori. If you want those bonus points, you have to find something worth it.

A burst of green light flared when the activator illuminated a long line of code that didn't match any of the open files. Squinting, Cheyenne clicked out of all of them until the screen flashed green again. Buried beneath everything else she'd wasted time reading was the only encrypted file in her student's attachment. She ran her decryption program, which prompted her for a password.

The activator lined up the letters of the password superimposed in her vision over the prompt, and she snorted. "Oh, that's cute."

But of course, she typed in the password: *Say_Please.*

The contents of the encrypted file practically exploded all over her screen, and the activator flashed wildly to the pieces it knew she was looking for.

Gotta love tech synced with magic. This thing can literally read my mind.

Most of the decrypted files were images. Cheyenne flipped through them one by one. Matthew Thomas sitting at an executive desk,

Matthew Thomas with a blonde woman, Matthew Thomas with a brunette woman, Matthew Thomas standing in front of a brand-new elementary school surrounded by hundreds of grinning kids.

She snorted. *Close.*

The next image made her freeze.

Her cyber-guru neighbor stood on the front steps of a huge stone house that rivaled Bianca Summerlin's. Beside him stood a tall, thin man in military uniform, clean-shaven and at least twenty-five years older. Cheyenne's gaze flicked at the caption: Matthew Thomas and his maternal uncle, Colonel Les Thomas, 2019.

But she didn't need the caption to know who his uncle was. "No fucking way."

Ember paused her show. "Oh, my God, is it Sir?"

"No. Oh, Jesus."

"Cheyenne, you're killin' me."

"Yeah, I'm gonna kill *someone*, all right."

"Seriously."

"Colonel Les Thomas." Cheyenne shoved her chair away from her desk and leaped to her feet. "One of Major Sir Carson's superior officers."

"*What?*"

"Not a benefactor of the FRoE, Em. He's *running* it."

"Okay, wait." With a flash of purple light, Ember swung her legs off the couch and floated off the cushions to hover in the living room, craning her neck up at the mini-loft. "Did you find a list of FRoE officers?"

"No, but I've seen this man before, in person." Cheyenne stormed down the iron stairs, her drow magic flaring at the base of her spine and taking over a second before her feet reached the floor. *I'm gonna wring that cursing bastard's thick neck.*

"What do you mean? Where?"

"When they interrogated me, Em. In front of Sir. The day everyone heard L'zar Verdys escaped from Chateau D'rahl again, and they thought it would be a great big help to ask his *daughter* where he is."

"Wait, wait, wait." Ember floated after the halfling and pulled up short when Cheyenne reached the kitchen island and spun. "Matthew's uncle interrogated you?"

"No, he didn't say a word. I *know* that's the same guy, Em. Plenty of officers in that meeting and one of them is the same asshole who's been feeding the Crown loyalists all this—" She shook her fists and stormed across the apartment. "Goddammit!"

"Okay, don't bite my head off or anything, but I'm still kinda lost."

"They've been playing me this whole time!" Purple sparks crackled across Cheyenne's fingertips. "They've been in on this deal between Combined Reality and the loyalists for *years*. Every single step, everything I've done, the FRoE's been watching. Not to keep me in line, but to fucking help *her*!"

Ember bit her lip. "Her as in—"

"Ba'rael, Em!" Cheyenne whirled again and barely noticed her friend's surprised gaze as Ember backed away. "No wonder those bullshead assholes kept finding me everywhere. The FRoE had their eyes on me and fed everything back to the loyalists. They didn't do a fucking thing to step in 'cause they were in on it too!"

"That's bad news." Ember watched her friend pacing and eyed the purple sparks flaring across the halfling's skin. "And you need to calm down."

"I'm calm," Cheyenne growled and paced away again.

"No, actually, you're dripping drow sparks on the rug."

"I can't believe I didn't *see* this!"

"Cheyenne."

"I'm fucking *calm!*" A burst of crackling purple sprayed from Cheyenne's hand when she whirled again. It smashed into the rug, consuming the black fibers along the entire edge in a puff of flame and producing an instant stink of burning fabric and plastic.

Ember reached toward the burning rug and clenched her fist. The fire snuffed out, but the burnt smell thickened with a few more wisps of black smoke. "Come on, Cheyenne."

"Damnit." The halfling stared at the rug and forced her loud, fast breathing into something resembling sanity. "Sorry."

"I don't give a shit about the rug." Ember studied her friend's face. "You're paying for it. I'll order a new one."

Cheyenne snorted. "Okay."

"Okay. You went revenge mode, and then you snapped out of it, so what's next?"

With another snarl, Cheyenne clenched her fists. "I'm gonna cut out the rot."

"Whoa, whoa, whoa." Ember floated smoothly across the floor, took her friend by the shoulders, and shook her. "You. Can't. Go. On. A. Killing. Spree. Do you understand me?"

"Let go."

"No."

A deep purple light flared behind the halfling's eyes. "Get out of my way, Ember."

The fae's hand slapped Cheyenne's cheek and whipped her head to the side. Cheyenne growled and stared at the floor.

"Shit." Ember floated backward and shook out her hand. "Forget listening to me, Cheyenne. Listen to *yourself*. Do you have any idea what just came out of your mouth?"

Cheyenne closed her eyes and focused on pulling her magic back under control. "I told you to get out of my way."

"Before that, you crazy idiot."

The halfling looked up at her friend and blinked. "What?"

"You said you're gonna 'cut out the rot.' Ring any bells?"

Cheyenne swallowed. *Those aren't my words.* "Did I say that?"

"Oh, yeah. You were this close to bursting into black fire and calling yourself the new drow prophecy. You need to calm down and think about what you're doing."

"You're right. Totally right, Em." Cheyenne turned and ran a hand through her hair, scanning the walls of their apartment like she'd find the right answer there. "I have to be thinking clearly. Be prepared before I do anything else. And thanks for slapping me. Again."

"Sure." Ember shook out her hand again. "If that's all it takes to pull a drow out of going homicidal, I'm honestly surprised I've never seen someone slap L'zar in the face."

"So far, I think Bianca Summerlin's the only one who's done that and lived."

"Oh, yeah. I forgot all about that."

"I wish I could." Biting her lip, Cheyenne looked up at the mini-loft again and nodded. "Good thing I have you around to get me back on track."

"I mean, it's in the job description, isn't it? Your *Nós Aní* conscience and everything. What are you doing?"

"Making a call." Cheyenne pressed the send button and lifted her phone to her ear. "To the FRoE asshole who thinks he's better than everyone else. Sir's my only access point to Colonel Thomas right now, and I'm gonna use him. See how *he* likes it."

"Uh-huh." Ember folded her arms and waited.

The phone rang over and over, then stopped with a click and beeped, presumably to leave a message. "Of course he's not answering. I can work around that."

The halfling's feet pounded back up the iron stairs to the mini-loft, and she didn't bother to sit in her chair before pulling up every command the activator suggested. Her search for Major Guy "Sir" Carson's personal details took her two minutes flat. *Of course, his first name's Guy. Here we go. Personal phone number. P.O. Box. Home address. If you don't wanna answer my calls, that's fine, but I'm not fucking around anymore, Major.*

She pushed away from her desk and ran back down the stairs again.

"Cheyenne."

"My head's clear and I'm prepared, Em. Nothing to worry about anymore."

"Where are you going?"

Cheyenne opened the front door and turned around to shrug at her friend. "I'm going to get answers. Depending on what Sir decides to tell me, I haven't figured out what I'm gonna do to him yet, but I'm a 'wait for inspiration to strike' kinda drow."

The front door slammed shut, and Ember let out a long, heavy sigh. "Be careful. We all still have to be careful." She floated around the back of the couch and paused in front of the burned edge of the rug. "I guess I'm the one putting out drow fires. There are worse things, like not replacing this rug."

CHAPTER FIFTY-ONE

At first, Cheyenne thought it would be a good idea to get in her beat-up Panamera and drive to DC to give herself time to cool down and form a plan. But she only got two miles up the highway before she realized she wouldn't be calming down anytime soon.

Not until I let him have it. Sir's been jerking me around for way too long, and I'm done holding back.

She pulled into the parking lot of a grocery store she never shopped at, grimaced at the warbling chirp of the alarm system when she locked the doors, and stalked toward the back of the building. Two seconds later, a blur of purple-gray, black, and white streaked across the lot and headed north toward the nation's capital. A deafening crack followed a second later and scattered fall leaves all over the pavement and the grass around the parking lot.

Cheyenne pushed herself faster than she'd realized she could go in drow speed. Glinting cars, headlights, taillights, trees and leaves, and asphalt—all of it streamed past her in one giant streak of indecipherable color. She didn't stop, even to catch her breath, until she reached DC's city limits, but it wasn't because she was tired.

The activator flashed in her vision and lit up with a large yellow arrow on her left. When the halfling dropped out of drow speed in a burst of wind and spiraling leaves, she looked left and found herself on the street she'd noted on the map of the city she'd pulled up before leaving her apartment.

My activator comes with built-in navigation. There's no reason to take this thing off.

A forest-green sedan honked at her as it sped down the road. Cheyenne darted into drow speed again and followed the activator's directional prompts to Major Carson's home. The shockwave of her departure made the driver of the green sedan lay off the horn and grab the steering wheel instead. The wheels spun, and he skidded to a squealing stop with two tires up on the sidewalk.

Cheyenne darted down side streets and through one residential neighborhood after the other until the activator zeroed in on the address she wanted. She dropped into normal speed again with another sharp crack, pulling her magic back to slip into human form as she jogged toward his driveway.

Look at that—cute little suburban cookie-cutter. I took the man for a cabin-in-the-woods kinda guy. Wonder how he gets along with the neighbors?

She hurried across the lawn. The huge dogwood tree and the hedges around the yard provided the perfect cover from the street, and she let herself slip back into drow form before focusing her gaze on the house. Gold light flashed around the walls, and she stopped. *That's not the activator.*

Cheyenne stared *through* the walls, seeing the hazy layout of the inside of Major Carson's house without having to close her eyes or touch a wall. *About damn time my drow sight leveled up.*

A quick scan of Sir's home showed no shimmering lights around humanoid bodies. No cars in the garage. Blinking quickly to clear the x-ray drow vision, Cheyenne looked back toward the road and the driveway-sized sliver of it visible on the other side of the hedges. *I can wait. Especially for something this worth it.*

Ten minutes later, a beige Toyota Camry slowed on the quiet neighborhood street and turned into the driveway. Cheyenne hid behind the huge tree, silent as she watched the driver's side door open and Guy Carson step out of his vehicle. For the first time since she'd met him when she was strapped to a hospital bed with dampening cuffs at the FRoE compound, Sir wasn't in his military fatigues. No uniform, just a pair of bright blue Levi's and a maroon polo.

She forced herself not to laugh when she glanced at his shoes. *White New Balances. Are you kidding me? He's taking this whole fake-civilian-life act over the top.*

With his arms full of paper grocery bags, Sir stepped onto his front porch, keys jingling. He didn't see the two golden eyes glowing at him from behind the tree in his front yard. He unlocked the door, opened it, and took two steps into the house.

Cheyenne made her move.

She darted across the yard and up the porch stairs in a blur. By the time Sir heard the noise and turned around, she'd dropped back into real-time so she could slam the door shut behind her without splintering it into a million pieces.

His keys and all the bags of groceries toppled from his hands and hit the floor. "Holy fucking rhino shit!"

"Almost," Cheyenne growled and snatched the front of his maroon shirt before slamming him against the opposite wall of the entryway. Her face stopped two inches from his, and she snarled, "We need to talk."

"You." The man's salt-and-pepper mustache bristled as he pressed his lips together in rage. "What the hell are you doing here?"

She thumped him against the wall again, not hard enough to hurt him but hard enough to make her point. Maybe even a little harder. "I'm the one asking questions! And you're gonna answer every fucking one of them if you want to leave this little chat with any of your limbs still attached to your body. No bullshit. Got it?"

His dark, beady gaze flickered from one of her golden eyes to the other. "You found me."

"I can find anyone. Now you know."

For a second, she thought the man was having a heart attack. His eyes bulged from his head, his face turned its usual deep crimson in rage, and he shook beneath the fist clenched around his shirt.

Cheyenne loosened her grip a little. *He's helpless. No phone, no dampening gear, no brain-washed agents to do all the dirty work for him. I guess rage and terror look the same on this guy.*

He finally managed to snarl, "Let go of me."

She thumped him against the wall again and raised her other hand between them in a warning threat, purple sparks dancing across her fingers. "Not until you tell me everything you know about Colonel Les Thomas."

"What?" Sir sneered at her. "You've lost your goddamn mind, halfling. Barging into my home like this and threatening to…what? Barbeque me with those cute little sparks?"

Her purple sparks flew down the hall and crashed against the far wall, leaving a huge charred hole in the drywall. Somewhere in the other room, china dishes rattled, and a picture hanging above the new hole in the wall slipped off the nail and crashed to the floor. "Not fucking cute now, are they?"

Sir stared her right in the eyes, his chest heaving beneath her hand.

At least he can look at me and not try to run away. Points for stupidity, I guess.

"Colonel Les Thomas is a superior officer in the US Marine Corps and a high-ranking FRoE officer."

"I already *know* that. What's he planning with the loyalists? He's already got them powering their machines with his nephew's cutting-edge tech program. What else does he know? How long have you been reporting to him about *me*, asshole? 'Cause at this point, it looks a hell of a lot like you've been playing dumb fucking grunt to this guy and making shit worse for all of us on *both* sides of the Border." Sir snorted, but his eyes widened when she slammed her free hand on the wall behind his head. Her palm left another hole in the plaster and drywall, sending white dust all over them both and two more framed pictures smashing to the ground. "*Speak!*"

"I'm not a goddamn dog, halfling."

"I'll *feed* you to a dog if you don't—"

Cheyenne froze at the sound of a second car rolling up the driveway. She glanced at the closed front door, then shoved her face right back into his. "You expecting company?"

Sir swallowed. "Just my wife."

She released his shirt and stepped back. A dozen other pictures lined the wall of the entryway. Sir in civilian clothes beside a woman in her late fifties with curly graying hair and a laughing smile. Sir and his wife at the park, a restaurant, in front of the house, standing on a beach. "Who the hell would marry *you*?"

"I asked myself that same question over thirty years ago." Sir sniffed, readjusted his shirt, and peeled his back away from the wall. His gaze darted toward the front door when a car door clicked shut outside, and all the fight he had left went out of him. "Don't drag her into this, Cheyenne. That's all I'm asking. Whatever else you wanna know, I'll tell you. Just leave her—"

The front door opened, and his wife stepped inside with a handful of mail. "Guy, I'm home. You went by the store, right?" She looked up and saw a human-looking Cheyenne standing beside her husband, both of them wide-eyed and silent. "Oh. Hi."

Cheyenne swallowed and took a step to Sir's right to cover the hole in the wall beside his head.

The woman smiled and glanced between her husband and the pale Goth girl beside him. "Aren't you going to introduce us?"

"Yeah." Sir cleared his throat and recovered enough to come up with lies. "This is one of my work associates. Cheyenne—"

"Blakely," Cheyenne blurted with a nod. Sir shot her a weird look, and she forced herself to smile at his wife. *We're not throwing my real last name around for fun. I don't care how long they've been married.*

His wife cleared her throat.

The words spilled out of Sir all at once. "Cheyenne, this is my wife Alice."

Cheyenne kept the oddly tight smile on her face and reached slowly toward the woman to shake her hand. "Pleasure to meet you, Mrs. Carson."

"Well, don't do that." Alice quickly shook the halfling's hand and laughed. "Just Alice, please." She looked at them and raised an eyebrow. "You must be a big deal at the office, Cheyenne. He never brings anyone over, even for drinks. Speaking of which, can I get you anything?"

Cheyenne almost burst out laughing. "Yes, please."

"What? No." Sir took a step and stopped when his foot hit a can of garbanzo beans that had spilled out of the grocery bag. "Cheyenne was just leaving."

"Don't be ridiculous, Guy." Cheyenne waved a coy hand at him like they'd been close friends for years. "I can't turn down hospitality like *this*." Sir sputtered and stared at her, one eye twitching. *Now I got him.* "Alice, I would *love* to stay for a drink. Do you have any whisky?"

"Ha. Do we have whisky." The woman winked and pointed at her guest. "I know for a fact my husband keeps a bottle of his favorite at the office, and I keep another bottle of it here. I don't see what the big deal is with Glenlivet, but I'm sure you two can compare notes. Want anything with it?"

"No, thank you. On the rocks is perfect." The grin Cheyenne gave Mrs. Alice Carson was as genuine as they came for the half-drow. "I'm gonna help your husband clean this up. I think I startled him when I showed up early."

Alice finally noticed the groceries spilled all over the floor and the broken glass from the fallen picture frames. She looked up at her husband. "What did you do?"

Sir grunted. "Stumbled."

"Okay." The woman looked him up and down, then smiled at Cheyenne. "I'll get the drinks. Make sure my husband doesn't hurt himself, won't you? His blood pressure tends to spike when he does a lot of physical work. Even picking groceries up off the floor." Alice chuckled and stepped down the hall. "It's still the worst on Mondays, isn't it, honey?"

Sir's lower jaw jutted out in aggravation. "Yeah."

"I'll be right back. Make yourself at home, Cheyenne. I'm glad we finally have company to entertain. You have no idea how long it's been."

"My pleasure." Cheyenne smiled after Sir's endearing wife until the woman returned her attention to the mail in her hand. The whole time, she felt Sir's glare burning into the side of her face and couldn't help but rub it in a little more. "I like her."

"Don't."

"You picked a winner there, Guy."

"I'm serious."

"Any chance she'll invite me to stay for dinner? I might take her up on that."

"Shut up and get out of my way." Sir dropped into a squat and reached for the can of garbanzo beans.

Cheyenne slipped into drow mode and tossed an arc of purple sparks at his hand. He snatched his hand back and scowled up at her. "I'll get it. Don't wanna spike your blood pressure, do we?"

Sir got to his feet and wagged a finger in the halfling's face. "I swear to every fat, fluffy, furball on legs, halfling, if you so much as *look* at her the wrong way, I'll—"

"Track my phone? Show up at my house? Try to blackmail me? Skip the halfling hierarchy and go straight to Bianca to prove a point?" Cheyenne clicked her tongue and felt her grin take the same shape she hated seeing on L'zar. "Come on, Guy. You're out of empty threats and you know it, so sit back and leave the thinking to someone who knows what they're doing, huh?"

He snorted. "You mean, you?"

The activator pulled up a series of commands from Cheyenne's magic when she glanced down at the spilled groceries. She flicked her fingers, selecting the offered levitation spell she couldn't cast on her own in a million years, and the grocery bags leaped from the floor to pile themselves neatly in her arms. Then she slipped out of drow form, cocked her head, and let herself channel Bianca Summerlin. "Well, I do have you at something of a disadvantage, don't I? I hope it's good whisky."

She stepped past him and headed down the hall.

Behind her, the man shoved the broken glass into a pile with the side of his white New Balance sneaker, spitting out curse after curse, not in Major Sir Carson's bellowing rampage, but in Guy Carson's small, hushed whisper.

This is way better than bashing in his skull. "Alice?"

"Yes?"

"Where's the kitchen?"

"Oh, turn left at the end of the hall. I'm almost finished with the drinks."

"Perfect."

CHAPTER FIFTY-TWO

Glass spilled out of the dustpan into the trashcan before Sir shoved it back into its place beside the fridge.

"You know, I wasn't a huge fan of those picture frames anyway. They were gifts. Really, honey, there's nothing to be embarrassed about. It's the perfect excuse to go buy new ones." Alice handed Cheyenne a rocks glass of whisky with two square ice cubes, then lifted her own glass of chardonnay and clinked it against the halfling's. "To meeting my husband's associates."

"And such fantastic hospitality." Cheyenne grinned at the woman and took a sip of Sir's favorite whisky.

He stiffly joined them at the kitchen counter, breathing heavily through his nose and staring at the glass his wife had poured for him.

"How is it?" Alice asked.

Cheyenne feigned hesitation and turned toward Sir.

"Oh, be honest." Alice chuckled and sipped her wine. "There aren't nearly enough people in this world with the gumption to tell my husband the truth. Honestly, I don't see why everyone seems so scared of how he'll react, but he *needs* it, Cheyenne. Trust me, you won't hurt his feelings."

Sir picked up his whisky, looked from the amber liquid to his wife, and smiled. "You make me sound like some kind of dictator."

Alice's easy laughter drowned out the sound of Cheyenne choking on her next sip. The whisky fumes burned up her nose before she swallowed. *Still worth it.*

Sir shot her a scathing glance and took a huge gulp.

"Honey, you know that's not what I mean." Alice waved him off and leaned over the counter splitting the kitchen down the middle to share a conspiratorial glance with Cheyenne. "Honestly, I think I'm the only one who ever questions him, and I don't see what the big deal is."

"Well, you should count yourself lucky." Cheyenne lifted her glass to toast the woman again. "At least he's his best self around *you*, if not everyone else. Some people don't treat their family any differently than their coworkers, and that can be difficult."

Alice blinked in surprise, and her smile grew with her admiration for the young woman standing in her kitchen. "I don't usually ask people this the first time I meet them, Cheyenne, so I apologize in advance."

"Don't worry about it. What do you want to know?"

"How old are you?"

Sir rolled his eyes and took another huge swig of whisky.

"Twenty-one."

"*Really?* And you landed a job in Guy's department already?"

"We've only been working together for…what is it, Guy? Two months?"

He grunted. "Something like that."

Alice shot her husband a playful frown. "Did he hire you personally?"

"He sure did." Cheyenne grinned at Sir and raised her glass. "Picked me right out of a crowd, didn't you? And you know what, Guy? I still haven't asked you what made me stand out above all the other applicants."

"Oh, yes." Alice turned toward her husband too, her eyes wide with interest. "I'd love to hear this story."

Sir blinked furiously beneath both women's gazes, smacked his lips, lowered his glass to the counter, and shot Cheyenne a quick glance. "I don't know."

"Don't do that." Alice sipped her wine again. "We both want to know."

"I liked her style. I guess."

Cheyenne had never worked so hard in her life not to break out laughing. Somehow, she managed to keep it all filtered into a grateful, composed smile. "That's so sweet."

He grunted again.

"Sweetheart," Alice said as she gently rubbed her husband's back and gazed lovingly at him, "it is. And Cheyenne, I don't mean for this to come off as offensive in any way, but we can talk all we want about how important it is not to assume things about people based on how they dress."

"Never judge a book by its cover," Cheyenne added.

"*Exactly*. It's so great to see young people like you following your dreams, applying to work in a high-level department like Guy's and still freely expressing yourself in a way that feels right to *you*."

"It *is* a nice story, isn't it?" The halfling wrinkled her nose in pretend glee and raised her glass toward Alice again. "Your husband didn't care one bit about the way I look. He's one of those open-minded, inclusive, forward-thinking people, you know?"

"Oh, Guy." Alice leaned toward her husband and placed a lingering kiss on his cheek. Then she gave Cheyenne a coy smile and a playful shrug. "That's one of the things I love most about this man."

"Among many others, I bet." Cheyenne smiled sweetly at Sir and batted her eyelashes. *I can go on like this all day, Major. Your move.*

He thumped a fist on his chest and grimaced. "We still have Tums in the cabinet, don't we?"

"Should be right next to your other meds, yeah." Alice watched him walk away, then fixed Cheyenne with a secret smile. "He gets embarrassed so easily."

"I would never have guessed."

"I know. Under all this pressure at work and the constant responsibilities. He's been in that department for about as long as you've been alive. Ha. Isn't that funny?"

"Just coincidence after coincidence."

"We'll give him a minute. Oh. I want to show you something." Alice stepped away from the counter, took a long drink of wine, then leaned over to set her glass down before heading into the hall again.

His footsteps pounded across the hardwood floor from the other side of the house, and he skidded to a stop in the hallway, his eyes wide. "Alice. What happened? I swear, if she—"

Alice frowned at him and pointed at the charred hole in the wall. "What's this?"

"Electrical shortage." Cheyenne stopped in the door of the kitchen and leaned against the frame, sipping her whisky. Alice turned toward her, and Sir scowled at the halfling behind his wife's back. "I saw a few loose wires in there when I walked by. Looks like something chewed through, maybe shocked itself. You might wanna check the place for rodents. You know," her gaze darted toward Sir, and she raised her eyebrows, "rats."

Alice glanced into the charred hole. "Honey, you still have the number for the exterminator we used last spring?"

"I'm sure I can find it." A vein throbbed in the major's temple.

"We should call them tomorrow." Alice glanced at her wristwatch and jumped. "Oh. Here we are chatting away, and I still have to get the steaks out of the marinade and put the rolls in the oven."

"Steaks." Cheyenne nodded. "Very nice for a Monday."

"It used to be almost every day of the week. I finally convinced him of what the doctors have been telling him for years. Less red meat. More greens. Easy on the booze." Alice chuckled. "We got two out of three, but at least the liquor doesn't have nearly as many calories as all the beer. Small wins. I'll take it."

Cheyenne raised her glass at Sir, whose face had darkened to the same shade as his maroon polo again, and nodded. "He seems to be doing fine."

"We both are, aren't we?" Alice rubbed her husband's shoulder and gave him a concerned frown. "Did you find the Tums?"

"Yeah." He stared at the wall and rubbed his fingers across his lips, ruffling his mustache.

"Give it a little while. I'm sure whatever it is will disappear before you know it and leave you alone so we can enjoy our dinner."

"Doesn't seem likely."

"Hey, remember what we talked about with Dr. Angstern? Our state of mind is as important as diet and exercise. Just a little optimism, honey. That's all it takes."

He ran his tongue over his teeth, and a small, tight smile spread across his lips. "I know. I'll be fine."

"Okay." She kissed his cheek, then clapped her hands together and smiled at Cheyenne. "Speaking of dinner, I need to get everything ready. I know it's rude with guests over, but Guy has to eat at a specific time, or he's up all night with indigestion."

"That's fine. Don't let me stop you." Cheyenne sipped at her drink.

"All right. I'll take your word for it. Honey, did you pick up a new tank for the grill?"

"It's in the car."

"You're the best. Cheyenne, would you mind helping him with that propane tank?"

"Physical activity. I get it. Come on, Guy. You open the door, I'll do the heavy lifting." The halfling walked down the hall toward the front door and nodded for Sir to follow.

"Thank you. I'll be out in a bit with the steaks. Feel free to make yourself another drink, Cheyenne."

"And I won't interrupt your cooking." Cheyenne opened the door and held it for Sir. "You want your drink?"

He nodded vigorously, then stormed into the kitchen to retrieve his whisky. Alice and Cheyenne smiled at each other, and when Sir returned, his glass was full again. "Then I'll show you around back and heat up the grill," he muttered.

"Sounds like *fun*."

Alice chuckled and headed back into the kitchen.

"Oh, and you could give me the grand tour of your lovely home if you like."

Sir pulled his face out of his rocks glass and snorted, heading through the front door without looking at her. "Fuck off, halfling."

Grinning, Cheyenne pulled the door closed behind her and followed him to his car.

CHAPTER FIFTY-THREE

The flames ignited on the grill in Guy Carson's backyard, and he scowled at them before stepping back and taking another long drink.

"Great yard." Cheyenne gazed at the half-acre behind the man's house, complete with a patio awning, two large trees with most of their leaves still clinging to the branches, and a well-maintained garden, despite the flowers having bloomed and died this far into autumn. "Aren't you and Alice the perfect picture of suburbia?"

He glared at her. "You didn't come here to talk about my personal life, you psychotic changeling."

"No, but it's so much fun."

"Get to the point."

"Sure. You know about the new portals opening because *I* told you about them."

He snorted and took another drink.

"I'm only telling you the rest of this because I don't trust you, and I want to see your face screw up when you realize you're fucked."

"Excellent opening statement. Ten points."

She gave him a deadpan stare. "Those new portals are opening because of some issues in Ambar'ogúl."

"I don't give a duck's corkscrewed dick about any of those glittering magical assholes on the other side."

"Shut up and listen." Cheyenne slipped in and out of drow form and narrowed her eyes. "Don't get too comfy playing house, Major. That's not why I'm here."

His nostrils flared as he studied her unflinching gaze, and he nodded with another grunt.

"Those magical assholes on the other side have been using those unregulated new portals to smuggle O'gúl tech across the Border. To Earth. Maybe you already know the stuff isn't supposed to work on this side, and I think you know that it does anyway."

"I have no idea what you're talking about."

"The machines, Major. War machines popping up out of the ground and digging their way into wherever the hell they're told to go. They're powered on this side of the Border by a program designed specifically for O'gúl tech. A man named Matthew Thomas owns the company and designed that program himself."

"Fucking woohoo for him." Sir sipped his whisky and smacked his lips, licking small drops from his mustache.

Cheyenne leaned toward him and studied every pulsing vein and twitching muscle in his face. *I'll find it. He's an especially shitty liar when his wife's around.* "Matthew Thomas was introduced to a group of extra-large magical assholes by his uncle Colonel Les Thomas. One of your commanding officers, isn't he?"

"Look, halfling. You can play glowy-eyed detective all you want, but you don't know a goddamn thing about—"

"I *know* he was at that little meeting you called when L'zar got out last week, and Matthew Thomas happens to be my neighbor, so I know a hell of a lot more than you think. I don't know who else is involved in this, but at the very least, Colonel Thomas has been using FRoE resources to send information to the other side. He's been funding an operation run by those assholes over here that will be the *worst* mistake of your life if you don't tell me everything else."

Sir snorted. "You're as crazy as your old man."

"Maybe. Is that a risk you're willing to take? 'Cause the crazy drow slipped out from right under your nose, Major. Twice."

He sucked his lower lip noisily and sneered at the heating grill.

"Assuming your cooked-up little conspiracy is true, and there's no way it is, what in the goddamn cosmos do you think I'm supposed to do about it, huh?"

"Set up a meeting for me. With Colonel Thomas."

"Ha! You did get the psycho gene from that slippery white-haired fuck."

"Hey, did you suddenly forget where we are and how easy it was for me to find you? This isn't a game."

"It's not true!" Whisky sloshed over the side of his glass when he spun toward her. "No way in hell, halfling. The FRoE doesn't have double agents. Shit, except for you."

She cocked her head.

"Everyone below and above me is squeaky-clean."

"Like Ranzig Ca'admar, right? 'Cause nobody smelled that one coming except for me."

"That was a one-time thing."

"No, it was not." Cheyenne glanced at the house when the clink of dishes rose from the kitchen inside the back porch. "I'm not making this up, and I'm giving you a chance to clean up your organization because it's rotting from the inside out. When the O'gúl loyalists with that program running their war machines get everything working the way they want, a few unexpected portals popping up around Virginia are gonna be a piece of cake in comparison. Those aren't normal machines, either. Your agents aren't regular O'gúleesh, and they don't have enough training or experience with this to know the first thing about how to take those machines down."

"Bullshit. My agents aren't the problem."

"The problem is Colonel Thomas!" Cheyenne stepped away from him and glanced at the house again as Alice opened the sliding back door and poked her head outside.

"I heard shouting. Everything okay?"

Sir and Cheyenne raised their hands at the same time to wave at his wife. "All good, honey. We're talking shop."

"You know how I feel about that."

"I'll rein him in." Cheyenne nodded and plastered a wide grin on her face.

"Okay. I'm almost ready."

"Grill's fired up and waiting." Sir winked at her with an equally tight smile. The minute Alice closed the door and disappeared inside, he spun toward Cheyenne again. "You've always been a pain in my ass, and now you've gone too far."

"You know what? I came out here fully intending to bash your head in if you didn't pull it out of your ass long enough to hear what I'm telling you. We have a serious problem. The FRoE isn't run by the same people you started it with twenty-one years ago, and Colonel Thomas is gonna bring the whole thing crashing down on top of you."

"It's impossible. That's it." Sir's face darkened again, his cheeks quivering furiously as he shook his head. "Not even. There's no way."

"It's true, and I can prove it. Why would I lie to you?"

"Huh, I don't know." He leaned closer and thrust a finger toward the back door. "You showed up at my home and threatened my life. I can think of a few reasons you'd wanna set me up and ship me out."

Cheyenne said, "More than a few, but ruining *your* life doesn't do anything to help all the other people on this side of the Border, the refugees at the reservations, or all the O'gúleesh on the other side. If we don't stop this, *everyone's* going down, not just you. That's what they want, and who do you think people are gonna blame when they find out about magic and the ruler on the other side sending her army out here to conquer Earth?"

"What are you, schizophrenic? You sound like it."

"And you sound like a piece of shit for thinking that's the right answer."

Sir stepped toward her and thrust a finger in her face. "Don't try to pin your problems on *me*, halfling. You did this to yourself!"

"You don't know half my problems. You're just the one I'm looking at right now."

"This is bullshit." Sir downed the rest of his drink, glared at it, and grunted. "I need a drink."

"Do I have to kidnap you from your own backyard?"

"Okay, okay. Shut up." The man sniffed and shook his head. "I like the sound of this whole thing about as much as I enjoy a hot poker up my ass."

"You kiss your wife with that mouth?"

"Fuck you. I'll look into it. That's it. I'm not signing a goddamn statement, Cheyenne, but I'll look. That's all I can do."

"Fine."

The back door slid open again, and Alice stepped onto the back porch with a long platter holding two well-marinated steaks. The stink of vinegar and spices made Cheyenne's nostrils flare. *I'm never touching vinegar again, not after Nor'ieth.*

"I'm sorry that took so *long*. The rolls have another five minutes in the oven, but these are ready to go." Alice set the platter on the grill's cold side-burner and stuck her hands on her hips. "Cheyenne, it's been great to have you here. Why don't you stay for dinner?"

"I can't," Cheyenne muttered.

At the same time, Sir said, "Fat chance."

"Oh." Alice blinked rapidly and shrugged. "Okay. Is everything—"

"Thanks for the drink, Alice. Excuse me." Cheyenne turned and stormed toward the gate in the fence. The wood creaked and snapped when she pulled the gate open, and she forced her anger and the brewing heat of her drow magic back under control.

Alice stared after her until their guest disappeared around the front. "Did something happen?"

The first steak sizzled on the grill, and Sir tapped the tongs on the grate. "Who knows with that one?"

She shot him a confused look. "I'll go close the gate, then."

"Excellent." He scowled at the grill, ignoring the smoke blooming up in his face as he slapped the other steak down beside the first. *I'm never leaving my gun at the goddamn office again.*

CHAPTER FIFTY-FOUR

Cheyenne stomped down the sidewalk through Guy Carson's neighborhood. *He can't seriously think I'm pulling all this out of thin air. The fact that I found him should've been enough.*

A dog darted toward her across the front yard of the house she passed. It stopped at the line of the invisible fence and jumped back and forth, hackles raised and tail wagging at the same time.

Cheyenne looked at the dog and let out a low growl. The barking stopped, and the dog's tongue flopped over the side of its open mouth as it panted at her, tail still wagging away. She kept moving.

I can't tell if Sir's mad face is his poker face, but he wouldn't have said he'd look into it if he didn't plan to. He's got eleven days. That's all the time either of us has. I'll be a little too busy to deal with his shit after that.

She didn't pay attention to where she was going, just walked down the street in the crisp, early-evening air to clear her head and put as much distance between her and Major Carson as possible without slipping into drow mode. *Then I'd wanna go right back and tear him apart.*

Her phone buzzed against her thigh, and she reached into the pocket of her trenchcoat to pull it out. *A call from Mom on the landline? I guess it's technically after hours.*

Cheyenne answered the call and put the phone to her ear. "Hey, Mom."

"Cheyenne! Oh, thank God. I didn't know when I'd get you to pick up. Have you been somewhere without service?"

"Eleanor?"

"Sweetheart, I don't know what happened. She was out there, and she wouldn't *listen* to me. I kept telling her to listen, to just come inside, and—"

"Whoa. Okay, Eleanor. Hold on."

"Cheyenne, if I knew anyone else to call, I… Well, I only know you, really."

"Hey, slow down a second." Cheyenne stopped on the sidewalk and stared blankly across the street. "Start over. Tell me what happened."

"Cheyenne, I can't even think! I don't know what to *do!*"

A loud rustling came over the line.

"Eleanor? *Eleanor.* What's going on?"

"You don't have to yell, halfling. I can hear you fine."

Cheyenne forced herself not to break her cell phone. "Rhynehart, what the hell is going on?"

"It's Bianca."

"What?"

"I know, kid. Shitty way to hear about it, but it's not like we have another way to get hold of you."

"Is she okay? What happened?"

"I don't know." Rhynehart sighed. "And I don't know. There's something wrong with her. I think."

"Quit screwing around and give me information, man." A car drove slowly past her, and Cheyenne briefly looked up before turning and pacing back the other way.

"She's just standing there, Cheyenne. Obviously, my team's still up at her place, keeping an eye on the black rocks. Bianca's been out here all day, standing in front of the ridge, and we can't get her to respond. She won't even move."

"*All* day?"

"Yeah."

"And no one had the bright idea to guide her back inside? Jesus, nobody has a brain anymore."

Rhynehart cleared his throat. "We tried, kid. Trust me. Moving her, I mean. Can't touch her, though."

"I don't have a clue what that means."

"Well, it means it fucking hurts."

Cheyenne's black Vans crunched on the leaves scattered across the sidewalk when she spun again, her heartbeat pounding furiously in her ears. "Seriously, what are you talking about?"

"I have no idea. Pretty sure I said that already. But I can tell you right now, Bianca Summerlin's sparking magic at anyone who touches her, and she's already fried a few of my men without lifting a finger."

"No way."

"Something you're not telling me?"

Cheyenne looked disbelieving. "Not about my *mom*. What the hell? That's *not* supposed to happen."

"Yeah, I had a feeling. You should probably get up here." Rhynehart lowered his voice. "Maybe bring somebody who knows how to handle this, huh? My guys aren't equipped for this kinda thing, and I'm not equipped to listen to Bianca's housekeeper shrieking in hysterics. Not for much longer, anyway."

"Yeah. I'll be there. Give me half an hour."

"You already on your way, or you gonna take the super-speed express?"

"If anything happens to her before I get there, Rhynehart, I will blame you for it."

"Yep. I probably would too. Don't take too long." He hung up before Cheyenne had the chance.

Shit. She shoved her phone back into her pocket and smoothed her hair away from her face. *Okay. Hang in there, Mom. I'm coming.*

Cheyenne headed quickly down the sidewalk, glancing up and down the street. When the last visible car passed her and turned the corner at the end of the block, she slipped into drow speed and took off with a burst of swirling leaves and a loud crack, heading for Henry County. The street swirled with kicked-up leaves and dry twigs. The dog who'd barked at her and probably would have rolled over if she'd stayed gave a high-pitched whine and sank to his belly in the grass.

She'd underestimated by ten minutes and stumbled out of enhanced speed twenty minutes later. The gravel drive in front of Bianca Summerlin's estate slid beneath her feet, and she almost ended up with a mouthful of pebbles.

From behind the house, Eleanor's frightened shouts echoed toward the front. "How could you let this happen? Why are you even *here*? You can't keep her safe. You can't keep any of us safe! Oh, my God. What if she never comes out of it?"

Fighting to catch her breath, Cheyenne staggered toward the bushes on the side of the house, her mouth dry and her legs trembling. *Okay, maybe I pushed myself too hard. Not like I had a choice.*

"Ma'am, please," Rhynehart pleaded as she staggered down the flag-stone steps toward the backyard. "I know I keep saying it, but the best way for us to handle the situation is if everyone remains calm."

"Calm?" Eleanor shrieked. "Does this look like something to be calm *about*? Listen to me, Mr. Secret Agent or whoever-you-are, I run this woman's life, and the fact that she hasn't moved from that spot in the last sixteen hours is the exact *opposite* of what makes me calm!"

"Eleanor," Cheyenne croaked. She pushed herself to move faster across the grass and raised her hand. "Eleanor!"

The woman turned toward Cheyenne and gasped, then practically shoved Rhynehart away before taking off across the manicured lawn. "Cheyenne. I'm so glad you're here. You got here so quickly."

"Come on, you know I can do that."

Eleanor grabbed the girl's shoulders and looked her over. "Are you okay? You look awful. Sweetheart, I have no idea what to do."

"I know. It's okay. I'll figure it out." Cheyenne gave the housekeeper's arms a gentle squeeze, then removed her hands and walked past her toward the portal ridge.

The pillars of black stone splitting across the pristine lawn of the Summerlin estate pulsed with waves of purple and green light. The colors mixed to give off a muddy brown glow that reflected in the FRoE agents' eyes as they watched the halfling slowly approach.

Bianca Summerlin stood in front of the line of portal stones, her arms hanging loosely at her sides, staring blankly at the pulsing lights in front of her.

"Mom?" A cold knot of apprehension coiled in Cheyenne's gut. "Mom, can you hear me?"

"I already told you, kid. There's nothing there."

She turned around and glared at him. "That's not true, and you know it. Don't say stuff like that."

"I meant, no reaction."

"Yeah, I know what you meant, but you need to work on your shitty delivery."

Eleanor clapped a hand over her mouth but didn't dare mention Cheyenne's choice of words.

Now I know *something's wrong.* Cheyenne turned back to her mother and swallowed. *She would've told me to watch my mouth.*

"Mom, if you can hear me, blink or something."

Bianca's eyes didn't move, let alone blink. The rise and fall of her slow breathing were barely visible.

"Mom? *Mom*! You have to snap out of it!"

Eleanor reached toward the halfling. "Cheyenne, don't!"

Rhynehart darted toward them. "Hey, I said—"

Cheyenne grabbed her mom's shoulder. A bubble of the same dark, muddy light bloomed around Bianca's entire body and blasted her daughter away from her with a zap. Cheyenne flew backward across the lawn, her skin and hair sparking. She hit the grass, slid another foot, and waited for the sting to fade from every inch of her skin. "What the hell?"

Rhynehart jogged toward her. "I know we've had our issues, kid, but come on. I wouldn't lie to you about something like that."

"Well, you definitely didn't lie about how much it hurts. I forgot about your warning." Cheyenne wiggled her jaw, her face feeling like it was moving all on its own, and accepted his hand.

The agent pulled her to her feet and nodded. "You okay?"

"I guess. Yeah. Does that happen every time?"

"Every time." Rhynehart turned to look at Bianca and the portal ridge with a grimace. "Had each one of my guys take a stab at it."

"Hey. *She* is my mom, not an it. Not a target."

"Sorry. You're right." He shrugged. "Everybody here tried helping your mom away from the portal, and everybody got their asses launched back just like you did."

Cheyenne brushed her hair out of her face and studied her mom's rigid, motionless figure. "I don't get it."

"Right there with you, kid, which was why I suggested bringing someone else. You forget about that too?"

She took a deep breath and pulled her phone out of her pocket. "I wanted to see what was going on first. I still have no idea."

"I seriously hope you know someone who *does* have an idea. She's not gonna last much longer standing there like that. No food. No water. No sleep. And those morphing-monster things could pop out of the stones at any time."

"Stop." Cheyenne looked up from her phone and glared at him. "You're the worst at making people feel better. You know that, right?"

"Still working on it." With a sharp nod, Rhynehart walked swiftly back to his team and left the halfling alone to make her call.

She pressed the phone to her ear and stared at her mom's silhouette, cast by the pulsing purple and green lights. *Come on, Corian. Pick up. Whatever you're doing, please pick up.*

"Where are you?"

A small sigh of relief escaped her. "I'm at Bianca's, and I really, *really* need your help. *She* needs your help."

The other end of the line was silent.

"Corian?"

"How bad is it?"

"Bad enough that I'm calling you less than five minutes after I got here. Please, can you get here or not?"

"Yeah, kid. Hang tight."

"Thank you." She swallowed thickly and felt like she could breathe again. "Hey, can you bring Ember with you? I have a feeling I'll need her too."

"That's usually how it goes. Five minutes, Cheyenne."

"Okay." She kept her phone against her ear for a full thirty seconds after he hung up. Then she blinked, slid the phone back into her pocket, and walked quickly back toward Rhynehart's agents and Eleanor the housekeeper, who was glaring furiously at all of them.

CHAPTER FIFTY-FIVE

"Who'd you call?" Rhynehart stopped beside Cheyenne and rocked forward on his toes.

She stared at her mom's blank, unchanging face. "You'll find out."

"Huh." He took a deep breath and folded his arms. "I have to ask, kid. Does this have anything to do with you running around and popping in and out of this thing?"

"No. That was one time, Rhynehart. And Bianca wasn't a part of it."

"Okay. If you're sure."

"I didn't have anything to do with this. I wouldn't risk anything happening to her." Cheyenne looked up at him and shook her head. "That was why I called you guys."

"I know. I'm trying to put together whatever pieces I can."

"Well, I don't have enough pieces, so you're outta luck."

They stood silently beside each other as the portal ridge pulsed with muddy light.

Then one of his agents shouted and stepped back, quickly followed by the others. A dark oval of light shimmered in the air behind Bianca, and Corian stepped out first. He didn't bother with an illusion this time, and he only spared the FRoE agents a quick, sidelong glance through narrow silver eyes before he headed toward Cheyenne.

"Christ," Rhynehart muttered. "Where'd you find *that* guy?"

"In a basement." Cheyenne met Corian halfway and shrugged. "I don't know what's going on."

"Show me, and we'll go from there."

She nodded at Bianca, then saw Byrd and Lumil standing in front of the portal, scowling at the FRoE agents. Persh'al came next, rubbing the side of his shaved head, then Ember floated through the portal.

Rhynehart rubbed a hand over his mouth and stared. "The whole damn circus."

"Who the hell is that?"

"Holy shit! It's him!"

"Get back!"

Eleanor's scream cut through the agents' startled shouts, and she fled back to the house, the strings of her apron left on that morning streaming behind her as she ran.

Cheyenne tried to ignore the agents running around like a magical bomb had gone off when L'zar Verdys stepped through the portal. "I didn't tell you to bring *him*."

Corian nodded. "I told him that. He refused to stay behind."

"Great."

"Goddammit, Cheyenne!" Rhynehart stormed toward her with a hand on the fell pistol at his hip. "You said you didn't know where he was!"

"Hey, did you see *me* walk through that portal?"

"You called the damn nightstalker who opened it! How am I supposed to believe you had no idea L'zar Verdys was with that cat-looking creep?"

Corian snarled, "Watch it."

Rhynehart stepped away from the nightstalker but didn't draw his weapon. "I have orders. I'm taking him in."

Cheyenne rolled her eyes. "Go for it. And have fun. I know *he* will."

"What?" The agent stopped and spun to stare at her.

"He's not playing 'imprison the drow' anymore, Rhynehart." Cheyenne gestured toward her father, who twirled both hands and gave the FRoE agents a flippant bow as they drew their weapons and waited for the order. "Seventy-five years in Chateau D'rahl was a *game* for him. Don't tell me you can't see that."

The agent bit his bottom lip and cringed when L'zar gave his crazed drow laugh and spun in a wide, slow circle. "Shit. I'd tell you to give me one good reason why I shouldn't put him away right now, but that's enough."

"Yeah, I know."

Corian watched the drow thief intently. "He might be the only one who can help her, kid."

"Let's go find out." Cheyenne shook her head and headed toward the gathered agents, who had all aimed their weapons on L'zar Verdys.

"Cheyenne!" He spread his arms and dipped his head. "What a welcome, huh? I haven't seen the end of this many toys in three-quarters of a century."

Rhynehart raised a hand toward his agents and shook his head. "Stand down."

"Are you insane?"

"Stand *down*, Walden!"

The agents blinked in confusion and eyed L'zar warily, but pistols and fell rifles lowered slowly under their team leader's command.

"So, you think you know what's going on here?" Rhynehart nodded behind L'zar at Bianca's motionless form.

"That depends. I'd love to hear what Ms. Summerlin has to say." When the drow thief saw Bianca standing there, his grin disappeared. "No."

"Huh." Rhynehart cocked his head. "Definitely *sounds* like he knows what's going on."

"Not in the good way." Cheyenne shot the agent a disapproving glance, then hurried toward L'zar. "What happened to her? Is she okay?"

The drow thief reached slowly toward Bianca, then pulled his hand away and pressed his fingers to his lips.

"L'zar. I asked you a question."

"Give me a moment, Cheyenne." One of his eyes twitched as he studied Bianca, moving in a slow circle around her. He stopped in front of her, his eyebrows creased in concern, and dipped his head toward her. "Bianca?"

Corian joined them and chewed the inside of his cheek. "Any idea what—"

"I said, give me a moment!" L'zar's fists clenched tightly at his sides, and his golden eyes glowed without leaving Bianca's face. "When I'm ready to tell you, I will tell you."

"Sure." Corian set a hand on Cheyenne's shoulder and drew her back. "Come on, kid."

"Wait, does he know or not?" She saw the warning in the nightstalker's eyes, combined with the strengthening pressure of his fingers on her shoulder, so she swallowed and forced herself to nod. "Right. He needs some time. Fine."

"Yep." Corian looked at L'zar warily, then turned with her and led Cheyenne away from everyone else. When they were out of earshot, he let go of her and stuck his hands in his pockets. "You're not gonna like what I'm about to tell you, kid."

"You know what this is."

"No, but he does." Corian glanced at L'zar, who leaned closer to Bianca, his expression changing from wide-eyed surprise to a concerned frown to disbelief and something else.

Looks a lot like sadness.

Cheyenne couldn't take her eyes off her parents. "Why won't he tell us what happened and how to fix it? I mean, he doesn't even have to do anything. *I'll* take care of it. I need to know what to do."

"I know. And he'll tell us when he's ready, kid. Whenever he comes out of shock."

"Out of shock?" Cheyenne gestured harshly toward her father. "That doesn't look like shock to me. He's studying her like she's some kind of experiment!"

"Trust me, Cheyenne. I've spent enough time with him to know his moods and what he's thinking. For the most part."

"Oh, yeah? You're gonna speak for him now? Then what the hell's he thinking?"

The nightstalker gazed at the grass and rubbed the back of his neck.

"Corian!"

"It's bad, Cheyenne."

She stepped away from him and swallowed. "Shit."

"The rest will have to wait. And then we'll do what we need to do."

Cheyenne's legs wobbled, and she staggered before letting herself sink to her knees. "That bad."

"Nothing L'zar Verdys and his halfling daughter can't handle."

She didn't have to look at him to hear the truth behind his words. *He doesn't believe that.*

CHAPTER FIFTY-SIX

Cheyenne knelt in the same spot in the middle of the lawn for the next half hour and didn't move. Ember sat beside her in the grass, though neither of them could think of anything to say as L'zar paced between Bianca and the portal ridge. The FRoE agents were nervous, keeping at least twenty feet between them and the drow who still had twenty-five years left on his sentence at Chateau D'rahl.

Probably more, now. Not like he's gonna serve it.

Lumil and Byrd stood on the other side of the portal ridge with their arms folded, staring at everyone else and muttering their thoughts aloud to each other. Persh'al sat cross-legged in the grass, his elbows on his thighs and his chin resting in his cupped hands as he watched L'zar watching Bianca Summerlin.

"How much can he figure out just by walking back and forth?" Ember muttered.

Cheyenne shrugged.

"It's an old habit," Corian explained.

"Whatever."

L'zar snarled and snapped them all back to attention. "To the death-flame then, huh? Fuck it."

He lunged toward Bianca and grabbed her by both shoulders.

"Don't!" Cheyenne leaped to her feet and ran toward him.

The drow thief shrieked in Bianca's face, the purple and green light sparking and flashing all over both of them, but he held on tight, his eyes flaring as deep purple replaced the flickering gold. The spell around Cheyenne's mom flashed brighter and brighter, and L'zar didn't let go until his scream ran out with his willpower.

He recoiled from the woman and spun away, sinking to his knees. Smoke and crackling flashes of purple and green rose from his upturned hands, and his chest heaved as he bowed his head.

Cheyenne reached him in seconds. "What did you do? Mom? Hey!" She stepped toward her father and forced herself not to hit him while he was down. "Say something!"

"It's all my fault."

"What?"

L'zar looked up at his daughter, his eyes shimmering with tears. "I was focused on the wrong thing." He swayed on his knees and lowered his gaze to the grass. His lower lip trembled as he opened his mouth and tried two more times to spit out the words. "I did this, Cheyenne. It's my fault."

Blinking furiously, she backed away from him and looked at her mom. Nothing about Bianca's suspended state had changed. "What do you mean, you did this?"

L'zar's eyelids fluttered as his palms filled with golden light. He closed his fists, and his burnt, smoking flesh healed in seconds. "I couldn't see all the way through."

Corian joined them, frowning at L'zar like the drow had murdered Bianca Summerlin instead of failing to help her. "L'zar."

"My fault."

"Get up."

"I should have known."

Corian hissed and shot a bright silver bolt of light at L'zar's chest. The drow thief choked and keeled over onto the grass.

"What are you doing?" Cheyenne shouted. "You think that's gonna help right now?"

The nightstalker blinked. "Yes."

"What's wrong with you?"

L'zar gasped and got quickly back to his knees. After another handful of deep breaths, he stood. "Right." His gaze flicked to Corian, then Cheyenne before he nodded at the grass. "Now we know."

Cheyenne felt Ember's presence beside her before she saw her friend from the corner of her eye. They exchanged quick glances and didn't have to say a word. *She slaps me in the face, and L'zar gets a bolt of nightstalker lightning. Different strokes, I guess.*

"No, L'zar." She stepped toward him and clenched her fists. "We don't know anything. You need to tell me what happened to my mother."

"Of course." His eyes twitched into narrow golden slits. "Apparently, Ba'rael's generous curse of exile or death passed through this portal." Long, slate-gray fingers gestured weakly at the ridge behind him. "I can't pretend to know how that worked over distance or time, but Bianca must have been standing right here at that exact moment."

"This happened this morning." Cheyenne folded her arms. "Your sister cursed you three days ago."

"Three days in Ambar'ogúl are not always three days on Earth, Cheyenne. If you didn't know that already, you believe it now." L'zar looked up at her, his lips pursed in concentration as he saw not his daughter but some piece of the magical puzzle only the drow Weaver could see.

"How?" Corian asked.

L'zar slowly shrugged. "Could have been the explosion of magic in Hangivol or Ba'rael's casting of the curse. Or any number of things that happened afterward—none of which we expected, of course."

"Hmm."

Cheyenne glared at the nightstalker. "'Hmm?' That's your response?"

"Do you have a better one?"

"Yeah. How do we fix this? How do we bring her back?"

L'zar smacked his lips and slowly shook his head. "I suggest you find your replacement as Crown as quickly as possible, Cheyenne. My sister needs to either step down or be cut down. Otherwise, your mother's state," he said, gesturing limply at Bianca but staring at the grass, "will only get worse."

Jesus, he sounds like he's talking in his sleep. "Get worse, how?"

The drow thief steepled his fingers in front of his face and tapped them against each other. "Well, to start, she won't be leaving this well-tended patch of grass."

"Seriously?"

L'zar dipped his head, and his eyes roamed everywhere but his daughter's face. "I'm going over there." He pointed vaguely at a different area of the lawn and moved in that direction.

"Do we need to worry about him too?"

Corian raised an eyebrow at the halfling. "When do we not?"

"I can't believe this." Cheyenne smoothed her hair back from her face with both hands, realized how often she'd seen L'zar do that, and instantly lowered her arms. "We need to do something."

"We *are* doing something. You'll find the best magical to sit on the throne in your place. L'zar and I will keep working on laying out those terms for his sister to accept, whether she likes it or not." He scratched his head as he stared at the woman frozen in front of the portal ridge. "It doesn't look like Bianca Summerlin's going anywhere until this two-week magical ceasefire is over."

"That makes no sense."

"I know."

Cheyenne laughed in disbelief, but it quickly died in her throat. "I need you to explain this, Corian. Ba'rael has no idea who my mother is. She had no idea Bianca would be standing right here when she cast that curse. She doesn't even know this portal leads into the fucking torture chamber in her fortress."

"I know, Cheyenne."

"So, how was this even possible?"

Corian raised his eyebrows and took a deep breath. His long exhale seemed to last forever. "Well, it shouldn't be, but that's pretty much at the core of everything we've been trying to accomplish, isn't it? Making the impossible possible."

Cheyenne glanced at Ember, who shook her head and shrugged, settling her luminous violet eyes on Bianca Summerlin's profile. The halfling closed her eyes and swallowed the anger threatening to burn its way out of her as drow magic. *He's right. Shit.*

"Okay." She turned to look at her father, who now sat cross-legged in the grass for another one of his meditation sessions. "I guess if anyone can do the impossible, it's us, right? Let's make it happen."

CHAPTER FIFTY-SEVEN

"So much for doing the impossible." Cheyenne Summerlin leaned over her crossed legs and stared across the manicured lawn. "I'd settle for doing *anything*."

Beside her, Ember tilted her head to one side. "Looks like someone's on the verge of doing something, doesn't it?"

"Yeah. Something stupid."

The FRoE agents stationed at her mom's house to guard the portal ridge had all but abandoned their duties at this point. The setting sun filled the sky with orange and pink, casting long shadows across the grass, and every operative in black fatigues and dampening vests, gloves, helmets, and carrying fell weapons stared nervously at the silent, immobile drow thief on the other side of the lawn. Hands tightened on weapon grips. Boots shuffled.

L'zar didn't move.

Cheyenne snorted. "They look like they're about to shit themselves."

"Guess it's a good thing he's unresponsive, then." Ember shrugged. "Would he fight them, do you think?"

"Probably not." Cheyenne glanced briefly at Lumil, who'd walked up to Byrd and now gave him a less-than-gentle nudge in the ribs with her boot. The goblin man slapped her foot away, and their bickering started up again in harsh whispers. The halfling looked at her mom, standing rigid and motionless in front of the Border portal in her backyard. "He's playing the victim card again, or as much of it as he can pull off."

"Really?" Ember raised an eyebrow as she studied L'zar's erect posture. "I don't know, Cheyenne. He looked pretty upset when he realized what happened to her."

"L'zar Verdys can look like a lot of things. Upset? Sure." Cheyenne snorted. "But not because he cares about Bianca Summerlin. That little display of remorse wasn't for her, Em. That was all for his own gain."

The girl turned to look at her friend with luminous violet eyes. "What, you don't think he has a heart?"

Cheyenne rolled her eyes. "Leaning toward no, but the jury's still out on that one."

"And the jury's waiting for what?"

"Proof." The halfling gestured at her father. "It's impossible to tell what's an act with him and what's real. Unless he smells like booze."

Ember snorted.

"Seriously, Em. I've only see L'zar freak out about someone else's wellbeing once before, the night this portal ridge exploded out of the ground."

"That dinner was going so well."

"Yeah." Cheyenne shot her friend a sidelong glance. *Mom really took a liking to her that night. I wonder how she'd feel if she saw Ember as a full-on fae.* "L'zar looked out-of-his-mind worried that night when he showed up in my head. He tried to pull it off as being worried about me, but it didn't stick."

"Most people would call that relief to see his daughter alive."

"Come on, Em." Cheyenne wrinkled her nose. "He didn't wanna make sure I was still alive because I'm his daughter and he loves me. He doesn't even know me. The only reason he freaked out that night was that me dying would've ruined all his plans."

"Right." Ember glanced at Bianca Summerlin. "And you think he fell to his knees and almost broke down sobbing because his plans were ruined again tonight."

"Total drow tantrum, Em. That's it."

"Hmm. I have a hard time seeing how the hell Bianca Summerlin would be a part of his plans."

Cheyenne shot another look at her father. "It's hard to see how the hell anything is connected inside that lunatic's head. L'zar Verdys doesn't do anything for anyone unless he gets something out of it too. Trust me, Em, I'm not the only one who sees that. There's no way that was genuine remorse and sadness without some ulterior motive."

Ember shrugged. "Unless it was, right?"

"I guess." With a sigh, Cheyenne closed her eyes and briefly shook her head, hunching over her crossed legs. "I don't think I can handle entertaining the idea that he's grieving over her being caught up in Ba'rael's curse because he cares." *Not after he spent one night with her and knocked her up, then left her alone with no help at all for twenty-one years. You don't do that to someone you care about.*

"There's no chance for him, then," Ember said to her friend and eyed the half-drow. "You'll drop him as soon as he's lost his usefulness, huh?"

"I know what you're trying to do, Em." In human form now that the immediate danger had passed, Cheyenne snorted. "I'm not L'zar. For now, I'll stick with thinking he's a selfish asshole because he keeps proving me right."

"Okay."

Cheyenne frowned at her *Nós Ani.* "What's that about?"

Ember feigned cluelessness. "What?"

"Come on. 'Okay?'" Cheyenne wiggled her head in a mocking impersonation. "Spit it out, fae girl."

"Ha." Ember shrugged and looked at the orange and pink sky stretching above the forest behind the Summerlin estate. "I'm wondering what you think would change if it turns out he's not. A selfish asshole, I mean."

"Huh. Not very likely."

"That's not an answer, and it's not what I asked."

Cheyenne snorted. "If he turned out to be anything else, Em, I guess I'd have to give him more credit. You know, for having a conscience." She gave an exaggerated shudder at the thought. "Not something I'm excited about." *He won't give me credit for anything, either. And I guess I'm falling in line behind all the other O'gúleesh who've made holding a grudge into a lifestyle.*

Rhynehart approached them slowly, his eyes narrowing as he looked at Ember. Cheyenne watched him with a raised eyebrow until he stopped in front of them and cleared his throat. "That asshole dad of yours and his minions are distracting my guys."

She shrugged. "Why are you telling me?"

"Hard to keep their heads in the game when the Chateau D'rahl's most wanted is sittin' over there like the drow Dalai Lama. Are these guys hangin' around forever or what?"

"I have no clue." Cheyenne stared at him until he cast her an uncomfortable sideways glance. "And I thought your guys were more professional than that."

Rhynehart swallowed and stared straight ahead at the portal ridge and Bianca's rigid form. "They are, and you know it. But this whole thing, whatever you're cooking up, goes way beyond professional, halfling."

"Deal with it." To prove her point, Cheyenne laid back on the grass and clasped her hands behind her head. "No one's going anywhere until L'zar comes up with an answer."

"To what?"

"Huh. I don't know, Rhynehart. I wonder why we're all sitting around in my *mother's* backyard." She closed her eyes. *He smells pissed off. Good.* "If you stay professional, your agents will have to suck it up."

Rhynehart grunted and studied the meditating L'zar. "What's he doing over there?"

"Meditating," Cheyenne and Ember said together, then the fae laughed.

Cheyenne grinned. "Only time he's not insane. You should try it sometime. How's your blood pressure?"

The agent looked down at her with a frown, but Cheyenne didn't open her eyes. "A hell of a lot lower than your housekeeper's, I can tell you that much."

"Shit." Opening her eyes, Cheyenne pushed herself up and looked at Ember. "She's in there all by herself. I need to go talk to her."

"I'll come with you." In a flash of violet light, Ember rose in one fluid movement to hover above the grass.

Rhynehart forgot all about the halfling rising to her feet as he stared at the inch of space between Ember's shoes and the ground. "What the hell is that?"

"Magic, man." Ember spread her arms and raised an eyebrow. "What else?"

His mouth opened silently but he didn't reply, and the fae turned to float after Cheyenne as the halfling stalked across the lawn toward the house.

"Hey." Lumil watched them leave and nudged Byrd again with the toe of her boot. "Deadly duo on the move."

"Huh?" The goblin man shot up off the grass and looked after Cheyenne and Ember. "You thinkin' what I'm thinkin'?"

"Man, I wouldn't step into your head for a lifetime supply of grog. A lifetime."

"Yeah, me too." Byrd scrambled to his feet, and the goblins took off after the halfling and her *Nós Aní*.

When Cheyenne reached the base of the flagstone steps that led up the hillside, she stopped and turned around. "What are you doing?"

The goblins froze six feet away. Byrd's shoulders sagged. "Aw, come on."

"We want a peek inside, halfling." Lumil nodded at the sweeping veranda jutting from the back of the house. "Place like that? I bet it looks even bigger when you're standing at those windows, am I right?"

Cheyenne rolled her eyes and followed Ember up the stairs. The goblins exchanged glances, then hurried toward the first step. A crackling sphere of black drow energy shot from Cheyenne's hand and struck the ground in front of them in a burst of dirt and grass. "Don't even think about it."

Lumil hissed at the hole.

Byrd rubbed his bald head. "Tough nut to crack, huh?"

"Yeah, like you even have any."

"What the hell?"

The goblin woman nodded at the house again. "What d'you think she's hiding up there?"

"Pshh. Everything."

"Yeah." Lumil squinted up the stairs as Cheyenne and Ember disappeared around the bushes lining the side of the house. "That's what I thought."

CHAPTER FIFTY-EIGHT

Before she even opened the front door of her mom's house, Cheyenne heard the sobs. "Oh, jeez."

"What's wrong?"

"Eleanor's finally had a chance to let it all sink in." The halfling opened the door and stepped inside. "Eleanor?"

A rising wail echoed beneath the high, vaulted ceilings.

Cheyenne and her friend exchanged knowing glances, and as she headed around the massive staircase rising up the center of the house, Ember flicked her fingers at the front door and gently shut it in a flash of violet light.

"It's Ember and me," Cheyenne called. "Wanted to make sure you're doing okay."

She turned behind the jutting rise of the stairwell and found the housekeeper in front of the wet bar beneath the stairs. Eleanor was sprawled on the polished hardwood floor, her forehead pressed against her arm as her body heaved with sobs. The glass cabinet beneath the bar was open, and an empty highball glass rested on the tray up top.

"What happened?" Ember asked.

Eleanor wailed again and shook her head. "I reached for the vodka first. For myself. Just like she always used to. It was her favorite."

Another sob escaped her, followed by a shuddering breath and a long, low moan.

"Whoa, okay." Cheyenne stepped toward the housekeeper and squatted beside her. "She didn't die, Eleanor."

"Oh, *God!*" The woman lifted her head just long enough for another keening cry before she doubled over in sobs again.

"Wrong thing to say, apparently."

Ember pressed her lips together and watched the housekeeper losing it.

"Okay, Eleanor. Come on." Cheyenne helped the woman up as gently as she could. The woman didn't fight the help, her face scrunched in distress. Her chest heaved, and she couldn't decide whether to breathe out or in.

Together, the halfling and the fae half-walked, half-carried Eleanor across the spacious dining room and deposited the woman on the chaise longue across from the sofa. Eleanor slumped onto the cushion and buried her face in her hands for more sobbing.

"You still want vodka?"

The housekeeper wailed.

Ember leaned toward Cheyenne and muttered, "Maybe stop talking 'til she's had at least one, huh?"

"What? None of that was insensitive."

"No, but I think she needs something stronger than words at this point." With a raised eyebrow, Ember returned to the wet bar and made Bianca's housekeeper a stiff vodka tonic with a freshly cut lime wedge on the rim of the glass. She floated smoothly back to Eleanor and bent in front of the woman. "Here you go. Focus on this for a second, huh?"

Sniffling, Eleanor looked up at the offered glass and wiped the tears from her cheeks. She froze when she saw Ember's hands, unnaturally pink for anyone but a fae. The woman slowly lifted her head and gazed at Ember's new full-blooded fae look. Her mouth dropped open. "Ember?"

"Hi, Eleanor." The fae set the glass in the woman's hands, and Eleanor raised the drink to her lips without looking away.

"What happened to you?"

"I mean, the short version is nothing. Technically."

"She's a fae, Eleanor." Cheyenne sat on the loveseat beside the chaise and propped her forearms on her thighs. "You already knew she was part of this whole world."

"I did." Eleanor took a long drink, stared blankly at the ice in her glass, then gazed up at Ember again. "I didn't realize you were… Are you like Cheyenne, then?"

"Um, beyond the magic part?"

"Part human."

"*Oh.*" Ember smiled at the woman and floated over to take a seat in the armchair. "Nope. Both my parents are fae, and I was born here on Earth."

"Earth." Eleanor took a long gulp of the vodka tonic. "Makes it sound like we're dealing with aliens."

"I'm pretty sure aliens aren't a thing," Cheyenne muttered.

"But do you *know?*"

"Well, no. Never crossed my mind, honestly."

"Hmm." Eleanor took another drink, and the vodka finally hit. She leaned back against the chaise and stared at Ember. "*Pink.*"

"Is it bothering you?"

The housekeeper barked a laugh. "Absolutely not. Can I be perfectly honest with you two?"

Cheyenne held back a laugh. "Might as well."

Eleanor slugged down another huge, boozy swallow. "I've always wanted to know more about your world, Cheyenne. I'm *fascinated.* If it weren't for your mother, I would've asked a lot more questions far sooner."

"Oh." Cheyenne cocked her head and couldn't help but smile. "I'm right there with you."

"She does have a way with off-limits topics, doesn't she?" Eleanor chuckled and stared into her two-thirds-empty glass. "Then again, the magical world didn't seduce me for one night and leave me with a child who can do *that.*" She gestured at Cheyenne with a flip of her hand.

"Ha. What's *that*, exactly?"

"Everything about you, sweetheart. Lord knows I love you to death."

"Love you too, Eleanor." Cheyenne and Ember exchanged quick glances, and the fae nodded. "She's gonna be okay."

"Cheyenne, if you're involved, I know she will be. It's a shock."

"I know. None of us expected anything like this."

The housekeeper sniffed and took a much more demure sip. "Do you know what happened to her?"

"Kind of, and I'm happy to tell you about it if you really wanna know." I have no idea what she thinks. Never got this far without Mom butting in and telling me to shut up about it Bianca-style.

"I have no problem with the topic, sweetheart."

"Okay. This is probably gonna end up being a giant conversation about magic, other worlds, and overthrowing asshole rulers. You sure you wanna hang around for it?"

When Eleanor finished downing the rest of her drink in one breath, she set the glass on the side table and turned to fix Cheyenne with an unwavering stare. "I've been working for your mother for over twenty years, Cheyenne. What *can't* I handle at this point?"

Ember grinned. "Wow. I *like* Eleanor and vodka."

"Don't think that's the vodka talking, honey."

The fae raised her hands with a soft laugh. "Not a chance."

"All right." Cheyenne nodded at the housekeeper, then took a deep breath. "Basically, Mom's been unintentionally cursed, I guess."

"Cursed."

"By someone in the other world, Ambar'ogúl."

Eleanor burst out laughing. "I'm sorry. I heard you say 'hamburger.'"

Cheyenne sat back on the loveseat and shook her head. "Close enough."

"Well, go on. Keep going." The housekeeper patted her graying bun and nodded. "I'll keep my comments to myself."

"Okay. The Crown cursed L'zar when we were over there, and somehow it slipped through the portal and hit Mom at the same time."

"The Crown."

"Oh, boy." Cheyenne ran a hand through her hair. "So, this is where things get weird. Fair warning."

Eleanor twirled her hand for Cheyenne to continue.

"L'zar's sister is the ruler of Ambar'ogúl."

"But not for much longer," Ember added. "Cheyenne's next in line."

"My God." Eleanor tilted her head and studied the girl she'd helped raise as if seeing her for the first time. "How long have you known *this*?"

"About four days."

"Four days! Is she sick or something?"

"What?"

"Your aunt."

Cheyenne grimaced. "I'm not calling her that, Eleanor. She's not really aunt material." *Come to think of it, L'zar and Bianca aren't parent material, either.*

"How are you next in line? Is there some kind of vote? An age limit?"

"She's been the Crown for a few thousand years, Eleanor. An age limit would be pretty pointless."

"We staged a coup." Ember grinned.

"Ah, yes." Eleanor frowned. "I'm sorry. I'm familiar with the term, but I still don't understand."

"We stormed the castle and took it by force. More or less."

"Oh." The housekeeper nodded, then stood. "I'll need another drink for this one."

Cheyenne and Ember looked at each other and held back their laughter. At least Eleanor was capable of pouring her own drink this time.

CHAPTER FIFTY-NINE

"And that's basically where we are now." Cheyenne finished her human-appropriate retelling of the last few weeks and crossed an ankle over her other knee. "L'zar's out there meditating on how to pull Mom out of that curse, and then we have eleven days to pull everything together before we go force Ba'rael Verdys off the throne and choose someone else to sit on it instead of me."

Eleanor blinked rapidly and lifted her glass. "Naturally."

"But the most important thing right now," Cheyenne continued, speaking more to Ember, "is focusing on what's happening with the FRoE."

"Oh, *yeah*." Ember nodded. "Did you find him?"

"I did more than that."

"Who, now?"

Cheyenne squinted. *Really, it's the least sensitive information I could possibly give her.* "Magical Special Ops, more or less."

Eleanor took a sharp breath and perked up in realization. "Those men in black you fought in the drive."

"Yeah. Same guys who are down there in the yard. Rhynehart's the one who took the phone from you when you called me. You met him before."

"Bianca's the one who remembers names and faces, Cheyenne. I just serve the drinks." Eleanor gave her a tight smile and lifted her mostly full second glass. "I'm amazed he even agreed to show his face on this property again after what happened last time."

"Well, they still owe me, like a lot. And Rhynehart's not the one who got the mental shit kicked out of him by Bianca Summerlin."

Ember snorted and spread out in the armchair with a grin. "I love the way that sounds."

"Well, whoever that other man was," Eleanor added, nodding sternly, "he was a real piece of work."

"Tell me about it."

"Why isn't *he* here again?"

Cheyenne scrunched her face and tried to keep her amusement to a minimum. *Ember's gonna lose it.* "I'm sure he's terrified of me at this point. Pissed-off and scared don't make for a threatening figure."

Eleanor chuckled. "Good. He *should* be terrified."

Ember grinned. "Now's your chance to tell *that* story. I've been waiting all day."

"The address I found was still good. It was his house." Cheyenne started to pull her legs up onto the loveseat, stopped when Eleanor eyed her black Vans, and drew her feet up to cross her legs beneath her anyway. *What Bianca doesn't know won't do shit. And she knows almost everything.* Eleanor raised her eyebrows and looked away with a smile. "I roughed him up a little. And yes, Em, by a little, I actually do mean 'a little.' I slammed him against the wall a few times. We got interrupted."

"At his house?"

"By his wife." Cheyenne licked her lips, trying to wipe off the smile. "He told her I was one of his work associates, and she asked me to stay for drinks."

Ember threw her head back and roared.

Eleanor didn't seem anywhere near as amused. The woman's face darkened as she met Cheyenne's gaze, then she lifted her glass to her mouth and muttered, "You should've killed him."

"Jeez, Eleanor." Cheyenne laughed in surprise. "That has to be the first time you've said that about anyone."

"I stand by my statement."

Ember laughed even louder.

"I think you're angry and don't really mean that," Cheyenne added, trying to keep a straight face. "So I'm gonna forget it ever came out of your mouth."

"I think your mother would agree with me, Cheyenne."

"Uh-huh. Okay." The halfling rubbed her lips. "As it turns out, he might be a little more useful alive than dead, unfortunately."

Ember twirled her hand. "Keep going."

"I mean, showing up at his house and having drinks with his wife was blackmail enough. She has no idea what he does for a living or the kind of person he is around everyone else. He clammed up quick when he saw how famously she and I got along."

Eleanor's scowl loosened. "Good girl."

"Yeah, I have Mom to thank for that. He said he'd look into Colonel Les Thomas for me. I have no idea what that means, and I can't tell yet if he's playing me until he can get out from under this or if he's finally starting to fire some neurons and realizes I know what I'm talking about."

"He wouldn't lie to you about it, right? I mean, you know his wife."

"I sure do," Cheyenne said, "and I'm starting to think I know Major Guy Carson pretty well too."

"Who's that?" Eleanor asked.

Ember burst out laughing again. "Guy? Sir's first name is *Guy*?"

"Believe it or not."

"Oh, man. Please tell me you called him by name every chance you got."

Cheyenne spread her arms. "You know me too well, Em."

Eleanor smiled softly as she watched the two young women sitting with her share a good laugh over something she didn't fully understand.

"Now I'm waiting to hear back from him." Cheyenne leaned over her crossed legs and studied the area rug beneath the polished coffee table. "I need to get to the colonel and make sure he's screwing around with the Bull's Head before we can do anything about it. If he is, we need to cut him out, or the loyalists are gonna keep getting everything they need and throwing it at *me*."

"Or both of us." Ember sighed. "They got my magical signature or whatever too."

"Right. I have a feeling they're not gonna stop with us, either. Whatever the Crown put them up to on this side, they'll do whatever they can to finish it." Cheyenne stopped short and blinked. "Oh, shit."

Eleanor snorted. "I haven't heard you curse this much in one sitting since your mother refused to let you apply to college three years early."

"Sorry." Cheyenne frowned at Ember. "Those missing kids, Em. The ones the FRoE took forever to believe me about. They were part of this whole thing Earthside too—Ba'rael stealing magic. Planning to wage war across the Border."

The fae's eyes widened, and she swallowed. "She did that to kids?"

"Well, just the one we found in that church. As far as I know."

"It's still disgusting."

"No argument there." Cheyenne slowly shook her head. "We need to find the Bull's Head and the rest of those machines. Tracing the machine signal didn't work. That name Matthew gave us didn't work. My guess is Les Thomas is a hell of a lot more on top of feeding the loyalists information than I thought. It shouldn't be this hard to dig up a couple dozen crates of smuggled O'gúl tech parts. I mean, seriously."

"I think the smuggling was the easy part," Ember muttered.

"I don't know what they're waiting for, Em, but we can't afford to find out. Any other time, I'd say the FRoE is equipped to handle magical issues, idiotic leadership notwithstanding, but they'll have a hell of a time trying to tear those things apart without tech of their own. Which none of them even know about."

Ember nodded. "Or they'll be ordered to stay back and not bother with a war-machine attack. You know, traitor in the higher-ups and everything."

"Yeah. It could go either way." The sitting area fell silent, and Cheyenne shrugged. "Eleven days, Em. That's all we have to shut down the war machines, put together those terms for Ba'rael, chose the next Crown, and get Bianca out of that curse-trap."

Ember gave her a small, knowing grin. "I feel like you can get more done in eleven days than anyone else in the history of the planet."

"Thanks, Em."

"Well, *this* planet, at least." The fae shrugged. Maybe not Ambar'ogúl."

"Thanks for the distinction."

"I'm just sayin'. I could be wrong. Once you whip Ba'rael's ass, you could be the drow on the throne who heals the world and turns things around for everyone in eleven days or less."

Cheyenne blinked at her friend and folded her arms. "You're thinking out loud, aren't you?"

"What?" Ember laughed in surprise. "I guess you're rubbing off on me."

"Don't get your hopes up, Em. If I'm gonna be the drow on the throne—"

"*When* you're the drow on the throne." Ember pointed at her and dipped her head. "We're staying positive here."

With a snort, Cheyenne continued, "It'll only be for a few minutes tops. Hopefully. 'Cause I'll be turning around and shucking that throne off on someone else. We have to find the right magical for the job, one who isn't hated by half of Ambar'ogúl, doesn't have a greedy-for-power streak, and isn't bound to a drow who can't cross the Border again and live. One who can fight, knows their subjects, sticks to the old laws, and won't try to kill me for suggesting they become the Crown instead of me."

Eleanor let out a low whistle. "That's some laundry list, sweetheart."

"Yeah, I know."

Ember leaned all the way back in the armchair. "So, who do we know who comes close to ticking half those boxes?"

"Maleshi and Corian are out. So are you, Em."

"That's obvious."

"Foltr's too old, and he doesn't want it anyway. Can't imagine a raug ruling a world built on super-advanced tech and not getting annoyed by the constant hum of the system around him."

Ember asked, "Constant hum?"

"You didn't feel that in Hangivol?" Cheyenne shrugged. "Maybe it's just me."

"Sorry to break it to you, *Aranél*, but a lot of things are just you."

Eleanor cleared her throat. "What's that?"

"What?"

"That word you called her. Did I hear you call her 'Ariel?'"

Cheyenne and Ember exchanged glances and tried not to laugh. Eleanor was drunk enough to start hearing things and sober enough to ask questions. *Hope she stops with drink two.*

Ember leaned toward the housekeeper and nodded. "*Aranél.* It's an O'gúleesh word, I guess. Right?"

Cheyenne nodded.

"It means 'princess.'"

Eleanor barked out a laugh. "Princess!"

The halfling playfully rolled her eyes and waited for the woman's fit of slightly buzzed laughter to die out.

"Oh, sweetheart. That's just… That's the most… Ha!"

Cheyenne almost lost it when Ember stared at the housekeeper in confusion. "Bianca used to freak out about pet names like that."

"She doesn't like 'princess?'"

"Try to picture it, Em. In what reality would Bianca Summerlin call a person anything other than their name? Unless she was pissed and started talking down to them, I mean."

Ember frowned in concentration, then shrugged. "Yeah, I'm getting nothing. What about 'sweetheart' or 'honey?'" The fae stopped when she got the same eyebrow lifted the same way by both Cheyenne and Eleanor. "Wow. No Christmas and no terms of endearment. Got it."

Cheyenne snorted. "That was my childhood in a nutshell, but we're not sitting here to talk about that. We're building a list of possible new Crowns, remember?"

"Got it." The fae rested her head against the high back of the armchair and stared out the massive house's floor-to-ceiling windows at the rear veranda. "What about that giant thing? Oh, man. What's her name? Red hair and horns and wings?"

"'*Wings?*'" Eleanor echoed.

"Nu'ek?" Cheyenne tilted her head in consideration. "Maybe. It would be a hell of a lot of work to keep her comfortable in the Heart, though. She can't fit through half the doorways at least. Maybe not ninety percent of them."

"Is that enough to make her the wrong magical?"

"I don't know. Might be enough to make her say no, though."

"Ooh, what about the ogre? Sakrit." Ember grinned. "He's cool."

"He's a rebel bartender, Em."

"Okay, fine. Do *you* have any ideas?"

Cheyenne sighed and slouched over her crossed legs. "I did before they all told me to piss off."

The sitting area fell silent again. Cheyenne stared at the area rug. *Why is this so damn hard?*

"Well." Eleanor downed the last of her drink and pushed up off the chaise. "While you two brainstorm, I'll have another drink." The woman swayed on her feet and giggled softly as she raised her empty glass in their direction.

"Not that I'm trying to tell you what to do," Cheyenne said as the housekeeper toddled to the wet bar, "but do you think that's a good idea?"

"Cheyenne, I can handle my liquor." Eleanor hiccupped. "I need more of it if I'm going to hang around and listen to you two naming creatures with horns and wings and ogres and I'm fine."

"Okay." Cheyenne watched her a moment longer, then returned her attention to Ember. *At least Eleanor's not sobbing anymore. Whatever it takes at the time, right?* "Anyone else even remotely come to mind?"

"I'm drawing a blank. It's not like we had a whole bunch of time to get to know every single magical in L'zar's happy band of rebels."

A loud, snarling shout rose from the valley behind the Summerlin estate, followed by an echoing burst of angry yelling in reply.

"Come on." Cheyenne stood. Either those magicals outside couldn't keep their shit together, or the portal ridge had another fun surprise for them. She couldn't tell which was worse.

"What's going on?" Ember floated out of the armchair and followed her.

"I'm about to find out." Cheyenne walked to the wall of windows and saw the magicals and the FRoE agents out beside the portal ridge. Two bright circles of red light appeared around Lumil's fists, followed by flashing green in Byrd's hands. No green fell bullets came from the FRoE agents' weapons yet. "Jesus, they're almost as bad as Maleshi or L'zar."

"What? Who?"

Ember joined the halfling at the windows as Cheyenne jerked the door to the veranda open and growled, "Tweedle-Dumb and Tweedle-Dumber out there. I'll tell you right now, Em, we're adding those damn goblins to the 'hell, no for the throne' list."

"Everything all right?" Eleanor turned from the wet bar and raised her freshly refilled cocktail.

Ember glanced from the half-drow darting onto the balcony to the housekeeper swaying beneath the stairs. "All good."

"I'll just be here, then." Eleanor took a long sip of vodka tonic and raised her eyebrows at the glass, then returned with it to the sitting area and relaxed on the chaise.

By the time Ember slipped through the open doors onto the veranda, Cheyenne had disappeared. Two seconds later, a blurred streak of slate-gray, black, and streaming white darted across the manicured lawn.

Ember stopped at the balcony and grabbed the rail to watch. *Here we go again. Might as well turn the Summerlin estate into a giant O'gúl fighting pit at this point.*

CHAPTER SIXTY

Cheyenne dropped out of drow speed between the magically threatening goblins and the team of FRoE agents scowling and shouting at them. Most of them flinched and backed away when the halfling appeared with a sharp crack and a burst of crisp evening air.

"Okay, whatever the hell's going on right now, cut it out."

"Turn that shit off, asshole!" an agent shouted.

Lumil raised both fists and snarled. "They started it. I'll finish it. What's the big deal?"

"You can't pick fights with the team I called here to protect us!" A low, warbling sound rose from the grass behind the goblins, followed by a dark, sinister laugh and a static-filled scream. "What is that?"

Cheyenne whirled to face the goblins. Byrd held balls of green fire at the ready, but he met Cheyenne's gaze with innocent eyes. Lumil scoffed and didn't look away from the agents. While the halfling waited for an answer, the shrill scream cut off, and a man's deep, spooky-sounding voice rose from the grass.

"Tonight's the night, ghouls and goblins. Join us for another six hours of Halloween fright as we take you through the darkest, most terrifying realms known to man and beast."

"Seriously?" Cheyenne scanned the grass behind the goblins, pinpointing the source of the sound before stalking past Lumil and snatching the goblin woman's cell phone off the ground. A livestreaming radio app was pulled up on the screen, displaying a blood-splattered picture. *I should break the phone.* She turned off the app and shook the phone at the goblins and the FRoE agents, fighting to keep a straight face. *This is ridiculous.* "You guys were going to tear each other apart over a radio show? Are you kidding me?"

"Tear each other apart?" Lumil barked a humorless laugh. "Don't give those Earthsiders more credit than they deserve, halfling."

Cheyenne scanned the lawn and found Rhynehart standing away from his team, his hand on the grip of his fell firearm. L'zar still sat perfectly motionless in his meditation, and Corian and Maleshi both watched the confrontation with barely visible smiles.

"Did nobody else think this was a bad idea?"

Byrd tossed a ball of green fire like it was a baseball. "Not our fault if the team you called up here turned out to be a bunch of pussies."

"Say that again, shitface."

"Make me!"

One of the agents stepped forward and drew his weapon from its holster. The others followed suit, readying again for a fight. Rhynehart finally stepped forward to intervene. "Stand down."

"Get rid of the spells." The jumpy agent glared at the spinning red runes around Lumil's fists and the green fire in Byrd's palms.

"You think you're scary, don't you?" Lumil sneered. "With your little toys, pretending to be a magical."

"Lumil, shut up." Cheyenne stepped toward her and pointed at the goblin woman's runes. "Kill it."

Rhynehart's grip tightened on his fell service weapon and he glared at the agent, who still hadn't followed orders. "I said, stand down, Borris. These clowns aren't worth a dishonorable discharge. Let it go."

"Who are you calling clowns?" Lumil spat.

Cheyenne rolled her eyes. "I swear to everything, Lumil, if you don't turn those spinning lights off, I'll shut them down for you."

Byrd's green fire immediately snuffed out. He stepped back and stuck his hands in the pockets of his denim jacket with a shrug. "Too easy anyway. That's a one-hit knockout right there."

Lumil sneered at the agents, but when Cheyenne took a step toward her, the goblin woman shook out her hands, and the spinning red runes disappeared. "Way to ruin Halloween, dipshits."

Corian chuckled, and Cheyenne shot him a warning glance.

She turned to the FRoE agents. "Just to put things into perspective, aren't you guys supposed to be the best on this side of the Border? You fought those things coming out of this portal right here, and I can't believe I have to tell you how much more deadly those are than a radio show."

"I mean, it did sound pretty creepy," Lumil muttered.

"Seriously, goblin, stop talking."

The agent, who still couldn't seem to settle down, turned from the goblins to Cheyenne. "Who do you think you are, halfling?"

"Excuse me?"

"You can't show up at a FRoE op and start telling us what to do."

"Hey, I called in this op, Borris." Cheyenne spread her arms. "You wouldn't even know about these new portal ridges if I didn't think you could handle yourselves out here."

"L'zar Verdys is sitting right behind you!" Borris drew his weapon and aimed it at Cheyenne.

"Oh, hell, no!" Lumil's spinning red runes burst into existence again.

"I said, stand the fuck down!" Rhynehart shouted.

"You're the one who brought him here!" Borris screamed at Cheyenne, gripping his fell pistol with both hands and aiming it at the halfling's chest. "How are we supposed to know you're on our side, huh? That drow's an escaped convict!"

"Yeah, that drow looks real threatening right now, doesn't he?" She gestured at L'zar, who still hadn't moved. "He hasn't lifted a finger toward any of you since we got here. You wanna know what side I'm on? Everyone's." *I'm so done with guns.* Cheyenne studied the weapon in his hands, and the activator still behind her ear picked up on every weak spot, every sliding mechanism, every separate piece. "That doesn't mean I'm gonna stand here and let you point your gun at me because you're trying to feel a little less like an idiot. Trust me, it isn't working."

Borris glared at her and readjusted his grip.

"So, I'm gonna ask you once." She spread her arms. "You gonna put that peashooter away or what?"

"Fuck you. You're a halfling. You don't even belong with those magicals. Who came here illegally, by the way."

Cheyenne accepted every action prompted by her activator. With two quick swipes of her fingers through the air, her tech-synced magic pulled the fell pistol apart, revealing the green glow of the fell firepower. The pieces thumped into the grass one by one. Borris struggled for a second to keep his grip on the pistol, but his eyes widened as the metal parts flowed through his fingers like water, and he stepped back.

The fell ammunition flared in a glowing green pile on the ground, and Cheyenne's activator gave her the perfect spell option for snuffing it. It left behind a puff of dissipating green smoke, and that was it.

She folded her arms and gave Borris a deadpan stare. "If we're gonna do what needs to get done, man, there are no sides. It's all the same. Now do you get it?"

Borris looked at Rhynehart.

Rhynehart frowned at the pieces of the fell pistol. "Cheyenne, how the fuck did you do that?"

"Nifty little trick I picked up in Ambar'ogúl."

"Trick."

Borris slapped a hand on his holster, forgetting that his firearm had been pulled apart in front of him. The other agents shifted nervously, and while none of them took their hands off their weapons, they were smart enough not to aim anything at the halfling.

"Technology, actually." Cheyenne stepped toward the agents and pulled the activator out from behind her ear, her eyelids fluttering at the small pinch. Every operative on Rhynehart's team stepped back.

"Whatever that is, keep it the hell away from me."

"We get it. You win."

"You made your point, halfling."

She stopped and held up the silver coil for everyone to see. "It's an activator. Top-of-the-line O'gúl tech that syncs with magic. Kinda hard to wrap your head around, I know, but it makes anything possible. Almost."

"Bullshit," another agent whispered.

Rhynehart's eyes narrowed. "If those things are so amazing, halfling, how come I've never seen one before?"

"They don't cross the Border." She shrugged and stuck the activator behind her ear again, cocking her head when the tech synced and made her eyelids flutter again. "Unless I'm the one ferrying it back across, apparently."

He chewed the inside of his lower lip. "Just you?"

"Well, there's a chance it's a halfling thing, but a few magicals went through a bunch of trouble to make sure no one on the other side could tell that's what I am." Cheyenne stuck her hands in the pockets of her trenchcoat and felt the thick silver cuff stolen from Ur'syth, the Oracle crone. "Most halflings don't have that luxury, do they?"

Rhynehart licked his lips, his gaze flickering over her. "So, you're the only one who can use that thing?"

"Earthside, yeah." She gestured at the magicals on his team. "And something has to change with the way you pick your operatives. Seriously. Or at least set them up with somebody who knows what the hell you're dealing with when refugees cross the Border. They're all clueless."

"Speak for yourself," a troll agent muttered, but he immediately stepped back and stared at the grass.

"No, I'm sure I'm speaking for all of you. Did anyone ever stop to think why your employer only takes magicals born Earthside?"

"Cheyenne." Rhynehart nodded away from his team and took off toward the house. "A word."

"Yeah." She gazed at the startled, confused operatives staring at her and shrugged. "Think about it."

When she joined Rhynehart in the middle of the lawn, the team leader folded his arms and leaned toward her, his chin dipped low. "What are you talking about?"

"Don't tell me you didn't know about the selection process for your agents."

"No, I'm well aware of that. The way you're saying it makes it sound like there's something else going on."

"Yeah, well, there is." She folded her arms in a nearly perfect imitation of his posture and leaned forward too. "The people running your organization don't want O'gúleesh on their payroll, Rhynehart, only Earthborn magicals. They know the cities and the way the human world works, and they're powerful enough to deal with whatever magical trouble pops up before you get shipped out to handle it. It also keeps every FRoE agent in the field dumb enough not to pick up on what's happening behind the scenes."

Rhynehart snorted. "You're walking a thin line, Cheyenne."

"I've been walking a thin line since we met. That hasn't changed. Now I don't care, 'cause I have a lot bigger problems to deal with."

"Spill it, then. What's happening behind the scenes?"

"Colonel Les Thomas."

The agent's frown darkened. "What about him?"

"Jeeze, I'm gonna know this story inside and out after explaining it to every single…" Cheyenne ran a hand through her hair and sighed. "Look. The colonel's connected to someone who wrote a program that works with old-school O'gúl tech. Not like my activator, but just as effective—and seriously dangerous in the wrong hands, which are the hands that have it right now."

"You're not making any sense."

"Okay. Let me put this into bite-sized chunks for you." Cheyenne ignored his irritated scowl. "Colonel Thomas is connecting O'gúl loyalists, magicals who came over here to organize seriously nasty stuff for the ruler of the other side, with the resources to make O'gúl tech that isn't supposed to function over here work. And it does. I've seen it, and I've fought it. I'm also sure he's been feeding everything about me right to those loyalists."

"What the hell is a loyalist?"

"The *bad guys*, Rhynehart!" She took a deep breath and forced her anger back down. "That simple enough for you? One of the FRoE's top officials is a traitor who doesn't give a shit about the Border regulation and is helping unregistered magicals build an army of war machines to use against us, and none of your agents is equipped to handle it because they have no idea how to fight this tech. Or even what it is. Because they were born here."

Rhynehart studied her face, glanced quickly at his agents milling nervously in front of the portal ridge, and cocked his head. "So tell me how to equip them."

"I don't know. Wait, you believe me?"

He shrugged. "I know what happens when I assume you're full of shit. And we agreed to trust each other at the very least, didn't we?"

"Yeah. Yeah, we did."

"Who else knows about Colonel Thomas?"

"Sir."

Rhynehart snorted. "You went straight to him, huh?"

Cheyenne couldn't help herself. She grinned. "Straight to his house, if you really wanna know."

The agent looked like he was choking. "His *house*."

"Guess he was off-duty today, or at least off a little early. He's supposed to be checking into Colonel Thomas, and I'm waiting to hear back from him so we can—"

"Back up!" one of the agents shouted.

Cheyenne and Rhynehart turned to see Corian standing ten feet from the frozen Bianca Summerlin. The agents were on high alert again, hands on weapons, unable to hide their fear of the first night-stalker most of them had seen. Corian lifted both hands and tilted his head. "I'm not interested in any of *you*. Not in the slightest."

"Doesn't mean you don't need to step back right now!"

With an amused look, Corian stepped away from Bianca, lowered his hands, and faced the agents who couldn't handle the unexpected company.

Cheyenne shook her head. "We need to make some changes."

"Yeah, your furry cat friend needs to get down off his high horse."

"Well, *there's* an image."

Rhynehart shot her an exasperated glance. "You gonna offer any suggestions, halfling? Or are you enjoying your new role as the drow who tells everyone else what to do?"

She scoffed. "Please. If I say I'm gonna do something, you know I'm good for it, whether you like it or not. And yeah, I have a suggestion. Things would be a lot less tense and way less dangerous if we had a shift change."

"I don't know that I follow."

"Fine. If *you* had a shift change." Cheyenne nodded at the agents, who were set more on edge by unregistered magicals than by fighting in-between monsters from a portal that shouldn't exist. "When I called in for help out here, Sir made sure you brought a team I didn't know."

Rhynehart grunted. "You picked up on that, huh?"

"Don't be insulting."

He smirked.

"These guys have no idea what to expect, and it's making them even more unpredictable. How about getting some operatives up here who know me and trust me, first of all, and who can handle the kind of attitude every single one of these O'gúleesh dishes out on a regular basis?"

"You want me to trade out this team that's been here for almost a week so you can hang out with your friends?"

Cheyenne cocked her head halfway in agreement. "Well, that's what we need right now, friends. If I need to call them that to get the point across, fine. They're my friends. And yeah, I want you to trade 'em out."

"Don't tell me you're feeling lonely."

She raised an eyebrow. "Very funny. I'm thinking about everybody's sanity here, Rhynehart. Not just my own. And physical wellbeing, too. Seriously, if those goblins start bashing your guys, none of your agents is making it out of here in one piece. Trust me."

"Hmm." The team leader squinted at his agents. "You know I'll have to put in a request for that, right?"

"Then put in a request." Cheyenne shrugged. "Sir's not in any position to deny me something like that."

"Care to explain how that's even remotely possible?"

"Just tell him I asked for this personally. If you're that skeptical, I'm happy to bet on it." She flashed him a tight, completely fake grin.

Rhynehart rolled his eyes, smacked his lips, and pulled out his cell phone with a long sigh. "I can't believe I'm doing this."

"Oh, you'll believe it. Don't forget to tell him." The halfling folded her arms and turned her back on the portal ridge, her cursed mom, the FRoE agents, and L'zar's rebels just to get a better view of Rhynehart's face. *This is gonna make so many things worth it.*

CHAPTER SIXTY-ONE

Rhynehart shot Cheyenne a quick glance as he waited for Sir to pick up.

"What is it?"

"Sir. I want to run a request by you."

"I'm not your goddamn wet-nurse, Rhynehart. That's why you have the job you have. You don't need a tit to suckle. Handle it yourself."

The team leader pressed his lips together and waited for the man to finish his relatively mild outburst.

"All right. Shit." Sir cleared his throat. "What is it?"

"Assignment change up at the Summerlin estate."

"What the fuck for?"

Rhynehart stuck his free hand in his pocket. "To give these guys a break. Mostly."

"Your attempt to cover that one up has whorehouse stink all over it, soldier. What's the other reason?"

"A personal request. Tate, Yurik, and Bhandi, plus—"

"Personal *request*? *Personal* request? Who the fuck do you think we are? The Make a Magical Goddamn Wish Foundation? If your team isn't laid out flat or hobbling away from that mansion in the middle of nowhere holding bleeding stumps where their heads should be, you're

415

not changing a goddamn thing about the assignment. Why the hell do you want to start switching it up now?"

Rhynehart pulled the phone away from his ear to keep from going deaf and blinked at Cheyenne. She nodded.

"Not a personal request from me, Sir." He swallowed. "From Cheyenne—"

"*Cheyenne?*" Sir roared on the other end of the line, followed by the smashing of glass and heavy furniture scooting across the floor.

The halfling stared at Rhynehart's phone. *And he didn't even put it on speaker.*

"That skin-changing freakshow needs to get her dark-elf nose out of our goddamn business! And *you*, Rhynehart, need to grow a pair! Santa Claus on a goddamn sandwich, man! A baby treefrog has a bigger sack than you do. You look that freaky face-pierced wannabe warrior of death right in the eye, and you tell her from me that I'm—"

"Give me the phone." Cheyenne extended her open hand.

"Yep." Rhynehart dropped it gently into her palm with a snort.

She lifted the phone halfway to her ear, which was plenty close enough to hear the string of nonsense metaphors and relentless obscenities spewing from the major's mouth. "Feel free to tell me yourself, Major."

Sir's voice cut off instantly.

Cheyenne pressed the phone against her ear. "You still there?"

"Go jump off a cliff."

"Well, I might. Just not quite yet. I could definitely use approval of Rhynehart's request, though. Of course, if you deny it, I'll probably have to stop by the base and grab new agents myself. Don't worry, I won't forget about paying you a visit either. It was so much fun last time."

"Better yet, I'll push you off that cliff myself."

"I'm sure you'd like to."

Sir snarled into the phone and thumped something beside him hard enough to make him hiss in pain. "Give him the phone, halfling."

This time when Cheyenne grinned at Rhynehart, it was genuine. She handed the phone back and stuck her hands in her coat pockets. *He caved a lot faster than I expected. Guess I made an excellent impression.*

Rhynehart frowned as Sir spent another minute grumbling into the phone. "Got it. Yeah. No, you don't need to—" Blinking quickly, he pulled the phone away from his ear and stared at the home screen. "Hasn't hung up on me in a long time."

"But you're good to go with the ol' switcheroo, aren't you?"

The agent slipped his phone numbly into the pocket of his black fatigues and turned to her. "What did you *do* to him, Cheyenne?"

She batted her eyes and emulated her mother's honed talent for delivering shocking news with grace and barely concealed enjoyment. "I had a lovely conversation with his wife."

"That asshole's *married*?"

"I know, right?"

"Jesus. I think my brain's turning inside-out."

"You'll get used to it." Cheyenne took a deep breath and glanced at the agent's empty hand. "You're supposed to be calling the new team, remember?"

"Oh, shit. Yeah." Rhynehart pulled out his phone again, cleared his throat, and scrolled through the contacts list. "You didn't happen to hear Sir's first name during that conversation with his wife, did you?"

"Many, many times." Grinning like a crazy person, Cheyenne watched him make the first call. *I'm not moving 'til I know we've got magicals I trust on the way, but I can really enjoy the fact that I know all about Guy Carson, and Rhynehart doesn't.* "If you put aside everything you know about how the FRoE works and help me take down Colonel Thomas and those war machines, maybe I'll tell you."

"Hmm. Turning against the best employer I've ever had, helping a drow halfling and her criminal father bash up a few *other* criminals, and finally figure out that bastard's first name. You know how much you're asking, Cheyenne?"

"Of course I do. Will it be worth it for you?" She pointed at him and tried not to smile.

Rhynehart cleared his throat again as the line rang and stretched his neck and shoulders like he'd been cramped in a box all day. "Kinda, yeah."

"Then it's not asking too much."

An hour later, the sun was well behind the horizon, but the sky was still streaked with fading orange light. Cheyenne's drow hearing picked up the sound of another black FRoE SUV making its way up the gravel drive in front of the house. She met Rhynehart's gaze and nodded. "They're here."

"What? How do you even know that?"

All she had to do was point at her pointy-tipped purple-gray ear poking out of her bone-white hair.

Rhynehart shrugged. "Can you handle briefing your friends on why they're here?"

"Someone has to."

"You know exactly why I didn't." He pointed at her and stalked over to his first team of agents, who looked dead on their feet. "It'll make more sense coming from you anyway. Probably."

"Yep." Cheyenne turned toward the house and saw Corian watching her. He stood beside L'zar now, who still hadn't moved, and pointed at the house in curiosity. "You'll see."

The halfling took off across the lawn, jogged up the flagstone steps beside the house, and hurried around the pruned bushes just as the newest FRoE vehicle pulled up behind the first in front of the Summerlin estate. Multiple pulses of soft yellow light shimmered behind the tinted windows, then the front passenger side door opened, and a grinning Bhandi leaped out of the SUV.

"Well, if it isn't everybody's favorite Goth drow! What the hell are *you* doing here?" The door slammed behind the troll woman.

"Dude, come *on.*" Yurik stepped out from behind the wheel and shut the driver's side door a lot more gently. "Every time. Lemme guess, slamming doors was a thing in your house growing up, wasn't it?"

Bhandi turned to the ridiculously muscular goblin with the massive bullring through his septum and snorted. "And I bet nagging was a big part of yours."

Yurik's yellow eyes narrowed, then he shook his head. "At least I'm *trying* to break old habits."

"Yeah, yeah, yeah." Bhandi waved him off. "Save it for the next time I need to be bored back into sobriety, 'kay?"

Cheyenne laughed and looked the troll woman up and down. "Please tell me you weren't called out of a bar to come out here."

"Hell, no." Bhandi approached the halfling and slapped a hand on Cheyenne's back. "Any of those assholes try calling *me* in when I'm off-duty, they've got another think comin'. That includes Rhynehart." She removed her hand when Cheyenne raised her eyebrow. "Yep. No touching the Goth drow. You hear that, fuckers? Hands off!"

"One of those things only *you'd* forget, Bhandi." Tate slipped out of the back passenger seat, the tattoos covering his neck, face, and bald head clearly visible in the low light of dusk. "The rest of us aren't stupid enough to get anywhere near that close." He jerked his chin at Cheyenne. "How you doin'?"

Cheyenne wrinkled her nose. "Not sure how to answer that."

"Okay. I bet it's easier to explain what you're doing at a tricked-out mansion in the middle of BFE. Better yet, maybe you can explain why *we're* here."

"Lemme tackle those one at a time, huh?" Cheyenne gestured at the front door at the top of the wide, curving staircase behind her. "This is—"

The black SUV shifted and wobbled from side to side. The door behind the driver's seat opened, and the huge ogre Jamal unfolded. He backed away from the car, stared at the massive estate in front of them, and grunted.

"Hey." Cheyenne nodded at the agent, who recognized her and responded with another grunt.

The goblin woman Payton climbed out after him. She slammed the door, making Yurik grimace, and headed around the car to join her fellow agents.

"Payton." Cheyenne nodded.

"Crazy-ass halfling." Payton tilted her head. "Didn't expect to see *you* here."

"Yeah, I can say the same about you. How long have you guys been up and back on assignment?"

Payton rolled her good eye. Jamal grunted and shifted the massive black dampening vest draped over his shoulders. "Few weeks."

Grinning, Yurik slapped a hand on the ogre's shoulder, which was even more muscular than his own. "Nothing a little healing juice can't fix right up. Too bad they couldn't fix your head, though, huh?"

Jamal stared at the beefy goblin until Yurik lowered his hand with a shrug. "I'll say this, halfling," he muttered, turning his yellow eyes back to Cheyenne. "Next time I hear you screaming to step away from something, that's exactly what I plan to do."

"Fuck our orders," Payton added without any expression.

"Well, thanks." Cheyenne gave them each a small smile. "Wish I could say we're done with boobytraps and explosions, but I honestly can't promise anything at this point."

Bhandi cracked up and shook her head, her scarlet braids flying around her shoulders. "Goddamn boobytraps, man."

Tate and Yurik stared at her. When she noticed the warning glances, she shrugged.

Tate gestured at Jamal and Payton. "Dude, they're standing right here."

The troll woman flipped him the bird. "They'll laugh about it eventually."

Neither of the magical agents who'd been more than severely injured by the Crown loyalists' exploding bomb-riddled construction site cracked so much as a smile.

Bhandi snorted and turned back to Cheyenne. "You were about to explain some shit, Goth drow."

Cheyenne smiled at the nickname and pointed at the house again. "Bianca Summerlin's house."

Yurik's eyes widened. "No shit."

"Who the hell is that?" Bhandi asked, shooting the muscular troll a surprised frown.

"Big name in politics. Kinda."

"Man, why the fuck are you into human politics?"

"Hey, when we're off-duty and runnin' around town with masks on, you think human politics don't apply?"

Bhandi shook her head, looking confused. "I don't give a shit what humans do."

"Well, you should. What's the point of—"

"Okay, assholes." Tate nodded at Cheyenne. "She's been trying to tell us what's up for the last five minutes. Let her finish a sentence before you try to kill each other, huh?"

"Yeah, and about that." Bhandi pointed at the halfling. "We get a call from Rhynehart to get our asses out here in the middle of nowhere, and nobody else could tell us shit about this assignment. It's not even in the ASS."

"The ASS?" Cheyenne licked a smile off her lips. "Please tell me that's an acronym like the BITCH."

Tate chuckled. "Assignment Safeguard and Surveillance. Cheesy as hell, but we're not the ones naming shit on base."

At least Sir and Rhynehart are keeping this off the record. If loyalists show up at this house too, I'll know exactly who fucked us over. Sir has to know that too.

"All right." Cheyenne gazed at the agents looking at her for an explanation. "Nothing's in the system 'cause I asked for you guys personally."

"No shit." Bhandi grinned. "Goth drow's running her own ops for the FRoE now, huh?"

"Dude, shut up." Tate punched the troll in the shoulder.

"Fair question, asshole." She punched him right back. Yurik met Cheyenne's gaze and shook his head.

"Not exactly." Cheyenne waited for Tate and Bhandi to give her their full attention again. *They're not half as bad as Byrd and Lumil. At least there's that.* "I wanted you guys up here, off the ASS, 'cause this is kind of a delicate situation."

Yurik smirked. "Delicate's not in our handbook, Cheyenne."

"Yeah, I noticed." She looked at Jamal and Payton, who watched her intently and didn't seem anywhere near as interested in why they were here. "Feel free to ask Rhynehart why this whole thing is undocumented. I'm kinda tired of explaining it at this point. Bottom line, I trust you guys, and I'm pretty sure you trust me."

"Damn straight."

"Bhandi."

The troll woman nodded at Cheyenne and ignored Tate's warning stare.

"And I wanted to be the one to tell you guys what you're about to step into," Cheyenne continued. "'Cause this isn't just a FRoE thing anymore."

Tate rubbed his bald and tattooed purple head and frowned. "Then what is it?"

"Well, it's kinda personal for me. It's a drow thing."

The agents exchanged confused glances.

Let's try this one more time. Cheyenne nodded at the house. "This is my house too."

"Ha!" Bhandi snorted. "The halfling's bringin' the hammer down, huh?"

"No, I mean literally. Bianca Summerlin's my mom."

Yurik's mouth fell open.

"And L'zar Verdys is sitting out back."

"What the fuck?" Tate stepped sideways in a fruitless attempt to peer around the corner of the massive mansion. "Does Rhynehart know?"

"Oh, yeah. Not that he's happy about it."

"No shit." Bhandi turned to look at her fellow agents. "And we're up here to what? Bring him in?"

"Not even a little. This is bigger than L'zar breaking out of Chateau D'rahl again. Trust me. You're up here to help him. Help us."

"Us as in L'zar and you?" Yurik pointed at the halfling.

"And a few other magicals who follow him, yeah."

"No fucking wonder this isn't in the ASS." Tate shook his head.

Cheyenne looked at each of the agents and shrugged. "Look. Sir approved it. Rhynehart approved it. Guess I better ask right now if this is gonna be a problem for anyone."

"L'zar Verdys is always a problem," Yurik muttered. "But not you."

"Told you we'd follow you anywhere, Cheyenne." Tate thumped a fist to his chest.

Bhandi shrugged. "Hey, blood and honor, right?"

Cheyenne cocked her head. "Where'd you pick that up? Blood and honor."

The troll waved her off. "Meh. Just somethin' I've heard the rez refugees toss around once or twice. Sounds pretty badass, huh?"

"Yeah." *Guess it applies to magicals everywhere, even if they've never stepped foot on the other side.* Cheyenne looked up at Jamal and Payton. "What about you guys?"

Jamal grunted. "No exploding crates, and I'm good."

"We're fucking here." Payton shrugged, her scarred face expressionless beneath the black eyepatch. "There's your answer."

"Cool." Cheyenne gestured at the side of the house. "Then let's get going."

"Hell, yeah." Bhandi marched after the halfling, followed closely by the rest of the team hand-picked to handle the weirdness of the whole situation.

Cheyenne led them down the stone steps. *Guess it pays to have friends in the FRoE. At least ones who don't think I'm full of shit.*

CHAPTER SIXTY-TWO

"Holy shit." Bhandi looked around the manicured lawn behind the estate house. "Not gonna lie to you, Goth drow. For a second, I still thought you were fucking with us."

Yurik shook his head and stared at L'zar, who was still sitting cross-legged on the lawn, unmoving and deep in meditation. "Just because you're always fucking around, it doesn't mean everyone else is."

"Damn, Cheyenne." Tate stared at the portal ridge. "Serious as a fell shot to the head."

"Come on." Cheyenne grinned at them. "Have I ever lied to you guys?"

The tattooed troll shrugged. "Well, you *did* tell us your name was Blakely."

"Necessary evil, man." Bhandi blinked. "So is this, apparently."

The other FRoE team noticed the new group of agents first, and the already high tension on the lawn thickened. "What the hell is this?"

"Yeah, nice to see you too, Gruner." Bhandi snorted. "You look like shit."

"You look like a clueless fucking troll."

Rhynehart shot Cheyenne a wary glance, then stalked toward his frayed, nervous, exhausted team. "New team to relieve you guys."

"What?" An orc with a thin strip of yellow hair down the center of his head scowled at Rhynehart. "What the hell for?"

"Didn't I say to relieve you?" Rhynehart stuck his hands in his pockets and nodded at the agents, who obviously didn't want to be here but were offended by being replaced. "You've done good work, and you've been up here long enough. Time to take a break and get the hell outta here."

The orc's scowl moved from his team leader to the agents walking across the lawn with Cheyenne.

"Hey!" Rhynehart shouted. "That was an order, people. Move."

Grumbling, the old team gathered their gear, slinging the straps of their duffel bags over their shoulders before heading out in a loose group toward the house and their car parked at the top of the hill. The new agents Cheyenne had asked for barely noticed the odd glances and frowns the other operatives shot their way.

Yurik had stopped to stare at L'zar's back across the lawn. Tate gaped at Corian and Maleshi, who stood side by side and watched the change of shift impassively. Bhandi scanned the portal ridge, cocked her head at the sight of Bianca standing rigidly in front of the jutting black stones tearing across the lawn, then turned her attention to Persh'al. "Who are you?"

The rebel troll glanced at Cheyenne and Bhandi and shrugged. "Who are *you*?"

She slapped the front of her dampening vest. "The gear and the human shouting orders over there didn't give it away?"

"Not really an answer."

Bhandi scoffed. "You know what? I don't need to explain myself to a fucking blueberry. What the hell happened to make you turn that color, huh?"

"Hey!" Lumil stalked toward them, her yellow eyes blazing in the near-darkness. "If anyone's gonna call this blue troll a blueberry, it's gonna be me."

Persh'al raised an eyebrow at Lumil and stepped aside. "Didn't know you cared so much."

"Yeah, me neither." The goblin woman stopped inches from Bhandi, who didn't move an inch as she eyed Lumil. "But then *you* showed up. What the hell is this, anyway?"

"You tell me." Bhandi cocked her head and stared at the thick scar encircling Lumil's throat. "Nice necklace."

"Yeah. Fucking rope burn. You should try it sometime."

Cheyenne frowned as she watched both sides of her life as a halfling converge in her mom's backyard. Corian approached her with his arms folded. "You trust them to handle this?"

"Yeah." She frowned. "Maybe I should've set up a meeting or something first, huh?"

"They'll either get it together, or they won't. Same goes for us."

"Holy shit." Byrd stared at Yurik. "There some kinda goblin steroids I don't know about?"

"How should I know?"

"How should you?" Byrd scoffed and rubbed his head. "Lumil. Would you look at the size of that motherfucker?"

For once, the woman didn't reply with a snappy insult. She and Bhandi were too busy sizing each other up.

"Keep staring at me like that," Bhandi muttered, "and this is the last face you're gonna see."

"Wanna bet?" The spinning red runes erupted round Lumil's fists.

Bhandi smirked. "I like bets."

"Jesus." Cheyenne ran a hand through her hair. "I thought this was a good idea."

"Like I said, they'll figure it out." Corian cast Jamal and Payton a sidelong glance as they stalked wordlessly toward the area where the previous FRoE team had set up their temporary camp. "Looks like those already have."

Rhynehart walked toward them with a scowl, gazing at Corian before stopping on the other side of Cheyenne. "So, now what?"

She folded her arms and shrugged. "We let them sniff each other's butts and figure out who's gonna roll over and who's not ready to play nice. Right?"

"First time I've heard anyone compare my agents to dogs."

Corian focused his gaze on the portal ridge. "At least it's not a comparison to cats."

Rhynehart snorted. "Bet you get comments like that all the time, huh, nightstalker?"

Corian's silver eyes flicked to the agent but didn't quite land on Rhynehart's face. "Careful, human. You're outnumbered."

"You think that scares me?"

Corian glanced at Cheyenne, then walked away to rejoin Maleshi. The general watched the meetup with a small, amused smile and didn't say a word.

"Some friends," Rhynehart muttered.

"They could say the same about all of you." Cheyenne cocked her head. "Already looks like an improvement."

"Aside from that atomic goblin over there." He nodded at the standoff between Bhandi and Lumil. The troll agent hadn't summoned her magic, and so far, Lumil's spinning runes were for show.

Cheyenne shook her head. "They said this assignment wasn't in the system."

"That was the plan, right?"

"Yeah. And I told them you'd explain why."

Rhynehart scoffed. "Great."

"Hey, that's your job. I guess I'm the mediator now or something."

"Well, as long as that psycho drow playing Buddhist monk over there doesn't lose his shit on my agents, we're here."

Cheyenne turned slowly to look at him. "You know I can't make any promises."

"I'm not asking you to."

She heard the doors of the other FRoE SUVs slam shut, then engines started, and the vehicles carrying the old team crunched down the gravel drive to leave the Summerlin estate, hopefully forever. "This is gonna be a weird night."

"We already knew that." Rhynehart watched Jamal and Payton set up their version of a temporary camp beside the Border portal. "I wanna know how the hell you pulled apart a fell pistol like that, Cheyenne. I don't care if you're the only one who can use it. You might not be."

"Trust me, if none of L'zar's friends from the other side could get it to work, your magicals sure as shit won't be able to."

"Not now. But what about that program running those war machines?"

"What?" Cheyenne frowned at him.

"If it's already been done, halfling, it can be done again, right? Think about it." Rhynehart marched off toward Jamal and Payton without another word.

Cheyenne stared after him. There was an idea—use Matthew Thomas' program to get working activators Earthside. Whether or not she was taking on this whole 'drow royalty on Earth' thing, there was still a lot of work to be done here. Not like magicals running around all over Earth with activator-synced magic wouldn't be an adjustment for everyone, especially if humans weren't supposed to know about it.

She looked at her mom's rigid form and grimaced. First things first. Get Mom out of this curse, then throw Ba'rael off the throne and finally finish this thing. *Then I can work on improvements here. Jesus, I can't believe I'm considering it.*

"Keep running your mouth, *dae'bruj*," Lumil shouted.

Bhandi spread her arms. "You know someone's insane when they start yelling gibberish at you."

"It's fucking O'gúleesh, you Earthside moron!" Lumil pounded one fist into the other palm in a flash of red sparks and spinning runes. "Sounds like someone needs to teach you a lesson."

"Oh, yeah?" Bhandi grinned, her scarlet eyes blazing as she lifted her chin. "That gonna be you?"

"Fuck yeah, it is." Lumil swung a red fist at Bhandi's face. The troll ducked and stepped aside before lashing out with a swift kick to Lumil's hip. "Eat shit, Earthsider!"

"Oh, come on." Cheyenne headed toward them but stopped when Lumil's glowing fist landed in Bhandi's gut.

The troll sailed across the grass with a grunt, and the other tense conversations stopped as both rebels and FRoE agents turned to watch the fight.

Bhandi didn't bother with the fell weapon holstered at her hip. Her hand shot out, and a red and purple streak of pulsing light burst from her fingers and swept Lumil's feet out from under her. The goblin crashed to the ground with a growl, and Bhandi scrambled to her feet to rush at her. She tackled Lumil just as the goblin got back on her feet, then they were rolling around in the grass, shouting and hissing and pounding each other with their fists.

"Tate," Yurik shouted.

"Man, I don't give a shit right now." The tattooed troll agent stood ten feet from Corian and Maleshi. "You ever seen one of these things before?"

Maleshi leaned away from the tattooed troll and grinned. "How cute."

"Dude, for real." Byrd smacked Yurik on the shoulder, then shook out his hand. "Damn. Like solid rock."

"You can stop touching me."

"Hey, what about that thing in your nose, huh?" Byrd pointed at the bullring through Yurik's septum. "How much did that hurt?"

"Not as much as I'm about to hurt you if you don't quit asking me stupid questions." Yurik eyed the other goblin and snorted. "How long have you been on this side of the Border anyway?"

"Shit." Byrd laughed and studied the other goblin's muscular physique. "Not long enough, apparently. Never seen a goblin your size, man."

"Well, now you have. And you can drop it."

"Sure, sure. Just as soon as you tell me—"

"Fuck!" Bhandi roared when Lumil grabbed a handful of the troll woman's scarlet braids and jerked them aside. Then she smashed her fist into the side of Lumil's face.

They stumbled away from each other, breathing heavily, and met each other's gazes. Lumil slowly looked down at her fists and the thin braid she'd ripped clean off Bhandi's skull. She dangled it in front of her for a second and chuckled. "Shit. I just pulled your hair out."

Bhandi lowered her hand from her head and stared at the blood on her fingers. "Fuck."

"Guess this qualifies as a catfight, huh?"

Wiping her bloody fingers on her black fatigues, Bhandi looked at the goblin woman and sneered. "Only if I call you a bitch."

"Ha." Lumil looked at the scarlet braid in her hand again and burst out laughing.

Bhandi shook her head and stared in awe at her hair in the goblin's hand, then couldn't help but laugh with her. In seconds, both of them had broken down in hysterics. Lumil tossed the braid into the grass and marched toward the troll agent to clap a hand on Bhandi's shoulder.

"You're all right."

"You're the craziest goblin fuck I've ever met." Bhandi nodded at Yurik. "And that includes the hulking green mountain over there."

"You mean, this guy?" Byrd pointed at Yurik, who rolled his eyes but couldn't hide a grin.

"Who the fuck else fits that description, asshole?"

Lumil flung her arm around Bhandi's shoulders and jostled her roughly. "You know what? I like you."

Bhandi laughed. "Kiss my ass."

"Ha! Damn, this is the time for a drink!"

When Lumil shot Cheyenne a questioning glance, the halfling shook her head. "No. No one's going inside that house, Lumil. I don't care how thirsty you think you are."

"Yeah. Worth a shot, though, right?"

"Tate," Bhandi shouted. "This psycho wants a drink."

"Good for her." Tate stared at Corian and Maleshi.

"Come on, man. Go grab it."

He ignored Bhandi and nodded at Corian. "I thought you guys had claws or something."

Maleshi raised a hand and extended four-inch silver blades from all five fingertips. "Like this?"

"Holy shit!" He laughed. "No one's gonna believe me when I tell them."

"She's used to being a myth," Corian muttered. Maleshi rolled her eyes at him and retracted her claws before folding her arms.

"Tate, I'm serious."

He whirled and shot Bhandi the middle finger. "Get it yourself!"

"Man, fuck you."

Jamal grunted and stormed across the lawn toward the front of the house. "Now *I* need a drink."

Rhynehart stared after him as the ogre marched past, then turned to Yurik and spread his arms. "You brought booze on an assignment?"

"Hey, you told us to gear up for a campout, man." Yurik shrugged. "Nothing else."

"You're on duty."

"Yeah, and you're standing there doing nothing when L'zar Verdys is sitting there like a statue."

Rhynehart glanced briefly at L'zar's back, then raised an eyebrow. "Watch it."

Yurik gave him a crooked smile. "You gonna join us?"

"No."

"Suit yourself."

"Lumil, I'm serious." Byrd pointed at Yurik as the two groups of magicals went from wary judgment to mingling in Bianca Summerlin's backyard. "Just look at the size of him."

"Man, shut up about it already." Lumil glared at him. "Big fucking deal."

"Yeah, *real* big."

Bhandi stared at Persh'al as everyone gathered by Payton, who sat beside their gear and glared at every magical, FRoE agent and rebel alike, with her good eye. "For real. Why the hell are you blue?"

Persh'al shook his head.

"You know what?" Lumil pointed at him. "You never told *us* why either."

"All of a sudden you give a shit?" Persh'al spread his arms. "It's not like I did it to myself."

"Yeah, but *something* had to make that happen."

Cheyenne closed her eyes. *They figured it out. I don't have it in me to deal with anything else right now.*

She headed toward the nightstalkers, who were slowly making their way over to the others. "I'm turning in."

"All right." Corian looked her over. "You okay?"

"Yeah." She glanced at the group of agents and rebels laughing and talking like they'd known each other forever. "Now that no one's trying to kill each other, I'm done. Keep an eye on my mom, huh?"

"You got it, kid." Maleshi gave her a small smile.

"And him." Cheyenne nodded at L'zar.

"He'll be sitting there all night, Cheyenne. Trust me." Corian stuck his hands in his pockets. "Whatever he's looking for, it's gonna take him a while to find it."

"Hopefully not too long. Let me know if anything changes, okay?"

"Of course."

"Thanks." With one more glance at the magicals throwing their own unlikely party behind the Summerlin estate, Cheyenne took off toward the house. She passed Rhynehart and shrugged. "Better than drawing guns on each other, right?"

"I have no fucking clue."

"No one goes into the house, got it?"

Rhynehart shook his head and stared at the magical party. "Don't get used to this, halfling. I still don't take orders from you."

"No. I guess you can call that a favor for a friend." She shrugged. "'Cause you owe me a lot of those at this point."

"Whatever." He shot her a sidelong glance and waited until the halfling was yards behind him before chuckling softly.

CHAPTER SIXTY-THREE

When Cheyenne rejoined Ember and Eleanor inside the house, she stopped beside the stairs and stared at the sitting area. The housekeeper sat on the chaise again, both legs propped up on the cushion and a fresh drink in her hand. Ember hovered in front of her, her fingers flashing with violet light as she spun some kind of magical design in the air between them. "And that's basically it."

The light fizzled out again. Eleanor grinned. "Well, isn't that something?" She tried to clap but spilled some of her drink, then took a long sip as if that would keep the rest of it from flowing out of her glass. She looked up and found Cheyenne watching them. "Cheyenne! Can you believe this? I've never—" She hiccupped and almost spilled her drink again. "I've never seen this kind of magic. Ember can…well, I have no —*hic*—no idea what she's doing, but it's—*hic*—beautiful!"

"Yep." Cheyenne raised an eyebrow at Ember. "Glad you two are enjoying yourselves."

The fae shrugged. "She wanted to see some magic, Cheyenne. I couldn't tell her no."

Cheyenne chuckled. "Yeah, that gets harder and harder to do."

"It's incredible!" Eleanor shouted. Her head thumped heavily back against the chaise's cushion. "All this time—*hic*—sweetheart. All this time, we never knew about anyone else." Eleanor lowered her gaze to her glass, and her lower lip trembled. "I wish your mother were here to see this, and then I remember it would only anger her."

"I know." Cheyenne sat on the loveseat again. "Probably a good thing she can't see what's happening right now."

"She would come undone!" Eleanor took a heaving breath. Another wail escaped her, and she broke down into sobs again.

"Oh." Ember frowned at her. "I thought we'd moved past that."

"I mean, it could be the booze."

"Yeah." Ember shrugged. "I wasn't about to stop her."

"Don't worry about it, Em. Not your job to babysit anyone."

Eleanor sniffled and took another drink. "I used to call myself a babysitter once upon a time, Cheyenne. When you were small and your mother—" Another sob escaped the woman.

"Okay." The halfling stood and gently approached Bianca's housekeeper. "I think it's time to get you into bed, huh? Maybe set down the drink."

"Cheyenne, I'm a grown-ass woman. I don't need you to coddle me."

Cheyenne stopped and raised her eyebrows, trying to hide her smile. "I know that."

"You stop worrying about me and you make it better." Eleanor fumbled in the pocket of her sweater and removed an already snot-soaked tissue before trying to blow into it again. "Just make it better."

"I'm on it, Eleanor." Cheyenne gently pried the half-empty glass out of the woman's fingers and handed it to Ember. "I really think it's a good idea for you to get into bed, at least. You know, sleep all this off?"

"I don't know anything anymore." Eleanor shook her head and weakly batted at Cheyenne's hands as the halfling tried to help her up. "What am I supposed to do without her, huh?"

"Who, Mom?"

"I'll be useless. Pointless." Eleanor sank back against the chaise, her eyes fluttered closed, and a startlingly loud snore escaped her open mouth.

Ember stifled a laugh behind her hand. "Only four drinks."

"Four drinks and the shock of seeing my mom caught in a magical curse from some other world." Cheyenne gestured at the windows looking over the valley behind the estate. "Plus everything else that's going on right now."

"True. Should we just leave her there?"

"Probably not. I'm imagining her rolling over in her sleep and right onto the floor."

Ember snorted. "Sorry. Not funny."

"I mean, it kind of is. Okay." Cheyenne leaned down and slipped her hands under Eleanor's body as gently as she could before lifting the housekeeper in her arms and heading for the stairs. "This is seriously weird."

"What, you mean watching you pick up a full-grown woman like she's a baby, or something else?"

"Well, yeah, that too. With all the drinking that goes on in this house, Em, I'm surprised I didn't have to do this sooner."

"Somehow, I'm having a hard time imagining your mom this wasted."

"Me too."

Ember floated behind the half-drow as Cheyenne trudged up the stairs, with Eleanor snoring loudly in her arms. She had to stop and wait for Ember to open the door to Eleanor's room, then they worked together to get the housekeeper under the blankets with her shoes off for the night. Then they left the woman's room, and Cheyenne closed the door behind her with a soft click.

"Whew." Ember raised her eyebrows. "Crisis averted there, I guess. Right?"

"Yeah, she'll be fine. Crisis averted out there too." Cheyenne nodded at the open doors of the breakfast room at the top of the stairs.

Ember glanced into the room, which flashed with soft, colorful bursts of light now and then. "What's going on out there?"

"FRoE agents and O'gúleesh rebels settling down for a magical picnic."

"A what?"

"I shit you not, Em. Go check it out."

Frowning, Ember floated into the breakfast room and up to the curving wall of windows above the jutting veranda below. From here, the view was even better, and they both took a moment to watch the gathered magicals out by the portal ridge. "Did they set up a picnic?"

Cheyenne snorted. "I have no idea what they're doing down there.

As long as they're not trying to kill each other and nobody's aiming guns at anyone else's face, I'm calling it a win."

Ember chuckled. "Your mom really would freak out if she saw this."

"That's a serious understatement, Em. But we're doing this for her. No one's going anywhere until L'zar figures out how the hell to get her away from that portal. And wake her up."

"You think he will?"

"I have to, right? Doesn't change how I feel about him in general, but if he can pull her out of that curse, I guess he gets points for it."

"When."

"What?"

"*When* he pulls her out." Ember nodded at her friend. "He will."

"Glad one of us has confidence in the Weaver."

"I wouldn't call it confidence in *him*, necessarily." Ember shrugged. "Just that everything will work out. It has to."

"Right." Cheyenne shook her head at the sight of Lumil raising a tin cup in the center of the magicals while the others stuffed their faces with O'gúleesh food. *Like they went for a quick shopping trip in Peridosh before coming up here. Yeah, right.* "This might be the weirdest thing I've seen in my life."

"Yeah, I gotta stop watching them." Ember yawned, blinked through the ensuing tears, and smacked her lips. "And go to bed."

"The guest room's still usable. Come on." Cheyenne turned away from the windows and headed toward the right curve of the second-floor hallway. She opened the guest room door and stood aside for Ember to enter. "Looks like everything's good to go."

"Thanks." Ember floated inside and grinned. "Gotta say, this is *much* better than trying to navigate your mom's mansion in a wheelchair."

"And no one had to carry *you* up the stairs." They shared a quiet laugh. "If you need anything, just—"

"Find it myself and let you sleep? Yeah, no problem." Ember nodded. "Go get some sleep, Cheyenne. We can focus on saving your mom and two whole worlds in the morning."

Cheyenne laughed. "Glad you're here, Em."

"Yeah, you better be. G'night."

"Night." The halfling turned away from the guest room before Ember softly closed the door. *And now I'm supposed to crawl into one of these beds and sleep like a baby, huh?* She looked over her shoulder at the closed door to her old bedroom and snorted. *Fat chance. I hate that room.*

She wandered slowly down the hall of the second floor, stopped by Eleanor's room one more time, and cracked the door open to check on her, despite the housekeeper's growling snores rising from inside. *Only took four drinks to get her to sleep. Not a road I wanna go down tonight.*

Feeling exhausted and restless at the same time, Cheyenne walked back down the hall and paused outside the open double doors to Bianca's bedroom. The king-sized bed was meticulously made, covered in soft, intricately decorated pillows in cream and beige and a shimmery golden-brown. The halfling stared at the bed, then peeked through the doorway out of habit. *Nope. Mom's standing outside by a damn portal. She's not in here.*

Her gaze fell on the bed again. *The first chance in my life to sleep on that giant-ass bed. Can't even bring myself to do it.*

Instead, Cheyenne reached out for the handles on the French doors and pulled them closed. Then she shuffled into the breakfast room, blinking heavily, and dropped into one of the cream-colored armchairs overlooking the back lawn, the forest, and the valley behind the Summerlin estate. Muffled laughter rose from the gathering beside the portal ridge. L'zar and Bianca remained in the same positions, unaffected by the drinking and lewd jests being thrown around the impromptu party. *Can't blame them for wanting to lighten the mood a little. Just as long as they can handle themselves when it's time to get shit done.*

She pulled out her cell and called Corian.

"What's wrong?"

"Nothing. I just didn't wanna walk all the way back out there for a thirty-second conversation." She watched Corian turn around and glance at the house. "Just don't let L'zar touch her without running it by me first, okay? The second he comes out of that trance or whatever."

"I'll let you know, Cheyenne. You have my word."

From where she sat in the armchair, it was impossible not to see the nightstalker's silver eyes glowing in the darkness at the other end of the lawn. "Thanks."

"Get some rest. You and Ember might be the only ones enjoying peace and quiet tonight."

"Yeah, you can handle it." She hung up and slipped her phone into her pocket. Then she settled back into the armchair and propped her arms on the armrests. Despite her heavy eyelids and a yawn of her own, she couldn't bring herself to look away from the group of magicals drinking and eating beside the scar of jutting black stone stretching out of the forest. *Probably couldn't eat, even if I was hungry. Sleep's looking just as impossible right now too.*

Cheyenne watched Bianca's unmoving silhouette and sank lower in the armchair. "Gonna be a long night for sure."

CHAPTER SIXTY-FOUR

"Wake up, Cheyenne. Now!"

She jolted at the shout and opened her eyes. She sat outside on the lawn in front of her father, his golden glowing eyes a foot away from her. "Dammit, L'zar! You gotta cut this out."

"I'll use the Don'adurr Thread when I have to, Cheyenne. You're the one who agreed to the connection."

"Yeah, 'cause I thought it was a one-time thing." She looked around, noting the blurred appearance of the grass and the tree line and the sky starting to lighten into dawn. "If this wasn't in my head, I'd be walking back to the house right now."

"Listen, I think I've found what we need."

Her gaze settled back on his. "To help Bianca?"

"Not directly, no, but it will greatly improve our chances of successfully forcing Ba'rael to accept your terms."

"Fuck that. You were supposed to be looking for the cure for this curse or whatever you wanna call it. Right now, I don't give a shit about Ba'rael or Ambar'ogúl or anything else. You need to fix this for my mom."

"I will, Cheyenne." L'zar stared at her without any trace of his usual annoyance. "My word might not mean anything to you at this point."

"You're right. It's pretty much worthless."

"But this is a huge step for us. I found it. It's right here on Earth. Ba'rael can't possibly refuse to step down when we bring this to her."

Cheyenne blinked. "Seriously? It took you this long to find something that was here the whole time?"

L'zar tilted his head. "Give me a break, all right? There's a lot going on in my head, and sometimes it takes longer than I'd prefer to dredge up what I want."

"You mean, like anything useful?"

They stared at each other, then L'zar took a deep breath and slowly let it out again. "Whenever you're finished berating me, I really would like to—"

Muted shouting rose through their astral-dream connection. The valley around them flashed with multi-colored lights, and Cheyenne was thrown out of the Don'adurr Thread with a jolt.

She gasped and sat bolt upright in the armchair in the breakfast room, wincing at the tightness in her neck and shoulders. "Ow. Shit."

Rubbing out the pain, she looked through the curving wall of windows to see every FRoE agent and O'gúleesh rebel on their feet, moving quickly and shouting at each other. The portal ridge flashed with multi-colored lights rippling between the formerly inactive columns of black stone.

Not inactive anymore. Shit.

Her gaze fell on Bianca, who seemed unchanged one second and started trembling violently the next.

"Mom!"

Cheyenne slipped into drow speed and sprinted through the house, racing down the stairs and slipping back into normal speed again only to open the glass French doors onto the veranda without shattering them. Then she darted in a gray and white streak to the balcony, leaped over the side, and sped across the lawn.

When she dropped out of enhanced speed right in front of her mother, Bianca's entire body bucked and jerked, her eyes rolling back in her head. "Mom. *Mom!* Come on. Corian!"

The nightstalker appeared beside her in a flash of silver light.

"What's happening?" Cheyenne reached out to Bianca, who made strangled choking sounds, but Corian jerked her hand away.

"Don't touch her."

"What's going on?"

"I don't know, Cheyenne, but it's not safe."

"Watch it!" Byrd sent a ball of green flames hurtling past the half-drow and the nightstalker before it burst on the portal ridge. "I'd get the fuck away from there."

Cheyenne and Corian spun to see a glistening black tentacle undulating between the fists of black stone. "Fuck."

"Nothing we haven't handled before, kid." Corian grabbed her arm and drew her away from Bianca.

"Stop." Cheyenne jerked her arm out of his grasp. "We can't just leave her there!"

"You wanna take yourself down trying to pick her up?" Glinting claws emerged from his hands with a metallic *tzing*. "'Cause that will happen if you touch her now."

"L'zar held on."

"L'zar's an idiot. We take out these things first." Corian turned to the FRoE agents and the rebels behind them and shouted, "No reason to hold back!"

"Damn right, there isn't." Lumil raised both fists and summoned the spinning red runes.

A sleepy-eyed Bhandi stared at the flashing portal ridge and her mouth dropped open.

Lumil turned to her and raised an eyebrow. "You ever fight one of those things?"

"I don't even know what the fuck it is."

"Fun stuff." Lumil let out a blood-curdling battle cry and darted toward the second tentacle sneaking out from between the black stone columns. Her first punch ruptured the in-between monster's appendage, which burst into millions of glittering black shards. "Huh. That was easy."

Cheyenne could only stare at her mom, who was still jerking where she stood, her feet magically glued to the grass beneath her. "Mom? If you can hear me, what the fuck?"

A black tentacle had snaked across the grass toward Bianca's ankle. Cheyenne sent a crackling sphere of black energy at the thing and shattered it. A warbling scream rose from the in-between creature trying to free itself from the portal, and the ground trembled.

"Was that thing reaching for your mother?" Corian asked.

"Yeah." Cheyenne summoned an energy sphere in each hand. "What the hell?"

He shook his head. "Doesn't change anything. Let's take 'em down."

The nightstalker darted away from her in a zigzagging streak of silver light and slashed at the next tentacle crashing toward him from the air.

As L'zar's rebel magicals darted into the fray, blasting in-between monster parts to small bits, Yurik stared at the portal ridge. "This is the weirdest damn thing I've ever seen."

Rhynehart drew his fell pistol. "Guess I forgot to brief you on this part."

"You've seen this before?"

"Couple nights ago. Get moving." The team leader stepped toward the ridge and fired shot after shot.

Another bellow from the in-between split the air, and a massive, constantly shifting form rose above the highest stone pillars. The FRoE agents unleashed their fell ammo at the wavering shapes. Corian and Maleshi darted about in flashes of silver light, slashing and severing tentacles into huge chunks that disintegrated into the air before they hit the ground. Byrd and Lumil screamed and fought together, punching with red fists and launching green flame into the portal ridge. Persh'al's whip of blue magic cracked against a huge pincer darting out of the portal and snapped one half cleanly off.

Cheyenne launched black energy spheres at the much thinner, faster tentacles snaking out of the portal and lashing at Bianca's arms and legs. *Why do they want* her? *She has nothing to do with this!*

A long, thin black barb shot from between two stones toward Cheyenne's face. She ducked and launched another attack. Glowing red eyes appeared beyond the wall of flashing lights in the portal, followed by a hulking, undulating mass without any real shape except for dozens of flailing tentacles and a mouth that looked like a blooming flower.

As she aimed an energy sphere at that mouth, the weirdly shaped feature burst open and sprayed a dozen more glistening barbs at the halfling. Cheyenne raised a translucent black shield in front of her and her seizing mother. The barbs pinged off it like metal pellets, and a second later, she felt the cold, tight grasp of a thin tentacle coiling around her ankle.

Snarling, she flung an energy sphere at the tentacle as it jerked her off her feet and sent her crashing to the ground on her ass. Blinking at the shock racing up her spine, Cheyenne unleashed orb after orb at the hulking black thing. The monster's scream of pain and fury was echoed by two more from farther down the portal ridge, where the other magicals battled the more easily shattered creatures.

Cheyenne tried to get to her feet and had to abandon that idea when another spray of barbs headed toward Bianca. She raised another shield in front of her mom and was whipped off her feet again by another darting tentacle. "Come *on!*"

Bianca let out an involuntary hiss as her body trembled on the grass. The flashing lights pulsed faster, growing brighter by the second. The rest of the in-between creature with the open petal-like mouth lurched between two stone pillars with not enough space for its body. The air filled with the sound of tearing flesh as pieces of the creature broke off. Cheyenne hurled attack after attack at it, trying to get to her feet and keep the lashing tentacles away from her mom at the same time.

The broken shards of the in-between monster rose into the air like hundreds of tiny flying war machines and buzzed in a swarm toward Bianca.

Cheyenne studied them and blasted them out of the sky at the same time, but most were fast enough to avoid her attacks. *And the activator's not picking up a thing? Does it only work on these in the in-between or what?*

The flying shards raced across Cheyenne's body, peppering her face and neck and the top layer of her trenchcoat with slicing cuts. She hissed and stepped in front of her mom, glancing briefly at the shredded sleeve of her jacket. *I'm so fucking done getting my clothes ruined by this bullshit.*

It only took a split-second's thought of the Nimlothar seed that had bonded to her before her drow magic blazed even hotter inside her. Black flames rippled across Cheyenne's flesh and burned behind her eyes. As she went to fire a column of drow fire at the emerging monster ripping itself to shreds to emerge from the portal, a streak of black and white darted past her.

A brilliant flash of purple light ignited *inside* the monster, then L'zar slipped back into normal speed and looked over his shoulder at Cheyenne. Shattered monster pieces spilled from his clenched fist like water. "They're trying to take Bianca."

"You think?" Cheyenne's voice didn't sound like her own, but she ignored it and shot a spray of black flames inches away from L'zar's head to join his purple magic blooming inside the monster. The second her magic hit his, the creature ignited in a burst of purple and black, spraying chunks all over the lawn and peppering the magicals fighting off two other hulking beasts emerging from the portal.

Hard chunks of glistening monster shell clattered against yet another shield Cheyenne raised in front of her mom. The in-between monster, or what was left of it, shrieked and withdrew into the flashing multi-colored lights.

"Fucking die!" Bhandi fired round after round of fell ammunition into the portal.

Jamal had opted for the one fell cannon the new FRoE team had thought to bring to the Summerlin estate. With a grunt, he hefted the launcher onto his shoulder and fired. A thick green burst of light flared around him and the heavy weapon as a concentrated fell rocket blasted into the portal ridge.

The monsters screamed together in dozens of voices, tentacles flailing and whipping around, claws and pincers and strangely shaped teeth clicking and breaking off. Squeals and creaking groans rose from the Border portal, then every remaining in-between creature slithered, thumped, or skittered back into the darkness between the jutting stone columns.

The wall of shimmering, flashing light flared once with blazing intensity, then winked out.

L'zar snarled and paced back and forth in front of the ridge, his golden eyes blazing with battle rage. He was the only one who didn't turn to look at Jamal, who dropped the fell launcher into the dirt and grunted.

The black flames racing across Cheyenne's body snuffed out, and she blinked at the superpowered FRoE grenade launcher in the grass. "Please don't tell me that's the most effective way to beat these things back."

"What?" L'zar hissed and spun to face the ogre, his eyes widening as he realized the portal ridge had shut down.

"Ha! Look at you, you giant fell-damn brute!" Lumil punched Jamal's upper arm and grinned.

He grunted, gave her the barest hint of a grin, and shoved her back. With a shout, Lumil flew away from him and skidded across the grass.

Byrd cracked up, one arm wrapped around his stomach as he pointed with the other at the goblin woman. "It's like you've never fought an ogre before!"

She sat up, shook loose grass out of her floppy yellow hair, and thumped her fist into the grass before her spinning red runes reappeared. "Sounds like you wanna get knocked the fuck across this portal too, *dae'bruj.*"

The FRoE agents joined Byrd in his amusement, snickering at the goblin woman on the ground. Even Payton cracked a crooked smile, but it disappeared as she stepped back and lowered the fell rifle strapped around her neck and shoulder.

"It wasn't the fucking bazooka," L'zar growled.

The laughter stopped. The O'gúleesh rebels waited for him to say more as the FRoE agents, including Rhynehart, stared at the drow thief finally on his feet and joining in their unlikely get-together.

"Then what was it?" Corian asked.

L'zar sneered at the columns of black stone, gazing from one jagged tip to the next. "They were called back."

"That doesn't make sense." Cheyenne shook her head. "You think Ba'rael—"

Bianca let out a strangled moan behind her daughter, and Cheyenne spun as her mom stopped seizing and crumpled to the grass.

"Mom!" She darted toward Bianca.

"Cheyenne, don't!" L'zar shouted.

At the same time, a deafening crack filled the air and echoed around the valley below the Summerlin estate. The ground trembled violently, then the black pillar in front of the unconscious Bianca split and started to fall.

CHAPTER SIXTY-FIVE

Cheyenne reached toward her mom, black tendrils snaking from her fingers. She coiled them as gently as she could around Bianca's arms before dragging the woman swiftly away from the crumbling pillar of stone. The top half of the column crashed into the grass with a thud mere inches from the soles of Bianca Summerlin's feet.

Retracting her tendrils, Cheyenne raced toward her mother and risked touching her. When the curse didn't blast her away, she lifted her mother in her arms, and turned away from the crumbling stone. "Mom?"

"Cheyenne," Corian called. "Get her to the house."

The ground bucked beneath them all, and every other thick, jutting black spear on the portal ridge trembled and splintered. Muted black light grew between them, buzzing and flashing in a way that seemed to suck all the dawn light out of the valley. Cheyenne turned toward the house and almost dropped Bianca when the ground shook one more time. The black light ballooned up from the portal ridge, then was sucked back through in terrifying silence.

Yurik raised his fell rifle in both hands. "What the—"

The portal ridge exploded, roaring like a violent windstorm and sending chunks of shattered black stone in every direction. The agents turned away, despite the helmets they'd tugged on before the fight.

Their dampening vests afforded them little protection. Corian, Maleshi, and L'zar darted away from the worst of the blast. Cheyenne gritted her teeth and raised a huge shield between the exploding portal and the magicals who could no longer fight back. She slipped into drow speed with Bianca in her arms and raced away, then gently lowered her mom to the ground.

"I'll be back," she whispered. "I promise."

She sent her black lashing tendrils whipping at the suspended debris to shove it aside and away from the others. Magic burst faster than it should have from within the crumbling portal and struck down her shield.

Then she saw the blight.

It was moving as quickly as they'd seen it consume the mountain village in Ambar'ogúl, snaking out from between the shattered chunks of stone to spread black sludge and shrivel the grass in its path.

Cheyenne saw Corian and Maleshi slipping into enhanced speed beside her, and their eyes widened when they saw the blight spreading from Ambar'ogúl through the in-between onto Earth. "What do we do?"

Corian gritted his teeth. "Get everyone as far away from that as we can. I told you to take Bianca to the house."

"There has to be something we can do." They all took a step back as the blight moved with surprising speed away from the shattered portal.

"We don't have time to look for alternatives, Cheyenne!"

"There's no way we can get everyone out of here." The halfling stooped to pick her mom up again and turned to the house. "And it's gonna keep moving. I can't take her to the house."

L'zar appeared with them in enhanced speed and scowled at the creeping blight. "Honestly, I did *not* see this coming."

"We have to move the others. Now." Maleshi headed over to Persh'al and lifted him under one arm like he was a cardboard cutout before running with him toward the hillside and the estate house.

"Go." Corian nodded at L'zar and pointed at the FRoE agents, Lumil, and Byrd, who were suspended in regular time.

"I'm not carrying anyone, Corian."

"Well, do you have a better idea? Because if *you* can't keep this shit from spreading, the least you can do is not be completely useless!"

Snarling, L'zar ran after Corian toward the other magicals to start the agonizingly slow process of moving them all in enhanced speed.

Cheyenne jogged across the lawn as Maleshi headed over to her again, trying not to jostle Bianca too much. *I don't even know if I can hurt her running around with her like this.* "What's next, open a portal when everyone's far enough away? Eleanor and Ember are still in the house!"

"Just keep moving. We'll figure it out, but we can't waste time talking."

Blazing purple light flashed on the veranda, and even with the drow and nightstalkers in enhanced speed, the light moved remarkably quickly above their heads. Cheyenne looked up at the source of the light bursting across the lawn and saw Ember standing on the balcony, both arms stretched toward the exploding Border portal and the blight spilling through from the other side.

"Whoa."

Ember's magic hit the creeping blight with an even brighter flare of light, sending up black smoke and sparks and a hiss like water splattering a hot frying pan. Corian, Maleshi, and L'zar raced across the lawn with FRoE agents, Lumil, and Byrd in their arms. Cheyenne set her mom down again and went to help Corian with Jamal because it took both of them to move the hulking agent more than a foot.

Ember floated over the veranda's balcony and sailed in a weirdly graceful arc toward the lawn. When the drow and the nightstalkers had gotten everyone to the grass beneath the jutting veranda, Cheyenne slipped out of drow speed and saw Ember dropping over the side of the veranda in a barely controlled descent. The fae screamed as she floated toward the portal ridge, then stopped. The place where her magic met the black sludge and withered trails of grass erupted in violet light and high-pitched ringing.

Cheyenne clenched her eyes shut and clapped both hands over her ears, doubling over beneath the aching pressure in her head. Then the light and the awful sound disappeared, and she only heard her heaving breath.

"Holy shit." Byrd scrambled to his feet. "I mean, thanks for the lift to safety, whoever it was, but a little warning next time would've been—"

Tate shouted in surprise and struggled to get to his feet, his head whipping from side to side as he tried to figure out how he'd gotten across the backyard in two seconds. Jamal grunted and looked down at his huge bicep. "Someone pinched me."

"Might've been me." Corian shot him a quick glance and shrugged. "Sorry."

Cheyenne removed her hands from over her ears and looked at Ember. The fae's hands dropped to her sides, her shoulders hunched, and her head drooped to her chest. "Ember. Whoa, whoa, whoa." She darted toward her *Nós Aní* and skidded to a stop in front of her. "Hey. You okay?"

Ember's eyelids fluttered, and she heaved a sigh. "I'm guessing my magic is stronger than my body. The floating spell's still up, or I'd be on the ground. Again." Her eyes closed heavily.

"You're not, though. You're gonna be okay." Cheyenne grabbed her friend's shoulders and gave them a reassuring squeeze. *How is that even possible? Healing Cazerel made her lose all her magic.*

"This is certainly a curious turn of events." L'zar stepped past them and continued toward the ruptured Border portal.

"That's it?" Cheyenne turned to glare after him. "That's all you have to say?"

"Hey, it's okay." Ember gave her a tired smile. "I didn't do it for his recognition."

"Yeah, I know, Em. Still not okay." Cheyenne turned to look at Maleshi and didn't have to tell the general to keep an eye on the still-unconscious Bianca. Maleshi nodded and squatted beside Cheyenne's mom, studying the woman's now much more peaceful expression. Cheyenne stalked after her father. "L'zar!"

He ignored her and kept moving toward the broken shards of glistening black rock lying in crumbled heaps across the lawn.

"Hey! Whatever you're so interested in, you wouldn't even be able to come look at right now if Ember hadn't cleared up the blight."

"I'm well aware of that, Cheyenne." He reached the edge of the fallen debris and walked slowly along it, hands clasped behind his back. "I'm sure we're all very grateful for her assistance."

"No, we owe her our *lives*. That wasn't just assistance."

"No, and this wasn't just a malfunctioning portal." L'zar stopped, looked slowly at his daughter, and grinned. "This was intentional."

"You mean because those things kept trying to grab my *mother*?"

"That's part of it, yes." L'zar squatted in front of a small pile of rubble and pointed at the shattered pieces. "And then there's this."

Cheyenne rolled her eyes. "Just tell me already. I'm really not in the mood for your guessing games."

"Come see for yourself."

She approached him and stepped to his right to look at the debris in front of him. "A mirror."

"A broken mirror." He looked up at her with raised eyebrows. "And that leaf."

Cheyenne's gaze settled on the glowing leaf she recognized from the last Nimlothar tree in the center of Hangivol. *A leaf and a broken mirror.* "Ba'rael sent those through, didn't she?"

L'zar chuckled, grabbed the leaf pulsing with faint purple light, and pocketed it as he stood. "Very good."

"I don't see how that's funny."

"It's not, Cheyenne." He turned to her with something like a sneer and cocked his head. "It's a combination of how amusing I find her failure and how much I enjoy watching you reason this out on your own."

As he stalked past her to rejoin the others, Cheyenne stared at the broken shards of stained, dented mirror and frowned. *The portal into her torture-chamber dungeon took us through a mirror.* Turning swiftly, the halfling followed her father, ignoring the fact that he made her jog to reach him as he moved swiftly with his long, casual stride. "She found where this portal opened on the other side."

"It would seem so."

"And she wanted to send a message? Destroyed the entire portal just to show you she knows how we got in?"

"I can only assume the message was meant for both of us, Cheyenne. If it was purely for you, I'm sure the Spider would've waited until you returned to offer your terms." L'zar cocked his head and searched the morning sky, which was filling with golden sunlight. "She knows I can't return, and she knows her curse extended through the in-between. Maybe not exactly where or how, but she knew she'd hit something other than my physical person with her sentencing me to exile."

"Other than your physical person? Are you kidding me? She hit a completely *different* physical person." They reached the other side of the lawn and the gathered magicals standing and staring in awe at the destroyed portal ridge and the blight Ember had healed and cleared away. The fae watched L'zar and Cheyenne approach, but she didn't move. "Hey, I'm serious. You need to answer me. If Ba'rael noticed she caught someone else in that curse besides you if she could—shit, I don't even know, control the in-between to look for Bianca, why the hell would she even *want* my mom? She's human."

"Hmm." L'zar turned slowly and eyed his daughter. "You know, I think your impressive reasoning skills must have been temporary."

"Fuck off. What's going on?"

"I'll be sure to let you know as soon as I do." His upper lip twitched in an irritating sneer, then he stalked to the flagstone steps on the side of the house.

Cheyenne turned to look at Corian and Maleshi, ignoring the FRoE agents' disbelief as they muttered in confusion and bombarded Byrd, Lumil, and Persh'al with questions none of the rebels could answer. The general sat beside Bianca, who still lay unresponsive in the shady grass, and looked up with a questioning frown. "What did he find?"

"A broken mirror and a Nimlothar leaf."

"And a destroyed portal." Corian narrowed his eyes at the piles of gleaming rubble in front of the tree line. "Ba'rael now knows how we got in without her picking up on it. New portals tend to do that, I suppose."

"Yeah, well, now it's a dead portal, and apparently, she was sending a message."

Maleshi looked back down at the unconscious Bianca and nodded. "Apparently."

"Why my mom?"

Corian cleared his throat. "It might've taken Ba'rael a few days to realize she had ensnared an additional victim in her curse, but she picked up on it. Then she tried to pull your mother through to the other side."

"I know that already." Cheyenne stared at her mother. "What I don't know is why Ba'rael would want my mom. I mean, seriously. Bianca would be useless there."

"No doubt. And it wasn't about your mother specifically, Cheyenne. Merely the extra prize in the Crown's curse."

"You're still not making sense."

Maleshi propped her forearms on her raised knees. "If anything got caught in her curse for her to grab and bring to the other side, kid, no matter what it was, Ba'rael would try to get it. Because whatever it was, it was something L'zar cares very much about."

Cheyenne's skin prickled with a cold chill. "What?"

"That's how this one works." Maleshi shrugged.

"Wait. You're telling me my mom's been unconscious for almost twenty-four hours because L'zar cares about her?"

Corian glanced at the drow thief standing by the edge of the forest at the base of the steps up the hill. "He can lie about it all he wants. Act like she means nothing and never has. But a curse doesn't lie, kid."

"That's bullshit." Cheyenne shook her head. "He couldn't care less about what happens to her as long as it helps *him*."

"You're entitled to your opinion." Corian shrugged. "I'm telling you what I know."

"Great." She scowled at him, then bent over her mom and scooped Bianca up in her arms again. "First time since we met that you telling me everything you know doesn't help me at all."

The halfling stormed toward the flagstone steps, refusing to look at her father as she passed him. He refused to look at her or her mother but turned instead to stare into the woods.

Ember floated slowly after the halfling. She tossed a hand weakly in the air and didn't stop to look at the rebels or the FRoE agents. "Don't worry about me, guys. I'm good. Just wiped the blight off the face of this planet for now."

By the time she'd disappeared up the stairs behind Cheyenne, the FRoE agents had recovered from their shock and started moving again, picking themselves up off the ground where the nightstalkers, Cheyenne, and L'zar had deposited them.

"So, I guess that means the assignment's over, right?" Yurik ran his hand over the yellow braid stretching down the center of his otherwise shaved head and looked at Rhynehart. "We goin' back to base?"

Rhynehart sat perfectly still on the grass, staring blankly at the wreckage of the portal ridge with his arms wrapped around his knees.

"Hey." Tate leaned over to their team leader and waved a hand in front of Rhynehart's face. "You okay?"

The human agent slowly shook his head. "If you don't get your goddamn hand out of my face, troll, I'll bite your fingers off. 'Cause either I'm crazy, or everything that happened was a hundred percent real."

The tattooed troll straightened and stepped away from their team leader. "I like my fingers, thanks."

Bhandi snorted, brushing bits of black stone and grass off her black fatigues. "So, what now?"

"Well," Lumil sniffed and looked at the floor of the veranda protruding from the back of the house. "I mean, it's not like we have a reason to stay here."

CHAPTER SIXTY-SIX

After settling Bianca in the master bedroom's king-sized bed and covering her with a throw blanket she couldn't remember being used in any capacity other than decoration, Cheyenne pulled together the French doors to her mom's room, leaving them open a crack just in case.

"Hey, Em."

"Yeah." Ember waited at the top of the staircase, her eyelids drooping.

"Wanna pinch me?"

The fae snorted. "Tempting, but I'm not sure I have enough in me for that."

Cheyenne stepped toward the staircase and cast one more glance at Bianca's room before heading down the steps to the foyer. "None of this makes sense."

"The part where you just tucked Bianca Summerlin into bed? Or the part where the FRoE's now working *with* L'zar Verdys and his rebels? *Or* the part where your aunt accidentally cursed your mom too because your dad cares about someone other than himself?"

"How about the part where you flew out of the house and healed the blight with fae magic? We can add that to the list too."

Ember chuckled wryly. "Not like that. I didn't *fly.*"

"Oh, I get it. Falling with style, huh?"

"Very funny. Levitation spell. Or hovering spell. Whatever. You know what? Corian didn't tell me what it's called when he taught me that one, but I figured I'd take a page out of your book and use it to keep myself from eating shit."

"I'd love to know what page of my book you're referring to."

Ember gave the halfling an exasperated look and raised an eyebrow. "Cheyenne Summerlin, drow halfling, overthrowing the O'gúl Crown and incapable of *not* jumping off every balcony she sees."

"Oh." Cheyenne laughed as they turned left at the bottom of the stairs toward the sitting area. "It's not like I see a balcony and go, 'Hey, I hope somebody needs me to clean up a shitty magical mess for them, 'cause I'd *really* love to jump off this thing right now.'"

"Yeah, I know. Wasn't something I analyzed before I did it either. So, now that there's no portal…"

"I guess the immediate danger's not so immediate anymore. Except for my mom." Cheyenne headed for the loveseat. "L'zar said something about finding what we needed to take to Ba'rael. You know, my terms and everything. And that it's here on Earth."

"Oh. That's odd."

"I know, right?"

"Shouldn't you be out there threatening him or something if he doesn't go get it right now?"

"I need a minute, Em. We almost stepped into seriously deep shit out there. Don't get me wrong. I'm super grateful."

"Please. Like I ever thought you weren't."

"I just want like five minutes before we head somewhere else, thinking we're wrapping up one thing and finding a dozen other things we have to deal with first."

"Sure." Ember nodded. "No problem. Want me to leave you alone?"

"Not really." Cheyenne snorted. "Only if you want to."

As soon as she sank into the loveseat's cushions, a crash of metal and a startled shriek came from the kitchen. The halfling and the fae looked at each other, then Cheyenne was on her feet again and racing toward the swinging door. Both girls barreled into the industrial-grade kitchen and found Eleanor bent over a pile of pots on the floor.

Cheyenne stepped hesitantly forward. "Everything okay in here?"

"Oh!" Eleanor jumped and straightened, slapping one hand down on the stainless-steel counter to steady herself and the other over her heart. "Cheyenne, I swear, one of these days, you're going to sneak up on me and make me keel right over."

"I didn't sneak." The halfling turned to the swinging kitchen door and shrugged. "Doesn't matter, I guess. Sorry."

"It's fine. It's fine." Catching her breath, Eleanor stooped again with a groan, picked up two pots, and set them gingerly on the counter, grimacing. "I'm sorry too."

"For what?"

"For sleeping so late, sweetheart. I'm usually up way earlier. You know that. It's this pounding headache. I'll have breakfast ready as soon as I can. I'm a bit slow."

Cheyenne swallowed a laugh. "Is that a euphemism for a hangover?"

Eleanor put a hand on her hip and turned slowly to shoot the halfling a warning look. "Most likely. It's the headache that woke me up. Still waiting for the ibuprofen to kick in."

Ember opened her mouth with a sharp breath and glanced behind her at the kitchen door, slowly settling into stillness again. "You *just* woke up?"

"Yes."

"From a headache?"

Eleanor frowned. "You know, I'm quite familiar with being hungover, girls, and as far as I can tell, I'm still perfectly coherent."

"You are, Eleanor. Hungover *and* coherent." Cheyenne shrugged. "You missed the entire showdown out back."

"Really?" Eleanor glanced at the kitchen door too, though the round window only looked out on the sweeping central staircase. "Was it loud?"

"Might be what made your headache worse. Mine too, actually."

"Well, do enlighten me."

<hr>

When Cheyenne finished recounting everything the housekeeper had slept through without knowing, she eyed the half-dozen eggs Eleanor had cracked into the skillet two minutes ago. "And you forgot to turn on the burner."

"No, I didn't…oh." Eleanor chuckled and then winced at the jolt it brought to her head before turning on the stove with a click and a whoosh of igniting gas. "I need to pay attention."

"Happens to the best of us." Cheyenne and Ember exchanged knowing glances. "You heard everything I told you, though, right?"

"Of course I did. My hearing's not the problem, sweetheart. I think I have a better appreciation for *your* sensitivity to loud noises right now."

"We might have to head out again pretty soon. One more time-sensitive thing, I guess."

"Oh. So you don't want breakfast, then?"

Cheyenne eyed the frying eggs. "I definitely do. Just let me see how long we'll be sticking around, and I'll let you know, okay?"

"Sure." Eleanor grabbed a spatula and poked the eggs with it.

"Like I said, Mom's upstairs."

"I *am* perfectly capable of watching her while I feel awful, Cheyenne. Of course, I'll look after her, and I'll call you the second something else happens. Assuming she doesn't disappear or…oh, I don't even know what else is possible."

"Anything, really," Ember muttered.

"What was that?"

Cheyenne shot her friend a sidelong glance and shook her head.

"Nothing."

"I'll let you know when we're leaving, Eleanor."

"Sounds good." The housekeeper looked up from her distracted cooking and managed a weak smile. "I'm glad everyone's all right."

"Yeah, so are we. Thanks." Cheyenne nodded for Ember to step out of the kitchen with her. Eleanor's moans of discomfort followed them through the swinging door.

"So, now that your mom's lying in bed instead of standing frozen in the backyard, Eleanor's cool as a cucumber, huh?"

"I guess so." Cheyenne stopped behind the loveseat and braced herself against it for a moment. "This isn't exactly the way I—"

The front door creaked open, followed by heavy footsteps. Lots of heavy footsteps.

"Holy fucking mansion."

"Dude, would you look at the size of this place?"

"How are we supposed to find her in here, huh? I bet you there are a million fell-damn rooms, and half of 'em are hidden or something."

Cheyenne jerked her head up and stared at the foyer, which was blocked by half of the huge central staircase. "No. No way."

"Yeah, you don't walk into someone else's house uninvited."

"It's not like I just didn't invite them, Em. I told them no. More than once." Cheyenne pushed herself away from the loveseat and stormed through her mom's house to the front door. "Hey. Nobody told you guys to bring the whole damn circus into the house."

"Relax, halfling." Lumil dismissed her with a wave and gazed around the foyer. "You're wrong."

"What?"

"Yeah, L'zar's the one who shipped us all off up the hill." Persh'al let out a low whistle. "Never thought I'd be looking at the inside of this place, kid."

"And you're not supposed to be." Cheyenne shook her head and tried to block them as Jamal, Payton, and the FRoE agents stepped inside. "This isn't L'zar's house. He doesn't get to decide who walks through that door."

Bhandi pointed at her and raised an eyebrow. "Not your house either, right?"

The halfling pointed at the open front door. "Get out."

"After we've all had a chance to sit down and chat face to face about what happens now," L'zar said as he stepped slowly inside. "Interesting."

Cheyenne rolled her eyes. "Nobody's gonna listen to me about this, are they?"

"Don't take it personally," Rhynehart muttered, stepping around L'zar in the doorway and skirting past the drow thief with a wary gaze. "I'll tell you one thing. I'm tired of sitting, standing, and sleeping on that grass. I don't care how soft it is."

"Pretty soft, though, right?" Lumil winked at Rhynehart and chuckled when he turned away from her to explore more of Bianca Summerlin's house.

"So, where should we *gather*?" L'zar's gaze lingered at the top of the wide staircase, then he looked at his daughter and raised his eyebrows.

Cheyenne closed her eyes and took a deep breath. "The dining room, I guess."

"Excellent. And that would be where?"

Grimacing at her father, Cheyenne gestured at the back of the house. "Under the stairs."

Bhandi gave the halfling a confused frown. "Say what?"

"You'll see." Rolling her eyes at Ember, Cheyenne brushed past the uninvited magicals and led them to the long dining table at the back of the house, which overlooked the veranda and the valley beyond it.

"Lovely." L'zar pulled out a chair facing the wall of windows, dropped into it, propped his feet on the seat next to him, and folded his arms.

Cheyenne stared at his shoes, stacked one on top of the other. *Mom would kill him if she saw that. Too bad she's passed out upstairs.*

The other magicals filtered around the dining table, scooting out chairs and thumping boots and chair legs on the floor.

"Hey, big guy." Persh'al nodded at Jamal and pointed at the head of the table. "Go ahead and take a seat."

Jamal folded his arms. "I'll break that chair."

"What? Come on. You don't know that."

"I can tell, troll."

Persh'al lifted both hands and shrugged. "Yeah, okay."

Cheyenne took the chair at the head of the table instead because it was the only one left open. *I'm not about to stand here feeling like I'm on the outside listening in. Who knows how long this is gonna take?*

L'zar smacked the table. "Now that we're all such great friends…"

Corian snorted. "What's this about?"

"I've found our next step."

"Which has nothing to do with breaking L'zar's curse on my mom." Cheyenne folded her arms and sat back in the chair, staring at her father.

"Which I also tried to share with you this morning before my sister and that portal had a little meltdown together. Incidentally, your mother's in much better condition now, isn't she? Tucked safely into her bed upstairs, I'm assuming."

Cheyenne cocked her head. "Don't."

"Then don't interrupt me." L'zar glared at her and turned to address the other magicals around the table. "I found exactly what we need next to bolster the irrefutable terms Cheyenne will be presenting to the Crown in a few days. No, it's not a direct solution to aiding the lovely woman whose home we currently occupy—"

The halfling snorted.

He ignored her. "But when the Spider steps down off her throne, the curse she never intended for Ms. Summerlin will end on its own."

"Don't say that's gonna happen if you're not sure," Cheyenne warned.

"Well, even if I wasn't sure, I'd still say it because I'd still have a hunch." L'zar leaned over the table and glared at his daughter. "But I'm sure."

"Hold on. Wait a minute." Yurik thumped both elbows on the table and lifted his hands for everyone to stop. "You said some stuff about a crown and a throne and a curse and…I don't even know. But I *do* know it all sounds like bullshit. What's really going on?"

L'zar clicked his tongue at the muscular goblin. "Pity you Earthborn have no idea where you truly come from."

"We come from right here, asshole." Bhandi jammed her finger on the table. "That's why we do what we do. To protect this world from everything else. Like you."

L'zar grimaced in distaste. "I assure you, if I wanted to destroy this world, I could very easily do so, and I am not the greatest danger we still face."

"Oh, yeah?" Tate folded his arms and sat back in his chair. "What's worse than you?"

Rhynehart cleared his throat and pointed at the wall of windows overlooking the backyard as he stared at the tattooed troll. "That. What we saw out there is worse than L'zar Verdys. Worse than him breaking out of Chateau D'rahl, worse than him leading us on a wild fucking goose chase. Whatever has to happen to make sure *that* doesn't repeat itself, I'm all for it."

Every magical around the table stared at the human FRoE agent and his sudden change of heart.

Cheyenne raised her eyebrows. "Gotta admit, man, that's not what I expected you to say."

He met her gaze and looked quickly down at the table, his nostrils flaring. "That makes two of us."

Bhandi narrowed her eyes at the team leader and leaned toward Tate, sitting beside her, to mutter, "You see him get hit in the head by any of those flying rocks?"

"Nope."

"Huh. Doesn't mean it didn't happen."

L'zar turned his golden eyes to Rhynehart and grinned. "This *is* a pleasure, though. Hearing those words from an operative of the FRoE. And a *human*." The drow thief wiggled his eyebrows, and Rhynehart glared at him. "I'm also glad you mentioned that wonderfully hospitable prison you people insist on believing you run."

Rhynehart stared at the drow thief. "Whatever."

"Not quite." L'zar rapped his knuckles on the table and leaned forward, peering at the odd collection of magicals with narrowed eyes. "I'm feeling rather generous today. One might even say my eyes have been opened to a larger, grander plan. Or perhaps I'm still riding the high of finally pulling something useful out of my head." He gave Cheyenne a pointed look. "Whatever the reason, I'll let all of you in on this next part of the plan."

"Oh, good." Tate nodded. "There's a plan."

L'zar stared at Rhynehart, the corner of his mouth twitching up in a sneer. "You're the one running this little Earthbound band of agents, if that's what you want to call yourselves, so let me make this perfectly clear. I *will* kill you if you try to stop us."

Cheyenne sat up straighter in the chair. "Wait a minute. L'zar."

"On the other hand," L'zar continued, "this might be an opportunity for you to make yourselves useful. I do hope you take it."

Rhynehart glared at the drow thief. "I'll make that decision when you quit playing games and tell us whatever the fuck you brought us here to say."

"Hmm." L'zar's lips parted in a lazy, crooked smile. "I always play games, human. I thought you knew that by now."

"Seriously, L'zar." Cheyenne shook her head. "Just spit it out already, huh?"

The drow thief grinned. "There's a certain—"

The rattle of dishes accompanied the swinging door on the south-east side of the house opening, and Eleanor bustled into the sitting area with a breakfast-laden silver tray. "Well, Cheyenne, since you never came to tell me you were leaving, I assumed I might as well make breakfast."

The housekeeper stopped when she saw thirteen magicals and one human staring at her from various places around the table.

Her mouth opened and closed silently until someone cleared their throat and snapped her out of it. "I'll just go make more breakfast, then." She spun and took the entire tray with her as she returned to the kitchen.

Cheyenne called, "Eleanor, you really don't have to."

"Carry on without me," the woman cried shrilly, then the kitchen door muffled her voice as it swung back and forth behind her.

Ember caught Cheyenne's gaze and leaned in to whisper, "She's not really gonna make breakfast for fourteen people, is she?"

"I mean, the kitchen was built for it." Ember gave her a sharp look, and Cheyenne shook her head. "No, Em. She won't kick us out, but she's not cooking for everybody." *Especially L'zar and the first FRoE agent to turn on me and try blackmail-via-Bianca on for size. Fairly sure Eleanor hates both of them.*

"Well." L'zar chuckled and laced his fingers behind his head. "Minor disruptions aside—"

"Okay, now *I'm* getting fed up with your posturing," Corian grumbled. "You've had your fun."

"Oh, see, that's just it." L'zar grinned at his *Nós Ani* with an extra flash of warning in his golden eyes. "The fun's just beginning because the agents at this table are going to help us break another inmate out of Chateau D'rahl."

CHAPTER SIXTY-SEVEN

Rhynehart jolted in his chair and leaned forward to stare at the grinning drow thief. "You're out of your damn mind."

"Naturally."

Corian frowned and stroked his tawny-furred chin. "Who is it?"

"Venga."

The nightstalker's mouth opened, but no words came out. Instead, he shut his mouth again and turned to Maleshi. The general raised both hands and slowly shook her head.

"That's the kinda reaction nobody likes to get." Bhandi shook a finger at the nightstalkers. "Especially from two—whatever the hell you are."

"Nightstalkers, dumbass." Tate scowled at her. "Seriously, only an idiot would fuck around like you are right now."

"You know what? I should've let that gang in Virginia Beach gut you like a fish."

Corian closed his eyes. "I swear, two arguing goblins were already more than enough. Now I have to deal with trolls too."

"I'll take care of them for you, *vae shra'ni*." Maleshi grinned at Tate and Bhandi and extended her claws from all five fingers with a metallic *shring*. "I have no history with *them*."

Tate lifted a finger. "Okay, wait a minute."

"*Everybody* needs to wait a minute," Cheyenne cut in. "For real. My mom's in some kinda magical coma upstairs, and we need to figure out our next steps right now. Save the bullshit for when no one cares about you wasting everyone's time, all right?"

The magicals around the table shut up and stared at the drow halfling. Persh'al giggled and covered his mouth up with a blue hand.

Cheyenne turned back to L'zar and raised her eyebrows. "Who's Venga?"

The drow thief chuckled. "Something of a friend, you might say. More or less."

Corian snorted and folded his arms, slowly shaking his head.

"That doesn't instill a lot of confidence."

"Well, at the very least, Cheyenne, he's far more of a friend to us than to the Spider."

"Okay." Cheyenne looked at her father and Corian. "Think he's someone I can put on the roster for potential new Crown?"

"For potential…ha! Absolutely not!" L'zar threw his head back and laughed. His dark voice echoed around the vaulted ceilings and glass walls of Bianca's stately home.

Cheyenne glared at him. *If that doesn't wake Mom up, she's definitely still cursed.*

When he'd finished laughing, the Weaver sniffed and gave her a condescending smile. "Not that kind of friend, but he *is* someone who can help us put down the loyalists on this side, at the very least. At the most—and here's to hoping for that—Venga will be able to access the rest of the information we can use as leverage against Ba'rael. An added bonus, you might say. Far more effective when it trades hands from one old friend to another."

"And he's a prisoner at Chateau D'rahl?" Rhynehart asked.

"Indeed."

"Then why the hell don't I recognize the name?"

"Oh." L'zar feigned surprise. "I wasn't aware you knew the names of every inmate in that hulk of rock, human."

"You're not aware of a lot of things, including how much time I've spent in that prison *beyond* chaperoning father-daughter visits."

"Of course." The drow thief gave Rhynehart a hideously fake smile of understanding and dipped his head. "Does the name Vinny ring a bell?"

Rhynehart stood abruptly from his chair with the loud screech of wood scooting across wood. "Fuck you. No!"

"No, you don't recognize the name?"

"No, we're not breaking that *thing* out of Chateau D'rahl! Goddammit. Just when I'm starting to think you might not be as crazy as everyone thinks you are!"

L'zar chuckled. "I'm flattered."

"That wasn't a compliment." The agent thumped a fist on the table. "Do you have any idea how much of our resources we put into keeping Vinny in there?"

"His real name is Venga." The drow gave Rhynehart a tight-lipped smile. "I'm sure you can understand an appreciation for calling something or someone by their real name, can't you?"

"I don't care if we call him Mary fucking Poppins. We're not breaking him out!"

Cheyenne and the FRoE agents shot Rhynehart confused looks. He was starting to sound like Sir. Another one bites the dust.

Rhynehart seemed to realize that, and no matter how deeply he frowned to try hiding it, the light flush creeping up his neck and into his cheeks was unmistakable.

"And I do know, by the way," L'zar added casually.

"Know what?" The team leader folded his arms and couldn't help but glance quickly around the table at everyone watching him argue with the mad drow thief.

"How much of your resources you put into keeping Venga locked up. I *should* know, at any rate. I spent seventy-five years in that sand-castle you call a prison."

Rhynehart scoffed and shook his head. "I don't think breaking him out is all it's gonna take to get the guy to agree to anything I'm involved in, at the very least."

"Why? Were you the one who put him away?"

"Something like that." Scowling, the operative slowly lowered himself into his chair and scooted toward the table again. "Why would he help us at all? Why would he help you?"

"Why, indeed." L'zar smoothed his white hair away from his face with both hands, tossed his head back, and interlaced his fingers behind it again as he stared up at the bright blue sky through the wall of windows. "Venga will help me because he used to be one of Ba'rael's most fervent disciples. And I believe he owes me a blood debt."

Cheyenne groaned. "Are you serious?"

Her father dipped his head and spread his arms, a sly smile playing on his lips.

"Who the hell is this Ba'rael?" Rhynehart grumbled. "You guys are throwing that name around like it's fucking candy."

"Yeah." Byrd snorted. "The poisonous kind."

Lumil frowned at him in question before slapping his shoulder.

"Ow."

When Cheyenne met Ember's gaze, the fae shrugged and shook her head. *Guess I'm running on my own counsel right now, like everybody else.* Rolling her eyes, she leaned toward Rhynehart. "Okay, let's get this over with. Ba'rael Verdys. L'zar Verdys' older sister. Technically, that makes her my aunt. And she's the Crown of Ambar'ogúl."

"The Crown?" Rhynehart raised his eyebrows and looked lost.

"Yeah. The drow dictator of the entire world over there, who's responsible for all the new Border portals, the war machines, that portal ridge exploding on us, the curse on my mom, oh, and the blight."

"Your *aunt?*" Rhynehart scrunched up his face and looked between L'zar and the thief's halfling daughter.

Cheyenne shrugged. "And I'm trying to kick her off the throne so I can take her place. Temporarily. Mostly to fix all the shit she's screwed up over the last few thousand years. So now you know." She stared at the table and slowly lifted her gaze to look at Rhynehart again.

The agent's aggravated flush had disappeared, taking what was left of the color in his face with it. He stared at Cheyenne, his Adam's apple bobbing up and down when he swallowed. He replied in a harsh, grating whisper, "Jesus fuck."

L'zar grinned at his daughter and folded his hands on the table in front of him. "This is so much *fun.*"

She shot him a warning glance and shook her head. "Yeah, fuck you too."

"Moving past *that,*" Maleshi said, waving a dismissive hand at Cheyenne, scowling above folded arms, and L'zar, grinning stupidly at his daughter, "how are we supposed to pull off something like this? *You* walked out of that prison on your own. Venga can't do that."

"Oh, no. He most certainly cannot. Which is where we come in."

"Yeah, obviously. That's the point of planning to break someone out of prison." Cheyenne snorted. "The only question I can even handle right now is whether or not all of us sitting around this table are equipped to do something like that without making everything worse."

"As in, can L'zar break back *into* prison?" Lumil snorted and let out a goofy chuckle.

"No, as in, do we need outside help?"

"You mean, like, call Sir and ask for his approval?" Yurik leaned back in his chair. "Just like calling us up here?"

"No." Cheyenne pointed at him and slowly shook her head. "Sir stays out of it. If he gets back to me with an answer about Colonel Thomas before we do any of this, and I can make sure he's not trying to fuck with me and go behind my back, then fine. Tell him whatever you want. But right now, we can't risk any of Sir's superiors getting wind of this, or we won't just be breaking some has-been Crown loyalist out of Chateau D'rahl, we'll be starting a war." She glanced quickly at the nightstalkers and shrugged. "Another one."

"You trust this human?" Maleshi asked, gesturing at Rhynehart. The man blinked furiously when he realized she was talking about him.

"Yeah." Cheyenne nodded at him. "Pretty much."

"Great. Thanks."

"He's the next highest in line with the FRoE? At least the ones we can get our hands on." Maleshi nodded. "He'll have to come with us to get this done."

Rhynehart looked sharply at the general and pulled his head back with another fierce scowl. "Fuck. That."

"That's cute." The nightstalker woman gave him a fierce grin. "You think you have a choice."

"Hey, just because I don't have magic and fucking *whiskers*, it doesn't mean I have to do what you tell me." Rhynehart spread his arms. "I don't *have* to be here."

"That's for sure." Lumil pushed to her feet and slammed her hands on the table. "If you feel like you need to get outta this, I'm sure I can find a river with 'Human asshole strangled, drowned, and chopped into tiny pieces was here' written all over it. Sound good?"

Rhynehart glared at the goblin woman and pointed at her. "You're pushin' it."

"Yeah, pushing your fucking face into the toilet. How long can you hold your breath?"

"You know how many times I've been threatened and cursed at by magical thugs stepping out of line? That's my *job*." He looked her up and down and waved a dismissive hand at her before folding his arms again. "And you aren't any different than the rest of them."

Lumil's chair screeched back across the floor as she leaped to her feet. "Oh, I'm a thug in your system you can't keep in line, huh? Okay. I can be a thug."

"Lumil," Corian warned.

The goblin ignored him and whirled to the wet bar behind the dining table. She grabbed a huge bottle of expensive gin in one hand and the unopened bottle of vodka in the other before stalking around the table to Rhynehart. "Let's go, little man. You wanna make this happen? I'll bash your head in and settle my nerves at the same time."

"Not here, Lumil." Cheyenne pointed at her, but the goblin kept coming. "Jesus, cut it out!" The halfling sent her black lashing tendrils at Lumil's hands, curled them around the bottles of liquor, and snatched them. The bottles shot into Cheyenne's hands, and she slammed them onto the table with a loud thump. "You're done. Sit down."

Lumil glared at Cheyenne, then looked down at her empty hands and snarled. "I'll stand right here."

"Look." Cheyenne met Rhynehart's gaze. "We can do this with or without you, but it'll be a hell of a lot less messy if it's *with* you. I gave you the CliffsNotes version of what we're trying to do on the other side of the Border, and you already know what we're facing here. If we don't get this done and stop Ba'rael sooner rather than later, that shit you saw spilling out of the portal right outside is gonna be everywhere, coming through every rez portal on this side. We both know there aren't enough fae Earthside to clean up that mess on a scale that large."

Rhynehart glowered at her but didn't say a word.

Cheyenne slid the bottles away from her on the table so she wouldn't have to stare at him through two thick pieces of glass. "You know I'm right, Rhynehart. And you know we have way more riding on this than you can possibly understand, no matter how many details I give you. We don't *need* your help, but if we have it, you won't need ours nearly as much after this."

The agent's lips parted in a grimace of frustration, then he thumped back against the chair. "If this is gonna happen, we're not just storming into Chateau D'rahl with magic blazing." His gaze slid slowly from Cheyenne to L'zar. "Something tells me that's a preferred method with you people."

"Magicals," Maleshi corrected.

"Huh?"

"With us magicals. You have your own people, but we most certainly are not *people.*"

Rhynehart blinked slowly at the general. "We need a plan. That's the only way I'll agree to help you break out that prison's most dangerous inmate."

"Most dangerous?" L'zar chuckled. "Come on now. That's hardly fair."

"Yeah, well, you aren't in that prison anymore, are you?"

"Touché."

"Great." Cheyenne slapped her hands on the table and pushed to her feet. "Now we're all on the same page. Now everyone needs to get the hell out of this house."

"I said, a *plan,*" Rhynehart grumbled.

"Sure. Let's make a plan. Not here." She shook her head. "I'm not turning my mom's house into our base of operations, okay? Not while she's lying upstairs for who knows how long. And there's no way in hell everyone's gonna hang out around here long enough for her to find out about it. Let's go."

"Well, then where else do you suggest we go?" L'zar grinned at his daughter. "I've heard wonderful things about your apartment."

"Don't even think about it."

Persh'al spread his arms. "Did everyone forget about the warehouse, or are we just going through the options that aren't really options for fun?"

"FRoE agents at the warehouse." L'zar stroked his chin and pretended to consider it. "Isn't that an unexpected turn of events."

"Quit screwing around." Cheyenne nodded at Corian. "No reason for us to stay here anymore. The portal's gone. Let's go."

"My pleasure, *Aranél.*" Corian dipped his head and stood.

Rhynehart glanced at him and Cheyenne. "What's all that about?"

"What? Nothing. I have to grab my stuff and tell Eleanor we're leaving. She's had enough surprises for a lifetime." Cheyenne turned from the table, stopped, and looked over her shoulder to point at the magicals staring at her. "Nobody touches anything. Trust me, I'll know." Then she headed quickly toward the kitchen and disappeared.

Ember floated over to Rhynehart and leaned in to mutter, "It means 'princess.'"

"What?"

"*Aranél.*"

The agent gave a wry laugh and shook his head. "Christ, could this day get any weirder?"

"Absolutely." Corian nodded at him as he stepped around the table to the open space between it and the wall of windows. "The day just started, after all."

"That was rhetorical."

"Was it?" Corian lifted both hands and muttered the spell to open a new portal right there in Bianca Summerlin's dining room.

CHAPTER SIXTY-EIGHT

Cheyenne stormed back into the dining area with her backpack slung over her shoulders and Ember's duffel bag swinging from one hand.

"What the hell is *that?*" Rhynehart stared at the shimmering oval of dark light that had opened in front of Corian.

"A portal." The nightstalker grinned. "Congratulations. You're the first human to ever go through one of these."

"Oh, fuck no. Uh-uh. I'm not stepping anywhere near that thing!"

Cheyenne stopped beside Ember and handed her friend the duffle bag. "Here."

"Thanks." Ember took it and held it against her chest. "You okay?"

"Oh, yeah. Sure. Just have to break up a fight before it starts every ten minutes. I'm great." Cheyenne joined the other magicals gathering in front of the windows and clenched her fists. *I knew it'd be weird to mix rebels with the FRoE, but this is getting ridiculous.* "Rhynehart."

"No fucking way, halfling." He pointed at the open portal and shook his head. "I said I'd help you, but whatever the hell that thing is wasn't part of the deal."

"It's *all* part of the deal. Get used to it."

Persh'al snorted and marched past the uneasy operative. "It's harmless, man. At least, this one is. Need someone to test it for you before you grow a pair?"

The blue troll ignored Rhynehart's growled protest and stepped through the portal into the warehouse.

Rhynehart stared at the shimmering light, his eyes widening when Persh'al turned around, spread his arms, and disappeared from view.

"Go ahead." Cheyenne nodded at the portal.

"You think I'm a fucking idiot?"

Lumil scoffed. "Yes." She shoved Rhynehart from behind and sent him stumbling and shouting through the portal. "Some friends you got, halfling."

"Yeah, I know." Cheyenne gestured for the other FRoE agents to step through. Bhandi, Tate, and Yurik looked at each other in hesitation. Jamal grunted and shoved past all of them before ducking beneath the top of the portal and stepping through. Payton followed quickly, then the other agents sucked it up and hurried after them.

L'zar grinned at his daughter as the rest of the magicals gathered in front of the portal to step through. "I was wondering when your knack for diplomacy would show itself, Cheyenne."

"It's my low tolerance for bullshit. Don't get too excited." She stepped into Persh'al's warehouse, with Ember close on her heels. Byrd, Lumil, L'zar, and finally both nightstalkers passed through, and the portal closed behind them with a soft pop.

"Don't ever put your hands on me again," Rhynehart shouted, pointing at Lumil.

The goblin woman snorted and stepped past him. "Then quit being a douche."

Bhandi snickered but stopped when Tate shot her a warning glance.

"So, then." L'zar rubbed his hands together. "Let's get on with this plan, shall we?"

"No. Not *shall we*." Rhynehart vigorously shook his head. "I don't have any information here. My agents don't have what they need. I have to get schematics, shift schedules, who's got what security clearance for which block in which wing of the prison. You didn't think about *that*, did you? You just pushed me through a goddamn portal and—"

"You need to stop before you hurt yourself," Persh'al interjected. "Or before one of *us* hurts you. I'm way ahead of you, man."

Rhynehart looked like he was choking as he blinked rapidly at the troll. "What?"

Persh'al stalked across the warehouse toward his computer setup at the trio of tables. "Hate to burst your bubble, human, but we've been here a lot longer than you."

"No shit. You all live to be, what? Like a million?"

L'zar chuckled.

Maleshi smiled at the human agent as she pulled a folding metal chair from against the wall and lowered herself calmly into it.

Persh'al looked up from behind his computer monitor and frowned at Rhynehart. "No. I'm talking about the FRoE. Come on. You didn't honestly think we didn't notice how conveniently the birth of your fun little organization coincided with L'zar's first *escape*, did you?"

Rhynehart spun until he found Cheyenne and scowled at her. "What's he trying to say?"

"It's coming through pretty clear to me." She shrugged. "You need to get your hearing checked?"

"How do they know so much about us?"

"We've had our eyes on the whole thing for a long, *long* time." Persh'al's fingers flew across his keyboard; he didn't even bother to sit in his swiveling desk chair before getting right to work. "Watching the Border reservations before they were called Border reservations. Before the FRoE had a chance to take over. And I've been *itching* to make a splash in Chateau D'rahl since that little gem popped up on the radar. When was that, L'zar? 1900?"

"1902, I believe." L'zar raised his eyebrows at Rhynehart. "No reason to be embarrassed. It was state-of-the-art for the times. I got my own personal tour in 1946, though I must say, the renovations were on the sloppy side."

Rhynehart stared at Cheyenne. "Are they for real?"

"Unfortunately, yes."

Persh'al looked up from his computer and nodded at Rhynehart. "You said you're part of it, human, so it's better to just—"

"Quit calling me that!" The agent clenched his fists and glared at the blue troll. "I have a name, assholes. Use it."

Persh'al looked at him. "Rhynehart's not your *first* name, is it?"

"Jesus Christ." Rhynehart pinched the bridge of his nose. "No, it's not my first name. Neither is 'human.'"

Cheyenne couldn't help it. She stepped over to him and leaned in to mutter, "You realize how long you've been calling me halfling, right?"

"That's different."

"Really?"

He looked at her and growled. "Get me out of here."

"Sure." She gestured at Persh'al's computer. "Just as soon as we have our *plan*. That was your idea, by the way. So come on."

Without waiting for a reply, she headed to Persh'al's tables and grinned when she heard Rhynehart's boots thumping across the cement floor behind her. *I get it. He's freaked out, and he's lost the upper hand. Can't say it isn't satisfying to watch him squirm.*

The other agents gazed around the warehouse. Bhandi stepped over to the piles of war machine parts. "This the kinda junk you keep around?" She kicked one of the metal hull pieces with her boot.

"*Don't.*" Persh'al pointed at her. "Don't kick the fell-damn machines. Don't touch anything in here, got it? Endaru's balls, man, it's like having a bunch of toddlers running around."

Bhandi scowled at him. "Say that again."

Yurik scratched the side of his face. "*Whose* balls?"

Ember snorted and tried to wipe the grin off her face.

"Oh, yeah." Bhandi nodded at her. "Funny fae girl has a laugh at our expense."

"Come on, guys." Ember shrugged. "You're in a whole new world here, okay?"

"Like we didn't already know that." Bhandi pointed at the metal husks shoved against the wall. "You been part of this world long enough to know what the hell this crap is?"

Ember frowned. "Those are O'gúl war machines."

"They're what now?"

"Same thing that dug its way into Peridosh and attacked everybody." Ember glanced from one FRoE agent to another. "Ring any bells?"

"Fuck." Tate looked at the pile of scrap metal. "Are you shittin' us?"

"No."

"This isn't the same one, right?" Yurik leaned toward the machine parts to study them from a full ten feet away. "Doesn't look like the same one."

"There are way more than that." Ember turned to the other side of the warehouse as Cheyenne and Rhynehart reached Persh'al and his computer. "Did nobody fill these guys in on what's happening?"

Cheyenne gave Rhynehart a deadpan stare. "I told you to explain the rest of it."

"You know what, half—Cheyenne." He cleared his throat. "I've been a little busy."

"Oh, sure. I have no idea what that's like. No problem."

"Well, shit." Lumil slapped her hands together. "If you Earthborn wanna grow up and play with the adults, somebody needs to tell you what's what."

Byrd snorted. "Yeah, like you know what that is."

"I know what your face is gonna look like in two seconds if you don't shut it." Lumil lurched toward him, and the goblin man flinched away with a snicker. "You wanna hear what's going on? I'll tell you. And don't ask questions, got it? That screws up my flow."

Tuning out Lumil's mostly accurate rendition of what they were up against on all sides, from the FRoE, the Earthside loyalists with war machines, and Ba'rael on the other side of the Border, Cheyenne studied Persh'al's center monitor and watched him work.

"Yeah, yeah. I know what you're thinking." The blue troll's fingers flew across the keyboard, and he shot Cheyenne a quick sideways glance. "You could use that fancy little coil behind your ear and pull up everything we need to know in two seconds. I get it."

She smiled. "Probably less than two."

"Don't even think about it."

"I'm not the one who brought it up, man."

Rhynehart folded his arms and swallowed thickly. "Somebody gonna tell me what the fuck any of that means?"

Persh'al shook his head and chuckled. "Cheyenne's gone halfling-tech-prodigy on us, *Rhynehart*. But *I'm* the one who pulled all this together. You don't get credit for all the hours I spent in this shithole, kid."

Cheyenne removed the activator from behind her ear, wincing at the pinch, and stuck it in her pocket. "Do your thing." *Can't focus when I can see everything way before he does.*

"That's exactly what I'm doing." O'gúl symbols flashed across his monitor as Persh'al kept typing. Then he slammed the last key with a flourish and grinned up at Rhynehart. "Voila."

The agent frowned at the monitor, then leaned forward in disbelief. "Fuck. This is everything."

"Yep."

"How did you get all this?" Rhynehart studied the information on the monitor, his eyes racing back and forth. "That's the layout of the prison."

"*I* know what it is. Come *on*, man. Just because Cheyenne doesn't get any credit for this, it doesn't mean *no one* does."

She chuckled. "Trust me, you get full credit for this. How long did it take you?"

"Meh." The blue troll shrugged. "About a month."

"Oh." Cheyenne tried to look surprised.

"Twenty years ago, kid, okay? Back when shit was a lot harder to set up. I've made a lot of improvements since then."

"I bet."

Rhynehart ran his hand over his mouth and shook his head. "Damn. You guys don't fuck around, do you?"

"Ha! There it is." Persh'al pointed at the agent and grinned at Cheyenne. "Out of everything he's seen in the last twenty-four hours, *my* system made a true believer out of the guy."

"What exactly am I a true believer *in*?" Rhynehart asked in a dull voice as his attention moved to the second monitor on the right and the list of guards and agents stationed in every cell block of Chateau D'rahl, organized by shift and day of the week.

"That we have what it takes, man." Persh'al folded his arms and watched Rhynehart's disbelief. "That you're steppin' up in the world. At least this one. You're runnin' with the big dogs now, my man."

"And the big dogs are taking on some serious shit." Rhynehart licked his lips and finally met the blue troll's gaze. "All right. If we're planning and you already have all this, any suggestions for where to start?"

Persh'al grinned. "Tons. You have no idea."

"Then let's hear it."

The troll interlaced his fingers and stretched them out, cracking all his knuckles at once. "We'll start with putting some of your guys on the inside. I'd go with the ogre and Eyepatch over there. They look like they don't put up with bullshit."

Bhandi turned toward them from the other side of the warehouse and raised an eyebrow. "And we do?"

"More than them? Yeah."

Payton turned her good eye on the blue troll and sneered. "The name's Payton, dickwad."

Persh'al raised both hands. "Okay."

"You want to give them shifts at security, or what?" Rhynehart asked.

"Fuck security. I can take care of that, no problem. What we need is someone right *here*. I can reprogram your access cards, which you won't have a problem handing over, right?"

The agent blinked. "Sure."

"Cool. That'll get you as far as this last checkpoint right here, right in front of what I call The Hatch."

"Huh. We call it the dunk tank."

Persh'al snorted. "Leave it to the FRoE to bring a carnival vibe into a max-security magical prison."

"Naw, I think you guys do a pretty good job of that yourself."

They stared at each other, and Rhynehart finally smiled.

"Whatever, man. We put the ogre and *Payton* right here, 'cause this door can only be opened from the inside. Locking mechanism's not in the system. It's manual."

"Sure." Rhynehart studied the schematics of Chateau D'rahl and picked at his lower lip. "Then what?"

As they went over the plans, Cheyenne stepped back, pulled out one of the folding metal chairs from beneath the table, and sat. *Look at everybody, playing nice.*

"I swear to the fucking deathflame, asshole," Lumil shouted, "if you don't shut the hell up and let me finish my story, I'll have one of these nightstalkers port you into *our* fucking dungeons. Capeesh?"

Corian pulled up a chair beside Maleshi and sat, shaking his head.

Laughing, Tate stepped away from the goblin and raised both hands. "You drive a hard bargain, greenskin."

"And you look like you let a fell-damn Asher draw those tattoos all over you in Sharpie. Shut the hell up."

The tattooed troll frowned. "What's an Asher?"

Byrd snickered and lifted both hands, tossing his fingers out to mime an explosion. "They scatter. A lot."

"What's that supposed to mean?"

"Maybe you'll find out if you quit wasting my time asking stupid fucking questions."

Cheyenne folded her arms in the chair. *Okay. Almost playing nice. That's close enough.*

CHAPTER SIXTY-NINE

After Rhynehart and Persh'al had finished hashing out their plan for breaking into Chateau D'rahl to break Venga out, the FRoE agent's temporary ease around the illegally crossed magicals—as far as the FRoE was concerned—faded. He grimaced at the·computer and stepped away. "All right. I need a day."

"What the hell for?" Persh'al asked with a chuckle.

"To get everything together. My agents need the right kind of gear to make this possible. I need to get you access badges. Can't believe I said that. And if I find any kinks, we have a day to work them out."

"Fair enough."

"Dude, this is insane." Bhandi snorted a laugh and thumped Tate on the shoulder. "You ever think this was in your future when you signed up for this shit?"

"Not part of the job description." The tattooed troll shrugged. "So no. Not really."

"I fucking love it!"

"So, who's getting us out of here?" Rhynehart asked.

Maleshi stood from her chair and quickly opened a portal onto the gravel drive in front of the Summerlin estate. "Your chariot awaits, assholes."

"You." Yurik pointed at her, then dropped his hand when she raised an eyebrow. "You're funny."

Maleshi followed him with glowing silver eyes and a predatory smile. "Okay."

"So, we walk through this thing again?" Bhandi pointed at the portal. "Man, somebody's gotta show us how to do this on our own. That'd make ops a hell of a lot easier."

Byrd and Lumil cracked up, practically falling over each other, then shoving apart again.

Bhandi gave them a clearly unamused grimace of a smile. "Yeah, these guys? Not so funny."

"Good fucking luck with *that!*" Lumil howled. "You hear that, Corian? The FRoE could use some fell-damn *portals!*"

"About fucking time!" Byrd staggered backward and nearly fell over, he was laughing so hard.

"Psychos." Yurik shook his head. "Every last one of you."

L'zar opened the door to his private office-turned-bedroom in the back of the warehouse. "Oh, I wouldn't go that far."

The FRoE agents spun to look at him. The mad-drow grin spreading across his face made Tate take a step back toward the portal. Jamal grunted.

"I suppose there are various levels of psychosis," L'zar said. "Wouldn't you agree?"

Bhandi scoffed and turned to Rhynehart. "This asshole's not coming with us, is he?"

"Unfortunately, yeah."

"Fuck."

"Hurry along now," L'zar crooned. "Go prepare."

Rhynehart flipped the drow thief the middle finger before stalking through the portal. His five agents followed closely behind.

"See ya on the other side, Goth drow," Bhandi called, tossing a hand in the air.

"Yep." Cheyenne stuck her hands in her pockets and nodded back.

Maleshi's portal remained open long enough for everyone to watch the FRoE agents pile into the last SUV in front of the house before Yurik drove them slowly out of view. Then the portal closed with a soft pop, and the general raised an eyebrow at Cheyenne. "Goth drow, huh?"

"I guess it has a ring to it, yeah." The halfling shrugged. "Hey, if it makes them feel more comfortable about this whole situation, why not?"

"Their comfort isn't our priority," Corian snarled.

"Yeah, but it makes all this a hell of a lot easier." Cheyenne glanced from the nightstalkers to L'zar. "So, what now?"

"Now we wait." Corian eyed L'zar as the drow thief spun slowly and headed into his box of a room. The door clicked shut behind him. "We're leaving a lot to chance by putting the next move in their hands, kid."

"Hey, it's not like I'm clueless, here." Cheyenne shrugged. "Chance doesn't play nearly as much into it with them helping us."

"You really think they will?"

She turned to look at Persh'al, who'd finally sat in his chair behind his computer and was typing furiously again, oblivious to everything around him. "I think Persh'al was right to show Rhynehart how much he knows about the prison and how long you guys have been watching it. Yeah, I think that's what convinced the guy this has to happen. Plus everything else we had to deal with this morning."

Ember snorted. "You're welcome."

"Hey, goes without saying, Em. We wouldn't be planning to break into a max-security prison for magicals without you."

"We wouldn't be planning a fell-damn thing without you, Healer." Lumil shot Ember the guns with both hands. "You're really comin' into your own these days."

"Great. Then maybe you'll take me seriously when I say drop the 'Healer' thing, huh?"

Byrd snickered. Lumil laughed too and didn't bother punching the amusement out of the other goblin. "I like your style, fae. Point taken."

Cheyenne glanced at the closed door of L'zar's room. "Looks like he's in a better mood too."

Corian dipped his head. "For now."

"You think the other shoe is gonna drop? If there even *is* another shoe?"

"Let's call it progress and leave it at that, huh?" Corian and Maleshi exchanged glances. "We could all enjoy a good distraction while it lasts."

"What distraction?" Cheyenne snorted. "There's nothing going on."

"Exactly."

"All right." She ran a hand through her hair and turned to Ember. "I'm ready to go home."

"I'll be right behind you." Ember gestured at the center of the warehouse, and five seconds later, Corian's newest portal opened there to take them back to their apartment.

"I'm assuming the human will get hold of *you* when everything's ready?"

Cheyenne raised her eyebrows. "I guess. We didn't cover that part."

Behind his computer, Persh'al snorted. "Well, don't look at me. I sure as shit didn't give him my number."

"Okay, then yeah." Rolling her eyes, Cheyenne stepped toward the portal. "I'll let you know when I hear from *the human*."

"It's much more fun to say than anyone's name," Lumil muttered. "Don't know why he has to be such a baby about it."

"See ya." Cheyenne tossed a hand in the air and stepped through the portal. Ember floated through behind her, and the oval of dark light in their living room disappeared.

"Whew." Ember ran a hand over her hair and shook her head. "How about the last twenty-four hours, huh?"

"You can say that again."

The fae chuckled. "But I won't. I know you get it."

"And I know what I smell like." Cheyenne sniffed at the front of her shirt and scowled. "Everything. I smell like everything, and I need to wash it off."

Ember turned toward the kitchen. "You know where the shower is."

Frowning at her friend over a surprised smile, Cheyenne cocked her head. "Yeah, I do. You know, maybe there *is* such a thing as me rubbing off on you too much."

"What, you can't handle the flippant attitude and the unnecessary comments?" Ember looked over her shoulder and grinned. "I'm starting to come into my own."

"Oh, jeez." Cheyenne turned toward the bathroom beneath the mini-loft.

"You want food?"

"Always, Em."

Ember pulled a frozen dinner out of the freezer and turned it over to look at the directions. "All right. I'll slave away for a full five and a half minutes in the microwave just to feed *your* drow ass."

"I'm so lucky." Shaking her head, Cheyenne closed the bathroom door behind her and turned on the shower to let the water heat up. Then she looked at herself in the mirror. *Not as beat-up as I usually am. And shit, I really liked this trenchcoat in one piece.*

She cracked the door open and shouted, "Hey, Em."

"Yeah."

"You think you can work a healing spell on my coat?"

The fae snorted, followed by the beep of microwave buttons and a low hum as it turned on. "Ask me again after I stuff my face."

"Yep." Cheyenne shut the door and stripped before hopping into her first shower in five days with hot running water.

CHAPTER SEVENTY

The next afternoon, Cheyenne entered the apartment and found Ember sitting on the couch, staring blankly at the wall beside the door. "Hey. You know the TV's still in its little cubby, right?"

"Yeah, yeah. Make fun of the fae girl who likes to veg out and binge-watch. I get it." Ember looked up at the halfling and grinned. "And I found something way more exciting than Netflix."

"Uh-huh." Cheyenne closed the door behind her, locked the dead-bolt without looking, and raised an eyebrow. "What's that?"

"Observe." Ember twirled her hand with a flourish and gestured to her legs, which were spread out fully on the couch as she sat back against the armrest. Her right foot twitched, then her calf lifted off the cushion by half an inch before dropping back again. Ember said, "Progress, bitch."

Cheyenne barked a laugh. "You talkin' to me or your leg?"

"What? Oh." Ember wrinkled her nose and grinned. "My leg. Obviously. At least when it's just you and me."

"Very funny." The halfling shrugged out of her backpack and dropped it on the floor beside the closest black leather armchair before she sank down into it. "That's awesome, Em. Moving your legs again."

"Yeah, a little. But it's a hell of a lot better than nothing." Ember rubbed her thighs, then sat back against the armrest. "I don't know how

484

the hell they did it, but the *olforim* really packed a punch when they helped me get my magic back."

"I don't think that was them. I mean, yeah. You said they drugged you."

"They *did* drug me. With weird fruit. Probably something in the water, too."

"Okay, but they did that to help you *see*, right? Isn't that what's supposed to happen with psychedelics or whatever?"

"You mean, you don't know?"

Cheyenne snorted. "The closest I ever came was when Corian mixed up some nasty-ass potion and made me drink it so I would forever have L'zar Verdys popping into my head at the worst possible time. And he failed to warn me about that last part."

"Well, whatever. If it was the *olforim* or just me, I don't know. But I'll tell you right now, I have *way* stronger magic than I did before I healed Cazerel. It's working on my legs, too."

"Obviously."

Ember grinned and made her left foot twitch before giving herself a break. "So, how was class?"

Cheyenne rolled her eyes. "Easy. Boring. I gave everyone an A for that Matthew Thomas assignment, even the kids who I think copied and pasted a Wikipedia page into their email."

"When did you have the time to go through their emails?"

"I didn't. I'm guessing, based on how much they annoy me when we're in the same room." The halfling grinned, and Ember burst out laughing.

"You're one hell of a college instructor."

"Thank you very much." Cranking the lever on the side of the recliner, Cheyenne leaned all the way back, her legs stretched out on the footrest, and sighed. "That Tori girl, though…"

"Who's that?"

"The one who sent me that picture of Colonel Thomas."

"Oh, right. The chick I have to thank for causing your crazy freakout and giving me the perfect opportunity to slap you in the face. Again."

"You can hold off on thanking her with that level of specificity, Em." They both laughed. "She might have some skills we could use later. You know, in a hypothetical world where I didn't have my activator and needed someone else's help and their skills."

"You mean, like how you asked all your students to dig into our neighbor's family ties for you?"

"Yeah. Like that." Cheyenne stared at the ceiling. "And now we're just waiting."

"Nothing from Rhynehart yet?"

"Nope. I don't know why it takes him this long to pull together some gear and access badges. I mean, the guy spent the last few months randomly calling me and expecting me to jump into a raid or whatever at the drop of a hat, and now he needs twenty-four hours to—"

Her phone buzzed in her pocket, and she pulled it out to read the text. "Well, speak of the human."

Ember laughed. "You really love calling him that, don't you?"

"You know what? It's not so bad. I endured months of being called 'rookie' and 'halfling.' Sometimes 'psycho drow.' It's only fair that we spread the name-calling around, right?"

"Oh, yeah. Makes everything fair and square, just like that." Ember folded her arms and nodded at her friend's cell phone. "Lemme guess. He's finally ready."

"Yep." Cheyenne sent a text to Corian to let him know and stuck her phone back in her pocket. "So now we just—"

The dark circle of light from Corian's portal appeared between her and the front door. Corian's tawny-furred face poked halfway through it. "Let's get a move on."

"Wow." Ember blinked her luminous eyes. "Everyone's got *perfect* timing today."

"That does only seem to happen when we're dealing with non-emergencies, huh?"

"I don't know, halfling." Ember rose in her sitting position from the couch in a flash of violet light, then her legs swung down together to hover over the floor. "I had pretty good emergency timing yesterday."

Cheyenne pointed at her *Nós Aní.* "True."

Corian's silver eyes widened. "This isn't a drill, by the way."

"Yep." The girls headed for the portal, which closed behind them as soon as they stepped through into Persh'al's warehouse.

"Hey, good to see everybody here." Cheyenne grinned at L'zar's rebels, who gathered around the new arrivals.

Lumil frowned and leaned away from her. "You feelin' okay?"

Cheyenne's grin disappeared, and she cocked her head with a deadpan stare aimed at the goblin. "Does this make you feel more comfortable?"

"*There* you go." Lumil wagged a finger at her. "That looks and sounds like the Cheyenne I know."

"You know, with the exception of Ember, there isn't a magical in this warehouse who can say they know Cheyenne."

Ember snorted and shot her friend a sidelong glance. "Talking in the third person now?"

Cheyenne shrugged. "Better or worse than plural personal pronouns?"

"I'll have to think about it."

Corian shook his head and stared at the halfling and her fae *Nós Aní*. "If I didn't know better, I'd say you two are trying to hide something under all this lightheartedness."

Spreading her arms, Cheyenne raised her eyebrows at the nightstalker. "Hey, just because I'm Goth doesn't mean I can't have a good day."

"With a serious attitude problem." Ember pointed at her and nodded. "Don't forget that part. Goth with a serious attitude problem."

"You're absolutely right."

Byrd frowned, his eyes widening in uncertainty. "Okay, now you're starting to freak *me* out."

Lumil elbowed him in the ribs. "I think this whole 'put the FRoE bastards in their place' thing went right to her crownless head."

"The *Crown* doesn't even wear a crown. What are you talking about?"

"It's a fucking figure of speech, man."

"Not when we're talking about literal crowns."

"Okay, stop." Cheyenne raised both hands and looked from one freaked-out goblin to the other. "You guys need to chill out. We're not fighting loyalists or infiltrating Hangivol or trying to hold back the blight. It's a simple magical-prison break-in. In comparison, this is a pretty good day."

"Simple, huh?" L'zar emerged from his room at the back of the warehouse and cocked his head. "You're starting to sound more like me every day."

"See, that's exactly the kinda thing that ruins a halfling's good mood."

The drow thief ignored his daughter's quip and joined the rest of them in the center of the warehouse. He nodded at Corian. "And the *agents?*"

"We're meeting them halfway between here and Chateau D'rahl."

L'zar settled his golden-eyed gaze on Cheyenne, and she shrugged. "Yeah. I passed along the information."

His brows flicked together in confusion. "I'm wondering why we agreed to go to them instead of the other way around."

Corian shook his head. "I can port them in and out of the warehouse all day, L'zar, but they don't get driving directions, and I'm not about to open a portal for all of us right in front of the prison gates. One magical surprise caught on camera twenty-one years ago was enough."

L'zar pursed his lips. "Hmm."

"Well then, let's go meet the super-agents, huh?" Snickering, Persh'al walked around his computer table, slinging a huge, heavy-looking square bag over his shoulder as he headed for the front door of the warehouse. He patted the hard-case bag thumping against his thigh. "Got this baby up and running, but I can't do shit until I get those access badges and a few other pieces. No one cares about the details. Got it."

Bright sunlight and crisp fall air streamed into the warehouse when the blue troll pushed open the door. The group of rebel magicals followed him out to his black SUV in the cracked, uneven parking lot overgrown with weeds.

Ember snorted. "Anyone else notice the Rebelmobile looks a lot like the FRoE wagon?"

"Ha. Good one." Lumil slapped the fae girl on the shoulder and brushed past her toward the SUV.

Blinking in surprise, Ember flicked her hand at the goblin. A burst of purple light bloomed on Lumil's back and shoved her into the side of the vehicle with a hollow thump.

"Hey! Who the hell thinks it's a good idea to start with the—" Lumil spun and found no one behind her. Byrd burst out laughing and pointed at Ember. "You too, fae?"

"If you're gonna hit people like it's no big deal, *goblin*, don't get pissed when someone hits you back. It's no big deal."

"Uh-huh. You're gettin' too big for your little magical britches, my friend."

Ember grinned. "There's a lot more where that came from."

Cheyenne leaned in and murmured, "I *knew* there was a reason you and I are friends."

"Oh, you're just now figuring that out?" Ember snorted. "Excellent."

The other magicals piled into the car, Persh'al behind the wheel, L'zar up front in the passenger seat. Corian pulled Byrd back by the collar when the goblin man moved to climb into the very back row of seats with Lumil. "Uh-uh. I'm not driving anywhere in a car where the two of you are sitting next to each other."

"You know you could say please instead of jerking me all over the place by my shirt, right?" Byrd ripped his collar out of Corian's grasp and tugged down the sides of his jean jacket. "Jeeze."

Corian shoved his face up into Byrd's. "Please and thank you." Then he climbed into the back seat after Lumil and stared straight ahead while Maleshi climbed in beside him.

Cheyenne, Ember, and Byrd sat in the middle row, and they made sure to keep the goblins on opposite sides of the car.

CHAPTER SEVENTY-ONE

The drive to the location Rhynehart had texted to Cheyenne only took them twenty minutes. Persh'al rolled the SUV to a stop and parked it beside a nearly identical black vehicle behind a maintenance building five minutes from the prison grounds. "Pros and cons of living in DC, right? Chateau D'rahl's just a jump away, but everyone's driving around in the same car."

Cheyenne laughed as she stepped out of the vehicle and pulled the back of the middle seat forward to let the others out. "Hey, at least we won't have any problem passing us all off as FRoE agents, huh?"

He snorted. "Says the halfling who doesn't have to play dress-up. And half of us aren't even going in, so don't blow it out of proportion."

"Still, it's convenient camouflage." Cheyenne folded her arms and watched Rhynehart and his agents hopping out of their SUV. "At least it's not an orange Kia Rio."

Rhynehart smiled as he caught the conversation. "Honestly, I'm surprised I haven't seen that car anywhere else around town."

She laughed. "That's probably because Sir drives a beige Camry."

He stared at her. "Where does he keep it?"

"Not at home. I can tell you that much."

"As fun as it is to watch you two talk about something with zero significance to our current objective…" L'zar gave them a fake smile and gestured at Rhynehart's SUV.

The team leader cleared his throat. "Right. On task. Bhandi."

"Quit naggin' me, man. I got it."

The troll woman grunted at the open back of the FRoE SUV and stalked over to the others with a pile of gear in her arms.

Cheyenne almost laughed out loud at Rhynehart's startled expression. "You let her talk to you like that all the time?"

"As far as I know, that's the only way she talks to anyone."

"Yeah, that's the impression I got too."

"Here." Bhandi chucked a dampening vest at Corian's face and slung one at L'zar, then eyed the others and shrugged. "Guess this one's for me. And you two are gonna have to wear a mask. You cool with that?"

As the troll woman tugged the vest on, Corian and L'zar studied theirs with barely concealed amusement. Lumil and Byrd cracked up.

"Are you kidding me?" Lumil thumped the side of Persh'al's SUV with a fist.

"*Hey.*"

She ignored the blue troll and pointed at Corian and L'zar. "You think those dinky little vests are gonna do anything those two can't do with their hands tied behind their backs?"

"Oh, shit." Byrd fought to catch his breath. "Man, I can't *wait* to see you boppin' around in one of those, L'zar."

The drow thief extended his dampening vest pinched between his fingers and looked it over. "Indeed."

"Those two," Rhynehart said, strapping on his own vest, "have to pass as FRoE agents. All of whom, by the way, wear these vests."

"And by mask, I'm assuming you mean a human illusion," Corian added, inspecting his own vest.

"Yeah." Rhynehart glanced at Bhandi, who shrugged. "That's what our magical agents tend to call it, and we don't assign magical agents to patrol Chateau D'rahl."

"Ha!" Lumil smacked her hands together. "You guys have to pretend to be puny *human* FRoE agents who think they stand a chance against —" She burst out laughing. "Against real magic!"

Rhynehart scowled at the goblin. "You know what? This gear's held up fine for the last twenty-one years."

Byrd chuckled, shooting Lumil a fleeting glance and stepping sideways as she flailed around in hysterics. "Yeah, against criminals and random O'gúleesh breaking all your rules. Not against soldiers from the other side."

When Rhynehart glanced at Corian, the nightstalker rolled his eyes. "Fine. We'll play the game." He pulled the vest on over his loose shirt and pants, and the goblins lost it all over again.

"A game. Yes." L'zar stared at Rhynehart and snapped his fingers. The dampening vest disappeared from his outstretched hand and reappeared around his body a split-second later. "Something I very much enjoy."

"As long as you're not playing your psychotic games with me, drow, I really don't give a shit." Rhynehart stared at L'zar and Corian. "We're not going any closer to that prison until you get rid of all the fur and gray skin."

Corian moved his fingers in a series of quick gestures. Silver light flashed around his hand, then his human illusion appeared, complete with black fatigues beneath the dampening vest. "I hope this will do."

Rhynehart looked him up and down and turned to L'zar. "Come on."

The drow thief widened his eyes at Rhynehart over a coy smile. "You really are a fan of details, aren't you?"

"I'm a fan of not being made by the people I'm supposed to be working with to keep assholes like *you* behind bars. If I have to turn against my own guys to get this shit done, you can look like a damn human for an hour,"

"Oh, it won't take us nearly that long." L'zar's fingers moved in a blur as he cast his illusion spell. His pointed ears disappeared, long white hair shrank into close-cropped brown curls, and he lost at least four inches in height.

Cheyenne swallowed. *Jesus. Just a few months ago, I was staring at that face on Mom's computer screen.* "You really think it's a good idea to walk around looking like the guy who turned himself in twenty-one years ago before he turned into *you*?"

L'zar playfully rolled his eyes. "No one's going to remember this face, Cheyenne."

"I did."

"Hmm." His fingers twitched again, and the bridge of his nose ballooned out into a sharp, angular hook as his hair went from brown to sandy blond. "There. I'm a new man."

Lumil shook her head. "Gotta say, L'zar. Not a good look for you."

"This isn't a damn beauty contest," Rhynehart grumbled. "Get in the car."

L'zar clasped his hands behind the thick dampening vest covering his back and strolled to the open back seat. Corian turned to Cheyenne and nodded. "Let's go."

"I can put on a mask too," Ember said, floating to the FRoE's SUV and getting ready to cast the spell. "I wanna see the inside of this place."

Corian shook his head. "Not a good idea."

"What? Why not?"

"Ember, if you have a reasonable explanation to give the guards in that prison as to why your feet don't touch the ground when you move, then by all means, come with us."

She glanced down at the inch of open space between the soles of her feet and the asphalt. "Shit. Okay, fine. I'll stay in this car."

Persh'al frowned at her. "You say that like we're a bunch of losers."

"Not what I meant. Sorry."

"It's fine." He opened the driver's side door of his SUV and climbed behind the wheel. "It's not like I'm sensitive about the tech geek always being shoved aside as the least cool one or anything."

Before Ember could say anything else, the troll closed the door and started the engine again.

"He's fine," Cheyenne reassured her friend. "And you'll have fun watching him work all that tech he rigged up to the back seat."

"I can't wait." With a snort, Ember opened the back door and climbed in beside the goblins. "See ya on the other side, Goth drow."

"Hey!" Bhandi slammed the trunk of Rhynehart's vehicle and pointed at the fae girl. "That's *my* line."

"Yeah, it's a good one." Ember grinned and pulled the door closed behind her, wiggling her fingers at the troll through the window.

Bhandi waved her off. "She's crazy, Cheyenne. You know that?"

"Why do you think we're friends?"

"Yeah, I like her too." They got into Rhynehart's car with Tate, Yurik,

L'zar, and Corian as Rhynehart started the engine. "She kick ass in a fight the way she kicked ass with that black shit at the portal?"

Cheyenne strapped herself in. "Yeah. She does okay." *If I told them about Ember blasting Ba'rael back through the portal at the binding ceremony, these guys wouldn't have a clue what that means.*

CHAPTER SEVENTY-TWO

Cheyenne watched Persh'al park outside the exterior gates opening into the parking lot in front of Chateau D'rahl. "We're all sure that's the best place for them to hang out and wait for us?"

"Persh'al's sure," Corian said. "That's all I need to know."

"Fair enough."

Yurik turned around in the front passenger seat as Rhynehart drove them into the parking lot. The brown eyes of his human mask settled on Cheyenne. "Has that troll really been watching this place?"

"Since it was first built," L'zar answered with a slow nod.

Cheyenne shot her father a quick frown. "What he said."

"And no one picked up on it. Huh." With a snort, the muscular goblin turned around again and thumped back against the seat. "Man, somebody needs to get this place some better security."

Rhynehart ran his tongue over his teeth in irritation. "So I've noticed." He parked the car, turned off the engine, and practically threw off his seatbelt. "Let's get this over with before I remember what a fucking terrible idea it is."

L'zar shot Cheyenne a playful grimace as Rhynehart slapped the driver's side door shut behind him. "*Someone's* a little touchy."

"I mean, with your track record, he kinda has a reason to be."

"I don't plan on jeopardizing this little jail-break, Cheyenne." He raised an eyebrow and opened the door. "I hope your friend can say the same."

She rolled her eyes and followed him out of the car. With Corian, Bhandi, Tate, and Yurik following closely, they headed after Rhynehart toward the front gates of Chateau D'rahl.

Bhandi leaned over to Cheyenne and muttered from the side of her mouth, "You've been here before, right?"

"Yep. Not that big a deal."

"For real?" The troll, whose human-illusion mask gave her bright blue eyes and dark auburn hair, clicked her tongue. "That sucks. We threaten to lock assholes up here all the time. Sometimes we even ship 'em here directly."

Yurik nodded and gazed at the top of the security towers on either side of the front doors. "Yeah, doesn't pack the same punch when you know the place you're threatening to send 'em isn't that big a deal."

"Sorry to burst your bubbles." Cheyenne snorted. "Would you rather have me tell you it's the most dangerous place I've ever been, and I hope we don't die on the extremely high chance that we get caught and we can't fight our way out of it?"

The agents glanced at each other, and each cracked a small smile.

"I mean, it kinda helps with morale, right?" Yurik wiggled his eyebrows.

Shaking her head, Cheyenne tried to hide a crooked smile as she stared at the front doors. "You guys are nuts."

"Come on, Goth drow." Bhandi elbowed her in the ribs. "You already knew that."

Rhynehart glanced at them over his shoulder and raised his eyebrows. "Do I need to find you a private room so you can hear each other better? No? Then shut up and pay attention."

Cheyenne frowned at the back of the agent's head. That better be his version of hardass superior bringing in new prison recruits. Could be real, though.

Bhandi stifled a laugh and rolled her eyes. "Here we go."

"Hey, Stevens." Rhynehart nodded at the guard in uniform, standing inside the security tower. Stevens nodded back and offered the gesture to the group of magicals in disguise. When he looked at Cheyenne, though, he frowned.

Cheyenne raised her fist and pumped devil horns his way before heading after Rhynehart, Corian, and L'zar. Gotta act like the angry Goth halfling who got in way over her head and has to pander to Sir and his fuckups. Easy enough.

When they entered the prison's front lobby, Rhynehart nodded at the guard standing at the counter on the left behind the pane of reinforced glass. "Crowley."

"Rhynehart." Crowley leaned forward as far as he could without pressing his face against the glass and took stock of Cheyenne and the five new agents on prison duty. "Something going on that I don't know about?"

Rhynehart forced a chuckle and headed for the metal detectors at the other end of the lobby. "Probably."

"Hey, I'm serious. What's goin' on?"

"Me doing my job," Rhynehart muttered. "What does it look like?"

"It looks like you walking in with a bigger team than usual. Mostly it's just you. And her." Crowley nodded at Cheyenne without any friendliness. "And I'm just doing *my* job."

"Big batch of new recruits, Crowley." Rhynehart turned around and spread his arms as he walked backward to the metal detectors. "I'd rather toss 'em in and indoctrinate them all at once instead of one at time. 'Cause, you know, my job has a bit more wiggle room than whatever you've got behind that counter."

Cheyenne shoved her hands into her coat pockets and raised an eyebrow at Crowley before following Rhynehart to the security checkpoint beyond the lobby. *Careful, Rhynehart. Not like anyone would suspect something if you're too much of an asshole. Don't snare us in stuff we didn't plan.*

Their party stopped in front of the metal detectors, and Rhynehart nodded at the guards behind the tables and scanning belt. "Hell of a day, huh?"

"It's hell every day." The guard shrugged at Rhynehart and gestured for the agent to step through the metal detector. Then the radio strapped to his shoulder buzzed with static.

"Hold on a minute, Mack. Don't let 'em through just yet."

Rhynehart stared at the radio.

Mack shrugged. "Guess you don't need me to relay that message."

"Jesus, what now?" Rolling his eyes, Rhynehart spun and headed to the door in the wall beside the glass-protected window just as Crowley stepped out into the lobby for a private chat.

The rest of the disguised magicals stayed where they were in front of the metal detectors. L'zar clasped his hands behind his back and rocked back and forth from his heels to his toes. Mack frowned at him. "You look right at home for a rookie on his first day."

The human-passing drow thief raised his blond eyebrows at the guard and smiled. "I'm happy to be here. "

Cheyenne forced herself not to roll her eyes and focused instead on Rhynehart's conversation with the guard no longer behind the window.

"We don't have anything in the system for new recruits today, man," Crowley said. "What's going on?"

"Exactly what I said." Rhynehart spread his arms. "New recruits. And L'zar's halfling kid. You remember her, right?"

When Crowley glanced over Rhynehart's shoulder at the halfling, Cheyenne wiggled her eyebrows at him. "Tell me you're not bringing her on to station her somewhere, man."

"No way. Are you kidding? She's here to help us look into where L'zar might be. You know, unique perspective and all that."

"I don't think hating L'zar's guts is a unique perspective, man," Cheyenne called from the other side of the lobby for everyone to hear her. "Trust me, I wanna see that asshole behind bars again as much as you do."

Rhynehart blinked at her, turned back to Crowley, and gestured at the halfling. "There you have it."

Corian lifted a fist to his mouth and forced out a cough.

Crowley shrugged. "Yeah, I know *she* comes in here without warning, but I don't get why you have five new recruits rollin' in here with you, and not a single thing pulls up in the system."

"Jesus Christ, man." Rhynehart pinched the bridge of his nose. "Look, I don't know what the hell's wrong with the system. Not my problem, and it sure as shit isn't my job to have to explain it to you."

"But it's not—"

"You know what? Fine. If you think this is seriously such a big deal, go ahead and call Sir. You can tell him all about how worried you are. That'll be a fun talk."

Crowley swallowed, cleared his throat, and glanced at Cheyenne and the disguised magicals again. "No, I don't need to call him."

"Good. Wanna get back to your post, or should I stick one of the new guys in there instead?"

Crowley shook his head and turned to the door leading back to his desk. "Guess it'd be too much to ask you to sign 'em in."

Rhynehart snorted and folded his arms. "Yeah, genius." He stalked to his waiting party and the guards at the metal detector. "Damn know-it-all, wasting my time. You know, I'm used to being in a shitty mood when I *leave* this place, not when I get here."

"Tell me about it." Mack slid a container across the table to Rhynehart, who emptied his keys, wallet, and phone from his pocket.

Rhynehart walked through the metal detector toward the guard on the other side and shrugged. "Fucking Wednesdays."

The guard standing there with his arms folded raised his eyebrows. "Nothing happy about Hump Day, I'll tell you that much."

The agent snorted and turned to stand beside the guard as his fake rookies dumped their pockets into the security bins and stepped through the metal detector. L'zar and Corian passed through no problem. Bhandi had to go back once and fish deep in her pocket for a dime she'd missed the first time. Yurik practically skipped through, grinning and nodding at the guards as he retrieved his things.

Tate pointed at the stack of plastic bins on the far side of the table. "I'm probably gonna need two or three of those."

Mack looked him up and down. "Just empty your pockets, and we'll go from there."

"I mean, not just my pockets, but that's cool." Just like Rhynehart, Yurik, and Bhandi, Tate removed his fell pistol from its holster and stuck that in the container. Then he lifted his black BDU shirt, untucking it from the waistband of his pants, and grinned at the guard. "This one's on here fairly good. Gotta keep the toys close, right?"

Mack's eyes widened when Tate removed an entire ammo belt from around his waist over his black undershirt. The thing was studded with small, round black disks that clinked together in the tray on top of his firearm.

Cheyenne folded her arms and stifled a laugh. *He brought a whole belt of fell grenades into the goddamn prison. I might have a new favorite troll.*

Tate started to walk through the metal detector, then chuckled and backed up. "Oh, yeah. Almost forgot."

He leaned down to remove a small knife from the inside of each of his black boots. Only one of them fit in the plastic container, and Mack had to pull another out of the stack for the second knife. Another fell grenade came from Tate's left boot, then he shoved his hands in his pockets and deposited a fistful of loose change, an extra magazine, a keyring, and a Bluetooth headset. Snickering, he removed the silver watch from his wrist, dropped it into the second bin, and raised both hands before stepping through the metal detector. Fortunately, it didn't go off.

Rhynehart raised his eyebrow. "You carry that on you all the time?"

"Hey. Couple years out in the field, and now I'm movin' on up to prison guard. Old habits, I guess."

"Yeah, well, leave that shit at home next time you come in, huh?" Rhynehart shook his head, looked Tate up and down, then shrugged at Cheyenne. "You comin' or what, halfling?"

She smiled at Tate, who was retrieving all his items on the other side of the metal detector. "Yeah."

When she stepped through, like she knew it would, the metal detector set off a harsh, beeping alarm and flashed a red light. Cheyenne turned to look at Mack. "Okay, I swear I'm not carrying a belt full of bombs like this guy."

"Yeah, I know." Mack stacked the bins and slid them aside. "We don't have to go through all that again. I know who you are. Good luck tracking down that shithole of a drow."

"Thanks." She pointed at him. "I like that description."

"Yeah, well, feel free to use it." Rolling his eyes, Mack gestured at the other side of the lobby, and Rhynehart turned around with a grunt and led the way.

"All right, rookies, listen up. And no, there won't be a Q&A afterward, so pay attention. I'm assuming most of you have seen magicals before and have probably popped a few scumbags in their otherworld faces, so if anybody shits their pants after what you're about to see, that's on you."

Bhandi snorted. "Literally."

Rhynehart glared at her, shook his head, and pulled his access badge out of his pocket to press it to the lock panel by the door. The mechanism buzzed, he slammed the handle down, and then he disappeared down the first corridor into the west wing of Chateau D'rahl.

L'zar slowed down as they moved through the hallway and fell in line beside his daughter. "You hate L'zar Verdys' guts, huh?"

She shrugged. "Hey, just trying to keep it realistic."

"I'm well aware of the intention behind it, Cheyenne. And impressed by your ability to lie so convincingly."

Cheyenne looked up at her father's borrowed blue eyes and gave him the sweetest, most innocent smile she could muster. "Who said I was lying?"

"No one."

CHAPTER SEVENTY-THREE

L'zar chuckled when they passed the doors into an inmate block. He paused beside a window with reinforced bulletproof glass on either side of fell-powered dampening mesh. "Cell Block Alpha. Hard to believe I was just here."

"And now you're here again," Rhynehart called from up ahead. "Move on. This isn't Memory Lane."

Still peering through the window, L'zar looked up at the guard station in Alpha tower above the glowing red light that stayed on twenty-four-hours in this particular cell block. The guard jerked his chin at L'zar's human-looking form and lifted a plastic mug in greeting. The drow thief raised his hand in a curt wave, then headed after the rest of their group. "This is fantastic."

"Enjoying yourself?" Corian muttered as L'zar turned away from the window to follow the others.

"I'm allowed a bit of fun every once in a while, *vae shra'ni.*"

The nightstalker snorted. "You find fun everywhere, Weaver."

"That doesn't make it any less entertaining."

Cheyenne watched them walking side by side, just two more FRoE agents in black fatigues and dampening gear. No one in Chateau D'rahl had any clue. *At least L'zar's dialed back on the crazy. Maybe Corian was right and the crazy comes straight from Ambar'ogúl. Not like we'll get the chance to test that again.*

Rhynehart's access card slapped against the next panel beside the door at the end of the hall. Another buzz, another flash of green light and turn of the handle, and they moved on.

"Maybe I'll come back for a visit next time," L'zar mused, casting Cell Block Alpha one final glance over his shoulder.

Corian snorted. "Just don't expect me to come busting in here to save your ass."

"I would never, *vae shra'ni.*"

Bhandi held the door open for the magical behind her. "So, what's the deal with you two?"

"Deal?" Corian raised his eyebrows and shot her a coy smile. "I'm not quite sure what you're implying."

"This guy's obviously been here before." She stuck her thumb out at L'zar. "What about you?"

Corian chuckled softly. "No. This is a first for me."

Tate laughed. "Guess you can rule out that cellmate theory, then."

"Can it, asshole."

"What theory is that?" L'zar asked.

"Nothing. Never mind." Bhandi sneered at Tate and punched him in the shoulder as they waited for Rhynehart to unlock the next door.

Corian turned and cocked his head at Cheyenne. "Do *you* know what she's talking about?"

"I stopped trying to figure out what's in her head after knowing her for an hour." The halfling shrugged. "Waste of time."

Yurik laughed and folded his arms. "Always knew you were a smart one, Cheyenne."

"Uh-huh."

Rhynehart shoved violently down on the door handle and jerked the door open. "You guys need to cut out all the side talk and pay attention, huh? If a single thing goes wrong in here—"

"Then we'll move from Plan A to no plan at all, and we'll be fine." Corian grabbed the door and held it open. "Please continue."

Gritting his teeth, Rhynehart stormed down the next hall.

———

Fifteen minutes later, the hallway ended in corridors branching to the left and right, but the magicals disguised as human FRoE agents headed for the door at the very end. The back wall was made entirely of double-paned glass with the same fell-powered dampening mesh between them. Through the large squares between the mesh, Cheyenne saw two FRoE agents standing behind the security booth in the room beyond.

"That's them, right?" Bhandi asked.

"Definitely Payton." Yurik stuck his hands in his pockets and nodded. "I've seen that mask before."

"I hope you're right. Seriously hope that's Jamal, too. He looks a lot bigger without all the hair."

"I think everyone looks bigger without hair."

L'zar rapped on the glass with his knuckles. The woman, who didn't wear an eyepatch in her human illusion, looked up from the monitor she'd been staring at, and scowled at him. He wiggled his fingers in greeting, then Rhynehart stepped up beside him with a grunt and pointed at the handle.

"This is why you guys are in there," he muttered. "Let's get this circus show on the road."

The female agent muttered something they couldn't hear and nodded at the door. The man with a thick brown ponytail stepped around the security booth, eyeing the line of seven presumably unexpected visitors to the security checkpoint right outside what Persh'al had dubbed the Hatch. He stopped on the other side of the glass door, punched in a number on the keypad, and pulled open the door to let them in.

"It's about fucking time you idiots showed up," the female agent muttered.

"Oh, yeah." Yurik snorted. "Definitely Payton."

"Good to see you too." Bhandi thumped her fists on the edge of the security booth's circular counter.

Jamal stood silently while everyone filtered into the final checkpoint and shut the door firmly again before punching in another code. The lock slid back into place with a metallic clink.

"How's it lookin' out there?" Rhynehart asked, stopping on Payton's left to peer over her shoulder at the security monitor.

The masked goblin agent turned her head and her shoulders to face him and scowled.

"Right. Sorry. I'll stand where you can see me." He stepped to her other side and shot her a sidelong glance. "Pretty damn hard to remember when you don't have that thing over your eye."

"Not hard at all to remember you're an asshole."

Rhynehart blinked quickly and shook his head. "Remind me again why we recruited you?"

Yurik stepped toward them, counting on his fingers. "Let's see. Earthside-born. Can see like a hawk with only one eye. Gets blown up and doesn't die. Oh, yeah. You had us on clean-up duty for way longer than we should've been, and she never complained."

"Yeah, but you did."

"Hey, I didn't sign up for this to play magical maid outside DC. Though that *was* how I met Cheyenne." The disguised goblin wiggled his eyebrows and extended a fist toward the halfling.

She eyed his fist. "You make it sound like we both showed up for maid duty."

"Come on. Don't leave me hanging."

Cheyenne rolled her eyes and bumped her fist against his.

"Ow. Shit." Yurik chuckled and shook out his hand. "You can dial that back any time."

"Sorry." She shrugged. "Guess I'm waiting for the minute something goes wrong and I have to use my fist for more than props from you."

"Aw, come on, Goth drow." Bhandi turned away from the two monitors mounted on the far wall and angled toward the security booth. "Have faith in us, huh?"

"It has nothing to do with you guys." Cheyenne shot L'zar a quick glance, but he was standing in front of the clear door they'd just entered, staring out into the hall. "Hey, if we start out with low expectations, we don't get nearly as disappointed."

"Yeah. And we end up punching our buddy's hands off. Christ." Yurik shook his hand out again and turned to the door on the opposite side of the checkpoint room. "This is the last one, right?"

"Yep." Rhynehart frowned and leaned closer to the monitors in front of him and Payton. "Just making sure that blue troll did what he said he could."

"He did." Cheyenne watched them studying the monitors. "Might've taken him a whole day, but if he said he hacked into the security system, he did."

"We're waiting for proof, Cheyenne." Rhynehart's eyes narrowed at the monitor showing the security footage for the hallway outside and the checkpoint where they all waited. The image of all nine of them standing inside the glass-encased booth shuddered, blinked off, and came back on with a recorded replay straight from Persh'al. Now it only showed Jamal and Payton.

"Damn." Rhynehart's said, "He got the timestamp to match up perfectly."

Payton studied Rhynehart, then looked back at the screen. "No, he didn't."

"I'm lookin' at it right here—"

The goblin raised both hands in the air like she was stretching and didn't look at the team leader again.

"No shit." Rhynehart looked between her and the monitor. "He erased the rest of us?"

Cheyenne couldn't help a wide smile. "Very nice."

"How the hell did he even do that?"

"O'gúl tech, man." Cheyenne shrugged. "Or at least a troll who knows enough about O'gúl tech to make the most of what we have to work with on this side of the Border."

"Yeah, sure." Rhynehart shook his head and leaned away from the monitor. "You make it sound like Earth's advanced technology is a joke." He looked sharply at Cheyenne. "Whatever. We're in, and he took us off the security feed. Time to go through that door."

Rhynehart pulled his access badge out of his pocket again and waited by the first door they'd come to so far that didn't have a window. It was all metal, thick, heavy, and dented toward them from the other side. "Hope that troll hacker friend of yours is as good with rewriting clearance as he is with erasing entire bodies from recorded footage."

Corian stepped up behind them to get a better view of their next move. "Persh'al wouldn't have told us he could do it if he couldn't. And we have no reason to lie to you about any of this."

"Well, hey. Forgive me if I don't take your word for it."

"Of course." L'zar spun away from the windows on the opposite side of the room and headed over to them. "I suppose you're waiting for us to prove ourselves one more time, hmm?"

Rhynehart ignored him and nodded at Cheyenne. "You're up."

"Yep." She pulled out the two extra access badges Persh'al had reprogrammed for this door specifically. *He said right one first, left one second.* She swiped the first badge across the security panel. The red light blinked yellow for two seconds, then flashed green once, so she swiped the second badge, and the process repeated. "You know, I'm really curious now."

"About what?" Rhynehart swiped his badge next, the last one they needed, and waited.

"How come we didn't need three different badges with high-level clearance to get to L'zar in the Dungeon?"

The agent raised an eyebrow as he stared at the blinking yellow light on the panel. "L'zar gave everyone a major headache."

Behind them, L'zar snorted. "I do love being spoken about as if I'm not here."

Join the club. Cheyenne watched Rhynehart intently.

"But he never put up much of a fight. So I guess no one expected him to."

"And Venga did, huh?"

Rhynehart pointed at the dent in the metal where it had been shoved toward them from the other side. "Case in point."

"Should we be concerned that the door still isn't open?" Corian offered, frowning at the panel.

The light still blinked yellow.

"Total faith in the troll hacker, huh?" Rhynehart shook his head. "If this doesn't go through—"

"Hey, he said he can do it. He'll do it." Cheyenne pulled the activator coil from her coat pocket and attached it behind her ear. Her eyelids fluttered rapidly during the split-second of syncing with her magic. "Just give it a little longer."

"What are you doing with that thing?"

"Just double-checking." The lines of code scrolling across Cheyenne's vision as she stared at the security panel didn't pick up any issues in the system's alarms. No warning signals. "Just let it run its course."

"Well, that course better finish up right about fucking now," Payton said, staring at another monitor in front of her at the booth. "We got incoming."

"Incoming *what?*" Rhynehart shouted, turning to stare at her.

The goblin shrugged. "Probably a real prison guard and not a fake one."

"This is my fate, isn't it? I'm surrounded by smartasses all the time."

"Don't act like you're not one of us," Yurik muttered.

"How much time do we have, Payton?"

"Forty-five seconds. Maybe."

"Christ. Were you gonna tell us any sooner?"

"You know what?" The goblin lifted both hands from the security booth and stepped away. "Feel free to come up here and play lookout yourself. I'm obviously fucking it up."

Rhynehart said, "Cheyenne, try the badges again."

"It's still thinking."

"Yeah, or it needs a reboot. Swipe the damn badges."

"No." Cheyenne's eyes darted back and forth as she read the scrolling code. "Persh'al's rewriting the security clearance as we stand here arguing about it."

"Why the hell would he do that?"

"Oh, I don't know. Probably so he can override all the other road-blocks in the system at the same time. We needed someone in here for him to finish the rest of it."

"Count's down to thirty now," Payton droned. "You know, just a guess."

"I can hide us," Corian offered.

"The fuck you can." Rhynehart whirled on the disguised night-stalker. "Everything on this side of that glass door is rigged to pick up magic. One little spell, and we'll be shouting at each other over breach alarms. Is that the Plan B you wanna go with?"

"I never said there was a Plan B."

"They won't be able to get to us in time anyway," L'zar said, lifting a finger toward the lock panel. "I just wanna get inside."

"Fifteen seconds, and they're turning the corner."

Cheyenne swatted her father's hand aside. "L'zar, don't."

"My patience seems to have run dry."

"It's almost—"

The light on the panel finally flashed green, the lock clicked, and the door popped open with a soft hiss.

"Lovely."

"Get out or get fucked," Payton growled. "They're coming."

L'zar, Corian, Cheyenne, and Rhynehart had enough time to slip through the heavy metal door into the chamber beyond. Cursing, Tate, Yurik, and Bhandi ducked behind the security panel as the metal door shut behind the others. The real FRoE guards passed in front of the checkpoint two seconds later. The closest one gazed around the room and spent an unusually long time studying Payton.

She stared back at him, both of her human-looking eyes moving together as she looked him up and down. "I got somethin' on my face, or what?"

Whether or not he could hear her, the guard jerked his chin at her, then frowned at Jamal and his long human ponytail before both guards kept walking down the hall and disappeared from view.

"I don't get it." Payton pressed her knuckles down on the booth's counter. "I have one goddamn eye, everybody stares. I wear a mask with two of the fuckers working like normal, as far as anyone can tell, and everybody stares. This is bullshit."

"Human, right?" Yurik asked from where he huddled under the counter. "Maybe he was into you."

"You *want* me to kick you in the mouth, or what?"

"Hey, I wouldn't mind watching that." Bhandi stood from beneath the other side of the circular booth and dusted off her hands.

"Kick the troll, Payton." Yurik chuckled and offered Tate a hand up to pull him out from under the counter. "Both of 'em, if you want."

Jamal stared at the monitors in front of them and grunted. "You three are stuck in here with us now."

"Yeah, thanks but no thanks, Jamal." Bhandi headed to the metal door and grabbed the handle.

The handle jammed when she tried to turn it, and she jiggled it up and down before snatching her hand away with a snort of disgust.

"Because the only magicals with fake security clearance are on the *other* side of the door. Awesome."

"They'll be fine." Yurik waved her off and sat in one of the hard, ridiculously uncomfortable plastic chairs against the wall. "Guess we get a laid-back day on the job, huh?"

Tate folded his arms and stared at the dented metal door, chewing the inside of his bottom lip. "We better be getting paid for this."

CHAPTER SEVENTY-FOUR

The second the door closed behind them, Cheyenne leaned her head on the metal door and listened. *No shouting. No running. No alarms.* "I think we're good."

"Unless someone does something stupid out there." Rhynehart scowled up at the four security cameras mounted high on the walls around the massive circular room. They'd all turned off the second Persh'al's manufactured security clearance passed through the lock panel and opened the door. "Which they might, knowing Bhandi."

"She's not as crazy in the field as she is in a tavern."

He snorted. "I wouldn't know."

"Yeah, well, I do. They'll just have to deal with it and improvise." Cheyenne turned away from the door and examined the huge chamber in front of them. "So, this is the Hatch, huh?"

"The dunk tank." Rhynehart folded his arms. "And we were supposed to have three more agents in here. Not exactly running smoothly."

L'zar strolled casually around the mesh walkway on the upper level. He stared over the narrow railing at a gigantic metal drum that took up the entire level below them and left only three feet of walking space around the perimeter. "You should relax."

"Oh, yeah?" Rhynehart gestured at Corian. "'Cause your furry friend over there just told me straight up there isn't a Plan B."

"Your agents are here as backup and support, Mr. Rhynehart. They aren't required for this part of Plan A."

The FRoE agent shivered. "Drop the Mr. part, huh? It's like none of you get it when someone tells you their name."

Cheyenne and Corian exchanged glances across the circular walkway.

L'zar stopped opposite the door they'd entered, where the walkway opened to a narrow, steep set of mesh stairs, and wrapped his long, slender fingers around the rail on either side of him. "You're not required for this part either, Rhynehart."

"Yeah, well, I'm here. And I really don't wanna be, so let's get a move on." The agent glanced nervously up at the security cameras aimed down at the giant metal vat with a heavy, hinged lid sealed tightly around the top.

L'zar took one step down the stairs, his gaze never leaving the thick steel wheel lock on top of the lid. "No codes or security clearance for this part, correct?"

The agent scratched his head and watched L'zar warily. "As far as I know, not needed."

"That looks manual to me," Corian added.

"Indeed it does. Let's go get our inmate, hmm?" L'zar headed slowly down the stairs, studying the giant metal vat. His shoes hardly made a sound on the metal mesh of the stairs.

"Wait." Cheyenne stepped to the rail around the circular walkway and looked straight down at the sealed lid of the metal tank. "They're keeping Venga in *that*?"

L'zar chuckled. "Honestly, if I were responsible for keeping him locked up, I'd put him in here too. This will be fun."

Cheyenne looked at Corian in confusion, and the nightstalker shook his head.

The drow thief reached the bottom level and skirted around the metal drum until he found the narrow metal ladder on the side and climbed up to the top. He moved like a spider up that ladder, easily reaching the lid and moving carefully around the narrow walkway encircling the top. He paused briefly and looked up at Corian with a secretive smile. "We didn't have a specific time limit on this endeavor today, did we?"

"Not that I'm aware of," Corian muttered. "What's wrong?"

"Nothing at all." L'zar's shoes clicked softly across the top of the tank's lid as he headed for the wheel lock at its center. "I would have enjoyed breaking a record with this one."

When he reached the wheel lock, a deafening, hollow bang came from inside the vat. Rhynehart jumped a little, Corian folded his arms, and L'zar chuckled. Cheyenne blinked and stepped away from the rail. "Maybe we should focus on what's inside that thing instead of how many records you can break. 'Cause this doesn't sound very—"

Another echoing bang from inside the metal drum, then another, followed by what sounded like sandpaper and a metal pick scraping the tank's interior wall. An involuntary shiver went down Cheyenne's spine.

The second L'zar's long fingers closed around the curving bar of the wheel lock, the noise inside the tank stopped. Grinning, he pulled fiercely on the wheel, which gave stiffly at first but then spun faster under his control. The lid's seal broke with a hiss, and the drow thief hauled the massive, heavy metal lid up and over to rest it on the thin rail surrounding the top of the vat. Then he got down on all fours at the edge of the opening and peered inside. "Hello, old friend."

A bellowing roar burst from the tank into L'zar's face. The drow snapped his fingers to remove his human illusion, and his white hair fluttered away from his high cheekbones, but he stayed where he was and grinned even wider.

The creature inside the tank snarled and thrashed, filling the multi-storied room with metallic bangs, scraping, and a long, drawn-out hiss. Then a deep voice that sounded more like a roaring bear than a voice echoed inside the vat. "Release me!"

"Yes, that's precisely why we're here." L'zar cocked his head as the thing inside the vat pummeled the metal walls, roaring and snarling.

Cheyenne frowned at the clink of metal against metal her drow hearing picked up beneath the ruckus. *They put this magical in a tank with no light or sound* and *chained him down inside?* She stepped to the rail again and peered over the edge into the open vat. A mass of green-brown scales, glinting claws, and thick iron chains writhed inside the tank, filling nearly the entire space. "Shit, he's big."

"Indeed." L'zar scrambled sideways along the opening and tilted his head in the other direction. "And pissed off."

"If you came here merely to laugh at me, Weaver," Venga roared, his voice crashing through the circular room, intensified a hundred times by all the metal, "*you* can piss off."

"Come now. I'm allowed to have a little fun."

Venga pounded so forcefully on the inside of the tank that a round bubble popped out along the smooth outer wall, filling the room with the screech of twisting metal.

"Get him out, L'zar," Corian warned.

"Oh, there's suddenly a time limit?"

"You know exactly how long we have."

Venga roared and thrashed beneath the thick, sliding chains coiling around his body.

"I'm well aware, Corian. Does anyone happen to have a key?"

Rhynehart's mouth popped open, and he glanced quickly at Cheyenne before shouting over the balcony, "Why the fuck would there be a *key*? It's not like anyone in this prison planned on letting him out!"

"Hmm. Well, then." Steadying himself in his crouch with one hand pressed firmly against the metal walkway, L'zar lifted his other hand in front of him and moved his fingers in quick, precise twists.

Rhynehart pounded on the railing. "Hey! I said no—"

A bright silver flash illuminated both L'zar's hand and the inside of the tank, then the mass of thick iron chains slithered off all at once and clanged noisily to the floor. Venga roared again and pounded both sides of the tank with his fists, buckling the walls outward.

The bright light filling the chamber cut off with a sharp pop, replaced by low red light and a blaring siren drowning out everything else.

"Goddammit!" Rhynehart gripped the rail and leaned dangerously toward the tank below. "What part of no fucking magic did you not understand?"

L'zar turned slowly around to look up at the agent and raised an eyebrow. "You didn't have a key."

"Fuck." Rhynehart vigorously scratched the back of his head and glanced at the metal door into the chamber while the security siren screamed at them. "We weren't supposed to have to fight anyone for this."

"Then I suggest we leave now." Corian vaulted over the rail and landed beside L'zar on the top of the tank with a metallic thud.

"Jesus." Rhynehart pushed away from the rail and headed for the door leading to the security checkpoint.

Cheyenne leaped over the rail and joined her father and Corian on the tank. They looked up at her with barely concealed smiles, then she glanced at Rhynehart. "You might wanna hurry down the stairs."

The second the agent looked down at the vat again, Venga erupted in another bellow and banged the tank with what sounded like a dozen fists at once.

"No." Rhynehart shook his head and grabbed the door handle. "Fuck that thing in there. Now my people know we're here, and I gotta go cover our tracks. Make sure at the very least this doesn't fall back on my agents out here. Hopefully not on me, either, but if you're serious about not fighting anyone—"

"Then go," Corian shouted over the obnoxiously blaring siren. "Let Cheyenne know when you're out of here."

"Right." Licking his lips, Rhynehart nodded at Cheyenne, then shoved the door open and stepped into the next room.

"Rhynehart, what the fuck?" Bhandi shouted on the other side, then the door closed, and that was all the conversation Cheyenne got to hear.

"Venga," L'zar called in a warning voice. "We're coming in there, and then we're getting you out. I would very much like to stand beside you in one piece, and I have no desire to have to fight you in order to break you out of this fell-damn prison. We're running out of time."

The scaly, upright-standing magical twice the size of Nu'ek the Golra stopped thrashing and looked up at L'zar with glittering all-black eyes. Cracked, scaly lips parted to reveal razor-sharp teeth, then the growling voice echoed up from the floor of the tank. "You have twenty seconds, Weaver. Then I rip you apart."

"That's plenty, thank you. Corian?"

"Yeah." They both jumped down into the vat beside Venga, who stood at least three times as tall as either of them, and sneered up at Cheyenne.

The halfling rolled her eyes. "Fine."

Her black Vans landed with a metallic thud on the floor of the tank, and she looked up to take in Venga's green-brown and light-gray scales and the four muscular arms above two legs as thick as tree trunks. Something smacked the other side of the tank, and Cheyenne peered around the giant lizard-thing to catch a glimpse of the source. *Is that a tail?*

"Here." Corian grimaced as his portal flared in front of the tank wall. He stretched his arms apart with a growl and ripped the shimmering window of light higher and wider to accommodate Venga's gargantuan size. Then he raised his eyebrows at Venga and snarled, *"Nineteen seconds. Go!"*

With a booming laugh that made Cheyenne think her brain would be permanently scrambled, Venga stalked through the abnormally large portal into the empty lot just outside Chateau D'rahl's property line. His tail whipped the tank as he moved. L'zar would have been flattened against the side if he hadn't darted out of the way at the last second. He grabbed Cheyenne's wrist and dragged her through the portal behind him.

"Hey." The halfling jerked her arm out of his grasp and scowled at her father. "I know how this works."

"I know, Cheyenne." L'zar took a deep breath and watched Venga, who stood stock-still on the asphalt, his glittering black eyes flicking to Persh'al's black SUV filled with his rescuers. The siren still blared behind them.

Cheyenne turned and waved Corian forward. "What are you doing? Come on."

"Go take care of your business with that one, kid." The nightstalker nodded at Venga's hunched, scaly back. "Let me take care of mine."

"What are you talking about?" The portal closed with a pop, and Cheyenne hissed, "Are you kidding me?"

"By the blood of Op'paro," Persh'al said, leaning halfway out of the driver's side door and staring at the massive magical standing in front of the SUV. "Nobody said shit about driving around a fucking *mountain!*"

"We can't fit him in the car," Maleshi said as she closed the door behind her. "But we can at least make him *look* like he'll fit."

L'zar shook his head. "We wait for Corian."

Lumil rolled down the back driver's side window and thrust a hand toward the huge complex of Chateau D'rahl a mile in front of them, which was mostly hidden by the high line of thick bushes that also hid their vehicle. "Man, that place is falling apart. Sirens. Flashing lights. And you just wanna wait!"

"We will wait." The drow thief pointed at the goblin and fixed her in his glowing golden stare. "Quietly."

Venga chuckled and crouched even lower in front of the SUV.

With a hiss, Lumil slapped the outside of the car and slumped back against the seat before rolling the tinted window all the way up again.

Cheyenne eyed the high-security magical prison going into lockdown and shook her head. "What the hell's so important that Corian had to stay behind?"

L'zar shrugged. "That's *his* business, don't you think?"

<hr>

As soon as Corian closed the portal into the empty lot, he lifted his hands again and cast another in the same place. The siren wailed overhead, echoing inside the tank as the red light spilled across the chamber. The red light fell through his newest portal too, streaking across the damp stone floor in an otherwise lightless room. It looked a little like blood.

The nightstalker gazed into the dark room, his silver eyes glowing brightly. Then he grinned. "Oh, you're going to *love* this. Time for a change of scenery."

CHAPTER SEVENTY-FIVE

The second Maleshi opened a much larger portal in the lot outside Chateau D'rahl, Corian's next portal opened in the air beside it, and he stepped quickly through with a feral grin. Behind him, the wailing siren was punctuated by panicked screams and incoherent pleas. The portal closed behind him with a pop, and the empty lot fell silent.

Cheyenne stared at him and folded her arms. "Do we have your permission to leave now?"

"I didn't ask you to stay." The nightstalker flicked bits of crumbled stone and what looked like a chipped claw off his shoulder and headed for the car. His silver eyes met Maleshi's gaze. "But I'm glad you did."

"And I'm done waiting here for everyone else to get their shit together. Warehouse." Though the general pointed sternly at the huge portal she'd opened in front of the SUV, large enough to fit the crouching, heavily breathing creature called Venga, a tiny smile flickered at the corner of her mouth before she stalked toward the extra-large window of wavering light.

Persh'al started the engine and rolled the driver's side window down to jerk his chin up at Cheyenne. "What about your FRoE friends?"

"They'll be fine. They deal with this kind of chaos all the time, and for the most part, they clean up pretty well."

In the front passenger seat, Ember leaned forward to meet Cheyenne's gaze. "Even with their *bosses?*"

Cheyenne snorted and flipped Chateau D'rahl the middle finger. "Those guys in there aren't Rhynehart's bosses. He can handle it."

With a shrug, Persh'al slowly drove the SUV through Maleshi's portal back to his warehouse. Cheyenne shoved her hands in her pockets and stalked after it.

"One more relocation, Venga." L'zar grinned at the enormous magical, craning his neck to meet the creature's gaze. "Then you and I will have an opportunity to chat."

"It will be more than that, Weaver." Venga grinned right back, his razor-sharp teeth covered with yellow flecks of who-knew-what. A glistening forked gray tongue flickered out between his teeth as he stooped over L'zar. "I look forward to it."

"Oh, as do I. Very much, in fact." The drow thief gestured at the portal, and Chateau D'rahl's only two escaped magical inmates walked side by side through the overlarge portal and disappeared.

When the portal closed behind them, Persh'al, Byrd, Lumil, and Ember stood beside the SUV, staring at Venga as he stomped his huge clawed feet across the cracked and overgrown parking lot of the warehouse. Dust and bits of crumbled asphalt kicked up beneath the creature's every step. Venga snarled and looked slowly around, the four shoulders of his tense arms curved in a perpetual hunch.

Persh'al rubbed his head. "I'll say it right now, man. No way we're getting this guy inside."

Venga's thick neck twisted sharply as he spun to face Persh'al, his head tilting almost ninety degrees before he took a crunching step forward. "I have spent the last five years inside a metal can, troll. You will not *put* me inside anything else."

"Hey, sure. No problem." Persh'al raised both hands and stepped back until he thumped against the SUV's hood. "Probably not the best idea for all of us to be standing *outside* the wards for everyone else to see, though. Just sayin'."

The scaly magical whirled to L'zar again. "We'll speak here, Weaver. I have a lot to do now that you've freed me."

"I have no doubt." The drow thief stared into Venga's black eyes, reached into his pocket, and pulled out the Nimlothar leaf, pulsing weakly with purple light.

Venga hissed and hunched even farther to peer at the leaf. "How did you get that?"

"It was sent to me. But that hardly matters, does it?"

"If you freed me from one prison just to keep me in another, L'zar, I assure you I have nothing to lose by ripping your grinning face off that tiny neck of yours."

Lumil sniggered at the threat but stepped slowly sideways to put the SUV's hood between herself and the giant magical in a stare-down with L'zar Verdys. Byrd shook his head and stepped away from her in the opposite direction.

"No more prisons, Venga." L'zar twirled the Nimlothar leaf between his fingers. The scaly magical hissed, his cracked lizard-like lips twitching into a sneer as those black eyes caught every movement of the leaf.

Cheyenne cocked her head. *If L'zar's breaking into hypnotism now, I'm done.*

"It's time for a trade, Venga." L'zar stared up into the hissing magical's face. "You get *this* when I get what I want."

One of Venga's four arms bent, and five-inch black claws twice as thick as regular fingers scratched the mottled scales of his chest. The scraping rasp made Cheyenne's nostrils flare. Even worse were the dead scales peeling from Venga's flesh and crumbling to the cracked asphalt with a shower of dirt, flakes of dead skin, and yellow-white clumps that looked a lot like maggots. Venga's eyes never left the Nimlothar leaf. "And what is it you want, Weaver?"

L'zar leaned away from the escaped prisoner and raised his eyebrows. "The Darkglass."

Venga grunted. "The Darkglass was not meant for you."

"True. But it's hardly being used as intended *now*, is it?"

"It rots with the rest of my endowments."

"Ah." The drow slowly lowered his hand and deposited the leaf back into his pocket with a shrug. "Well if we're bringing your *endowments* into this—"

Venga hissed viciously and extended all four arms as he took one more crunching step toward L'zar, all four clawed hands outstretched.

Looks like that promise to rip off L'zar's head is about to be a real thing. Cheyenne shot Corian a questioning glance. The nightstalker lifted a finger for her to wait and shook his head slightly.

"What other price have you set?" Venga snarled at L'zar.

The drow thief cocked his head. "None so far. Other than the Darkglass, of course."

"Do you know how I came to be wrapped in chains and darkness, Weaver?"

"I have a vivid imagination, Venga. I can imagine. I'm offering my assistance in reclaiming what was taken from you. Do we have a deal?"

The huge magical's spine cracked like snapping branches when Venga drew himself to his full height. His long, broad shadow fell across the SUV, and Persh'al shrank against the hood. A shuddering laugh escaped the blue troll, then he glanced quickly at L'zar and slid away from his vehicle before darting to the warehouse door.

"I'll accept your assistance, Weaver," Venga hissed. "And your token. Everything else we may find belongs to me."

"Done."

Venga's thick tail bashed the cracked asphalt of the parking lot. Chunks of broken black rock sprayed up around him and pelted the SUV like hailstones. Persh'al didn't say a word. Then the giant magical turned to eye everyone staring at him. "Has anyone heard of Felgar's Horn?"

Corian shook his head. Persh'al, Lumil, and Byrd were frozen where they stood, staring at Venga as if they'd never seen a magical. Maleshi looked at L'zar. "No word of it."

"Then nothing has changed much while I've been contained." Venga snorted, and a spray of thick yellow-white mucus shot from his flat nostrils to splatter the asphalt. "I'll take you there. My endowments and the Darkglass have become well acquainted, I imagine."

"Yes." L'zar kicked out one heel and bowed at the waist, gesturing at the open street beyond Persh'al's abandoned warehouse. "Then by all means, do lead the way."

"Uh, *hello?*" Persh'al glanced nervously up and down the street. "Escaped convict bigger than a bus, here. Does nobody see an issue with this?"

"No issue." Maleshi stepped over to L'zar and Venga. "Until what belongs to you is returned, I can at least make you *look* whole."

A low growl escaped the ex-prisoner, but he didn't object or move away from the general as she slowly raised her hands. With a quickly whispered incantation and a brief twist of her fingers, Maleshi's spell bloomed from her fingertips in a web of silver light. Venga's eyes narrowed. The light engulfed him, and when it faded, it left behind a thin, pale, hunched man with scraggly gray hair falling over his shoulders.

Venga raised his human-looking hands, studied them, and scowled. "Far less than whole, General Hi'et."

"And the rest of the world will be none the wiser." She dipped her head and clasped her hands behind her back. "Where are we headed?"

"Felgar's Horn is two miles south of the DC city line." Venga's human hair swung beside his haggard face when he turned to look at Corian. "I cannot hide my trail."

"We'll do it for you." The nightstalker nodded and opened another massive portal.

Persh'al groaned and stepped away from the warehouse door. "It's like nobody even cares about being seen out here."

L'zar shrugged. "We're keeping our eyes on the much bigger prize, Persh'al. Let the rest work itself out."

"Oh, sure. Yeah. Work itself out while we get ported across the state fifty times in one day." The troll stalked over to the portal and tossed his hand at it. "So, who's leading the way?"

Venga's scraggly gray human eyebrows drew together as he looked Persh'al up and down. "You don't listen very well, do you?"

"I guess that's you, then. We'll follow the old man." The troll clapped his hands together and waited for everyone else to move toward the portal. The other magicals cast their human illusions again.

Cheyenne slipped out of her drow form and met Ember's gaze as the fae reached into her pocket and slid on the illusion-charm ring. Her pink skin and luminous purple eyes disappeared, but when she glanced down at her feet, they still hovered half an inch off the asphalt. "Here's hoping nobody notices."

"Trust me, Em. Out of everyone in this weird-looking group, you'll draw the least amount of attention."

Byrd and Lumil followed hesitantly. The goblin man pointed at the shadow moving across the asphalt behind Venga, which stretched three times longer and wider than it should have. "He didn't really shrink, did he?"

Lumil elbowed him in the ribs. "Man, Maleshi's not stupid enough to even *try* shifting someone else. Especially not that hulking pile of scales."

Venga headed for the portal, and though it stretched at least six feet over the top of his human-looking head, he ducked and hunched his shoulders even tighter before passing through. The rest of L'zar's rebels followed quickly and quietly. L'zar wore his usual grin, though no one else seemed to find this odd turn of events amusing in the slightest.

When the portal closed behind them, they stood in the center of a relatively quiet DC neighborhood, the street empty in the middle of the day. Cheyenne looked at Maleshi as the general walked up beside her. "You had to cast an illusion *for* him?"

"Oh, good." The general cocked her head. "I'm glad that was what it looked like."

"Huh. Guess I'm not the only magical who can't cast spells."

Venga's hooked human nose was the first thing she saw before his head turned farther so he could look at her over his hunched shoulder. "Did you leave your magic behind in an O'gúl vessel too?"

"Uh, no."

"Hmm." He stared at her for a moment, then turned around again and shuffled slowly down the street.

Cheyenne shot Maleshi a sidelong glance and whispered, "Magic in a vessel?"

"Everyone's got different ways of dealing with their issues, kid."

"I have no idea what that means."

Ember cleared her throat. "What exactly is this Felgar's Horn place we're going to?"

Venga hissed, which was weird coming from a stooped old man with long, stringy hair and dark circles under his eyes. "The Bull's Head Earthside vault."

CHAPTER SEVENTY-SIX

Ember cocked her head and stopped in the middle of the residential street. "The what now?"

"That is Felgar's Horn," Venga grumbled. "And that is where we will all find what we seek."

"And by 'we,' you pretty much mean you and L'zar, huh?"

The newly liberated prisoner didn't answer. Cheyenne waited for Ember to catch up with her so they could all keep moving.

"Is this guy for real?"

Cheyenne shrugged. "Wish I could say magical prisoners broken out of Chateau D'rahl have no reason to lie about something like this, but my only experience so far is with L'zar."

"Yeah, but," Ember leaned in to whisper, "The Bull's Head Earthside vault? I mean, I can't even pick which part of that is the most disturbing."

"I know. But if Venga can take us right to the Bull's Head, we're hitting two birds with one stone, right?"

The fae cast Cheyenne a sidelong glance. "That was a missed opportunity."

"For what?"

Ember shrugged. "I would've gone with something like 'hitting two magical deals with one vault raid' or something. Maybe that sounded better in my head."

Cheyenne snorted. "Well, however we wanna say it, if Felgar's Horn is still where Venga thinks it is, and the Bull's Head is still there, we get the chance to wipe them out, handle the war-machine problem, *and* snag this last piece L'zar seems to think is so important for me to dictate my terms to the Crown."

They followed the rest of the group in silence for a moment, then Ember muttered through the side of her mouth, "I seriously hope we can trust this escaped convict a lot more than the last one."

"That makes two of us, Em."

The group of magicals disguised as an odd assortment of humans following an old, hunched, homeless-looking man walked another three blocks through the neighborhood before the streets started to narrow. Then Venga pointed a crooked finger down the next intersection and turned right. "This way."

A blue Ford Focus parked on the corner squealed and wobbled as Venga took the right turn. The front wheels slammed up onto the sidewalk, but the ex-prisoner kept moving and paid it no attention. Cheyenne frowned at the car and turned behind the others down the much narrower side street, which was practically an alley. As Venga passed down the center, cars on either side of him squealed and indented, shoved aside by an unseen force. Two car alarms activated and blared.

Lumil gestured at a Subaru parked by the curb. The car's back fender crumpled and the vehicle bumped the car parked in front of it as Venga moved past it. "Anybody else see something wrong with this?"

Maleshi flicked her fingers at the crashed cars, and the alarms stopped. "Nothing to *see*, really. Can't change the guy's size, just the way it's perceived."

"Well, that's great." Persh'al staggered across the narrow side street as the rear tire of a Chevy Malibu on the left burst with a hiss, throwing shreds of rubber in their path. "Here we are, in broad daylight, following an old geezer who'd rather bash into every car than take a shower."

"You saw how big he is," Byrd muttered. "I'm amazed he can walk down this street at all."

Corian turned around to walk backward with the group and raised his hands. Quick, precise movements and a few muttered O'gúleesh words brought a dimly strobing light to his fingers. The crushed, dented, and scraped cars flashed too, and the metal sides reworked themselves.

Cheyenne looked over her shoulder at the sideways-parked cars, many of them with their headlights and taillights broken out. The Malibu's rear passenger tire was still nothing but a flap of rubber. "You missed a few."

"If I stopped to clean up every little spill, Cheyenne, we'd never make it to where we're going." Corian turned around again and raised an eyebrow at her. "But at least now it doesn't look like a rhino stampeded through the neighborhood."

"Right. Just a bunch of vandals smashing taillights."

"By the time anyone gets here to investigate," L'zar added, moving casually behind Venga at a safe distance to avoid the huge bashing tail none of them could see, "we'll have what we came for, and we'll be long gone."

"That's the extent of your optimism, huh? Cut a path through a narrow street where people live, but as long as we're gone by the time anybody figures out something's wrong, it's okay?"

"No one's getting hurt if that's what you're worried about." The drow thief nonchalantly studied a fire hydrant knocked halfway over by a car rocking against it as Venga passed. Water sprayed from the hydrant in an arc, splattering the car, the sidewalk, and half the street.

Cheyenne raised a shimmering black shield against the water before sloshing through the quickly growing puddle in the street. "We should keep it that way." *I'd bet most people can't spring for a brand-new car when reckless magicals bash in their old ones.*

"Quiet," Venga hissed. He stopped almost at the end of the street, glanced up to sniff the air with his hooked human-illusion nose, and turned left down a wider street where the neighborhood ended and rows of run-down commercial buildings began. "We're here."

Persh'al gazed around. "Here's hoping we don't have more massive cover-ups after this."

"Is that even something you guys do?" Cheyenne pulled the activator from her pocket and stuck it behind her ear, then she raised her eyebrows at the blue troll as everyone followed Venga down the next street.

"Sometimes. I guess."

"We usually take enough precautions that we don't *have* messes to clean up afterward," Corian added, squinting at the commercial buildings with wary curiosity. "Your FRoE friends are the ones who handle that side of things, aren't they?"

Cheyenne said, "When it's their magical messes, sure. I don't think anyone will be sent to help us out with this one." *That's one phone call to Sir I can't even pretend would go in my favor.*

Venga stopped on the left side of the street and scanned the boarded-up windows of the storefront. "Felgar's Horn."

"Looks pretty abandoned to me." Persh'al looked up and down the street, then returned his attention to the closed storefront with the faded marquee sign that marked the place as a record store. He pulled out his cell phone and tapped it. "All right. I'll head around back and take a look inside. If those assholes have war machines up and running, I can at least pick up on their system, maybe throw in a few—"

"Weaver." Venga clenched his fists at his sides as he glared at the glass front door, which was boarded up like the windows. "I would do this as myself."

"By all means." L'zar's quickly cast spell unraveled Maleshi's illusion.

Venga's old-man figure fell away, his size ballooning again into the hulking mountain of scales and claws. Cheyenne moved aside when she realized she'd almost stepped on the scaly magical's tail. With an ear-splitting bellow, Venga raised a fist and smashed through the boarded glass door. When he shouldered his way into the three-story building, he took another six feet above the doorway with him. Brick and plaster and splintered wood rained down over the hole in the wall, and L'zar darted inside after him.

Both nightstalkers disappeared through the crumbling doorway in streaks of silver light. Cheyenne slipped into drow speed and joined them, a sphere of crackling black energy at the ready in her palm. Ember floated through right after her.

"Oh, sure." Persh'al stuck his phone in his pocket and rolled his eyes as Byrd and Lumil rushed past him into Felgar's Horn. "Well-planned attacks are so last week."

He flicked his wrist and summoned his magical whip, then darted into the not-so-abandoned building to join the fray.

Venga roared and swung all four arms violently, crashing against lights hanging from the ceiling and swatting down half a dozen hovering black orbs blinking blue and green light.

Cheyenne's activator lit up another four dozen floating metal orbs in her vision. She ducked a spray of yellow energy spewing from the flying war machines and sent her energy sphere hurtling toward them. Her attack caught three orbs in one go and they crashed to the ground, shuddering and spitting yellow sparks.

A much thinner version of the crawler Ember had borrowed from the raugs scuttled across the floor toward the magicals, each narrow leg clinking loudly. A black rod emerged from the body and blazed with crackling green light before launching an attack like a shower of automatic gunfire. The first burst of it peppered the back of Venga's thick leg, shredding what was left of the stained gray rags passing as a prison uniform. The huge magical roared and spun toward the crawling war machine.

Lumil let out a screaming battle cry, her fists blazing with the spinning red runes, and charged the attacking war machine. Before she could get in a good hit, two of Venga's arms swept the machine off its thin metal legs and sent it crashing against the far wall of the building. It thumped to the ground, legs twitching like a spider's.

"Hey, asshole!" Lumil snarled. "Maybe leave something for the rest of us, huh?"

Thick black cables uncoiled from the ceiling and swung at Venga, sparking with charged bursts of magic as they lashed his scaled head and neck. The second he wrapped his giant hand around some of them and jerked them free of the ceiling, another swarm of tiny flying war machines fell from the rafters to join the fight.

Cheyenne ducked another spray of yellow attacks, then raised a translucent black shield on her other side against the second wave of incoming yellow pellets. They pinged off her shield and knocked several flying war machines out of the air.

Three metal wheels rolled toward them from a back room, stopped at the end of the hall, and unfolded before firing red and green bursts of magic in every direction.

"What the hell?" Ember shoved a wave of purple light at a hissing, magically-sparking cable snaking down from the ceiling toward her. Her magic caught the cable mid-swing and blocked its firing mechanism, and the thing lurched and exploded. She ducked beneath the flying fragments of metal cable and turned to the rolling war machines spewing lights in every direction.

Persh'al and Byrd fought off another spider-like crawler, dodging attacks from the flying metal orbs as the blue whip and bursts of green fire pummeled the rod on the top of the crawler and ripped it to pieces.

Corian and Maleshi darted around the building in streaks of silver light, their extended claws slicing through dangling cables and war-machine legs. Cheyenne raised a shield in front of her to ward off the bursts of green magic spewing from one of the rolling machines at the end of the hall that had apparently decided to focus on her. She pushed the shield, moving it forward step by step as the green bursts pinged off her magic and ricocheted around the room.

The back of her calf erupted in a sharp, burning sting, and it climbed up her leg. Snarling, she looked back and found two much smaller spider-machines moving up her legs, piercing her thick black pants and her flesh with every stab of their needle-like feet. She blasted them off with a crackling black energy sphere, then ducked under her shield and reached out to the rolling machine with her black tendrils. They coiled around its curved, segmented metal back and she stepped aside and pulled, flinging the thing through the air.

Venga roared and brought a fist down on top of the sailing war machine, which was still firing green bursts across the room. The roller slammed into the ground and jerked Cheyenne with it before she released her tendrils, stumbling to catch her balance. She snarled at Venga and blasted another trio of floating metal orbs out of the air. "Should we have let you come in here on your own instead?"

"Right?" Lumil dropped to one knee and brought a spinning red fist against the underside of a crawler scuttling toward her. It jerked when her fist pierced its undercarriage, then she pulled out a handful of gears and metal pieces and stood. "At least let the rest of us get in a few hits." She kicked the shuddering, sparking hull of the crawler, and it sprawled on the floor.

L'zar stood to the side of the crumbling hole in the front wall and batted aside every flying orb darting his way, his hands moving in a blur of purple light.

Byrd shouted in surprise when the end of a dangling cable pierced the back of his jacket collar and lifted him off the floor. "What is it with picking me up by my fell-damn shirt?" Struggling and kicking his legs a foot off the floor, he reached up behind him, grabbed the cable with both hands, and sent a flare of green fire racing up it. The metal segments fell apart in a rain of hollow metal rings, and the rest of the tangled nest of cables dropped from the ceiling and buried the goblin man beneath their weight.

"What are these supposed to be, snakes?" Lumil grabbed fistfuls of cables and ripped them apart as bursts of green flames exploded from the mass on top of Byrd.

Persh'al's blue whip cracked into the legs of a second roller that was spewing red magic across the room. The machine wobbled and tilted sideways but kept firing. Corian appeared behind it and sliced his claws through the segmented back. The roller shuddered and burst apart, sending shrapnel flying.

Cheyenne raised another shield in front of Ember, ducked beneath a flying metal back segment, and sent a black energy sphere at the third roller. The machine dodged her attack, curled in on itself, and rolled toward her. Four more flying orbs swooped at her head, and she swept them aside with a telekinetic burst. The roller stopped two feet in front of her, uncurled, and exploded in a burst of green light and metal shards when Venga stomped it into the ground with a clawed, scaly foot.

He snarled at the mess of war-machine parts beneath him, then turned glistening black eyes on Cheyenne.

She looked up at him and shrugged. "Okay. Thanks for that one."

"Whoa, whoa! Easy!" Lumil reeled back as Byrd shouted and snarled, blasting green fire in every direction and twisting back and forth to free himself from the writhing mass of metal cables tightening around him. "If you blow my head off, you idiot, I can't help you!"

"You're *not* helping." Byrd kicked the cables and extended both hands to shoot columns of green fire at the tangled nest around him.

A high-pitched squeal rose from the cables as they heated quickly under his magical attack.

Cheyenne frowned. "I think you got 'em, Byrd."

The goblin roared and spun, spewing green flames from his hands. The nest of cables shuddered and jerked, the high-pitched squeal grew even louder, and Lumil stepped away with wide eyes. "You're gonna—"

A silver streak darted over to the nest of cables, and Byrd grunted as Maleshi snatched him up and deposited him on the other side of the room.

"Whoa, shit." Cheyenne cast a shield around the nest of flaming cables a split-second before they erupted in flaming, sparking rings of black metal. The sound of so much shrapnel pinging against the inner wall of her domed shield was deafening. She gritted her teeth against the sound rattling her skull and focused on holding up the shield until it was over.

When she dropped it, the only sounds left were the hollow clinks of metal pieces settling, the sparks and hisses of the last few war machines to die, and the heavy breathing of every magical in the room.

CHAPTER SEVENTY-SEVEN

Byrd pushed away from the wall and straightened his denim jacket with a snort. "Way to be fast on that one."

Maleshi raised an eyebrow at him. "To whom are you referring?"

"I mean both of you, I guess."

Clenching her eyes shut against the ringing in her ears, Cheyenne straightened and took a deep breath. "That's all of them, right?"

"It fucking better be." Lumil turned slowly and eyed the destroyed front room of Felgar's Horn with a scowl, red runes still spinning around her fists.

"Looks like they've beefed up their security," Persh'al grumbled. "Without even having to be here."

"Just security, huh?" Cheyenne took stock of the scattered war-machine parts. "There's no way this is everything they smuggled Earth-side in those crates."

"Of course not." L'zar smoothed his hair back with both hands and stepped over a fractured pile of useless metal orbs. "This is their vault, not their headquarters."

"So, you weren't expecting to fight any Bull's Head loyalists."

"I wasn't expecting anything in particular, Cheyenne." He shot his daughter a brief glance. "Though I will say I'm a little disappointed not to see any bodies."

She snorted and shook her head. "Yeah, me too. Now we have to track down the rest of the Bull's Head to rip out whatever they've been using to control these machines from somewhere else."

"Not yet." L'zar stepped past her, his attention focused on Venga. The former prisoner was stomping across the room toward the hallway leading to the back.

Ember bent over one of the crushed rollers with a frown. "Okay, I *know* there's no TV on the other side. I mean, science fiction isn't fiction over there, but somebody please tell me I'm not the only one who thinks these things were pulled right out of *Star Wars*."

Cheyenne stifled a laugh. "*That's* what bothers you the most right now?"

"It's more than a little weird. Whoa." Ember straightened when Venga's shadow fell over her, and she looked slowly up at the scaly magical glaring down at her with all-black eyes. "Uh, hello."

"Move."

She raised an eyebrow and floated slowly back across the floor before folding her arms. "A please goes a long way, you know."

Lumil snorted. "You moved without it, didn't you?"

Venga ignored them both and bent over a large, rusting metal crate bolted to the wall beside the hallway. He grabbed the heavy iron lock at the front of the crate and ripped it off in one jerk before tossing it aside. Persh'al ducked the flying lock and scowled.

The crate buckled when Venga slammed a huge fist into it, then it opened easily, and he rummaged inside with two hands while his other two propped him against the wall.

Cheyenne glanced at Maleshi and gestured at the trunk. "His endowments, I'm guessing."

"Your guess is as good as mine, kid. Right now, we're here for backup."

"Obviously."

A low chuckle escaped the gigantic magical, and he straightened. The glinting object in his hand caught the harsh light as he turned it back and forth. His black eyes widened, and cracked, dry lips peeled back to reveal his stained teeth in a crazed grin. "There you are."

"More tech?" Ember asked.

"Not quite," L'zar said, also grinning, his golden eyes fixed intently, not on the round object that looked like a twenty-sided ball of glass, but on Venga's grotesque smile. "Are you satisfied?"

Venga chuckled again, his black eyes flicking to the drow thief. "Almost." He opened his mouth, tossed the orb of black glass into it, and crunched down with powerful jaws.

Lumil and Byrd grimaced and leaned away. The goblin man passed a hand over his mouth. "That can't be good for dental hygiene."

"Man, the dude was locked in a *tank*. You think those fuckers tossed him a toothbrush?"

"He's eating *glass*!"

"Yeah, but not to clean his mouth." Too far away from the goblin across the room to punch him, Lumil waved him off instead and rolled her eyes. "Just don't talk."

The noisy crunching of glass and Venga's grunts of satisfaction almost made Cheyenne look away. But she noticed the small, shattered fragments of glass spilling from the ex-prisoner's mouth and disintegrating in the air before they reached the ground. *Not just glass, then.*

With a violent swallow, Venga closed his eyes. When he opened them again, the glistening black was replaced by a flash of blazing green light, and he opened all four clawed hands. Green and black smoke wafted from his palms, and he let out another dark chuckle. "Much better."

He flicked the scaly fingers of one hand, and his massive form shrank until he stood only three inches taller than L'zar instead of three times the drow thief's height.

L'zar dipped his head. "Magic restored, my friend. Now for—"

"The Darkglass." Venga looked sharply at the drow. "Don't think I've forgotten how to fulfill my end of a bargain, Weaver. I deal with much darker forces than yours."

Kicking his heel up, L'zar spread his arms and bowed once more. "I'm well aware."

Venga's tail thumped the floor, scattering broken war-machine bits, then he stalked over to the far side of the room and raised all four hands. A low, guttural chant rose from his scaly throat, and green and black sparks wafted from his fingers and palms, stretching to a metal panel set high on the wall. The sparks flickered across the panel, and it flashed white and pushed itself away from the wall.

Metal panels and sliding gears unfolded all the way to the floor, forming a cabinet wider at the base than the top. Venga flicked his hand at a central panel, which opened under his command like a drawer. Then he reached in with two hands and gingerly pulled out an object composed of black metal and glass panes.

"As promised." He turned and offered the rectangular object to L'zar.

"You always keep your promises, Venga." The drow gingerly took the box of metal and glass and grinned at the scaly magical. "You have my thanks."

"It's not your thanks I want, Weaver." The ex-prisoner tilted his head, and his eyes flashed green again.

"Of course." Nestling the Darkglass delicately beneath one arm, L'zar pulled the faintly pulsing Nimlothar leaf from his pocket and set it in Venga's outstretched hand. "I don't have to tell you to use it wisely, do I?"

Venga growled and stalked back to the open trunk. He pulled out a black leather jacket and a pair of worn, baggy jeans before stripping off the rags of his prison uniform and changing right there in front of everyone.

Ember blinked furiously and turned away. "Guess privacy isn't an issue when you're chained up in a tank."

"Apparently." Cheyenne stuck her hands in the pockets of her trenchcoat and shrugged. "Honestly, I'm waiting to see what he's gonna do with that leaf."

"He's not gonna eat that too, is he? That was weird."

Corian chuckled. "Endowments and a Nimlothar have two different uses for a scaleback."

"Oh, yeah?" Cheyenne forced herself not to look at Venga tugging on his jeans and slipping his thick tail through a tailored hole in the back. "What does he get out of something from a drow tree?"

"None of your business, *Aranél,*" Venga grunted and slammed the dented lid of the trunk closed. He slipped the Nimlothar leaf into his jacket pocket and headed back to L'zar. "I don't remember this many questions being part of our arrangement."

"They're not." L'zar waved a dismissive hand at his daughter. "She's still learning."

Cheyenne stepped toward them. "Okay, wait a minute."

"Our business is completed," L'zar said, nodding at Venga and lifting a finger to silence Cheyenne. She folded her arms and glared at him. "But you now have the opportunity to repay the Crown for what she's done to you."

Venga's forked tongue flickered from between his scaly lips. "An opportunity I'd be more than happy to accept."

"Excellent." L'zar turned to Cheyenne with a pert smile. "Then when it's time, you'll be making the crossing with my daughter."

Cheyenne stopped. "Wait, what?"

Venga turned his black eyes on her and sneered. "Agreed. Now let's go. I'm hungry."

"Hungry?" Ember frowned at him as he stalked across the destroyed Bull's Head vault to the front entry hole in his former shape and size.

"For the last five years, fae, my meals have been highly unsatisfactory."

"What did they give you?"

Venga snapped his fingers, and a haze of green smoke bloomed around him before he masked himself in a human illusion with short-cropped black hair, a neatly trimmed goatee, and brilliant green eyes. Two hands instead of four slipped into the pockets of his leather jacket as he stepped through the doorway. "You don't want to know."

Ember's eyes widened, and she stepped aside to let the other magicals pass through, pulling up their illusion spells again.

Cheyenne headed over to her father as he strolled casually across the room, his hands clasped behind his back again. "L'zar, I don't think we need to keep adding magicals to the list."

"Of course not. But it's done. Think of him as your personal bodyguard. I can't be with you when you return, and Venga may even be a better choice. He wants to see the Crown fall as much as we do." He chuckled. "Perhaps more."

"How am I supposed to trust someone who stashed his clothes and his magic in a place run by the Bull's Head?"

"You don't need to trust him, Cheyenne. Just let him join you." They stepped outside onto the sidewalk, and L'zar cast a brief glance at Corian and Maleshi, who were discussing lunch options with Venga. "At the very least, his presence will make a much more convincing argument than mine. Ba'rael's never had much luck with necromancers."

"With *what?*" Cheyenne leaned away from him, her eyes wide.

L'zar tossed a hand in the air. "He's one of the best. Deals with death magic and the spirits of those beyond the deathflame. To tell you the truth, it's something I've never cared to dabble in."

"Oh, great. You're sending me back with someone versed in magic too dark for even *you* to touch. That's supposed to make me feel better?"

"It's not, but the look on Ba'rael's face when she meets you with Venga at your side will be more than worth it." L'zar grinned and closed his eyes, taking a deep breath. "I do regret not being able to see *that.*"

Venga grunted. "Cheeseburgers."

"Ah." L'zar stepped away from his daughter, ignoring her scowl, and gestured down the street. "If that's what you want, we're happy to assist you."

"Something I missed very much, yes," Venga said, smiling as L'zar patted him on the back. They led the rest of the startled magicals down the street to the closest burger joint.

Ember stuck her thumb out at the destroyed building behind them. "We're gonna leave the place like this?"

"It's not our problem anymore." Maleshi joined them. "Think of it as a message for the Bull's Head. The tables have turned."

"Yeah, and they'll know exactly who broke into that trunk to pull out his magic and eat it again." Lumil snorted and slammed a fist into her other palm. "I'm done fighting shit I can't hear screaming in pain."

"Jesus." Cheyenne shook her head. "Have you always been this sadistic?"

The goblin grinned at her. "Have you?"

The halfling shrugged. "I just wanna know why it's so hard to pin down these loyalists and finally stop them. All of them."

"That's why you're trying to get in with the colonel, right?" Ember tossed her hair out of her face and floated gracefully beside them. "If he's the one with connections to the Bull's Head, you'll find them through him."

"He's the one, Em." Cheyenne pulled off the activator and stuck it back in her pocket. "I'm waiting for proof from Major Sir Carson. If I'm gonna nail Colonel Thomas, I gotta do it the right way. Take the right steps."

"Listen to you." Maleshi fought back a laugh. "Cheyenne Summerlin's going by the books to root out the thorn in all our sides."

Ember chuckled. "Yeah, but there *isn't* a book for dealing with traitors in the FRoE."

Cheyenne laughed. "I'm making it up as I go along." So far, it's taking way too much time. Sir better not be screwing around.

CHAPTER SEVENTY-EIGHT

"This is too weird." Ember lifted her burger to her mouth with both hands but couldn't stop staring at Venga, who was sitting at the table next to them. "Just sitting here like this. In public. With everyone."

Cheyenne took a bite of her own burger, leaning forward as sauce and chunks of fried jalapeños hit the paper wrapper. "Just as long as the necromancer doesn't do anything crazy in public, I think we're good."

Ember closed her mouth and lowered her burger to the table as she stared at the halfling. "Sorry, it sounded like you said 'necromancer.'"

"Yep." Cheyenne took another bite and stared at the table.

"Yeah, that makes me feel so much better." The fae eyed Venga, who'd devoured two double cheeseburgers and was now on a third, ignoring his illusion goatee covered in ketchup and mustard. "Well, he sure is eating like someone who came back from the dead."

Maleshi chuckled as she sat across from them with her tray of food. "That's not quite how it works."

"Yeah, I bet." Ember abandoned her burger for the paper cup she'd filled with iced tea and took a long drink. "I'm just trying to talk myself into pretending any of this is normal."

"It isn't." Corian sat beside Maleshi, grabbed a handful of fries, and jammed them all into his mouth at once. "Neither is necromancy, but Venga is one of the best."

"I'd go so far as to say *the* best." The general snatched a handful of fries off Corian's tray and dropped them on hers. "Which made him that much worse when he served the Crown."

"L'zar said she wasn't a fan of necromancers."

"Ba'rael?" Maleshi snorted. "She's not, but she appreciated what he could do."

Ember set her drink down with a grimace and eyed Venga, her nostrils flaring at the sound of him gobbling his burger and chewing madly with an open mouth and satisfied grunts. "What, she made him talk to the dead for her or something?"

"Ha." Venga swallowed his last bite and washed it down with half his cup of root beer. Then he sighed and sat back in his chair. "The Spider never *made* me do anything."

Sitting across from the escaped prisoner, L'zar clicked his tongue. "Not to your knowledge."

"I was content to serve the Crown just like the rest of us, Weaver." Venga gestured at Maleshi, who rolled her eyes. "Until she turned on me. Her mistake."

"Oh, indeed." L'zar popped a fry into his mouth and folded his hands on the table.

Sitting farther down at that table, Lumil slapped Byrd's hand away from her tray. "If you wanted French fries, asshole, you should've ordered some."

"Aw, come on."

"No."

Ember leaned back in her chair, already wary of the answer as she stared at Venga's sauce-smeared goatee. "What did she do to *you*?"

"She sent me Earthside," Venga grumbled and unwrapped the fourth burger on his tray. "Of course, that was only *after* she'd gotten what she wanted from me."

"Which was what?" Cheyenne took another sloppy bite of burger and leaned farther forward, propping her forearms on the edge of the table.

"There is alchemy involved in my work, *Aranél*. Transformations and reallocation of magic. The Spider tasked me with channeling the excess magic she took from others into something that would solidify her power."

L'zar grinned as he watched Venga digging into the last of his abnormally large meal.

Ember frowned. "You mean, like that huge glass container thing in that room full of black sludge?"

Venga swallowed and shook his head, sucking mayonnaise off his fingers. "That was a conduit."

"Well, your conduit exploded before we left Hangivol," Cheyenne muttered. "Spewed extra magic everywhere, and we had to—"

"Get creative in cleaning it up," L'zar finished for her. He shot his daughter a warning glance as he sat back in his chair. Then his grin returned.

Oh, of course. Don't tell the necromancer about the *Sorren Gán*. That'd be going way too far. She snorted and took another bite.

Venga gulped down more root beer, then rattled the ice around in the empty cup and stared at it. "That wasn't *my* work. I'm not surprised it didn't hold the way she wanted."

"So, what *was* your work?" Ember asked. "'Cause we saw a lot of messed-up crap in the capital."

"I'm sure. No, I crafted an overflow of sustained dark magic spread as far from Ba'rael as she was willing to go. And the rest of it was left to its own devices. I'm sure by now, it also isn't holding the way she expected." Venga grunted at his empty cup. "There is little I enjoy more than this sweet Earthside beer. How much of this would it take to be as strong as a tankard of grog?"

Lumil snorted. "All the root beer in the world couldn't hold up against grog, man."

Beside her, Byrd laughed and stole another of her French fries. "You should go ahead and try it. I'd like to see that."

"I want more." Venga scooted his chair back and stood.

Ember pointed at him. "You didn't say what you made for her."

The escaped prisoner looked around the restaurant before his gaze settled on the soda machine. "I called it the Undoing, and from what I hear, it has been quite effective." He took off to refill his drink.

Ember slumped in her seat and rolled her eyes. "How hard is it to get a real answer out of that guy?"

Cheyenne took a long sip of her bottled water and looked at the nightstalkers sitting across from her. "Why do both of you look like you're hiding something?"

Maleshi raised an eyebrow and stared after Venga. She slowly slipped a fry into her mouth and shrugged. "He calls it the Undoing."

L'zar chuckled. "And we've been calling it the blight. Honestly, I prefer his name for it."

Cheyenne choked on her next sip of water and fought not to spray it all over the table and the nightstalkers sitting across from her. Swallowing quickly, she coughed and leaned over the table to whisper harshly, "Are you fucking serious?"

Corian looked at Maleshi, and the general shrugged before stuffing her face with another huge bite of food.

Ember bowed her head and ran her fingers slowly over her eyebrows. "Are you saying we're sitting here eating bacon cheeseburgers with the mad death-magic scientist who engineered the blight?"

"Death-magic scientist." L'zar chuckled as he pointed at the fae with a floppy French fry. "An accurate *and* entertaining description."

Cheyenne dropped the rest of her burger and clenched her eyes shut. "When we agreed to break this guy out of prison, L'zar, it was under the assumption that Venga would help us against Ba'rael. Because that's all you told us, not that we'd be unleashing the mastermind behind the shit that's killing your world and trying to slip into this one."

L'zar chomped on the fry and dusted off his fingers. "The two aren't mutually exclusive, Cheyenne."

"In what universe do you think I'm stupid enough to believe that?"

"Hmm." The drow thief shrugged. "All of them?"

"We should take him back." Ember looked at the nightstalkers and nodded. "Just drop him off in front Chateau D'rahl and let *them* handle him."

Maleshi shook her head. "I don't think that's an option at this point, Ember."

"Why not?" The fae gestured at Venga, who was still standing in front of the soda machines. He'd already downed another cup of root beer and was now filling it for the third time. "I mean, forget the necromancer part, whatever the hell that means. He made the fucking blight. He has to be insane."

"They say there's a fine line between insanity and genius," L'zar replied. "I love that line. It applies to so many facets of—"

"No one asked the nutjob's opinion on insanity, okay?" Ember raised a hand, turning her head to L'zar but not looking him in the eye.

Corian chuckled. Maleshi kept eating her burger. Byrd's mouth dropped open in the middle of chewing up more stolen fries. On the other side of him, Persh'al shook his head and flipped through something in his cell phone.

Ember shot L'zar a quick glance. "No offense."

He raised an eyebrow at Cheyenne and laughed softly. "If I were less aware of the finer nuances here, Ember, I most likely wouldn't believe you."

Cheyenne closed her eyes and couldn't hide a small smile. *About time someone else stood up to his bullshit. I'm glad it's her.*

"Still." The fae cleared her throat. "I can't see a single good thing about bringing Venga back to Ambar'ogúl with us. What's to keep him from turning on us the minute Ba'rael snaps her fingers?"

"Well, first of all, I'm not a dog."

Ember jumped and spun in her chair. Venga gazed down at her with his straw between his lips and gulped down more root beer.

"You do not see the full scope of what was done, so I'll tell you." Venga walked between the tables and returned to his seat. The other magicals went back to eating their meals, anticipating the necromancer's story. Ember swallowed and stiffly lowered her hands into her lap. After another long drink, Venga finally put down his cup and let out a contented sigh. "Yes, I crafted the Undoing. Yes, it has had far more drastic effects than I anticipated."

"It's consuming Ambar'ogúl," Cheyenne muttered. "That's pretty drastic."

"It was not meant to go so far." Venga folded his arms. "Once my work was finished, once I'd convinced Ba'rael of the Undoing's efficacy, she sent me here to 'prepare our sister world for the dawning of a new age,' as she put it."

Ember snorted. "Said every genocidal dictator ever."

"I made the crossing," Venga continued. "I convened with the Bull's Head, already very much established on this side. And I fulfilled my purpose here in certain instruction of those loyal to the Crown."

Cheyenne stared. "*You're* the one who brought all that black magic shit across the Border."

"If you mean knowledge of how to craft and utilize it, *Aranél*, then yes. The first of it, at least."

"Okay, now I'm with Ember on this one."

L'zar shushed her. "Let him finish."

Venga blinked. "If they do not wish to hear the rest of it—"

"No, no. Please." Cheyenne gestured for him to continue before folding her arms. "You're building a really strong case for yourself."

Maleshi snorted and wiped her mouth with a napkin.

Venga gazed at the halfling. "I did what I was ordered to do in this world, and when that was finished, the Bull's Head did what *they* were ordered to do. They turned against me, used the knowledge I'd shared with them to siphon my magic into the endowments, and left me at a scene of their destruction to be picked up by the FRoE."

Cheyenne blinked at him. "They framed you."

"And I spent five years in that fell-damn tank because of it."

"Damn." Byrd rubbed his bald head. "That's some next-level betrayal shit right there."

"That is what Ba'rael the Spider does to those with powers greater than her own." Venga stuck his straw in his mouth and guzzled down more root beer as he gazed around the tables of magicals.

"To those she fears," L'zar added and slapped a hand on the table in delight. "Which is exactly what makes you a perfect candidate for escorting Cheyenne back into the Heart."

"And if she dies of terror when she sees me again, I cannot say I'll be disappointed," Venga snarled. "At the very least, I mean to make her piss herself."

Byrd and Lumil burst out laughing, drawing looks from the closest human patrons.

Venga met Cheyenne's gaze and grinned, his tongue flicking out between his teeth despite it no longer looking forked or nearly as threatening. "Perhaps more than that, if the *Aranél* permits."

"Well, let's take that part one step at a time when we get there, huh? If you can scare the Crown enough to make her step down, that's really all we need. But if it comes down to a fight—"

"I cannot involve myself." Venga raised his super-sized soda cup toward the halfling and nodded. "I am aware of the old laws. I'm merely extending a suggestion for *after* the Spider crawls willingly down from her web."

"Sure." Cheyenne nodded. "I don't give a shit about what happens to her afterward."

"Excellent." Venga's green eyes narrowed, and he stuck the straw back into his mouth to gulp down more soda.

"What about the blight, though?" Ember asked.

The goateed magical raised his eyebrows. "The what?"

"Whatever you called it. The Undoing. If you created it, you know how to get rid of it, right?"

"Hmm. Perhaps. I imagine the Undoing has developed its own agenda, more or less. That happens when a necromancer's work is left unchecked for so long without its master."

"But you can help us reverse it."

"I'm not certain it *can* be reversed."

"Oh, yes, it can." Ember leaned across her uneaten burger and pointed at her chest. "I pulled your fucked-up experiment out of a Raug chief to save his life, and I beat it back across a Border portal that wasn't supposed to exist and definitely wasn't supposed to be spewing the blight all over Cheyenne's backyard."

"Technically not *my* backyard."

Ember rolled her eyes. "The point is, it *can* be reversed. It can be healed out of magicals and out of the earth. So if you're coming with us to get revenge on the Spider, you sure as hell better do whatever you can to clean up the mess you left behind."

Venga set his drink gently down on the table and held Ember's gaze. "You are merely one fae."

"No shit. Unfortunately, my magic isn't strong enough to pull a necromancer's poison out of an entire world. This is on you."

"I will try."

Ember scoffed and turned to Cheyenne. "A little help here?"

"Hey, you're doing a pretty decent job all on your own."

"Cheyenne."

The halfling fought back a laugh and shrugged. "What do you want me to say, Em? He said he'll try."

"That's not good enough. He needs to promise."

"I cannot give my word before I've seen what has become of the Undoing," Venga muttered, his root beer now forgotten as he frowned at Ember. "Nor will I make a vow to some fae who seems to think I am a hatchling she can order around."

"'Some fae,' huh?" Ember folded her arms. "Do you know who I am? Why I'm sitting next to this drow who already started the turn of a new Cycle?"

Cheyenne wiped her lips to cover a surprised smile and watched the showdown. *She's pulling out the Nós Aní card. Somehow, I get the feeling that's not threatening to a necromancer.*

Venga stared the fae down and raised his eyebrows. "Enlighten me."

Ember sneered at him. "If you can't figure it out, I don't think your head's in the right place to make the crossing with us. You know, too much time spent in an isolation tank."

"Then promise to give the order," Persh'al muttered as he tapped his cell phone. Every magical at both tables looked at him.

"What order?" Cheyenne asked.

When Persh'al realized everyone was staring at him, he shrugged and slipped his phone back into his pocket. "Fighting about what he is and isn't willing to promise before we even get there is pointless. When Ba'rael steps down and Cheyenne turns her new Cycle, she can give a fell-damn order to anyone, even a necromancer. Problem solved. Can we move on, or what?"

Ember opened her mouth to reply but thought better of it and sat back in her chair again.

"Okay." Cheyenne pointed at Venga. "I agree with everything Ember said, so this is fair warning. I'll order you to clean up the Undoing when we're done with Ba'rael. Sound good?"

Venga stroked his goatee and turned his head to eye her sideways. "As long as it's not the Spider, *Aranél*, I am happy to serve the Crown."

"Good." Cheyenne gently nudged Ember's shoulder. "Taken care of, right?"

"As long as he follows through. Sure."

"Cool." Cheyenne met Persh'al's gaze and nodded. He nodded in return before grabbing his burger again and stuffing what was left of it into his mouth all at once. *Guess it pays to have a blue troll around for breaking up heated discussions. Good to know.*

"Here." L'zar whisked a napkin off the table and offered it to Venga. "You're dripping."

The necromancer grunted and took the napkin before roughly wiping his mouth and chin.

"You know, when all this is over and done with, I would very much like to hear about your work."

Cheyenne tuned out her father's voice and pulled her buzzing phone out of her pocket. "Great."

Ember turned to her and glanced at the screen. "What?"

"It's Sir." Cheyenne grabbed her bottle of water off the table and stood. "I gotta take this. Be right back."

As she headed to the restaurant's door, she heard Byrd sniggering behind her. "Super-private conversation, huh?"

"More like she doesn't want the whole restaurant to hear the guy screaming at her," Ember replied.

CHAPTER SEVENTY-NINE

Cheyenne pushed open the door and stepped onto the sidewalk in front of the restaurant. *Ember's got it down.*

Then she accepted the call and raised the phone to her ear. "That was fast."

"Which goddamn part, halfling? You taking after your lunatic sperm donor of a dad and breaking felons out of Chateau D'rahl, or me smelling the stink of your halfling bullshit all the way from here?"

"Actually, I was expecting a call from you about Colonel Thomas."

"Fuck Colonel Thomas! What kinda fucking joke were you trying to play, leaving those assholes behind?"

Frowning, Cheyenne stepped away from the front door and turned around to look at the other magicals through the window. "Not sure what you're talking about."

"Don't give me that shit. I talked to four goddamn guards at that prison who all said they saw you in there two hours ago."

"Well, yeah, Guy. I'm pretty easy to remember when I walk into a room. Or a prison."

Sir growled on the other end of the line, followed by a clang of something heavy smashing against the wall. "I don't know how the hell you did it, but I *know* you didn't do it alone. You better have a coherent explanation for why a dozen beat-up, bloody, shit-covered magicals that aren't in our records are sitting at the bottom of the dunk tank where Vinny used to be in chains."

"Vinny?"

"The fucking giant lizard with four arms, Cheyenne!"

She forced back a laugh and pulled the phone slightly away from her ear. "Right. You're not gonna like it, but I don't have an explanation."

"I swear on every single strand of hair growing from—"

"Your wife's head? You know, I'm not sure Alice would appreciate being the center of so much swearing, Guy."

"Shut the hell up. Who are the goddamn dipshits in that tank, halfling?"

Cheyenne looked at Corian through the window, and he met her gaze. "Trust me, they're all the kind of criminals you want in that prison."

"Criminals."

"Yeah. And I bet they're really good friends with the same assholes who kidnapped all those kids. You're welcome. Now tell me you have something useful to say while you have me on the phone."

"Shit." Sir grunted, and the clink of ice swirling in a glass came over the line. "I'd rather eat my Aunt Bertha's two-week-old meatloaf than tell you this."

"But I'm right about the colonel," Cheyenne muttered, a small smile blooming on her lips.

"I think you might be onto something, halfling. *Might be.* Don't get the two confused."

"What did you find?"

"It's what found me." Sir took a long sip of what she could only assume was his early-afternoon whiskey. "As soon as I heard about our second escaped convict in the last two weeks, both of which I'm pinning on your halfling ass, by the way, I got a call from Colonel Thomas. He wants to talk to you. In person."

Cheyenne turned away from the restaurant to stare across the street. "No shit."

"No shit." Sir growled something unintelligible into the phone and knocked back his drink with a loud gulp. "The meeting's been scheduled for seven o'clock tonight on base. You better believe he'll be grinding your ass into the floor to figure out what you know about this goddamn prisoner escape. Maybe I'll get in line."

"Honestly, you'll probably be waiting a while."

"Don't fuck this up, Cheyenne. And don't conveniently forget to tell me whatever the hell you find out at this little meeting, you hear me? If you find anything that *proves* your theory, I sure as shit better hear about it."

"Yeah, I hear you."

"Promise me, halfling."

"Hey, I'm not making any promises 'til after I get a good look at the guy." *Great. And now I sound like Venga.*

"Well, make sure you bring your goddamn glasses, then!" With a roar of frustration, Sir slammed the phone down, and the line went dead.

Cheyenne stared at her cell. *Colonel Thomas works fast too, apparently. So now he gets to try to figure out how much I know, and I get to prove he's a traitor asshole who's been selling me out to the Bull's Head the whole damn time.*

The glass door to the burger joint opened, and Corian led the procession of human-disguised magicals out to the sidewalk to join her. "How did *that* conversation go?"

She stuck her phone back into her pocket and folded her arms. "Peachy. How many Crown loyalists did you port into that giant tank to leave as a parting gift?"

The nightstalker shrugged. "All of them."

"All the magicals you guys tortured and locked up in the warehouse basement?"

He leaned in and whispered, "Yes, Cheyenne. All of them. I wanted them off my hands."

"Well, you picked the right way to do it. Better than sending them blind and deaf across the Border or dead."

"We both know I don't need your approval for these types of decisions, kid."

She scoffed. "Obviously."

He held the door open for the rest of their group and nodded. "But I'm glad I have it."

"Yeah, okay." Shaking her head, Cheyenne nodded at Ember floating out of the restaurant, and her smile faded. "You okay, Em?"

"Me? Sure." The fae shrugged. "I'm not a huge fan of walking around outside DC with our new death-magic friend, but whatever."

"Well, if it helps at all, I think it's awesome."

Ember shot her a confused look. "What's awesome?"

"That you jumped into this thing with both feet. That you were about to start threatening the magical who engineered the blight so he'd promise to clean up his mess. Your Healer's showing, Em."

"Very funny." Ember floated past her but couldn't completely hide her smile. "So, how did *that* conversation go?"

"With Sir?" Cheyenne shrugged. "Well, it got me a meeting with the colonel, so I'd say overall, it was fairly productive."

"Wow. That was fast."

"Yeah, that's what I said. Gotta be on base at seven tonight. I was asked for by name, apparently."

Maleshi joined them on the other side of Cheyenne. "Anything you need from us before that happens?"

"You mean besides nobody else getting broken out of jail or sucked into curses or exiled from places where it would really be useful to have them around?" The halfling snorted. "I don't think so, but thanks."

"All right, kid. Well, when you know what needs to happen next, make sure you tell somebody. I hope it goes without saying, but none of us want you heading after the rest of the Bull's Head on your own."

"Oh, come on. I'm not *that* reckless." Cheyenne pursed her lips when Maleshi and Ember gave her skeptical looks. "Anymore. Okay, yeah. I promise I won't go after them on my own."

"That's all I wanted to hear." The general clapped a hand on Cheyenne's shoulder and gave the halfling a little shake. "'Cause I'm really looking forward to taking down as many of them as I can before it's time to go border-hopping again."

"Yeah, me too. And while we're on that topic, I should get back to the apartment. Set up a few fun things to get ready for this meeting, you know?"

"Sure." Maleshi gazed at L'zar and Venga, who were talking and laughing like Ba'rael Verdys' betrayals and the time served in Chateau D'rahl had never happened. "I'll fill everyone in later. Might as well make a clean break while you can." The general stopped in front of a narrow alley between storefronts and summoned a portal into Cheyenne and Ember's apartment. "Good luck with the colonel, kid."

"Well, the chance that I'll have to fight the guy is lookin' pretty slim, but thanks. I'll let you know."

Maleshi turned away from the portal as Cheyenne and Ember moved through it and disappeared.

Cheyenne headed for the iron stairs up to the mini-loft.

Ember hovered behind the couch and watched her friend practically run up the steps. "You obviously already have a plan for this."

"Yep." With a quick punch of the power button, Cheyenne got Glen cycling up to full processing speed and dropped into the desk chair. "If I can find a few golden nuggets of traitor bullshit in the next few hours, I'll at least have a bargaining chip or two."

Ember floated around the couch and sprawled on the cushions. "There's a visual."

"Exactly what I'm hoping for, Em." Cheyenne pulled out her activator and placed it behind her ear before vigorously rubbing her hands together. "I'm so ready to make this asshole squirm."

Ember grabbed the remote off the coffee table, and the flat-screen TV rose out of the entry table with a soft hum. "However you end up doing it, you have my full support."

"Thanks, Em." *Wish I could say I'll be getting rid of Colonel Thomas tonight, but I have a feeling this is a practice run. The guy should've taken pointers from Sir. I don't screw around.*

CHAPTER EIGHTY

The activator guided her every step of the way as she searched the dark web for as much information on Colonel Les Thomas as she could find. *What better place to hide his slimy friendship with O'gúl loyalists, assuming the man's more tech-literate than Sir.* Cheyenne chuckled. *Not very hard.*

Once the activator located Colonel Thomas' personal drive on the FRoE's multiple servers, she stopped to consider what she was about to do. *Somebody should tell them they have a gaping hole in their firewall, but it's not gonna be me.*

She dove into the server and pulled up the IP address and physical location of Colonel Thomas' operating system. *Yep. Right there at the base.*

His system hadn't been used for the last hour, so she poked around in his files to see what she could dig up. The activator lit up in her vision with a flashing yellow light superimposed over the scrolling window of code across a folder labeled *Friends of the Bull.*

"Very cute, Colonel." Cheyenne clicked the file open and was met by three more folders inside, each of them heavily encrypted, but she couldn't focus on reading the folder names or the quickly moving code illuminating the encryption data. The activator let off an annoyingly persistent alarm in her head, not terribly loud but not quiet enough to ignore. As if that wasn't enough, bright red letters flashed across her screen.

Unauthorized access detected. Do not proceed.

"Okay, okay." Cheyenne grimaced and waved her hand in front of her to turn off the activator's ridiculous alarm signal. "Jeez."

"Find something?" Ember asked.

"Just a warning from the activator to—"

A hard, fierce knock came at the front door.

Cheyenne pulled out of Colonel Thomas' desktop system, turned off her monitor, and stood. "We're not expecting anybody, right?"

"Not unless you planned some kinda surprise." Ember sniggered and stared at the TV. "Which honestly wouldn't be that big a surprise if you think about it."

"I didn't." Cheyenne was hurrying down the metal stairs when whoever stood outside their apartment knocked harder and louder. "Whoever it is needs to chill the hell out."

She slipped out of drow form when she reached the front door, slid the deadbolt lock aside, and slowly opened the door to peer into the hall.

"Cheyenne."

Cheyenne narrowed her eyes. "Matthew."

"What are you doing?"

"Hmm. Well, I *was* minding my own business, but now I'm curious why you look like someone found out all your secrets and laid them on the table for the whole world to see."

Their neighbor took a step back and ran a hand through his hair, breathing deeply through his nose. "If you're still pissed at me, I get it. But this is serious."

"It is, huh?" She cocked her head and gave him a fake smile. "What happened?"

Matthew tried to peer around her into the apartment, but she pulled the door toward her to block his view and only opened it again when he gave up. "I got a security alert on my phone, Cheyenne. Someone tried to hack into my uncle's computer."

Oops. Cheyenne raised an eyebrow. "They must not have been very good."

"I built that security system, okay? I know how efficient it is."

Matthew grimaced and stared at the door instead of meeting her gaze. "And it traced the user's IP address right back here."

"No way." Cheyenne's eyes widened, and she decided to pile on the exaggerated surprise. *If he could prove it one hundred percent, he would've kicked me out of the FRoE server. All he has is a general location and a hunch that I'm the only person in this building who knows how to get into tight spaces.* "That's confusing."

"Look, I wouldn't normally say anything, but whatever you did, you didn't cover your tracks very well."

"Hey, I know how to cover my tracks, okay? And I'm telling you right now, I didn't—"

Matthew pulled his phone from his back pocket and lifted it toward the narrow crack in the front door. He stared at her with deadpan skepticism.

Cheyenne blinked quickly and read the information on the screen: her IP address, her name, her address, and a timestamp of her double-click on Colonel Thomas' *Friends of the Bull* folder. *Damn. He's good, or I was hasty and stupid.*

"Please don't deny it again." Matthew's phone went back into his pocket, and he folded his arms, glancing nervously down the hall at the elevators. "This is embarrassing enough."

"Maybe your uncle shouldn't be sticking his lying nose where it doesn't belong. You ever think of that? Same goes for you too, neighbor. You said he was an investor. Conveniently forgot the part where he sits at the top of the damn FRoE pyramid, didn't you?"

Her neighbor's blue eyes flicked back toward her. "What?"

"Colonel Les Thomas, Matthew. He's not *funding* the FRoE, he heads it. Calling a lot of the shots, and I gotta say, he's doing a really shitty job right now."

"That's not right." He took a step back and shook his head. "My uncle retired six years ago. He's not active in anything. Definitely not as a colonel."

"Well, at the very least, he's been actively lying to you."

"No. No way. He's retired, Cheyenne."

"He's really not." She gave him a tight smile and cocked her head. "I honestly don't care whether or not you believe me, but don't say I didn't warn you. You know, when you find out your uncle's been leading a double life, and he runs out of excuses to feed you."

Matthew turned away from her, tried to look inside the apartment again, and pointed at her. "I came here about the hacking, Cheyenne."

"Don't worry about it. I called off my hounds, and you won't get another alarm. Promise."

"Okay." Wrinkling his nose, he gritted his teeth and turned without another word to stalk back across the hall to his apartment.

Cheyenne had her front door shut and locked again before he'd even opened his. "That was seriously weird."

"His own uncle." Ember folded her arms and scowled at the closed front door. "Is he really that freakin' clueless?"

"Maybe." The halfling looked up at her desk in the mini-loft. "Maybe not. It *is* kinda hard to believe the cyber-security genius, Matthew Thomas, couldn't pull any of that information up on his own."

"That'd leave something of a mark on his reputation." Tilting her head, Ember settled back against the armrest of the couch and shrugged. "Then again, who thinks they have a reason to vet their own family members?"

"Yeah, fair point." Cheyenne drummed her fingers on her thighs and scanned their apartment. "Hypothetical neighbor ignorance aside, the only thing I care about right now is that I can't get into the colonel's computer before our little chat tonight."

"You don't think you can talk circles around him until he spills his guts about the Bull's Head without even knowing it?"

"Ha. I like how confident you are." Cheyenne stepped across the living room and slumped into one of the black leather recliners. "I probably *could* do that, but I need proof this time around, Em. Hard evidence that Les Thomas is giving classified FRoE details to the O'gúl loyalists and actively funding their bullshit with the war machines."

"Okay. Then you could sneak into his office when he's not there and poke around in his computer physically, right?"

"I don't think me being at the base after hours without a good reason to stick around is gonna go over very well with any of the higher-ups. Even Sir." Cheyenne cranked the lever on the recliner and pushed the chair as far back as it would go. "But I don't need to touch his computer."

Ember sighed. "You're gonna try to hack it again, aren't you?"

"Yep. Not from Glen, though."

"Okay, you lost me."

Cheyenne chuckled and spread her arms. "Hey, if I'm standing in his office and reading his files with the activator, there's no other system involved. It's technically not hacking into anything."

The fae's mouth opened in realization. "You're right. That's more like borrowing someone else's computer to send an email."

"I'll get him, Em. Might take a little longer than I wanted, but this meeting won't be totally useless. That's for damn sure."

CHAPTER EIGHTY-ONE

At 6:54 p.m., Cheyenne parked her dinged-up Panamera in the FRoE compound's parking lot and didn't bother locking the thing. Instead, she pulled out her phone and texted Rhynehart as she headed for the front doors.

Got called in for a meeting about the missing lizard. Probably a good idea for you to stay away from home base for a while. Shit might get pretty weird.

She watched her phone until the text was sent, then stuck it back in her pocket and opened the first glass door into the compound. *If he doesn't know what that means right away, I can't do anything to help him.*

The second she stepped inside the front lobby with all the empty cubicles, she found Sir standing in front of the hallway on the left. He scowled at her, arms folded. "You're late."

"I'm on time, and you know it." Cheyenne headed in and grinned when he nodded at the hall behind him. "So I get to have a little sit-down with the colonel. Making me do all the heavy lifting for you, huh?"

Sir glanced quickly around and grimaced in irritation. "We're not having this conversation here or now, halfling, so you can fuck right off into his office. First two left turns, and the elevators are at the end of the hall. He's on the third floor."

"A rain check, then." She shot him a syrupy smile and walked past him. "That'll be a fun talk."

"Fat fucking chance," he grumbled and stormed across the lobby.

Cheyenne followed the fairly simple directions to Colonel Thomas' office. The halls were empty of FRoE agents, as were the elevators. Almost the entire third floor was dark, except for one office on the left at the very end.

Still might be a chance this is a setup. If it is, I'm pretty sure I can handle a few FRoE officers trying to take me down all together. If it comes to that. And Sir gets to skip out on the whole thing. Don't wanna spike his blood pressure.

Her black Vans moved silently across the carpeted hallway of the mostly dark, mostly empty third floor. The door to Colonel Les Thomas' office was wide open, spilling warm yellow light on the opposite wall. Cheyenne stuck the activator behind her ear and slipped into drow mode before she reached the office. *Just so this asshole knows exactly who he's dealing with when I step inside.*

She turned the corner into the office and found herself in a room very much like Bianca's personal study. Clearing her throat, she knocked firmly on the open door but didn't expect much in response.

Colonel Thomas sat behind the massive oak desk at the far end of the office, his arms folded and one ankle crossed over the opposite knee. "Cheyenne Summerlin, I presume?"

"Colonel." She stuck her hands into the pockets of her trenchcoat and strolled casually into the room. "A little birdie told me you wanted to have a chat. Face to face."

The colonel snorted. "More like a screaming, cursing birdie, but I get the point. Please, take a seat." He gestured at the two leather captain's chairs in front of his desk.

Cheyenne shook her head. "I'll stand, thanks. This won't be a long conversation."

"Really?" Colonel Thomas opened the center drawer of his desk and pulled out a tobacco pipe and a book of matches. "Why's that?"

"Because you want me to tell you about the *other* break-in at Chateau D'rahl, and I can't help you."

The man tamped a pinch of tobacco into his pipe, then struck a match and puffed as the dried leaf strips caught. He shook out the match and set it gently on his desk. "Can't or won't?"

"Not much of a difference when they have the same result."

Les Thomas chuckled and puffed on his pipe again. "How's L'zar?"

He's testing me, but I've been perfecting my poker face since I was eight. "You'd get a more accurate answer if you asked him yourself."

"So, you don't know where he is?"

"Right now? No. Your fellow officer asked about him the last time I was called in for a meeting."

"Sounds like you have an issue with answering the same question more than once."

"It's a waste of everyone's time because the answers haven't changed." Cheyenne raised an eyebrow and scanned the code the activator brought up in her vision. Every time she glanced at the colonel's computer sitting off to the side of his desk, a new prompt revealed itself to dig deeper. *Helps that this thing jumped right onto FRoE wi-fi. I don't even have to see the screen.*

"Well then, let's move away from L'zar Verdys, shall we?" Thomas' executive desk chair creaked when he leaned back in it. "I wanted to talk to you about the break-in this afternoon anyway."

"So I heard." With a mere thought, Cheyenne moved the visual her activator fed her to center over the top of the colonel's head instead of on his screen. *And there's that encrypted file. Time to dig in.* "I'm surprised this is a one-on-one meeting, Colonel. How come *you're* the only one who wants to talk to me about this other little mishap?"

"Ah." The man blew a thin trail of smoke from between thin lips. "We're more concerned about the security at Chateau D'rahl than the prisoner who slipped past it this time around. He has no magic, as I understand it."

"Hmm." Cheyenne cocked her head. "Then it must be pretty awful security." The activator flashed quickly in her vision, sending scrolling code across the top half of Colonel Thomas' forehead before the message she'd been waiting for flared in bright yellow letters:

Full system scan complete. File Folder Friends of the Bull download successful.

Gotcha, Colonel.

"That's the thing, though, Ms. Summerlin." He rocked back and forth in his swiveling leather chair. "In 2000, after L'zar Verdys escaped the confines of his cell at Chateau D'rahl and surprised us all by returning to custody three days later, I personally headed the team that designed and integrated the prison-wide security upgrades, so as you can imagine, I'm intimately familiar with the way that prison operates when it comes to assessing potential threats. There's nothing wrong with the security."

Cheyenne gave him a pert smile and flicked her fingers at her side to wipe away the activator's scrolling code from her vision. "Except for the second prisoner escape in the last two weeks."

"This wasn't a solo attempt, Ms. Summerlin. While L'zar apparently finds it amusing to test our patience with his antics, it's impossible for an inmate to break out of Chateau D'rahl on their own. Especially an inmate who was brought into custody without magic or the ability to use it. Unless they had help."

"Huh. Maybe L'zar helped him."

Colonel Thomas tilted his head toward the tip of his pipe held loosely in his hand. He puffed three times and smacked his lips. "Where were *you* this afternoon when the prisoner escaped?"

Yep. He's fishing. Persh'al wiped all the security cameras. Cheyenne gazed around the room and assumed her best nonchalant expression. "I'm not sure, Colonel. When exactly *did* he escape?"

"The system alarm activated at 1:13 p.m."

"Okay. I was at my apartment in Richmond. I got home from teaching a VCU undergrad class at about twelve-thirty. Feel free to look me up there if you haven't already. I didn't leave my apartment again until I headed here for this stimulating exchange of useless information."

"Is that so?" Thin plumes of smoke rose above the colonel's head, dampening the light.

Cheyenne clicked her tongue. "You know, if my apartment building ever thought to install security cameras in the hallways, I guess you'd have proof. Not that I'm advocating for security cameras on my floor. There are only two apartments up there. And I enjoy my privacy as much as the next halfling, you know?"

"I'm sure." He scanned her with narrowed eyes.

If he knows about his nephew living right across the hall from me, he'll find that proof and lay off the hunt. Matthew's cameras don't show me stepping in and out of my living room through nightstalker portals. Points for a nosy neighbor with way too much free time. I guess.

The colonel looked down at a piece of paper on his otherwise pristine desk and touched it briefly with a fingertip. "You've spent a lot of time in the field with Agent Rhynehart, as I understand it. Is that correct?"

Cheyenne almost laughed. "Yeah. He's a real shithole, too. He the one who put it in your ear to bring me in and try to interrogate me again?"

"Would it matter, Ms. Summerlin?"

"Not really. I'm keeping a running list of all the times Agent Rhynehart's thrown me under the bus. Part of me wonders why I stick around to help you guys."

The man's lips twitched into a smile devoid of amusement. "As it stands, perhaps that's because we still have plenty to offer each other in this working relationship. I think you'd agree."

"I don't know. I've never offered you anything, but if you're speaking for the FRoE in general, then sure. Maybe."

He sighed. "It's been a pleasure, Cheyenne. Do let us know if you hear from your father or any other convicted prisoners from Chateau D'rahl. It's in your best interests to continue cooperating with us to the best of your ability, you understand."

That almost sounded like a threat. Cheyenne dipped her head. "It's perfectly clear, Colonel. Have a nice night."

She spun, stalked out of his office, and headed down the hall to the elevators again. *Okay, that came a little too close for comfort. Even with tampered security footage, the guards still saw me at the prison. And Rhynehart. But it doesn't mean shit if nobody can prove it.*

The elevator doors opened, and she stepped inside before stabbing the button to close them again. Then she pulled up a summary view of the encrypted folder she'd snagged from Colonel Les Thomas' personal desktop. *I'm the only one with proof. Just gotta crack this baby and decide how I wanna use it.*

CHAPTER EIGHTY-TWO

The second Cheyenne re-entered her apartment, Ember bombarded her with questions about the meeting. The halfling gave her friend a distracted summary before heading back up to the mini-loft.

"And he let you walk out of his office. Just like that."

"Yeah, Em. If we hadn't had Persh'al for our prison-break adventure today, I'd probably be telling you a different story right now. Or maybe no story. Who knows?"

Ember grinned. "You know, that troll's all right."

"Yeah. The troll's all right. Les Thomas thinks I had something to do with the great escape. He brought up Rhynehart too." Cheyenne snorted and turned on her monitor before sitting in her chair. "He's probably shitting himself, wondering how the hell he's gonna pin either of us down when it's hearsay from a few FRoE guards who couldn't even stop a magicless scaleback from breaking out of a tank."

Ember draped her arm over the back of the couch and laughed. "It's enough to piss anyone off."

"He'll have a lot more than that to be pissed off about when I'm done. I just need a little time to open up all his files, and then it's game over, Colonel Thomas."

"You're looking awfully proud of yourself."

Cheyenne peered through the iron bars of the rail around the mini-loft and grinned at her *Nós Ani*. "You know what, Em? I *am* proud. I walked into a mostly civil meeting with a guy I'm already ninety-nine-percent sure is responsible for all my issues with the Bull's Head, and I didn't lose my shit. See? Totally possible for me to handle something delicately first without blowing anything up."

"Uh-huh." Ember tried to fight back a laugh. "Tell me you're not looking forward to blowing stuff up, though, and I *will* call you a liar."

"Come on." Cheyenne scoffed. "I'm always down to blow stuff up. You know that."

While Ember turned her latest show back on, Cheyenne selected every command the activator offered to sync Colonel Thomas' down-loaded files onto Glenn's drives. *Time to break your secrets wide open, Colonel. I hope they're good.*

She sent the encrypted files into the Bunker and gave her custom program as long as it needed to run the decryption and scan everything for malware or any hidden cyber-landmines.

Twenty minutes later, the Bunker's notification popped up with the all-clear. Cheyenne rubbed her hands together. "Here we go."

The first three files held the same information Matthew had given them, more or less: names of magicals, locations, and when they had their first meeting with Colonel Thomas. Cheyenne skimmed through the written accounts of those in-person meetings, which pretty much corroborated what Matthew had told them. *Okay, but I don't give a shit about Les hooking his nephew up with the Bull's Head. That's old news at this point. Show me something I can use.*

Her activator skimmed through the file content and flagged the information she wanted in under two minutes. Cheyenne clicked through each suggested file source and went right to the activator's search results. "Holy shit."

"That sounds like the good kind," Ember called from the couch. "It's the good kind, right?"

"I mean, I found what I wanted, so that's a plus." Cheyenne scrolled through the files, her mouth falling open. "I was fucking right."

"The FRoE's been playing you this whole time?"

Cheyenne forced herself to look away from her computer. "Almost."

"Okay, that's not what I expected."

"It's not the whole FRoE, Em, just the colonel. I've got lists of every meeting he's had with them. All the login and security information for the private fucking server he's been sharing with the Bull's Head—courtesy of his ridiculously accommodating nephew, of course. Jesus, this guy's in deep."

"It's just him? All on his own?" Ember shrugged with a sheepish grimace. "I mean, I at least figured Sir would've had *something* to do with it."

"I don't have anything on Major Guy Carson." Cheyenne shook her head and let out a wry chuckle. "And I don't really give a shit about the major right now. At the very least, Les Thomas has been tracking *me* using old-school tech from the other side, or he was until I came back from Ambar'ogúl with my very own activator that isn't supposed to work over here."

"Damn." Ember lifted the remote and turned off her show before tossing the thing back onto the coffee table. "What, he just stopped keeping tabs on you now that you have the activator over here?"

"That's what it looks like, yeah. Nothing from the Crown, though. I don't know what I'd do if a human was dealing with Ba'rael Verdys from the other side."

"Ugh." Ember shuddered.

"But everything the FRoE has on me in their stupid system was fed to the Bull's Head. Locations. Assignments. Shit, even my mom and her address are in here."

"Okay, that's a reason to blow shit up."

"Yeah, but I have something even better, Em." Cheyenne tapped her monitor and grinned. "Looks like Colonel Thomas set up an emergency meeting with those assholes this morning. Ha. It's on Sunday."

"Whoa." Ember clenched her eyes shut and took a deep breath. "So, we have four days to figure out how we wanna deal with this human traitor batting for the wrong team."

"More than enough time. We still have a little over a week to put everything together for the Crown before we make the crossing again. We need to lay low until Sunday, crash the colonel's private party with those idiots who don't even know Ba'rael's on her way out, then skip on over into a different world and overthrow a drow monarch. We're golden."

"Oh, yeah. Sure." Ember rolled her eyes and chuckled. "Piece of cake."

Cheyenne shrugged. "I mean, really, though."

"Actually, that does sound a lot simpler and easier than most of the weird crap we've done in the last week."

"Exactly, Em." Removing the activator from behind her ear, Cheyenne dumped all the stolen files back into the Bunker to keep them hidden and powered Glen down. *Don't want our nosy neighbor getting too nosy with my IP address and a phone call or two from his uncle about a Goth chick in his apartment building.*

Ember rose from the couch and floated into the kitchen. "I'm kinda feeling it right now, but I should double-check just in case. This is totally something worth celebrating a little, right?"

"For sure." The halfling hurried down the stairs, her black Vans clanging on the metal grates. "I mean, not as celebration-worthy as finally wiping out the Bull's Head and getting Colonel Les Thomas off my back, but this is good, Em. Like, we're finally figuring stuff out before we go and level the playing field."

Ember snorted. "More like turn the whole playing field into a massive smoking crater, but I get it."

"Very funny." Cheyenne joined her friend in the kitchen. "You were saying something about celebrating?"

"Basically, I'm saying screw takeout." Ember opened the fridge and pulled out two pints of ice cream. "Chocolate Chip Cookie Dough or Double Fudge Mint?"

Cheyenne barked a laugh. "And I thought choosing someone to take my place as the next O'gúl Crown was hard."

"Laugh it up, smartass." Ember flicked her hand at the cabinet. The door swung open in a burst of purple light, and a large glass mixing bowl sailed into the fae's outstretched hand. "Then I'll choose for you. We're going half-and-half."

"Very nice."

With another flick of Ember's hand, both lids popped off the pints of ice cream. Two spoons flew from the suddenly open drawer, and the fae snatched one of them out of the air without looking. The other dug into the pint of cookie dough ice cream, and Ember pointed the spoon at her friend. "And I'm not afraid to use it."

"So, I'm gonna have to get used to things flying all over the apartment now, huh?"

"Only if you want ice cream for dinner."

"I think I can deal with it." Chuckling, Cheyenne watched her friend scoop heaping spoonfuls of mint ice cream into the bowl first, her tongue poking between her pink-tinted lips. "What are the chances of you teaching me your flying-spoon spells?"

"Zero, halfling." Ember dropped her spoon in the bowl and got to work scooping out half the other pint on top of it. "You said it yourself. We both know how much you like blowing shit up, and I'm not sure flying spoons are worth the trouble."

"You drive a hard bargain, Healer."

Ember snorted and slid the bowl of mixed ice cream across the kitchen island to Cheyenne. "Shut the fuck up and eat your dinner."

With a warning glance at the halfling, she scooped up both half-full pints and took them with her to the couch.

Cheyenne ran her fingers over her lips to wipe off the smile and snatched up the bowl and the spoon. "Yes, ma'am."

***

Two hours after slipping beneath the black satin sheets on her bed, Cheyenne dreamt she was in her mom's house again, walking down the hall and passing the open French doors into Bianca's bedroom. She stopped to peer into the room at the crisply made king-sized bed like she had two nights ago, only her mom was in the bed this time.

Bianca's ratted, tangled hair lay scattered across her shoulders, framing her face in an unkempt halo of auburn curls. The woman was sitting up, her legs covered by the thick quilt. Her hands rested on top of the quilt beside her thighs, making her look peaceful until Cheyenne noticed the bunched fabric in her mom's tightly clenched fists.

The worst part was that Bianca Summerlin looked like shit.

"Cheyenne," she whispered fiercely, her eyes wide and glistening with fearful tears.

"Mom?" *This is a dream. It has to be a dream. No way would she let me see her like this.* Cheyenne stepped into the bedroom without meaning to. "Are you okay?"

"Cheyenne, help me." Bianca started to tremble, her knuckles white with the fierceness of her grip on the quilt. "I won't make it without you. Help me, Cheyenne." She swallowed and looked desperately around her bedroom, her eyes flicking left and right as she panted. "You have to hurry."

"I'm right here." Cheyenne took another halting step toward her mother's bed. "What's wrong?"

"I'm begging you, Cheyenne. Help me. Right now. Come right now!"

The sudden buzz of Cheyenne's cell phone on her bedside table jerked her out of the dream. Her eyes flew open, and she blinked in the darkness against the bright light behind the screen. "What the fuck kinda dream is *that*?"

Groaning, she rolled over beneath the sheets and slapped at her phone. It took her three tries before she picked it up and pulled it over to her. The single word on the screen woke her up the rest of the way: **Home**.

"Shit." Cheyenne answered the call and propped the phone against her ear. "Hello?"

"Cheyenne, sweetheart."

"Eleanor?"

"I'm so sorry to call you so late, but I didn't know what else to do. Something's very wrong."

"Whoa, okay. Slow down a second." Cheyenne pushed up off the pillows and gripped the phone tighter to be sure she didn't drop it. "What happened?'

"It's Bianca. Honestly, beyond the fact that it's obviously bad, honey, I have no idea *what* to tell you."

"Well, try, okay? Please?"

Eleanor took a shuddering breath. "At first I thought it was a seizure again, or a fever. Then these weird designs showed up. They're on her *skin*, Cheyenne. There's no way in hell I'm calling a human doctor to make a house call for something like this."

"No, no. That's probably not the best option." Cheyenne blinked furiously and slapped her cheek to clear the cobwebs of sleep.

"Are you all right?"

"Just waking up. Is there anything else happening? With Mom?"

"Well, not that I can *see*, but I have a feeling that doesn't really mean anything at this point. Cheyenne, I need you up here to tell me what to do. *We* need you."

"Yeah. Yeah, I'm coming." Cheyenne threw the purple velvet bedspread off and swung her legs over the side of the canopy bed. "I'll get there faster if I have Corian's help."

"Sweetheart, there were over a dozen magic people sitting at our table last night. I think we're past the point of walking on eggshells when it comes to bringing them into the house again. Just get here as soon as you can."

"Give me a few minutes. Thanks for calling, Eleanor."

"Well, don't thank me just yet. See you soon."

Shit.

CHAPTER EIGHTY-THREE

Practically launching herself out of bed, Cheyenne dialed Corian's number, turned on speakerphone, and tossed her cell onto the bed as she darted to her black dresser.

He answered on the fifth ring.

"I normally don't get much sleep, Cheyenne," he croaked, "but you call me on the one night when—"

"Something's wrong with Bianca." She shook out a pair of relatively clean black jeans and slammed her pants drawer shut with her hip. "I need you to port me to her place."

"What?" He cleared his throat. "What happened?"

"Weird designs on her skin, Corian. That's straight from Eleanor. How much you wanna bet they're O'gúl runes in the shape of that drow bitch's curse?"

"I'll be right there." He hung up, and Cheyenne pulled on a blood-red shirt with black satin strips crossing the chest.

After she finished tugging on her clothes, she snatched a hair tie off her dresser, twirled her hair back into a loose bun, and grabbed her trenchcoat off the bench at the foot of the bed. Her phone went into her back pocket, keys jingling in her coat as she stormed out of the room. She didn't bother to shut the door behind her.

"Em?" A low groan came from her *Nós Aní*'s bedroom. "I know it's late, but I'm yelling 'cause there's something wrong with Bianca."

"What?"

"I'm about to leave, so if you—"

Ember shrieked, and a gust of purple light flared beneath her bedroom door. Cheyenne raced to the fae's room and flung open the door just as Ember found her voice again.

"What the fuck's the matter with you, asshole?" Ember pointed at the door but glared at Corian, who was standing in the middle of her bedroom. Her other hand clutched her sheets to her chin.

The nightstalker shrugged. "Figured I'd make sure you both were awake."

"Nobody gave you permission to pop into my personal space whenever you think it's a fun fucking idea! Get out!" Ember waved her hand at him, and another burst of purple light propelled Corian backward through the doorway. The bedroom door slammed shut, and Corian staggered across the kitchen.

Cheyenne blinked at him. "You think you're really cute, don't you?"

"It was an honest intention to help us get moving a little faster, kid." He rubbed his chest and grimaced. "A naked fae doesn't interest me in the least under the best of circumstances."

"Right. Good thing we don't have a cat."

Corian glared at her, then Ember's door flew open again and cracked against the wall. She floated into the kitchen and flipped him the middle finger with both hands. "Don't ever wake me up like that again."

He dipped his head. "I'm sorry. Can we go now?"

Ember gestured for him to continue, and the nightstalker conjured a portal straight to the upstairs hallway of Bianca Summerlin's house.

The French doors were open just like in her dream, and for a second, Cheyenne thought it was Bianca sitting up in the huge bed when she walked through the door. *No, that's Eleanor.*

"We're here."

"Oh!" Eleanor jumped off the side of the bed and turned around, her hand tightly gripping Bianca's pale, limp fingers. "That *was* fast."

"Not something we can take our time with, huh? Sorry if I scared you."

"Sweetheart, everything's scaring me right now, and somehow, I'm still alive." The housekeeper pulled Cheyenne into a fierce hug, then released her and swallowed thickly. "Take a look for yourself. I have no idea what to make of this, but maybe the three of you can put your heads together and figure something out. Is this everyone?"

"For now." Corian nodded and stepped over to the unconscious Bianca, lying on the right side of the bed. "May I?"

"I should hope so." Eleanor's voice rose in volume and shrillness. "Otherwise, what would be the point?"

"It's okay." Cheyenne set a hand on the housekeeper's shoulder as Corian approached her mom. "We'll figure it out."

"Oh, look at me." Eleanor clasped her trembling hands together and clenched them hard. "Like a scared little girl."

"You're not running away screaming," Ember added. "That gets you serious points."

The woman chuckled weakly.

"Cheyenne." Corian turned from Bianca's side and nodded for the halfling to join him. "You need to see this."

Shit. Cheyenne and Ember exchanged tense glances, then the halfling joined Corian at the bedside. "Do you know what's happening?"

"Well, why don't you tell *me* what it looks like?" He peeled back the top layer of the bedspread and the neckline of Bianca's nightshirt.

Cheyenne grimaced. "Looks exactly like I expected, honestly. Only I didn't think the O'gúl runes showing up on my mom's skin would have a cattle-brand effect."

Eleanor gasped behind her and covered her mouth with both hands.

"Sorry, Eleanor. I'm processing."

The woman staggered back, reaching blindly behind her until she lowered herself into a satin-striped armchair the same color as the bedspread.

Ember joined the other magicals at the bedside and bit her lip as she studied the raw, blazing red runes growing darker and more pronounced across Bianca's flesh. "So, what does this mean?"

Corian tapped his lips with his thumb and forefinger. "If I had to guess, I'd say—"

"Shit. What's happening? Mom?" Cheyenne grabbed Bianca's hand as the woman seized on the mattress. The halfling pressed her mom's shoulders and collarbone down lightly, then grabbed her arm again and looked at Corian with frightened eyes. "*Fix* this!"

"I don't—"

Ember shoved him aside and took his place beside the bed before pressing both hands on Bianca's chest. She closed her eyes, took a deep breath, and focused as much of her healing magic as she could into Bianca Summerlin's being.

Cheyenne's mom jerked again, her head twitching from side to side, and small choking sounds spilling from her parted lips. Ember frowned and pressed harder against the woman's chest before snatching her hands back with a hiss. "Ow!"

"What?" Cheyenne leaned over her mom. "Em, please start talking."

"The invisible hot iron is apparently contagious." Ember opened her hands to reveal fresh O'gúleesh symbols burned into her palms, but they faded within seconds. "But they only stick to her."

"Wait." Cheyenne peeled her mom's silk nightshirt farther down along her collarbone and almost couldn't find her breath. "Oh, fuck."

Corian saw the new symbol appearing swiftly below Bianca's collarbone. The four-pointed star magically branded into the woman's flesh was streaked with black instead of red.

"Why is the Verdys bloodline's symbol showing up on my mom's body, Corian?"

"It's another message, kid."

"Meaning *what?*"

The nightstalker's silver eyes darted over Bianca's body. "We have to move. It has to be now."

"Now is *not* the time for fucking riddles!" Cheyenne's eyes flared with purple light as the Nimlothar seed bound to her lent its power to her fury.

He glanced quickly at her and bowed his head. "If you want to save your mother, Cheyenne, you're making the crossing again. Now."

"As in, the crossing straight into Hangivol?"

"The very one. Our two-week timeline has been shortened by a bit more than half. Let's go." Corian turned to summon a new portal.

"Shit."

Ember smoothed the hair away from Bianca's sweat-slickened forehead and closed her eyes again. "At least let me help her settle. Just a little peace and calm, right?"

"Yeah, Em." Cheyenne looked at Eleanor, who leaned forward in the armchair with her fingers steepled against her lips. "Thanks."

Golden light bloomed under Ember's hand and seeped into and around Bianca's face. The woman's furrowed eyebrows and tightly clenched jaw relaxed, and her residual trembling ceased. "There you go."

Ember stepped away from the bed, and Cheyenne grabbed her mom's hand before leaning over the unconscious woman. She kissed Bianca's cheek and whispered in her ear, "I'm gonna fix this, Mom. I promise. I'll make sure you're safe."

"We need to go now." Corian said it firmly, but he dipped his head and took a sharp breath. "I'm sorry."

"Don't be. I get it." Cheyenne squeezed her mom's hand a final time, then let her go and turned to the others. "Eleanor—"

"*I'm* not going anywhere." The housekeeper shooed them off with both hands. "You have a job to do, sweetheart, and so do I. You're not the only one who prides herself on not giving up."

Cheyenne tried to smile, felt the grimace on her lips instead, and gave up. "We'll be back soon. Couple days at the most."

"And after that," Corian added, "you should see a marked improvement. Take care." He gestured at the newly opened portal.

The halfling looked over her shoulder to see Eleanor approaching Bianca's bedside again, then she stepped through the shimmering window of light into Persh'al's warehouse.

"You okay?" Ember muttered.

"Yeah, Em. I'm just wondering if we're even ready for this."

Corian shot her a sharp look. "Don't tell me you're worried about missing one of your classes."

"Fuck my classes. This is my *mom*. I'm talking about *us*. The terms for Ba'rael. Everything we thought we still had ten days to prepare for."

"I can tell you Venga has been *very* helpful." Corian peered around the main room of the warehouse as small lights clicked on in corners and over makeshift beds. "Trust me, kid. We're as ready as we'll ever be."

"Anyone wanna explain why the hell you're throwing a party at two-thirty in the fell-damn morning?" Lumil grumbled, pushing out of a sleeping bag beneath Persh'al's computer tables. Her yellow hair was plastered over her eyes, and she smacked it away with a floppy hand. "What gives?"

"Time to move on the Heart, goblin."

"Very funny, nightstalker. Try that joke again when it's not the middle of the night."

The door to L'zar's small box of a private room flew open with a bang, and the drow thief stormed into the center of the warehouse. "What happened?"

"It's Bianca." Cheyenne forced her voice into a volume resembling reasonable and swallowed. "The curse is getting worse."

"It's scarring her, brother." Corian tapped his chest. "With the four-pointed star now too."

L'zar's golden eyes widened, and he cast his daughter a sharp glance. "Then it has to be now."

"Yeah, that's why we're here."

"And you're ready?"

Cheyenne puffed out half a breath in disbelief and shrugged. "As soon as you hand me what I need to push Ba'rael off her damn throne, yeah."

"Good." He looked her up and down, then clapped his hands together. "Everybody up!"

His voice boomed through the warehouse, magically intensified to a volume that made the bare lightbulbs hanging from the ceiling sway and dust rain down on the cement floor. All around them, the rebel magicals camping in Persh'al's warehouse roused themselves out of sleep.

"Endaru's balls, L'zar!" Persh'al half-climbed, half-fell off the sagging couch against the wall behind his computer table. "It's too early for—"

"It's time, Persh'al." L'zar nodded. "We're moving up the turning of the new Cycle to tonight. Cheyenne needs all of you, so pull your shit together and fulfill your vows as they were meant to be fulfilled."

Byrd snarled and slapped both hands on the cement floor before pushing himself unsteadily to his feet. "I knew you were impatient, drow, but this is—"

"This isn't about me." L'zar ran a hand down his face and turned slightly away from the others, then gestured at Cheyenne. "Ask her."

"It's about Bianca," Cheyenne muttered. "The Crown's curse got worse. A lot worse. We have to bring Ba'rael down now before my mom—" She swallowed and couldn't finish the sentence. *That's not gonna happen, Cheyenne. Pull your shit together and make sure that doesn't happen.*

Ember put a hand on the halfling's shoulder and gave it a little squeeze. "She'll be okay. We'll make sure she's okay."

"I know, Em. Thanks."

Corian stuck his phone back in his pocket, and two seconds later, Maleshi appeared through a portal. "How you doin', Cheyenne?"

The halfling shook her head. "How do you think?"

"Good. If you said you were prepared for this, I'd think you'd lost your mind."

"Not sure I haven't."

A low growl rose from the corner of the warehouse opposite L'zar's room, then Venga's hunched form rose from a pile of thin woolen blankets. He saw everyone gathered on the warehouse floor and snorted. "And here I thought I would have to wait."

"Not anymore, old friend." L'zar smoothed his hair away from his face and nodded, staring at the cement floor. "Which portal will you take?"

Venga chuckled, hiking up his loose jeans with two scaly hands and scratching viciously under an armpit with a third. "You say that as if there were a shortage of options, Weaver."

"Technically, there is." Maleshi folded her arms. "The portal leading into the Heart was destroyed, and the portal ridge the Bull's Head used as a smuggling port is still down. I checked."

"So, no more secret portals to Ambar'ogúl." Cheyenne rubbed her forehead and turned in a tight circle. "Look, I know it was a sore topic last time because L'zar was with us, but now he can't make the crossing again. Our only option is one of the reservations, right?"

The warehouse fell silent. Then Venga burst out laughing and slapped the scaly belly showing beneath his unzipped leather jacket. "Indeed!"

Ember pressed her lips together and stared at the scaleback. "Like I said, total mad scientist."

"I find it very amusing, fae. The organization trying to keep all us magicals in line, trying to keep us away from the Border, is the very same institution that will fall if we do not deceive them for this."

Byrd snorted. "More like you're gettin' off at the idea of stickin' it to your jailors. Am I right or what, scaleback?"

Venga grinned, his forked tongue flickering between his lips. "Perhaps that plays a part in it. A small part."

"So, which rez will it be?" Cheyenne asked. "The only one I really know is Rez 38."

"It's as good as any." Corian sniffed and stepped away from the group to summon a portal into the FRoE regulated reservation for O'gúleesh refugees from the other side.

Only this time, we're the ones hopping across that portal at the edge of a cliff. That'll be fun.

"Cheyenne." L'zar turned halfway to her, his golden eyes roaming everywhere but her face, and crooked his finger. "A moment, if you will."

"Sure." Cheyenne exchanged confused glances with Ember but followed her father to the other side of the warehouse. "What is it?"

"A few necessities for your journey. If all goes according to plan, I imagine this will be your last crossing for quite some time."

"Well, nobody's exiled me with a curse just yet."

"Yes. Very funny. Wait here." He darted into his tiny bedroom in a blur of white and gray, then reappeared in another burst of air where he'd just stood. "The Darkglass, of course. We went through a bit of trouble to procure this."

Cheyenne cocked her head. "Just a bit."

A humorless chuckle escaped L'zar as he lifted the O'gúl case of black metal and glass to her. "I took the liberty of making it travel-sized for you. It's what this device carries that's important."

She reached for the miniaturized Darkglass with both hands and couldn't help but stare at the pulsing white light suspended at its center. "That's the metal star you made of—"

"Neros' magic, yes." L'zar bowed his head as he released the device. "Our little visit to your cousin wasn't everything I'd hoped it would be, but it wasn't fruitless, either."

Cheyenne swallowed and turned the Darkglass over in her hands. "What do I do with this?"

"Ah. Think of it as an O'gúl voodoo doll." He gave her a thin-lipped smile. "Significantly more advanced but essentially the same premise."

"You're telling me to torture Neros with this thing?"

"No, no, no. This is blackmail, Cheyenne. With everything else in your favor, I should think it highly unnecessary for you to use the Darkglass. Ba'rael will know what this is and what it does. You won't have to say a thing. Just make sure she sees it."

"Okay." Cheyenne tucked the shrunken Darkglass carefully into the pocket of her trenchcoat and shrugged. "What about the terms?"

"Yes, of course." Clasping his hands behind his back, L'zar bowed his head and cleared his throat. "There's the Darkglass, naturally. And the fact that we found her son before she realized he could be found. Tell the Spider she is to step down immediately and remove herself from Hangivol, never to return. The rest of our world is fair game for her after that, though it's a fitting punishment for her crimes in many ways." His lips twitched into a morbid smirk. "She hates Ambar'ogúl almost as much as I do, and she has far fewer friends."

Cheyenne blinked at her father. "It took you a week to come up with that three-item list?"

"Hmm. Be sure to mention the last Nimlothar in the Heart. She receives no alms from that tree, Cheyenne. That must be made perfectly clear."

"No touching the tree or taking anything from it. Got it."

"And be sure to offer her *Nós Aní* the option of remaining in Hangivol as part of your council once you turn your new Cycle."

Cheyenne frowned. "Who's her *Nós Aní?*"

L'zar's characteristically sly grin spread slowly across his lips. "Ruuv'i."

"Seriously? The other *drow?*" She shook her head. "I thought he was her husband or something."

"The O'gúl equivalent of it, yes. Surely it doesn't surprise you that my sister would bind another drow to her for eternity, both by magic and by law. He's the father of her child, Cheyenne, but as her *Nós Aní*, he can never rule as the O'gúl Crown."

"Christ. And Ruuv'i agreed to that?"

"He had little choice in the matter. As part of your terms, you will be offering him a rather weighty decision." The drow thief stroked his hairless chin and tilted his head from side to side. "If I had to put money on it, I'd say Ruuv'i will gladly accept the new Crown's offer to remain in the only home he's ever known *without* Ba'rael commanding his every move, and that will isolate her. She won't roll over easily or quickly, Cheyenne. Be firm. Don't give her an inch, no matter what kind of tantrum she throws."

Cheyenne snorted. "Guess that runs in the family too, huh?"

"Hmm. Among so many other things." He looked past her at the magicals gathered around Corian. "And don't forget, you have Venga with you now. If he doesn't put the fear of the dead in Ba'rael Verdys' already rotting heart, nothing will."

"Okay. And that should be enough?"

"That is everything I can offer you on such short notice and without my physical presence." L'zar tried to smile again, met her gaze briefly, and ducked away almost as if it hurt to look at his daughter. His throat clicked when he swallowed. "I will be with you in spirit, as the saying goes."

"I sure as hell hope not." She pointed at him and raised an eyebrow. "No Don'adurr Thread while I'm trying to overthrow a drow dictator. Got it?"

"With perfect clarity."

"Okay. Thanks." She eyed him, but the drow thief merely bowed his head and took a step back. *What did I expect? It's not like he's gonna give me a fucking hug before I leave.* Cheyenne turned to Corian and the others, feeling the weight of the Darkglass in her pocket like she'd filled her jacket with stones instead.

"*Aranél.*"

She stopped at the sound of her unwanted title spoken by her father. Raising her eyebrows, she slowly looked at him over her shoulder. "Weaver."

L'zar lifted his chin and met her gaze. His golden eyes blazed with determination and a seriousness she'd seen there only a few times. "This is your birthright. Your *blood*right. You are the blade that will cut out the rot. The chains will shatter, and blood and water will flow through Ambar'ogúl again as one. Don't forget that."

Cheyenne pursed her lips. "Somebody's been paying too much attention to prophecies that don't belong to him."

Her father chuckled softly, his nostrils flaring. "What else would you expect from a thief?"

"Nothing."

Before she could turn her head again, he stepped urgently over to her and stopped, his need to protect her at war with his knowledge of what lay ahead. "You are the heir to everything I am, Cheyenne, just as you are the heir to everything I am not. Surviving this final stage is a greater legacy than all the rest of it. If nothing else, claim *that.*"

He can't just come out and say it, can he? Cheyenne nodded slowly, trying to hide a smile that forced itself onto her lips anyway. "A simple 'good luck and don't die' works pretty well, you know."

His eyes widened in surprise, then his low, dark chuckle built in the tense silence of the warehouse. "Good luck, Cheyenne. And don't die. Please."

"That's the plan, Weaver." With a final nod at her father, Cheyenne joined the other magicals waiting to make the crossing with her.

Ember bumped the halfling with her shoulder. "You okay?"

"Totally." Cheyenne shot her friend a sidelong glance. "Let's go pull down the Spider's web and blow some shit up."

Lumil let out a low whistle. "Damn, halfling. If that's the last morale-boosting pep-talk I ever hear before an epic battle, it's not half bad."

"It better not be the last." *Just the first. Guess I'm a better leader than I thought. But I can lead like this from anywhere, and it sure as hell won't be the Heart of Hangivol.*

Corian's portal shimmered in the air in front of them, and they stepped through into the night on the other side.

CHAPTER EIGHTY-FOUR

The bright lights mounted on the exterior walls of the black metal outbuildings on Rez 38 took some adjusting to. Cheyenne blinked against the glaring halos and stepped lightly away from the portal inside Q1.

"We are going to the cliff," she whispered, slowly raising her hand to point at the massive portal tower of black stone at the back of the reservation. "And then we cross."

"Let's be quick about it." Corian crouched beyond the pools of light, and the group of magicals snuck through Rez 38 without a sound.

The instant Cheyenne's foot pressed down on the trampled dirt two feet away from the base of the portal tower, a crack like a snapping tree trunk split the air, and three massive floodlights illuminated Q1. An alarm siren blared from the gate tower by the reservation's entrance, followed by shouted commands and footsteps thudding across the ground toward them. Doors slammed, fell weapons withdrew from holsters and clicked into place, and the first floodlight swept across Cheyenne and the rebel magicals sneaking onto the rez.

"Breach!" a guard roared. "By the tower!"

"Shit." Cheyenne broke into a jog and snarled, "Guess a quick, quiet crossing was too much to ask."

"Get to the cliffs," Corian growled as the guards' rising shouts grew louder and closer. "We're not here to hurt anyone."

A fell charge crackled through the air just in front of the nightstalker's face before crashing into a stunted tree on the other side of Q1. The bark exploded in a burst of green light, and Corian rolled his eyes.

"But if we have to, we will." Lumil smacked her fists together and summoned the swirling red runes around them both as they ran. More fell weapons fire filled Q1 with green light, and the magicals darted between buildings and away from rez guards trying to stop them.

"Just keep moving!" Cheyenne ducked a spray of fell shots and raised a shield in front of Persh'al and Ember as they ran behind her. The green fell shots ricocheted off it, and a guard somewhere screamed.

Lumil threw her head back and cackled when two guards cut them off at the opening between two outbuildings.

"Hands up where we can see 'em!"

"You mean these?" The goblin woman raised both fists in the air and dove across the dirt, sliding toward the guards like a batter sliding into first base. Her right fist cracked into the first guard's ribs and sent him flying into his fellow. Without missing a beat, Lumil leaped to her feet and kept going. "I've been wanting to do that for decades!"

Maleshi and Corian darted across the dirt in flashes of silver light, tossing startled guards aside to give the rest of their party a clear shot to the cliff. Cheyenne raised another shield beneath a heavy spray of fell shots and shoved aside a stack of metal crates with a toss of her other hand. The crates flew out of their path and cracked open against an outbuilding, spilling FRoE weapons and dampening gear across the dirt.

Ember stopped when a guard jumped out at her from behind the next outbuilding and trained his fell rifle at her chest. The goblin guard snarled when he saw a fae hovering two inches above the ground.

"It's not *that* weird!" She flicked her fingers at him with a flash of violet light, and the guard's yellow eyes rolled back into his head before he dropped. "We should all be used to magic by now. Fuck."

The siren blared louder as the rebels fled to the edge of the cliff.

"Stop them!"

"Bring 'em down!"

"They're going for the portal!"

Green fell fire whizzed through the air. Cheyenne raised a shield behind her, stretching it as wide as she thought was necessary for all eight of them. Her feet skidded to a stop at the edge of the rugged ledge of gray stone jutting past the portal tower and over the crashing waves of the Atlantic Ocean below.

Ember stopped beside her, breathing heavily. "So, where's the portal?"

"Down there." Cheyenne grinned at her friend and shrugged. "Leap of faith, right?"

"Kowabunga!" Byrd leaped off the cliff, his arms flailing as he vanished into the darkness.

"The fuck?" Lumil slowly shook her head and jumped off after him.

"This is it, kid." Maleshi winked at Cheyenne and stepped nimbly over the side.

Persh'al snorted. "I hate heights."

He disappeared just as Corian jumped into the Border portal.

Venga roared with maniacal laughter and shook all four fists at the star-studded sky. "Blood and honor, or the deathflame take us all!"

Grinning, he slapped Ember's back and sent her tumbling off the edge of the cliff with a yelp. Then he flicked his forked tongue at Cheyenne and jumped.

"Don't move," a guard shouted behind Cheyenne. "You don't have permission to step through that portal!"

"Yeah, you've never seen a drow before." *That'll change.* Cheyenne flipped the guard the middle finger as she spun to face the blinding lights and green fellfire. Grinning, she leaned back and let herself fall off the cliff toward the crashing waves.

She never hit the water. All the breath was squeezed agonizingly out of her lungs, and her awareness returned with the feeling of both knees pressed against something hard and her hands buried in a substance half sponge, half cold mist. Choking for breath, she snatched her hands away from the invisible ground of the in-between, focusing only on that first raw, searing inhale. Then she looked up at the place between worlds she barely recognized. "Holy shit."

"See this?" Ember offered Cheyenne a hand up but glared at Venga. "This is what happens when you screw around with too much magic and not enough magical space!"

"Incredible." Venga gazed around them, taking it all in. Not that there was much of anything to take in. The entire in-between was now coated with thick black smoke.

Or maybe all the light's gone, and this isn't smoke. Cheyenne let Ember help her to her feet as she caught her breath. *Maybe it's absolute nothing.*

"There." Persh'al pointed at the opposite doorway for this Border portal. "Don't ask me how it got that close, but there's our exit."

"Everybody move." Maleshi stalked forward, sneering at the blackness swirling around them. Their vision blurred with every step, the darkness sometimes blocking the other magicals from view, only to reveal them again the next second. But the outline of dampened light around the portal doorway remained bright enough to see at any given moment.

"Somebody's shrunk this place," Lumil muttered. "I don't like being in a box."

Venga hissed at her. "This is nothing like being in a box."

"Well, sure. I meant metaphorically." The goblin rolled her eyes at him and shook her head. "Asshole."

"Picking up the pace would probably be our best bet," Persh'al muttered. "You know, with shifters at three o'clock and everything."

"Really?" Cheyenne squinted through the blackness, looking for in-between monsters. "You sure? 'Cause I don't—"

A pair of burning red eyes materialized in the black smog two inches from the halfling's face.

"Holy flying shit!" She leaped back and blasted the thing with two orbs. The ground shook beneath them as the shifting monster bellowed. Cheyenne slapped her hands over her ears and blinked against the tears welling in her eyes.

"Yep, loud as fuck!" Ember grabbed her friend's arm and tugged her to the doorway. "Can't stop now, Cheyenne."

The halfling stumbled across the spongy, slurping ground, throwing energy spheres and purple sparks at anything with red eyes that moved.

Lumil bashed at the giant pincer sweeping toward her and splintered the hard carapace into thousands of tiny pieces. The in-between monster shrieked and withdrew. "You'd think these things would grow a few brain cells and learn to recognize us by now."

"No brains, asshat!" Byrd unleashed green fire at a swarm of black, glistening wings flapping overhead. "And yeah, I might be talking about you too!"

Persh'al reached the doorway first, his sparking blue whip writhing from his clenched fist, and turned back to wave the others forward. "Come on! Let's go!"

A thick tentacle lashed at him from the top of the doorway. He cracked his whip into the shimmering black flesh and split the thing clean in half. The severed end thumped on the ground, and he kicked it away with a grimace. "Fucking disgusting."

Ember and Cheyenne hurried toward him and the shimmering doorway. The halfling turned to blast more energy spheres at the point of a razor-sharp beak dropping toward Venga. Her attack splintered the beak, but the creature simply rearranged itself and spilled a nest of writhing tentacles from within the dangling husk that had been its mouth.

Venga roared and shoved two scaly fists into the wriggling mass. His other two fists rose high above his head, palms open, and jagged claws extended. Green light flashed across his all-black eyes as he shouted a spell, and the tangled tentacles hovering over him burst to smithereens in his grasp.

"Everybody through. Come on!" Persh'al waved them forward again, lashing every striking black appendage until the space in front of the doorway glowed a constant blue.

Byrd and Lumil darted through the doorway first. Then Maleshi raced past, skidding across the ground as she slashed at a striking tentacle and split it into five ribbons with her claws. Venga stalked toward them, throwing up plumes of black smoke with every heavy step and tossing incoming black monsters aside with all four arms.

Corian darted through the doorway, dragging Venga the rest of the way with him. Ember tugged Cheyenne's arm to get her to move. "Persh'al, come on!"

"Go!" He stepped in front of the doorway and cracked his blue whip at a spider-like creature with a dozen red eyes at the center of not eight legs but nineteen. His whip lashed leg after skittering leg before any of the sharp, barbed ends had the chance to stab their intended targets, namely Cheyenne and Ember.

The fae finally managed to pull Cheyenne through the doorway, and they stumbled across the portal exit two seconds before Persh'al. The blue troll shouted as a severed spider's leg morphed into a barbed claw, and he dove through the doorway to skid unceremoniously on his stomach across loose, charred dirt. The in-between monster shrieked and retreated through the doorway, and then it was over.

"I really hate those things." Persh'al shoved himself off the ground and slapped the coarse dirt off his clothes. "Now what?"

Corian pointed to their right. "Now we get the hell away from here and *that.*"

Everyone followed his gaze to see the blight's black tendrils snaking across the land, sucking the life from the few rare scraps of plant life remaining this far in the Outers. Venga scratched his hairless head with one hand and stroked his scaly chin with another. "That's it, then?"

"That's it." Ember glared at the necromancer. "Feel free to let inspiration strike. We could really use suggestions from the magical who created that."

"Come on." Maleshi nodded at the portal she'd just conjured, then looked over her shoulder at the quickly approaching blight. "I hope I don't have to tell anyone how important it is to be *quick* about it!"

The magicals slipped through the shimmering oval of dark light. Less than ten seconds after the general's portal disappeared with a soft pop, the snaking tendrils of the blight's corruption spilled across the soil. It cracked the earth beneath it, filled the empty spaces with black, oozing sludge, and kept going.

CHAPTER EIGHTY-FIVE

"Anyone else think it's weird that the crossing took less than five minutes?" Ember straightened her sweater and gazed at the shimmering magical dome surrounding the capital city of Hangivol in front of them.

"My guess is the in-between acts rather like the Outers these days," Corian muttered. "With ever-changing boundaries."

"You're not complaining, are you?" Lumil grinned at the fae.

"Not even a little. I was under the impression that the portal door-ways were farther apart, that's all."

"They usually are." Maleshi lifted her chin and stared across the dark silhouettes of Hangivol's rising towers in front of them. "And this city usually isn't on fire."

Cheyenne squinted at the green and purple flames that looked like they were engulfing the highest towers in the center of the city around the Heart and the Crown's fortress. Thick pillars of smoke billowed into the night sky, which was just starting to grow lighter with the coming dawn. "That's not the city burning."

"Oh, joy," Byrd muttered flatly. "Then what's burning?"

"That look like the *Sorren Gán*'s fire to anyone else?"

"Huh." Maleshi cocked her head. "Good eye, kid."

"That thing kept its promise, huh?" Ember folded her arms. "I honestly didn't expect it to."

Venga studied the fae, his black eyes glistening in the starlight. "Am I to believe you summoned a *Sorren Gán* to your will and sent it to Hangivol?"

Ember scoffed. "Don't be ridiculous; that was L'zar. But you better believe that giant fiery asshole with wings came here to clean up *your* mess, necromancer." She pointed at him. "Anything goes wrong with the *Sorren Gán* feasting on magical leftovers, that's on you."

"Indeed." He glanced at her one more time and stalked toward the city. "When we've achieved our purpose here, I would very much enjoy speaking to such a creature."

"Hey, if you can make yourself smell like a drow, Venga, you're probably in," Cheyenne said while the goblins sniggered at her comment.

"Perhaps raising your ancestors would grant me an audience with the *Sorren Gán*," Venga replied. "You know, the dead ones."

"Oh." Cheyenne shrugged. "I guess that'd work too."

"We need to make this as quick as possible," Corian muttered. "Not because *we're* running out of time, but to give Bianca a—"

"I think we all know what's at stake, Corian. Thanks." Cheyenne forced herself to look straight ahead. "This time, we can just roll into the fortress without having to be sneaky or fight off the Crown's army to put any drow coins on a damn altar, right?"

"That's it, kid." Maleshi flexed her fur-covered hands and let out a low growl as they stalked toward the city center and the rising towers of the inner circle around the fortress. "And this round, the Spider can't do shit to lift a finger against us."

Ember grinned. "I like that part."

"Yeah, it has a certain ring to it, huh?"

* * *

The group made their way up the various levels of Hangivol's circular tiers. None of the O'gúleesh who lived here bothered them, and there wasn't a single Crown soldier in sight.

Cheyenne nodded at a group of ogres standing at the entrance to a tunnel breaching the level's outer walls. *Feels a lot safer now that L'zar's not with us. Big surprise, right?*

The entrance to the Crown's inner circle was unguarded, and the rebel group walked swiftly across the dark courtyard where Hangivol's drow citizens lived. Maleshi reached toward the closest door, intending to open it with a spell. Venga beat her to it by stalking over to the sheet of metal and bashing it inward with two fists. The general lowered her hand and glared at the sheet of metal wobbling and clanging on the floor, ripped off its hinges. "You realize we've taken the Heart by surprise once already, don't you?"

Venga flicked his forked tongue at her. "Of course, General. But breaking down even one of the Spider's doors pleases me very much."

Maleshi rolled her eyes and gestured at the now-doorless opening. "By all means, then. As you were."

Everyone else followed the necromancer inside, and they moved swiftly down empty corridors of stone and metal crafted to look like stone. Cheyenne stuck her activator behind her ear and studied the scrolling lines of code racing across the surface of every wall in green, blue, and yellow. "Doesn't look like anyone knows we're here."

"Or they haven't started talking about it through the system yet," Corian muttered. "Either way, I particularly enjoy the silence."

"You're right." Ember gazed from the walls to the high ceilings of the corridor and down the other side. "You'd think it would be super-creepy to walk into a place this big with this much nasty dark magic in it, but it's peaceful."

"Not for long, Em. I wouldn't count on it." Cheyenne studied the lines of code scrolling across the black metal walls and reached out to an access point illuminated by her activator. Using that, she sent an encrypted message to the Four-Pointed Star, which was hopefully still stationed somewhere beneath the city.

We're early. Come join us for the new Cycle.

The activator alerted her ten seconds later that the message had been received, and then she got her reply.

Expect our arrival.

Cheyenne smirked. At least they were ready to roll with the punches and change up a few things on the timeline.

Not having to follow L'zar down hidden route after hidden route through the Crown's fortress meant they cut their time to nearly a quarter of what it had taken them the first time. Sooner than she expected, Cheyenne found herself staring up at the tall, vaulted ceilings of the courtyard at the Heart. The magical dome over the city spilled gray light into the courtyard, barely illuminating the twisted, gnarled Nimlothar tree sprouting from the burst stone at the Heart's center.

The courtyard was empty.

Cheyenne approached the last Nimlothar and frowned. "This thing looks a lot worse off than the last time we were here."

"Not much of a surprise." Maleshi studied the tree's almost-bare branches and its few fluttering leaves, pulsing weakly with purple light. "This thing's been used a lot more than it should have been for Ba'rael's magic. It might be taking a necessary break from overloading itself."

"Used?"

Corian turned from gazing up at the stone walk on the upper story and met Cheyenne's gaze. "How do you think that leaf got through the portal in your mom's backyard, kid?"

Cheyenne's nostrils flared. "She's been stealing magic from the *tree*?"

"'Stealing' might be a strong word," Maleshi said. "From what I understand, a Nimlothar will lend its power to a drow—any drow, regardless of what their intentions are."

"Just because the tree has no idea it's being robbed, it doesn't mean it's not being robbed."

"No one's arguing in her defense, kid." The general spread her arms. "I'm just saying that tree is giving of itself willingly because it doesn't know any better."

"Look at it." Cheyenne reached toward the twisted bark, then pulled back her hand. "It doesn't have anything left to give."

"Not true." Corian folded his arms and glanced at Maleshi and Cheyenne. "There is plenty more left in this tree. It just has to be used the right way."

The halfling gazed up the length of the twisted, gnarled trunk. "What do you know about using this the right way?"

"Don't forget who I've been bound to for centuries, Cheyenne. I've learned at least as much from him as he's learned from me." With a curt nod, the nightstalker approached the Nimlothar and gently set his hand on the twisted bark. Faint purple light pulsed beneath his touch. "We still have to move quickly if we want to make this work. For everyone."

"Kinda hard to give the Spider my terms when there's no Spider in sight."

Corian blinked at her, then nodded at the tree. "Put your hand there."

"Why?"

"We're going to summon the Spider together, Cheyenne. I imagine that's as far as I can take you before you face the rest of it on your own. Now close your eyes."

With her hand on the rough bark, which vibrated slightly beneath her palm, the halfling did as she was told and took a deep breath.

"Call her to you—silently, aloud, it doesn't matter. Just call her."

Sure. Just call the drow who'd rather kill me than step down. No problem.

Still, Cheyenne forced herself to picture Ba'rael Verdys' face. Beside her, Corian muttered a spell in O'gúleesh, and the Nimlothar's purple light grew stronger and pulsed faster.

"Say her name, Cheyenne."

She took a shuddering breath. "Ba'rael."

The doors burst open at the other side of the courtyard, and in stormed a scowling Ba'rael Verdys, the Crown of Ambar'ogúl, cloaked in thick black robes. Behind her was Ruuv'i, glancing dubiously from one of L'zar's rebel magicals to the next.

Of course, he'd be with her. *That's better for me, though, isn't it? I'll only have to state the terms once.*

Ba'rael stopped when her golden eyes settled on her niece's hand resting against the Nimlothar. "Giving up so soon, Cheyenne? You still have plenty of time."

"But you don't." Cheyenne removed her hand from the tree and stepped in front of it, almost as if she were protecting the Nimlothar from yet another mad drow ruler. "I'm surrendering the rest of my fortnight to offer you my terms right now, Ba'rael. The new Cycle turns today."

"Oh." The Crown tilted her head, then let out a lilting chuckle. "Such a grand speech for an infant."

"I'll start then."

"Yes, by all means." Grinning, Ba'rael looked over her shoulder at

Ruuv'i, who did nothing but scowl at the visitors to the Crown's court. Then his gaze fell on Venga, and when Ba'rael saw the fear in her *Nós Aní*'s eyes, she spun. A shuddering breath wracked her chest.

The necromancer erupted in booming laughter, his voice echoing through the Heart. "Ba'rael. You worry too much."

"I most certainly do not." The drow woman swallowed and spared Cheyenne a quick glance. "I worry exactly the right amount. Child, what chewed through your brain and convinced you it was a good idea to bring this death-dealer back to my gates?"

Cheyenne raised her eyebrows. "Mostly just to see that look on your face. And because we all know how much you hate it. And because he's useful. To me."

"You foolish—"

"You screwed with the wrong drow, Ba'rael."

The Crown snarled. "L'zar's not even here!"

"I'm not talking about L'zar. Shouldn't be that hard to pick up on." Cheyenne rolled her eyes. "You know, I *could* just let Venga kill you right now. That'd solve all my problems. You'd be out of the way, and we'd have a new Crown just like that, no votes and no arguments. Having a necromancer on the throne might take some getting used to, but it's better than—"

"No, no!" Ba'rael staggered forward, one hand outstretched to stop her niece and the other tightly clutching at the bodice of her black robes. "I will hear your terns, Cheyenne. That is the least of it."

"Excellent."

Footsteps echoed through the courtyard, and the rest of the Four-Pointed Star emerged from the archways leading from the tunnels. Nu'ek, Foltr, Elarit, Sakrit…one by one, they lined up around Cheyenne and the other rebels, eager to watch the exchange and the turning of a new Cycle.

Cheyenne took a deep breath. *Didn't realize how much better I'd feel with more magicals standing behind me than her.* "So, here are my terms. You'll step down as Crown. Obviously. And leave Hangivol. There's no coming back for you after this. Ever."

Ba'rael blinked slowly.

"When you leave, you take nothing from the Nimlothar with you. Not a leaf, not a twig, not even a scrap of bark. You'll be on your own.

Ruuv'i has a standing offer to peel himself away from you like a scab. He can stay here if he wants as part of my council."

The courtyard was quiet. Ba'rael stared at her niece, then burst out laughing. The sound rang through the courtyard. Cheyenne put her hands on her hips. *Okay, the heartless bitch has a pretty laugh. We get it.*

"You can't be serious." Ba'rael composed herself and shook her head, chuckling softly. "That's all? You've had nearly a week, and that is all the Weaver handed you to deliver to me?"

"Almost." Cheyenne reached into her pocket and pulled out the shrunken Darkglass with the metal star forged from Neros' magic hovering at its center. The silver light in that four-pointed star pulsed brighter than ever. "I also have this. If you refuse my terms, Ba'rael, I will use it."

The Crown's eyes narrowed, and her jaw clenched in fury. "You wouldn't."

"Try me."

The drow's eyelids fluttered closed as she tried to find words. "How did you find him?"

"Doesn't really matter, does it?" Cheyenne shrugged and tucked the Darkglass back into her pocket. "What matters is that I've got a lifeline to him right here in my pocket. I know where to find him again if I have to. I mean, obviously, if you accept my terms and step down, I won't ever have to—"

"No."

The single word rang through the courtyard. Cheyenne cocked her head with a frown. "No?"

"I do not accept your terms, *Aranél.*"

Ruuv'i stepped toward the Crown with a hiss. "Ba'rael, this isn't—"

"I'm not playing games with you, Cheyenne." The drow tossed her head and spread her arms. "You brought me your terms, and I reject them in favor of combat. If a new Cycle turns today, dearest niece, it will not be yours."

The halfling let out a shaky sigh. "I did not see that coming. Fuck."

CHAPTER EIGHTY-SIX

The Crown's soldiers swarmed into the courtroom from all sides, grunting and snarling and banging their weapons against metal armor and what little metal existed within the Heart.

Cheyenne spun to look at Corian and shook her head. "That didn't work the way we wanted."

"She never planned to consider your terms." The nightstalker's gaze flicked to Ba'rael. "She just wants an audience. Cheyenne, I'm sorry this is what it's come down to."

"What?"

"You have to fight her."

"Are you fucking serious? Hey, in no way did I prepare for this!"

"Not true, kid." Maleshi gave the halfling a firm nod and a gentle smile. "You know what you're doing. Just go do it."

"I can't!"

A powerful force knocked Cheyenne forward, and she spun around.

Ba'rael laughed, her arm outstretched toward the halfling, that same crazed determination behind her golden eyes as Cheyenne had grown used to seeing in L'zar's. "This *will* be fun."

"You pushed me."

"I'm merely waiting for the *Aranél* to begin."

Gritting her teeth, Cheyenne lunged and threw a sphere of crackling

594

black energy at the Crown.

Ba'rael swatted it aside with a black light of her own and chuckled. "Please tell me you're offering more of a challenge than the last time we fought in front of this tree. I really was hoping for something a little more."

Cheyenne unleashed another energy orb, then another, and another. Each time, Ba'rael dodged her niece's magic, deflected it, or ignored it.

"Hmm. I think your fear's affecting your aim."

"I'm not afraid of you." Cheyenne dipped her chin and glared at her aunt. "I'm just annoyed."

"Oh, is that all?" Snarling, Ba'rael lunged into enhanced speed and struck Cheyenne's cheek before darting away again. The blow made the halfling reel back, flailing to catch her balance. Her jaw and cheek burned furiously. "See? I said it would be fun."

The Crown disappeared again in a blur of white and black. Cheyenne darted into drow speed to meet her, and Ba'rael sent a telekinetic wave hurtling against the halfling's chest. Cheyenne grunted, skidded back across the cracked stone floor, and watched Ba'rael streak back across the courtyard before slapping her niece on the other cheek.

Cheyenne glared at the darting blur, following Ba'rael with her gaze and moving nothing else. "Just fucking fight me already."

A screeching laugh erupted in the courtyard before Ba'rael charged into the halfling and threw Cheyenne back again. The halfling's back slammed into the thick, rough bark of the Nimlothar. She felt a pain that didn't belong entirely to her coursing through her body, and when she blinked away the dizziness, she saw three purple leaves flutter to the ground. They landed at her feet and pulsed weakly, like the tree's final plea to cut out the heart and the rot and let it live.

"Fine." Cheyenne pushed off the tree and staggered forward, clenching her jaw against the pain in her back. "You wanna have fun, Ba'rael? I can make this fun."

"Oh, now you want to play, do you?"

"No." Cheyenne thought of the Nimlothar seed within her and the pulsing cries of purple light from the leaves behind her on the ground. Her eyes flashed purple, then erupted in black flames, and drow fire raced across her flesh. "Now I'm pissed."

Ba'rael's eyes widened above an unsure smile, then Cheyenne

unleashed a column of black fire at her aunt.

The Crown darted away but wasn't fast enough to avoid a blast of black fire against her shoulder. She spun sideways, cried out, glanced at the charred flesh through the hole in her robes, and snarled. Her hand lashed out with a burst of black lightning. Cheyenne lifted a shield and sent the attack hurtling up to the walkway around the courtyard. Then she stepped forward and launched another spray of lightless flames.

"You think you have it in you to stand against me?" Ba'rael shrieked and sent two more bolts of black lightning at the halfling. Cheyenne deflected one with another shield, then caught the other with her lashing black tendrils and whipped it back at the Crown. Ba'rael ducked and screamed in fury. "You may have my brother's blood, *Aranél*, but I have all of Ambar'ogúl."

"No, you don't." Cheyenne pounded her fists together, then drew them apart and sent black fire arcing around the courtyard to converge where Ba'rael stood. "You only have yourself."

Screaming, the Crown threw the flaming attacks aside with her own shield of howling wind and acrid smoke. The black fire snuffed out, then she charged Cheyenne again with another sizzling attack of black lightning.

This time, Cheyenne reached out and plucked the magical bolt from the air, the black drow fire protecting her as Ba'rael's magic buzzed and shuddered in her fist. *She only has her own magic right now, not everything she stole. If I could punch L'zar in the face, I can take her down.*

The sight of her black lightning bolt clenched in Cheyenne's fists snapped what was left of Ba'rael's sanity. She screamed and threw her arms out to her sides, her mouth opening far wider than her jaw should have been able to manage. The courtyard shuddered. The Nimlothar tree swayed from side to side as if standing against a cyclone. Dust and chunks of rock fell from the domed ceiling all around them, then the Crown darted into enhanced speed once again and launched blazing purple darts at her niece at dangerously close range.

Cheyenne tried to dodge the spikes but couldn't move faster than she already was. She raised a shield, but Ba'rael tore it down and kept firing. Two of the purple spikes hit their target. One grazed the side of Cheyenne's neck, instantly drawing blood, and the other pierced her chest beneath her shoulder.

The halfling's scream erupted through the courtyard as she dropped out of enhanced speed and fell to her knees. Black fire flickered along her body, racing up and down, but it did nothing to protect her from the purple dart of Ba'rael's magic that had stuck her like a spearhead. Lifting a trembling hand, Cheyenne peeled her shirt away from the weapon in her flesh and groaned at the thin black lines snaking away from the dart and spreading quickly across her purple-gray skin.

"Cheyenne!" Ember surged forward, but Corian darted in front of her and pushed her back.

"You can't get involved, Ember. I'm sorry."

"That bitch is gonna kill her!"

"We don't know that." He wrapped his arms around the panicked fae girl and leaned in to mutter in her ear, "But I do know that if you step in to intervene, you won't make it out of here alive. The old laws still stand, Ember. It won't be me or Ba'rael or Cheyenne. Ambar'ogúl will kill you for getting involved."

"That's insane."

"That's the way this world works."

Swallowing thickly, Ember nodded and stopped fighting him. Corian sniffed, gently released her, and turned around again to watch a fight that looked like it was almost over.

"*This* is why you will never be the Crown, Cheyenne. You're too young." Ba'rael sent a purple dart into her niece's other shoulder. The halfling screamed again and tossed a stream of black fire at Ba'rael, but the drow woman ducked and kept advancing. "You're too *soft*." Her next purple spear struck Cheyenne's right hip, right where her first bullet had struck her.

Shrieking, the halfling lost what footing she'd regained and dropped to her knees again. Her hip screamed in pain. She could barely feel her shoulders anymore. Whatever those black lines were burned through her veins.

Breathing heavily, her golden eyes ablaze with crazed victory, Ba'rael approached her wounded niece and loomed over Cheyenne like a hungry predator. "You are far too much like my failure of a brother, Cheyenne."

"No." Cheyenne swallowed thickly and lifted her head, trying to keep herself from falling forward and slamming her face into the stone. "I'm exactly who I'm supposed to be."

"Hmm." Ba'rael grinned and clapped her hands together. When she drew them apart, a blazing circle of black light bloomed between her palms, spitting and hissing with drow magic and all the force Ba'rael could muster behind her final spell.

Oh, fuck. This is it. We all knew I wouldn't make it through this. At least I'm not laid out on the ground.

"Pity your father isn't here to see you burn like the rest of his spawn, but I'll send him a message. In great detail, child. Don't you worry about that."

Despite facing her end, Cheyenne found herself laughing. "Trust me, the last thing I'm worried about right now is that lunatic."

Sucking in a sharp breath, Ba'rael pulled her hands all the way apart and prepared to deliver the final blow.

A massive crack rent the air, and the black stone wall at the end of the courtyard behind Ba'rael the Spider ripped open. A violent gust of wind swarmed through the Heart. Ba'rael turned around and staggered back, her mortal spell suspended in the air in front of her.

White light filled the tear in the stone wall, then a warbling screech echoed across the stone courtyard. The thick flap of wingbeats followed, then a shimmering blue beast soared through the tear in space and entered the Heart of the Crown's fortress.

On the back of the glowing blue *luré* stood Neros, his white hair and robes whipping around his washed-out face and body. His eyes glowed blue with the pulsing light of the flying stingray beneath him.

Ba'rael gasped and glanced at Cheyenne. Inside the halfling's pocket, the Darkglass flared. The Crown looked back up at the pale-skinned drow and made the connection.

"I have seen enough!" Neros shouted. His flying mount dove toward the drow women.

Roaring in fury, Ba'rael turned away from Cheyenne and raised her trembling hands toward Neros. The crackling wall of black energy she'd summoned grew stronger as her son approached. His glowing blue eyes were focused on his mother.

The *luré* screeched again and pulled out of its dive as Neros leaped from the creature's back and lunged toward Ba'rael. The Crown screamed and unleashed the attack that was meant to take her niece's life, not her son's.

Neros threw his arms around the Crown, his burst of white magic colliding with hers. Neros, his *lurè*, and the screaming Ba'rael burst into millions of glittering lights. The Spider's last vengeful scream still echoed within the stone walls. Tiny particles of what had once been two magicals locked in an embrace fluttered away on a soft breeze, disappearing like ash. Then there was nothing at all.

Cheyenne stared at the empty space where they'd just been. Everything hurt. Everything was numb. She swallowed and tried to stand but only managed to get one foot squarely planted on the stone floor instead of both her knees. "What. The. Fuck?"

"Oh, my God." Ember raced toward her and bent over Cheyenne's wounds. "You're okay."

"I'm okay."

"I can't believe it, Cheyenne. You're not fucking dead!"

"I'm okay."

"This is probably gonna hurt."

"What...*ah!*"

Ember ripped the first purple dart out of Cheyenne's shoulder and tossed it aside. "Sorry. You've had worse, right?"

"Sure, Em." Cheyenne swayed where she knelt. "Loads worse. Ah, *fuck!*"

The second dart clattered across the stone floor, shedding a thin trail of halfling blood behind it.

"Now, this one in your hip."

Cheyenne snatched the girl's wrist in one hand and jerked it away from her hip. "Touch that one, Ember, and I'll throw you the fuck across this room."

"Whoa." Ember glided back and raised her hands. "Noted. Don't touch the hip." She did, however, offer Cheyenne support to get to her feet. Then the halfling turned slowly around to watch every other magical in the Heart staring at her in stunned silence.

Yep. Everyone thought I would die today.

Maleshi stepped forward and cleared her throat, then turned to address the witnesses gathered in the courtyard. "Ba'rael Verdys, the Spider Crown of Ambar'ogúl, has met the final deathflame. The new

Cycle has turned today. It moves for Cheyenne Summerlin. The Black Flame of Ambar'ogúl. The new Crown."

Ba'rael's soldiers fell to their knees as one, their metal axes and swords and maces clinking against armor as they bowed their heads. One by one, the members of the Four-Pointed Star did the same. Some of them closed their eyes. Most had recovered from their shock and now grinned at Cheyenne, nodding and thumping their hands and feet against whatever metal was within reach.

Byrd and Lumil shoved each other until they were both on their knees. Corian thumped a fist to his chest and knelt as well. Persh'al and Venga both did the same, until finally it was just Maleshi standing in front of Cheyenne and Ember.

The general pressed her fist to her chest as well and held Cheyenne's gaze. "May the Black Flame reign."

"May the Black Flame reign." The echoing response rose from every mouth in the courtyard.

Maleshi raised an eyebrow at Cheyenne as she lowered herself to one knee and nodded.

"Okay, so we have two options here," Ember muttered.

"What's that?"

"I can either bow like everyone else and drop you and we'll all be on our knees, or I can keep holding you up like this so everyone thinks you can stand on your own."

"You know what, Em? I'm sure a *Nós Aní* is exempt from the whole 'bowing to the new Crown' rule."

"Okay, sure." Ember nodded and tightened her hold on her friend. "We'll just stand here, then."

"Yep." Cheyenne grimaced and tried to ignore the pain flaring through her body. "I guess we have a little time to let it all sink in."

The fae snorted. "The Black Flame, huh?"

"Shut up. You know it's badass."

"For sure." Turning to meet Cheyenne's gaze, Ember grinned. "May the fucking Black Flame reign."

Cheyenne's adventures don't end here. Join her as her story continues to unfold in *The Drow Hath Sent Thee.*

Get sneak peeks, exclusive giveaways, behind the scenes content, and more.
PLUS you'll be notified of special **one day only fan pricing** on new releases.

Sign up today to get free stories.

or visit: https://marthacarr.com/read-free-stories/

I've been working with my old trainer from Chicago – over Zoom. One of the strange benefits of a very strange year. Laura was my favorite trainer I've ever run into because she bothered to research physical hindrances I had with credible sources and came up with creative solutions. They were challenging without being dangerous and lead to progress. Never had anyone before or since tailor something to me that much and so effectively. Also, she's got a wicked sense of humor, which is a big plus.

It turns out Laura has added a new element of mindfulness around exercise. I've been practicing mindfulness around food for a couple of years now and it's changed the way I eat in ways I didn't think were possible. Basically, the short version is that I became more aware of whether I liked what I was eating or not (you'd think that would be obvious but turns out, nope) and whether I was hungry or full.

I wondered when I started that journey just how much it could change decades old habits. Turns out, it could change them to the point where I can actually eat just one. And I quit doing the old seesaw of eating perfectly or throwing caution to the wind.

How do you do all that with exercise? When we started, I had no clue.

I'm kind of all or nothing with exercise too and generally, I don't like it most of the time. There are aspects of it I like and certain exercises I like more, but how do I get to mindfulness? (Laura likes to say there are certain exercises I dislike less. Semantics.)

Some of my instructions have been to use a short meditation before I start working out. To take an approach of building at a moderate pace to something. To make up a list of ways to blow off steam – the naughty list – so I already know what I'd like to do on days that running seems like too much. (Actually build in that there will be those days and be ready, instead of acting like maybe this time that won't happen). And to make a list of the exercises I like – or dislike less till there are sixty or more for me to choose from.

Mind blown. So obvious but I never saw any of this before. Makes me think that there's a chance I could learn to incorporate regular exercise in my life without long stretches of doing nothing but walking the dog. I'll let you know. More adventures to follow.

AUTHOR NOTES - MICHAEL ANDERLE

AUGUST 12, 2020

Thank you for allowing me to work in a profession that feeds my need to be creative. That is to you the reader, and companies such as Amazon (and others such as Apple, Google, Kobo, Barnes & Noble etc.) which have created the distribution methods we indie publishers use today.

Without readers such as yourself willing to take a chance, I wouldn't have the honor to chat (even in the back of the book) with thousands of people.

So, I just got off the phone and did something I've NEVER done before. I reached out to Martha and asked her to add to her author notes.

I had to explain that mindfulness (the concept) is something my brain doesn't understand (nor the corollary be-in-the-moment.)

I heard the term hundreds of times, but never have I had someone explain what the @#%@# it meant in a way I could grasp.

And Martha did it.

But, I couldn't follow all of her comments without trying two or three times to unpack her thoughts. So, I reached out and asked if she would EXPAND her author notes.

You know, to author block me because she needs my help to accomplish that little feat (she does not.)

I appreciate her explanation for a concept I am going to be able to use. I'm 52 years old. Maybe I've got 10 years, maybe I've got another 50 years (my grandmother was 100 when she passed) but I now understand when someone tells me to be in the moment.

Don't even ask what I said to those people in my head after about the 10th time. Even Bethany Anne might be impressed with the purity of the cursing.

Since I didn't say anything out loud, I nodded my head politely and still went away confused. So, if you haven't read Martha's author comments in this book (and don't understand 'mindfulness') go back and give it a read.

It's pretty freaking useful as a core tool to use to help you make your life better.

I'm looking forward to another chance to talk in the next book!

Ad Aeternitatem,

Michael Anderle